FROM TORMENTED TIDES OMNIBUS

THE COMPLETED SERIES
FROM TORMENTED TIDES
ON TWISTING TIDES
ACROSS TORN TIDES

VAL E. LANE

Wave Song Publishing

Letter From the Author

Dear Reader,

I am so excited for you to dive into my world of paranormal pirates, siren curses, romance, and adventure. From Tormented Tides will always hold a special place in my heart as my debut series, and these characters are like family to me. FTT began as a vague idea many years ago, about a girl with a necklace that somehow tied her to a curse of her lover, causing him to die the same death each night. This fuzzy idea remained just that—an idea—until one day it took shape in the form of a college girl and a ghost pirate, which was partly inspired by a childhood story from my dad about a piece of wood washing up on the shore that he pretended came from a pirate ship still out sailing the ocean somewhere. The funny thing is, I never intended for this book to be more than a fun publishing project for myself, and never could have guessed it would reach as many readers as it has. I certainly never imagined it would become a three-book series! But now that it has, I am so proud of how far this little paranormal pirate series has come, and I hope Jack Sparrow would be honored. But in all seriousness, I want to thank you for picking up my series and giving it a chance. My love of writing is why I started, but the readers are why I continued. And I hope to write many more books to share with you all in the years to come!

These characters are pieces of me and my strange imagination, and I hope you get to experience the thrills, mysteries, joys, and pains of their stories through their eyes as I have. So set sail and embark on these adventures as you battle inner demons with Katrina, face the past with Milo, and rewrite the future with Bellamy.

And most importantly, never stop looking for magic in the ordinary. You might be surprised what you find.

Keep a weather eye on the horizon,

THE PAST IS ANYTHING BUT DEAD

FROM
TORMENTED
TIDES

VAL E. LANE

FROM TORMENTED TIDES

BOOK I

VAL E. LANE

Wave Song Publishing

"The heart of man is very much like the sea. It has its storms, it has its tides, and in its depths it has its pearls, too."

Vincent van Gogh, The Letters of Vincent van Gogh

Playlist

Scan the code or click to listen. Each song corresponds to the chapters in order, plus additional songs at the end. You can also search for the playlist on Spotify by book title.

Prologue: "Caller of the Tide" by Dmitry Ustinov, Atom Music Audio

1. "Watercolor Eyes" by Lana Del Rey

2. "Devil on My Shoulder" by Faith Marie

3. "Astronomical" by SVRCINA

3.5 *BONUS OMNIBUS CHAPTER "The Ghost on the Shore" by Lord Huron (at the bottom of playlist)

4. "13 Beaches" by Lana Del Rey

5. "Bad Dreams-Stripped" by Fauozia

Unravel the past.

Break the curse.

Pass midterms.

And don't fall in love with dead pirates.

Prologue

I should have expected tragedy when I met him. After all, he was meant to die centuries ago, yet here he still stood—the phantom of a past that refused to die.

I think some part of me always knew he would break my heart. I just didn't know it would be like this.

Even in my nightmares, I'd never dreamed he could resort to this.

He pressed the cold cutlass blade to my throat as the captain looked on from the deck. My silent tears trickled down, mixing with the raging seawater below.

"Don't do this," I whispered, quietly enough that the rest of the crew couldn't hear me.

"I have to." He spat out his words through gritted teeth. I could feel the steel blade shaking against my skin as his hand trembled.

Could he really bring himself to kill me after everything else he'd lost? I knew that he was driven by his pain, but I'd still trusted him this far. We were two broken hearts, both fated to a dismal end, but betrayal wasn't supposed to be part of it.

I was going to die in my first semester of college. And I had accepted that.

But even 300 years still wasn't enough for him. He wasn't going to let me save him.

He loosened his hold around me just enough to allow me the freedom to turn my head. Turning my face toward his, I looked up into his eyes one last time. I prayed that somehow my desperate gaze would be enough to turn the tides of his will. He blinked through his own tears and swallowed, and I thought—for just a breath—that he might change his mind.

And he did.

He tightened his grip and lowered the edge of the sword to my chest, right over my pounding heart.

The dreams, the visions—they were right. I knew the sea would bring my downfall. But I thought it'd be different. I thought I'd drown beneath the waves, not be brutally murdered by pirates.

Yet here I stood, betrayed with a blade at my chest as the waves battered the ship's hull, heralding the coming maelstrom. And one taunting phrase echoed in my head, louder than the sound of the storm and the creaking of the ship—a cruel warning I should've heeded from the beginning.

Never trust a pirate.

KATRINA

"*Was it another bad dream, Mom?*"

I could still hear myself, clear as day. The haunting echo of my nine-year-old voice.

How could I forget it when the memory hung right over my bed? A moment forever held by watercolors on canvas, from a past I'd worked so hard to leave behind—an all-too-common night in my childhood home, captured in hues of inky blue midnight, where a dark-haired woman knelt at her bedside, arms wrapped tightly around the small girl who'd crept in from the doorway.

To the casual onlooker, the scene portrayed a child coming to her mother's room seeking comfort from a nightmare. Almost no one would think to consider it might be the other way around.

I stared at the little girl, awoken all too many times by her mother's sobs, and the worry painted in her sleepless eyes.

My eyes.

It was that age when I started to understand why my mom had to drink herself to sleep. But understanding didn't necessarily come with forgiveness. No matter how hard I'd tried to find it at the tip of my paintbrush.

'Nightmares,' I'd titled it.

And now it hung here in my dorm at Isabel College of Arts in Constantine, Florida, far from my home back in Arkansas.

Despite the unfortunate circumstances that inspired its creation, it was the only reason I was here. It was the piece that had earned me my scholarship here, and I was once proud of each painstaking hour spent layering the watercolors on the page, and the accomplishment of finally signing my name in the corner of the finished piece—*Katrina Delmar.*

But sometimes it was just another reminder that Mom wasn't home—just like my 19th birthday just three days ago, when she didn't even bother to call or text.

Not that I'd expected any different.

And with each passing day since, I wanted to rip that picture off the wall and hide it away. So, I stood there, remembering a past I was trying to bury, until I decided I didn't want to remember anymore. With one last look at the canvas, I pulled it off the wall and slid it underneath the bed frame with bitter mixed emotions.

Happy Halloween, Mom.

With the memory out of sight, I returned my attention to what I had come for—my birthday gift from Dad. I strode to my dresser where it lay, still nestled in the small box it had arrived in.

A necklace.

Careful and slow, I picked it up by its delicate chain and then made my way back toward McKenzie's side of the dorm where we were getting ready for tonight's party.

We had attempted to style my hair, but I knew that my out-of-control waves wouldn't be so easily tamed in a place where the sea breeze never relented. The rich loose curls of a brunette shade so dark it was nearly black framed my heart-shaped face and tumbled to my waist—a treasured feature I liked to believe came from my half-Cuban blood.

Overall, I looked a lot like my mother, much to my disdain. I always thought she was beautiful, but everything else about her blinded me to that.

McKenzie's costume of choice was a "sexy cheerleader," and to be honest it suited her well, her ginger hair tied in a half-up half-down style tied with a big navy bow, garnet red lips, and mini skirt complementing her slender figure.

I, on the other hand, felt like my deep brown eyes and dark hair clashed with the starch-white dress and wings of the costume McKenzie had loaned me from last year. My olive skin had darkened a touch since I arrived, thanks to the endless sun, and the short white dress only enhanced the tan.

"Don't forget your halo." McKenzie placed the fluffy halo-on-a-spring headband on my head before I could object.

I felt exposed in the tight satin dress that just barely reached the middle of my thighs. It wasn't exactly what I would have chosen for a Halloween costume, but I was in no position to be choosy. Until more of my paintings sold at the antique store downtown,

I was at the mercy of luck, McKenzie's generosity, and my quickly dwindling savings account.

But I was still determined to add something of mine—only mine—to make it feel a little more like me. To remind myself to keep my head above water and stay focused, my own special good luck charm in this new place that still felt like uncharted waters. To remind myself no matter how bad the nightmares got, I wouldn't deal with them the same way Mom did.

So I secured the clasp of the necklace around my neck with a nod, and glanced at myself in the mirror.

McKenzie stood behind me, and her bright blue eyes caught on the necklace in my reflection. "Oh my God, where did you get that?"

"My dad," I said. "He sent it for my birthday. And honestly, I'm just as impressed as you are," I breathed out, twirling the peculiar pendant hanging perfectly past the groove of my collarbone. "He usually just gets me something like paint supplies or some weird car accessory. You know, typical dad gifts. Something like this was...unexpected."

My stomach knotted with a pang of guilt as I thought of him. I'd promised him I wouldn't make him worry. That I'd stay out of trouble, and that especially meant staying away from alcohol.

But I'd already failed. Just two weeks ago at a dorm party, I drank. I drank far more than I should have.

I wanted to see if it would really work—if it really would stop the nightmares like Mom said, or if she'd just been using it as an excuse.

Turns out she was right.

But I refused to let my dad think I was following in Mom's footsteps.

The pendant caught the light as I shifted, dazzling blue and white like sunlight on water. Secured on a silver chain with simple silver prongs, it was almost reminiscent of a seashell. But it wasn't a shell, or a jewel, or even a stone. It was unlike anything I had ever seen before, and yet looked somehow natural, despite its ethereal beauty. It shone like glass, through a thin pearly glaze, shimmering with an array of colors anywhere from an icy blue to hints of green to white silver.

I couldn't shake the strange sense of Deja Vu I felt while looking at my reflection wearing it, as if the weight of it around my neck felt all too familiar.

McKenzie nudged me with her elbow. "Well, looks like he really upped his game this year. It's gorgeous! Maybe next time let him know when it's *my* birthday."

I chuckled weakly. McKenzie's energy could sometimes be enough to power a rocket launch, which made me thankful for the large dorms on the East Wing of ICA, with small separate bedrooms on either side and a tiny, shared kitchenette in the middle.

McKenzie flashed a toothy grin as she tugged at my arm and held up her treasured vintage Polaroid camera. She carried the thing around everywhere and took every opportunity she could to add an instant-print photo to her clothespin collection hanging from string lights over her headboard.

"Let's get a pic while our hair and makeup still look good," she chimed. "Once we're out on the yacht, the wind will probably ruin it."

"Yacht?" My voice rose and my throat went dry. "You said the party was on the beach."

"Well, it *is* on the beach," she cooed. "It's just...further out."

"What is that supposed to mean?" I folded my arms, disappointed in myself for even letting her talk me into another party after last time.

McKenzie bounced throughout the space between rummaging for her keys and touching up her makeup. "Well, Ty convinced his parents to let him use their yacht for the Halloween party. I know you hate the ocean, but we won't technically even be touching the water. It's not like we're going swimming."

"Right," I huffed, trying to soften my sarcasm as a flash of my last nightmare darkened my thoughts. "Not touching the water, just completely surrounded by it. With no escape."

"Please don't bail. Pleeeeease. This will be the last party I ever drag you to. I promise," McKenzie squealed.

I knew that wasn't true. Deep down, McKenzie had a heart of gold, but it ran entirely off emotions.

"You said that last time," I reminded her, tucking in my chin. "I know you're just trying to help me find my place here, but you have to admit, most of the time it backfires."

"I know. I know. I know." The words rushed from her ruby lips. "But tonight will be different. It's a costume party on a fancy yacht, not just some random dorm party. Totally legit."

I stared at McKenzie in silence for a long minute before speaking. Then my focus shifted to the space between my feet.

"It's not the parties. It's not even the yacht, really. It's just that..." I closed my eyes and took a deep breath. "I just can't risk drinking again tonight. Not even one drink, okay? I don't want to do that again. I don't want to have to be carried back to my dorm because I can't stand up straight. Maybe that makes me a buzzkill, but...I just can't."

"Oh." McKenzie set down her tube of lipstick. "Well, yeah, okay. I totally get that. Do you think it'd be better if you just...didn't go?"

The thought triggered me.

I *didn't* want to go. I didn't want to get on a yacht and be surrounded by the very thing that was the source of my nightmares.

But if I didn't go, what did that mean? That I was truly just as hopeless as my mom? That I couldn't face my fears, so I just ran from them like she did?

I could be stronger than Mom. I *was* stronger than Mom.

"No. I'm already dressed. I'm not staying here." I said, more to myself than to her. "I'm going."

"Yay!" McKenzie clapped her manicured hands together as fast as a hummingbird flapping its wings. "I owe you a cinnamon chai latte from Sea Dogs for this! You won't regret it, you'll see."

I shook my head, the reality of what I'd just agreed to setting in—a night on the ocean, surrounded by people I didn't know or care to know.

I hoped if anything, it might give me some spark of inspiration for the fall semester student art showcase. Because the blank canvas in my room was a reminder that my creativity had stalled out since moving to this coastal town that seemed to bring out my deepest fears.

I was still struggling to make it all mean something. And I didn't know if I could paint something again that had quite the same impact as the painting under my bed that brought me here.

I reached for my necklace and clutched the pendant.

"So what are we waiting for? Let's go," I said. "You said it yourself. Tonight will be different." I held onto the words, determined that I would make them reality. It didn't help that I couldn't stop thinking of my last nightmare and I'd be tempted to do almost anything to forget it.

But I wouldn't.

Because I swore I wouldn't get drunk again just because I was terrified of dreaming about drowning in the sea.

KATRINA

Tonight will be different.

I repeated the thought to myself as we slid into McKenzie's convertible.

We headed straight for the harbor, only a few blocks from the far side of the campus, where most of my art classes were held, opposite our dorms beside Matanzas Bay. Crossing the campus meant a breathtaking tour past towering Spanish rooftops and the elegant colonial statues nestled throughout the cobblestone pathways. Manicured palms lined the walkways that twisted through the grounds, swaying with the breeze from the bay. The older authentic buildings echoed their history of a golden age of exploration, and the newer structures were built to match. It was hard to deny the romantic feel of the old castle-like buildings, especially when the sun lit their colors on fire in the golden evening hours.

I stared at the bay, which flowed along the border of St. Constantine, and its neighboring, more renown city of St. Augustine, separating both towns from the Atlantic beaches. My watercolor eyes couldn't help but drink in the last bit of golden sunlight dancing across the indigo ripples as the anchored boats bobbed up and down. Gulls perched along the stone wall that lined the water, mocking me with their calls before taking flight just to soar back to the top of the bridge over the bay.

Just beyond that bridge was the vast ocean that I'd spent every moment avoiding since I arrived here. Nothing terrified and captivated me more.

I gazed up at the arched sign above us as we walked onto the docks. *Gull Marina*, it read in pink faded letters, once red before the Florida sun had sapped them of their vibrance.

Here we met Ty, a playboy sophomore and McKenzie's latest situationship. He winked at her from across the docks as he ushered some friends onto his family's luxury cruiser.

As we neared the water, my pulse sped up and my chest tightened, suffocating me with each hesitant step toward the yacht. When I made the mistake of glancing down at the roiling water on either side of the docks, a knot formed in my stomach, a sickness creeping upward, and I did my best to swallow it down. I took a deep breath as we boarded, but it felt like breathing through a snorkel.

With trembling steps, I was careful not to lose my balance as we crossed the gangplank onto the boat. I was glad that I chose to wear my sneakers, instead of the white pumps McKenzie had insisted on. My palms were sweating from my nerves, and the fact that it was eighty-three degrees on October 31st wasn't helping.

The yacht was impressive, even being one of the more compact vessels, the open deck on the back of the boat could easily hold an entire party. A straight stairway along the side of the ship led from just behind the bow of the boat to a higher deck up top. The inside cabin boasted a lounge area, where a dozen or so unfamiliar faces sat, drinks in hand, laughing and commenting on each other's costumes. Music boomed with MJ's Thriller first up on the playlist.

McKenzie got invited to all sorts of things like this. She knew everyone and everyone knew her. But I felt like a square peg in a round hole in these places. I had made a few acquaintances at Isabel, but so far, we had toured the entire length of the boat without seeing another face I recognized.

As the yacht left port, the faintest remnant of orange glow faded behind the blue horizon. When the salty air filled my lungs as we began moving out to sea, my nerves welled up in my chest. My heart fluttered as the small ship bobbed up and down in the wake, picking up speed. I tried not to think about the fact that there was nothing but vast ocean surrounding us with nowhere to go but down.

It was just a dream, Katrina.

I fought back my fear. But no amount of inner pep-talk could banish the clarity of the nightmares that had held my thoughts captive lately. As I stared down at the black water it all came back to life in my head.

A mammoth wave curled over me, sucking me under as if I was no more than a piece of seaweed. Water collapsed down on my chest like a crushing boulder. It was all a blur of blue, crystals of foaming bubbles swirling in a frenzy around me. I tried to swim back up, kicking furiously, but I was no match for the current. The surface glimmered tauntingly above me, ever out of reach. The sound of my own racing heartbeat thundered in my head. My searing lungs felt like they would explode, but I knew if I tried to draw a breath it would be my last.

Yet I could no longer resist the burning need in my body to breathe. The urge to inhale was a raging fire consuming me from the inside, and at last, it won. Opening my mouth to gasp for air that wasn't there, I braced for the sting of salt water that would rush to fill my lungs...

"You okay?" McKenzie's voice snapped me back to reality. She must have noticed my white-knuckle grip on the railing of the hull where we sat looking at the water trailing along the side of the boat.

"Yeah. I'm fine." I nodded, but my shaky voice betrayed me. I didn't expect to react this way, but old fears were resurrecting that I had forgotten were so strong.

"Ty's been boating since he was a kid." She tried to reassure me. "He's got this. Nothing is gonna happen...except a good time." She patted my hand playfully, batting her eyelashes.

I nodded unconvincingly. I tried to enjoy myself, but none of this felt like me—the skimpy costume, the booze, the crowd. I was just a nobody from Ozark, Arkansas suddenly trying to blend in with elite art students whose allowances probably rivaled my dad's yearly income.

I redirected my thoughts to the whole reason I was here—my full-ride scholarship and a chance to focus on my art and leave the baggage behind. To leave Mom behind. Yet somehow, I kept ending up in places that reminded of everything I was trying to escape from.

Just a moment later, McKenzie saw someone else she knew and waved her pom-poms at them from across the boat, springing up to head over in their direction.

I tried to focus on the beauty of the water instead of my fear of what it could do to me. As I watched the water rolling beneath the boat, its unstoppable nature captivated me. Gold and neon blue lights from the ship danced in the ripples as the boat glided smoothly. For whatever inexplicable reason, for just a moment, I felt more intrigued than afraid.

"Who's ready for Boozing for Apples?" Ty's voice shattered my calm. He stood at the helm, dressed like a gladiator, throwing up his hands like some kind of Roman Caesar demanding cheers from his subjects. I couldn't help but roll my eyes. That seemed like a horrible game to play on a moving vessel at sea.

The guests cheered and scurried to participate. McKenzie returned and sat down beside me just in time as everyone began the game, but her interest was clearly divided. The thought that she was only staying with me out of pity made guilt wash over me like the sea spray misting up from the side of the boat.

For a second, I missed home. Though Arkansas held nothing for me and reeked of stale friendships, small-town gossip, and painful memories, in that strange moment I missed it. I missed the cool Octobers, I missed the orange and red leaves peppering the mountains as the grip of autumn strengthened, and I missed Dad's store-bought chocolate cake every year on my birthday.

But breaking cycles meant leaving the familiar behind. And this all felt anything but familiar.

While the partygoers carried on, chomping their teeth at apples floating in a bowl full of spiked cider that was sloshing over the sides with the boat's movement, a pretty girl with cat-eyes and a perfect sleek ponytail came by and gestured to the crowd. "Ty says the island is just a few minutes out. We should be there soon."

McKenzie glared at the girl as she disappeared into the crowd, and I shot a panicked look at her. "What is she talking about? What island?"

McKenzie pulled her bottom lip between her teeth and squinted, her shoulders shifting away from me.

"McKenzie! What is going on?" My voice cracked.

"I—I didn't know," she stammered. "I mean...earlier I heard Ty say something about making a bonfire for a few hours and hunting for ghosts...but I didn't think he was serious—or at least, I thought he meant when we got back—I swear Katrina, I didn't know." Her whole body tensed and her eyes narrowed again. "But apparently that girl did."

I sucked down a breath deep into my chest to keep calm. "So what does this mean then? What island is he taking us to?"

McKenzie's glower became something unreadable, and I wasn't sure if she understood the severity of the fear all this stirred up within me. "Well, the thing is, Constantine has some urban legend about a tiny little haunted island off the coast." Her face softened and her voice lifted again, as if she'd just made the problem go away with that explanation. I crossed my arms, and she went on. "But it's just an island. There are seriously so many ghost stories and creepy legends here. You know that's what this area is known for, right?"

"I mean, yeah, I know they do ghost tours through the old town, but this...." my voice trailed off as I chewed my lip in distress.

"This isn't any different. And I guess Ty thought it would be cool to go check it out and spend part of the night there. Ya know, make a bonfire and look for spooky shit. I mean, it's Halloween, after all!"

"McKenzie, this is not what I agreed to." I groaned.

"I know, I know. And I'm sorry." She dipped her head, and then raised it with that signature beaming smile back on her face. "But don't worry. I promise, it's going to be fine!" Her ponytail bounced as she shrugged dramatically. "I'm pretty sure no one has actually seen a ghost there or anything. It's all just scary stories."

"Is that supposed to make me feel better?" I muttered. "You know I don't like the water, ghosts or not."

"Well, maybe you can stay on the boat. And I'll go out there just for a little while, but I'll come right back so you won't be alone." I wanted to believe she meant it. She was even giving me puppy dog eyes. But I could tell by the nearly empty solo cup in her hand that she was already a little tipsy, so I tried not to take anything she said too seriously.

And now I was powerless to do anything but regret my choice to come here. I inhaled slowly, bracing myself to accept my fate and survive the night.

With another wave from some obscure figure across the deck, McKenzie's attention drifted away. She told me she'd be back again in a minute and stood up to scurry over to another group of people.

I stayed in my spot on the seats along the railing and glanced back around to stare out at the dark horizon, wondering what awaited at the island.

I blinked when I noticed something looming on the surface. The more I strained to see it, the more I could make out the silhouette of a massive ship with sails, drifting in the shadows of the distant horizon, with not a single light to illuminate its path. Looking back over my shoulder, I checked to see if anyone else saw it, but everyone was too immersed in the party to notice.

When I turned around, the shadow ship was gone.

Land Ho

3

KATRINA

"Land ho, ladies and gents!" Ty shouted, a careless edge in his voice.

I watched him from my seat as he maneuvered the wheel at the helm, clearly intoxicated. He had gotten us this far on the water without a problem, but as he inched the boat closer to the island, I started to feel uneasy. It was no small number of beers I had watched him slam down since before we had left the marina.

The crowd on deck became livelier, voices and spirits lifting as they turned their attention to the dark mass ahead. Illuminated only by the boat's single headlight, the little island stood as creepy as ever, as if levitating in the fog on the ocean's surface. As everyone excitedly rushed to the edge of the boat to see their destination, the boat rocked as it struck something solid underneath. I grabbed the railing to keep my balance, looking around for McKenzie to no avail.

The yacht's groans vibrated through my bones as the underside grated against the sand. I gripped tighter, trying not to panic as the ship grew silent.

"Shit. We hit a sandbar!" Ty called out to everyone.

Close to where I thought I'd seen the shadow ship, the visible edge of the island skirted just a few meters away. Thankfully, the lights from the mainland back in Constantine were still visible behind us, reminding me that we hadn't entirely disappeared into a void. But still, the lights were tiny dots barely shining in the distance, and they didn't change the reality that we were much farther out than I thought we would go. And now we were stuck.

I stood up to get a better view as the boat chatter resumed with a new kind of tension in the air. McKenzie came bounding down the steps from the top deck and hurried over to me. How she managed to keep her balance while running in her high heels on a tilted boat deck was something I never figured out.

"Are you okay?" She exclaimed.

"Yes," I said, still holding the railing. "But just so you know this is not making things better." I tried to sound playful, but I certainly wasn't kidding.

"I'm sure Ty will get us out. I'll go see what the plan is." McKenzie scurried away before I could even begin to think of a response.

I stood, braced against the railing, watching the water rippling below against the now stationary boat. A couple of frat boys appeared at my side, pushing each other with incredible energy, as though they were trying to urge each other toward me.

"Hey, gorgeous." One of them cleared his throat as though holding back a laugh, leaning onto the railing next to me. "Looks like our captain's screwed us, huh?" He snickered as the string lights along the boat caught the sheen of his slicked-back copper hair. He wore an F1 driver suit, with a helmet tucked under his arm. His friend's face was obscured by smudged makeup drawn to look like a skull, but it wasn't enough to hide his smug expression.

When I simply nodded and half-smiled in reply, Race Car inched himself closer. I let go of the railing and closed my arms around myself.

"Hey, I remember you from that party a couple weeks back. We practically had to carry you to your dorm you were so trashed."

I didn't remember them. I only remembered McKenzie telling me I needed help making it to the door and up the stairwell back to our dorm. Was it really these two jackasses who did the honors? I recoiled, embarrassed.

"Well, don't worry, I won't be needing any help getting off this boat tonight. I can't believe I even got on in the first place." I couldn't tell if the twisting in my gut was from watching the water too long or the two obnoxious goons flanking my sides.

Skeleton boy now stood on my left side and took a puff of his vape before blowing it in my face.

"Whatever's out there, babe, I promise it's not as interesting as what's on this boat." He grinned in a way that mismatched his teeth's alignment to the white skull lines around his jaw.

I kept my gaze fixed on the sea, but they persisted.

"So then, if you didn't want to party, why'd you come?" Skull Face leaned in.

"I—well, I thought maybe a night at sea might give me some painting inspiration." I didn't owe him an answer, but I didn't know what else to say.

"Painting," he repeated flatly. "That's cool, I guess."

"Well, we are at an art school," I added, swallowing down a lump of self-doubt. I was holding onto the railing again, twisting the skin of my palm against it nervously like throttling a motorcycle. I didn't like to talk. I didn't *want* to talk.

"Yeah, but who's thinking about that at a Halloween party? It's like bringing homework on a vacation." Race Car laughed, his voice rising and falling.

A slew of cursing came from the direction of the helm, catching his attention. "Well, uh...see you around. Guess we'll go start the bonfire since we clearly aren't going anywhere soon."

"Guess so," Skull Face nodded. "Looks like we're stuck here till the tide rises, watercolor girl."

I shook my head. The yacht engine sputtered uselessly in the background. We were really weren't leaving.

Until the tide rises.

Interestingly, the notion of being run aground on a haunted island seemed to stir up more excitement than concern as the others leaped and crawled over the side of the yacht into the ankle-deep water below, splashing their way to shore where a small fire was already sparking.

I, however, was not at all enticed by the idea of fumbling through the surf, no matter how shallow. Looking down over the boat's edge, my mind whipped up memories of the nightmare, and there was nothing I couldn't do to convince myself to follow everyone overboard. I told McKenzie I was staying put when she came to try to persuade me otherwise.

I watched her follow the crowd off the boat and onto the island. Some part of me felt bad for being such a drag, but it didn't seem to dampen her spirit in the slightest.

I wished she understood. I didn't want to be afraid. I didn't want to feel out of place.

But I did.

Distant cheers and laughs arose from the shore as the bonfire bloomed. Someone turned on a radio.

As I sat there on the empty yacht, I ran through ideas for my showcase piece.

Should I use regular watercolor paper? Or maybe go a little less traditional and prime a canvas for watercolor? It all depended on what I would create...

I studied my surroundings for inspiration. I looked at the glowing cinders rising into the night sky from the fire, the glitter, and colors of the costumes, the midnight canvas of the sea and sky that blended into one dark endless void.

But nothing felt quite right.

I glanced at my phone to check the time – a quarter past ten, and an earlier missed text from Dad.

-Happy Halloween, Trina. Te amo.

He almost always told me he loved me in Spanish. Even after living in Arkansas for over twenty years, a slight remnant of his Cuban accent still decorated his words when he spoke. Halloween was our favorite holiday, and I knew he was probably home alone reminiscing about carving pumpkins together.

My thumb hovered over the keyboard as I went to reply. I wanted to tell him I loved him, too, and to thank him for the necklace, and to tell him I decided to enter the showcase after all.

But I'd typed out two words before realizing I had no cell service. And I still hadn't spoken to him since my birthday.

I laid my head back on the railing, pulling the halo headband off my head. As the stars twinkled overhead, the sound of the waves lapping at the bottom of the boat was drowned out by the noise from the island beach, which reverberated with loud music, talking, and laughter.

By now the tide had crept up a bit and some of the partygoers were having quite the time wading around in the now shin-deep water and dancing around on the shore. I started to wonder if McKenzie was as concerned with getting stuck out here all night as I was. I glanced over the edge of the boat. The sand bar was completely underwater now, and it didn't look like it would be much longer before the boat would be lifted free.

But that also meant a lot deeper water to wade through. The window for getting back to the boat safely would be slim...and soon.

My stomach sank at the realization that with no cell reception, I would have to go find McKenzie if I wanted any hope of getting everyone back safely before the tide became too high.

I placed my phone on the seat next to my halo and removed my shoes before hoisting myself onto the edge of the boat. I made my way down the ladder, grimacing as I forced myself to dip my toes into the water.

Come on, Katrina. You can do this.

I didn't grow up near the beach. In fact, I never even visited it as a child. I would have happily lived my whole life without ever going near it—but then the scholarship happened, and fate had other plans. It didn't care that the ocean scared me, that I cowered at the thought of its power and strength. There was no telling what secrets lie within its trenches. And I shuddered at that.

The thought of getting back to dry land was all the encouragement I needed to take one step further down and let myself slide feet first into the water. It was higher than it had been an hour earlier, but not so much that I still couldn't wade through it. In that moment I was thankful for my super short angel dress, as its hem was well above the water line. A knot formed in my chest as I entered the water with trembling hands, but as I stepped forward, the fear eased a bit.

Something about the water against my skin, as foreign and unnerving as it was, stilled my breathing as I realized it wasn't pulling me under. It was nothing like the sea in my dreams. That version was brutal and relentless, using all its force against me. But this placid glass water was gentle, encasing my frame delicately as it lapped up lazily along my legs. For a moment, it wasn't so bad. But then I started moving forward into a black abyss into which I could not see below.

And then I wanted to scream.

Gritting my teeth, I trudged through the water, trying not to think about what I might be stepping on as my bare feet scraped the sand, I finally made it to the island's edge. With a long sigh of relief, I marched forward towards the crowd on the beach, the bonfire's glow flickering off their dancing bodies. I could see McKenzie's bright cheerleading dress even from there, and I dashed toward her.

I didn't see anyone "ghost hunting." I figured they had either forgotten about it or chickened out, as the rest of the tiny island was quite dark and foreboding.

"Aww yay! You came! Couldn't stay away from where the fun is, could ya?" Her words came out slurred.

"No, I came to check on you." I responded a touch more sharply than I had intended. "And also to make sure Ty has a plan for going back to the boat. The tide is rising pretty fast. Everyone needs to be ready."

"Oh, well yeah, I'm sure he knows. Stop worrying, Katrina. Just have fun!" She spoke, trying to dance, stumbling in the sand, while not even looking my way. And that's when it all felt futile.

It occurred to me that I might be stuck here, completely at their mercy for returning. This was, without a doubt, the last party I would ever let McKenzie talk me into.

I turned away, determined to get back to the boat before the rising water made it impossible. As I stepped back into the water, it felt much deeper than it had been just a moment ago. The water curled around my hips like a warning signal that our time was running short. I closed my eyes again, trying not to look at the dark water below. But this time, my toes didn't touch the bottom with my next step forward.

The sudden drop off the sandbar sent me stumbling, and the stupid wings on my costume acted as sails in the current that sucked me out further into the sea and made it awkward to swim. I fought the current, but quickly found it was no use.

I tumbled amongst the torrent, saltwater splashing around me. Panic welled up in me as I remembered the dream from the night before. Had it been a warning for this very moment? Was I about to drown out here while no one even noticed?

I opened my mouth to cry for help, but no sooner had my lips parted than the seawater rushed over my head with a quick lap of a wave, stinging my eyes and forcing my scream back down. And I could've sworn I heard the pulse of drum pound in my ears and rattle my bones.

I was fully under, my soaked wings now heavy and weighing me down. I wasn't the best swimmer, as I'd never had many opportunities to practice, so the drenched feathers at my back only added to the difficulty of trying to fight against the rip current. My arms grew tired as I fought, but I could tell I wasn't getting any closer to the surface. If anything, the hidden torrent was washing me farther and farther out. My heart beat so fast it felt as though it could've been heard all the way to the ocean floor.

Terror pulled me under as fast as the current. Just as I thought I'd never make it back up above the water, I felt something lift me from the bottom. Arms, strong and sturdy, raised me up back to the surface, and somehow we were right back at the island's edge. In the dark I couldn't see my rescuer, but they lifted me gently to the sandy shore of the island, on a side far enough away from the party that I could catch my breath in peace. After I coughed up the seawater caught in my throat and rubbed my eyes to soothe the salty sting, I glanced around, looking towards the partygoers, to find whoever it was who had brought me here, but I didn't see a soul who seemed close enough to have managed such a feat.

But I knew without a doubt someone saved me. And whoever it was had vanished.

Once I caught my breath, I stood, tearing the heavy, dripping angel wings from my back and tucking them under my arm. They had almost been the death of me, and I certainly didn't plan on wearing them on the way back.

I began to make my way toward the party in the distance, but then I decided I'd rather not get caught up in all that again. I needed a moment to come back to myself, and going back to the yacht alone was not an option after what had just happened. In search of a place away from the chaos, I wandered away from the bonfire and walked along the edge of the shore.

The island wasn't very big, likely too small to appear on any maps. It could probably have been crossed on foot in no more than five minutes if you could manage to get through the thicket of trees condensed in the center.

I was thankful for those trees as I walked around the corner, hidden by wild unkempt palms and wide-leafed brush that acted as a barrier to the chaos behind me. I plopped down into the sand, exhaustion settling into my bones. With the light of the fire blocked by the trees and the moon hidden in the sky, it was quite dark there in my little corner of the island. But I didn't care.

I leaned my head back with a deep breath and looked up at the stars nestled in the black heavens stretching as far as the sea. Out here they looked brighter than I'd ever seen, and they appeared clustered together, feathered by wisps of starlight. For nearly the first time since I'd come to Isabel, I felt like myself as I sat there alone beneath the night sky.

Right before an unfamiliar voice made me jump.

(BONUS CHAPTER)

MILO'S POV

I knew I shouldn't talk to her. It was best that we kept far away from the living. Especially after what happened just a handful of decades ago. I swore that night I would never show myself to anyone with a heartbeat ever again.

But no one with a heartbeat ever came here. And if they did, they certainly didn't sit alone at the island's edge like this girl was doing. If only she knew what was in those waters. If only she knew what happened to the last pretty girl to venture into our depths. And by the looks of her wet hair and soaked clothing, she'd already been close to finding out.

She hadn't even noticed me. Even from here I could see the emptiness in her eyes as she sat lost in thought. An easy target if she wasn't careful. And the people who'd come here with her wouldn't be able to help her if the worst happened—if the captain saw her and got another stupid idea in his twisted head. My mind knew better, but my heart saw an opportunity to clear my conscience. If I could keep this girl safe, maybe it would undo the guilt I carried for the ones I couldn't, and for the ones I should've tried harder to save.

After all, I was here, too, staring at the same stars. This was as close to an escape as I could get. Perhaps it was the same for her.

I knew I shouldn't talk to her. But as I walked along the shore she called to me, like the promise of redemption I'd been chasing for centuries. So against my better judgement, I sat next to her, waiting for her to realize I was there. It would be fine. I would talk to her until I knew she was safe to leave, and then I'd never see her again. Whatever happened might at least distract me from the pangs of hunger and thirst that never eased, or the phantom sensation of saltwater burning in my lungs.

I knew I shouldn't talk to her. But I couldn't help myself. I was already damned anyway.

KATRINA

"**A**re you looking for constellations?"

I whipped my head around to see a guy, close to my age, maybe a junior or senior, sitting in the sand a few feet from me. I had no clue how I didn't notice him sitting there before.

"Not really…Just catching my breath," I replied, squinting to see him in the shadows before looking back up at the sky. It was difficult to see his features clearly, but I could at least make out his light brown hair that was just sun-kissed enough to appear golden. "But I'll admit, I've never seen stars this clearly before."

"Then you need to get out on the sea more. No better way to stargaze," he chuckled.

I couldn't help but notice his accent, which held a timelessness about it, not quite American, but not quite English, and felt like soft satin against my ears.

"No thanks." I shook my head and tilted my chin back toward the crowd. "I can't even believe they talked me into this."

"It's not wise to come here." He hesitated for a breath. "The tides here are…dangerous."

The night sea breeze sent a small chill over my bare arms and legs, and my mini dress did little to offer much warmth. I brought my knees up to my chest.

"You're telling me." I mumbled. For a moment I thought perhaps he'd been the one who rescued me from the water. But his clothes were still perfectly dry.

"Nice costume," I said, noting his pirate attire. "Though you could really pull it off with a peg leg or an eye patch."

"Well fortunately I've never had need of either," he laughed, and the sound of it was pleasant. "And what are you?" he asked.

"I was supposed to be an angel." I gestured at my destroyed pair of wings and my soaked dress.

"Hmm," he purred. "This is certainly no place for angels."

My eyes narrowed at him with a flick of my head, and before I could respond, he was on his feet. "You look cold."

I was shivering.

He strode over, his boots padding against the sand, and offered me a blanket that he produced from seemingly nowhere.

"Where did that come from?" I took the blanket from him and quickly wrapped it around my bare shoulders.

"I brought it with me from the ship. It can get cold out here on the water."

"Well, at least someone came prepared. Why aren't you over there with the others?"

He glanced over toward the party behind the trees and flashed me a smirk that made me blush. "They're not really my crew," he said. "I just needed to get away for a bit, find some peace."

"Same," I sighed. "I'm glad someone else gets it. And thanks for the blanket."

"Of course."

There was another minute of silence between us as he sat back down beside me, propping an elbow on his knee. I felt a strange comfort with him, and I didn't even know him.

"What's your name?" he asked lowly, not taking his eyes off the horizon.

"I'm Katrina."

"Lovely to meet a fair lass like you, Katrina."

"*Fair lass*?" I laughed "You are *really* committed to your character, Will Turner."

"My name is not Will Turner," he said smugly, looking out at the ocean.

"Sorry, did you prefer Jack Sparrow?" I giggled, amused.

He sighed and shook his head, and his chuckle rumbled low. "Well, excuse my attempts at flattery. You did say you were an angel after all."

I rolled my eyes playfully. I certainly didn't mind flirting with him. A few more notes of laughter escaped us both until I brought the conversation back.

"So, what is your name then?" I asked.

"Milo." His voice sent a wave of warmth through me that made me nuzzle deeper into the blanket.

"Milo," I repeated under my breath. "Nice to meet you."

He looked at me, as if he was going to say something. But then he hesitated, and I followed the way his gaze dropped from my face to my neck, where he suddenly glanced away and tossed a broken piece of seashell into the waves at our feet.

A strange silence stretched between us after that, until I was finally the one to break it.

"Back home I used to sit outside on summer nights to watch the fireflies near the woods behind our house." I leaned back onto my hands, shifting the blanket to cover my legs, and kept my gaze fixed on the sky. "That's what the stars remind me of."

Even with the echoes of the party music behind us, the only sound that caught my attention was the gentle gurgle of waves rolling at my feet. And that smooth, husky voice peppered with the sea air.

"Can you locate the North Star?" he asked.

Locate.

Something about that sentence—about the way he spoke altogether—sounded poetic, as if he carefully weighed his words before speaking.

"I honestly have no idea," I laughed. "Sorry."

"Don't apologize." He inched closer, pointing into the sky. "Right there to the left a bit—That's it."

I nodded as my eyes locked onto the bright dot in the sky.

"Impressive," I said. "So how does it work?"

"You use the angle between the skyline to the north and the star, and that will tell you the ship's position. Any good sailor can find it." He glanced down and pulled up his sleeve, revealing a navigational North Star tattooed down half the length of his muscular forearm. "And the best of us carry it with us."

"You must spend a lot of time out on the water." I lingered on the design before looking back up at him long enough to really notice the small scar above his left eyebrow, a unique mark on a handsome face I found myself wanting to admire longer.

"You could say that," he said lowly, that intense focus slowly sliding back down to my neck. I touched a finger to the pendant on my necklace protectively, and he snapped his gaze away once more.

I swallowed. "Why do you keep—"

The sound of McKenzie screaming my name and the thud of footsteps in the wet sand cut me short. Glancing up, I saw her barreling towards me. Without so much as a glance at Milo, she grabbed my hand and yanked me up.

"C'mon, we gotta get back to the boat before the tide gets too high!" she said.

"That's what I was trying to tell you," I snapped.

Without response, she pulled me back in the direction of the party. I turned around to make sure Milo was coming, too, but when I looked over my shoulder, he was gone. I clutched the blanket he had given me and inwardly hoped I would see him again back on the yacht.

The rising waves were lurching closer to the shore, snuffing out the last bit of dying embers from the bonfire. It was time to move, or we would be navigating some dangerously deep water back to the boat.

The icy water was nearly to my thighs now, and I held onto McKenzie's hand tightly from behind as she led the way forward, but her stumbling made me anxious. As I stared down into the water, I was grateful for the light on the front of the yacht that illuminated the now fully submerged sandbar.

Cheers and applause erupted as the last person climbed up the ladder back onto the boat. As we waited for a little while longer to allow the tide to peak, McKenzie whipped out her Polaroid from her bag.

"You might not think so now, but you'll want to remember this night, Katrina!" She laughed loudly. "Smile!"

I flashed her a forced grin as she snapped the photo. The camera spat out the film with its iconic whirring sound to reveal the still-developing image of my smiling headshot against the eerie dark sea, my necklace a clear pop of blue in the overexposed picture.

McKenzie's fingers had barely pulled it from the printing slot, when a powerful burst of wind tore the photo from her grasp and whipped it out to sea. My gaze followed the little white rectangle as the gust carried it back toward the island. I shuddered, unsettled at the thought that some small part of me was now forever bound to the ocean's mercy.

"Oh well, it should've been a selfie anyway," she shrugged, turning the lens on herself and tugging me closer into the frame.

I fake-smiled again, my mind completely adrift as the yacht's engine fired up. I wondered where Milo was and looked around, hoping to catch a glimpse of him.

"Hey, McKenzie." I touched her shoulder to get her attention as she smiled at her newly printed selfie. She knew everyone. She'd know how to find him.

She glanced up at me, mascara smudged beneath her eyes from a mixture of sweat and sea, but her aquamarine eyes still sparkled with vibrance as I asked her. "Do you know a guy here named Milo? Pirate costume?"

She bit her lip and scanned the crowd, tapping a finger to her chin. "Hmm, doesn't sound familiar. As far as I know, there's no one at ICA named Milo."

Anchors Aweigh

5

KATRINA

"He was right there with me," I said. "When you came to get me. Didn't you see him?"

McKenzie cocked her head and scoffed, but then her grin disappeared. "Wait, you're serious?" she said. "Katrina, there was no one there."

"Then...then you just weren't paying attention," I muttered. "He was there. I talked to him. We have to go back for him." I clambered to my feet and pushed through the crowd, desperate to make sure he'd made it back safely with the rest of us.

"Wait!" I cried over the engine's gurgling rumble. "We're missing someone!"

The crowd quieted down and exchanged quick glances, muttering softly.

I could feel Ty's glare on me. "Everyone here?" he snapped at the crowd before turning back to the wheel. "Good. Let's go."

"No! We left someone on the island!" I rushed to the helm, McKenzie in tow, calling my name as I denied her a further explanation. She stared at me, her expression a mix of disbelief and concern.

She trailed me up the deck as I ran to Ty, pushing past the group surrounding him. "Someone is missing. I'm sure of it," I huffed out at a glassy-eyed Ty who whirled around with one hand still clasped around the ship's wheel.

Ty's mouth curled into a scowl as he tossed me a life vest. "Well then go get them. But your ass better hurry."

"Ty—" McKenzie started, placing a hand on his bicep.

"Look, I'll try to keep the boat from drifting out further, but you're on your own out there. If you don't get back fast enough it'll be two of you left behind." He pulled a flashlight from a compartment beneath the wheel and shoved it into my hands. "So be faster than the tide."

"Sorry for the trouble. I'll try," I muttered beneath my breath, dashing for the ladder at the stern. I waded back, half-swimming through the waist-deep water, and this time it almost seemed to guide me gently, weightlessly, as the current pulled me toward the shore. Once my bare feet touched dry sand, I rushed back to where I'd sat with Milo, passing the eerie sight of empty glass bottles and the dying embers of the bonfire, the flashlight illuminating my path.

I called out for Milo, pacing the area where we sat together, watching how far the tide rolled up the shore and knowing my time was short.

There was no one. No sign of him anywhere.

Maybe he did make it. Maybe he was fine back on the yacht, while I was risking my safety for some guy I just met. Either way, I couldn't waste any more time.

Just as I turned around to head back, the sand beneath my feet shifted, and I stumbled. A strange, unsettling breeze blew in from the ocean, a frigid air lingering on my skin.

A faint whistle in the wind grew into a wailing groan of creaking wood and wind. The gentle waves lapping along the island's edge began to grow, attacking the shore, rolling and churning until they peeled back like petals to reveal an opening in the water's surface.

Something unearthly gripped me and held me frozen in place, watching. The water spiraled and sprayed salty mist into the air, catching in the ray of light from my flashlight like fog. Something menacing burst from the water, the sound of wood aching under pressure splitting my ears. The winds blew stronger, chilling my damp hair and ripping feathers from what was left of the wing remnants along my shoulders. Violent gusts bent the trees so strongly I thought they would snap in half.

I was paralyzed by the scene unfolding before me—a ship—a rotting, massive wooden ship was emerging from the ocean right before my eyes, like a whale springing up to the surface.

The faint moonlight gave me just enough clarity to make out the endless layers of barnacles climbing up the hull, coating the long-corroded mermaid carved into the bow. Saltwater gushed down in waterfalls off the edges as the ship righted itself onto the water. The waves died down and the winds steadied, but a ghostly chill still hung in the air.

Worn sails unfurled from the masts, the edges mottled with tears and rips that made them dance in the wind like wraiths. A gruff voice yelled out from within the ship, with an edge like something from another time.

"Hoist the colors and man the sails!"

A tattered flag slowly rose along the mast, equally ravaged by time as the battered sails, and every bit just as haunting. As it peaked at the top, the wind peeled it back to reveal a black flag with a skull and crossbones.

A pirate flag. An actual pirate flag.

On a ship that just surfaced like a dead man from a grave.

More voices called out. They were those of men, but I couldn't make out what they were saying. But I realized they could probably see me.

I turned off the flashlight with trembling fingers and made a break for the island's foliage. From behind a palm tree, I peeked out, desperate to see the ship to confirm what I was seeing was real. To convince myself I wasn't hallucinating.

I wasn't drunk. I wasn't high.

I wasn't Mom.

The ship was there, floating on the water, bathed in moonlight. And now a shadowy figure stood looming at the bow, overlooking it all.

He was brooding and overpowered every other human on the deck, and his stature alone would be enough to send someone running in the other direction. The tails of his blood red captain's coat caught the wind and fluttered back, revealing the pistol strapped to his chest and the sword at his hip.

He could've been my dad's age, and the harsh brow over his steely eyes made him look as though he was enraged with the world and ready to take it out on whoever had the misfortune of speaking to him next. Tilting his black captain's hat from the wind, he looked in my direction.

My blood ran cold when the moonlight hit his face. With the empty eyes of a broken man looking like he'd lost it all—and was furious about it—he stared in my direction. Terror rippled through me as his unnerving expression remained unchanged, and I prayed he didn't see me.

And then the song started, something cold and haunting that crept into my bones. The ship voices rose, together as one, into a monotone, hollow tune comprised of words that made my blood curdle.

"Yo ho, we rise again
Upon this cursed tide.
The siren's woe
Has bound our souls
To sail another night."

As the dreadful shanty ended, I noticed the captain himself hadn't been singing, but instead had been looking right in my direction the whole time. His stare pierced through the trees as my heart pounded in my chest. His deathly gaze only broke when a voice below called him to attention.

"Starboard side is clear, Cap'n, and anchors aweigh! Where we be sailing tonight?" Through the clink of metal and chains, the gruff sailor's question broke through clearly.

"Drop that anchor back down!" The captain ordered, his words pouring out like smoke as he looked back at the shore separating us. "No sailing tonight. Not until we've combed every inch of this island for her."

And that's when I had the sense to turn and run. My fear of the water was far overpowered by the fear of what I'd just seen and heard, and I leapt into the tide without hesitation. My life jacket kept me afloat as I awkwardly flailed through the water back toward the boat.

I was frantic, soaked, and out of breath when I made it to the ladder, and I slipped trying to climb up. McKenzie rushed to help me up, along with some others.

I couldn't look at anyone as all eyes lingered on me in hellish silence. My body shook from the cold seawater and from the horror of what I'd just witnessed as I shuffled to a corner of the boat and plopped down, ignoring the stares.

And I knew if I said a word about what had just happened, they'd think I was crazy.

So I sat there, in shock, staring at the floor of the yacht as I huddled for warmth into the blanket Milo had given me.

"Did—did you find him?" McKenzie asked. A shivering nod was all I could manage. I contemplated telling her, but the world was still spinning. And she wouldn't take it seriously anyway. Not right now. Not as she giggled over herself between her genuine looks of concern.

I looked back to see if I could still catch a glimpse of the ship—of any shred of evidence that it'd happened, hoping there was a chance everyone might've seen it from the yacht. But this was the opposite side of the island, and it must've obscured whatever the hell I'd just seen from everyone else.

"Are you okay?" McKenzie asked, some real concern in her voice. "You look like you saw a ghost."

"Well...what would you say if I said I did?" I managed to squeeze out between breaths.

"I'd say I can't believe we wasted all this time because you had to go back for your imaginary friend." Ty sneered as he revved the boat engine. "Anyway, Happy Halloween everybody! Afterparty on the beach when we get back! No ghosts invited this time!"

We jolted forward and a roar of laughter erupted across the deck. To avoid further making a fool of myself, I kept my mouth shut the rest of the night, aching to get back to land and away from that creepy island. And with that frightful captain's gaze still haunting my memory, along with the strange things Milo said, I decided maybe I'd better start believing in ghost stories.

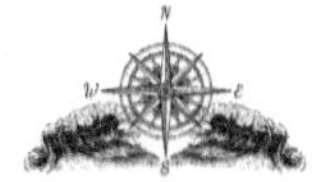

It was sometime after midnight.

My skin was sticky from the night on the sea. Strands of wild hair clung to my arms and neck from the humidity. I was itching from the sand in my dress scraping against my skin. I longed to get back to our dorm, take a shower, and fall asleep in my bed.

I knew McKenzie was in no shape to drive, so I took the keys from her bag and placed myself in the driver's seat. She plopped down into the passenger's seat like a wet noodle and without objection.

My hands still shook as I drove back to campus, but I couldn't get there fast enough. I practically jumped out of the car once we parked and started speedwalking to our dorm building.

We were one of the few inhabitants on the top floor. The privacy couldn't be better, but it also felt a little eerie sometimes, like tonight, when not a single other soul wandered the hallway overlooking the bay across the street. And eerie was the last thing I was in the mood for.

As I unlocked the front door, McKenzie put a hand on my shoulder and whispered, "See? Tonight was different. You didn't end up drunk. It was my turn this time..."

Her voice faded out into a giggle, as she shuffled inside and toppled onto her bed, still fully clad in a cheerleader costume, and within seconds, I heard gentle snoring. I exhaled and kept walking.

I slunk wearily into the hot shower and felt sweet relief as the warm water rinsed away the salt on my skin and the chill of the night. I felt like throwing up, but this time at least I knew it wasn't from drinking.

Slipping into an oversized T-shirt, I crawled into my bed and wrapped myself in the covers.

But I couldn't sleep. There was a churning in my stomach and a whirlwind in my head. I couldn't stop thinking about the pirate ship and its captain and the last thing he said.

Not until we've combed every inch of this island for her.

Who were they looking for?

And worse, I couldn't stop worrying that it was all one big hallucination. It certainly wouldn't be the first in my family, and that foreboding possibility haunted me more than any ghost ship ever could.

I climbed out of bed and tiptoed outside. The cold stone against my bare feet contrasted with the heavy, wet heat that engulfed me as I walked out. Underneath the hall's open archway, I leaned on the twisted iron railing and stared out into the blackness of the bay.

Our dorm building in the East Wing of the campus was so isolated from everything else that it made the sky and sea appear that much darker. A faint glow from the town's lights hung in the air like a phantom fog. I slid down to the floor with my back pressed against the stucco walls, staring out into the void. I half expected the ship would reemerge in front of me again on the bay, and some part of me kept watching just in case, until the distant sound of the water crashing lulled me to sleep.

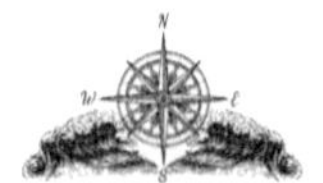

"Did you sleep out here all night?" McKenzie's voice woke me. It was morning.

I sat up, rubbing my eyes that were dry from the salty air.

"Is this about last night?" she asked. "Are you mad at me?"

"No, McKenzie, I'm not mad." I sighed through a yawn, holding my head. "I'm just...freaked out, I guess."

"About last night?" She knelt next to me. "Listen, I'm sorry about all that. I promise I won't ask you to go to any more parties."

"It wasn't just the party. I mean—it was, but not what you think." I pushed my hair back behind my ears and placed my hands in my lap, focusing on a discolored part of the floor. "And if I tell you, it's going to sound absolutely insane."

She leaned in and squinted at me through the thick frames of her glasses. She only wore them in the dorm.

"Well good thing I like insane."

I took a deep breath before word-vomiting up everything that happened to me on the island.

"It was a ship, McKenzie. A whole ship and a crew and everything. It just came up out of the water."

Her eyes grew wide. "You're one hundred percent sure you saw this?"

"No, actually," I stuttered. "I wish I could say I know what I saw...but, my mom saw a lot of weird stuff, too. I...I don't know if any of it was real, or if I'm just going crazy like her." I looked down at my fingertips, reassuring myself they were real. "You're sure I didn't have any drinks or anything?"

When I looked up, McKenzie was watching me intently. She put both hands on my shoulders. "I'm sure," she said, forcing me to meet her gaze. "You absolutely did not drink. And listen to me—you are not going crazy. And you are not your mom. You're Katrina, and you're awesome and brave and hot."

I cracked a tender smile.

"So, you believe me?"

"Well yeah!" She grinned. "Especially on Halloween. Consider yourself lucky. You're the only one of us who got to see anything cool last night." She tilted her head, as if thinking and uttered under her breath with fascination. "But damn, I guess those stories don't come from nowhere..."

"So, what are these stories exactly?" I leaned in, and my words came out faster than I meant for them to. "What the hell happened on that island?"

"Well, everybody knows Constantine is famous for all the spooky sea stuff. They say pirate ghosts haunt the coast or something. And the island is supposed to be especially haunted because some girl mysteriously drowned out there a long time ago, but nobody knows how she got out there or why. So people just started making up stuff, of course. Now there are so many stories around it no one knows what really happened." Her lips pursed as she exaggerated the last two words and stood, pulling me to my feet.

"Well I guess that kind of tracks then." I said flatly, thinking about the pirate captain and his desperation to find "her," whatever that meant. Maybe he was still looking for the poor girl who drowned there. Maybe she was his long-lost lover or something. That always seemed to be the way ghost stories went.

"Thanks, McKenzie." I smiled weakly, glancing around the empty hallway. "But can you please just not tell anyone about this?" I pleaded. "I already feel like enough of a freak around here."

"Got it." She straightened her shoulders and pretended to zip her lips with her fingers. "Your secret's safe with me."

I shrugged with a chuckle as she ushered me back into the dorm. She smacked her lips and placed her glasses on the table. "Now come on, get dressed. I've got a killer headache, and I still owe you that latte."

All at Sea

6

KATRINA

Monday was hell. My nightmares now included pirate ships in addition to drowning, so I was fighting through my lecture in Art History on very little sleep.

I would've given anything to nap that afternoon after classes, but I had a paper due the next day that I had completely forgotten about due to ghost pirates and parties. That meant I'd be working on finishing it for the next few hours.

I carried my laptop and backpack out to the South Lawn, where it wasn't uncommon for students to set themselves up at a picnic table or hammock and hang out or study, even well into the evening hours.

Picking a spot under a tree, I opened the document, staring blankly at the screen. I'd started on it last week, but so far had only managed to get down a paragraph. Five more pages to go. I sighed.

It took everything in me to push away thoughts of haunted coastlines and the feeling that someone was watching me. But I had to get something down, and once I finally started, I found the writing to be a nice distraction.

By the time I was finishing up the last paragraph, dusk had darkened the sky. My mind was spent, and I hadn't even stopped to realize how incredibly hungry I was. After packing up my things, I made my way toward the campus library to print my essay for our old-fashioned professor who demanded hard copies.

But I didn't mind. Queens Library was right across from the Lawn, and as far as I knew, it was open late most nights.

My steps were brisk as I crossed the great cobblestone courtyard at the center of campus and the antique stucco buildings inspired by Spanish architecture. I was eager to get this over with and silence my growling stomach, though I still couldn't shake the feeling of being followed.

As I strolled past the towering palms around the front of the building and entered the arched doors, the last ghostly glimmer of daylight dipped behind the building.

I printed the paper quickly, and then headed for the door, but something caught my eye in a corner of the library—a section of books titled "Constantine History." I wondered if it might contain something about the myths and ghost legends surrounding the town—or even better, the island. Even my rumbling stomach couldn't dampen my curiosity.

I strode to the shelves, nestled away from the main lobby. My eyes scanned the titles, hoping one of them might look promising for island ghost stories.

Glimpses of St. Constantine

Constantine Under Three Flags

Stories of Old Constantine

Castillo de San Romero

The Hidden History of Constantine

St. Constantine Legends

The last one caught my attention. I snatched it up, flipping through the pages in my hands. I saw accounts of the Old Constantine Jail, the Castillo de San Romero, and others, but there was nothing about the island off the coast. I turned to the back of the book where the last page closed with a note:

Constantine is one of the US's oldest cities, and as such there have been various reports of people seeing figures, ghosts of soldiers, pirates, and others. This nearly 500-year-old city has a history of haunting!

And then a sinking feeling weighed on me that maybe I was just spooked and paranoid. Maybe my anxious mind exaggerated everything. Maybe I was just one of the countless people who came here and thought they saw something lurking in the shadows. Maybe I was just being a little ridiculous. What did it matter anyway if I'd seen a ghost?

I needed to stop worrying about coastal ghost lore and focus on the real problems in my life.

"Interesting book?" A velvety voice from behind startled me.

I glance over my shoulder to see a tall, attractive man with raven black hair and piercing blue eyes looming beside me, leaning on a bookshelf. He was half-smirking, brows raised teasingly as though he was eager for my reaction.

He was quite beautiful in a striking kind of way. The icy blue of his eyes complemented his sharp, shadowed jawline, like the color of the sea among white jagged cliffs. I couldn't help but notice the small silver hoop in his ear, and his unique all-black ensemble of a shirt, vest, and jacket with pants half-tucked into black leather boots.

"Not interesting enough," I muttered, sliding the book back into its place on the shelf.

"Oh? What were you looking for?" He asked, his accent smooth in ways I couldn't quite place. Maybe Australian?

"Just browsing..." I said, and then for some reason added "...for ghost stories."

"Ghost stories?" he rumbled softly. "Maybe I can help. I've been here a while, you might say."

"Oh?" I raised my brows, turning my attention back to the bookshelves. "I just started here this semester."

"I can tell," he chuckled.

"What's that supposed to mean?"

"Nothing," he stammered with a tilt of his chin. "It's just that I haven't seen you around before. I'm Bellamy."

"Katrina."

"Pleasure to meet you, Katrina." He said in that charming voice of his. "If you need anything this semester, I'm always around."

I slowly stepped out of the book aisle and Bellamy took up stride beside me. It was only then that I noticed the black serpent tattoo coiling up the side of his neck.

"Okay...thanks. I'll keep that in mind," I said, not sure what he was getting at. "So, are you, like, a foreign exchange student?" I asked.

"Not exactly." He slid his hands into his pockets with a laugh. "My parents are from Europe, and dear old dad brought me here. Guess he thought I needed some sun and sand."

"Must've been quite the move," I said quietly, still looking ahead as we passed through the library doors.

"It certainly was." He paused, brushing his bottom lip with his thumb. "Will I be seeing you again?"

I stopped walking at his brazen question. However, I hated to admit that some part of me wouldn't have minded seeing him again.

"You might," I responded, curling the corner of my lips into a small smirk. "But no promises."

"When and where are my best chances?" he asked.

I hesitated, glancing around, suddenly aware of my growling stomach.

"Well, I have classes tomorrow, and after that I—"

"I can promise a good ghost story," he cooed with a smile.

I blinked. That certainly got my attention.

I shifted my feet, swaying a bit as I considered. "Any chance you could meet me on the Lawn tomorrow evening? Eight-thirty?" I brushed my hair behind my ear nervously.

"I'll be there," he grinned, then turned to leave.

As I watched him walk away into the night, a chill crept across my skin. "It better be a damn good ghost story." I called out, only half-joking.

He stopped and looked back with some kind of twinkle in his eye. "Don't worry. It will be."

Walking back to my dorm, starving and convinced it was the reason I felt more anxious than I should have, my phone rang.

It was Dad.

I'd completely forgot to text him back all weekend. I hadn't even thanked him for the necklace.

I was such a crap daughter. He had to be worried after not hearing from me for so long, I couldn't blame him for calling so unusually late.

"Hey, Dad. I've missed you. Sorry, I've been busy." I picked up, expecting his usual upbeat greeting, but something in his voice sounded strained.

"Trina, I need to tell you something."

"What is it?" My steps quickened. "Dad, is everything okay?"

There was an uncomfortable pause before he spoke again.

"I found your mom."

T he words came through the phone like knives into my chest. I felt a twisting in my stomach.

"I...I didn't know you were still looking for her." I squeaked out.

"I know, *mija*. I wasn't exactly looking," he said. "Well...I did try to call her on your birthday...but she came back on her own. Said she's been across state lines, trying to let things settle."

I was silent, not sure what to think, my thoughts racing a million miles an hour.

"I just wanted you to know that she's safe and she...she says she's doing better."

I finally spoke. "That's...good, I guess."

It was difficult for me to take in. I was glad to know she was safe, but the resentment was still so strong.

I also didn't believe her. It wouldn't be the first time she'd disappeared to "let things calm down."

"She—" Dad started up again after another long silence. "She's actually here and would like to say something to you."

I huffed in surprise. "Um...okay."

"Katrina...Trina, sweetie." The sound of her voice on the other end was surreal, nearly giving me chills. I couldn't remember the last time I'd heard her so clear and coherent, instead of slurring her words.

"What, Mom?" I said coldly.

"I—I just want you to know that I'm sorry for everything. I never meant for things to go this way."

I didn't respond. She kept going.

"I had to go away for a while. I didn't tell you where I was because I was trying to keep you and your father out of it. I know you're tired of it, and I know you won't believe me, but I'm telling you anyway," she pleaded, "I hope you can understand that there are things I can't control."

"Oh believe me, Mom, I know that," heat rising in my veins and a lump forming in my throat. "You've reminded me for years that there are things you can't control." I didn't mean to be so harsh, but I had nowhere else to direct the anger inside me. It just came bubbling over without warning.

She didn't respond. I exhaled and squeezed my eyes shut, trying to calm myself before saying anything else I'd regret.

"Where were you?' I finally asked bluntly.

"Trina, I was trying to get sober. I didn't want to come back until I could—"

"Where were you?" I repeated the question, slow and enunciated.

No answer. Not for a minute.

"I was...in a program. In Louisiana. A really good one. It was helping. It was working."

"Was?"

"It was. It did...I did the full program, and then they wanted me to go on some retreat at the end of it, but I realized I needed to come back to you both instead. Because I think I'm okay now."

"I'm glad you're okay," I said. "But we were worried. For a whole year, Mom."

"I know."

My chest felt tight. "Can I talk to Dad?"

"Of course, sweetie," she said, sounding defeated and tired.

There was some rummaging on their end of the phone and then my dad's voice broke through once more.

"I just thought you should know, Trina."

"Thanks." I paused. "So, is she staying at home?"

"For now, yes." Dad breathed. "But try not to worry about any of this. Everything's fine here, I promise. It'll take some time, and we can talk more later, but you focus on yourself for now, *claro*?"

"Sure thing, Dad," I uttered.

"We both love you, *mija*. Mom says goodnight."

"*Te amo*, Dad."

I hung up, my thoughts and feelings a mosaic of confusion.

Mom had vanished with no trace for an entire year, and she just thought she could walk back in like nothing ever happened. My high school graduation, being accepted for the scholarship, two whole birthdays—she wasn't there for any of it.

The last memory I had of her was when I'd walked through the door after my senior art club show to find her passed out on the couch, empty bottles lining the floor around her. She'd promised to come, and I was stupid enough to believe it finally would happen. Dad was pissed, and they fought about it, like usual.

Then two days later, she was gone.

I bit my lip so hard it nearly bled as I mindlessly walked up the stairs to my dorm, thinking about how I'd worked so hard to let Mom go. And now she wanted back in.

With heavy steps, I trudged through the door to find McKenzie lying across the couch in the shared area.

"You're out later than usual." She looked up from her phone. "See any more pirate ghosts?"

I shot her a playful glare, aware that I was already in a foul mood from the news about my mom, so I was almost glad that her teasing had directed my thoughts back to Bellamy.

"Actually," I said, "I met someone at the library."

A grin stretched across McKenzie's face, and she shot up from the couch like a bullet. "You met someone?"

"Yeah, his name was Bellamy. He said he's been here a long time. Do you know him?"

McKenzie tapped her chin with a dramatic tilt of her head.

"Hmm, must be a senior. Did you get his last name? I'll see if I can look him up."

"I didn't even think to ask."

She slumped back down onto the couch. "Well, there can't be too many guys with a name like Bellamy here. I'll find him."

Right away, McKenzie got to sleuthing on her social media.

"Well, you let me know when you find him," I joked.

I headed to my side of the dorm, and tossed off my clothes, eager for a hot shower to wash away the day.

Once I was in an oversized T-shirt, some cotton shorts, and my freshly-washed hair wrapped tightly in a towel, I emerged from my bedroom to find McKenzie still on the sofa, desperately trying to dig up something on her phone.

"Find him?" I asked.

"Come here and look. Are any of these him?"

I shuffled over to check her search results. "Nope, none of those."

"I give up!" McKenzie exclaimed. "Just get a pic of him soon!"

"It's nothing serious. I'm not even really sure what I think about him."

"Is he hot?"

"Yeah, he is actually," I chuckled, thinking about that cool, casual way he looked at me in the library. "But I don't know, he just seemed a little...strange."

McKenzie made a little face, scrunching up her nose with a grin full of mischief. "Well, if you want to dig up any real dirt on him, just get me his full name. My dad's a lawyer, and my ex's mom works for the PD, and she still loves me, so I have my sources if he turns out to be a serial killer."

"Well, at least I know if I go missing, my death won't be another mystery in this town with you on my side."

McKenzie cackled, and I laughed, too, as I headed for my bed, but weirdly enough, nothing really felt all that funny.

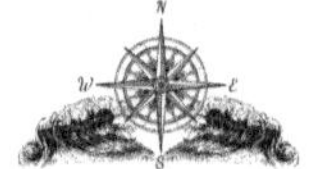

I woke up from a nightmare, my fist clenched around the necklace as I gasped for air. I hadn't taken it off since the night of the party, because it brought some strange sense of comfort. A symbol of tides of change in my life.

And as I held the pendant against my skin, I thought of Mom, and drifted back to sleep, where I saw her in my dreams drowning with me.

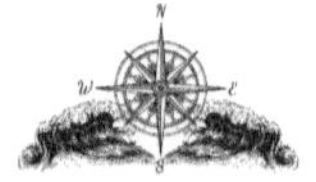

The next day, every class was a blur I barely remembered because I was too anxious about meeting Bellamy that evening, wondering if I'd made a mistake by letting him lure me in with his charming promise of ghost lore.

But mistake or not, I had a feeling he would find me again either way. At least this way I could be prepared.

I scampered from my last class to the dorms, putting together an outfit in my head for tonight, ignoring that ever-present feeling that someone was always lurking nearby.

"No wild parties tonight, I hope." The groundskeeper, Russell, called out to me as I passed through the wrought-iron gates to East Wing. I vaguely smiled at him to hide my embarrassment as he swept stray mulch from the first-floor corridor.

"No," I said. "Just a date...I think."

He dipped his head with a nod and went back to sweeping. I shrugged and went on my way.

I'd often noticed that he kept a watchful eye out for the students. Something about his quiet, humble demeanor in this extravagant place made me feel more connected to him than most other faculty, even despite the fact he'd never spoken to me before now.

I found the dorm empty. McKenzie's keys weren't in their usual spot on the table by the doorway. I figured she must be out on one of her own adventures, so I took advantage of the emptiness to sit and stare at my blank canvas, begging some source of inspiration to strike.

I happened to glance over at the blanket Milo had given me, still lying at the foot of my bed where I had dropped it that night upon coming home. His words—his voice came flooding back all at once.

"It's not wise to come here."

"This is certainly no place for angels."

He'd been trying to tell me. It was a warning. And he—he was one of them. It was the only explanation.

He was an actual pirate. I'd spoken to an actual ghost.

And yet, I'd enjoyed every minute of it. Every little passing glance, every awkward joke, and every star he pointed out.

"Can you locate the North Star?"

No, I couldn't.

But I could paint it.

Dipping my wet brush into a buttery smooth block of blue, I slid the brush across the canvas and laid the foundation for a night sky reflected in the sea below—a sea that would mirror the beauty above it.

I finally had something.

As I mixed some blue and white pigments, creating lines and creases on top of the thin layer I had already applied, I vividly recalled the star as Milo had pointed out, twinkling unwaveringly over the horizon. I wanted to amplify the vision in my head with my colors, to make the ocean waves reflect the starlight in waves melting into silver.

By the time I thought to check the clock, night had fallen. It was ten minutes past eight, and I still had paint on my hands and my hair thrown in a messy bun.

I tossed down my brushes and rummaged my closet for something to wear. It was hotter than it should be in November, so I grabbed a simple black sundress, and there was no time to think twice about it as I threw it over my head and let my dark tresses tumble down.

I reached for my mascara and a neutral shade of lip color, knocking over handfuls of crumpled receipts, granola bar wrappers, and the small gift box that had once held my necklace. I made a mental note to tidy up later.

I reached down to pick up the necklace box, and that's when I saw the writing on a paper no bigger than a notecard tucked between the gift paper—a note I'd missed when I first unwrapped it.

It's your turn to have this, Trina. Always keep it with you. I don't know if I believe in magic, but something about it helps lessen the nightmares. I don't think I need it anymore. Whatever you do, don't lose it. It will help you keep your head above water until you figure out how to free yourself.

I didn't know what to make of the message. But I knew Dad didn't write it. It sounded just like Mom. I'd heard so many similar hallucinatory drunken rambles that I'd lost count. And.I knew her well enough to recognize her handwriting. But what the hell was she talking about? Magic was a stretch, even for her.

I shook it off for the time being. There was no time to give it more thought or try to solve one of Mom's crazy puzzles. I'd deal with it later, but for now, I was running very late to my meeting with Bellamy.

I scurried outside and headed to the South Lawn, my nerves coiling up like springs inside me. I even considered turning around for a second or two.

What if he really is a serial killer?

As I followed the cobblestone sidewalk, I noticed Russell struggling with some boxes he was loading into a parked van.

"Do you need some help?" I asked shyly, hoping not to offend him.

"I'm fine, missy, you just worry about staying out of trouble now." He uttered in his raspy voice. I liked to think his voice was weathered by the sea air from some past life in his younger years as a fisherman, but the truth was I had no clue who Russell once might've been.

"Katrina!"

I glanced over my shoulder toward the voice that called my name. Bellamy approached, dressed in dark attire like the day before, but this time he wore a black jacket that reached past his hips—a vintage flair that flattered him.

He walked up, nearly blocking Russell, who was still wrestling with the boxes.

"Let me lend a hand with that," Bellamy offered, taking one of the containers from Russell's hands before he could answer.

I couldn't help but notice a very peculiar moment between them, as Russell narrowed his eyes at Bellamy, who repaid him with a piercing glower, almost threatening.

"What are you doing?" Russell growled under his breath.

"I'm just helping you, *sir*," There was an edge to Bellamy's voice, despite the formality.

The tension was overbearing, like a crushing weight that I couldn't ignore. Russell shot Bellamy one last glare before turning around to climb up into the driver's seat of the van.

"That was nice of you," I said. "Do you two know each other?"

Bellamy shrugged. "He's a...an old friend of my dad's. They aren't on the best terms at the moment." He paused after that sentence, then changed the subject. "Hope you're hungry."

"Well, I painted so long today that I forgot to eat, so I'm actually starving." I smiled at him, only now actually feeling the pangs of my empty stomach.

"Come on then. Where would you like to eat?"

"I'm new here, remember?" I said. "You said you've been here a long time, so you choose the place."

"Well, if you insist." He nodded, turning away. "I think I have a place in mind."

I followed him off campus and through the hustle of Constantine's central historical hub, just a mere two blocks from ICA's grand entrance. Within minutes we were surrounded by the tender glow of streetlamps on stone-paved roads and the chatter of bustling tourists, the ever-steady view of the bay at our side as we walked. We small-talked along the way, about the weather, about my annoyingly old-fashioned professor, and about Bellamy's favorite beaches.

The moon shone brightly above. Palm trees along the sidewalk swayed in the evening breeze, carrying the scent of salt and fish to our nostrils. Tourists typically flocked the streets here, but now that it was autumn, vacationing season was dying down, leaving a more intimate feel.

Before long, a quaint outdoor cafe overlooking the bay with cozy lights and metal tables came into view. A hanging wooden sign over the entrance portrayed a cartoon labrador with a fisherman's hat.

"This is Sea Dogs." I breathed. "I love this place."

A low sound rumbled in Bellamy's throat, like he wasn't quite surprised, and something about it unnerved me. We seated ourselves, picking the spot closest to the water and directly beneath the string lights.

He ran his hand through the trimmed messy black waves turning in every which way across the top of his forehead in an untamed sort of way. A faint shadow of equally dark facial hair bordered his jaw and chin, enhancing his sculpted cheekbones. His features possessed something seductive that delved deep, tugging at the devil in me.

"So, Katrina Delmar," Bellamy began, placing both elbows on the table. "Who exactly are you?

A slight flush of embarrassment rippled through me, though I wasn't sure why. I wasn't even sure how he knew my last name. I didn't remember telling him.

"Well, I guess the simplest way I could put it for the time being is that I'm a girl who hates the ocean and just moved to a seaside town." I glanced down with a nervous laugh.

Bellamy interlocked his fingers and leaned in. "You hate the ocean?"

I let the question linger for a breath. "No," I looked up. "I don't hate it at all, actually. I like to say that I do, because it terrifies me. But to be honest, I sometimes feel...drawn to it."

"Are you always drawn to things you're afraid of?" he cocked his head.

"I just don't like to be controlled by fear. So, when I got accepted here for art school, I wasn't going to turn it down because of a few beaches."

"And what kind of art is your specialty? Music?" Bellamy's eyes shimmered. "I'd bet your voice is as beautiful as the rest of you."

I cackled at the thought as warmth flushed my cheeks. "No, never. I paint." My confidence rose greatly as I proudly spoke of my passion. "Mostly watercolors."

"A watercolor artist who doesn't like the water." His lips twisted into a playful smirk as he toyed with the salt and pepper shakers.

The server appeared in her ketchup-stained apron to take our orders, yanking us both out of the moment with her sandpaper voice. "What'll it be, folks?"

"I'll just have a kale wrap with fries, please," I requested. "And iced tea with lemon."

"And for you?" When the waitress looked at Bellamy, he seemed almost surprised.

"I'll -em...I'll just have the same."

"That makes it easy." She snapped her notepad shut and sauntered off. Moments later she returned with our plates, impressively fast.

"So, what are *you* at an art school for?" I prodded, taking a bite of a crisp, hot French fry.

He huffed, as if my question was funny. "I guess you could consider it foreign language studies...with a minor in history." He said, stirring his tea with his straw, but not taking a sip. "I do a lot of traveling...or at least I once did."

"Do you miss it?"

"I do." He looked out across the bay. "But nothing lasts forever."

The way he voiced that last sentence caught my attention. Like he was alluding to something painful he was harboring. I noticed he still hadn't even touched the food on his plate.

"Maybe not," I said softly, pressing my lips together. "But maybe you can travel again someday, and put those foreign language skills to use." I kept going, hoping to ease the tension. "My dad's Cuban, so I know a little Spanish. I kind of wish he'd taught me more, but he had no one else to speak it with after he married my mom, so I guess I can't hold it against him."

"Ha, I have a whole list of things I'd like to hold against my dad. But that's a story for another day." Bellamy leaned back and stretched, removing his jacket and revealing a shirt with sleeves rolled up to his elbows. I noticed the tattoos on his arms, including a flying sparrow and an anatomically correct heart pierced by two arrows. "But speaking of stories...I suppose I still owe you a ghost tale."

I nodded with a half-smile. "That's the whole reason I came."

"You mean you didn't come to admire my ink?" he snickered. I blushed, realizing I was still staring at his forearms. "So what's got you so curious about the things that haunt this coast?"

"The island..." I said plainly, "I ended up stuck out there a few nights ago, and I saw...something. At least, I think I did."

"That island and anyone on it..." he said through his teeth. "...is very dangerous. Sometimes the tides get out of control around that area. You shouldn't have been out there."

"Trust me, I found that out the hard way. I don't plan on ever going back there."

"That's for the best," he said solemnly.

"I don't disagree, but if it wasn't for that creepy island, I wouldn't be here right now. I was hoping one of your ghost stories might have something to do with it. Did a ship sink there or something?"

"There are rumors." He leaned back in his chair.

"Rumors of what? Tell me." I demanded, getting anxious.

He sat up and made a motion with his finger for me to come closer. I leaned over the table, tired of playing his game, but desperate for answers.

"Some say," he began, his voice barely above a whisper, "there was once a pirate captain who fell in love with a siren. But he betrayed her right here off these coasts." His gaze drilled into mine as he spoke. "So she cut off her own tail and summoned a maelstrom. It sunk the ship, taking down the captain and his crew, and the siren trapped them between life and death, cursing them to relive the same fate for eternity. Legend says they're damned with their ship at the bottom of the ocean and resurrect with the tides each night."

A morbid chill coursed through my veins as I remembered the pirate ship, and all at once, I believed in ghosts again. Once more I was certain of what I had seen.

"And what happened to the siren?" I asked.

"Without her tail, she became human, and dove into the sea as the ship went down. No one truly knows her fate."

I'd eaten most of my meal by now, but Bellamy still hadn't so much as touched a thing on his plate or taken a drink. And after the siren story, I felt uneasy.

Then, to my surprise, Bellamy began to laugh.

"That's the legend anyway. Something like that." He said, slapping his hands on his thighs as if he hadn't just reeled me in like a fish on a hook.

"So…a pirate pissed off a mermaid?" I asked, twisting a lock of my hair around my fingers.

"Mermaid. Siren. Whichever you prefer."

"How do you know so much about this?" I moved from fidgeting with my hair to gently tugging at the chain around my neck, twisting the blue pendant back and forth.

Bellamy's gaze dropped to the necklace, and he became strangely quiet. He appeared distracted, entranced—almost the exact same way Milo had—and then he snapped back out of it. Something shifted in that moment. Something tangible.

"Why did you bring me here?" I urged him on. "Was all this really just to tell me a ghost story?"

"I brought you here to tell you that it's not just a ghost story. It's history. And now you're part of it, like it or not."

My blood ran cold.

He reached into his pocket and pulled out something before gently slid it across the table to me. There under his finger was the picture of me that McKenzie had taken with her Polaroid the night of the party, the one that had been whisked away in the wind. My heart nearly stopped.

Stalker. Serial killer.

"How—how did you find this?" I asked, still shocked.

"Well let's just say it sort of found *me*," he paused, eyes still locked onto mine. "Back on the island you're so curious about." His words slithered out, and I suddenly felt dizzy.

Disbelief, shock, horror. They all hit like tidal waves. And I feared I was going completely insane.

"You—you were there on the island that night?" The question stammered from my lips.

"Who do you think pulled you out of that rip current?"

My breath caught in my chest. It was all impossible.

He went on. "When I saw this picture, I realized that you might be in possession of something that is putting you in grave danger. Now I know my suspicions are true."

"What the hell are you talking about?" I stood up, ready to leave, ready to run.

"The sea claimed you for a reason." Bellamy held up the photo, stood, and took a step toward me. "I was there that night. We all were, just as we are every night. When I saw this picture—saw what you have around your neck—I knew I had to find you before *he* did."

"We? He?" I squeaked. "Who is *he*? And how were you on the island—unless…"

Unless Milo wasn't the only one who was a ghost.

"Listen to me, Katrina."

I pressed my fingers to my temples. "I'm listening. But it doesn't make sense. What does any of this have to do with me? Why am I in danger? Who is trying to find me?"

Bellamy closed the space between us and pointed to my throat. "The necklace you wear, it's something special, you're aware?"

"Well yeah, I guess so, it was a birthday gift."

"Sure, but do you know *what* it is?"

I was silent. Bellamy's voice dropped to a whisper.

"It's a scale. A siren scale."

"I'm sorry, what?" I bit back a sarcastic, nervous laugh at the thought that my date might be more delusional than I was.

"I've seen my fair share of siren scales," he said. "Enough to know that is one around your neck."

"You've seen mermaid scales," I repeated for confirmation. "You're serious right now?"

"You believe in ghost stories but you can't believe in mermaids?"

I scoffed, backing up. "How do I know you're not crazy? Or that I can trust you? It's not easy to believe any of this."

Bellamy stretched out an open hand toward me. "Then let me help you believe."

I hesitated and stepped forward, my heart pounding in my chest as everything inside me screamed to turn away.

Then I reached out with uncertainty to take his hand.

8

KATRINA

His grip on my hand was steady, but not forceful, as he pulled me along toward the bay.

"We can't just leave without paying," I argued, reluctantly following his steps.

I caught a glimmer of mischief in his eye as he looked back at me over his shoulder. "It's a way of life for some of us, love."

"Love?" I coughed with a scowl.

He winked before looking back ahead. "Don't worry, I left a tip."

I spun around and squinted towards the table, to catch the gleam of an ancient-looking gold coin on the table we'd just left behind. My jaw hung open as I glanced back around, bewildered.

A lock of his midnight hair caught in the wind and ruffled. "Up for a walk?"

"To where?" I hooked my thumbs in the pockets of my dress and tilted my chin.

"The shore. I can't show you here on the bay with all these people," he uttered.

"Show me what?"

"Everything."

He didn't offer any further explanation as we trekked across the bridge over the bay and to the nearest beach entrance.

My focus settled on Bellamy's forearm, noticing the subtle, pronged star tattoo just beneath his elbow. The same tattoo Milo had, only much smaller.

He shot a glance at me. "See something you like?"

"No," I snapped. "I just recognized your tattoo, that's all."

Bellamy's eyes darkened. He flexed his jaw and looked ahead. "You've met him then."

It wasn't a question.

I didn't respond. Something sinister clawed at me. But there was no escaping now as we approached the beach ramp and trudged past the dunes to the empty shoreline.

"You're not gonna kill me, right?" I asked, only half-joking.

"Oh, Katrina, I'm more of a gentleman than you think." He smirked.

We stood along the coastline, waves crashing inches from us, creeping up the sandbanks. A tender glow of city lights created a haunting aura far in the distance. Miles of sand stretched parallel to the water as far as the eye could see, devoid of any sign of life besides the two of us. The cool night breeze carried the promise of salt and secrets, a phantom messenger of the tide.

"Why did you bring me here?" I asked, tasting salt on my tongue.

"The ocean brought you here." Bellamy's voice was a rumble over the waves as he let go of my hand and stepped into the rolling surf. "It brought you to *me*, just as it did before. But this time, I'm not letting you go."

He turned around to face me as his words chilled me to the bone. He stepped backward, letting the foaming water consume him until he was half-way submerged.

His form became like mist, a specter watching me from the waves, transforming into a vision of the past. His clothes changed before my eyes into a naval black coat over a billowing shirt and trousers that hung loose from the tops of worn tall boots—a true pirate's uniform—complete with a cutlass at his side. A shadow of salt and sea.

He reached out to touch me, and I was too shocked to move. When his fingers touched mine, I recoiled at an otherworldly sensation that jolted through my veins like ice

"You're really one of them—the crew the siren cursed." I swallowed the dry lump in my throat, my voice a hoarse whisper.

Bellamy offered no response, only a serpentlike sneer, as though he was amused by my terror. He stepped forward out of the water, and like the first brushstroke of watercolor on paper, the hues of moonlit flesh rushed back into his being. And even in the darkness, his winter-blue eyes pierced like arrows.

I stumbled, backing away from him like he was a rabid animal. "So you're ghosts. You and Milo, and everyone on that ship. What—what does this have to do with me?"

"Because you're the one we've been waiting on for 300 years, Katrina." He closed whatever distance I tried to create between us, and he didn't waver, even when I tried to run. He closed in on me, and pulled me to him, bringing his lips to my ear. "And that means I had to find you before they did."

I flinched.

He held me against him, his hand clasped at my waist. I couldn't fight him off. I couldn't even budge him. He towered over me, looming and seductive and threatening all at once. I couldn't breathe. I couldn't move. I just stood there, fixated on his handsome face and that devilish gaze that slowly slid down to my collarbone. He dragged his finger beneath the silver chain of my necklace, and then twirled the pendant between his finger and thumb.

His scent of earthy spices, woodsmoke, and rum filled my nostrils. I didn't like that some part of me found it intoxicating.

"What...what do you want with me? Why won't you explain what is you want?"

Bellamy's lips curled into a grin as he tightened his grip on me. "I want the siren scale...and that heart of yours wouldn't be so bad either."

He tugged on the necklace, and I thought he was going to rip it from my neck. I reached up to stop him. But something else stopped him instead.

"Let her go!" A deep voice roared.

A figure in the shadows pulled Bellamy off me, knocking him to the sand. I tumbled to the ground beside him.

"You followed me here?" Bellamy seethed toward the figure as he leapt to his feet, leaving me on my own. He and the mystery attacker circled each other, just steps away, and the ocean's edge lapped at my side.

"You left me no choice. I'm not going to trust *you* with her." The familiar voice growled in a way that called to some hidden memory of mine.

"She's not yours to claim. I found her first." Bellamy hissed.

I clutched my necklace and stood to my feet, trapped between the ocean and the two men arguing before me.

"She's no one's to claim," The shadow closed in, stepping in front of me, further blocking my path to escape. "And for the record, you didn't find her first...I did."

I knew that voice. The sound of it hit me all at once as those last two words rattled every fiber of my being.

"Milo?" I gasped.

He threw a glance back at me over his shoulder, the moonlight illuminating his face.

He peered at me with hazel-brown eyes that no longer held the same softness from the island, but instead simmered with something disquieting.

"You think she'll just go along with you, mate?" Bellamy called. "You think you can convince her to throw herself into the sea for you?"

I stumbled, stepping backward into the icy surf and shuddering as it swallowed my ankles. "What is he talking about?"

"The curse. You're the one we've been looking for," Milo muttered, loud enough for Bellamy to hear as he stared him down. "But not for the same reasons."

"Don't listen to him, Katrina. What he wants from you will get you killed." Bellamy glared at me and stalked forward.

"You don't know that." Milo bit back, shielding me by blocking Bellamy's path. "You're the one trying to control her."

"What?" I screamed.

"I'm trying to protect her."

"No, you're trying to protect your interests." Milo bellowed. "I've more than paid for my sins. I won't keep paying for yours, too. Not all for *your* selfishness."

Bellamy grinned. "What is a pirate if not a little selfish?" He drew the sword at his hip. "Since I can't ever seem to win the battle of superior morality, let's settle this another way."

Milo reached for the cutlass hanging from his side that I hadn't even noticed until then, the curve of the blade catching the moonlight. "There's nothing to settle. But I'll happily keep you busy so that you stay away from her," he breathed. "Katrina..." He glanced back at me, a loose strand of hair lining up with the scar over his eye.

I held my breath.

"Run."

Bellamy lunged. Milo charged toward him.

Their blades met with sparks that lit up the darkness. The sound of metal striking metal split my ears as they danced across the sand, swords crossing with each breath. Bellamy was fast, but Milo was faster, and they whirled around each other like two clawed predators in the night. A glimpse of an age long past, the two undead pirates dueled beneath the moonlight in a scene resurrected from time itself.

I saw my chance and took off running, ignoring the sting of broken shells beneath my bare feet when my slick sandals slipped off in the sand.

Just as I made it to the dunes, I heard a cry that made me turn around, and I strained to see in the shadows.

Then I gasped, trying everything to convince my mind this was just another bad dream as Bellamy swiped his blade against Milo's arm, drawing dark blood spatters that painted the sand, before swinging again towards his head. But Milo dodged swiftly at the last second and plunged his sword through Bellamy's stomach.

I couldn't suppress the scream that tore from me. Blood bloomed at Bellamy's center, and he grimaced with fire in his eyes as he ripped the sword from himself and tossed it into the sea.

He uttered something I couldn't make out to Milo, then dropped to his knees as the ocean rose and a wave curled over him. I could feel his eyes on me, even as he went under.

"Don't give him the scale, Katrina!" He called out. "Unless you want your nightmares to become a reality." Then, he vanished beneath a swirling black mist in the water, like the smoke that shrouds a freshly put-out candle.

My breath hitched, and my heart hammered so hard against my ribs I thought it would explode. I should never have turned around. I closed my eyes, telling myself none of this was real. It couldn't be. I was just seeing things.

But then I opened my eyes to see Milo striding toward me, his brown loose-fitting shirt billowing in the wind to reveal his muscular tattooed chest. I spun around to unclasped my necklace with trembling hands and shoved the coiled silver chain into my pocket. Whatever either he or Bellamy wanted with it, I still didn't understand.

But they were willing to kill each other for it—for me. And that made me want to guard it for dear life.

Calm Before the Storm

9

KATRINA

"Are you hurt?" Milo asked, his voice husky from the sea air.

"You—you just killed him!" I managed to exclaim between breaths, fighting back a lump in my throat.

"I just saved you from getting your heart ripped out." Milo said flatly. "And I didn't kill him. We're already dead, remember?"

"Then what happened to him? Where did he go?" I recoiled, a chill overwhelming my body. I couldn't take the confusion of it all much longer. "And what do you mean getting my heart ripped out?"

"It's what happened to the last girl he thought was a siren. I'm just assuming you were next."

I eyed him suspiciously, questioning each and every word that left his mouth. And questioning my sanity along with them.

The battle on the beach had left more than a few loose strands of his mid-neck length hair sweeping across his forehead. He brushed a hand over the dark-golden locks, tousling them back in a way that softened his rugged, scruff-shadowed jawline.

"You didn't answer me." He moved closer. "Are you hurt?"

"No, I'm not hurt." I simmered, crossing my arms and twisting away from him. "But I don't know what the hell is happening. I watched a pirate ship rise up out of the ocean, I'm being stalked by dead men who want to rip my heart out, and somewhere in all that I'm supposed to believe the necklace of my deranged, recovering alcoholic mom is a magical mermaid scale."

"Aye, that about sums it up. And as long as you have that scale, we won't stop coming for it—coming for you."

I blinked in disbelief at his words and the way it came out so hollow. Like he was just telling me the weather instead of throwing out an ominous threat.

The note from the necklace box flashed in my mind's eye, like some kind of supernatural warning.

Always keep it with you.

"Well, I don't have it, see?" I pointed to my empty neck. "Bellamy must've stolen it when you pulled him off me."

Milo arched a brow. "You're lying."

I shook my head with a groan that rivaled the ocean's crashing in the distance. "So if I give you my necklace, you'll all just…go away?"

"That depends." Milo pretended to study his knuckles, smiling a sultry crooked smile that made me want to look at him longer. "If the siren scale alone is enough to break our curse, then yes. Though I have my doubts."

"And if it's not?" I raised my eyebrows.

"Then our captain will want you, too," he uttered.

I noticed how he glanced out to the shoreline from time to time. Like he was waiting—or watching—for something.

I positioned my back to him and started walking, trudging through the last bits of sand before my feet touched the wooden walkway connecting the beach to the empty parking lot.

"Wait—"

I whirled around. "I'm one more cryptic threat away from calling the police."

"And tell them what? That Constantine's ghost stories spooked you a little too much?" He held up his hand, and it dissolved into shadow. "We've been haunting these coasts for a long time. We know how to remain unseen."

I pursed my lips, and scowled, refusing to meet his gaze.

He was right. The cops would just think I was crazy—or worse, a drunk college kid on the beach. And maybe they'd be half-right. Either way, I'd make a fool of myself, and I'd still be haunted by pirate ghosts. I might as well save myself the trouble and skip the first part.

And if I tried to leave Constantine—if I tried to come back home suddenly—Dad would think I was coming back for Mom, and he'd blame himself, and I'd never be able to explain the truth. Not to mention it would mean forfeiting my scholarship.

"Bellamy told me not to trust you. You told me not to trust Bellamy. And that leaves me trusting neither of you." My throat was scratchy from thirst, irritated further by the salty night air.

"As you shouldn't." Milo grinned. "Never trust a pirate."

"So then who do I trust?" I scoffed with a roll of my eyes.

"Yourself."

I cocked my head at him, noting the subtle twinkle in his brooding eyes. "So let me make sure I understand...You and your crew think my necklace will break your curse—the curse that came from a mermaid—"

"Siren."

"—siren—which Bellamy thinks I am, so he wants my heart for some reason. And if I don't give you the necklace, you'll hunt me down and take it anyway."

"Most of that was correct," Milo nodded. "Except I have no plans to take the scale from you unless you offer it willingly—because most likely it's useless without you. And I will protect you from Bellamy and the rest of the crew until you do." He flicked his gaze back toward the ocean again, his body tense.

"Why would you do that?" My gaze followed his, a sense of nervousness rising. Something was wrong.

"Because on the slim chance there's something waiting after this life, I'd prefer not to damn my soul on the other side, too, when the curse finally breaks and I die for real." He leaned in, his voice low as he stared into my eyes. "And you just might be my last shot at redemption."

"So...it's not because you actually care, it's just because you want to save your own ass? That's cheating." I shifted, partly disgusted with his unbothered, dull expression. It still baffled me that this was the same kind, charming man who'd been so tender to me on the island. He'd shown me the stars and noticed I was freezing. He'd listened to everything I had to say. He was the first person here who had actually made me feel home.

And now he didn't care at all. I was just his insurance.

"That's a pirate." He gestured to himself with a shrug.

I sighed. "And what makes you so sure my necklace is the answer to your curse?"

"Sirens' magic came from their tails. That makes the scale magic. The curse was clear: *'By siren's blood and magic done.'* So, it only makes sense that it would take the same to undo it."

"And the blood part?"

"That's where you come in. If you're a siren, you can activate its magic." He paused to glance back at the shore, then continued.

"Why the hell would I be a siren?"

"Why else would you have a siren scale? Our only hope these past 291 years has been that maybe the siren who cursed us wasn't the last one—that maybe some survived, living out their days on land. And *you* might be descended from one." He looked down at me from the corner of his eye, his focus still on the sea's black horizon. "And if that's really a siren scale in your pocket, you hold power greater than you know."

My body went rigid. Silence stretched between us as I digested his words. He knew exactly where I had the scale, and he hadn't so much as tried to take it. He could easily overpower me and save himself. But he was standing here explaining everything instead.

Unless he was lying to earn my trust. And I was just a complete fool.

"Come on," he said suddenly, ushering me forward with a gentle nudge of his palm at the small of my back. "Let's get away from the shore before you're spotted. Captain Valdez won't be as cordial about all this. And if he finds you, there'll be no chance you make it out alive."

"And you're willing to defy your captain?"

My eyes drilled into him as we walked further inland beneath the eerie glow of street-lamps as soft sand turned to cold, cracked asphalt beneath my feet.

"I consider it a rare and necessary pleasure." He nodded. "He's a desperate man. The most dangerous kind. He's weary of our torment, and there's no line he won't cross to end it. That's why he sent Bellamy to bring you back. And I volunteered to find you if he couldn't."

"And yet neither of you plan to take me to him?"

"No. Not if we don't have to. But Bellamy has his own intentions with you, and even I'm not quite sure what he's capable of anymore after—" he stopped himself there, stretching tall as he looked back out toward the beach. "We need to get you out of here. They'll be looking if Bellamy's come back wounded."

"Will he tell them about this? About what you did?" I stole a peek at the sea, nothing visible to my eye in the void of darkness it had become.

"Not likely. He doesn't want them to find you either, so I'm sure he'll prefer to keep this a secret." He quickened his pace. I followed, nearly tiptoeing across the pebbly surface.

"Will he...heal?" I asked, part of me wondering why I cared to ask.

"Yes, by the next tide. Our bodies have endured far worse."

I smoothed back stray locks from my face, daring to look up at him as he walked beside me through the desolate sand-dusted parking lot. Loose bits of gravel dug into my soles, and I tried to hide my wincing.

"What's it like?" I asked, trying to focus on anything but the jagged terrain that slowed my steps. "The curse, I mean. Being immortal must have some perks, right?"

"Aye, you mean like the sensation of your lungs burning as you drown without dying, as the current drags you down and feels as if it's tearing you apart." I shrunk back as he went on. "Never aging, never dying, never feeling the simple pleasures of life that remain just out of reach. Knowing each sunrise brings the same end. Begging for death from those tormented tides until the night takes pity on us."

"So, at night you get to be…normal?"

"Well, sort of. The first night of our cursed existence, we quickly realized we could still set foot on land and walk among the living. But then we tried eating and drinking, only to find the satisfaction of it all eludes us. There's only emptiness," he uttered with a broken smile, as if he was wishing it was all just a sad joke. "And every night for three centuries, we wait for the tide to pull us from our purgatory. A temporary, cruel reprieve."

"And you think I can change that?" I swallowed, trying to wet my parched mouth as my words came out dry. "If I return the scale to the ocean, it'll set you all free from this?"

Milo shrugged. "Perhaps if you really are a siren's descendant. But only Cordelia—the siren that cursed us—truly knew what her curse demanded."

"Then let's try," I said. "Let's just put it in the water. Maybe it's just as simple as making the ocean believe it's returned." I took a step back towards the shore.

Milo snorted. "You can't fool the sea, starlight."

I shot him a withering look, ignoring the unexpected nickname I didn't care to start up another argument about. "I can try." I stomped back toward the beach, pretending it didn't hurt with each step, and ignoring Milo's calls after me.

When my toes touched sand again, I rushed to the surf and knelt at the edge of the waves. After glancing over my shoulder, I pulled the necklace from my pocket. There in the moonlight, the "scale" pendant shimmered with a pearly blue iridescence. If my family wasn't known for hallucinations, I might've even sworn it was glowing. Even if it wasn't magical, it certainly looked the part.

"Katrina! Don't!" Milo's voice neared, along with the hurried thud of boots across the damp sand.

I dangled the pendant by its chain over the water, careful to keep my grip on it. I looked back at Milo, who skidded to a stop behind me, and almost fearful look in his eyes. I braced myself for whatever might happen when I lowered the necklace into the water—to see him vanish before me or get sucked into the sea. The unsettling truth was that I had no idea what to expect, and by the wide-eyed expression on Milo's face, neither did he.

After all, I had never broken a curse before.

Batten Down the Hatches

10

KATRINA

I let the chain slip through my fingers, dipping the pendant into the lapping water. I held it under for a moment or two.

A soft aura glowed in the water around it, and a reverberating pulse thrummed through the water and into my veins, sending out an unseen force beneath the water that even forced back the waves. The same drumming force I'd felt when I went under at the island.

I yanked the necklace up with a shriek.

"Are you crazy? I told you it's not safe out here!" Milo spun me around by the shoulder. "And now you've just alerted the crew to your presence—again."

I whirled around, tearing myself from his grip. "Do you want your curse broken or not?" I snapped.

He sighed and knelt beside me, hanging his head over the water's edge. "Of course I do...but not if it means they kill you. I prefer not to add any more innocent deaths to my tally."

"Doesn't that make you a bad pirate?" I asked.

"Perhaps," he tilted his head toward the shadows. "But it doesn't make me a good man either. I deserve every bit of what's happened to me for the things I've helped Valdez do. That's why I won't sacrifice you to save me."

I glanced up at him. "One last shot at redemption...right?"

He shifted uneasily and looked sideways. "Right."

I stood up and placed the chain back around my neck, keeping a guarded position as Milo watched me secure the clasp.

"Well, sorry that didn't work," I muttered. "But maybe this thing can at least help one of us."

Milo drew his brows together inquisitively. "What do you mean by that?"

"I mean that I sort of have a curse of my own to deal with—nightmares...and now hallucinations it would seem." I waved my hand toward him. "And I'm starting to think maybe there really is something to this necklace—something that can stop them before they ruin my life like they ruined my mom's."

Maybe Mom really did know something about it. Maybe it could help. Maybe the answer to breaking the pirate's curse was breaking mine—because if I could stop dreaming about and imagining all this, it would all go away. All of this had to be in my head, just like the women who came before me.

I stood up, determined to uncover the truth about the pendant at my chest.

"I'll take you home." Milo offered, drifting at my side. "You can't walk all the way back like that. Don't think I didn't notice you limping across the rocks."

My bruised feet ached as I marched toward the parking lot, where I braced for the sting of gravel. "I can walk, and I will." I said numbly over my shoulder. "Don't you have a ship to catch?"

I'd just taken a step onto the asphalt when I was swept off my feet.

"Stubborn as you are, I'm not leaving you here." Milo growled into my ear as I squirmed against his arms. But he was unshakeable.

"Put me down!" I hissed, slapping my hands against the flying bird tattoo peeking out on his broad, bare chest. He only pressed me closer, so close that I could feel his mist-dampened shirt through the fabric of my dress. I paused at the unexpected sensation—my palm against his skin. "You're warm," I noted.

"Were you expecting otherwise?"

"Well, you are dead, or whatever."

"Or whatever," he repeated. "Maybe I *will* take you to Valdez, on second thought."

I rolled my eyes as he flashed a cunning smile and then carried me through the parking lot despite my growing protests.

There was not a soul to be found—only a single rusty truck parked beneath a fluorescent streetlight, probably a late-night fisherman's, and a deserted old motorcycle parked in the shadows. Milo effortlessly carried me over to it and lowered me down.

"Get on." He gestured to the bike, a vintage-style racer.

"I'm not stealing a motorcycle with you." I crossed my arms.

"Who said anything about stealing?" Milo swung a leg over and the engine's roaring rumble startled me.

"It's—it's yours?"

"You think I haven't found a way to have some fun in 300 years?" He tilted his head, a strange sight astride the purring bike. But the more I thought about it, his leather boots and vest over his sea-worn clothes strangely didn't look all that out of place on a motorcycle. "I found it a long time ago, and I've had all the time in the world to learn how to get it running."

"Great. So you're a not just a ghost pirate, you're a *biker* ghost pirate." I snorted out. "Would it be crazy of me to say this is probably the weirdest part of it all so far?"

Milo shook his head with a rumbling laugh, tongue in cheek, and then narrowed his eyes at me. He jerked his head toward the backseat, few tresses of hair flicking across his eyebrows. "Get on." He repeated.

I hesitated, my mind clambering for more excuses. But then I leaned a little too heavily on a crag in the asphalt.

"Fine," I mumbled. "None of this is real anyway." I swung a leg over behind him and plopped down into the seat, my bare thighs wide open with his backside filling the space between them. And his body was still every bit as warm against mine as I never expected it to be.

Then, I didn't know what to do with my hands. "Hold on to me," he ordered over the engine's growl.

I hesitated to wrap my arms around him, having to scoot even closer and lean into his back. But once my hands were on his body, pressed into his hard, flexed sides, he flicked his wrist at the throttle, and we surged off into the night.

A breath of ocean air rushed over my cheeks and through my tangled hair. The lights of the sleeping town blurred by and the moon was a silent watchful eye above, a lone witness to my strange secrets. I buried my face lower, closer to Milo's back as the night air chilled me, and picked up the faint scent of salt and leather.

We crossed the bridge over the bay and were all too quickly back in front of the college. Milo turned off the bike, the heat from its engine warming my bare legs. I braced against his shoulders, careful not to touch the wound where Bellamy's blade had sliced, and lifted myself off the seat. I scrambled awkwardly to stand on both feet again.

Milo stayed seated on the bike and wasted no opportunity to once again remind me of the rules of his game. "The longer you keep the scale, the more danger you're in. You *cannot* be near the water at night. Valdez may decide to come looking for you himself, but until then, Bellamy nor I will let on that we know where you are."

"So you and Bellamy—your enemy—are going to work together to protect me."

"Correct, lass, but it's more of a convenient consequence of conflicting interests."

"Your interest being potentially saving your soul from eternal damnation, and Bellamy's being stealing my heart—literally?"

"Aye." He nodded.

"You're both the strangest pirates I've ever met."

"Ah, but you *have* met us." Milo smirked. "There are few who do."

"I guess brooding ghost pirates aren't a common hallucination." I sneered, turning to go.

Milo called out to me. "You still think this isn't really happening? You think it's all in your head?"

"There's no other explanation. I must've gotten home after my date with Bellamy and not remembered falling asleep."

"Katrina, this is all very real." Something grave overshadowed Milo's face.

I shivered and took a small step back, no longer certain what to believe.

"Find out what you need to about the scale. Soon." He said plainly. "I'll buy you some time by keeping the crew off your trail. But stay away from the sea at night. It's dangerous. They'll be looking for you, and they won't stop until they have that scale—and you."

"And if Bellamy comes back for me?"

Milo's eyes darkened. "Then I'll have to kill him again."

Uneasiness crashed into me like a wave as I stood there, lost for a response. And with that he disappeared into the night, leaving me standing in front of the gilded campus gates of Isabel.

IN DEEP WATER

11

KATRINA

I lay in bed tucked beneath the covers. A shadowed figure stood over me, and I was paralyzed. It loomed throughout my room, watching me, waiting. It neared, stretching out an arm. Reaching for my heart—

My eyes flew open at the sound of my alarm. I clamped a hand on my chest and clutched the pendant at my throat, reassuring myself it was still there as I drew a deep gasp to calm my breathing.

It was all a dream. Just like I knew it had to be.

Just another bad dream.

"It was just a dream." I finally said it out loud, trying to make myself believe it. But when I looked down to see I was still wearing last night's sundress, a trickle of doubt crept up my spine.

I had English Comp at eight-thirty. But class was the last thing on my mind. Dream or not, last night had solidified one harsh truth for me—I couldn't avoid Mom forever. I had to figure out whatever power it was she believed the necklace held. And why exactly she'd sent it to me after showing back up out of the blue.

If there was any hope it carried of helping me not end up like her, I had to know it. Because judging by the way things were going, I would need to be admitted to a psych ward before my next birthday.

I crawled out of bed and stumbled to the kitchen to find McKenzie there already, sipping on a coffee at the table and scrolling her phone.

"Katrina, oh my god. Why didn't you answer your phone last night? I texted you a million times!" She leapt up. "I was about to call the cops if I didn't see you this morning."

I rubbed my eyes. "What?" I hadn't even checked my phone since—I didn't even remember the last time I'd looked at it.

"You were gone all night! You didn't come home until just before sunrise." She gestured toward the door, her voice rising with each word.

"I—I did? I barely even remember walking through the door."

"Oh no…" McKenzie's shoulders dropped and she reminded me of a timid, startled lapdog. "You were with that Bellamy guy. Where did you go with him? Did you drink?"

The mention of his name sent last night flooding back. Dread curled around me like a claw, and I swallowed down a thought that shook me to my core—that it was all real.

My gaze slid down to the gray tile floor where I lifted my foot with slow reluctance and peeked at the underside. My soles were smudged with charcoal stains of asphalt.

The room seemed far away all at once, and I sat down to steady myself from the dizzying despair that washed through me.

"Trina, are you okay?" McKenzie was at my side in seconds, begging me to take a sip of her coffee that she held at my lips. "It'll help you sober up so you can try to remember what happened." Her usual lilting voice was almost shaking. "I'll kill him, I swear. If he hurt you, you just tell me—"

"He didn't hurt me." I rubbed my head with my hands. "He actually um…got in a fight with someone and got hurt, and his…" My voice trailed off as I lingered over the choice of word. "His friend took me home."

McKenzie's blue eyes bore into me in a way that looked like topaz gems burning beneath her ember locks. "You better not be lying to me," she threatened. "I will hunt him down. You just say the word."

I grabbed her shoulders. I knew she was trying to help, but in that moment I just needed it all to stop. "I promise you, I'm fine." I lied, trying to smile. "Nothing happened."

I glanced at the clock on the wall.

Eight-forty.

"I'm late for class." I muttered. McKenzie backed up and I stood to go clean up and change. I knew I should've been hurrying, but the world felt like it was slowing, and I was watching it all from a bubble—an airtight, delicate bubble that could pop any minute and leave me to drown.

I had to call Mom. And I would.

After class.

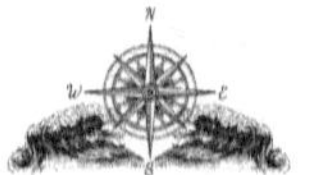

I fought to stay awake. The tip of my pencil scratched back and forth as I found myself sketching tiny North Stars on my notebook paper. A vibration from my phone made me tense, because I was already so on edge. I pulled my phone from my pocket, paranoid to check the sender.

I breathed a sigh of relief to just see a notification from Housing that I had a package waiting for me to pick up.

After class I shuffled to the student mailroom and checked my box. There was a small package for me, addressed in Dad's handwriting, marked as delivered two days ago.

I tore open the package. It contained a cheesy birthday card and a gift certificate to a chain art store—exactly the type of gift I would expect from my dad.

I touched the scale pendant around my neck.

Mom's gift.

Like everything she'd ever given me, it had brought its own slew of troubles. Some part of me almost wanted to tear it off and stuff it in a drawer forever. But I couldn't be careless with it now. It might've been the only think standing between me and my own curse threatening to drag me under.

It will help you keep your head above water until you figure out how to free yourself.

The thought of having to call Mom—of having to ask her to explain everything—made my stomach turn. It was hard enough just talking to her without feeling like some part of me was being chiseled away at, piece by piece. Like I was talking to a version of myself I was destined to become, like every woman before me eventually did. She was a mirror of a future I wanted so desperately to deny.

But I was going to have to force myself to look.

Ignoring the hollow twisting in my chest, I walked back outside and dialed her number. I pressed the phone to my ear. With each taunting ring, I felt sicker and sicker.

I almost hung up before the fourth ring, my heart beating more nervously than made sense.

"Trina, sweetie...Hi." The surprise in her voice was obvious, and the sound of it was almost unreal.

"Hi, Mom." I uttered tensely, shuffling my way over to stand beneath the shade of a tree on the Lawn, more paranoid than usual that someone might be listening—or watching.

"It's so good to hear from you, baby. I'm just working on some sketches." I'd almost forgotten my mother was as artistically inclined as I was, though she preferred the drier medias. She went on. "I—I don't know what to say. How are you?"

I almost laughed. "I'm…tired, if I'm being honest, Mom. I've been having trouble sleeping here."

"Oh no, sweetie…" Something cracked in her voice, something that almost felt safe.

"That's actually why I called. I wanted to ask you about the necklace you sent me. Why didn't you ever tell me about it before? What did you mean in your note about it helping with the nightmares?"

There was a long, uneasy silence that felt tangible even through the phone. My mom finally shattered it.

"I'm glad to know you got it. I was wondering." She exhaled deep, and I heard things rummaging around in the background, like she was scooting a chair out from our old kitchen table. "I never gave it to you before because I wanted to be completely sure I no longer needed it. You know, the whole 'put on your own oxygen mask first in a crashing plane' metaphor. I knew I couldn't help you until I helped myself."

She must've learned that in rehab. I'd never heard her say something that made so much sense before. She continued after another deep breath. "Your grandmother told me before she died that when it's time to pass the necklace on, the nightmares always come back worse. And that's why I went away. I was bracing myself for that.

"I saw how the dreams were getting stronger with you. I saw you starting to struggle the same way I did. And that's when I really knew I had to do everything in my power to overcome mine—to be better, so that losing that necklace by giving it to you wouldn't be the end of me."

"So then…it really did help with the nightmares?"

"It does seem that way. Not completely, but wearing it does lessen them—it at least makes them easier to live with. Without it, the hallucinations and dreams become a lot more…severe."

"So…you don't need it anymore?" I swallowed.

"Well, I don't think I do. I came so far in the program in Louisiana. I spent a whole year learning to manage the anxiety and depression—and how to hold on to reality even when the delusions come. And I really think I did it, Trina. I think I finally did what my mother couldn't. So I figured it was time for the necklace to go to you."

"I'm really glad, Mom," I blinked back a sting behind my eyes. "I really hope that's all true. I'm proud of you. But why didn't you finish the program?"

"Oh you mean the final retreat?" she asked, her tone shifting. "Well, I know this might sound ridiculous, but it was going to be down on the beach and you know I've never been comfortable with that. I figured I was good enough without it. The last thing I wanted to do was trigger old fears and undo how far I'd come."

"You're...afraid of the ocean? Is that why we never took beach vacations when I was a kid?"

She chuckled. "Yeah, I know you probably think that doesn't make any sense, but—"

"No." I said. "I don't think that at all, actually. After moving here, I get it." My chest tightened. "The ocean's...intimidating, to say the least. There's a reason they call it monster soup."

Mom laughed softly on the other end, and it was a sweet, strange echo that unlocked memories too far and few between. I was suddenly aware that I couldn't even remember how long it'd been since I last heard it. So I joined her and we chuckled together—something I never thought we'd do again.

"So then, you think you're really better, Mom?" I quavered. "Like for real this time?"

"I really think so," she said. "And if it turns out I'm wrong...then at least I know I did everything I could."

I swallowed. I wished she hadn't felt the need to add that last part, but I understood. It was a terrifying thing to think you'd outrun your darkness, only to turn around and find it catching right back up to you. And it made it that much harder to believe it was real when the light finally broke through.

But maybe it finally had. Maybe she'd finally found her guiding star.

A screen door creaked on her end. "Oh, sweetie, your dad just came in from the shop. I totally lost track of time. We're going out for Mexican tonight, so I'll talk to you later."

"No tequilas," I chided.

"No tequilas. I promise...and Trina?"

"Yeah, Mom?"

"I love you."

The opportunity lingered for me to say it back, but I froze instead. Those sacred words felt alien and ancient and foreign, despite how I'd longed to hear them.

Then the line went silent.

For the first in a long time, a small glow of hope felt within reach, like a lighthouse in the distance. I was starting to wonder if the necklace might just be the key to mending the broken pieces between us. Maybe ancient siren curses weren't the only kind of curse it could break. Maybe, in some ironic twist of fate, the sea would finally be the thing to save her.

Even if it was the very thing that was trying to destroy me.

I'd barely reached the other end of the Lawn when my phone buzzed in my hand as I watched a text come through.

Not from Mom, but McKenzie.

-Grab a coffee with me at the usual?

I fought back a yawn, suddenly all too aware of the exhaustion weighing on me. I knew better than to spend what little money I was holding onto, but splurging on a cappuccino sounded far from the worst choice I could make given the circumstances.

-Sure, be there in five

I rounded the corner to head for Sea Dogs, replaying the same steps I'd taken along the weathered path with Bellamy at my side last night, before everything spiraled into a tempest I couldn't escape.

I ran through every part of our conversation, dissecting meaning from everything he told me, trying to find some clue as to what he might want with my heart. And shuddered to think what he might be willing to do to get it.

A gray mist shrouded the sky as a steady drizzle fell, leaving the cobblestone streets slick and shining. Thick fog obscured my path, like a perfect metaphor for the uncertainty I faced in real life. I fixated on the soft, familiar glow of Sea Dogs' string lights in the distance, merely orange halos through the mist. I just had to keep moving toward them, and everything would be fine.

I chose a table inside the cafe this time, trying to keep as much distance between me and the bay as possible. It looked ever foreboding now, in this dank, dull weather, lapping at the sides of the stone wall rhythmically like a heartbeat. Goosebumps rose along my arms as I considered where it led—that far beyond where the bay spilled into the sea, an entire crew was drowning somewhere in a shipwreck from 300 years ago.

And they thought I could save them.

McKenzie rattled through the door soon after I sat down, her freshly curled orange tresses bouncing with each step. She hadn't even dropped her notebook on the table and her designer handbag on the floor before the words flew out of her mouth.

"I'm worried about you."

I forced some semblance of a grin. "I told you, I'm f—"

"Hold that thought." She waved toward the barista counter and scurried over to grab the already prepared drink she must've ordered ahead.

Each of her steps back toward the table filled me with dread. What exactly was I supposed to tell her? I didn't even know where to begin, and I certainly wasn't going to tell her about Milo and Bellamy.

"Anyway," she resumed, plopping down into the chair across from me. "Are you absolutely, positively sure everything is alright? You've been acting a little weird since the Halloween party." She blew on the lid of her steaming lavender Earl Grey tea. "Is it still the island ghost thing?"

I tilted my gaze upward, focusing on the ambient lighting fixtures overhead as I strung my thoughts together. "Yes—I mean, no. I mean..." I bit my tongue and leaned back with a deep inhale. "I'd be lying if I said it hadn't caused a few new nightmares."

McKenzie scooted forward, pressing her elbows over the table as her eyes begged me to go on.

"But mostly, it's my mom. Turns out she's the one who sent the necklace for my birthday."

The barista shouted my name, breaking my train of thought.

"I'll grab it. Stay here." McKenzie shot up before I could object and then within seconds came gracefully floating back with my iced cappuccino in hand.

"I thought your mom's not around." She set the drink down before me, and I slurped the cold vanilla foam off the top.

"She wasn't. But she came back—the same night I met Bellamy in the library. Which is probably why I forgot to tell you." I stared out the window at a tourist horse carriage rolling through the streets, finding some unique comfort in the clip-clop of the sound of hooves on cobblestone.

"Well that's a good thing—right?" McKenzie leaned in, demanding my focus.

"I think so, but...she's done similar things before."

"Well surely, she understands how much she put you through. Has she at least apologized?"

I smiled at the question. McKenzie's relationship with her parents seemed so perfect, and yet she was trying so hard to empathize with mine. They took her on extravagant family vacations every winter and summer, gave her a credit card with a seemingly infinite limit to use while she lived on campus, and she called them every weekend. I didn't know if she had ever even fought with her mom.

"Yeah, she apologized. She apologizes a lot, actually." I stirred my straw in my coffee, watching the ice cubes swirl around. "I can't count how many times she'd swear she'd stopped drinking—she'd even pour everything down the drain. And then one bad night of dreams and she'd be back at the liquor store, drunk before she even left the parking lot. So I don't know what to think this time around. Trusting her is just so...hard." I sighed, silence hanging between us. If I'd shared too much, I no longer cared.

"Well, maybe the necklace means she's serious this time. Like a peace offering." McKenzie straightened up in her chair, her face lighting up at the mere idea.

"Maybe." I shrugged, hanging onto her words more deeply than she knew.

Perhaps she could sense I was done with the topic, because McKenzie quickly switched the topic from me to her most recent manicure experience, explained how they didn't get her cat-eye gel polish just right on her left pinky finger. And then she reached for her handbag when her phone chimed.

"Ooo, Ty just asked if I want to go mini golfing." She looked at me with pleading eyes, as if asking my permission to leave the table.

I flicked my head toward the door and smirked. "You go ahead. I have some studying to do tonight anyway."

"You're the best, Trina. See you later." She leapt to her feet with a squeal, tossing her phone back in her purse before she paused. "Oh yeah—" she dug around in the handbag. "You must've left this on the dorm kitchen table. It's got your name on it. Wasn't sure if you needed it for class or anything."

She held out a folded up paper that I took from her hand with surprise. She whirled around and was to the door before I could thank her.

Now alone, I studied the eloquent, unfamiliar penmanship that spelled out my name. The paper was mine—*my* watercolor paper. I unfolded it and gasped.

My paper.

But not my drawing.

I felt the blood drain from my face as I stared at a sketch of a heart with two arrows.

Bellamy's tattoo.

And then my eyes dropped to the words scribbled below the image.

Do North Stars still guide broken hearts? I'll be patiently waiting for you to learn the truth about me...and about you. Give Milo my regards.

Bellamy.

The shadow in my room.

He *was* there.

A deathly cold curled around me like a steel curved hook. The weight of it all came collapsing onto me like the monstrous waves in my dreams. An undead pirate who wanted to cut out my heart had been prowling around in our dorm...and now he was taunting me.

Terrorizing me.

And he knew exactly where to find me.

Three Sheets to the Wind

12

KATRINA

In the dorm that evening, I obsessively checked the locks on the door while McKenzie showered after returning from mini golfing. I didn't even know if locks could stop a ghost pirate, but it was the only sense of control I could cling to. Once I confirmed the door was locked for tenth time, I closed myself up in my room.

I told McKenzie I would be studying. And I would be.

Studying the past.

While Mom might have been of little help that day, I didn't intend to let that stop me. If she was going to send me a cryptic note and a creepy family heirloom, I was going to do some digging on just who all might've had that heirloom before me.

I remembered years ago as a kid, the first time we checked Mom into a rehab facility, I'd overheard her talking about her mom and grandmother's hallucinations. I knew it ran in the family and blessed every daughter that came through Mom's line. But what I didn't know was why. And if I could figure out how far back it went—how long the women in my family had been carrying this burden, maybe I could understand how it all tied to the strange things haunting me on the coast.

Leaned against my headboard, Milo's blanket draped across my lap, I opened my laptop and began an ancestry search for any records available under the only clue I had to go off—Mom and Grandma's name: Grace and Lydia Gatlin.

I typed the names in the search bar, and when something promising appeared in the results, I clicked to find it blocked behind a paid subscription to an ancestry database. Desperate, I signed up for a free trial I fully intended to cancel. I certainly didn't have enough money to spare a month's access.

The results unlocked to reveal dozens of family records with the same surname. I narrowed mine down, eager to find anything that might offer a clue. I searched through marriage records and birth dates of a long line of daughters that spanned back nearly two centuries. Maybe one of them had married a pirate or a sailor, I thought. Maybe the connection would be clear.

It would've been a lot more helpful if the last names didn't change with every marriage that forced them to take their husband's name. Damn patriarchy.

But regardless, based on the records, Mom's ancestors were anything but seafaring people, having never even settled near the coasts. If anything, they seemed to have stayed concentrated as far inland as they could manage.

Disheartened that I couldn't find more, and feeling the weight of sleep tugging at my eyelids, I jotted down the last name of the farthest back in the line I could find, complete with her birth and death dates just like all the others. Maybe if I saw Milo again, I could ask him if any of the names sounded familiar, for whatever that was worth.

Lydia Gatlin – 1959-2003

Nelda Gatlin Harrows – 1932-1971

Esther Graves – 1906-1952

Alma Whitlock – 1880-1922

Edith Barnes – 1853-1890

Sarah Adams – 1829-1872

Marina Smith – 1800-1839

Elisabeth Shores – 1771-1813

Marina Eversong – 1750-1796

That was as far back as I could dig. I lingered on the unique last name of Eversong, finding beauty in the way it sounded, and finding no evidence it ever existed outside of Marina.

But something more made stomach turn. An unsettling pattern I noticed—not in the names, but the dates.

The death dates, to be exact.

After calculating carefully, double-checking and triple-checking my math, I came to a chilling conclusion.

Not one of those women had lived beyond the age of forty-six.

Mom was forty-five.

I grasped the necklace at my collarbone, desperate for some sense of hope, and some sense of connection to the ill-fated names before me.

Questions raced through my mind.

Did all of these women hold this necklace in their possession at some point? Did they all cling to it in desperation that it would free them from the prison of their own mind? Did they all sleep with it each night, hoping it might just have the power to keep even just one more tormented nightmare away? And if they did, why did they even believe that it could in the first place?

My eyes grew heavier and heavier until they felt like anchors. I finally surrendered to the call of sleep, tucking my necklace close to my chest, and glancing at the locked doorknob one last time before I slid down beneath the sheets.

And I wondered whose eyes I felt watching me that night.

I'd talk to Mom again tomorrow.

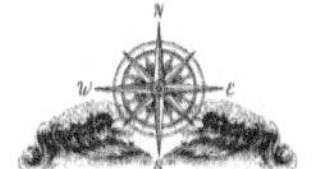

The next morning, I woke up just as tender orange sunlight leaked through my blind, compelled by a rare sense of inspiration that I didn't want to let escape. Despite the exhaustion in my soul, I sat up, got out of bed, and reached for my paint brushes and some water. I needed to paint. Just for a little while, to keep myself grounded.

And because if I survived not getting murdered by ghost pirates, I still had every intention of entering the fall student art showcase.

I swiped a fingertip across the paper to be sure the last layer had dried properly, and then sat down to work on it. The star had already begun to take form, but I needed to do so much more with the blending and layers to really make it "shine" on paper. With the ocean's surface filling the landscape at the bottom, I decided to add a tiny depiction of hope—a lone lighthouse out in the sea. I selected one of my finest-tipped brushes to create its towering figure in the distance. It might have easily been missed in the painting at first glance, but it was there, buried in plain sight, a hidden secret in the middle of a dark night at sea.

KATRINA

Things were quiet the rest of the day, but I couldn't help looking over my shoulder at every turn as I crossed the campus after class, books in hand, thinking of too much at once.

Mom. The necklace. Next week's exam.

But strangely enough, I couldn't stop thinking about Milo and whatever he might've done to keep my whereabouts hidden for this long. And the fact that I had no choice but to trust that he would.

Then my thoughts sailed to Bellamy, and I wondered why, if he really wanted my heart, why he hadn't cut it out when he'd had the chance in my room while I slept.

I barely heard the voice shouting at me from across the grounds. "Hey!" It was Russell, hobbling over in his worn khaki coveralls that contrasted against his deep umber skin.

I whipped around, thinking I was in trouble for stepping on some forbidden freshly pruned landscaping.

The groundskeeper neared, picking up speed as I gave him my attention. "What's your name again, missy?"

"Katrina," I said, bracing for the verbal lashing.

"Katrina...Do you have a minute?" he asked.

"Um..." I arched a brow and scanned my surroundings. "Sure."

Nothing could have prepared me for what came next.

He placed a weathered, thorn-scarred hand on my shoulder, and met my eyes dead on.

"The man you were with—he's dangerous. You're not safe anywhere near him."

"You mean Bellamy?" I asked, thinking back to the tense exchange of glances between them that night.

"I mean *either* of them." He drew in a breath and looked around. "They are not of this world."

"I know," I hesitated, still in disbelief that this conversation was happening, but equally relieved once more that I wasn't the only questionably delusional one around here. "I know that they're...dead."

"They're demons!" A vein popped in his forehead, and his jaw flexed so hard that I backed up a step. "And believe me, they do not have good intentions with you."

I glanced down at my sneakers before speaking again. "What do you mean? How...how do you even know about them?"

"I knew you'd ask that." He shook his head. "Let me show you something." He plunged a hand into his khaki pocket and pulled out an antique watch on a chain. "Open it." He placed it in my hand, a glassy, tearful look between the creases of his eyes.

"I don't understand," I confessed.

"Open it and look inside." His voice wavered as he gestured towards the tarnished vintage clock in my hands. I pressed the mechanical pin that freed the clasp, and the tiny metal plate opened like a book to reveal a yellowed, faded picture of a beautiful smiling young woman.

"Am I supposed to know who this is?"

"Serena. She's my daughter. And they killed her." His voice had gone stone-cold.

"What?" I asked.

"The cops said it was a suicide drowning after they recovered her body. But I know that she was murdered by those pirates," he stammered. "They couldn't prove it. But I *know* what I saw."

My pulse quickened, and I shifted uneasily at the mention of the mystery girl who died off the coast. "And what did you see?" I asked.

"She loved to freedive. Best damn swimmer around." He looked away, leaving me hung on each word before he picked up again. "One night, she went to the shore by the pier—I don't know why, she of all people knew how dangerous those tides get—and they took her. I was at the same pier fishing earlier before she'd gotten there, and I was packing up to leave at high tide. I heard voices below, and I looked down to see that boy—Bellamy—he was sneaking around the shore, arguing with another fellow with him—the one who brought you home on a motorcycle."

I blushed, thinking back briefly to having my arms wrapped around Milo from the backseat of his bike and how many times I'd reimagined the feel of him against me since. Russell went on as I pushed the thought away.

"They were talking about a girl, about how she wasn't the one they needed, or something like that. But Bellamy said he didn't care—that he wanted her heart anyway. I didn't realize at the time they were talking about Serena, but it all makes sense now. She was reported missing from the pier not even an hour later."

My stomach twisted into knots. I took a deep breath in through my nose. How painful this must have been for him to relive this incident right now as he described it to me.

"I immediately went out looking for Serena on my fishing boat. I was out on the water all night. Just before morning, I found her by the island, floating in the water, bloody. The bastards cut her open." He drew out an imaginary cut across his chest with his finger, a tangible ache in each motion. His lips trembled as he went on to finish the story. I stood there, speechless, my breath stuck in my chest.

"Then out of nowhere that cursed ship was right in front of me. And the captain—he was the devil himself—told me to go back to shore. Said he'd kill my wife and son, too if I ever came back. I fired at him with my speargun. It pierced him right through, but he just laughed and screamed that he couldn't die. And your two sniveling pirate boys were right there on the ship alongside him—absolute bloody messes—staring at me like they weren't covered in the proof they'd just carved out my daughter's heart."

A pit formed in my gut. I could barely process the mental image, much less the thought that Bellamy and Milo wanted the same with me as Russell continued.

"Of course, when I told the police about it, they never believed me. The ship had disappeared along with everyone on it. They thought I was crazy. My testimony didn't mean much. So her death was ruled a suicide by drowning. Said her body must've got caught on a reef or was found by a shark to explain why she was cut open. Closed, just like that."

Russell snapped his fingers as he uttered the last sentence. Then he paused for a long moment. I couldn't find words to fill the silence. So I handed him back the watch instead.

"My Serena." He ran his thumb over the curved edge of the metal. "She was barely twenty. And so much like you, always looking closer beyond the ordinary."

The combination of what he was saying and the tortured expression on his face shook my nerves. Who could have possibly suspected that this sweet old man who watched over the campus was harboring such a dark burden all this time?

"Russell, I'm so sorry. I don't know what to say." I croaked out.

"Don't say anything," he snapped. "Just have the sense to stay away from them before the same thing happens to you."

Another long bout of awkward silence hung in the air as I glanced at the ground once more.

"Do you know why they wanted her heart?" I finally uncovered the courage to look up and ask.

"I only have my guess that it has to do with some old sailor's lore that a mermaid's heart can grant eternal life." A prickle rose in Russell's voice. "Serena was the closest thing to a mermaid these coasts have ever seen. But at the end of the day, she was just a girl who gave her heart to the sea."

I stared at a withering flower on a bright green bush next to Russell's boots, my mind devoid of any fitting response I could possibly offer. So I asked a question instead.

"Have you ever seen this necklace before? Did Serena have anything like it, by chance?"

When Russell was silent, I began to turn away, but then I looked back when I had a sudden thought. "You wouldn't happen to know anything about this necklace, would you?" Russell examined the pendant at my neck for a moment.

"No, I don't recognize it." He shook his head. "And I don't believe Serena would've either."

LOOSE CANNON

14

KATRINA

That night, I couldn't stop mulling about Russell's dire warning. I also wanted to be anywhere but in the dorm, where both Milo and clearly Bellamy had me caged like an exotic bird. And now, after everything I knew, I couldn't help but fear they were taking their time with me for a reason. Like predators toying with their prey.

I still had no real proof they murdered Serena. It didn't fully make sense. But I was also taking Milo's words to heart—Never trust a pirate.

"Do you want to go window shopping in the old town?" I asked McKenzie, desperate to escape the walls that were starting to feel like a prison of my own invention.

"*You're* asking *me* to go shopping downtown? Who are you and what have you done with Katrina?" McKenzie teased with that bubbly cackle of hers.

"I'm serious," I said with a half-smile. "I just need some air—and *not* ocean air."

McKenzie sauntered over to the door and grabbed her purse. "Okay then, let's go."

Within minutes, I'd thrown on a pair of jeans and a tank top, and we were strolling through the campus and out into the old historic district, where the crooked stone streets and weathered rooftops greeted us like a kiss from the past. The seagulls were strangely noisier than usual at this time of night, and cool, balmy autumn air made the palm trees dance beneath the moonlight. I was grateful the lingering hot, humid nights of long past summer months were finally coming to an end.

I knew I still had to figure out what dark secrets my necklace held before the pirates returned for me if I wanted to avoid meeting the same fate as Serena. But tonight I just wanted to forget it all for a while and breathe.

At least that's what I told myself. So then why couldn't I stop searching up Serena's name online, reading old ghost forum threads with made up theories about the famed Constantine island drowning?

McKenzie and I walked the same paths over, stopping in boutiques and jewelry stores for her to browse—and buy—whatever caught her eye.

We were passing by a bustling restaurant with a canopied roof and an open patio when a scream pierced the air. My body went rigid and I stood on edge, whirling around towards the sound only to realize it was an old friend of McKenzie's sitting at the bar tucked beneath the awning, dramatically shouting her excitement into the night at spotting her. She waved at my roommate and called her over, and I flashed her a grin as I told her to go catch up with her.

She tried to persuade me to follow her inside and make a new acquaintance, but I was more than happy to wait for her outside the restaurant and stare at the sky.

"I'll try to be quick, but Jade loves to chat." McKenzie tossed a perfectly styled curl over her shoulder and lifted her chin. "Be right back."

I stood outside the patio, where few people passed by, as it was getting late and businesses were starting to close for the night. My gaze drifted upward, where I found myself studying the stars, their angles, and their places in the sky, even through the thin clouds that veiled them. And I found the North Star, all on my own, and I hated that it made me think of him—the ghost I couldn't get out my head. The dead man who'd made me feel most alive. The pirate who wagered his soul on my life. And who I stupidly refused to believe wanted any part of cutting out my heart.

"Have your lovely friend bring out some rum, will you? Ship's been fresh out for a few centuries."

I recognized that serpent-like voice instantly, as a shudder crawled up my spine. I turned to face Bellamy where he stood, a shadow at my back.

"Why?" I seethed.

"Why what?" He leaned against the building and lifted a brow. "Why is the rum gone? I'd think that'd be more than obvious." He smirked.

"Don't play games with me." My voice hardened. "Why are you stalking me and leaving notes in my dorm? Why are you watching me when I sleep? Why haven't you taken my necklace and cut out my heart already?"

"Just because I'm after your heart, love, doesn't mean I plan to cut it out. I think I can steal it just fine from where it is."

I failed to suppress a scoff as he inched closer, those blue winter eyes sliding over me as he positioned himself between me and the wall.

"Don't use your pet names on me," I backed away until my shoulders met damp stucco. He flashed a handsome smile, the charming picture of deceit unbothered and infuriatingly cool in the face of my wrath.

"It's truly fascinating how easily Milo managed to turn you against me."

"He didn't turn me against you." I corrected, my pulse fluttering in my ears like the moths on the street lamps. "You did that all on your own." I dashed to the left of him in an attempt to walk past his brooding figure, but he blocked my path with his arm.

"Milo isn't the only one trying to rewrite his destiny. Just so happens we both need you to do it. What makes his reason any better than mine?"

"I don't even understand what it is that you want with me."

"Revenge, love." He smiled accentuating the last syllable. "Against your dear Milo, and against our captain, for a priceless treasure they stole from me."

"You're insane." I bit my lip and bit back a lump in my throat.

"Am I? For wanting to awaken the power that you don't even realize lurks in your veins. I'd say that makes me resourceful," he purred, dragging a finger beneath my chin to lift my face to his. "And I like to protect my resources."

"Is that what you told Serena?" His shoulders stiffened at the name. I held my gaze on him, his face half-cast in golden shadow from the streetlights. "Before you killed her?"

Even for a ghost, he'd gone deathly pale. I used his reaction as my chance to break free and shove past him.

Without looking back, I could feel his eyes on me as I stormed away to place myself in the middle of the street, where I at least had a better view of the restaurant—and where they'd hopefully have a view of me, if I were to be kidnapped by a cold-blooded ghost pirate.

"I didn't kill her." His words had gone hollow, and they gripped me like ice. I braced for him to offer some sort of further excuse or attempt an explanation. But none came.

When I turned around, he was gone. And the hurried tap of Mackenzie's heels on cobblestone stole my attention.

"Who was that guy?" She gasped.

"That," I grumbled, "was Bellamy."

"Well, damn." McKenzie squinted toward the street with her hand over her eyes. "You weren't kidding about him being hot. Was he bothering you?"

"No," I sighed. "Just saying hello."

"Mmm hmm, sure. Is that why you look so nervous?" She took up stride beside me as I started walking the other direction.

"I just...didn't expect to see him here," I uttered, looking out at the bay. "But anyway, we should probably head back to campus. It's getting late. And there's a storm rolling in."

I'd noticed the thick black cloud in the distance, earlier, and now low thunder rumbled close by. The breeze had picked up, and soft lightning bursts revealed the silhouettes of billowing clouds.

As we hurried back along, the smell of salty rain hanging in the air, I glimpsed a painting hanging in the storefront of a small antique store that caught my eye. I stopped to admire it—a scene of a woman at a cliff's edge, with only a single lantern to light the dark as she looked down upon a dark raging sea. On the horizon drifted a lone ship that might've been coming or going, but regardless, remained the woman's sole focus. And in the corner, the artist's signature—Elisabeth Shores.

I studied the piece, so skillfully crafted in watercolors, and goosebumps rose along my arms. Looking at it felt transcendent, like a voice was calling me home, singling me out in a world that otherwise didn't see me.

"She...she was a painter, too," I murmured low, a strange smile overwhelming my face.

She was a painter. And she painted the sea—a glimpse of a vision that must've become significant enough that she had no choice but to give it life.

"Who?" McKenzie fluttered to my side after she'd noticed I'd stopped.

"The artist. I can't believe it. She...she was one of my relatives from a long time ago." I flicked my gaze to the door. "We have to go inside. I need to see it up close."

McKenzie balked. "But the storm—"

"It'll be quick." I didn't wait for her answer as I rattled through the door, the tiny bell overhead chiming as I stepped foot inside.

It smelled like old books, like dust and roses, and only a few vintage orange floor lamps kept the store illuminated.

"We're closing." A voice from the far end of the store said matter-of-factly. "Come back tomorrow."

"I'm not here to browse. I saw what I want in the window, so if I can just grab it really quick—"

"You can come back tomorrow. I already closed out the register." A guy about our age appeared from a back counter and moved to turn off another lamp, as if making his point.

To my surprise, the bell chimed behind me as McKenzie appeared at the door. "Come on Trina, we can just come back tomorrow."

I hesitated, reluctant to leave the painting behind, even though I knew I was being unreasonably obsessive. I strode over to the window display, passing old record players and an assortment of Victorian-era furniture, and reached for the canvas. I strained to read the writing on the back in the dimly lit shop as thunder clapped outside.

Elisabeth Shores-'The Sea Draws the Heart,' 1803. Ten years before her death.

"It's this," I said, the words jumping up my throat. "How much for this?"

The guy strode over and crossed his arms, his deep brown eyes and rounded jaw vaguely familiar. "Check the sticker."

I searched the painting and found the white rectangle sticker with the price, and my heart sank. "Sixty."

"Good job. Now come back tomorrow."

"No, it's...it's okay," I mumbled, defeated as I placed the painting back. "I can't swing that right now."

"Okay," he whistled, unenthused, heading for the door and jangling a set of keys.

I turned to leave, and a long streak of lightning illuminated a small display on a dusty leather trunk by the front counter, where I swore I saw Serena's face. My heart skipped a beat.

As my eyes adjusted to the darkness, I leaned forward, looking closer to see a collection of old newspapers—some clippings, some entire articles—of notable events in the town, dating to as far back as 1940. And there in the center stack of them was Serena smiling back at me—the exact same picture that was in Russell's watch—on the front-page headline about her death.

And the sticky-note sign on the trunk read in plain messy handwriting: *$2.00-5.00 each.*

I picked it up. "I'll take this. Right now." I dug into my purse and pulled out everything I had on me—exactly five crinkled dollars. The shop guy stared at me, his face emotionless as he threw a dull glance toward the door and then back at me. "Great. I'll ring you up tomorrow."

"Hey now," McKenzie butted in. "Is it really that much trouble to just ring her up?"

"Yeah, it is. Because it's raining outside and my Bronco's open." He rolled his eyes and I was all at once aware of the sound of rain on the rooftop. "For God's sake just take the damn thing. Nobody's buying that old crap anyway."

I clutched the newspaper. "Thanks."

"Yeah whatever—just...stay here while I put my top up and I'll come back to lock the doors."

Without another word he spun on his heel and bolted through the door. We followed, halting beneath the awning sign of Bay Side Relics, watching him fumble with his 70's Bronco's canvas top in the downpour.

Seconds later he came sprinting back, soaked to the marrow, and cursing with each step as he fumbled with the keys in his hand.

"I hope you two have a short walk. Because this isn't clearing up anytime soon," he panted through raindrops rolling down his forehead.

McKenzie looked at me. "We...have to make it back to ICA."

The shop guy glowered at the both of us. "Do you need a ride? I pass right by the campus on my way home." The question came out in a breathy exhale, like it took everything in him to make the offer.

"I don't know," McKenzie drawled out. "You're not very nice."

"I'm offering you a ride so you don't have to walk home alone at 10:00 PM in a thunderstorm."

"Yeah, but you could be a creep," she said. "What's your name?"

"It's Noah." He flashed a hollow smile as he turned the lock, his gleaming white teeth a stark contrast against his dark skin. He blinked a few times before speaking again. "Look I'm sorry I was a bit of an asshole," he sighed. "It's just been a rough day at the shop. I completely understand if you don't want a ride and I don't blame you at all for turning it down. I can go look for an umbrella in the store at least." He moved to unlock the door of the shop he'd just fought so hard to close down.

I looked at McKenzie and shrugged. I truly didn't get any weird vibes, and if anything, I'd much have preferred to the keep the Serena newspaper as dry as possible, because I planned to comb through it from back to front. Besides, if I could handle undead pirates, I could handle a grumpy shopkeeper.

"We'll take the ride," she nodded. "It's just a few blocks."

"Whatever," Noah sighed. "Just...please don't scratch the leather."

We piled into his Bronco and the ride was mostly silent until he started asking more and more casual questions directed at McKenzie. I noticed the way he kept glancing at her in the rearview mirror, and I thought I saw him blush when he caught her looking back.

Five minutes in and she had managed to turn the grouch into a ray of sunshine. I let them chatter on while I focused on the newspaper in my hands.

It was old, and weathered by the Florida climate. I could feel the layer of dust and mold settled into the pages, as I pressed my fingers against the underside of the yellowed paper. Swallowing, I glanced down and read the headline, dated July 19, 1988.

Local Freediver Drowns at Sea

I read through the article, the story much the same as what Russell said it would be. A naïve young girl found herself caught in a riptide and the case was closed. But what Russell hadn't specified was that Serena wasn't just a freediver, but also a coach for others learning to do the same. At a place called Vista Laguna Diving School.

While rain battered the soft top, I searched the company name on my phone out of curiosity, yielding a handful of results. It had closed down not long after Serena's death. But there was an old address still listed for the company that made me more than curious—I recognized the street name.

Bay Lily Road—an overgrown gravel road I passed sometimes when I took scenic drives on backroads to clear my head. I'd never thought much of it, but now I wondered if the old diving school might still be there.

I wasn't one for snooping, but something in me itched to see it for myself. If for nothing more than to confirm that this—like everything else unraveling my sanity—was real. To see if there was anything left behind that might connect me to the past and the truth.

Because Bellamy's words still lingered in my mind as thunder shook the sky.

I didn't kill her.

Some part of me almost believed him.

And I could certainly use a drive to clear my head soon.

HIGH AND DRY

15

KATRINA

Noah dropped us off in front of the campus entrance just as the thunderstorm waned into a light, steady rain. McKenzie waved to Noah before shuffling through the gates, and I was right on her trail—until the undeniable shape of a motorcycle caught my eye in the shadows.

Milo's motorcycle.

My thoughts spun in a million different directions. I didn't want to believe Milo was capable of what Russell said. I didn't want to think that anyone could be.

But my weakness for wanting to assume the best in people might just have been the thing that would get me killed by two manipulative, cunning pirates. And if there was anyone I should trust, it certainly shouldn't be the pirate who'd already warned me against it.

Unless...he knew by telling me not to trust him, it would ultimately make me *want* to trust him, which is how he could get me to play into his hands. I couldn't distinguish if he was being honest with dishonest intentions, or perhaps the other way around. Either way, the mind games were taking their toll.

The cold hard fact was that I didn't know what he really wanted or truly planned to do with me.

All I knew was that he was here somewhere.

And I couldn't risk leading him right back to our dorm on the slim chance he didn't already know where it was. So I made up some excuse to McKenzie, telling her it would be best if she went on ahead because I needed to get something from my car in the student parking lot.

And when she was out of sight, I veered around the corner and began my search for the man I refused to let have the upper hand. I would find him first. And I would not put McKenzie in danger if I could help it, even if I had to stay out there all night.

I searched every corridor, every breezeway, and every dark corner of the campus sidewalks. As I snuck quietly past Russell's fresh landscaping, the newspaper still in my hand, something rustling in the bushes made me look up. I held my breath, staring at where I'd heard the noise, feet planted as a large white bird took flight out from behind the shrubs and soared towards a gazebo across the Lawn.

It disappeared behind the gazebo into the night, and by some inexplicable lure, I followed. As I crossed the deserted campus, I noted a shovel left behind where Russell had been working earlier, sticking upright out of the fresh dirt, and instinctively grabbed it for protection.

With my shovel raised and my steps calculated, I crept toward the gazebo, unable to shake the feeling that something—or someone—loomed in the shadows there. I stood at the entrance, blinking in the rain, staring into the darkness beneath the covered archway.

I could almost feel his presence. A sensation welling in my chest that became impossible to ignore—like a magnet pulling me towards the gazebo. I tightened my grip on the shovel handle, every muscle in my body stiff and coiled.

"Why are you here?" I finally demanded, tossing my voice into the darkness.

Silence taunted me, except for the gentle patter of raindrops on cement, and I took a nervous step forward. "Tell me why you're here. Why can't you just leave me alone?"

"I thought we've already been through this," Milo's voice cooed from the shadows. "I'm ensuring Bellamy never finds his way to your room again."

He stepped out of the gazebo and into the dim warm glow of the sidewalk lanterns, and I raised my shovel like a weapon, my grip slippery.

"Stay back!" I shouted. "I want both of you to stay away from me. You're killers. You're liars. For all I know you're probably working together to kidnap me like you kidnapped Serena."

He narrowed his eyes at the name and cocked his head, as though more curious than offended. "Who told you that name?"

"It doesn't matter!" I waved my shovel and tossed the newspaper at him, watching it hit his chest like a brick wall.

He glanced down at the paper as it dropped to his feet, unfazed by the shovel I prodded into the air by his head.

"All that matters is that I know. I know what happened. I know what you did!" I seethed. "So, stay away from my college, and stay away from me."

He raised a hand, palms open and eyes pleading. But I wasn't going to keep falling for the quiet charm. "Katrina, it's not—"

"Stop it! Just get away from me!" I repeated. "You told me not to trust you—well, this is me not trusting you."

"If you would just listen—"

"Listen to you? You're a pirate!" I growled. "And that's the problem, isn't it? I could listen to you all night and I still wouldn't know what to believe. But I *will* learn the truth. And until then, stay the hell away from me! You told me not to come to the beach, and I haven't—so don't you dare come back here!"

He started to stammer out something once more, and I slammed the end of the shovel on the ground in front of him so hard I thought it would break off the handle. "Leave. Me. Alone." I drew out each word, long and low.

He stared at me for a long time, brows knit tight together, before he finally offered something like a half-nod. He carried on, as if he expected me to look away.

But I refused. I held my gaze on him, watching, unblinking, every single step he took back across the campus. And I waited until the sound of his motorcycle faded into the distance, drowned out by the sound of steady thunder, before I relaxed enough to let go of the shovel and retrieve the loose, wet pages of the newspaper.

And with my heart heavy and my nerves firing hot beneath the cold rain on my skin, I waited a long time before I felt safe enough to trudge back to the dorm, where I silently checked every lock and window more times than I could count.

Fathoms Below

16

KATRINA

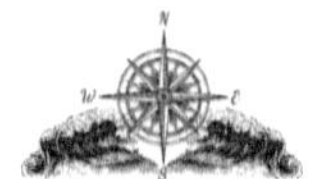

My dreams found me as Elisabeth, standing on that cliff above the sea as the waves rioted below, walking toward the edge, unable to stop whatever strange tide was pulling me toward it. And Milo's voice, a far away echo in the raging wind.

"You need to leave. They're looking for you."

McKenzie had already left for class. I had class that morning, too. But I had already made up my mind that I wasn't going.

Instead, I grabbed breakfast from the kitchenette, gulping down the sugary cereal as I imagined what I might find waiting for me at the old diving school, and trying hard to forget last night's encounter with Milo.

I slid into my Jeep, the engine clanking to life after a few prayerful turns of the key. It never failed me. And just as I rolled out of the parking lot, the hopeful glint of white morning sunlight after a night of storms bouncing off Matanzas Bay, a short string of separate texts from Mom chimed.

-I remembered something last night. About the necklace.

-Got me thinking after you asked.

-There's a box that goes with it...I think. It's a jewelry box for a single necklace with a locked compartment, so idk what else it would be for. I remember seeing it when I was cleaning out Mom's things after she died.

I went on high alert, both at the mention of the jewelry box but also of my grandma's death. She struggled with nightmares and hallucinations just the same as us, and she took her life when Mom was still a teenager. I'd never made the overarching connection—or understood it—until now. And the dates of all those women's deaths flashed before my eyes, a haunting reminder that Mom—and that I—would be next, if I didn't overcome the same curse that plagued us for generations.

I texted back at a stoplight.

-Please tell me you didn't throw it out.

She replied at the next turn.

-Of course not, Trina.

-It's somewhere packed away. I'll look through the attic and see if I can find it.

I thumbs-upped the message, and then refocused on the road. I was almost to the stretch of swampy backroads I found so intriguing.

Nearing the empty street that led to Bay Lily, I thought what I might find when I turned my wheels down that unkempt hidden dead-end drive, barely wide enough for a vehicle. I pictured pulling up to a dilapidated, abandoned facility entangled in foliage and weathered by the sun and salt.

But the further I traversed through the uneven, gravel drive, the condition of the area actually seemed to improve the closer I got to the end of the road. Before long, water came into view—a lake or lagoon, surrounded by mangroves and tall seagrasses—and on its shores, right at the end of the driveway—a small house with a rusted motorboat parked beside it. There was a car parked beneath the carport, and the house was clearly maintained.

Someone lived here.

As luck would have it, a woman was standing outside on the porch of the little yellow watering plants that hung between a small Puerto Rican flag dangling from the railing. She glared at me suspiciously as my Jeep slowed to a stop and I turned off the engine.

I stepped out and approached cautiously, surprised by own nerve.

The woman looked to be in her thirties and tired, her toffee-colored hair dangling in a loose bun. She flashed an uncertain smile, more like a quick, awkward show of teeth. I threw up my hand to gesture a wave in a failed attempt to ease the tension.

"Hi, good morning!" I tried to sound as sweet as possible, wishing my voice was as charming as McKenzie's at that moment. "I was just...looking for the old diving school? Is this where it used to be?

"Technically, yes." The woman released her hold on the trigger of the hose nozzle and the shower of water ceased. "Why are you looking for it? You one of those weirdos who post videos online of themselves exploring abandoned places? I thought I'd seen the last of you all." There was an edge in her voice, like she was waiting for me to say the wrong thing so she could rip me apart and send me on my way.

"Well, no. I actually...I—" I thought of something fast and braced myself for the lie. "I'm...working on a research project for school, and I was hoping to learn more about the dive school's...impact...in the area."

"Well, you found it."

"This is the school?"

"Yes. My mother ran the admin side of the business out of her house. You don't need much of a building for training people to swim in the sea." She nodded toward the boat. "And when she did, she just made use of different facilities in the area." She turned back to watering her plants.

I stepped closer, a foot on the porch steps. "Is this...still her house? Is she here?"

The woman paused, looking at me as though I had just asked a forbidden question that shouldn't have dared left my lips. She tossed down the hose, and her gaze burned through me like embers.

I backed away, withering into myself, car keys in hand. "I'm sorry. I didn't mean to—"

"*Que está pasando*, Denise?" The creak of the house door caught my attention. A frail elderly woman huddled in a pink robe and holding a coffee mug pushed her way onto the porch.

Denise flashed me a look of aggravation as she dropped the hose and stepped toward the old woman, taking the mug from her, and attempting to usher her back through the door.

"It's *nadie*, Ma. Go back inside." Denise threw a glance back my way, her lips tight and jaw tensed. "She has Alzheimer's," she hissed so quietly she nearly mouthed the words at me.

My briefly piqued hopes sank. Time had ravaged the one thing I needed from here—memories.

The old woman resisted and slipped past her daughter, much more spryly than I would have imagined her capable of. She squinted towards me with eyes that were already nearly pressed closed by sagging skin and wrinkles.

"Serena, is that you?" Those wrinkled eyes widened, and joy sparked on her face as she stumbled through her words. "I...I haven't seen you...since Christmas."

"Actually, I'm Katrina." I corrected, stepping forward. "But I know Serena. Or at least—I know about her." The old woman's look of excitement crinkled slowly into one of confusion.

"Look what you did," Denise snarled. "You're going to get her going."

The old woman gestured to me with a trembling hand etched with creases. "Come here, *reina*."

I crept cautiously up the wooden steps to meet her on the porch. She took my hand, her speech suddenly a bit smoother.

"Oh *reina*, you remind me so much of Serena. She would love to meet you." Her voice fawned at the mention. "Are you here for a diving session? The boat goes out this afternoon."

"No, Mrs...." I pulled a gulp of humid air into my lungs and glanced at Denise

"Gutierrez," she said curtly, arms crossed. "Cynthia Guirierrez."

"Mrs. Guiterrez," I said. "I was wondering if you had a minute. If you could tell me what you remember about Serena?"

"Oh, hmmm..." she uttered. "And when did you get here? Who...who are you?"

"I'm Katrina." I reminded her.

"Oh. W—where's Serena?" She let go of my hand and looked around.

"Serena's gone, Ma," Denise groaned.

Mrs. Gutierrez went silent, staring dead ahead out over the lagoon.

"*Mamá*?" Denise put a hand on her mother's hunched shoulder.

A strange trembling tune emanated from the old woman's lips, as she still looked out at the water, bewitched by something unseen. It began as a mumble, but then her voice grew until the words were clear. She sang each lyric perfectly, without one stumble or stutter.

Down by the shore
Meet me once more
By the light of the moon
Love me, then leave me
With the dawn rising
Haunt me forevermore

I clutched my necklace instinctively as the song ended. The pendant tingled in my hand, and I released it as a phantom shiver coursed through me.

"Not that song again, Ma," Denise rolled her eyes and then flicked her gaze to me. "She hasn't sung that for a long time. And now you come here and—"

"What's the song?"

"Serena used to sing it. All the time. In fact, she was singing it right before...right before..."

"Before what?" I didn't mean to keep interrupting; I couldn't let the opportunity pass just when it seemed something might be finally rising to the surface.

The old woman turned her head to face me, her eyes now clear and focused. "Before she was taken."

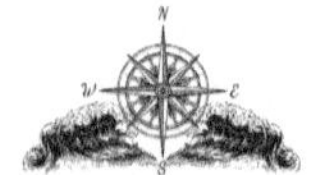

Mrs. Gutierrez invited me in for a cup of Café Bustelo, much to Denise's disdain. The old woman was small, but she was a spitfire even her own daughter couldn't contend with. In my mind, she was everything I imagined the grandma I never got to meet might've been.

"You really remind me so much of her..." Her voice trailed off as she patted my hand from her place across the table. My lips couldn't help but curve into a smile as my gaze roamed the little kitchen. The old cherry red wood of the table contrasted the pastel yellow cabinets and the frilly white curtains in the best way. The smell of baby powder and coffee grounds filled my nostrils.

"You seem like you were fond of her. She must've been a good diving coach." I said, blowing on the piping hot drink in my mug.

"Oh, she was absolutely the best freediver we ever had. And she loved her job so much." Mrs. Gutierrez closed her eyes. "You would've thought that girl was born underwater. I've never seen a better swimmer." She put a pruned finger to her cheek. "I think I have some pictures, come to think of it!" She turned to Denise. "*Oye, hija.* Get the little photo album from the bookcase. The blue one."

Denise shook her head and stood to do as she was asked. Returning with the book, she set it down in front of her mother, who grinned with delight, the pink lipstick cracking across her creased lips. But then it faded as quickly as it had come.

"Why...what is this?"

"You asked for the picture book, Ma."

"I...is the coffee burning? Did you get the groceries yesterday?"

Denise looked at me, defeated, and sighed, "Maybe you should go."

"Don't be rude," Mrs. Gutierrez snapped. "Show me the pictures."

Denise thumbed through the photos in the booklet until her mother stopped her..

"*Mira*, right there" she said, pointing. "Oh, look at Serena. Orange...she loved orange. And she'd always have little flecks of gold in her braids...Let me tell you, she even looked like a sea queen. A real *reina*."

I leaned over the table, admiring the photograph. Even though it was a bit fuzzy from age, I could easily make out the image of a beaming girl waving from the water, a young student grinning beneath goggles beside her, her coral two-piece swimsuit a bold pop of color against her delicate brown skin.

For a moment it was almost hard to even imagine her terrible fate.

Mrs. Gutierrez shook her head with a breath of laugh. "She even had this crazy idea to start a mermaid school program for the kids—found a place to make the tails and everything. But we never got that far..." Her voice trailed off.

"She looks so happy there," I said softly.

The old woman leaned back. "She was—as long as she was in the water. And if she wasn't working, she was in it anyway, out on the beach from dawn till dusk...sometimes even after, despite my warnings." She frowned.

"Is...is that what happened to her?" I asked timidly, taking out the newspaper from my bag and placing it on the table. "She went out in the water at night?"

The old woman's eyes grew distant. "Yes. She drowned herself." I noticed the way she locked up. The way her whole body stiffened when she said it. As if there was far more to the story that she wanted to say. "It says it right there in your newspaper, *claro*."

"But," I inhaled, "do you really believe she drowned? You said she was such a good swimmer..."

"She drowned? Who? No...she wouldn't. Serena wouldn't drown. Is she alright?" She glanced around, calling her name.

I couldn't shake the feeling that this little old lady knew more. I believed she knew something—if I could just get it out of her. I needed to guide her to another spurt of clarity. And then I recalled Russell, how he said Valdez had threatened him if he told anyone. Maybe it was the same for Mrs. Gutierrez. I mustered the courage to ask.

"Mrs. Gutierrez, is there any chance you know what really happened that night? This night?" I pointed to the newspaper clipping.

Denise shot up, nearly tipping her chair over. "Okay, that's enough."

But, to my surprise, Mrs. Gutierrez raised a hand and motioned for her daughter to sit back down.

"I couldn't...I can't prove what happened. No one believed me. No one...No one is going to believe me." Her drooping eyes welled with tears.

"Serena's father would believe you. He knows she didn't just drown. He knows the police just gave up on her because they couldn't piece it together." I paused, and I don't know what kind of courage came over me to do so, but I gently placed my hand on top of hers from across the table. "And I think you know that, too."

The old woman buried her head in her hands and began sobbing.

Denise cursed under her breath and then stood up again. "Girl, whoever you are, you need to leave. Look what you are doing to her! You come in here asking her questions about all this weird shit, bringing up a past she barely remembers—"

"Oh no, *hija*," Mrs. Gutierrez sniffed, trying to compose herself. "I remember it well. Too well. But they think I'm *loca*. You think it, too." She paused, looking at her scowling daughter. "But now, maybe here is someone who will listen."

I hung onto her every word, leaning forward as I silently pleaded for her to continue.

Mrs. Gutierrez settled herself in her chair and began to stare into a spot on the floor beside her.

"It was a Friday. Serena hadn't shown up for her shifts, which was unlike her. I knew she liked to freedive at the pier, even knowing how dangerous those currents get. She had a personal goal of proving herself—proving she belonged to the sea by facing the most dangerous parts of it." She paused. "What did I tell you already? I...I'm sorry."

"You said it was Friday and Serena hadn't shown up for work."

"Oh, yes...I went looking for her at the pier, and I saw her there—just standing there watching the waves. Like she was waiting for something. Then..."

Her voice trailed off and her eyes began to shine. I nodded to reassure her.

"She started singing that song. The one from earlier. And when she stopped singing, a man appeared from the water, like a shadow, right out over the ocean, and walked through the waves right up to her.

She'd talked about her mystery man all the time—about how they would meet by the sea under the moon, and about how he'd give the world for her. But I never imagined she was talking about a...a..."

"A ghost." I finished for her.

"See, *mija*?" She turned to Densie, who looked horrified and annoyed all at once. "She gets it."

"Could you see what he looked like?" I pressed.

"Oh yes," she said. "Black hair, nice face, all that. I remember he had a snake tattoo on his neck."

Bellamy.

"I was hiding a ways back, behind the last leg of the pier the tide hadn't reached yet, watching. They kissed and held each other, and then Serena started walking off into the water, while her mystery man screamed after her and followed. And then another man came running across the shore through the water—he came from nowhere—yelling to both of them so loud I could hear it over the waves. 'You need to leave! They're looking for her!'

"But before he even reached them, a ship came up out of the water, right there on the surf. I can't explain it, but it did. And a man like *el Diablo* himself walked right through the water and grabbed Serena. The other two men fought him—they did everything to pull her away from him—and they were screaming things like 'She's not the one! She's not what you think she is!' But the devil man had brought a whole crew with him, and he ordered them to beat the two men and tie them to the masts as he dragged her onto his ship."

Mrs. Gutierrez hung her head, her voice quavering.

"I wanted to help her. But what could I have done? The tide was rising so fast it was going to take me out with it, so I ran to get help. I found the police, but by the time I led them back, all of it—Serena, the ship, everything—was gone. And they thought I was a lunatic."

"Did...did you get a good look at the other man who tried to help save her?"

"Not really. It was all happening so fast in the dark. He looked about the same age as her mystery man. Hair like honey. I think I might've glimpsed a big star tattoo along his arm, but I can't be for certain."

Milo.

Denise looked back and forth between me and her mother. By her expression, I could tell she thought we were both unstable. Mrs. Gutierrez wiped a teardrop that was threatening to roll down her wrinkled cheek. "And I couldn't prove any of it. The idea of a kidnapping or murder was thrown out along with my testimony. No evidence."

I searched for words to respond, but they wouldn't come. I'd accused Bellamy and Milo of the very thing they were trying to prevent. And it made my stomach twist in knots.

Then just like Russell did, Mrs. Gutierrez shattered right in front of me, her sobs filling the silence.

"I'm so sorry," I said softly. "And I'm sorry about Serena. She didn't deserve what happened to her."

I squeezed her hand and she looked up to meet my gaze, composing herself.

"There's someone else who needs to know the truth," I said. "Serena's father thinks her lover killed her. It might help him find some closure to know that all this time he tried everything to save her."

Mrs. Gutierrez nodded and pulled a handful of pictures of Serena from her photo album. "Take these pictures to him and tell him what I told you. Tell him who I was. If he still doesn't believe you, you can send him here and I'll tell him...I'll tell him myself."

"Thank you so much, *Señora*," I told her as I took the photos from her. "I'm glad to have met you and your daughter. It means a lot to me that you took the time to talk to me. Thank you, again."

Denise, arms crossed, still looked at me as though I was a nuisance, but I flashed her a genuine smile anyway.

"No, *Sirena*," she said. "Thank you."

"I'm Katrina," I gently reminded.

"I know." She flashed a tender smile. "Not *Serena. Sirena.*"

I brushed off the shudder that threatened to trickle down my neck, as she and Denise walked me back outside where we exchanged goodbyes once more.

No sooner had I taken one step off the porch than Mrs. Guiterrez's voice rang out. "Are you leaving so soon, lovely? I don't believe we've met. I must've been upstairs while you were visiting. Who are you?"

"I'm a friend of Serena's." I called back.

With a warm smile and a new light in her eyes, she closed the door. And as I backed away, I couldn't help but look at the little white house on the lagoon, with its creaky screen door and hanging flower baskets, and think what a secret it was harboring all these years.

And if there was one thing I was sure of about Constantine, Florida, it was that nothing was ever as it seemed.

DIRE STRAITS

17

KATRINA

A creeping weight lingered in my chest from what I uncovered at Bay Lily. My first thought was to find Russell and tell him everything. I only hoped he would believe me.

I wandered around campus, looking in all the usual places where I often saw him. I finally spotted his golf cart parked off to the side of the school's grand fountain, loaded with shovels, tools and buckets full of trimmings and hedge clippings. I rushed over, clinging to the photos Mrs. Gutierrez had given me.

He emerged from around a cluster of trees, pushing a wheelbarrow. The smell of mulch and fresh soil greeted me as he neared, walking with the same short step he always did, and that tender, quiet look in his eyes.

"Russell" I started, striding over, unsure of how to start the conversation. Luckily, I didn't have to, as his eyes wandered down to my hands, and he recognized the pictures of his daughter in my grasp. I offered them to him, and he took them in silence, a solemn question written on his face.

"I...I talked to the owner of the diving center where Serena worked. She went looking for her that night when she didn't show up for work." I started, having to clear my dry throat just to get the words out. "The captain attacked her, but Bellamy and Milo were only trying to stop him. They were covered in blood because they were beaten for trying to save her. Cynthia Guitierrez saw it all."

I waited for him to say something, but he only kept his gaze fixated on the photos in his calloused hands. He rubbed a thumb along the edges of the top picture—a photo of Serena standing on the dive boat.

I waited for him to say something. I wondered if I should mention Bellamy and Serena's relationship but then thought better of it. Something told me he already knew. There was nothing left for me to explain. He only had to decide whether to accept it.

The seconds felt like eternity, but Russell never looked up, and he never spoke. I watched him processing it with such reverence, and I realized there was nothing more for me.

After moments that dragged on in uncomfortable silence, he looked up at me through eyes glistening with welling tears.

"Thank you," he muttered with a small nod. He turned away slowly, but stopped to look over his shoulder to offer four somber last words. "Please, just be careful."

The only option I had left was to walk away, too, hoping he had believed the truth.

Within the next few minutes, I was scurrying up the stucco-textured steps to my dorm with a newfound vibrance. All at once, I had hope that maybe things weren't all as foreboding as they seemed. Some strange weight had been lifted off me, and I could only hope that Russell now felt some sort of closure, too.

And I felt strange relief at the thought that if I saw Bellamy or Milo again, I knew the dark truth between them. Because now I had a small glimpse of the men behind the masks that somehow kept luring me deeper into their world. And now, strangely enough, I knew their secrets—maybe even better than I knew my own.

And yet, I didn't see either of them again for days. No notes in my room, no motorcycles parked in the shadows, and no eerie dreams to follow. Just the haunting feeling of the stillness they had left behind.

It should have been a relief, but something unnerving lingered—the thought that just because they weren't showing themselves, didn't mean they weren't still around. And I couldn't help but glimpse over my shoulder every time I walked to and from class. I'd all but threatened them both the last time I'd seen them. I'd accused them of terrible things, and I'd made my mistrust for them clear.

Especially Milo. He had reason enough to decide I wasn't worth the trouble of protecting—to lead his captain right to me since the night I forbade him from coming back to see me. I'd been so harsh to him, I couldn't blame him if he'd at least considered it.

And so I kept my head on a swivel, constantly fighting the sensation that someone still lurked in the shadows—watching and waiting for the right time to surface again. But as each day passed, the paranoia eased—until the nightmares returned, and I all at once felt like I'd been tossed to the waves once more.

Even during classes, I felt like I was drowning, my head swimming far too fast to focus. Like some sense of unnamed, impending doom was right upon me like a slow storm blowing in. So, one afternoon after class, when the creeping thoughts and memories wouldn't subside, I knew I needed to escape them the only way I knew how, just for a little while.

I needed to paint.

I passed McKenzie on the way up to my dorm, and she looked even more dolled up than usual.

"You look cute." I smiled. "Going out with Ty?"

Something mischievous flashed across her face. "No, actually, I…I have a date with Noah."

"Noah?" My brows lifted. "As in, grumpy Noah from the antique store?"

"Yeah," she laughed. "He's actually really sweet under that mean exterior. But anyway, I just thought I'd let you know so you don't wait up for me tonight."

"You got it." I nodded with a grin, thinking even Noah on his worst day would have to be better than Ty. "Have fun."

Back in my dorm, I stared at the wall. With every passing shadow, I flinched. I imagined noises. I was convinced someone had watched me walk across campus. In a rare twist of fate, I felt more afraid of being awake than asleep.

I had to quiet my mind. I had to silence the paranoia, the anxiety, and the never-ending loop in my head trying to fill the gaps between Serena's story and mine. Maybe when my mom found the box…maybe that would bring more answers. Maybe it held the key to breaking whatever curses I was tied to.

But until then, I had to calm the raging storm in my head. I turned on my low-light lamp and crept over to my unfinished painting.

There was hardly more than a week left until the gala, and the scene before me still felt lacking.

The North Star shone gloriously, casting its hopeful aura down onto the waves. But the ocean beneath needed a nod to the darkness—something that hinted at something sinister beneath the surface. I smudged some black and charcoal grey into the indigo waters, adding dimension to the abyss.

And then I traced an outline of a ship, sunk deep below the water, before filling it in with soft colors that pulled the faintest light of the star all the way down into its dreary grave. A small ray of hope breaking through to even the darkest depths.

And as I lost myself painting for hours, I thought of him—bound to the depths by day, and rising with the tide by night.

MAKE UP THE LEEWAY

18

KATRINA

My phone buzzing against my thigh stirred me awake. I sat up in a dark room, realizing I'd nodded off at my table, bits of dried paint clinging to my skin and hair.

I reached for the phone and blinked as my eyes adjusted to the bright screen—2 AM.

And Mom was calling.

My pulse jumped as my blood became icy. Middle-of-night calls from her only meant one thing—she was drunk.

Unless maybe this time it was different. Maybe she'd just found the box and whatever was in it was so important she just had to tell me now. Maybe this would have a happy ending.

I fed myself the lie as I answered the call.

"Mom?" I breathed.

"Hello? Oh, Trina...I'm surprised you're up this late..."

"I—I wasn't. You woke me up," I said, my voice void of emotion.

There was a long, heavy silence as she breathed into the phone. Swallowing, I forced out more words.

"Everything okay, Mom? Did you find the box?" McKenzie was surely sleeping on the other side of the dorm, so I kept my voice low.

"What box?" she repeated with a giggle.

"The necklace box. From grandma," I stated.

"Ohhhh that..." She smacked her lips. "Yes, actually—well not exactly. I found it but turns out it's—well, you'll never guess."

"What?" I pressed the phone to my ear. "Just tell me, Mom."

"Well, it's locked," she snickered. "And I have no idea where the key is. Isn't that just like me? Always soooo close, but never close enough...never close enough." Her eerie laughter faded into some form of sorrowful sing-song tune as she repeated herself. Like her own voice mimicked the void I could sense her falling back into.

"You're drinking again, aren't you, Mom?"

"Katrina..." she mumbled, barely coherent.

"Mom, I know you're drunk."

"I was doing so damn well, Trina" she breathed. "I *was* sober...I was. I even had some nightmares since I've been without the necklace, but I still didn't drink. But then I found that damn box...and it's like a dam broke." She coughed, as if trying to disguise the shiver in her voice. "Your grandmother was right...It's all come back—worse than before...the dreams...the voices...the things I see—it's never been this bad. Even the alcohol doesn't drown it all out anymore..."

"Mom," I said, trying to slow her down. "It's okay, we...we can talk about this. We can still fix this."

But she went on saying things, and the more she spoke, the more frantic she became. "I should have tried sooner...I couldn't do it. I couldn't figure it out on my own. I'm weak like all the rest of us. But now it's your turn...I couldn't, but maybe you can. You...you're smart. You're better than me." Her words came between sobs. Her sentences were slurred and disconnected, every word uttered through a tremble.

"It's okay, Mom. Try to stay calm." I no longer cared if I woke McKenzie. I didn't care if I woke the whole world. I sprang to my feet and rushed out to the hallway, desperate for fresh air.

"Right now, Trina, I'm scared to sleep...But it doesn't matter anyway. I see it—I feel it—even when I'm awake. I can't drink it away anymore..." she gasped. "I'm going to drown."

"Mom, what—what do you see? In your nightmares and the hallucinations?" The words spilled out like a raging river. My heart was thumping through my chest. "What do you mean you're going to drown?"

"It's...it's always like... like water. I'm always drowning. Always."

An icy grip squeezed me, like a serpent choking out the air.

"Mom—"

"I know it sounds.... sounds crazy, doesn't it? Why—why do you think...why do you think I never took you to the beach? I thought it was a warning...I was so scared when I heard you moved to Florida."

I stared out at the black nothingness leading toward the bay, paralyzed as I clung to every word of her drunken breakdown.

She went on, her speech more garbled than before. "The rehab, the meds...they just numbed everything...but it was never strong enough without the necklace. It will never be strong enough. I don't know what to do...anymore. I just...I don't know how much more I can take." Then her words cut through me like a steel blade. "We're all meant to drown."

Suddenly, the anger I'd harbored towards her for so long vanished, replaced only by a twisted, strange sense of compassion. And fear for her as much as myself.

All this time she was drowning. All this time we were both at the mercy of the exact same kind of torment.

None of this was coincidence.

This was by design.

"Try to get some rest, Mom. Please. We can fix this. We can fix this."

"I...No, I don't know. I'll try. I'm trying," she hiccupped through sniffs and sobs. "You're a good girl, you know. You're not too far gone yet. You're smart. You've got a chance...You need to be careful...Whatever you do...don't take that necklace off. Don't ever love someone enough that it might give you a reason to let it go. Be selfish. Just let our line finally end so you never have to pass it on. So you can live your life."

"Mom, wait," I begged. "Please stay with Dad. Is Dad with you?" I could hear my own desperate breaths in the static of the phone.

She didn't answer.

"Mom, please...just don't let yourself be alone. It's going to be okay." I forced myself to reassure her, needing to hear the words myself.

An uncomfortable silence followed, and then she repeated that cruel, awful phrase. "We're all meant to drown."

And she hung up.

I called my dad, desperate to know he was with her. But before I could even find his number, he was already ringing through. I answered as I rushed back inside the dorm to grab my keys, as if there was somewhere I could go—as if there was anything I could do from here.

Dad's voice on the other side offered me some sense of grounding. "I've got her, Trina. I've got her, don't worry. Get some sleep. *Te amo*."

"Okay." I nodded, even though he couldn't see me, and bit back tears stinging my eyes. "*Te amo*, Dad."

My chest hollow and my thoughts shaken, I put down the phone and stared at the empty space above my bed where my painting of Mom once hung.

And then I went under.

SAILING CLOSE TO THE WIND

19

KATRINA

The undertow pulled me farther, as I fought to swim back up. Salt water not only burned my eyes and lungs, but the open wounds on my skin. My blood turned the water red as I suffocated beneath its weight like a wet towel from which I could not untangled myself. The ocean tossed me mercilessly, drawing the life from me as I bled out into it, fading deeper. I looked up, sinking, to a white glimmer of light breaking through the surface, before the ominous shadow of a ship's hull passed over, blocking the light, and sealing me beneath the cold darkness below it.

I gasped at the feeling of my own hand at my throat, squeezing the necklace for dear life, cold sweat chilling my skin. I was still there, staring ahead at the wall, and the nightmare still vivid in my mind.

Only, it wasn't a nightmare.

I hadn't fallen asleep. I was still standing perfectly upright. I checked the clock just to be sure—and not even five minutes had passed since Mom's drunken call.

That could only mean one thing, and it shook me to my core—I'd truly just hallucinated a vision.

And the necklace hadn't stopped it.

Mom was right. If I'd found a way to escape the visions in my sleep, they would find me when I'm awake. And if there was truly no escaping any of this—if this damn family curse was going to drag Mom under and now it was coming for me—then why was I still running?

Why should I believe I would be any different from all the women before me, who'd all drowned in their darkness in the end? Maybe the fact that I'd even ever briefly considered I could, made me more delusional than all of them.

I was tired. Tired of fighting the current. Tired of trying to save Mom when I was drowning myself.

So I stood up—my motions numb and automatic—trudged to the secret cabinet where McKenzie stashed her alcohol, and I grabbed the first bottle I saw.

And then I walked to the sea.

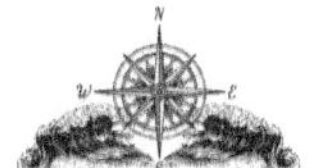

The ocean wind whipped my dark curls wildly as I closed in on the shore. Soft sand beneath my feet greeted me and I collapsed on its moonlit surface, pressing my lips to the bottle. The drink stung, and I winced as it burned the whole way down, but I didn't care. I took as long of a pull of it as I could stand before I stared out into the black horizon, watching the waves roll at my feet like hands reaching for me.

Looking at the sea felt like looking at Mom. I hated it and loved it all at the same time. And even when I knew the pain it could bring me, I kept coming back to it.

I was all out of answers or explanations.

With another gulp of the liquor, I pulled the silver chain from around my neck and felt the pendant's weight in my hand. And then I looked out once more at the waves as they beckoned me to let them take this burden from me.

A strange wind blew in, caressing me like frostbite, reminding me of the one I had felt on the island when I saw the pirate ship rise for the first time.

"I told you not to come here."

I didn't turn around at the voice. I knew it well enough now.

"You also told me not to trust you, Milo." I said blankly. "And you told me Bellamy cut out Serena's heart. But that's not really what happened, is it?"

"No. It isn't. And I never said Bellamy cut out Serena's heart. I said he wanted to cut out yours."

"You know, before tonight I might've asked why," I muttered. "But now, it doesn't matter. None of it matters. And I might as well go ahead and let your captain kill me. I'm right here waiting."

Footsteps neared as Milo slid down next to me in the sand. He took the bottle from my hand and drank a long pull before meeting my gaze. "Were you trying to lure him with the rum?"

I looked away. "I didn't even know it was rum. I just took the first thing I saw."

"Why?" he leaned in. "Why are you here drinking your sorrows on the beach, starlight?"

I flinched at the name. "Why do you care?"

Silence.

"Why did you come?" I asked. "Especially after everything I said to you the last time I saw you."

He didn't answer, and I refused to look at him.

He chugged the rest of the rum and then tossed it into the sea.

"Hey!" I shouted, grabbing his arm all but too late.

"You and I both know you don't need that. You came to give something to the sea—let it be that bottle."

I shook my head, my jaw clenched as I fought through the warm buzz in my body to choose my words carefully. "I know all about Serena. I know Bellamy loved her, and she died anyway. I know you tried to warn them, and she died anyway. And now I know my mom tried everything to save herself, but she's going to die anyway."

There was another long pause, the only sound between us the lulling of the night tide. Until Milo finally spoke, his voice quiet and gentle. "My mother died when I was young. I would've done anything to save her. So, I don't blame you one bit for wanting to save yours." He went quiet once more.

I turned the necklace in my hand, twisting the chain around my finger as I fought the urge to release it to the waves. I could feel Milo's eyes on it—on me—in every movement I made.

"Cordelia's curse has taken something from all of us." Milo said. "But if you throw that out there, we all lose. The scale means nothing without you. You can't escape this without it."

"It seems to be the thing that brought me into it." I sighed. "You're so sure I have something to do with this Cordelia's curse...You and Bellamy think I'm a siren. What if you're both wrong? What if I'm just a broken girl with a broken mind?"

"Far better than a broken heart," Milo uttered, his gaze sliding to mine. "But it seems to me that if you were anything less than a siren, you wouldn't be here right now at the edge of the sea, luring me to you like a moth to the flame."

Heat rushed through me, and I told myself it was just the warm tingle of the rum.

"Then you should hate me, siren hunter." I murmured, giving him a sideways glance. "Isn't killing sirens the very thing you helped your captain do?" Part of me almost didn't want to know.

"Yes, and I regret it every day," he said, voice low as he fixated on a sand dollar between us. "I was fifteen when Captain Valdez forced me into his crew. My father was a merchant from Nassau who ended up working with pirates for survival. I'd spent my whole life sailing with him, until an agreement between my father and Valdez turned sour."

"What happened?" I whispered.

"My father refused to transport a pair of sirens for him. So he killed him in cold blood and forced me aboard. My navigational knowledge of my father's charts, maps, and trade routes were invaluable to him." He swallowed, and I saw the muscles in his neck tense. "And so were my skills with a blade."

"You cut out the sirens' hearts..." I almost choked on the words as the salt in the air stung the back of my throat.

"Once," he breathed. "And then I told Valdez I'd sooner kill myself than ever do it again. And I suppose he needed a navigator more than he needed a butcher."

I shuddered. "So that's your redemption? You killed a siren, so you think protecting one will undo it?"

"Something like that, starlight," he chuckled, a sound like low thunder deep in his chest. "The truth is, I know the terrible things I've done can never be undone. Which is why I won't ask you to save me unless you find me worthy. Because every pirate knows his own soul's not worth saving. But a siren, perhaps, might be a better judge." His hazel eyes slid to mine, and I could've sworn something like desire flickered in them for a half-second.

But then I remembered the rum.

His eyes snaked down slowly and followed the curve of my neck. Then they fell lower, hovering across the rest of my body. I tried, without success, to suppress the wave of warmth that flooded into my cheeks and settled into my core.

"You could take the scale right now. You could snatch it right from my hand and disappear." I uttered hoarsely, my gaze flicking between his eyes, his lips, and the bit of muscle peeking out from his billowing, half-open shirt.

"Don't think I'm not tempted," he whispered, lifting a hand to my neck where he slid his calloused fingertips over my skin. I tingled at his touch.

He traced gently downwards, caressing the skin along my collarbone and down my arm, where every inch of me tingled with shameful delight. I stared at his rugged, handsome face, his wind-blown hair and brown scruff softening his harsh, angled jawline.

When his hand reached mine, he uncurled my fingers and slowly took the necklace from my open palm. I was either buzzed or bewitched enough that I didn't even resist.

I watched his motions, waiting for him to take it and run or vanish into the sea.

But he held it up by either end of the chain, dangling it before me, and then leaned forward to wrap it around my neck.

He secured the clasp, and with tender, intentional motions, untucked my hair from underneath it. He worked his fingers through my thick brown locks, and let them linger far longer than was necessary before pulling away entirely.

Only then did I notice I was holding my breath.

Milo looked out at the sea for a moment, and I noticed the way his body went rigid.

"We need to get out of here. Valdez is looking for you, and he can raise the *Siren's Scorn* almost anywhere off these coasts."

A somber sensation crept over me like a shadow at the sound of the ship's name. I squinted to see its haunting black figure framed in the moonlight, sails billowing like wraiths on the distant waters.

Milo leapt to his feet and pulled me up without warning. "Come on. I know of a place you'll be safe for tonight."

I stumbled, my balance compromised by the alcohol and the tide pulling away the sand from under my feet. Milo steadied me, holding me up each time I faltered, and I found myself leaning into him even when I didn't need to.

It had nothing to do with the fact that the warmth of his broad, muscular body felt like laying on sun-warmed sand, or that his strong, tattooed arms felt like a safe harbor in the midst of a raging sea.

No. I was simply intoxicated and lacking better judgement.

He led me away from the rolling surf, each step more hurried than the last, toward the motorcycle parked somewhere between the ocean's edge and the sleeping town behind it.

He guided me onto the backseat and then swung a leg over in front of me, settling deep between my thighs.

"Can you hold on?" he glanced back.

I nodded, hooking my arms under his shoulders and across his chest, where I expected to feel a heartbeat, but there didn't seem to be one.

"Then don't let go." He ordered just before sending the bike forward, the engine roaring to life. We sped down the coast, following the shoreline for miles that passed in a blur, as the wind roared in my ears and the damp chill of night caressed me.

We left the distant haunting view of the *Siren's Scorn* back on that beach, and somehow it felt like I'd left everything else there, too. And though I didn't even know where we were going, I relished the escape, and in the way it made me feel like maybe everything might actually make sense one day.

And as I flew with Milo under the stars, racing the tide along an endless road of glistening wet sand, it felt as if the world stood still for just us. And for a moment I might've been a ghost, too, because I believed no one in the world could ever find us.

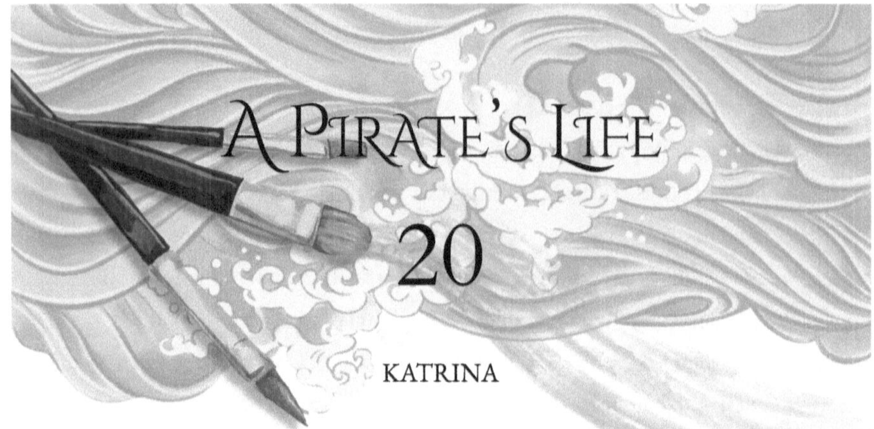

KATRINA

I'd been staring out at the water, mesmerized by the way it never changed no matter how far we traveled, when our soaring came to an end.

"They won't find us here." Milo's voice pulled me back.

We rolled to a stop at the base of a rocky coastline that looked unlike any shore I'd ever seen in Florida—crags and jagged boulders formed a peculiar haven around a towering stone structure that stretched toward the night sky. Waves lapped at its ravaged base, and the night air howled through crumbling cracks that climbed up the structure like vines.

"What is this place?" I asked, tasting the salty mist on my tongue.

"An old lighthouse." Milo lifted himself off the bike and then held out his hand to me.

I lifted myself off the motorcycle, captive by the gentle touch of Milo's hand as he guided me across the rocks and towards the lighthouse. "Older than you?" I sniffed, my eyes watery from the coastal winds.

Milo huffed low and deep, something like a laugh. "Not quite that old."

"Speaking of," I said, the question nagging at me as I picked my way through ledges of sand and stone. "How old are you—or *were* you, when you…um…died at sea?"

"Just a week shy of my twenty-second birthday," he said without turning around.

I was quiet as we reached the lighthouse, and I placed a hand against the cool stone of its base, enchanted by its haunting presence. I wondered briefly what sort of dreams had been stolen from him. What kind of life he would have sought for himself had he not been forced to become something he didn't choose.

"You're sure the ship won't follow us here?" I asked, reassuring myself as I glanced out at the low fog settling over the sea.

"These waters are unforgiving, even for a ghost ship."

"Why don't you just stay here then?" I blinked, wiping sea spray from the side of my face. "What happens if you just don't go back to your ship? Couldn't you just stay and claim this lighthouse as your haunting ground or something?"

Milo laughed so hard it caught me by surprise. "It doesn't work like that."

"How does it work then? Tell me." I pressed.

"We're not ghosts," he finally said, his tone solemn now. "We're something caught between life and death. And when that first light of dawn peeks over the horizon, the sea drags us back no matter where we are. Believe me, we've all tried to outrun in at some point all these years. But the sea is no one's fool. And it gives no mercy to the damned."

I grew quiet, the faint whistle of the wind the only thing between us. "That...sucks." I finally said. "I know you say you deserve it, but...but maybe you don't anymore."

"Don't take pity on me," he growled, looking out to sea. "I could have defied Valdez. I *should* have defied him. I had nothing left to lose. But I was still just a boy...and a coward."

"Beating yourself up for the past won't fix anything. Believe me." I tilted my head, noting the clench of his fist as we stood side by side at the lighthouse's looming entrance, a hollow black tunnel leading upward into nothingness.

He only huffed and looked up, and my gaze followed.

"I bet the view is amazing up there," I said softly, dreaming of what artistic inspiration might await at the top.

"It is." Milo said. "I've spent many a lone night here waiting for the ocean to pull me back. I've never felt closer to the stars than here."

A powerful burst of sea mist sprayed me like a cold shower, and I shuddered. Milo stepped forward into the darkness of the entrance, and I followed, staying close to him as we climbed the spiraling staircase in near pitch darkness.

I lost my footing halfway up, and before I could even try to reach for something to balance on, Milo had me in his grasp.

"I'm not usually this clumsy," I said, still tasting the rum on my breath.

"You'd downed half a bottle when I found you. I'd expect nothing less," Milo teased as he helped me right myself.

I clung to him as we scaled the staircase in silence the rest of the way. And once we reached the top, my breath caught in my chest as I tilted back my head to gaze at the map of stars above me.

"You weren't kidding. It's beautiful," I said, feeling like I could reach out and pluck the North Star right out of the sky. I glanced over to see him looking at me. "And none of your crew knows about this place?"

"No."

I stepped closer to the edge. "Not even Bellamy?"

His eyes darkened. "Especially not Bellamy."

"I can't imagine how you two managed being on a crew together with as much as you hate each other."

"Our rivalry is far from rooted in hate," he breathed. "You'd be surprised to know Bellamy was once my closest friend. He sort of took me under his wing once I joined the crew—shielded me a bit from his father's wrath."

"He's the captain's son?"

"Yes. But that has not spared him from Valdez's cruelty." He drew in a breath. "After Serena, Bellamy's grief consumed him. He blamed me for not warning them sooner and even accused me of leading Valdez to her—but I knew he didn't really believe any of that. He was just blinded by a broken heart, trying to make sense of his loss. But he's still convinced himself that I'm somehow to blame, despite the fact that I tried everything to save Serena and was flogged to shreds right along with him for it."

I envisioned them both, bloody and bound to the mast, just as Mrs. Gutierrez had said, and chill crept beneath my skin.

Milo walked to the edge of the lighthouse, leaning on the rim next to me, and looked down at the sea before continuing.

"Believe it or not, Bellamy was once more desperate to end our curse than any of us. He spent decades searching the coasts relentlessly for the one who could finally free us—it's how he found Serena in the first place. He fell in love with her, even after I warned him of the danger it would put her in.

"And after her death, he no longer wanted our curse to end. He still doesn't, because he wants Valdez to suffer forever, even if that means he suffers with him."

"So…" I tucked a disheveled lock of hair behind my ear. "He wants to keep me from breaking the curse?"

"Aye. And above all, he wants your heart—your loyalty. As revenge. Against Valdez…and against me."

"And how would Bellamy having my heart give him his revenge? What is it about these siren hearts that's so invaluable?"

"Eternal life. The very power to cheat death." Milo breathed, a grim shadow falling over his face. "There was a rumor on the seas that anyone who possessed a siren's heart could live forever..."

Russell was right.

I reached up to touch my chest, as if making sure my own heart was still beating, and then my fingers brushed the necklace. "That's why Valdez wanted Serena's heart. He thought she was a siren and he could cheat his curse?"

Milo nodded. "He thought sacrificing her to the sea would end our curse, and that possessing her heart would spare him from the death that awaits us. And he still believes that. The only difference is—this time we've found the right girl." His gaze slid to me uneasily. "Bellamy will do anything to keep you from trying to break our curse. And I don't believe he wants your heart so much as he just wants to keep it from Valdez...even if that means he must steal it for himself. That, and he swore to make me feel his pain one day. And he's trying to use you to do it."

"Okay, so I understand why Bellamy wants to use me as revenge against his father." I exhaled, closing my eyes before looking back toward him. "But how exactly is stealing my heart revenge against you? Why does he think that would hurt you so much?"

Milo's gaze fell away, as if I'd struck something uncomfortable. As if I'd asked a question he'd rather not answer.

"Well?" I prodded, gripping the thin barrier around the lighthouse's edge and stretching myself across it to try to force him to meet my gaze.

Milo sighed and clasped his hands together, shaking his head. "Because in Bellamy's twisted mind, you're my Serena." He still wouldn't look at me.

I pulled back, steadying my feet against the stone surface of the tower. I swallowed a gulp of cold air and stepped back. "Well...am I? Is that why you came and found me on the beach? Because you actually do care?"

"I told you the reason I'm protecting you," he snarled, voice low and brow tensed. "And it has nothing to do with caring for you—nothing to do with love. I'm not foolish enough to damn myself a second time."

"Glad to where the line in the sand is—nothing more than your redemption and Bellamy's revenge," I muttered, some part of me strangely wounded, though I knew it made no sense for it to be. I stepped away from the ledge and pressed my back to the lighthouse, aware that just inches above my head creaked rusty metal and salt-weathered stone from which a beacon of light once turned. "Have you ever loved anyone?"

I didn't know why I was pressing. Maybe it was the rum making me bolder than usual. Maybe I wanted to pass the hours by hearing whatever tales this undead man would share. Maybe I wanted to learn if his heart had truly died along with him.

Milo scoffed. "Nothing more than a few meaningless flings with port tavern girls." I thought that would be it, but he went on after a long pause. "Love is like fool's gold. It looks like treasure at first, but it only leads to pain. Bellamy and Valdez alone are enough proof of that."

"That depends, I guess," I said, pulling my knees up to my chest. "Did Valdez ever really love the siren he betrayed? Or was he just using her the whole time?"

"I don't know. I think it started out real enough...but then his greed took over, and she became his key to fortune and power on the seas. Once he learned that siren's scales held their magic—and that he could track them using Cordelia—he built an empire around hunting sirens for their tails and hearts for the wealthy and elite—until the sea had no more to give. That's when Valdez tried to capture her for himself, and she turned on him."

I closed my eyes for a moment and breathed in the briny air. "Bellamy said she turned human—that she gained legs and jumped into the ocean. Do you think she survived?"

Milo pushed himself off the railing and turned around to face me, leaning with his elbows back against the ledge. "I don't know if she even wanted to. She was the only one left. She was distraught with guilt once she realized she'd help destroy her own kind. So much that she destroyed all the evidence and records of Valdez's mermaid trade before she gave herself to the sea. She stole his most prized possession with her, too—a chest—a box he kept locked in his quarters. It had been her gift to him years before. Whatever was in it, she must've wanted it to die with her."

My ears perked up. "A box? What was in it?" My pulse sped up at the far-fetched possibility that it could somehow pertain to the same box Mom had found.

"I don't know. None of us did," he said. "Whatever Valdez valued the most, I assume."

"So many secrets..." I mumbled, filing the idea away for later and all at once reminded of Mom. "Let's talk about something else. Show me some more constellations or something."

"Very well. Lay down."

"What?" I gasped.

Milo crouched down and lay flat on his back. "It's easier to see the whole sky at once that way."

I shrugged and crawled next to him on the narrow platform, lying across from him so that our heads were side by side but our bodies opposite each other's direction.

Milo pointed to the heavens as I settled on the cold surface. He began to tell me all about the patterns in the sky and how to look for them. He described how the stars moved from east to west, and how every sailor worth his salt knew how to watch their movement. I listened carefully as he described the tricks of celestial navigation.

Just as I was mesmerized by the enthusiasm in his voice—almost something like joy—he stopped pointing at the corner of Ursa Minor and turned his head to me. I looked back at him when I noticed he'd gone silent.

"What?" It was only then that I realized how close we were, his face inches from mine when we turned our heads toward one another.

"Nothing." I smiled through a snicker. "It's just that you really light up when you talk about stars—pun intended."

For once, I seemed to have been the one to have left *him* speechless. He blinked slowly in surprise as the edge of his mouth lifted into a smirk.

"What can I say? It's in my blood. I was born a sailor, pirate or not." He laughed. "No doubt you have a passion of some kind yourself."

I chewed my bottom lip for a second.

"Painting," I finally muttered.

"Painting?" He crossed his arms over his chest and peered at me through a rogue lock of hair in front of his eyes. "Okay. Your turn. Tell me all about it."

"Well," I shifted my shoulders against the hard stone at my back. "I've done a little of everything. But watercolor is my favorite. It's kind of... chaotic and peaceful at the same time, if that makes sense. But it can be tricky, because if you make a mistake, it can bleed over into everything else pretty quickly. But I think that's part of the challenge—trying to keep everything together, trying to control something as fluid as water. And of course, there are ways to blot out some slip-ups, but you have to know what you're doing. It can be unpredictable if you're not careful—" I suddenly realized how much I was talking. I'd been rambling on about paint so long I'd lost track of everything else. I rarely rambled—in fact I often went out of my way to avoid conversation—and I had certainly never spilled out so many facts about watercolors in one sitting.

And yet Milo urged me to continue, his eyes shining as though he was listening to directions to buried treasure. "And?" he prompted.

"And..." I inhaled. "I guess I like unpredictable things."

Milo smirked. "And what's your favorite thing you've ever painted?"

"I...I think I'm painting it right now." I said, my heart fluttering, though I didn't know why.

"And what might that be?"

"I'm not sure I trust you enough to tell you—you are a pirate after all." I smiled. "If you want to know, you'll have to come see it for yourself."

I swore I could almost feel the rumble in his chest as he chuckled low and shook his head. Was I...flirting with him? Was I really batting my eyelashes at an undead man from the 18th century?

"That has to be the rum talking." He whispered, but he was still smiling.

"You would know." The words half-sputtered from my lips, my eyelids feeling heavy and the sound of crashing waves starting to sound like a lullaby.

"Don't get too comfortable," Milo warned. "I have to take you back soon."

I didn't know why the thought of leaving bristled me the way it did. But I sat up, shaking off the sleep that threatened to pull me into its clutches. I didn't want to fall asleep. I didn't want to go back to ICA. I didn't want to lose whatever this was.

But I knew as well as he did that it wouldn't be much longer until the sun rose. And I couldn't imagine getting stuck on this lighthouse alone and watching the sea reclaim Milo.

So I followed him groggily down the long staircase, a somber walk of silence. We crossed back through the mist and the rocks on the shore, and we soared once more along the coastline, back to the heart of St. Constantine.

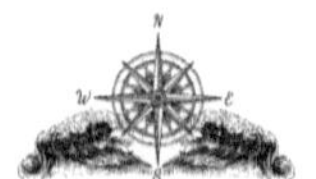

And the whole way there I thought of what'd just happened at the lighthouse—of how I'd caught a glimpse of the Milo I'd met on the island. The Milo who cared, and listened, and made me feel home. And I couldn't stop asking myself why he was doing this. Why did he come find me drunk on the beach? Why was he pulling me out of my shadows to remind me of the light? Was it all truly just to redeem his soul from the terrible things he had done as a pirate? Or was there a reason beyond that?

Because the way he looked at me tonight made me wonder if he yearned for more than just his soul's redemption.

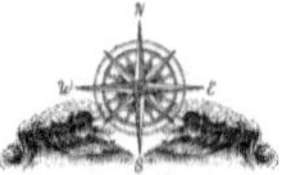

This time he didn't drop me off at the campus gates. He walked me to my dorm, his steady arm my support the whole way.

And when we stood in front of the door to my dorm, he finally spoke again.

"Go rest."

"What if...what if I need you again?" I swayed in the doorway, and he caught me as I fell against the threshold.

"Then call me. Use the stars."

I was confused, but far too tired to clarify. He knocked on the door, and I heard McKenzie's startled voice from a million miles away as she ushered him inside and directed him to my side of the dorm.

I didn't even remember him picking me up, but he was carrying me to my bed, where he laid me down gently and turned to go.

"Wait..." I said, fighting the sleep overtaking me. "Will you tell Bellamy I'm sorry...sorry for what I said to him last?"

He glanced back as if I'd struck him with an arrow. "I will," he said. "Now sleep."

GET UNDERWAY

21

KATRINA

"Hey...heyyyy..." McKenzie's voice came to me in a dream, breaking through the fog in my head as I came to. "I know you probably need to just sleep it off, but you have class in thirty minutes."

I rolled over, the shame of it all flooding over me. I'd made such a big deal out of not drinking at the Halloween party weeks ago, and now here I was, half-hungover after staying out all night with some guy McKenzie had never even met. I knew I must've looked like the world's biggest hypocrite.

I'd almost given up. I'd almost let myself go—almost thrown it all away at the edge of the ocean and accepted my fate as well as my mom's. But someone had pulled me back from the edge. Someone had reminded me to keep my head above water, just a little bit longer. Someone saved me from drowning again.

I shot upward, a pulse of pain thrumming through my head.

"Milo," I gasped.

"Yeah, he brought you home last night," McKenzie patted my back. "Guess you really weren't making him up. But I don't know where you keep finding these hot guys."

A small laugh sputtered from my lips. I eased myself from the bed and glanced in the mirror. I looked like hell, with my wind-blown hair tangled and framing the smudged mascara in the corners of my eyes.

"I've gotta run to class," McKenzie said, inching toward the door. "I just wanted to check on you before I left this morning. There's hot coffee on the table."

"Thanks," I smiled softly.

"Don't thank me. God knows how many times you've done the same for me." She blew me a kiss and fluttered out the door.

I showered, my senses coming back with each second the hot water washed over me, taking the sand and sticky salt from last night down the drain. Ignoring the dull pounding in my head, I thought of lying there with Milo beneath the stars, hidden with him from the troubles of both the land and the sea. And I wondered, foolishly, for a moment, what it might be like to feel him—not just pressed against him on the back of a motorcycle, or leaning on his arm stumbling across the sand—but to truly touch him, and be touched by him.

Then as I turned the shower knob, I tossed the thought away with a flick of my wet hair. It was absurd. He was a dead man.

And yet my mind couldn't stop drifting to him in every movement I made. As I crept from the bathroom to my closet, sunlight spilled into the room and made the white walls gleam. I felt a twinge of something I couldn't name as I thought of the *Siren's Scorn* at the bottom of the ocean, where Milo and Bellamy had by now long returned to endure their daily damnation.

It was futile to attempt to concentrate in the lecture hall. I found myself in a daze looking up at the intricate gold and wooden dome ceiling through most of it. And as the professor droned on about medieval literature, my thoughts were still spinning around Milo and what he'd told me about the chest Cordelia had stolen from Valdez. If there was any chance it was the same box—or more importantly—if it contained some answers to what Mom and I were truly up against, and how the necklace was supposed to help us defeat it.

I snuck my phone out, keeping it tucked in my lap, and wrote out a quick text to Dad.

-How's Mom?

He must not have been working in the shop. Or if he was, he was taking a break. Because he answered quickly.

-She's okay. But I haven't been able to leave her alone. She's really scared to sleep. But I'm keeping an eye on her, I promise. If I have to take her somewhere, I will. But for now, I don't want you to worry. You've got a lot to focus on.

I read the text three times before I could put together a response.

-Okay. I'll be home soon and maybe I can help. Somehow.

-We can't wait to see you. Mom keeps talking about you, especially at night.

-Should I call her?

There was a long stretch of time before his answer came through.

-I wouldn't.

His response was a bit unnerving, but at the same time not unexpected. I knew how this worked. If Mom was at least manageable for the time being, it wasn't worth triggering something worse.

I just had to get through the showcase gala—which was now only two nights away—and then I could go home for Thanksgiving break. I could give Mom the necklace to help her until I could figure all this out. I could find the box and...and—

The sound of books slamming shut, chairs screeching across the floor, and clattered footsteps tore me from my sea of thoughts. Class was over, and I had a lot to do before the gala—part showcase prep and part digging deeper into the siren's curse—and into mine.

I rushed back to my dorm, my headache thankfully subsided, and plopped down at my canvas. I needed to ground myself, to find calm waters in my mind before I dove into the depths of my bloodline's past one more time.

I reached for my detailing brush, watching the way sunlight danced on the wall through the slits in the palm fronds waving outside our window. I could feel the colors of the light—gold like warm sand, and shadows like white misty foam. My hands trembled as I dipped the brush tip into water.

I mixed colors until I had the shade of grey blue that reminded me of the sky just before a storm. And I added flecks of that stormy blue throughout my haunting seascape, adding the details of foaming white waves and silver starlight. And then I stepped back to admire my star above the sea, finally complete.

I left the painting to dry for the last time before I would take it to the showcase venue.

And then a text from Mom shattered the peace and triumph of it all, and reminded me of the work still to be done.

-Trina, are you okay? I keep seeing visions of you drowning. Please don't go to the beach.

-I'm okay, Mom. I promise. Don't worry. I'm just in my room painting.

-That helps a little. I'm trying so hard not to drink. But it's the only thing that stops the dreams for a while.

-I know. Just hold on a little longer, Mom. I'm coming home the day after tomorrow. Please, stay near Dad and try not to think about the dreams. That's all they are. Dreams.

Suddenly I was nine years old again, calming my mom's nightmares at her bedside. I sighed, trying to reassure myself, and sent one more.

-Everything will be okay. I promise.

And yet I knew I couldn't really promise that at all. But I could promise that I would try—I would try to break us free from this generational curse, whatever it meant.

So flung open my computer and started typing. I started with the names that held the most history—Marina Eversong and Elisabeth Shores. And I searched until the sunset painted my room an orange the shade of embers.

Marina was like a ghost herself, with very few records of her life and name at all. Even her name—Eversong, seemed to have come out of thin air. There was no tracing it anywhere.

So I focused on Elisabeth, finding a vague record in the ancestry database of her checking into an asylum, but little else. But because she was a painter, there were some small snippets of her life and career scattered throughout the other search results—and one specifically that snared my attention.

It wasn't even an article about her—but rather, a short entry about a Spanish naval officer posted between St. Augustine and St. Constantine who was engaged to her briefly.

But they never married.

An electrifying chill sent goosebumps down my arm.

That was when I realized the internet would only take me so far. I needed more. Something dedicated to the history of these seaside cities. I needed what could only be found right here at Isabel—the archives in Queens Library.

I rushed to the library, repeating the naval officer's name in my head to ensure I didn't forget it, and still trying to believe it— David Fernando Del Mar.

It was practically my dad's name—David Delmar—and it took everything in me to convince myself I wasn't hallucinating it.

I hurried up the coquina stone steps and burst through the great library doors, barely catching my breath before I slid to the nearest computer and searched the database.

The officer wasn't well known. His name appeared in a single book, in the farthest corner of the library's historical archives, in a letter that was documented as an artifact of Spanish military presence.

I scurried to the archives, pulled a heavy leather book from its shelf, and sucked in a breath when I found the picture printed in on the thick, stuck-together pages.

An image that bore the caption: *A Spanish naval officer's diary entry lamenting his forthcoming relocation.*

I skimmed the letter, where David talked about his duties, the ship that would be coming to take him across the sea to his reassigned post in Cuba, and the fiancé he was leaving behind—Elisabeth.

Though I loved her with all my being, Elisabeth and I will not be wed. Her mother's state of mind is dire, and in her stead, her heartless grandmother has become her guardian. She keeps her from me, forbidding her to be with a seaman. Elisabeth will not depart these shores with me, because she has been taken far away where I cannot follow by a woman I do not trust with her wellbeing. If Elisabeth is found to be unwell, or disappeared, or changed for the worse, let it be known that Cordelia Eversong is responsible, and should be held accountable, for she has sentenced her granddaughter to a life she does not choose.

The name shook me to my core and my pulse quickened as I read it again and again.

Cordelia was Elisabeth's grandmother—and she forbade her from following her love to the ocean, no doubt bitter from her own betrayal by a man of the sea. It must've been the story behind Elisabeth's haunting painting of her standing on the sea cliffs.

And that meant...Bellamy and Milo were right.

I was descended from a siren. And not just any siren, but the very siren that cursed them.

I was a great-granddaughter of Cordelia.

And maybe all of this was just as much up to chance as my parents being long lost descendants of forbidden lovers who couldn't be together the first time around.

And maybe if I knew how being a siren's descendant made me capable of breaking the curse, I'd be willing to do it, if I knew it would save us all.

But that was still the great mystery—and my last hope of an answer lay in a locked box back in Arkansas.

Turning Tide

22

KATRINA

I nearly dropped the book as my trembling hands slid it back into place in the archives.

I needed to talk to Milo. I had to tell him about the box and about what I'd discovered. If there was anyone who might know how to open it, maybe it'd be him—or maybe it'd be Bellamy or Valdez—but he was one step closer to either.

One step closer to learning how to save my mom and maybe even the two pirates who swore my blood was their salvation—and who had begun to steal a small part of my heart more than I cared to admit.

I sprinted across campus to the parking lot and leapt into my Jeep, turning the key frantically as if it would stir the engine to life that much faster. I floored it across the bridge over the bay as dusk faded. I had a place in mind where I planned to follow Milo's advice—to call him with the stars.

The pier.

I rummaged through my Jeep, looking for something—anything—I could use to summon my immortal pirate the only way I knew how. I reached for a partially unzipped bag of old painting supplies in my back floorboard, and out rolled some old brushes and a palette knife. I snatched the knife and ran, aware that my time was dwindling to safely be on the very same shore where Serena was taken.

Ten deep breaths carried me from my car to first supporting beam beneath the pier, where the edge of the tide was already beginning to creep upward. I quickly carved a North Star into the beam, cutting through the corrosion and barnacles, and then removed my necklace. I dipped my scale pendant into the water, where I felt its magic ripple outward like each time before.

And then I watched the last bit of golden light flash behind the sea's horizon.

Racing back to my car, I hoped my plan had worked. My necklace would draw the pirates to the pier. And Milo would see the star carved into the beam, and know that I needed him to find me.

Now I just had to get out of there before his bloodthirsty captain did.

By the time I'd made it back to the Jeep, I already heard booted footsteps behind me.

I ran faster, faster, and faster, until I was reaching for the door handle with a chill scouring down my back.

And I leapt into the driver's seat, locked the door, and then turned to see Milo sitting in the passenger seat, half obscured in shadow.

"Don't talk. Just drive," he ordered.

I started the car and peeled out of the beach lot, and only then did Milo prop an elbow on the armrest.

"You called me."

It wasn't a question.

"Yes," I gasped. "I...I didn't know what else to do. You're the only one I can talk to about this, and selfish or not, you have a reason to care about what happens to me." I concentrated on staying on the road, driving as far inland as I could.

"Aye," he said, voice low and almost weary. "But what you did was dangerous."

"It worked didn't it. What else was I supposed to do? How the hell was I supposed to know what 'use the stars' meant?"

I noticed the way he didn't look at me. He hadn't met my gaze even once, and kept his face turned toward the window. "The star was enough. You didn't have to lure them right to you."

"Why do you care?" I asked. "If they find me and Valdez cuts out my heart and kills me, that's on them, not you. And then you'd have your curse broken. If they catch me because I'm stupid enough to let them, why would you still care?"

"Because I promised to protect you." I could hear the edge in his voice.

"Yeah, well, what good is the promise of a pirate?" I asked. "There's nothing binding you to it."

"You make a fair point, lass."

I gripped the wheel, twisting my palms against it, my mind snagged on the strain in his voice.

I stretched forward and looked over at him, desperate to see why he was avoiding my gaze, and I gasped. The right side of his face was covered in blood that had dried in a stream trickling down his shoulder, which was also bleeding down the length of his arm. I almost slammed on the brakes, but had the sense to keep going.

"What—what happened to you?"

Milo drew in a long breath. "Valdez knows I'm helping you. He knows I've been lying about not knowing where you are. And this was his way of dealing with it. A few lashes with the scourge to remind me to keep my priorities in order."

"So you took that...because of me?"

"I took it because I refuse to be Valdez's puppet. Besides, he can't exactly kill me."

"Yeah, but...can't you still feel pain?"

Milo laughed in a way that made my blood run cold. "That's the only thing we feel." Before I could respond he looked away again. "So, now that I'm here, what do you need?"

"The box," I said, turning down the next road to Isabel. "I need to ask you about the b—"

"Don't go to the college," Milo ordered flatly. "We can't risk them finding out where you live."

"The lighthouse then?" I huffed.

"No, we can't get there in this." Milo shook his head, his jaw tense. "There's no road that leads to it."

I chewed my lip and thought of all the secluded spots I knew of that were least likely to be frequented by ghost pirates. And then it struck me.

"I think I have an idea."

I veered around, heading for the backroads still fresh in my memory from my hunt for Bay Lily before. There were many offshoots from the path branching off towards the lagoon long before I reached the house on the water.

I drove there quickly, my headlights fighting through dense fog the nearer we got to the road leading to the cove. The gravel beneath my tires sounded like sweet relief as I nestled my Jeep down in a hidden bank by the lagoon's edge.

I shut off the engine, ensuring there were no lights to alert anyone to our presence, and breathed a deep exhale.

"Okay," I said. "Now the box. The one you said the siren stole from Valdez. I think it could have something to do with me—with all of this. And I think it might be back at my childhood house a thousand miles away."

"I'm listening," Milo leaned forward, shifting in the seat as he peered at me from across the center console, such a strange sight it was—this rugged, tattooed bloody man straight out of a history book sitting in the passenger seat of my Jeep.

"You said the siren's name was Cordelia," I said. "I found a letter from a long time ago naming a Cordelia as one of my great grandmothers. She wanted to keep her granddaughter from marrying a naval officer. And she took her far away to do it. I think that's how my family must've ended up so far from the sea. She didn't want us near it.

"All this time I thought we were all born afraid of the sea—born to hate it. But I think maybe it's been calling us to it through memories—memories of Cordelia jumping into the sea during the storm that sank your ship."

Milo's eyes darkened. "If you truly have Cordelia's blood...then that means..."

"I can break your curse. And maybe mine. I just don't know how. And I wonder if the box—if it's the same one—might have the answer..." I fiddled with the necklace on my skin, feeling its weight.

And then I looked at Milo, and wondered why he wasn't as excited as I was. In fact, he looked every bit the opposite, tense, and brow furled, like I'd just given him the worst news imaginable.

"Why are you looking at me like that?" I asked. "Why aren't you glad to hear this if it means I can break your curse?"

"Because if you're Cordelia's descendant, I fear breaking the curse won't be enough for Valdez." Milo spoke low, his voice a husky whisper in the dark. "Centuries of torment have made him into a madman. Reason is lost on him. He will want your blood. He will want to do inconceivable things to you to enact his revenge, to feel that he had the final word."

My heart stuttered as I digested his words. Suddenly the stale, suffocating air in the vehicle became unbearable as a trapped, hollow feeling squeezed the air from my lungs. Milo's words swirled around in my mind like a haunting mist, and my chest all at once felt empty.

I opened the door and jumped out, humid, cool night air filling my lungs as I walked toward the edge of the lagoon, stopping where the ground turned soft and marshy.

I didn't turn around at the sound of the car door slamming shut behind me as Milo attempted to follow.

"He was going to try to cut out my heart anyway, wasn't he?" I said. "That's why I thought I would figure out how to break the curse without him...with you. I thought that was the point of protecting me all this time."

"The point of protecting you was to keep you from Valdez until you gave up the necklace—the only thing allowing him to track you down." Milo's appeared beside me as I stared through the overgrown grasses lining the water.

"And after I gave up the necklace, then what?" I breathed.

"I...I hoped that would be enough."

"What do you mean? What about your redemption and all that?"

Milo sighed deep, and even from the corner of my eye I could see the way he hung his head.

"It may have started out as a chance for redemption. Because I hoped the scale would be all it would take to free us from our curse. I thought you'd be begging me to take it from you once you learned what it truly meant—once you learned what was at stake. I thought it would be the only way to make sure I never saw you again. But..."

I closed my arms around myself and looked over at him slowly, waiting for him to continue as he struggled to say the rest.

"But instead, it only drew you closer—inevitable, like the tide pulls the moon. And now I don't know how to let you go."

I took a step backward, glancing at the moon above, watching the way the water rose and lowered at my feet. "What are you saying, Milo?"

"I'm saying that I think breaking this curse may demand a higher price that we bargained for."

I shook my head, shutting him out. "Then I guess no matter what I do, I'm doomed."

Milo cocked his head and looked at me inquisitively.

"If I give you this necklace, it may save me from Valdez, but it won't save me from myself."

"What are you talking about?" he asked, his voice rising.

"Why do you think I was drinking on the beach that night? My family...Cordelia's line—we all die young. And the older I get, the more I understand why. The dreams, the hallucinations, the visions, the memories—it all becomes too much. And the only clue of how to stop it—how to save my mom and myself before it's our turn—is this damn necklace somehow." I thumped my chest with my palm. "And that damn box that might just hold the secret."

"You're sure Valdez's chest has the answer?"

"The only thing I'm sure of is that it's the last hope I have. I'm going home the day after tomorrow, and I will do whatever it takes to get that box open." I choked. "And if I'm wrong..." the words lingered on my lips as I turned to face him. "If I'm wrong, I'll give you the necklace to take back to Valdez. Because none of it will matter anymore."

Milo arched a brow, his broad arms crossed over his chest as his gaze flickered between my eyes and the pendant at my neck. "You're going to need the key to open that box," he said. "If Cordelia had anything to do with creating it, I'm sure there's no way around it, or someone would've done it by now. Siren magic is powerful."

I locked eyes with him, my heart sinking a bit as he brought up the obvious obstacle I still had no idea how to overcome. "There's no key, so I have no choice but to try."

"Oh, but there *is* a key." Milo rubbed his jaw with his thumb as he spoke. "And I think I know where it is."

KATRINA

"**Y**ou do?" I swallowed. "Where is it"

Milo straightened his shoulders as he held my gaze, and I braced for whatever he was about to say. He pulled his lips together and let his eyes wander away from mine.

"Valdez's quarters."

"As in...on the ship?" My throat suddenly felt dry.

"Yes. He keeps everything he owns secured in there. It has to be in there somewhere." He shuffled his feet in the dirt. "I'll look for it during the next tide and bring it to you one night."

"We don't have that kind of time. I have my art showcase tomorrow night and then I have a flight home the next morning." I stepped toward him, eyeing his bloody face, arm, and the slashed open shirt and skin along his shoulder. "And also, if he did this to you just for helping me, what will he do to you if he finds you stealing his key?"

"It doesn't matter. I can't die."

"But you said you can feel pain." I argued. "I won't ask you to be tortured for me."

Something splashed in the water just a few feet from where we stood. Milo pulled me back with one smooth motion of his arm. "We did not outrun my crew tonight just for you to get eaten by an alligator," he said smugly.

He was right. If a semester in Florida had taught me anything, I knew that it was a death wish to be standing so close to a brackish body of water like this in the middle of the night.

"You're probably drawing them to us with that blood all over you." I marched back toward the Jeep, opening the trunk. "Maybe I have something in here to clean you up."

"Katrina—"

"Come here," I said, as I grabbed a wadded-up beach towel and an unopened plastic water bottle from weeks ago.

Milo rolled his eyes and walked over reluctantly. But the closer he got, his steps steadied, and I motioned for him to sit on the edge of my trunk.

He hesitated, but he did it. And I went to work pouring water on the towel and then reached forward to dab the side of his face.

At first I stopped myself, my hand hovering just over his skin as I realized I wasn't breathing. I was so nervous to touch him—to do something so intentional and intimate to him as he sat before me—and I didn't know why.

He stared at me as I leaned towards him, the moon shining in his eyes, as if waiting for my touch while pretending he didn't want it.

I slowly pressed the damp towel to his temple, wiping away the blood and studying his face all at the same time—the scar on his left eyebrow, and the brooding, tender eyes of sunlit moss and amber that seemed fixated on me. The strong, crossed jaw beneath a crooked, sultry smirk that only made me want to keep looking at his lips.

I dabbed the blood away gently, adding more water as needed, and found myself tracing his jawline with my gaze, down his neck where a small tattoo of a ship flexed when he swallowed, all the way down to his deep collared shirt that hung even more loose since one sleeve was torn open, revealing a tan, well-muscled upper arm beneath the blood.

I had to say something, or he was going to notice the way I couldn't stop staring at him. Or worse, he'd notice the way I kept wiping the same spot on his skin because I was too distracted by the heat pooling in my core.

"You said you can only feel pain," I finally asked. "Is that true? Can you really not feel anything else?"

"It's true," he murmured. "Just another one of those immortal perks."

"I'm...I'm sorry." I looked down, dabbing one last section clean before lowering the towel and tossing it in the trunk.

"Thank you," Milo's eyes softened and he brushed a thumb against the side of his face I'd just wiped. "Now...the key."

"Yes," I cleared my throat. "Back to the key. I want to come with you—on the ship—and look for the key."

"Might as well go ahead and let the alligators have you. Absolutely not." He stood up and wiped his hands together, striding back over to the edge of the lagoon towards a patch of tall reeds.

"There's no other choice. I need the key by tomorrow night. I'm not letting you risk yourself for me." I stomped down to where he was, noticing him dragging something from the grass, something heavy. Something I hadn't noticed earlier.

With one more tug, he slid it out from the reeds—a wooden rowboat. He gestured to it. "You want to get on a boat, there you go. But I'm not letting you get near Valdez's ship."

"Why?" I scoffed. "You'll need someone to help you watch your back. We'll lure the crew to shore and then sneak on."

"You're out of your mind. No, Katrina. It's too dangerous."

"Why not?" I asked louder than I meant to, something like frustration coiling up inside so hard I clenched my fists. "Why are you so afraid of me getting hurt?"

"I've told you a thousand times—"

"Told me what?" I snapped, looming over him as he stooped over the boat and nudged the bow into the water. "That it's your path to redemption? No, I don't believe that bullshit anymore, Milo. Because this goes beyond redemption. You're protecting me and helping me and now taking floggings for me. No. This seems like way more than you just clearing your conscience. This feels more like...like you care."

Milo stood up straight, facing me, mere inches away, and drilled his gaze down into mine as I stared back up at him. "I won't let you do this for me. Not alone. And especially as long as you keep lying about why."

"Get in the boat," he finally said. "And I'll tell you the truth."

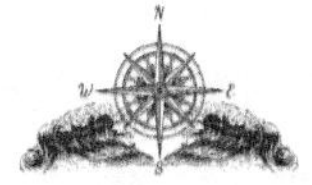

I carefully stepped into the boat, Milo's hand grazing mine as he steadied me on the wobbly surface. I settled into the wooden seat and Milo plopped down onto the other, taking the oars in each hand and rowing us out into the open water.

The rhythmic sound of the oars tapping the water and the song of frogs and crickets serenaded us. A heron perched in the shallows, and fireflies twinkled above the water's surface like tiny golden stars.

Milo rowed us through a small inlet leading to a cove surrounded by wild oaks and mangroves, where Spanish Moss draped from their branches and shielded us from the outside world.

I propped my chin on my hand aggressively and leaned forward. "I'm waiting."

Milo sighed deep. "You want the truth?" He gave one more sweeping row with the oars before letting us drift. "The truth is...the siren I helped kill haunts me in my dreams. I've always heard a voice calling to me ever since...and sometimes when you speak, it reminds me of that voice—the one that has been drawing me to its call for centuries. And sometimes it feels like...like I was always meant to find you. Like if this curse was meant to lead me to you, maybe it was all worth it just to know there's at least one person who will know I'm no longer the same cowardly boy who killed a siren while his captain held a lash at his back."

I stared at him in silence until my gaze dropped to the floor of the boat. "And what if I don't know that? What if I still think you're just a selfish, lying pirate who doesn't believe in love." I whispered.

He leaned in toward me. "Then I'd say that's the smartest thing you've said all night." He smirked and picked up the oars again. "Believe me or don't. But often we tell ourselves we don't believe something is real because it's easier than admitting we want it to be." His voice was a strange warmth in the darkness.

I didn't know what to make of it. I didn't know if he was just toying with me, or if he really meant it all. But the way he watched me like I might vanish from the boat, the way he leaned in closer with every word—and the way he'd spent each night defying his captain for me—made me wonder all the same how he possibly *couldn't* have meant it.

He finally spoke after I'd been silent for far too long. "I know what it's like to lose a mother. What's a few more days in the depths to me if it means you have a chance to save yours?" He said, voice low as he held my gaze, rowing us gently through the mossy haven. "Go figure out how to save her and then if you see fit, you can come back for us filthy pirates. But if you try to go with me to get that key, and something happens to you, then everything I've done will have been for nothing."

I stared at the fresh scars across his body. "And you're sure you can get the key?"

"With a little planning, I have no doubt of it." He cocked his head. "Tonight may be the last night before Valdez comes ashore to find you himself anyway. He's not a patient man, and he made it clear that he plans to search inland if I return empty handed again tonight." I winced at the thought. Milo continued. "I'll search his cabin while he's gone and bring the key to you just before dawn—that way if Valdez realizes it's gone, there won't be time enough for him to do anything about it before we get dragged back down to Davy Jones' Locker." He rolled his shoulders as he spoke, as if trying to loosen stiff muscles.

"Does he know that Bellamy also knows about me?"

"No. For once, Bellamy's thirst for vengeance is proving quite useful. He'll do anything to keep Valdez from getting his hands on the scale, and consequently—you." He shot a quick glance at me through that untamed lock of hair that swept across his face. "He's been leading the crew in circles searching along the coasts a few leagues out, so I trust he will do the same if Valdez comes ashore. He's been desperate to keep them from finding you, which thankfully also keeps him away from you."

I looked down. "Did you tell him?"

"Did I tell who what?"

"Bellamy. Did you tell him I'm sorry? For accusing him of killing the girl he loved."

Milo released the oars once more and put his elbows on his knees. "Yes," he groaned. "I did."

"What did he say?"

His eyes darkened and his jaw clenched as he looked up at me. "That I'm a hypocrite for doing the exact same thing I warned him not to do."

I straightened, noticing how eerily quiet the sounds of the night had become. The frogs hardly chirped, and a few soft splashes filled the silence where they lacked. Even the fireflies had dimmed.

And then a great white bird—far more massive than any seagull, heron, or egret—burst from where it was hidden among the seagrasses, a fish flopping in its beak, and soared just above our heads, wings grazing my shoulder even as I ducked down. The motion tossed the boat, sending it rocking side to side, enough to throw me off balance.

Milo's hand grabbed mine just before I was slung over the side of the hull.

I watched the majestic bird disappear through the branches and into the moonlit sky, the song of crickets and the glow of fireflies returning all at once again. And I realized it was the same bird that had led me the gazebo that night.

"What was that?" I gasped.

"An albatross," he said. "Very rare to see one on Atlantic shores. It was said that they carried the souls of dead sailors. They were also thought to bring good luck."

It was then that I looked down and noticed Milo's hand was still holding mine. And I didn't pull away. Instead, I leaned in closer.

"What's it like holding my hand?" I asked, surprised by my own boldness. "If you can only feel pain, does that mean you can't feel me at all?"

"Something like that," he huffed, trying to make light of it, but I could see the misery in his eyes.

I took his hand in mine and lifted it to my face, pressing his calloused fingers to my cheeks. My own skin tingled at his touch. "Can you feel me? Any of me?" I whispered.

He leaned in, his gaze burning into mine before it dropped to my lips.

"I...I can feel the ache of how badly I wish I could," he said low, his face now an inch away from mine. "And it's enough."

"Enough for what?"

"To make me want you." He clasped the other side of my face, guarded and uncertain, caressing me in some fragile, forbidden embrace as he drew close enough to brush my lips with his, barely a breath between us. "As if looking at you wasn't its own cruelty enough, you tormented, beautiful creature."

My breath hitched, but I didn't pull away. Something in me wanted him there—wanted him closer. I wanted to feel him, even if he couldn't feel me.

My hands found their way up his arms, sliding along the tense muscles until my fingertips touched his chest, where they lingered, feeling him breathe and the place where his heartbeat should've been.

A wild, searing ache coiled up in me, and my own heart thumped in my ribs like something rabid. I trembled, my fingers stiff and aching to reach up and bury them in those disheveled locks of golden brown. My lips parted softly, begging to feel his as he traced the shape of my mouth with his thumb. I wanted him to know that I wanted him, too.

My body arched toward him like a tide pulling me in. His knuckles caressed the curve of my ear, and he looked at me as if I was the only anchor still holding him to this world. And in that moment, it was all I longed to be.

We collapsed against the bow together, slowly, awkwardly, lowering our bodies as the vessel swayed. I crawled to keep my balance as I nestled beside him where he leaned against the curve of the boat. My gaze was tethered to his as he combed his fingers through my hair and back across my cheek, stroking softly with his thumb, as if studying every feature of my face like a new constellation. A small tremor betrayed me as his calloused palm slid down my neck, tender and gentle just before he pulled away, leaving me feeling empty and chasing the ghost of his touch.

"I should never have let you get so close," he whispered, a hollow look in his eyes as he leaned his head back and stared up at the arching mangroves overhead. "I'm sorry."

"Sorry?"

"Yes, because there is no happy ending here, Katrina. I'm dead now and I'll be gone when the curse breaks. There is no sense in forming attachments."

Something sinister gripped my heart. He was right. He was only meant to disappear in the end, one way or another. And yet I couldn't help that relentless drift toward him, like a lost vessel at sea. He was dead, but I'd never felt more alive than when he touched me. He was temporary, and yet nothing else had ever felt so permanent.

"I think that ship has sailed," I said hoarsely. "This is our curse, now."

"Katrina—"

"Come to my art gala tomorrow night before you steal the key. I want to show you what I painted. I want—" I hesitated. "I want you there with me."

He scoffed so hard I felt his body tense from it. "Are you sure you haven't been in the rum again?"

"I'm serious," I laughed. "It'll be a special last night before I leave for the holiday. And Valdez won't find us there—there'll be way too many people."

"Which is exactly why I should not be anywhere near there." Milo's shoulders went rigid.

"Come on," I begged, turning my head to look at him. "I'll be alone without you."

He seemed to consider it for a moment, closing his eyes before finally saying something. "I...I can't, starlight." He exhaled. "In another life—in another time—I have no doubt you were meant to have been mine, Katrina. But fate is already cruel enough. I won't be selfish enough to hurt you, too."

"Then you never should have sworn to protect me," I said. "You should have let me find my own way without you."

"And let Bellamy sink his hooks into you?" Milo closed his arm around me protectively.

"At least Bellamy is honest enough to admit he wants my heart."

"And I'm honest enough not to break it."

"Well," I sighed. "I am a siren after all. Maybe I can just sing to you and make you do what I say." I teased, running my finger along the boat's weathered interior, noticing the tiny cracks in its dense surface.

"Sing for me then." He chuckled. "The alligators and I would appreciate a lullaby."

I froze, bracing against his warmth to fight off the chill I felt at the thought of singing. "I don't sing."

"And you don't like the ocean," he breathed. "Yet you can't seem to stay away."

"That's different..."

"Is it? Just try. Sing something simple. It doesn't even have to have words. Just hum a tune."

I tried to think of something, not sure why something so simple paralyzed me so much. And inexplicably, the only tune that came to mind was an old lullaby my mom used to hum to me when I was small. So I pressed my lips together and quietly began to hum the melody.

It was a haunting sound, lying there with our backs against the bow of the boat drifting in complete solitude. And the longer I hummed, the more I realized the tune I carried almost sounded tragic.

And then, as I reached a high note, the pendant at my neck glowed a faint white and blue. It felt warm against my skin, like it would fuse itself to me if I didn't remove it fast enough.

Horrified and confused, I yanked it from around my neck, desperate to get it away from me.

"What just happened?" I dropped the necklace onto Milo's stomach, where he clamped a guarded hand over it. It was no longer glowing, but I didn't care.

"The magic is in the scales. That's why Valdez cut off the sirens' tails. He'd sell jewelry and fine trinkets made from the scales, sometimes the whole tail if the rich wanted a trophy."

Nausea rose in my stomach at the thought. "So when I sang just now..."

"You just proved, without a doubt, that you have siren blood."

A pit formed in my stomach, and all at once the boat might as well have been sinking out from under me. "That was my mom's lullaby," I said under my breath.

"It was Cordelia's, too."

A long tense silence hung the air, thick as the humid fog around us, everything I'd learned about sirens and sea curses coming together into a single, merciless moment.

"I...I can't put that necklace back on tonight." I could hardly believe what I was saying. "It just felt...terrifying. Like I became someone else for a split second."

"Didn't you say you need the necklace to help you sleep? That it wards off your nightmares?"

"I do...but I guess I'll just have to face them tonight. Because right now reality is scarier than whatever my dreams can come up with. I hardly expected to get any sleep being out here all night anyway."

"You'd be surprised how easy it is to drift off on the water. It's like being rocked to sleep. If not, I doubt I would've ever slept after joining Valdez's crew. My own nightmares started after he killed my father."

"You get nightmares?" My brows rose as I tilted my head back to look at him.

"Not so much anymore. But that probably has something to with being a damned immortal who doesn't sleep."

I snorted a small laugh, feeling my body relaxing once more as I leaned against him. I rested my head in the crook of his shoulder and watched the last few remaining fireflies dance around us lazily. Then my eyes drifted to where Milo still carefully held the necklace against his lap.

It made no sense for me to be there with him. It made no sense for me to want it, either. But the fact was, he'd ignited something in me, and I couldn't seem to douse it no matter how hard I tried. No matter how futile I knew it was to fall for an undead man who belonged to the sea.

I blinked, trying to make sure I wasn't trapped in different sort of bad dream—one that would dissolve the moment I realized it and leave me hollow and broken. I needed to keep talking or I was going to spiral far too deep into my never-ending cyclone of thoughts.

"What would you have done if Valdez never forced you to join his crew? If...if you never became a pirate?" I asked.

He was quiet for a moment before he answered. "I would've left Nassau. My father had little choice but to work with the pirates to stay afloat there, quite literally. It was a booming island, but I wanted something quieter, simpler. After my mother died, I planned to get out of there when I was old enough—to work until I could afford my own ship and then make my own luck on the seas. I don't know why, but I always imagined I'd settle in Cape Cod." I could feel the way he eased beneath my weight, a flicker of a dimpled smile creeping at the corner of his mouth, like for once he was thinking of something pleasant. And then the light dimmed in his eyes once more, as though he was all at once aware again that he was talking about a dream that was forever past and out of reach.

"And what's your dream?" Milo asked.

I hadn't expected the question, so I hesitated at first. "I...I just want to paint. I never thought beyond that really. It'd be amazing if I could make a living from it, but I can barely manage enough money for gas with how little I sell at the studios and antique stores that were nice enough to let me sell them there." I sighed. "I guess I've never thought beyond college because...because this seems to be the age where we all fall apart. I figure by the time I graduate, maybe I'll hallucinate it all away." I blinked away the sting of tears I dared not let surface. "I never planned to fall in love, or have a family, or grow old with anyone—because I would never want to knowingly put someone else through the pain of having to watch me fade. Why would I do that?" I swallowed. "Why would anyone do that?"

Milo was quiet for a minute. "You're right. Why would anyone do that?" He finally repeated the question so low I barely heard him, and I was almost convinced he was asking himself.

I found myself drifting, just like he said I would, as the boat rocked softly and I rested propped against him, my head on his chest, breathing in his familiar scent of amber, leather, and sea salt as I strained to hear something behind that hollow ribcage.

"You don't have a heartbeat." I finally uttered lazily, my eyes already closing.

"Aye. It stopped beating 300 years ago."

"Do you miss it?" I asked through a heavy yawn, hardly even sure what I was saying anymore as my eyelids fluttered shut.

"You're just fighting sleep now, starlight. Sleep you clearly need." Milo laughed tenderly, and I felt the warm vibration in his chest. "Don't worry, I have the necklace right here. I'll watch over you and if you seem to be having a nightmare, I'll put it on you or wake you. But either way, I'll be here."

"So now you're going to fight off my bad dreams?" I snickered drowsily.

"I promised to protect you—that means even from nightmares." He was so tender—even his voice was like a cozy blanket, a deep, husky nightingale lulling me into a sleep I could no longer resist.

"But what good is the promise of a pirate?" I mumbled.

He brushed aside a lock of my hair from my face. "A pirate's word is everything...when it concerns his treasure."

Before I could question what he'd whispered against my ear, I drifted into nothingness.

As the Crow Flies

24

KATRINA

I was sure it was a nightmare. It had to be.

Cold water trickled along my skin as the sound of roaring waves approached, and my eyes flew open.

I scrambled to right myself, to see Milo slouched against the edge of the teetering boat, looking at me with a morbid dullness in his eyes.

I glanced around, looking for the sound of the rushing waves, but there was nothing but placid water on either side of us. But around Milo, water gushed at his feet as if filling a sinking ship, encompassing only him. I could feel the spray of it, and the whipping wind it brought, but the water touched only him, rising around him far too quickly.

There was a tinge of light in the sky now, the shade of burning cinders in a haze of lavender.

Dawn.

"The ship's going down. And I must go down with it." He stared at me with hopeless, empty eyes as he became icy mist and shadow. I reached to grab him, but the waves creeping up to form a wall around him pushed me back.

"No," I uttered, watching ghostly seawater emerge from nowhere, wrapping around him like vines, pulling him under a surface I could not see. "No!"

The waves crashed back into themselves with a deafening hiss and erupted in an ethereal display of mist. Then it all dissolved, leaving nothing more than raindrops scattered on the lagoon's undisturbed surface.

Milo was gone.

I sat there, alone in the rowboat and stared at the empty seat across from me—the oars left unattended in their keepers, and the morning's silence more deafening than the waves that had dragged Milo to the depths.

With shaking hands, I reached forward to touch the space in the boat where we had been—where he had held me as I slept—trying to convince myself it had been real. As my heart hammered in my chest, I felt for the chain of my necklace, driven by some instinct.

It was there, clasped around my neck.

I didn't remember any nightmares. So either the entire night was a dream itself, or Milo had put the necklace on me right before the sea demanded him back.

As I rowed myself back to shore, I couldn't get that vision of Milo out of my head—of the aching dread in his eyes and the flinching brace of his body as he was torn from me and sent back to suffer another day in some merciless, underwater hell. It haunted me, and for the first time, I truly wished I knew how to save him. And I was hopeful that maybe I could.

Because Milo just became one more reason to ensure I got that box open.

I hurried to my Jeep as the sun rose. I had to get my painting to the showcase gala venue and pack my things for the flight home. I cursed as I realized I hadn't even planned what I would wear tonight. But it was to be expected—I'd been more than a little distracted these days.

As the orange light of dawn burst through a wall of grey clouds, I pressed my foot to the pedal, fully aware that I probably looked like death from sleeping on a lagoon all night. I had to get back to my dorm, hopefully before McKenzie woke up and freaked out that I was still gone—again.

As I drove, squinting as the morning Florida sun beamed through my windshield, my phone rang, and I answered without even looking at the screen.

"I'm on my way back to the dorm, don't worry. Everything's fine, McKenzie. I'm fine." The words spilled out of my mouth like rushing water. And then my chest tightened at the voice on the other end when I realized it was not McKenzie.

"Trina, what? You were out all night, *mija*?" My dad asked, his voice rising with urgency.

"Dad, no." I backtracked, my thoughts muddled and racing. "No, I left early to...to pick up some last-minute things for the showcase. I'm on my way back to the dorm with some supplies."

"You had me worried for a second there." He laughed, but there was still a nervous edge in his voice.

"You have *me* worried," I said. "Why are you calling so early? Is it Mom?"

His long sigh filled me with dread. "Yeah," he finally muttered. "She...um...she's not doing well, Trina. She snuck out of bed last night and hit the liquor hard. I found her a few hours ago and couldn't wake her up, so I took her to the hospital."

"What?" I swallowed. "I'm coming home right now, Dad."

"No—that's what I was afraid you'd say," he said. "She's stable. She's okay, but they're going to keep monitoring her overnight. To be honest, she's probably in the safest possible place she could be right now."

I didn't say anything. Dad didn't know about her expiration date. He didn't know Mom might be destined to die before the next year—that she was going to follow the pattern of those before her.

Or maybe he did.

And maybe he knew by now he was powerless to stop it.

"I wanted to update you, but I don't want this to ruin what you've worked so hard for all semester. Don't throw away the showcase tonight. Your flight leaves first thing in the morning. She'll be fine until then. I promise. I wouldn't be telling you this otherwise."

"Dad..." I hesitated, my heart being pulled in a hundred different directions.

"*Mija*, listen to me. Do not let this take anything more from you. Your mother is fine here. I'm staying with her at the hospital, and I promise you, if something changes and I think you need to leave immediately for any reason, I will let you know."

I let his words hang in the air like a crushing weight.

I knew my dad. He wouldn't lie to me.

So I nodded, finally letting out the breath I'd been holding. "Okay, Dad. Thanks for letting me know. Watch over Mom. *Te amo. Los amo a los dos.*"

I love you both.

I did my best to clear my head, to brush aside everything, even if for just a few short, desperate moments. I rolled down the windows and let the sticky morning breeze take over, the faint sound of "The Boys of Summer" playing on the radio.

When I rolled back onto campus, it all came flooding back.

But I didn't have time to drown.

I rushed up the steps to the dorm and quietly turned the handle in hopes McKenzie might still be sleeping.

She wasn't. She was in the middle of dragging a rolling suitcase to the door, still wearing her fluffy pink pajamas and her hair in a vibrant messy bun I rarely witnessed.

"Good morning. Have fun with Milo?" She raised a brow with a flirty smirk.

"Yes...I mean no...I mean—yeah, but I still have to get everything ready for the show-case."

"Well, you better hurry," she cooed. "Before they close off the venue to start decorating."

"Yeah. I know." I panted as I hurried through the kitchenette and into my dorm. I cringed as I glanced at my reflection in the mirror, but there was no time to clean up or smooth out my hair or put on a fresh sundress that wasn't wrinkled and smelled like sea algae.

Not until after I'd moved the painting from my bedroom to the venue.

I took a breath as I stepped toward the canvas, the North Star shining at me like some unspoken promise.

I snatched it up and scampered toward the door, muttering to myself all the things I still needed to do. I paused just as my hand touched the doorknob, a sudden sense of despair looming over me enough to make me freeze.

"You good?" McKenzie asked, her scrutinizing stare eating through me.

"I'm just..." I stammered, my fingers curling around the knob. "I'm just second guessing if I should even be doing this because my dad just called to tell me my mom is in the hospital after he found her blacked out in the middle of the night." I sighed. "And I don't even know what the hell I'm going to wear."

"Oh," McKenzie's shoulders slumped. "I'm so sorry about your mom. But..." she said.

"But what?"

"But not showing off your incredible art isn't going to fix her. Give her the day to sober up and then you can see her tomorrow." McKenzie pointed to the door. "But today, you're gonna go to that gala. Get your shit set up and then come right back here."

"McKenzie, I—"

"And you think you don't have anything to wear? It's like you don't know me at all."

"But—"

"Okay fine," McKenzie snapped, marching toward me. "Forget setting up. They can wait. Right now, we're going to solve at least one of your problems, and if you still don't want to go after this, then you can back out."

She linked her arm with mine and practically dragged me to her room, so forcefully that I stumbled trying to keep up with her.

"Stand here." She adjusted me with a hand on each of my shoulders and then twirled around to her closet. "We are pretty much the same size. Remember how that angel costume fit you like a glove?"

I silently shuddered at the mention of that Halloween night and the memory of everything that'd been haunting me since I stepped foot on the island and nearly drowned in its waters.

"Okay, what are you getting at?" I sighed, watching her whip an analytic gaze over each piece of clothing in her bottomless wardrobe as she slid them along the rack.

"I think I may have the perfect thing. I bought it for a debutante ball at the country club last year, but I ended up wearing something else. It just didn't quite feel right on me. But I think you'll like it. It's much more *you*."

My eyes lit up at the gown my roommate pulled from her closet and held up before me. I was no fashionista, but I could certainly recognize a high-end dress when I saw one.

The sleek silver-blue evening gown glittered like the night stars as she flipped it back and forth in her hands, the fabric flowing through her fingers like liquid. I had never seen such a gorgeous thing.

"Let's see it on you!" She tossed the dress towards me like it was a T-shirt, hanger, and all.

I handled it as delicately as possible, admiring the extravagant beading covering nearly every inch of fabric that dazzled in even the faintest light. I pulled the garment from the hanger and quickly stripped down to my underwear. McKenzie wandered over to help me pull the gown up over myself and zip up the back. Then she stepped back and grabbed my arms, positioning me in front of her full-length mirror.

My mouth hung open at the sight. The dress enhanced every gentle curve I possessed, hugging my figure all the way down to my thighs, where it then gently blossomed out into a cascade of glittering glacial blue-silver fabric that brushed the floor like a waterfall. It reminded me of moonlight on a calm sea just before dawn.

"You're a queen." McKenzie grinned.

I turned to her, speechless.

"Don't you dare say you're not going. No excuses now! Milo's not going to be able to keep his hands off you when he sees you in this."

"I'm sure he would, but he can't make it." I swallowed and smoothed the dress down along with a sudden pang of disappointment. "He um...he had something urgent come up."

"Damn, that's a bummer," she said. She had made her way over to her dresser mirror and began carefully applying mascara as she spoke. "Whatever happened to that Bellamy guy?"

"That's a good question." I winced, twisting my arm to reach the zipper behind my own back. "I haven't seen him since that night in town. Probably for the best."

Guilt crept up my spine at the thought of Bellamy. I wouldn't know how to face him again after the last thing I said to him. But some foolish part of me hoped that wouldn't be the last time I ever spoke to him. Some part of me believed Bellamy was just far more broken than he wanted to admit, and maybe if he could just reconcile with his past—with Milo—he could begin to heal.

McKenzie pouted with her bottom lip as she tucked her mascara wand back into her makeup bag and peered over at me. "Well, you know I would totally be your date if I didn't have to head back home to my parents' tonight. But Surfside is almost a four-hour drive."

"I know you would." I smiled half-heartedly. "Don't worry, though. I'm a big girl. I can handle it on my own. I'll just be standing there by my display anyway. I'm sure it will be kind of boring."

I slipped out of the dress, desperate to get cleaned up before I let it touch my skin again, and threw on a pair of jeans and T-shirt. I grabbed my canvas once more.

"But if I don't get this painting over there, I'm not going to get to go anyway. I'll be right back."

"Go!" McKenzie nodded, shooing me out the door.

On the way to the venue, my stomach did flips, and each step felt like I was rising and falling in waves. I felt guilty for being here when Mom was back home falling apart, and Milo was about to risk himself for me to get the key that I didn't even know for sure could save her. But I knew as well as anyone there was nothing about either that I could change at this moment. And maybe the best way to move forward was just that—to keep moving forward.

I hurried up the gilded steps of Valencia Grand Hall, the showcase gala venue. This particular building of the school had once been a hotel for the elite in decades past, and it was now open to the public as a tourist attraction when it wasn't being used to host the school's extravagant events or being rented out for high-end weddings.

I didn't have many reasons to venture to this area of the campus often, so it was an entirely new world for me as I hurried across the gleaming cobblestone pathway, around the elaborate marble fountain and up the clean white steps into the ballroom. As I entered the building, still catching my breath, my eyes took in the sight of people scurrying to and fro, ensuring the finishing touches were in place as they prepared for the evening. I walked up to the rectangular table in the corner where a lady with a perm piled high on her head and thin lips sat with a pile of papers and a sign that read *Artist Check-In*.

"Hi, I'm Katrina Delmar," I stepped up to the table, scanning the papers for my name.

"You just about missed your chance, hun." Though she looked a bit like she had just tasted something sour, her extreme southern drawl sweetened her face.

"I know. I'm sorry for being late."

"Well, you're only *almost* late. And that still counts," she shuffled some papers around as I scribble my signature on a line on the page. "Did you want to put your artwork in the charity auction? A percentage of the sales goes to the art program, but the rest goes to the artist."

I almost laughed, knowing the likelihood anyone would bid on my piece. But I thought it was worth a shot to earn some extra gas and coffee money.

"Sure," I feigned a smile.

The lady glanced down at her paperwork and made some adjustments, then glanced back up at me through wire-framed glasses that hung low on her nose. "Looks like you got spot number twenty-four."

"Where is that exactly?"

She pointed with her pen to the hallway next to her. "Right through those double doors on the left. That's where the art displays and the silent auction will be."

I nodded and followed her directions. Painting in hand, I pushed through the lane wooden doors to find a wide-open room carpeted in scarlet and gold, with art displays lined up along the wall and a few placed throughout the rest of the room museum-style. It didn't take me long to find my empty spot, as most of the other displays were already filled. I pulled out my painting and placed it in the glass frame that sat on a pedestal near the end of the room.

My soul swelled with pride as I stepped back to admire the canvas that had started out so simply and yet had come to mean so much to me. And I wished Milo could've seen it—could've seen what he'd inspired by a simple conversation on the island that night.

But then I pulled my head out of the clouds and reminded myself to focus. The goal here was to show off my skills as an artist, nothing more. I reminded myself that this was why I came to Florida in the first place—to escape the past and focus on my art—not fall in love with a dead pirate.

Rogue Wave

25

KATRINA

I returned to the dorm with everything squared away, and wasted no time attempting to rid myself of the weight of the world in the shower.

As the steam rose and the water smacked my skin, I found my thoughts drifting once more to Milo—of his hand on my face, stroking my cheek, and of the last thing I swore I heard him say as I fell asleep on his heartless chest.

His treasure.

I must have misheard him. I was half-conscious after all.

But the more I thought about him, and remembered the way he looked at me, I drowned in him all over again. I ducked my head beneath the hot, running water to distract myself. But I could still feel the trace of his touch on me—the warmth of his body holding mine in that rowboat, the graze of his breath against my lips—and I imagined those lips on mine completely. I imagined those calloused hands caressing the skin down my arms once more, but not stopping. I slid my own hand down along my waist, my fingers brushing over my hips, resisting the urge to let my imagination run further.

I breathed in deep, steam filling my lungs, and slowly released the tension through an exhale. I had to get Milo out of my head—and out of my heart. He was part of another age, another time, another world. He was an immortal caught between life and death.

He was a selfish pirate who didn't believe in love. Who swore I was nothing more than his condemned soul's second chance.

And I was an idiot who thought he called me his treasure.

I emerged in my towel, hair freshly washed and smelling of apricots, and McKenzie insisted we have one last latte at Sea Dogs together before our week apart. I obliged, happy for the distraction, and for a genuine date with my always-exuberant roommate.

McKenzie talked about her plans for Thanksgiving—how her massive extended family gathered at her parents' lavish estate for a three-day get together. Some part of it sounded lovely, and another just sounded overwhelming. But I supposed it would be far better than what I had to look forward to—seeing my mom in person for the first time in over a year, in a hospital room, with no one by my side but Dad.

Like nothing had ever changed.

Like it was just further reassurance that even ghost pirates and curses couldn't drag me down deeper than staying in the hopelessness that had attached itself to the place I left behind.

By the time afternoon rolled around and I'd packed my things for the morning, McKenzie offered to stay a bit longer than she'd planned so she could help me with hair and makeup. However, I called dibs on the eyeshadow.

With a careful hand, I worked the brush over my eyelids to create a natural shadow that enhanced my dark eyes and sun-kissed olive skin, with just the faintest touch of shimmer to match the dress. I watched my reflection, hardly recognizing the elegant girl in the mirror. My hair cascaded down my back in a frenzy of loose coils pinned half-up by an ornate twist in the middle. And of course, the opalite mermaid scale dangled from its thin, silver chain around my neck, an eerie reminder of its glowing presence the night before. Despite how apprehensive it made me feel, it looked as if it was made for the sparkling ensemble.

"Ugghhh, I am seriously considering just driving home tomorrow so I can go with you tonight." McKenzie squealed, doing an excited little sorority squat. "You look so gorgeous."

"I'll be fine on my own. I probably won't even stay that long anyway." I reassured her. "Thanks for being my fairy godmother." I smiled sweetly at her as I wrapped my arms around her in a hug. I truly hoped that the next time I saw her my world would be less complicated and I wouldn't have to feel like I was hiding half of myself from her.

"You know I've always got you." She winked, an unusual tenderness in her voice.

We shared one last goodbye. And the last thing she did before walking out the door was whip out that vintage Polaroid camera, press her cheek against mine, and snap a picture of our grinning faces. She handed me the printout, and all at once the memory of Bellamy sliding my photo across the table flashed before me.

And I silently realized I had so much to blame on that stupid little camera.

The minutes crept near to six-thirty. In the late autumn, nightfall came early, so the golden glow of sunset was already fading to indigo when I arrived at the showcase. I slid out of the driver's seat, my dress slinking across the floorboards behind me. There was no way I intended to walk the four blocks from East Side to the Grand Hall in the silver heels strapped to my feet.

The other artists were arriving in similar fashion in their exquisite gowns and pricey suits, and they looked like mostly juniors and seniors. Though tonight I looked the part, I was not one of them. As I watched the Porsches and BMWs rolling in, I felt a prick of embarrassment at my beat-up old Jeep with a patched tire from months ago. It was moments like this that reminded me just how life-altering one scholarship had been.

Scurrying past other guests, I made it my mission to simply get to my artwork quickly and take a picture for Dad. The fountain from earlier now served as the centerpiece of the entrance with gold lights strung above, hanging in drapes like curtains of fireflies. I lifted my dress to walk up the stairs, careful not to bump into any of the other gala attendees.

When I entered the ballroom, my jaw dropped at the glamour before me. I stopped with wide eyes as I shifted in my stiletto heels to keep from slipping on the polished floor. The area that had merely been a half-decorated venue this morning was now transformed into a fairytale setting. The shining floor reflected the gleaming lights of the massive diamond chandelier overhead. Sophisticated archways lined the walls alternating between strong white columns of marble. A gentle melody of violins teased my ears over the chatter of the room. The hotel's history was manifested in this elegant display like nothing else I'd seen, and I could have believed for a moment that I had stepped back into the 19th century.

I weaved through the guests as delicately as possible, making my way to the silent auction room down the hall. When I got there, the bid sheet next to my piece already had a couple of offers, but I didn't even look at them. Thirty percent of the winning bid would go to the school, and the artist would pocket the rest. but I assumed my offers would be too low this early to really make a difference, so I didn't even bother looking. It was really the least of my worries.

As I stood by my work, after snapping a picture to send to Dad of the display, people began to stop, inundating me with the same questions. They'd ask if I was the artist, or if I could explain the technique I used to create the rippling reflection effect, or how long it had taken me to paint.

One stunningly beautiful woman who looked like a middle-aged millionaire stopped and lingered for a while, running her piercing eyes over the painting what seemed like a hundred times. Her thick hair was raven black, pinned up elegantly atop her head. She glittered with jewels and her silk blue dress rippled like liquid as she walked, reminding me of the sea. She finally spoke, introducing herself as the owner of a wealthy beach club and local marina.

"I'd love to have such a piece in one of my resorts," she said, her delicate, lofty tone reminding me of the dramatic way 1940s movie stars used to speak.

"Thank you." I smiled. "I'm flattered. Of course, you can bid on it at the auction if you'd like."

"Of course." She nodded with a subtle tip of her regal chin.

She studied the painting once more and finally asked me a question I hadn't received yet—where I had found the inspiration for such a piece. I hadn't prepared an answer, stupidly, but I did my best to come up with one. I straightened my spine and breathed in.

"I...I used to be afraid of the ocean," I said. "Until I met someone who showed me the stars and told me how to use them to find my way. And I realized, a little while after that, I wasn't so afraid anymore."

If only it was truly that simple. If only I could somehow put into words every piece of me that had bled into the paint on that canvas.

The woman simply nodded, her face unreadable, and walked on, moving like liquid into the crowd.

I felt myself blush with embarrassment. I probably sounded like a complete idiot. And something about her reaction had left a bad taste on my tongue.

My stomach turned and I wanted to escape, especially as I noticed the time and thought about the impending plan for Milo to steal the key. And another thing haunted me in the back of my mind—that he'd said Valdez planned to come ashore to look for me. Being there, especially alone, suddenly felt...unsettling, even though I knew it was probably the safest place I could be.

I decided to leave the room to get a breath of fresh air. All the glittering enchantment around me couldn't mask the troubles drowning me inside as I stood there alone. I glanced back at my painting as I exited the auction area and made my way through the ballroom, the only direct path to a small patio outside, where the moonlight gleamed like a beacon.

Pushing through the throng of people, I headed for the open door, but stopped still when I heard a familiar voice say my name from behind. An icy sensation gripped my chest as I found the courage to look back, just before I fully turned to see him standing there amongst the sparkling crowd.

Bellamy.

26

KATRINA

He took a step toward me. The air shifted, tense and almost tangible, each breath noticed, each movement heavy with intent. Everything around me—the grandness, the chatter, the orchestral music—faded into the background as I watched Bellamy move toward me with the sleek precision of a predator, devastatingly handsome in the black suit he wore, holding one end of the jacket casually tossed over his shoulder.

Why the hell was he here?

His ice blue gaze never left mine, and when he was one last step away, his eyes dropped from mine to my neck.

My fingers curled around the necklace, quick and instinctive. Surely, he wouldn't try to take it in a place like this, not with all these people. I stared up at him suspiciously, the top of my head reaching just above his chin.

"Don't worry," his voice smoothed over me as he took the hand that covered my necklace in his. "I'm not here for that this time."

"Then what are you here for?" I asked.

"You."

I could barely hear his soft whisper over the melody of violins. He reached for my other hand with a gentle motion and guided me towards him.

"I'm a terrible dancer." I bit my lip, turning my head away. I couldn't look him in the eyes any longer. I was too bothered by what I last said to him.

"And a terrible judge of character."

My gaze dropped to the floor.

"I'm sorry," I said "I had no idea. What happened to you—to Serena—was—"

"I don't blame you for expecting the worst from me, love. I am, after all, just a dirty, no-good pirate." He smirked with a wink.

Before I could gather a response, my footsteps were following his along the dance floor, slowly stepping in time with the music.

"You're not so bad," he chuckled, glancing down between us.

"I'm just following your lead."

"Good." His eyes darkened. "Where else would you follow me?"

He was intoxicating. And it was maddeningly confusing. His scent of sweet rum and salt filled my nostrils, and his touch made my body tense. Something about him always made me feel like a trapped mouse being taunted by a cat.

But I couldn't bring myself to pull away.

"Don't try to get inside my head." I took a breath. "What are you saying?"

"I'm saying, listen to me. You possess the power to manipulate a hundred men with your voice and that scale around your neck. You could avenge the sirens by claiming that last remnant of power for yourself, and I could help you do it. After what my father did to your kind—think about it. He exterminated them, one by one. Just like he wants to do to you. But you could become more ruthless than him. He can feel pain—you could control his every moment, even when we've surfaced. You could make it truly endless for him."

"Valdez will meet his justice as long as my heart stays in my chest. If I break the curse, he dies, just like he was meant to 300 years ago. And what he did to Serena...he'll never be able to do it again to anyone else. Isn't that vengeance enough?"

A shadow fell across Bellamy's eyes. Our dance slowed, and I held his gaze, losing myself in his unreadable expression as I thought about what I was saying. "Bellamy, you could finally be free from this heartache that tortures you. If I can break the curse, you won't have to suffer like this anymore. You could finally rest."

"Will I?" His voice cracked. "Because every pirate knows his true place is in hell."

"You're already in hell. Your own personal kind. You're miserable, and you are willing to stay that way just to see your father suffer. You want to steal my heart just to hurt Milo, and because you want whatever power you think I have as your personal weapon. Do you hear yourself? Do you really want to be trapped this way forever?"

"I want my father to pay for what he's done. And this is the only way I can ensure that." Bellamy brushed my hair behind my ear with a gentle finger. The upbeat tune from the orchestra clashed with the grim topic we were discussing as we twirled across the dance floor.

I shook my head. "You don't want what's real, Bellamy. Everything you think you want is an illusion. And you're the one paying the greatest price."

He leaned in and lowered his voice as we swayed in rhythm, and he pressed me closer. "It's no illusion that Valdez and the crew would've found you by now if it weren't for me. The real illusion is that you think Milo's protecting you, when in fact, he's going to get you killed, despite whatever he's made you believe."

"I know you blame Milo for what happened to Serena. But he came to warn you. He tried to help save her." I snapped back, keeping my voice low. "You hate him, but why do you want me to hate him, too?"

"Because he's a hypocrite." Bellamy seethed. "And that's never been clearer to me than the night he spoke to you on the island. We agreed never to let what happened to Serena happen again. And yet, he broke the code by speaking to you."

"That's why you disappeared after you saved me from drowning, isn't it?"

The look in his eyes was confirmation enough. "I never want to see my father released from his torment. He's earned every second of it. Even if it means we're damned along with him. To release him from this curse—to offer him the sweet escape of death—would be a mercy I cannot afford to grant him. Not after what he's taken from me." Bellamy paused, crossing his jaw as he looked away for a fraction of a second. "Milo wants to end our curse, as I once did...because he's never had someone worth suffering for." He moved his hand from the curve of my waist to the small of my back.

"So? He's never pressured me to end the curse. He's helping me break my own."

"He's making you fall in love with him."

My pulse quickened, and I stumbled as our dance hastened aggressively.

"No, that's not—"

"Just like Serena loved me." Bellamy purred. "So much that she believed she could convince the sea to let me go...by giving herself to it."

"I'm not going to give myself to the sea. Not for Milo. Not for Valdez. Not for anyone. I'll figure out how to use the scale to undo the curse after I fix myself and my mom."

"Right," Bellamy rolled his eyes. "Milo hasn't told you the whole curse, has he? I assure you it's not just as simple as you singing some song over the scale in deeper waters." He laughed through his teeth, low and disconcerting. "Milo told you he wants redemption, I'm sure. But what he hasn't told you is that you'll die for it."

His words hit me like a wave, like a far-away ringing in my ears, and my chest hollowed out all at once. I blinked a few times, looking past his shoulder to ground myself. "No," I said. "He's kept me safe all this time. He wouldn't..."

Bellamy's grip on me tightened. He squeezed my fingers together as his eyes drifted to something behind me. "Ask him yourself."

He twirled me outward, so that I caught a glimpse behind me of what had caught his attention—the brooding, tall figure standing in the open doorway, half shrouded in moonlight and staring right at me—Milo.

It was a flash of him standing there, only a glimpse before Bellamy reeled me back into his grasp.

"It's hard to believe just how easily you bend to him." He whispered against my ear, holding me to him in a way that was obviously intended for Milo to see. "Do you think he really cares about you?"

"You don't hate him, Bellamy. You just think you do." I breathed. "He told me you were once friends."

"That was long before he stole the heart of a siren from me." Bellamy leaned into me, dipping me backward in time with the music as his solid, powerful arms held me in place. He pressed his lips to my neck and kissed me right above the scale pendant. His voice crawled across my skin like a whisper in the dark. "But I'm a pirate, after all, so I intend to take it back...one way or another."

"You're out of your mind." I snapped, realizing he was still looking at Milo, a burning hatred in his eyes like fire melting ice.

I craned myself around once more to see Milo approaching, parting the crowd as he moved forward like a thunderstorm rolling in, walking cooly with slow steps, but fists clenched at his sides.

"Katrina." Milo was looking at me, but he briefly flicked his gaze toward Bellamy.

"I thought you weren't coming," I said, trying to suppress the sound of my relief.

His jaw flexed as he looked down at Bellamy's hand on my waist and then back up at me. "I suppose that siren song worked on me after all."

"She sang for you?" Bellamy growled, letting go of me as I turned toward Milo.

"She sang for herself." Milo shot back. He slid his hands into the pockets of his dark blue suit that I couldn't help but wonder where he'd gotten, and drilled his gaze into Bellamy's once more. "Why aren't you with the crew, leading them away from her? You know Valdez intends to come ashore tonight."

"Oh? Must've slipped my mind." Bellamy pretended to look surprised, then met Milo's stare with a threatening look of his own. "Or perhaps I felt the greater threat might already be here." He switched his gaze between the two of us. "Don't worry, I'll catch up to them. But while I'm busting my ass to keep her safe, why don't you tell her all about the curse you've got her so convinced she's meant to break, hmm? Specifically, that last line."

Without another word, as quickly as he had appeared, he stepped between the two of us and vanished into the crowd, but not before pecking me on the cheek. The way Milo watched him, I thought he might go kill him again.

And if Bellamy was a dark, opulent wine, Milo was milk and honey.

"It's hard for me to believe you two ever *weren't* enemies." I said.

"There was a time," Milo uttered, his voice flat. Then he looked at me, pausing for a breath as he swept his eyes over me and the music shifted to a tender, lilting ballad.

"You look...like starlight." He drew near, his eyes softening as he stretched out a tattooed hand to me. "One more dance?"

My lips curved into a smile. "I think I have one left in me."

We danced across the gleaming floor, waltzing, and swaying as sweet songs guided our movements, everything around us fading away. The music swelled, and I might have been floating. I leaned into Milo's touch, savoring the feeling of his palm over the small of my back, pressed against the bare skin my open-back dress left revealed. And for the fleeting length of a song, the world made sense.

There was so much to worry about, but for now, I chose not to let any of it matter. Everything that haunted me would have to wait until the song finished. Whatever horrors were awaiting at the end of it, I would deal with then, but for now, I was stealing back my peace in the midst of a melody I'd never forget.

By the end of it, our bodies were pressed against each other, and Milo's fingers closed around mine as if he might never let go. And I looked up at him, waiting for his explanation.

"Why are you here tonight?" I asked. "You're supposed to be getting the key."

"And I intend to. Once the ship is unattended," he said softly. But then he dipped his head, and he closed his eyes for a moment, as if bracing for something. "There's something I need to tell you, Katrina." He released my hand and pulled away slightly.

"Is...is it about the curse? About what Bellamy was saying?"

"That's...that's part of it, yes. It's unfortunate that Bellamy got to you before I did. But it doesn't change what I came to say." He nodded toward the open doors leading to the patio. "Let's go somewhere we can talk."

I followed him outside, where a small stone courtyard awaited with another ornate flowing fountain in the center. The damp night chill was enough to ward off most people, but I didn't mind.

Lights twinkled behind us and overhead like stars. The gentle trickle of the fountain prevailed over the muffled hum of the music from inside.

It was just us.

"Katrina," Milo started, his voice low and hoarse. I had never seen him look so uncertain as he fumbled trying to say whatever was next.

"Yes?" I leaned forward. "What is it?"

He hesitated, his lips parting briefly before he'd stutter on a word and then close them again.

"You're leaving in the morning," he said matter-of-factly.

"Yes, that's right." I said, arching a brow and leaning in. "Milo, what—"

"Good. Don't come back," he muttered, almost too quickly, too harshly for me to process.

I blinked. "What?"

"Promise me you won't come back," he said. "Promise me you'll stay far away from here. And never come back."

Now it was me who was lost for words. "Milo, this doesn't make any sense. If you're worried about Valdez finding me, we've already talked about that. I'll go home and figure out how to break the curse once I get the box open, and hopefully then I'll understand everything—I'll understand what I'm supposed to do to break the curse."

"I'm afraid I already know what you're supposed to do to break the curse..." he said, his voice creeping into something formidable—something regretful. "And that's why I've changed my mind about everything."

"What do you mean?"

"I mean I haven't been entirely honest with you. I haven't told you that there's more to the curse..."

I urged him to continue, his words like a hook carving through me as he began to recite the full siren's curse.

"*By siren's blood and magic done,*

This curse of lasting flesh and bone,
The sea will hold your bodies bound
'Til siren's blood again be found.
The depths shall never set you free.
'Til she returns her magic to the sea."

A deathly shudder swam down my spine as he emphasized the final line and his expression turned grim.

"None of us fully agree on what it means, but Valdez believes it's clear enough—that you must be returned to the sea. Not just the scale—you. The magic is only activated by your siren blood, just like you saw last night. The curse demands you—and in every way. The only difference between he and I is that I believe it means you must do it willingly."

"So was Bellamy right then?" I looked away, focusing on the trickle of the fountain as something stung inside me. "Has all this just been a ploy to get me to fall for you and give myself to save you?"

Milo took a step closer, something like fear in his eyes. "It was never my intention. I spoke to you on that island even when I knew I shouldn't. Because I was drawn to you like the tide itself. But after that, I swore to stay away from you. I never thought I'd see you again...until I learned the crew knew about you, too. And then I had the idea—the selfish, disgusting idea—that maybe you might choose to save me. Because, yes, Katrina, a few weeks ago, I still wanted nothing more than to end my own torment. But now, after everything...I don't want you to break the curse. Because I don't want to lose you."

"So everything..." I swallowed. "Was any of it real? On the beach...the lighthouse...the lagoon? Did you mean any of that?"

Milo hung his head, and I thought I might break right there.

"I meant every damn word," he said, closing whatever space was left between us. "And that's the problem. I have no doubt that makes me a terrible man, and an even more terrible pirate. Because in trying to win your heart, I lost mine to you." He looked to the sky and closed his eyes, breathing in before speaking again. "And now, my only desire is to know that you are safe from Valdez. Safe from the crew and the curse. And...safe from me."

I glared up at him, my lips pressed tight together as my response simmered inside me. Until I couldn't keep it in any longer. "So now you want me to leave you—and Bellamy—suffering forever at the bottom of the sea? Even if I'm the only chance you might ever have at breaking free from it? Now you just want me to give up everything here and leave?"

"I want you to be safe. And I want you to free yourself."

"While knowing you're spending the rest of forever in hell." My lips could barely utter the words, my throat closing as I choked them out.

"No." Milo breathed steadily. "The real hell would be knowing what it cost you. There is no promise of redemption or rest that is worth losing you. And if that makes you my damnation, so be it." He touched my chin tenderly and tilted my face up towards his.

"I thought you didn't believe in love. That it's all just...fool's gold." I muttered snidely.

"I didn't," he breathed, holding me captive with his gaze. "Because I'd never found anyone worth burning for...until you."

I could barely see him through the blur in my eyes.

"Milo, you absolute prick." I sniffed, unable to hold in a tear. "You don't know for sure that sacrificing myself is what I have to do. Maybe there's another way."

"There isn't," he said bluntly. "And even if there is, Valdez will never stop hunting you. And he will give you to the sea regardless, after he's done carving out your beating heart and ensuring he enacts his revenge upon your bloodline. Which is why once I get this key, I want you to take it and never return to these shores."

"I've wondered what it would be like..." I confessed, a tear tickling my cheek as it rolled down. "When I finally broke your curse and it made your death final. I guess some part of me always knew eventually I'd have to face the fact that I'd never see you again. I just didn't think it would be like this."

"You don't need me, Katrina. You never did. I was the one who needed you. I needed light, and you were the dawn." He glanced down at my lips, hesitated, and then pulled away. "You have no idea the depths to which I care for you."

I grounded myself, struck by the weight of it all, and the rollercoaster of emotions that had left me breathless. I wanted to argue with him. To stand there and throw back every stupid reason I could think of that might change the outcome. But I knew it would be futile. Because everything he said was true—and the sinking realization of that was slow current from which I could not escape.

"Fine." I agreed, an idea forming in my head that I knew would sound as reckless as the sea itself. "I will promise to never come back here—on two conditions."

Milo sighed so deep his shoulders slumped. "You're going to bargain?"

"I am."

He cocked his head, his brow tense. "And what are your demands?"

"First," I sucked in a breath, "I come with you to steal the key. It's the only way I can be sure you'll do what you say."

"That is absolute madness," Milo groaned. "No."

I crossed my arms. "Then I'll be right back here after Thanksgiving."

"Damn it, Katrina," Milo shook his head, nostrils flaring as he looked away and curled his fingers at his sides. "I get it. You don't fully trust me, and after everything, I don't blame you. But if you come anywhere near that ship, you *have* to trust me and do everything I say if you want to make it out in one piece."

"Now you want me to trust you?" I raised my chin, emphasizing the wariness in my voice with a narrowed stare into his hazel eyes.

"I want you stay alive." Milo huffed, returning my glare.

"Fine."

"And what is your second condition?"

I nodded towards the bustling gala behind us. "I want you to see the painting."

Milo looked toward the ballroom, his jaw relaxing into the faintest beginning of a what was almost a smile before his eyes fell back on me. "That one I'll gladly agree to."

I reached for his hand, pulling him back into the room where once more the air pulsed with melodies on violins and cellos, where fine suits and satin dresses painted the room in colors, and the scent of perfume and champagne engulfed us. Nothing at all had changed in that ballroom, meanwhile it had felt like time had stopped in the courtyard just steps outside of it.

We drifted through the crowd with purpose as I led Milo to the auction room. I didn't know why it meant so much to me that he saw the painting. I didn't know what I was hoping it would change—or if I hoped it would change anything at all. But perhaps some part of me wanted Milo to know that whether he'd realized it or not, he'd changed me, too.

For better or worse, I wasn't sure yet.

He stayed close to me as I pulled him along, careful to position him at the display. And when his eyes found the painting, his eyes widened, something almost like reverence sparking in them.

He took a step closer to the canvas, the look on his face so captivated that I almost thought he would reach out to touch it. His gaze hovered over the sunken ship in its dark bleakness for a long time before drifting up toward the star's light breaking through the surface.

"You...you painted us," he finally said.

I blinked slowly, my coiled emotions masked beneath the faintest nod. "Yeah...I guess I did."

And then a tidal wave hit. Suddenly I was suffocating once more. The room, the gala, the glow of the golden lights, all seemed to be swimming around me, distorted visions and blurs in a cage that felt like being underwater, and I couldn't find the surface.

And there I was, drowning in a cyclone that felt like it was tearing me to pieces, blood pouring from my heart in an undertow of crimson. And I was swimming, but my legs were tangled beneath me, useless against the weight of the glittering blue-silver dress anchoring me down. And above me, standing on the surface and looking down at me—my mom.

I snapped back to the present moment, seeking the feeling of the floor beneath my feet as I stumbled from the horror of the vision that left me reeling and gasping. Milo steadied me, and others glanced my way with a few concerned murmurs leaking through the room.

I assured everyone I was fine—that I simply hadn't eaten much and felt a little light-headed. But inside, my stomach was in knots from anything but hunger.

"I need to leave." I uttered beneath my breath. "I don't want to be here anymore."

"I've got you." Milo escorted me to the door, his hand never leaving the small of my back. "What did you see?"

I described the hallucination to him, and he rushed me through the doors.

"Maybe it's a warning that Valdez is near—that he's begun his search on land," he said under his breath. "We should get you out of Constantine."

"We have to get the key." I reminded him.

"And we will," he said. "But we still have a whole night to survive until then. If you insist on coming with me on the ship, then we must wait until the absolute last hour of darkness. If something goes wrong, we need the dawn on our side."

I trailed him down the building's steps and to a small lot around the corner, where the shadow of his motorcycle filled the space. He gestured with an open hand and without a word I swung a leg over the back seat, grateful for the high slit in the dress that allowed me to do so.

He removed his suit jacket and laid it over my bare shoulders to shield me from the wind. Then he slid down in front of me, and without a word I locked my arms around him, not bothering to ask where we'd go.

Because I knew the only place left.

So we sailed into the night, back along the coasts, until we reached the cragged shores of the old, abandoned lighthouse.

LIGHTHOUSE

27

KATRINA

We picked our way across the rocks, the waves smacking the shore more quietly than last time. I pulled Milo's jacket around me as the salty breeze raked over my skin, and focused on my two feet in front of me.

"We'll wait out a few hours here," Milo called over the wind.

"How will we know where the ship will be?"

"I have a good idea where Valdez intends to anchor. A spot unlikely to be noticed."

I shrugged and huddled deeper into the jacket, a chill from something other than wind biting at my bones.

"Where did you get the suit?" I asked, trying to shift my mind's direction.

Milo's only response was a quick glance behind me with a mischievous curve of his mouth.

"You stole it?" I pressed.

"Don't sound so surprised, starlight," he snickered, taking my hand as I short-stepped over some lumpy ground in my stilettos.

"Why do you call me that?" I asked.

"Starlight?" He repeated "Well, just look at you."

I glanced down at the sparkling train of my dress, and was once more reminded of that vision, where this same silver-blue skirt rendered my legs useless.

"The hallucination," I muttered, closing my arms around myself. "I don't think it was a memory. I think it was the future. I...I was wearing this—or something like this. I can't stop wondering if it meant I'm going to die tonight, or if it was meant to keep me afraid, to keep me from doing this."

Milo turned to me, waves rolling in rhythmically just steps away as the breeze tugged on the hem of my dress.

"You don't have to do this, Katrina," he said, sitting down on a tall rock beside me where I stood, facing the sea. "I promise you I will find that key, whatever it takes. If that's the reason you're doing this—because you don't trust that I will—don't let my foolish mistakes make you risk yourself."

"It's not just that." I reached up and smoothed a fingertip across the siren scale. "I think I need to do this...to see the ship one last time. I need to take something from it—I need to take the key myself—so that it will forever be proof that all of this was real before I leave it all behind."

Milo nodded, his pensive stare piercing the dark horizon. "Then take all the proof you need." He stood up and made his way to the base of the lighthouse, where he stooped to pick up something hidden in the shadows of the entrance. "I had a feeling we'd end up here tonight, given Valdez is out hunting you. I brought this for you."

He tossed a bundle of fabric my way. I caught it, looking at the strange, otherworldly thing in my hands. A simple pale-colored dress, with long flowing sleeves and an ankle-length hem, woven from thread long from another time.

"What is this?"

"A change of clothes. You don't have to wear it, but if you're planning on sneaking aboard the *Siren's Scorn*, it's probably best if you aren't shimmering like a diamond."

I eyed him carefully as he tucked his own pile of clothing beneath his arm and pulled out a pair of seaworn leather boots.

"You knew I would end up sneaking onto the ship with you?"

"With how cleverly stubborn you are, it wasn't hard to anticipate." He winked with a tilt of his head as he began undoing the buttons of his suit shirt. "If anything, you'll certainly look more like someone who belongs on a pirate ship than a university student."

"Hmm," I made a face, holding the dress out in front of me. "Do I want to know the fate of the woman aboard who this once belonged to?"

"You do know her fate," Milo uttered. "It was Cordelia's. Before Valdez betrayed her, she spent many nights aboard the ship with him."

"Lovely," I crooned. Something haunting washed over me as I considered the dress in my hands.

I glanced over to where Milo stood with his back against the threshold of the lighthouse as he undid the last button. He straightened his shoulders, casually removing the shirt and tossing it aside like it was crumpled paper.

My breath hitched as I saw him, my gaze hung on his powerful form. His muscular abdomen tightened as he turned my direction, drawing my attention to his center and the carved physique that promised more of the same below.

I knew I was blushing. I knew I should've looked away.

But I didn't.

He stepped forward, and I found I couldn't stop watching him. His tan skin glistened in the moonlight across his broad, muscled figure. Tattoos trailed from his chest down his arms, depicting various symbols. Sharks, anchors, bits of rope, ships—but my favorite was still the star inked across the sculpted ridges of his left forearm.

I swallowed a mouthful of dry air. "I'll...um...I'll go change around the other side." I sputtered.

Still flushed, I moved behind the curve of the lighthouse wall and stretched my arm back to reach the dress's zipper, only to find it snagged in place no matter how much I tugged and wiggled. With careful steps, I strode back around into the open where Milo still stood shirtless, the top button of his pants undone.

Then I turned my back toward him more quickly than I meant to, the words tripping their way out of my mouth. "Can...can you unzip me?"

His footsteps closed in. I felt his heat against my back. And every muscle in me tensed as I felt him take hold of the zipper. With one slow motion, he pulled it down and the bodice relaxed its fitted grip around me. And I finally released the breath I was holding.

And then, with him still looming at my back, the question spilled out before I thought it through. "Did you call me your treasure that night on the boat?"

He chuckled, a deep rumble that ignited something in me. "You were asleep. You weren't supposed to have heard that."

"Well, I *did* hear it."

"Well, I did call you that. For the same reason I call you starlight."

"Because I'm glittering?" I sneered, tapping the sides of my dress.

"No..." Milo breathed, leaning in close and letting his words brush the tip of my ear. "Because when I'm in the abyss, you're the only thing I see when everything else looks like darkness. You are the light that guides me to the surface when the tide rises. You are my North Star."

His words hovered somewhere on that shore just out of reach. I heard them, but I needed an extra moment to understand exactly what they meant to me. My pulse quickened as they settled and swept my heart into their pull. I opened my mouth to say something, but nothing came. Any words of my own might as well have been lost to the sea in front of us, as I stood there all too aware of how long I'd gone without answering.

Until he finally broke the silence, his voice like a ghost at my back.

"And if you keep standing here in front of me with your dress unzipped, I might not have the strength to keep myself from you any longer."

I turned my head to peer at him over my shoulder.

I shouldn't have wanted him. He was a scheming pirate, spinning tangled promises and half-truths into the same breath. He was a man bound by no rules or limits, no doubt as reckless as the sea that had shaped him.

It was insanity to want him. And I knew that if I let myself have him, the inevitable heartbreak would only be that much stronger. Because he was never even supposed to know me. He was meant to be long gone at the bottom of the sea.

And yet here he was, with me, like he'd been so many nights before, whispering strange promises in my ear.

I didn't walk away. I kept standing there as he watched me.

I didn't move when he stepped closer, closing whatever little space was left between us.

I didn't flinch as he traced the skin of my back with his finger, drawing a line where the zipper had once covered.

And I didn't move as he touched his lips to the skin of my shoulder, and planted slow kisses along the side of my neck.

I sucked in a trembling breath and leaned into him, neck tilted toward him, as his mouth slid along my skin softly. When he pulled away, I turned to face him.

"Why did you stop?" I breathed.

"Because I promised not to hurt you."

"It doesn't count if I'm asking you to," I said. "Kiss me."

He stared at me for a long moment, his hand creeping up toward my face, where he wiped a tear with his thumb. And then he leaned down and pressed his mouth against mine.

Milk and honey. Our breaths danced together, tasting one another under the stars. His tongue traced my lips before I parted them, inviting him to deepen the kiss.

His hands slid down, exploring each curve along the way as he tucked them both beneath the smooth of my hip and lifted me off the ground, spinning me around to the edge of the lighthouse, where he placed me down with my back against the stone wall.

He kissed me again, deeper, holding my face in his hands as his mouth teased mine, the taste of his tongue sending sweet ripples of heat through my core.

His hands slid down to my neck, then along the curve of my waist where I felt his calloused fingers tease the skin of my back once more. He moved lower and curled them inward, gripping me like I was meant for him. Sparks ignited under my skin at his touch.

I gasped as his hand curled around my thigh, lifting it slowly through the slit in the dress. He crouched down at my feet, both hands sliding down the length of my leg with a touch that made me tingle from head to toe.

He drew my leg toward him, his fingers hooked around the back of my knee, and brushed his lips along the length of my thigh, his breath trailing upward as his fingers followed. The tease of his lips on my skin, of the salt and amber scent of him blown in on the sea breeze, made me throw my head back with a soft gasp that left me aching.

"Consider this your proof," he said. "That this is all real. That I'm real." His voice was a hoarse whisper as he looked up at me, caressing my exposed leg propped on his lap. He kissed the inside of my thigh, leaving me breathless and tense as he worked his way closer to the end of the dress slit.

He was so close to the core of me, I could feel the warmth of his breath against me, against the center of my body that throbbed with desire to feel more of him everywhere. I leaned back against the wall, giving myself to the feel of his lips suckling my skin, teasing my nerves with every careful planted kiss.

He moved closer, hesitating for a breath before he lingered just beneath me, promising to give me something I couldn't name. His fingers traced me, delicate and careful, until each moment stretched, building a deepening need in me that grew with each tender touch. I burned above him, desperate and aching from a growing pull that left my body charged, until the silent rhythm of his closeness made it almost too much to hold inside.

He pulled away slowly, and slid his hands back up along my body as he stood, his eyes fixed on mine, shadowed by hazy moonlight. "I don't need to give you another reason not to trust me."

My own fingers curled into the bare skin of his back, feeling the tight muscles that flexed with each of his movements—and uneven jagged lines that I presumed to be scars—until I raked my fingers through his hair and stared up at him, begging him to finish whatever unspoken thing he'd stirred up in me. The tenderness of his mouth, the scent of him, the warmth of his breath, the strength and gentleness of his hands along my body. It took me to a place I'd never been. And it felt like I could stay there forever.

But a sharp pang pierced my heart, and I remembered we didn't have forever. We didn't even have tonight.

He was a wall around me, his arms pressed against either side of the lighthouse with me in between them. I was invincible and powerless all at once as my unzipped dress inched further and further down, until it slid completely off the top half of me, catching only at the widest part of my hips and leaving the rest of me exposed. Our hands took turns wandering each other like ships on uncharted waters.

He pushed himself against me, and I felt the solid hardness at his center against my stomach. I reached for him, but he stopped my hand with his, an edge like sadness in his voice. "No," he hushed. "Tonight is for you. I won't feel your touch anyway. But you can feel mine." It drew a quiet moan from me as he pressed his lips against mine once more, his hands drifting up to tenderly tease my breasts with the rough skin of his palms. I trembled like palm fronds in a hurricane. My heart raced, thumping louder than the crashing waves below us. The fire between us fought away the damp chill on my skin.

I had never been this vulnerable with anyone before.

And I wondered if it broke him as much as it was breaking me.

He touched me once more, drawing out that silent, yearning pull from earlier, his fingers navigating my body like a map he knew by heart. I shuddered against the lighthouse wall, all the things I hadn't said earlier trickling out in a single quiet surrender from my lips as I breathed out his name.

I pressed my forehead to his, savoring the scent of him and the salt of the sea. I placed a hand on his chest and began tracing the bird tattoo underneath his collarbone.

"What does this one mean?" I asked, my voice quivering.

"The swallow," he said softly. "It's the mark a sailor gets when he's traveled five thousand miles at sea."

"And the anchor?" My eyes drifted to his upper arm.

"A merchant's mark. Or a mark for those who have crossed the Atlantic. I've done both so I suppose I especially deserve this one."

I smiled, still breathless at the feeling of his body so close to mine. "Do you have the heart and the arrows?" I asked. "Like Bellamy?"

Milo's gaze hardened.

"No," he uttered. "That tattoo was personal for Bellamy." He took my face in his hands, and kissed me gently on the lips once more. "We should finished getting changed."

I nodded, pulling the bodice of my glittering gown back up around me as I scrambled to find the dress I'd wear on the ship.

It was a wrinkled pile on the ground, nestled among the rocks and reeds. I snatched it up and walked to the other side of the lighthouse, pulling it over my head and silently asking McKenzie to forgive me for leaving her sparkling gown out here on the coasts of nowhere.

When I came back around the corner, Milo stood staring at the ocean in his billowing ivory shirt cinched at the waist and dark loose trousers tucked into boots.

I joined him at the seaside, and his eyes wandered over me in the long-sleeved vintage dress that hung to my feet just as it caught in the wind and rippled behind me like a ghost. He smiled, and I caught a twinkle in his eye.

I smiled back, but a dark thought intruded all at once as I glanced back out at the foaming waves. The warmth within me suddenly turned to frost.

"Milo," I uttered. "What will Valdez do to you once he realizes you took the key."

"It doesn't matter what he does to me."

"I know he can't kill you. But there are some things worse than death." I swallowed. "Those scars I felt across your back...were they?"

"From the floggings," Milo said, his face unreadable. "Valdez's preferred tool of punishment."

I leaned against him, touching a hand to his back and feeling the deep, raised lines on his skin through the fabric of his shirt.

"I can't let you endure that...forever." I shook my head, a lump rising in my throat. "You've already suffered enough."

"It is not suffering to know you are safe." He never looked at me, only held his empty stare on the horizon.

No matter how he tried to convince me, the guilt would always sting like salt in a fresh wound. But what choice did I have but to leave? At least until Mom was safe...until I fixed all this somehow...somehow.

Somehow.

I stared out at the endless black sea before me, wondering where the *Siren's Scorn* drifted at this very moment. My heart turned in my chest. I didn't know what was more foolish—going with Milo aboard the *Siren' Scorn* or thinking I could truly be the first in my bloodline to change everything. To save those of us left before the sea's curse claimed us, too.

"Katrina," Milo's voice called my attention as he started ambling across the shore to the parked motorcycle. "We need to head back soon. But please just promise me you'll be careful aboard the ship and that you'll do what I ask once we're there. We cannot risk Valdez seeing you, no matter what."

"Aye, aye captain," I muttered. "I promise I'll be fine."

"Be careful making promises you can't keep, starlight." He said without turning around.

I followed him to the bike. We stole a few last kisses under the moonlight, and then set off for the distant shores of Constantine Beach, where the *Siren's Scorn* awaited behind a cloud of dark fog.

Close Quarters

28

KATRINA

The silhouette of the ship bobbed just offshore in the eerily calm waters. There was a single lantern on the deck casting a yellow glow on the tattered sails, but otherwise, it was difficult to determine what the rest of the ship looked like if you didn't know what it was.

Even still, these coasts were entirely quiet at 4 AM. No one would be out here looking for a pirate ship.

No one except us.

Milo parked the bike in the shadows and told me to wait behind it. He quietly walked across the sand to the five wooden dinghies parked ashore and checked to make sure no one was watching or returning to them, and then motioned for me to follow once he determined it was safe.

"I guess this is where the saying 'the coast is clear' comes from?" I joked, though inwardly I was nauseous from the thought of being ferried out into the ocean in such small boats.

I studied the size of the dinghies. They looked as though they could hold at least half a dozen men each. Valdez must've had a crew of close to forty with him. And they were all ashore somewhere looking for me. I wondered how such a phenomenon had existed for so many years without anyone noticing. But then again, some *did* notice, just like Russell and Mrs. Guiterrez, but no one believed them.

And that was enough to explain all the ghost stories and legends shrouding these coasts.

"You're sure no one is on the ship?" I stammered.

"No, I'm not sure." He hesitated. "I can only hope Bellamy was able to lead them all ashore." He leaned over to adjust the rowboat of choice and then looked at me. "You don't have to do this, Katrina. You could stay right here. You could hide and wait for me."

"Not a bad idea, mate. Leave her here in some capable hands." Bellamy's lofty voice startled us both.

He appeared from seemingly nowhere, and it was the first time since the beach that I'd seen him in his long black pirate's coat that nearly reached the tops of his boots.

Milo cocked his head, stomping toward Bellamy. "You've been following us?"

"Quite the contrary. I just came to see the spectacle."

"Aren't you supposed to be leading the crew off my trail?" I threw in.

"Already done, love. You've got nothing to worry about." He paused to look up at the moon. "At least not yet."

A long silence weighted the air. Milo touched my arm, pulling me aside as he stepped between me and Bellamy.

"I'm not leaving her alone with you."

"We don't have time to argue about this. I'm going with you," I snapped.

"You heard the lass." Bellamy clapped his hands together. "Time to go."

"Why are you *really* here?" Milo grumbled.

"Why do you think, *old friend*?" Bellamy spat the last words, opening his coat to pull out a pistol from the leather strap across his chest. I stepped back as he flipped it once in his hand. "Neither of us wants Valdez anywhere near her. I'll keep watch from here. Anything suspicious happens and I'll fire off a warning shot."

Milo glared at him, his jaw crossed and body rigid. "I'm supposed to trust you?"

"What choice do you have, mate?" Bellamy grinned.

"Fine." Milo inhaled, brushing back his hair from his forehead as he stepped back toward the dinghy.

"Okay, enough. It's settled," I said, annoyed with them both. "Now let's go."

With a shudder, I stepped into the boat in front of Milo. The wood was ancient and splintering.

I gripped the edges as Milo pushed the vessel out into the water and quickly leapt in. As the waves crested, they lifted us. The dinghy rocked back and forth with each stroke of the oars, the sounds of the sea the only thing keeping silence at bay. The ocean was a void on all sides of me, and I was at its mercy.

Once we reached the ship, I could see its rotting exterior much more clearly. It looked just as fearsome as it had the night I first saw it rise up from the ocean. Cannons lined either side, barnacles growing up the side of the hull. The Jolly Roger flag flapped hauntingly in the breeze. As we neared, Milo let the dinghy drift closer before leaning over the edge and securing a tether to the ship.

"Ready?" he asked, a pleading look in his eye.

I sucked in a breath of air heavy with the scent of brine and fish and nodded.

"Remember—trust what I say, no matter what," he whispered. "I'll go first, just in case any of the crew stayed behind."

I watched with fascination as he stood in the rocking boat with perfect balance and reached up to grab the rope ladder dangling from the ship's starboard edge. With the grace of an acrobat, he heaved himself upward and climbed.

Once at the top, he peeked over the deck before climbing back halfway down to offer me his hand. Standing in the swaying boat was enough to make my heart jump into my throat, and I struggled to find my balance as I reached for him. But he pulled me up with ease, and I grabbed onto the thick, algae covered knots of the rope. My grip nearly slipped as the ladder bent to our weight, dangling from the ship's edge like a pendulum.

Milo climbed up quickly, and I gritted my teeth and followed, taking each rung of rope at a time, careful not to get entangled in my skirts.

When we reached the top, I surveyed the deck before us. The smell of salt, rotting wet wood, and iron overtook my nostrils. The masts towered over us, their dark sails gently billowing like looming wraiths. It was still nearly impossible to believe it was all real. And yet, there I stood, bare soles flat against the cold, damp deck of a 300-hundred-year-old pirate ship wearing the dress of the siren that sank it.

"Valdez's cabin is there, in the quarter deck." Milo shifted his gaze to the left toward a door nestled near the back of the ship. He held a finger to his lips before he stepped toward the rickety steps leading to the door. He knocked once, then gently pushed it open to peer inside.

"All clear," he muttered, pushing forward.

I stepped forward into the cabin, and he glanced behind us. "We'll have to look carefully and make sure we leave everything exactly as it was. Valdez likes his order. He will notice if his quarters have been searched."

I held up a hand. "Then maybe one of us should look, and the other should keep a lookout."

"That's not a terrible idea," Milo nodded, stepping back. "I'll stand watch. They won't suspect anything if they see me on deck. If anyone comes while you're in there, I'll knock three times. You shatter the window in his quarters and escape."

"Then he'll know someone was here—"

"And I'll deal with it." He stood squarely at the door.

I nodded, feeling sick to my stomach. But I had gotten myself into this. I wanted to come. I had gotten this far, and I wasn't about to abandon ship—literally. I whispered once more to Milo before I closed the door. "If anything happens, be careful."

The door groaned and took half my strength to close it shut. And then I was standing alone in the captain's quarters.

My feet were as heavy as lead. I willed them to carry me forward, a damp chill blanketing me down to my bones.

The floorboards creaked and swayed beneath my feet, shuddering with the ocean's movement in a way I wasn't used to. A sense of suffocation crept upon me in the darkness, warded off only by the moonlight and the flame of a lone candle on a writing desk in the corner.

A rolled-up hammock swung gently in the farthest corner of the room, over a solid bed draped with tattered linens once of the highest quality. A large leather chest sat against the wall, rotting away beneath a blanket of algae and barnacles. Beside it was a small bookcase of maps and parchment, strangely in better condition. A deteriorating ornate table and broken chairs occupied the center of the rounded room, and there was sea sludge coating every corner of the walls, casting an eerie green glow about the room.

I let out an audible breath, reaching up to feel my necklace. It was still there, of course. But it felt as though a phantom might appear to snatch it away at any moment.

I approached the writing desk first. On it, there were maps—hundreds of years old, a compass, sextant, and a spyglass. But no key.

I wondered what use Valdez could have for these things now. Maybe they only served as reminders of a time long past. Maybe he was using them still, searching for an end to his curse. It was impossible to know.

I carefully opened a drawer, my movements delicate, as if it would shatter into pieces if I pulled too quickly. Blank parchment, some quill pens. But something different did manage to catch my eye.

It wasn't a key, but a scribbled note on some crumbling parchment. I was careful not to touch it. It looked ready to disintegrate. But I leaned close to decipher the words written—the same words Milo had recited to me hours ago. The last two lines of the mermaid's curse:

The depths shall never set you free.
'Til she returns her magic to the sea.

Beside it there were stacks of papers, with notes and annotations, particularly about the wording in the last line. From the looks of it, Valdez had been racking his brain about the meaning for decades, probably longer. He was desperate to find the answer, to shatter this unbreakable spell on him and his crew. Who knew how many innocent souls had been caught up in his quest to free himself?

I thought of Serena.

And now me.

Who else throughout all those centuries had he dragged into this?

I pulled my thoughts away. There wasn't time for these ominous reflections. I had to focus on finding the key. I searched the other drawers, keeping everything in place as best I could. But it wasn't in any of them.

Next, I moved to the big chest. I opened it, but found nothing but clothes, glass bottles, gunpowder, a few swords, and blunderbusses. I unfolded each piece of clothing, searching in the pockets for anything that might resemble an old key. But I had no luck with that either.

I was beginning to worry. Milo was silent on the other side of the door, and I assumed that was a good thing, but I couldn't help but feel unsettled by the creaks and groans of the old ship.

I searched the bed last, pulling the blankets away slowly to keep from wrinkling them. It didn't take long to realize the key wasn't there either. I huffed and twisted my hair over my shoulders, thinking. As I surveyed the room before me, the eerie moonlight poured in through the foggy glass window, lighting up an area I hadn't noticed before. From this angle, beside the bed, I saw a thin drawer on the side of the desk that looked oddly out of place, as though it had been added in after the desk was built.

I tiptoed over, the molded wet wood beneath my feet sending a shiver through my body. Goosebumps rose along my arms as I reached for the drawer, sliding it open as though I expected a snake to jump out.

When I looked, I saw a small stack of letters never sent—all addressed to Cordelia. My curiosity got the best of me, and I couldn't ignore the urge to read at least one.

My dearest Cordelia,

How cruel and ruthless of you to leave me suffering for so long. But of course, the same was often said about me. Perhaps we really were meant to be together, just like you wanted. I know there is no mercy for me, and I wear that proudly. I regret nothing that I've done. Only that I chose too cold and clever a siren for my own good.

Still, I'm offering you a proposal. Release my son from this curse, at the least, and you can have my soul forever. Let Bellamy die once and for all, and I'll stop trying to escape your punishment.

Once yours,

Captain James Valdez

I nearly dropped the letter at the mention of Bellamy's name. Of course, I knew Valdez was his father, but there was something all too real about the words on the page that made me shudder.

And I was perplexed. Did Bellamy know that at some point his father had been willing to give up himself to end his pain? Or did Valdez merely write the letter to trick Cordelia back to the ship?

Or maybe he just hadn't known where to send it. The possibilities were endless, but I couldn't help but wonder if I had just glimpsed a small sliver of evidence of Valdez' humanity—or perhaps nothing more than the clever manipulation tactics of a cold-blooded pirate.

That letter was one of many unsent. But it was the only one not sealed with the captain's wax signet seal. Most of the others were made out to a "Maria," but I didn't dare break their seals to read them.

I knew time was short, but I was running out of ideas and there was nowhere in the room left to search.

I glanced down once more at the letters. That's when I noticed one of them seemed just a bit thicker than the rest—like there was something wrapped between the folded parchment. I didn't want to break the seal, but it was the only way. I pulled the wax from the paper, and the iron key slid out. I cradled it as though it was precious treasure, still in disbelief that it was even real. The seconds were ticking, but I opened the letter, thinking I could at least skim it before putting it all back.

Cordelia,

You may have sent me to hell, but maybe now they'll call me the devil himself. Don't forget how you turned on your own, leading the sirens right to me, one by one. You betrayed the sea, not me. The blood of your sisters is on your hands. And for that, you have a debt to pay as well. And what consoles me each morning when this ship sinks to those god-forsaken depths, is knowing that you'll still never possess what you wanted most—my love.

Yes, I loved you once. Maybe some part of me always will. But Maria needed me...and I betrayed you both.

Captain James Valdez

Of course, I had no way of knowing how much of the letter was true, but it made me suspect Cordelia could have very well been as formidable and conniving as Valdez.

The more I read, the more I got the feeling Valdez might not have been the only one cruel and unpredictable. If Cordelia was truly a siren willing to betray her own kind for what she thought was love, it was no wonder such tragedies followed when the two of them collided.

A sudden muffled explosion outside made me jump. A bang like a distant gunshot.

Bellamy.

Whatever other secrets lay behind Valdez' past would have to wait for another time, because my time was up.

I tucked the key away into the small dress pocket making sure it was snug. As quickly as my trembling fingers would allow, I moved everything back into place. I gave one last glance over the room to ensure nothing looked out of place and strode back to the door.

Milo had never knocked or responded to the gunshot, so I expected to see him waiting for me, ready to head back to shore. But when I opened the door, what I saw made my stomach turn and my knees go weak.

Milo was waiting for me—and flanked by a small crew of pirates. They encompassed the cabin door so there was nowhere to go. And stepping out from the middle of them, grinning at me with a wild-eyed stare, like an animal ready to tear into its prey, was a giant of a man in a scarlet red coat. He loomed over me, peering at me down the barrel of a blunderbuss. His voice was like steel on steel and made the hairs on the back of my neck stand up.

"Pleasure to finally meet you, lass." He tipped his hat at me, then addressed Milo. "And thank you for arranging the introduction, Master Harrington."

Troubled Waters

29

KATRINA

Afraid to move, I stood, planted in place, glancing back and forth between Milo and his captain. In some strange way, he could have almost been handsome, but his menacing presence overshadowed even that. His accent seeped out like black smoke, and the insidious, guttural tone of his voice rattled my bones.

"You bested my own son, Harrington." He curled his lip beneath cold and empty eyes, slapping Milo across the shoulder. "And you finally redeemed yourself for that cowardice you showed all those years ago. Perhaps you are a worthy siren hunter after all. Perhaps you won't show so much remorse for this one." Valdez tossed a cutlass toward Milo, who caught it by the hilt with ease.

Milo stood at Valdez's side, his face unreadable as he watched me and turned the sword in his hand. He averted his gaze the moment I locked eyes with him. He'd betrayed me, and now he wouldn't even look at me.

My racing heart began to sink, further and further until it hit the bottom of a part of myself I didn't even know existed until now. Tears simmered behind my eyes for the fool I had been. For the sickening anger I felt. And for the trust I had given—for the thought that a filthy pirate could care about anything more than himself.

Valdez stepped forward, still aiming his pistol at me. I fought with all my strength to keep my terror from showing, but my panicked short breaths gave me away. He stared at my throat like he was hypnotized. I glanced down at my necklace, careful not to make any sudden movements, trying to think of a way out of this.

"Aye, men." He pulled in a heavy breath through his nostrils, the rest of his mouth obscured beneath his thick, dark beard. "That'd be a siren and her scale without a doubt."

A crewman spoke up from the back, his voice a dry, desperate question. "Then what are we waiting for, Cap'n? Take the scale and spill her blood into the sea!"

The men grumbled in accordance. Valdez held up his hand with command.

"Patience, you bilge rats," he grunted. "We have a striking beauty aboard our vessel. It'd be a shame to waste the chance to indulge in the pleasures so long denied us…" He licked his teeth while eyeing me in a way that made my skin crawl. Every muscle in my body flinched, rigid and defensive. Whistles and obscenities erupted from the crowd of pirates looking on.

Trembling, I glanced over once more at Milo, who remained expressionless. But I noticed his free hand coiling into a fist at his side, and his knuckles white as he flexed them around the hilt of his sword with the other.

"There's no time, Captain. Dawn is just on the horizon." Milo spoke to my surprise, his voice as dull as his eyes. "Just let me cut out her heart for you so the rest of us can end this."

I blinked in disbelief at him. Rage smoldered in my chest, every inch of me drowning beneath the weight of betrayal and disgust.

"How could you do this?" I hissed at him.

He only looked away, up at the mast overhead, which only infuriated me further.

"You deserve every damn bit of this curse." I said, each word more bitter than the last.

"You'll not be disrespecting my crewmen like that, lass." Valdez's tone carried a cruel amusement. "Let's see you on your knees for that. I think it's high time you learned some manners."

I stood tall, repulsed, and resisted his order. He moved toward me, hand lifted as if to strike me, and Milo cut in just before he did.

"Wait!" he shouted. "Best take her heart and get it over with, Captain. You won't feel anything anyway. There's no pleasure to be gained this way."

Valdez turned to face the crew. "What you all fail to understand is that this is hardly about feeling or pleasure. It's about power. About revenge. It's about knowing even the last siren on earth couldn't escape me. And I can't imagine Cordelia, being the traitor to her own she was, would've wanted any less." Valdez's wicked glare found me once more as he pointed at me and then back at Milo, who stood locked in place. "So, I tell you what, Harrington. I'll let you at least have the honor of undressing her—to ensure your cuts are clean, of course." A blood-chilling grin twisted across Valdez's face.

A sickening cheer rose from the crew—from all except Milo, whose empty eyes offered me nothing—no hope, no strength, no answers. Only a slow blink as he swallowed, something like nervousness breaking through for a fraction of a section.

I trembled, tempted to run past him and toward the side of the ship. But there were too many of them. I stepped backwards, remembering the window in Valdez's quarters. But the pirates had closed in, encircling me entirely with not even the smallest gap left open.

There was nowhere to run. No escape.

"On your knees, siren." Valdez snapped.

Milo circled me, drawing his sword at my back. "Get on your knees. Captain's orders." He clasped a hand on my shoulder. "Get down."

There was something peculiar about the last command. It wasn't threatening, but urgent, like he was pleading with me to do as he said. And then he tapped the tip of his sword on the wood of the deck with three distinct beats.

I looked at him, eyes widening as I realized the message, and then thought to conceal my understanding beneath the coldest scowl I could manage. I lowered myself to my knees, pretending to buckle beneath the strength of Milo's hand, though there was no real force behind it. Valdez put his pistol away.

Milo stood angled behind me, the edge of his blade still pressed to my back, as Valdez glowered at me from only a few strides away.

"You remind me of her in that dress, you know—beautiful and cruel. Powerful, too, with a deadly song. It's really stirring up some...unpleasant memories, to say the least." Valdez gestured to the deck. "Do you know she gave me this ship? She could enchant any man to obey her, and she sent an entire naval crew overboard with just her voice. All for me. And she stood right where you stand now. Except, if I remember correctly, she stood there without a stitch of clothing on her and hadn't an ounce of shame about it."

I assumed he spoke of Cordelia. He continued peering down at me from beneath thick, dark eyebrows as he drew closer.

"But you, lass, you're nothing like her. You're shivering like a scared dog in the rain. Like you've got something to be ashamed of. Like you've got something to be *afraid* of."

I gripped the necklace with both hands and drew into myself. His boots rattled the wooden floor with each step. Nearer. And nearer.

"Go on and cut that dress off her already, Harrington, before I do it myself."

He'd hardly taken another step before Milo grabbed me from behind and pulled me to him, one arm locked around me and the other holding his blade to my throat.

"You won't lay a finger on her, Valdez. She goes free," he seethed, pulling me along as he guided me near to the ship's edge. "She goes free...or I kill her. And I'll destroy the scale along with her." I flinched, trying to resist his hold, confused, terrified, and unsure once again what was happening.

Milo leaned in close, brushing his lips over my neck and up my ear. I barely managed to catch the whisper, but I heard him clearly.

"He needs your heart still beating. It's our only leverage. Trust me and hold on as tight as you can." He pulled me back once more, yanking me toward the hull, against some rigging secured on pulleys.

"You fool, Harrington. You'll damn us all." Valdez cocked his pistol, closing in.

Milo whirled me around, his body shielding me as Valdez fired.

"Hold onto me!" he yelled over the horrifying sound of boots stampeding as the crew charged. I threw my arms around his shoulders as he reached for the rigging with one hand and sliced his blade through a single taut rope with the other. The rope snapped upward, part of the mast whipping around and hoisting us up with it. We zipped up past the sails, and Milo managed to direct us toward the crow's nest.

We leapt, the force sending us rolling onto it. Wood splintered around us as lead bullets pelted the rickety platform, and the smell of gunpowder filled my nostrils.

I looked at Milo as we ducked for cover, catching my breath.

"I almost thought that was real. I really thought you set me up." I panted. "What happened to 'knock three times?'"

"I had to improvise. Valdez had a boat waiting behind the ship. By the time Bellamy saw them they were already here. It was an ambush." Milo shook his head. "It was a trap."

More gunshots fired and pirates tossed out profanities from below, Valdez's booming voice clearer than the rest. Milo winced as he shifted.

"You're shot." I said, only just now noticing the blood stain blooming at his side.

He pressed a hand to the wound, pulling his palm away slick and red with a smug expression. "Yes, and I'll be fine tomorrow."

"No...no, Valdez is going to torture you. He's going to—"

"None of that matters." His voice was sharp as steel "It's almost sunrise. They're coming for you. We have to get you off this ship."

The pirates below shouted threats, and two were beginning to climb the mast. The rest of the crew had arrived on rowboats, clambering up the ship like insects. More pistol shots rang out.

I looked at him, then at the blood soaking through his shirt, horrified and trembling. "Don't worry about me." He took my hand in both of his and pressed his lips to them. "Did you get the key?"

"Yes." I nodded, my movements fast and nervous.

"Good." Milo's eyes softened. "Now, leave and never return to these coasts. Never, Katrina. Do you hear me? You can never come back here."

"But—"

"Never," he repeated. "But if by some miracle I ever find a way out, I'll come back to you. I'll find you, wherever you are. I promise."

"Weren't you the one who told me not to make promises you can't keep?" I asked, my voice cracking.

He gave no response—only pulled me to my feet and glimpsed over the edge into the water at a dinghy in the black surface below.

"There's your ride," he muttered.

"What?"

He didn't explain.

As one of the pirates began to reach the underside of the crow's nest, swinging his cutlass, Milo kicked him down. The man toppled to the deck below with a curse and a grunt. But there were more coming. And Valdez had his pistol locked onto us—onto Milo, who I noticed was breathing harder and moving slower.

Milo reached for the rope that still hung by a loop in the mast rigging. "Don't let go until I tell you." He plunged his lips forward into mine and I whimpered, melting into him as he held me close as if to remind me it would be the last time. And then we leapt, soaring past the sails as the first light of dawn cracked through the horizon.

The rope was a pendulum, and we were the counterweight, sweeping over the deck as the crew clamored below and fired a few aimless shots. I felt Milo's body rigid with strain as he pushed for momentum, and we swung just over the edge of the ship, where a small boat bobbed in the water below.

Those last few seconds in the air, Milo brought his lips to my ear, his voice humming against me like low, gentle thunder.

"You will always be my North Star."

He dropped me into the dinghy and let the swinging rope carry him back to the deck, where swords begin to clang and men cried out in violent rage.

As Milo's words still rang hauntingly in my ear, I pushed myself up off the floor of the boat to see Bellamy sitting across from me.

"Grab an oar, love. It's almost dawn," he ordered calmly.

I did my best to assist Bellamy in rowing back to shore as fast as possible. The faint light of sunrise began to take over the horizon, and the sound of the chaos on the ship drifted away as we distanced ourselves from it. I could hear the maelstrom forming as it began its ravenous ritual of plunging the ship into its depths.

But we were silent.

Something was different about Bellamy.

He let the boat drift to the shore with gentle, weary nudges of the oar. His usual air of confidence was missing, and instead, he wore a broken expression I had not seen before.

"Bell—"

"Don't." He lowered his head and looked down at the water. "I know you love him. Don't say something just because you pity me."

"Love him? I don't—" I tripped over the words, unsure how to finish. "I...I just wanted to say thank you."

"No need to thank me." He leaned on his knee with his elbow and raked a hand through his black hair. "Looks like Milo and I finally managed to agree on one thing."

"And what's that?"

"That you're very much worth protecting."

I flashed him a tender half-smile. Did he know Valdez had written about sacrificing himself to free him from the curse? Did he know that there was a chance perhaps that his father hadn't always been a monster?

There was no time to mention any of it before Bellamy began to fade before my eyes. In the same way that the phantom waves had come for Milo before, the water rose around Bellamy to swallow him down.

The little boat slowly vanished after him, becoming nothing out from under me, and I leapt out into the water that was just shallow enough to wade in. When I turned around, I saw the last glimpse of the ship in the distance as it was pulled beneath the surface. And then the beach was silent—normal—and the sun was coming up. As if none of it had ever been there at all.

DOWN IN THE DOLDRUMS

30

KATRINA

I zipped the key into my carryon as I made my way through airport security. Some part of me dreaded this trip.

I was excited to see Dad, but I dreadfully anticipated seeing mom for the first time in so long in a hospital room. And there was still the looming fear of what I would find in that box, or if the key would truly even open it. And now I had the added weight of knowing what I'd left behind in Constantine—two ghost pirates who wanted nothing more than to suffer on my behalf and the part of my heart I'd left with them at the bottom of the sea.

-On my flight! Should be landing this afternoon.

I sent the text to Dad right before the plane departed, but I didn't wait for a reply before closing my eyes and leaning my head back. I was exhausted from the night before, and who knew how long it would be until I could truly rest again.

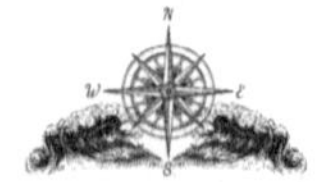

When I awoke, the plane was landing.

How was I supposed to just step off the plane onto Arkansas soil like everything was back to normal? Like my life hadn't drastically changed from one impossible encounter no more than a month ago. Hours ago, I was nearly murdered by pirates after kissing one. And yet, now I was just a college freshman returning home for Thanksgiving Break.

And if I kept my promise to Milo, I was supposed to stay here—to forfeit my scholarship and somehow explain that to my exuberantly proud father.

But I had all week, at least, to figure that out.

For now—for today—my priority was the box and, hopefully, saving Mom.

As I hustled out of the terminal and through the crowded airport, I rubbed my eyes with one hand. The space between my forehead throbbed with pain from sheer exhaustion. Adrenaline had fueled me all night, and my brief nap on the airplane did little to combat the crash I was feeling now. But I ignored it as best I could, fumbling to haul around my duffel bag and carryon as I scanned for Dad's truck in the pickup area.

The familiar brisk November air brushed against my skin, but I hardly noticed as I sped up to see Dad waiting to greet me. He placed my luggage in the truck bed, and then I flung myself into his open arms as the old truck engine hummed beside us.

"I missed you," I muttered into his shoulder. He smelled faintly like diesel and grease, and it was the most reassuring smell in the world in that moment.

"I missed you so much, Trina." He drew in a deep sigh. "It's so good to have you home."

I could hear the weariness in his voice. The sure sign Mom had been wearing him down. And I knew based on his silence that something was wrong as he opened the door for me and I hoisted myself into the passenger seat of his old Dodge.

Dad asked me about school as we pulled away from the airport. I told him classes were going well. I told him the showcase was fun and unforgettable—which was technically true. I told him that McKenzie was still the same as last time I described her. And then I broke the tension he was trying so hard to ignore.

"How's Mom?" I asked, shifting in my seat and fidgeting with my fingers.

Dad exhaled and tapped the steering wheel with his thumb. "To be honest, Trina, she's...she's in bad shape."

"W—what do you mean she's in bad shape?" I leaned in.

"I mean this morning she was...crying...screaming...hysterical. She was absolutely out of it, screaming about drowning, and seeing water filling the room. I couldn't shake her from it. Neither could the nurses. Whatever this is, it's worse than usual. Something's wrong."

I swallowed. "She's hallucinating..." I said under my breath. "Is she awake now?"

"She might be coming to now," Dad said. "They had to sedate her. I don't know what she will be like when she wakes up."

For a minute or so we both sat there in silence, and I stared at the lines on the highway and fought to ignore the heavy shift in the air.

"I tried so hard to shield you from everything, *mija*," Dad finally added. "You shouldn't have to be worrying about all this."

I breathed, weighing my words carefully before I said them out loud. "I have no choice but to worry about it, Dad. You know Mom isn't the first in her family to go through this. I have to worry about her. I have to hope there's some way to help her...because I have to know there's hope for me."

"Hope is the best thing we have, Trina. *La esperanza.* Whatever happens, don't stop hoping."

I nodded quietly and offered him a weak smile as he drove forward to the hospital, twisting my fingers together as Dad maneuvered out of the airport traffic.

Breathe.

"I can't help but feel this is somehow my fault." I pressed my forehead to the glass window. "Maybe if I'd just never left. Maybe if I stayed here instead of moving to Florida, I could have stopped her from doing this...if I'd just been here."

"*Mija*, no," Dad reached over and put a sturdy hand on my shoulder. "We've been through this. It's *never* been your fault. "

"I know," I breathed.

It wasn't my fault. But it was sure as hell my curse to carry.

When we arrived at the hospital, I stared upwards at the entrance. It had been a long time since I'd been here.

The last time was when Mom had broken her wrist stumbling up our porch and falling after a typical night of drowning away her demons. She had made it home just after dinner. Dad had rushed to take her there, and I left my high school homecoming game early to stay with her that night. The memories were anything but good, and they were flooding back now, perching in the back of my mind like a threatening shadow.

As we approached the front desk, I wondered what I would feel when I saw her for the first time, conscious or not. She had been away for over a year, and though I had heard her voice many times over the past few weeks, I hadn't actually *seen* her in what felt like ages. Would my anger towards her return? Would I feel just as helpless as her?

A few turns down the hallway and we were at the entrance to her room. I held my breath as Dad opened the door. Mom's eyes were closed, and her shoulder length hair was pulled back in a ponytail to one side. A menacing thought snaked its way into my head as I watched her—that she'd done this on purpose. That she wasn't drinking just to stop the dreams and visions anymore.

She was drinking to end it all.

I stood over my mother as she breathed like she was sleeping. Was she at peace, I wondered? Or could the nightmares find her here, too? I couldn't explain the way I wanted to hug her and hate her all at the same time. Attempting to dam up the tide of emotions within me, I bit my lip as tears fought their way to the surface.

"Grace," Dad uttered.

But Mom didn't respond. There was only the quiet of our breaths and the beeping of the monitor connected to her. I feared I didn't have much time left to figure out how to save her before she was pulled under completely.

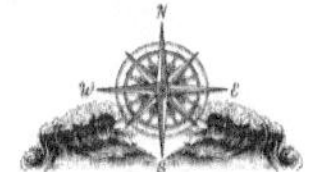

We stayed with her as the day turned into evening, taking turns staying at her side. Dad refused to go home, but he offered to take me to the house to get some rest for the night. I ached for sleep, but I planned to spend my time alone in the house searching every corner of the attic for that box. I thought about telling him about the box and the death dates, but how could I possibly explain what I knew? There was nothing he could do to stop it anyway, and he was carrying too much already. If he only knew how the clock was ticking...

But he didn't need to know.

On the ride home, I stared at the road ahead, focusing on the yellow lines on the pavement sweeping up underneath the truck headlights as we passed over them. Gray soft clouds billowed overhead, creating a horizon of shadows and gloom. The leaves had mostly all fallen now, but a few remaining gold and crimson stragglers still clung to branches for dear life.

"So, what happens, now?" I turned to Dad. "What if Mom doesn't get over this one?"

"Don't say that, *mija*. Don't give up hope. Not yet." I clung to the steadiness in his voice.

Hoping wasn't enough. For so long I *did* hope. I hoped Mom would change for so many years. I hoped we could be a family. And when that didn't work, I hoped I could forget about it all and start over on my own. When I finally thought I had left the past far behind, it caught right back up to me. But it was becoming clear to me, in more ways than one, that the past was never dead, just buried beneath the surface for a little while.

I had let go of hope a long time ago. Now I was scrambling to get it back like a child chasing a runaway balloon before it floated away for good.

As I pondered all this, Dad took a turn along the same road I used to drive to school. For a moment, I was back in 11th grade, a socially awkward nobody just trying to make it to graduation and find a fresh start, applying for art scholarships around the country. How I had so desperately wanted to escape from this small town that had caged me for so long that I would've gone anywhere—and it was Constantine that called me.

And now nowhere felt safe, and oddly enough, something primal in me longed for the security of my boring little home in my boring little town. But what I wanted didn't matter. There was nowhere I could go to outrun the struggles I faced any longer. They would always be there. In Arkansas. In Florida. Literally at the bottom of the sea, even.

And it was time to stop looking for a way out. I couldn't run any farther. Instead, I was ready to swim against this tide head on.

X Marks the Spot

31

KATRINA

The diesel engine of Dad's truck growled steadily as we rolled into the driveway of the little one-story ranch-style house. I had never known a different home beyond those walls until moving to my dorm this year.

Once he turned the engine off, nothing but the sound of crickets remained as the silent night sky looked down upon us. I wasn't wearing a jacket, and I shivered as the cold, dry air clawed at my skin. Stepping through the front door was like being wrapped in a cloak of familiarity.

Everything looked identical to the day I left, with the bright green fake plants contrasting sharply with the out-of-date wood paneling on the walls. Baby pictures of me and some old wedding photos of my parents hung throughout the house. I stepped into my old room, so much of my artwork still pinned to the wall, right where I left it. Pairs of mismatched socks were still strewn across the floor. The wall behind my headboard featured my own attempt at Van Gogh's 'Starry Night,' stretching from floor to ceiling. I hand-painted that wall when I was in middle school. Turns out I had liked sleeping beneath the stars for longer than I realized.

I tossed my bag across my bed, failing to stifle a yawn. My body was weary, and my mind was murky. My dad stood eyeing me in the doorway.

"I'm going back to the hospital once you're settled in." He gestured to the bag on my mattress. "Please don't think I don't want to spend time with you, Trina…"

"It's okay. Trust me, Dad. I know. Someone should be there with Mom." I reassured. "I'll be there tomorrow. You can pick me up in the morning." I whirled back and around and began pulling my things from the bag. I scattered my clothes out across the bed, not bothering to keep them folded.

When I was met with only silence, I glanced over my shoulder. "Go. Don't feel bad, Dad. She needs you."

"I don't want you to think I'm not happy to see you."

"Dad, of course I know you are." I stood to face him, holding my elbow with my opposite hand. "But right now, you are the one Mom needs. You've always been there for her, and I'm the one who gave up on her. If she wakes up, you are the one she'll be looking for. I'm still not even sure I'm ready."

The last part was partially true. I wasn't ready, but for more reasons than just that. I needed time to search for the box hidden in the house somewhere. And that made me more than eager for him to leave.

"*Bueno*, Trina," he finally said. "I'll leave you to get settled then. But if you need me for anything, no matter how small, you call me."

I hugged him one last time before he finally made it out the door, and once he was gone, I hurried back to my luggage and pulled the key from my carryon. Fighting another yawn, I cradled it in my hands. It was the first time I had the chance to really study the ancient thing.

I analyzed the exterior, darkened and roughened from corrosion and salt as I turned it over in my palm. The rusted iron was crafted with intricate swirls molded into the handle, similar to the wave-like swirls on the prongs of my necklace.

After everything it had taken to get it, I silently hoped it was worth it. Milo had committed mutiny for it, knowing the price he would pay. And I was the reason.

I needed proof. And now I needed answers. Answers that would finally show me the way to end my family's curse.

But some part of me secretly feared I might not like the answer, if there even truly was one. What if my mother really was just a hallucinating alcoholic beyond saving? What if this destiny was unavoidable for both of us?

The cyclone of voices in my head spiraled without relenting. The questions. The fears. This little key in my hand was summoning them all. Determined not to waste any more time, I started for the attic, where I had only visited once before as an uninterested child.

I tugged on the cord, watching the steps expand out before me in welcome. With no one else in the house, an eerie feeling befell me as I crawled into the dark attic space alone. I backed away and retreated to the kitchen for one of Dad's many emergency flashlights. It didn't take long to find one in the junk drawer, and I was back at the base of the steps within seconds, clutching the light in my hands.

The stale air from the attic ambushed my lungs. It was musty and stuffy, and I was more than thankful it wasn't summer. There in the corner, I saw the pile of toys I had carried up with Mom eleven years ago. Among other things, old chairs, small, grimy car parts, and random house decor that looked like it belonged in an old lady's living room claimed nearly all the space in the cramped attic.

Mom said she had found the box...but where did she leave it? The daunting heap of disorganized junk before me made my chest tight. It could take forever to find it. I didn't even know what it looked like.

I pulled down cardboard boxes from everywhere and moved every object I physically could. I opened every container, unpacked every single thing, only to put it all back to make space to do it again. I checked every corner, every crevice, and every possible space I could find until minutes turned to hours that had me checking the rest of the house as well. But nothing. There was no sign of this legendary secret treasure chest.

I crawled back up to the attic, telling myself to check one more time—that maybe I'd missed something. And so, I did, my body aching for sleep—only to be disappointed once more.

I plopped down onto the floor, resigned and exhausted, a stirring in my chest building like a wave. And then the ocean I'd been holding back for so long finally came crashing over me. The broken wail that escaped from me echoed off the hollow walls of the attic. My teardrops dotted the dusty floor as I fell forward with my face in my hands, my sobs fast and heaving. I lay down and hugged myself tightly, trying to catch my breath as I stared up at the empty ceiling in the darkness.

I couldn't do it. I couldn't save us. And I was so, so tired.

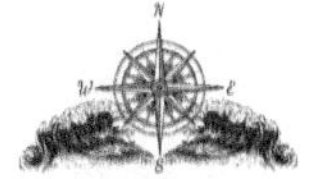

I dreamed of Milo—of the *Siren's Scorn* rising beneath a full moon that cast its glow down to reveal him bound on the deck, hunched over and shirtless, the skin of his back flayed open by countless whips of the lash. Thick crimson blood dripped from the wounds, pouring at his feet and washing away in the salt water that soaked the deck. The crew jeered around him, and two of them even held him steady as Valdez readied the whip once more.

He cried out in agony as the lash struck again, and again, and again.

And each lash scar spelled my name.

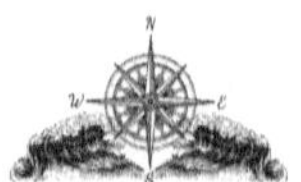

The horn honking outside woke me up with a gasp. My eyes adjusted to the dark, and I suddenly remembered I was lying on the attic floor. I must've slept there all night.

The horn honked again. I scrambled to my feet and quickly rushed downstairs to the bathroom to brush my teeth and shower.

"Trina, I'm here!" I heard Dad call through the hallway.

I peeked my head out from the bathroom door. "Sorry, Dad...I slept in. Must not have heard my alarm."

Dad didn't mind waiting on me to finish getting ready, and I tried my best to act more rested than I felt.

Back at the hospital, I turned over every inch I'd searched in the house and the attic in my head. There was nowhere left to look. What could I have possibly missed? I planned to hunt for it once more tonight, but first I was hoping maybe there was a chance Mom could tell me where she'd found it.

But my hopes of that were dashed quickly upon arriving at her room. She was still sedated.

The nurse told me that whenever she awoke, she became erratic and dangerous, clawing at the air as if trying to fight her way to some invisible surface. If she could just come out of whatever it was that had pulled her under—even for a moment—maybe I'd have a chance. But instead, I watched her, waiting by her bedside for any sign she could give me that I hadn't lost her yet.

When dusk came, I curled up in a spot by the window in the hospital room. I studied the horizon, noticing the way the pale oranges and gray hues clashed together like waves in the sky as the sun crept downward. The wisps of color were woven across the sky like silk threads, making me yearn to have a paintbrush in my hand.

But the closest thing I could get to that for now was the sketchbook stuffed in my duffel bag. Watching the moon take the sun's place, I allowed my heart to guide my hand as it began to trace an outline of a face. From the strokes of my pencil came tousled hair, a strong jawline, and smoldering, fierce eyes staring back at me from the page. As I shaped his mouth, I silently recalled the rum and nectarine taste that still lingered on mine. Those rough, sturdy hands that I could still feel tracing my body...

And then the pleasure turned to horror as his scream echoed in my mind from the dream in the attic—a nightmare that even the necklace couldn't keep away. Because it hadn't come from the curse.

It was real. And it was all mine. Every guilt-ridden, brutal second of it.

The smell of marinara sauce and garlic tore my focus from the sketch. Dad entered the room, carrying a pizza box and placed it on the small table, casting his gaze my way.

I noticed him eyeing my drawing. "Who's that?" he asked.

"Oh...um." I quickly turned the sketchbook to obscure his view, feeling my face flush. "It's no one."

"Well, I don't believe that for a minute," he laughed. "I've never seen you draw a person like that. Usually, it's butterflies or flowers or clouds."

"Dad, I'm not seven anymore."

He had a point, though. Occasionally I sketched and painted people, but portraits weren't typically my thing. Especially portraits of attractive men.

"Trina, you don't have to tell me, but don't think your papá can't figure it out. I've been in love for a long time." He grinned, flashing a set of pearly teeth beneath his dark mustache as he flicked his gaze to my mom. "And I know you well enough to know *you* don't just fall for anyone. He must be something special to make it into your sketchbook."

He was right about that too. I had a boyfriend in high school, but it was nothing that lasted very long. I was too afraid to get close to anyone—too afraid they'd abandon me, too if I let them see the deepest parts of me. So, I never let anyone close. I'd certainly never let anyone make me feel the way Milo did. The way he'd kissed me on the shore, and touched me at the lighthouse...

And that was the strangest part of it all—I knew he would have to leave me, one way or another, and yet I still couldn't shake away whatever it was that kept drawing me back to him like an unseen tether.

Heat flushed my cheeks red. My lips were dry as I swallowed down the sensation and croaked out a reply. "He's definitely...different...from other guys."

"And what's his name? Actually, wait—you don't have to tell me. I'm fine with *secretos*." He chuckled.

"Well, his name is no secret," I sighed in surrender between something like a huff and a giggle. "It's Milo."

"Well tell Milo if he causes any problems, I may be a fourteen-hour drive away, but I know how to get there in three if I need to."

I shook my head and playfully rolled my eyes. "Don't worry," I said. "He's great." My half-smile faded, and I pressed my lips together. "But he couldn't stay around long. I doubt I'll ever see him again."

"That's too bad, *mija*. If he knew what was good for him, he'd stay."

"He didn't have much of a choice," I mumbled. "And honestly...I don't know if I do anymore either." My gaze slid to Mom, watching her eyelids gently tremble and I wondered what she was seeing. "I'm not sure if I can go back to St. Constantine. Especially with Mom like this..."

Dad leaned back and crossed his jaw, as though choosing his next thought with intention. "That choice is yours alone to make, *mija*," he said. "But don't do it because you think you have to, or because you think someone will be disappointed in you if you don't. Don't do anything unless it's what you really want." He paused, glancing over at mom, staring at her all the while as he continued. "Sometimes doing the right thing for the ones we love hurts—and sometimes, we learn to love ourselves through it. Because many times when we don't know the next step, that's where love pays the balance. That's when we let our heart have a say in our decision."

His words settled over me like the heavy, humid fog of ocean mist in the morning—something I realized I'd come to miss.

Then with a complete shift of mood, as if he didn't just drop the deepest, heartfelt advice I'd heard in a long time, Dad reached for the pizza box.

"Now I don't know about you, but I'm starving. Pepperoni and pineapple. Still your favorite, I hope?"

I nodded. "Of course."

Dad put an arm around me and lightly kissed my temple, probably noting the dullness in my voice. "Don't worry, *mija*. Everything is going to be alright in the end. I promise."

The bold strength of such a confident promise reminded me of McKenzie in that instance. It was the same thing she'd told me on the yacht—that everything would be fine. The blind, enduring optimism offered some kind of foreign reassurance I had never been able to give myself. I only hoped that someday I could know what it felt like to so easily believe in happy endings.

After we ate, Mom stirred in her bed, groaning a bit. Dad had nodded off in a chair, snoring gently. I reached for my mother's hand, but I didn't know exactly why.

As I watched her, her eyes began to flutter open and quickly shut a few times. She took in a gasp for air and tried to lean forward, opening her eyes again, in a panic, as if suffocating.

Dad jolted awake and I released Mom's hand.

"I'll get the nurse." He whipped out the door, calling for help.

My eyes stayed locked on her, my nerves leaping back and forth. She sat up and grabbed my wrists with both of her hands, clinging to me with a white-knuckle grip. Monitors beeped out of control, like shrill sirens in the background of her desperate gasps.

"Just let me drown. Please. Please. The water's getting too high to keep fighting. It wants me. It always has..." She squealed the words out between choked breaths, but I heard them clearly.

"Mom!" I cried. "Mom, where is the box? Where is it?"

She looked at me, her grey-blue eyes dancing back and forth between mine.

"Underneath," she whispered.

"Underneath?" I gasped. "Underneath what?"

Then just as Dad burst into the room with two nurses trailing close behind, she let go of me, her eyes closed once more, and she fell back against her pillow, the beeping pattern of the monitors slowing alongside the rhythm of her breathing.

I *had* to find that box.

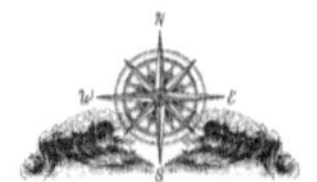

Once Dad dropped me off at home again, I practically ran to the attic, this time with no regard for the mess I made as I searched in desperation, pulling out objects and sliding boxes across the floor in the dark. I strained to pick up an old rocking chair that had a bin of my grandmother's collection of hand-painted ceramic figurines beneath it. I'd seen it before, but I hadn't truly looked at the tiny sculptures within. This time I rummaged through them, noting the theme among the tiny porcelain figurines my grandmother had painted throughout her life—ships, mermaids, and seashells.

I laid them out on the floor, silently admiring them one by one. And it was then that I noticed a slight unevenness in one of the floorboards beneath them.

Underneath.

I moved to pull up the board where it lifted higher than the rest, but the wood was wedged too tightly. With more certainty than I'd felt in a long time, I rushed down to Dad's garage and found a crowbar, desperate to uncover the buried secrets calling to me through the floor. I jammed the metal between the floorboards and pulled, prying up the loose board with a crack that made me cringe.

My heart stood still as I aimed my flashlight down into the empty space and stared down at something wrapped in faded, moth-eaten silk. I pulled back the fabric to reveal a wooden, intricately-carved chest—a box with a salt-rusted iron lock that matched the etched designs on the key from Valdez's quarters.

BURIED TREASURE

32

KATRINA

T he lock groaned as it clicked into place for the first time in centuries with a careful turn of the key. The weathered hinges threatened to crumble as I lifted the chest lid with gentle hands, only to reveal a stack of stiff, yellowed papers, ravaged by time and neatly held together by a string that was ready to disintegrate upon the slightest touch.

As carefully as I could manage, I lifted the papers out, trying to untie the rigid, shriveled string, but it snapped immediately.

The papers that fell out ranged from old letters and merchant records, documenting where the *Siren's Scorn* had made port, and a map to show each location. Eerily enough, a small few of them bore the signature of Daven Harrington, who I supposed was Milo's father selling or transporting on behalf of Valdez.

But the majority of the papers were notes—notes about sirens and their manipulative nature, about how to cut out their tongues to incapacitate their song, about how to harvest and preserve their scales and tails, and about how best to remove their beating heart while they were still alive. Things about a mermaid's abilities to acquire legs and live on land once out of the water too long or if they'd lost their tail.

Some papers bore scribbled details about where to find them—specific coded spots throughout the Caribbean, in the Atlantic, and even some as far as the Baltic Sea.

And all of it was in Valdez's handwriting—the same as the letters on the ship.

He must've been documenting everything he learned from Cordelia about sirens, and she must've taken it all back out of spite.

I shuffled through the sales records and business notes, but the last letter was the document of most intrigue. The handwriting was immaculate and elegant—distinctly different from Valdez's, and my eyes swept over it, pulled in by each word.

My dearest love, Captain of my heart,

What you have asked of me is no small task. I bear the burden of turning over my sisters in exchange for your love. But if the fleeting moments we have spent together are any indication of how it will be to love you forever, I consider it a worthy exchange. I trust you will leave Maria and the boy, as discussed. I shall be the only one who holds your heart, my love. And with this single piece of me, I give you my promise, that as long as you are mine, I shall continue to share my power with you so that you may conquer, and when you someday rule the seas, I will be your queen. With this, you are bound to me.

Forever yours,

Cordelia

And beneath it, all was a hollowed-out spot with the remnant of a dark velvet surface that had long been worn away—a spot carved out for a necklace.

With trembling hands, I reached behind my head to take the necklace off and placed it in the mold. It fit perfectly, down to each individual imperfect edge of the scale.

My breath caught in my throat. My chest tightened as the space around me suddenly felt far too small.

None of it should've been a surprise. I already presumed I carried the blood of Valdez' betrayed scorned siren. I'd even seen the scale glow when I sang.

But now, inside my own house, so far away from the cursed shores of Constantine, it strangely felt all the more real. The letters, the necklace box, the magic in my veins—it was here all along.

Milo and Bellamy were right—I truly was the one they'd been waiting for.

But even with the bone-chilling confirmation, none of it explained how to stop my own curse—how to save myself and Mom.

Then, as if on cue, the bottom of the chest gave way to a separate secret compartment carved into the bottom, seemingly added later in some DIY fashion.

And jutting out from there was a journal, well-used. It looked like it could have been at least a hundred years old, with its worn leather binding and chipped, weathered pages. I longed to delve into its pages of secrets. Perhaps it held the answers I needed.

I ran my finger along the crinkled edges of the old journal, careful not to damage the brittle pages.

Just as I opened to the first page, Dad texted that he was on his way to pick me up. The hospital was about fifteen minutes out. Fifteen immensely valuable minutes. So, I made myself comfortable on the floor, adjusted my flashlight onto the pages, and began to read.

MAYDAY

33

KATRINA

I've never been much of a writer. I much prefer to tell my tales with the tip of my paintbrush. But those who come after me whether in birth or matrimony must know...

Cordelia is a cruel woman. She is no loving grandmother or mother. Something dark festers in her. I know it sounds crazy, but I have no other explanation—I suspect she must be a witch. A witch who has cursed this bloodline. She hardly even ages.

First, she took me from my beloved David, and far from the sea where I met him. She chastised me greatly for wanting him, for wanting to return to the coasts to sail away with him. And she is forcing me to marry some brutish, controlling blacksmith here instead.

And when I found Mother at the end of that noose—her own daughter dead by her own hand after one dreadful vision too many—Cordelia did not shed a tear.

She only looked at me and said that Mother had been weak. And then she told me, "You will always yearn for the sea, but you will fear it with all your heart...because that's the only way to keep you from breaking it."

By the mention of David I knew it had to be Elisabeth. I checked the date—*August 1793*. Ten years before she painted The Sea Draws the Heart.

I was reading Elisabeth's journal.

The rest of the entries were descriptions of her own nightmares. They started out slow, like mine—sporadic and manageable. But each year they grew worse, haunting her even in her waking hours.

And just like mine and Mom's, she described the same thing—crushing waves, violent waters, lungs weighted with salt and sea, and eventually visions of herself and her mother drowning in the abyss.

She wore the necklace to keep her sane, until Cordelia threatened to take it when she became too defiant for her liking—when she became a mother herself.

I told her I would never stop trying to find him again—even if I had to crawl back to the edge of the sea and wait for him. I knew she'd take the necklace away, so I hid it before she could. So that you would have it someday when you need it, Marina.

She hid away the necklace. She kept it from Cordelia—all for her daughter. And then something grim fell over me as I realized what that meant for her. I turned the page with five minutes left until Dad arrived. More descriptions of the dreams, each one worse than the last.

Until one day—one paralyzing entry, written many years later, that left me feeling hollow.

My dearest Marina,

This is the most difficult thing I've ever had to write. But I never want you to think any of this was because I do not love you.

I, too, was weak. And now I know why your great-grandmother didn't want me to cross the sea with my first love. It would've saved me. It would've saved all of us. She knew it was calling me. Knew I would have dived right in.

But instead, here I am now, locked in an asylum, about to end it another way, drowning in a bathtub of my blood instead of the sea where I belong. Where WE belong.

My daughter, if you find this, please don't let her keep you from the sea. Go to it and free yourself. Go to it, and free us.

I love you.

I shuddered. The answer I'd been waiting for rang like haunting church bells in my head.

Go to the sea and free us.

Exactly the opposite of what I'd promised Milo. The very thing I'd been fighting to stay away from—was the answer to everything. And something deep within me knew that it only made perfect sense.

Cordelia was every bit the villain Valdez was. The same curse meant to torment Valdez was the same curse tormenting our minds for centuries. In damning the pirates, Cordelia damned her daughters as well. Our blood—our hearts—were always drawn to the ocean, but our minds had been taught to fear it, keeping us far from the sea so that we might never free the man who betrayed her—and in turn, free ourselves.

To save both Mom and Milo, the answer was the same—I had to return our magic to the sea—even if it meant breaking my heart.

The sound of Dad's brakes squealing in the driveway whisked me back to the present. I scurried to my feet, carefully keeping the journal close to my body. With a jumpiness that wasn't typical of me, I climbed back down the attic stairs and managed to shut the entrance just as Dad opened the front door, the light of late morning a harsh greeting after so long in the attic.

"Morning, Trina." He smiled, but there was exhaustion in his eyes. Exhaustion he didn't deserve. Mom wasn't just going under—she was dragging him down with her. And I supposed the perhaps it was impossible for him to tear himself away because he was in love with the descendant of a siren, whether either of them realized it or not.

I could tell he was trying to act as if things were normal, but something was wrong, and the issue at hand just hung in the air like a dark fog.

"Has Mom ever woken up—normally, I mean?"

Dad hung his head, his hands deep in his pockets. "No..."

"What is it? What are you not telling me?" I said, facing him at the door.

He fumbled, glancing around before finally giving me an answer. "Every time she wakes, her monitors fly off the charts. Her heart is stressed—like she's stuck in a panic attack she can't come out of. She's on the verge of a cardiac arrest. And they said if it comes to that, then she..."

"She what?" I leaned in.

"She might not survive it." Dad drew in a breath and leaned his head against the wall, rubbing his forehead. He wouldn't look at me. "Her heart's weak, Katrina," he said lowly. "When I found her that night—she hadn't only drunk herself half-to-death. She...she'd overdosed on something...on some old pain pills I forgot to throw away. They practically revived her at the hospital. And at first it seemed like she'd be okay...but it's clear she's not." Dad was silent for a long, torturous minute, as I stared at him with my mouth open in disbelief, choking on any word that might've tried to come out. "I...I should've told you, but I was so scared myself."

It felt like the breath had been knocked out of me. I blinked to hold in the tears fighting their way to the surface.

It was all exactly what I had been afraid of. And I only hoped it wasn't too late to change the course of things.

"So, then...what do we do?" I asked, my voice cracking.

"I really don't know, *mija*." It was unusual to hear him say my full name, and it meant things weren't good. "It's just one step at a time. Like it always has been."

I nodded, the room spinning as the reality settled over me of what I knew I needed to do.

"I—I think I want to stay here today." I finally said. "I think I just...need some time alone to process. Maybe go hike and clear my head or something."

The lines in Dad's forehead softened, his lip curling into his mouth as he stood a little straighter. "That's not a bad idea, Trina. Some fresh air would do you some good." He turned toward the door, his movements slow and burdensome. "Just call me if you need me."

"Will do, Dad." I croaked out through the tightness in my chest. "*Te amo.*" I muttered softly, unsure when I'd have the chance to say it again.

Because for quite possibly for the first time in my whole life, I knew what I had to do.

I couldn't tell Dad right then. I couldn't bear to tell him to his face after what he'd just told me. I didn't have time to try to explain either.

So, I'd do it later, when it was far too late to change my mind.

I watched him pull out of the driveway, and once his truck was out of sight, I eyed Mom's gray sedan. Things couldn't wait another few days for my return flight. And my Jeep was back in St. Constantine, where I needed to be.

I changed out of my jeans and into Cordelia's dress once more, shaking away the memories of the last night I'd worn it. I grabbed Mom's keys from their place by the door and walked outside, locking the door behind me.

It would make me look heartless, to suddenly up and leave right before Thanksgiving with Mom in the hospital. But what choice did I have? Hurting Dad was the only way.

I started Mom's car and drove away from the house, the steering wheel against my palms slippery with sweat, and my heart pounding like a war drum in my ears. I felt faint. I hadn't eaten, but if I had I was sure I would have thrown it up.

With each passing mile, I tried to find the courage to call Dad. Every time I would reach for the phone, I'd be hit with a wave of dread and panic and ultimately chicken out.

Five more minutes.

But then five minutes turned into an hour. I was on the interstate heading south. I could imagine my dad's broken expression. It was going to darken his world. When he texted me to ask if I was okay—if I'd gone out hiking—I knew it was time.

I called.

"Dad." I started, trying to control the shakiness of my voice. "I have to leave for a little while. I took Mom's car."

"What do you mean, Trina?" A subtle panic rose in his voice. "Where are you going?"

"There's something I have to do back in Constantine."

"You're going back to Florida? Now?"

"Yes..." I swallowed the lump in my throat. "Yes, because I can't keep looking at Mom the way she is right now. She made this choice, and I'm tired of always being the one who gets hurt." My chest ached as I forced out the lies I'd rehearsed in my head for the past hour.

"I—I thought you were okay. You said you were okay."

"Yeah, well that was because I was trying to make you happy. But I'm tired of having to hide how I feel. You told me to do what I really want. So, I am. I need to get away for a while. I'll be back when I'm ready."

"Trina, this is serious. Your mom is—"

"I don't care, Dad." I fought to keep from crying. My words came out like venom. "There. I said it. It's always about Mom. It's always been about Mom in this family. I'm over it."

It was unusual for my dad to be left speechless, but he wasn't saying anything. I knew I had just destroyed him. If I tried to speak another word, tears were going to flow like a flash flood.

So, I hung up.

I allowed myself the consolation of crying, careful not to let my tears blur my vision too much as I drove along the freeway. The sky was overcast, darkening my spirit even further, reminding me that I had fourteen aching hours ahead of me. It was a long road, and I wasn't entirely sure what awaited me at the end of it.

I just knew I had to go.

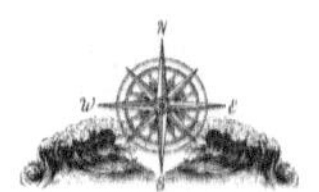

I reached Constantine a few hours after nightfall. Fighting my tiredness from the long drive, I parked at the pier, hoping it wasn't too late to find Milo one last time. I had to tell him everything. About the chest, the journal, and Cordelia.

Maybe he'd already known. But he'd given me the chance to discover it for myself, and I was grateful for that. He'd quite literally carried me part of the way, so that I could finally learn to save myself.

If for nothing else, I owed him for that. I would set him free, even if he thought he didn't want it anymore, even if he'd made me promise not to. I would end his curse and mine.

But I still wanted the chance to tell him goodbye first. To tell him that he didn't have to steal my heart, because I realized I'd already given it to him. And when he was gone, a piece of me would go with him.

I stood alone on the pier, wrapping my arms around myself to keep warm as the wind clawed at the hem of my dress. Bitter cold air swept in from the dark, billowing clouds in the distance, and the waves were choppy and fierce as a storm brewed out at sea.

By some instinct I had developed, I checked that the scale was still secured around my neck every few moments. If I hadn't tried it already, I would have tossed it into the ocean below, but it was clear that just throwing it into the water was not enough, as I had discovered before.

The tide was high, and the churning water made it far too dangerous to attempt climbing down below to carve my star into the pier beams or dip the necklace into the surf.

I didn't know how I was supposed to let Milo know I was here. But I needed him to understand why I broke my promise. I needed to beg him to let me break the curse, to end his suffering. I needed him to want to die again.

I needed him to come to me.

As if by some strange magic, a hauntingly familiar melody began to play in my head. I followed it, singing aloud the words into the mist of the dark sea. Into the wind, as the waves swelled, and the stars disappeared, I sang this strange song to the tune of my mother's lullaby. Serena's song.

"Down by the shore

Meet me once more

By the light of the moon

Love me, then leave me

With the dawn rising

Haunt me forevermore."

As the last chilling note escaped my lips, the mist over the water seemed to thicken, and the outline of an albatross came into view through the rolling fog before disappearing. My necklace began to shimmer with a soft iridescent glow. I felt a warmth, a small pulse of power, radiating from it against my skin.

I breathed a sigh of relief as I felt footsteps behind me on the wooden pier. I closed my eyes as the steps drew nearer, and warm breath touched the back of my neck. Soft lips grazed against my ear as strong arms reached forward around me, pulling my trembling frame into an embrace. Leaning my head back to rest against his chest, I breathed in him in, expecting to inhale the warm scent of amber, but instead a familiar dark spice infiltrated my nostrils.

"I never thought I'd hear that song again. You almost sounded just like her, you know." Bellamy spoke delicately, and I could feel each movement of his lips along the tip of my ear.

I pulled away from his hold with a gasp. He stood smirking at me with smoldering blue eyes.

"I had no idea you could sing so beautifully," he added in a voice like rich velvet, "but I guess it only makes sense, siren."

"Don't call me that," I pleaded. "What are you doing here? Where is Milo?"

"Tsk, tsk, Katrina," Bellamy shook his head, taking a few steps towards me. "I really thought you'd be happier to see me after all we've been through. Don't forget I helped you escape. It wasn't all Milo, you know."

"I am glad to see you..." I admitted, putting a hand to my head. "I'm sorry. I'm just worried about him. About what Valdez might do to him..."

"Don't worry," Bellamy said coolly. "He can't kill him, remember?"

"Exactly, so I can't imagine what kind of torture he might have in mind as an alternative."

"Well, I'll tell you where Milo is, and what has become of him since you left, if you tell me why you're here."

"Really?" I blinked tears back down and pressed my lips together. I couldn't cry, not now. "You're going to blackmail me? Didn't Valdez punish you for helping me, too?"

"He doesn't know it was me who got you back to shore. Besides, he tends to turn a blind eye to his son."

"So it seems." I crossed my arms.

"It's too bad I'm not so willing to return the favor for him. Guess I didn't quite inherit his gracious mercifulness," Bellamy sneered with sarcasm.

The wind picked up, blowing my hair all around me as I raised my voice to talk over the sound of the roaring waves.

"I know that you want him to pay for what he did, Bellamy. I get it. But this curse must end. You have to let go."

"Ah, as I expected." Bellamy's eyes darkened. "So that's what you're here for. You've finally decided you're going to try to break the curse. Just like Serena, you think you can reason with the sea—you think you can save the ones you love."

"Well...yes, I *am* going to break the curse. By siren's blood and magic done," I sputtered the first line of the curse, never taking my gaze off Bellamy. "Serena couldn't. But I can. Because...because I'm Cordelia's great-granddaughter."

"And you thought I was just making up fun pet names." Bellamy smirked, closing the space between us, and lifting my chin with his hand. "You see? You *are* a siren."

"No." I squeezed my eyes shut. "It doesn't mean that. Maybe Cordelia was my ancestor but that doesn't make me an actual mermaid. I think I'd know by now if I had a fish tail." I spat the words out as if they were sand in my mouth. "Now, I told you why I'm here. Tell me where Milo is."

"He's aboard the ship, love."

"Take me to him."

"I don't think so," Bellamy leaned back on the railing of the pier. "Do you have any idea what will happen to you if you go aboard that ship again? If Valdez knows you're truly descended from Cordelia..." his voice trailed off, lost to the sound of crashing waves. He stared out into the water, looking past me, but then his blue eyes moved to capture mine. "You're practically making me beg."

Bellamy straightened, leaving his position along the railing. He stepped towards me once more and took both my hands in his. "Let me destroy the scale. Go back home so you're safe, just like Milo wanted. Let Valdez get what retribution is due to him. Let him spend his eternity hopeless, just as he's left me."

"No!" I shouted, voice quivering. "Can't you see? If I don't break this curse, my mom will die! I will die! Cordelia didn't just curse your crew. She cursed her bloodline. We all descend into madness until we kill ourselves. It's all connected, and it hasn't failed a generation." I didn't expect Bellamy to look so surprised as I went on. "The sea called each one of us, but we never knew how to answer—until now. I do know how to answer." I pulled in a breath of sea air and steadied myself before speaking again. "And if I don't answer, I watch my mom die and Milo goes on suffering forever. He doesn't deserve to suffer anymore. And neither do you, Bellamy."

For the first time since I'd known him, I swore I saw raw emotion welling up in Bellamy, his eyes glassy, and his jaw flexed tightly, as though for once he was too afraid to speak. For just a moment, his witty, arrogant persona was gone, no longer there to act as his armor.

He pulled me closer, until we were mere inches apart. But I didn't back away this time.

"Please," I whispered. "Let me save you,"

"I wish I could." He let go of my hand and traced my cheekbone gently with his knuckles. My chest fluttered, in a strange way. I became rigid and unsure, as was the usual with Bellamy. My body leaned into him slightly, but my mind and heart were divided.

As I studied his handsome face in the shadows, charmed by him like a fool for just a fleeting moment, I lowered my guard—and failed to notice what he had done until it was too late.

He backed away, looking at me through a pained but unwavering gaze, with the silver chain wrapped around his fingers and the pendant tucked tightly into his closed palm.

"No!" I screamed, grasping at my bare neck.

Then something struck from above, swallowing me whole—wet and smothering, forcing me to the ground beneath its weight. A net, soaked through and so heavy it was impossible to lift off myself.

As I fought the entanglement, I strained to peek through the dripping seaweed stuck in the net holes, and I saw that Bellamy was trapped beneath, too.

A group of men—pirates—emerged from the darkness. They ignored Bellamy's insults and attempts to fight them from within the ropes. I groaned, pleaded, and did everything I could to work my way out from the tangles, but it was too heavy, and they were too quick. They yanked me along with one swift tug of the net, and I screamed as they dragged us as though we were lifeless piles of fish. But no one heard my screams there on the empty pier.

After hoisting us over the edge and dropping us onto a different wooden, slick surface, they pulled back the nets, and I took in my new surroundings.

We were aboard the *Siren's Scorn*.

The crew held us both at gunpoint with their pistols and swords. My eyes frantically scanned the deck to see a bloodied figure tied in front of the mast, each wrist bound by a rope pulled taut to the rigging on either side. His scarlet-stained shirt was torn to ribbons, and he was on his knees, his head hanging so low that his matted hair obscured his face. He looked up at me weakly, hazel eyes peering at me from a face smeared with both fresh and dried blood.

Milo.

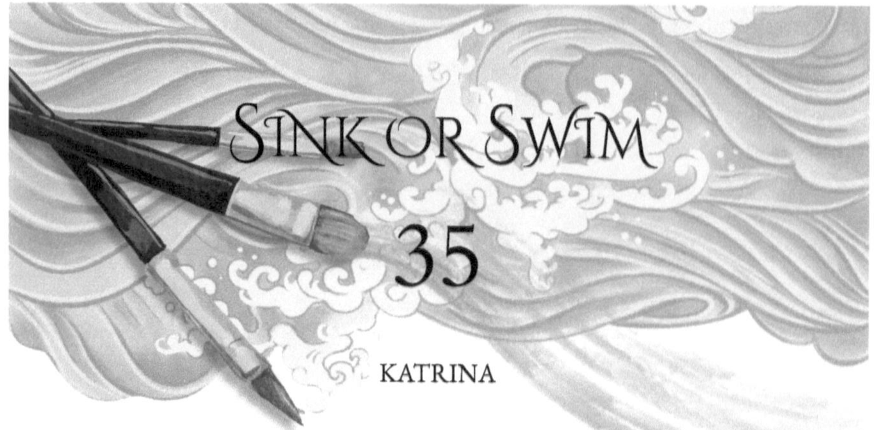

SINK OR SWIM

35

KATRINA

"**M**ilo!" My scream tore through the air as I lunged forward, resisting the crew member who held me in place by my arm.

"Don't worry, lass. He's still alive, of course." Valdez stepped out from the throng of pirates looking on, his men parting the way for him to stand in their midst. "One good thing about this damned curse—it allows me to treat traitors accordingly. Over and over again. Your dear Harrington here has chosen mutiny.

"At first, it was promising. He played his part well—romancing the naïve siren to lure her to her fate. Until she managed to steal his heart for real. And he proved once again that he is naught but a coward." Valdez's voice carried over the entire ship as he slowly made his way across the deck to where Milo was bound.

He jammed the tip of his boot into Milo's jaw, and I winced, resisting against my own captors as Milo recoiled, spitting blood in defiance at Valdez's feet. The captain went on, looking at me. "So many nights he spent leading my men off your trail, charting our course in the wrong direction—when he wasn't sneaking off romancing you of course. Had us all fooled for a long time, he did." Valdez drew his sword from his hip and slashed Milo's thigh wide open. The blade cut deep into muscle, sending blood spattering across the deck as it swept through cloth and skin. Milo was silent, but even from here I could see how his teeth were gritted in pain.

"No! Stop!" I pleaded. I thought I had run out of tears by now, but I was wrong. My vision blurred as I watched Milo slump further forward. I imagined he would've fallen over by now, but the thick ropes pulling his arms taut kept him dangling in place.

Valdez only laughed, a menacing rumble in his throat, and took a step towards Bellamy and me.

"But to be honest, I should be thanking Mr. Harrington for wasting all this time. If he hadn't, we would never have learned about that shocking secret of yours, Katrina." With the bloodied tip of his sword, he moved a stray hair from my face as he came close enough that I could feel his breath on my skin.

"Cordelia's great-granddaughter. Hmm..." he purred in a way that made my blood curdle. "How charming to know she made such a lovely legacy for herself on land while she damned me to these pits of hell."

"As you deserve." Bellamy spat. His back was pressed against mine, and up until now he had been silent.

"Boy!" Valdez tore himself away from me and crept to Bellamy, his footsteps creaking against the rotting wood of the deck. "I've put up with your insolence long enough. I ought to have you strung up with Harrington over there. This wench has had you wrapped around her finger all this time—just as is her nature."

Members of the crew scattered along the deck nodded and voiced their approval in unison. Valdez turned back to me, his cold eyes narrowing as they searched my chest and neck.

"Where's the scale, whore? Will we have to take the pleasure of stripping you down and searching you for it?"

"Don't you dare touch her!" Milo shouted as he wrestled against his bindings, his voice like blazing fire in the night.

Valdez twisted his lips into a grin. "Or will I have to gut your beloved in front of you to make you talk?" The tears streamed down my face faster than I could blink them away.

"No, no! Please...don't hurt him anymore!" My voice cracked as I cried out in anguish. "I came here to break the curse. I'll do what you want if that's what it takes. But I can't give you the scale...because I don't have it." I explained frantically. "I don't have it, I swear. Bellamy took it from me—just before you kidnapped us."

My whole being shook as I watched Valdez stew over my words until he finally looked at Bellamy.

"Is that true?" he asked. "Hand it over, boy."

"I—I dropped it," Bellamy stuttered. "It must be back on the pier." I couldn't tell if he was telling the truth or not, but either way I felt my heart sink at the thought of him having lost the only source of siren magic I was capable of using.

"He's lying," Milo uttered weakly. "Are you really so blinded that you can't see that your own son despises you? He's lying."

"Shut him up," Valdez ordered coolly. A pirate at Milo's back flicked the lash, and another jabbed him in the face with the blunt end of a pistol. I flinched at the crunching sound of bone and the tearing of flesh. And my tears fell hard, flooding the deck alongside his blood.

Valdez watched both me and Bellamy with snake-like eyes, reminding me of a vulture as he circled us. "Men, throw these two in the brig for now and go back to search the pier."

A man grabbed me, and another took Bellamy, pointing swords at our backs as they forced us across the ship and towards the opening to a galley beneath the deck.

Bellamy went before me, disappearing into the darkness below. As I passed Milo, he looked up at me.

I fought against the man pushing me forwards, begging for just a moment to speak to him. As if he found some inkling of compassion within himself, he let me stop long enough to meet Milo's broken gaze.

My heart shattered.

"Why did you come back?" he groaned, squirming against his ropes and the sting of his wounds.

"I had to," I whispered. "Because...because I—"

"—because she's fool enough to think she loves a worthless, filthy pirate." Valdez interrupted, placing himself between us. "Don't worry, Harrington. I'll take good care of that heart of hers while you and the rest of the crew sink to the depths for good. You can rest in peace with that, aye?" He grinned a cruel, devilish grin and pulled a dagger from his belt, running his finger along the edge.

I shuddered as my blood turned to ice.

Milo ignited, tearing against his bindings like a feral animal, shouting with each breath. "If you hurt her—if you so much as touch her, Valdez, I swear on my father's grave—"

Someone shoved me forward and the galley door slammed shut behind me, muffling the rest of Milo's desperate cries. The pirate behind me led me down to a dark cell, ravaged and rusted with barnacles clinging to the bars. He threw me into the cell with Bellamy, who stood at the far end, in a corner obscured by shadows, with his back to the wall.

The pirate locked the cell door, and then retreated up to the deck. I whipped around and grabbed the salt-crusted bars, shaking them in an attempt to break free. When that didn't work, I desperately checked every edge and corner for anything I could use to break out, ignoring the sickening smell of algae and the dripping of cold water on my skin. But there was nothing in the cell with us except a rusted bucket likely once used for waste.

I noticed Bellamy wasn't moving or speaking. He seemed entranced as he stood staring into the wall. I felt the ship lurching forward.

"Bellamy, please. Help me," I begged. "Your father is going to—"

"He's not my father!" Bellamy spun around to face me, his eyes flashing with anger even in the darkness. "I refuse to see that monster as my father!"

He stomped towards me, and I stepped back, afraid of what he might do. He pinned my back against the cell bars, his chest heaving as he growled. "He's taken everything I ever cared about from me. And now he's doing it all over again." His voice became eerily calm as he stared into the deepest part of me.

I trembled as I spoke to him, afraid of what he might do next. "I—I found a letter from Valdez to Cordelia, Bellamy. He wanted to save you. Before he went mad from the torment." It was all I could think to say in hopes of keeping him from succumbing further to his rage.

Bellamy said nothing, but let my words linger in the cold, damp air around us, his silence unsettling as he leaned in closer so that his eyes were inches from mine. Then, he straightened his shoulders and his throat rumbled with a low, quiet laugh that chilled my bones. He pointed to his tattoo of the bleeding heart pierced by two arrows.

"Do you know what this tattoo means?"

I shook my head.

"The first arrow to my heart was when Serena was killed. The second…Well that one's for my father. He's dead to me."

"I know Valdez is horrible…but I think in his own way, he loves you. I think he always has. In the letter, he was begging her to come back to free you from the curse." My voice grew hoarse.

"You mean the letter never sent? You think that man cares about me? That was just a pathetic attempt to trick Cordelia into coming back. But even she wasn't so stupid," he sneered. "If he cared about me, do you think he would want to tear your heart out for himself just so he can go on living while his son pays the penance for his sins?"

The walls of the cell spun like the thoughts and emotions in my mind. I didn't know what to say or do next, and I grasped for some sense of hope, but I couldn't find it. I thought of Milo up on the deck, and my mom slipping away in the hospital. I was failing them, and it was tearing me apart.

Bellamy still had me pressed to the bars between his arms. He was still breathing hard, as if containing some raging beast within. He was hardly the charismatic charmer I'd met in the library so many nights ago. Now he was a broken, confused, and out of control shell of himself.

And all I could do was hope he still had the necklace somewhere on him. But I worried that if I asked him for it, it would send him over the edge. I couldn't afford to risk it.

If he had it, it had to be somewhere on his person. But it could've been anywhere. The only option I had left was to manipulate it out of him. I finally spoke.

"I know you're hurt and angry." Though it pained my conscience, I reached for him. "This doesn't have to be the end, Bellamy," I whispered as seductively as I could manage. "You were right. There is no way out of this. Unless we figure out how to use the scale's magic." I slid my hand around his waist, underneath his loose-fitting shirt, feeling his skin and discreetly searching for anything that felt like the necklace. "Maybe we can figure out how—together." I leaned forward and spoke softly against his ear. My fingers trailed up his chest, and then along his neck until I was caressing his face.

The way he looked back at me as I touched him struck something within me. I'd never witnessed him break the way he did that moment—as if he was in disbelief that I was offering my affection, and he refused to believe he deserved it. He was looking into my eyes, but he stared right through them, as though he was elsewhere. As though they were someone else's. With short, slow breaths, he leaned into me and gripped the cell bars on either side of me.

Then his eyes softened in a strange sort of way. I thought he would kiss me, but he didn't. With trembling, calculated movements, I pulled my hand from his face and sent it trailing down with the other, exploring his body for any sign of the necklace. I forced myself to appear calm and unwavering as I slid my hands down farther than I had hoped to go, caressing the skin beneath his trousers, praying for the feeling of a small chain or pendant to graze my shaking fingers.

"Serena," Bellamy breathed, closing his eyes, and pressing his lips to my neck. I nearly jumped back from the sudden mention of the name, but I held my ground. When Bellamy's eyes opened, they were soulless blue voids, as deep and endless as the sea.

I hadn't even noticed that someone had entered the room until I heard the lock clicking behind me. The door to the brig swung open, causing me to stumble backward as I had been leaning against it. Bellamy snapped from his trance and grabbed my wrist with a ruthless grip. Without warning, he twisted around toward the crewman who'd opened the door and connected his fist with his jaw, then snatched the man's sword from its holster.

"You think I don't know what you're trying to do, Katrina?" Bellamy bared his teeth at me. "Seems you've learned a few too many tricks from us dirty pirates. Or maybe you're just finally realizing what a siren can do."

He pulled me to him, his arm across my body and the other holding the sword at my neck. I resisted, but he only pushed the blade against my skin, further, and unlike when Milo held me the same way in order to save me, it was clear that Bellamy was serious.

He forced me up the steps to the brig, keeping the sword at my throat the entire time. I could see that the ship had sailed far from any point of land now. We were back in open water. And Valdez was waiting for us at the top of the deck.

"Well, well..." He spoke with a voice like thunder, standing at Milo's side, surrounded by his crew. "We searched the whole pier and didn't find the scale, son. Where is it? It's nearly sunrise, so speak up."

"I'm never giving it to you." Bellamy choked. "I'm never giving *her* to you either."

"Bellamy, let go of her! What the hell are you doing?" Milo's voice pierced through the sound of the rioting waves below. The ocean breeze blew my hair against my face, plastering loose strands to my tear-soaked cheeks.

Bellamy turned his gaze on Milo. "If I had to watch the girl I love die, it's only fair that you should, too. If I don't kill her, Valdez will. And I won't let him win again."

I couldn't have imagined Bellamy would do this. I never dreamed he'd let his pain take him this far.

"Don't do this," I whispered, quietly enough that the rest of the crew couldn't hear me.

"I have to." He spat out his words through gritted teeth. I could feel the blade shaking against my skin as his hand trembled.

He blinked through his own tears and swallowed, and I thought, for just a second, he was going to change his mind. And he did. He tightened his grip and lowered the edge of the sword to my chest, right over my pounding heart.

"Go on, boy." Valdez's midnight voice hummed as he smiled, seemingly entertained with the whole scene. "Go on. Cut her heart out. Take it for yourself. At least I'll die with pride seeing you finally become as ruthless as I always hoped you'd be."

Bellamy hesitated, pulling my head back as if to give himself more clearance to my chest. I thought I would faint if he weren't forcibly holding me up. I was dizzy, and my vision blurred from crying. I could only trust what I could hear.

I heard Milo screaming, pleading, begging Bellamy to stop. I heard Valdez laughing. I heard Bellamy's quivering breaths coming fast as he kept me frozen in this horrific moment of anticipation.

"Go on, Bellamy," Valdez urged once more. "Take the heart. Maybe you can even use it to bring back that lass of yours."

I felt a shift in Bellamy as his father's cruel words took hold and his face went pale. He gripped me tighter. So much that I struggled for each breath. The blade pierced my skin, just enough to draw a tiny bead of blood.

"Bellamy..." I choked. "Don't be like Valdez. This isn't you. Serena wouldn't want this." He loosened his grip and eased the blade against my chest, but kept it aimed at my heart. I turned my head to look into his face. "You have the scale, Bellamy. The ship is about to go under with all of us on it. The scale's magic is going to go to the depths either way. Along with me and every last drop of my blood. It's too late to stop it."

"I can destroy it. Or...what if...what if I *can* bring her back?" he said shakily, as if trying to convince himself, his empty eyes red and bloodshot with strain.

I shook my head softly. "No. No...you can't..." In a moment of courage, I took his hand holding the sword and lowered it. He offered no resistance. I leaned forward, whispering as quietly as I could. "But you can finally be with her," I uttered.

And then I pressed my lips against his, tasting the salt from both our tears as we stood locked in a dark, deep kiss of surrender.

The sword fell out from his grasp, clattering on the wooden floor below. He slid his hand into mine and closed his fingers, and I kissed him until he pulled away. And when he finally let go, I clenched my fist at the feeling of something thin and metallic, realizing he had tucked the necklace into my closed palm.

Valdez roared in anger and cursed the air as Bellamy pushed me aside, raised his sword with a primal, fervent cry—and cut Milo's ropes free.

The Devil and the Deep Blue Sea

36

I ran to Milo, collapsing at his side as he plunged to his knees. Bellamy stood over us, facing his father.

"I'm so sorry," I cried, pushing the hair back from Milo's battered face. "Look at you...I wanted to tell you goodbye. But not like this..."

He grasped my face between both hands. "You shouldn't have come back."

There was too much to explain. I couldn't tell him everything I'd learned in such a fleeting, desperate moment. So, I simply said, "You had to know I wouldn't stay away. The sea draws the heart."

He smiled that crooked smile through blood and bruises, but then it faded, and he shook his head. "I was supposed to protect you."

"And you did," I said. "It was my choice to come back here. I knew what would happen."

He pressed his lips together, weariness weighting his every movement. "This can't be the only way," he groaned. "You have to save yourself."

"I am." I pressed my forehead to Milo's, breathing in his scent mixed with blood and brine.

The ocean howled below, growing more deafening and unruly as the first light of dawn threatened to break through. The air had shifted the same way it had on the island weeks before. Water spun slowly, drawing the ship in as it rocked beneath the raging water. The maelstrom was forming.

"Katrina." he sighed my name as though it brought him relief just to say it. "I love you. You were my missing piece. And that will forever be my freedom." My heart stood still, cracking into pieces as each word from his lips soothed my battered soul.

"Milo...I..." I sobbed, my words caught between my breath and the ache in my chest, refusing to come to the surface, and when they finally did, it was too late.

"Give me the scale!" Valdez ordered, snatching my wrist as he towered over me.

With my free arm, I stretched out my hand, my fingers still curled around the necklace. And just as I dared to open them—to give the scale over to Valdez—some distant voice in me screamed not to. That he would not truly give it to the sea for whatever vague ritual the curse demanded.

I would be the one to break the curse, by my power and my will alone—to ensure he didn't somehow cheat his way out of it.

Because I wanted to.

Because of love.

"No!" I shot back, sneering with some strange new burst of courage. "I know better than to trust a pirate."

I twisted, heaving myself against his vice-like grip. As he dragged me forward, my heels dug into the deck wood, and Bellamy grappled him from behind, fighting to pull him off me. Milo leapt forward, pulling out a concealed dagger from his boot. Before I could even register the motion, he struck Valdez's arm, piercing his forearm with the blade.

The captain yelped in pain, his howl slowly twisting into distorted laughter, and I managed to slip from his grip as Bellamy wrestled with him from behind.

My whole body wobbled from both my trembling and the sway of the ship, but I forced my feet to carry me swiftly to the edge of the ship. Leaping up onto the hull, I grabbed the netting fastened to the sails for balance.

I thought I was going to be sick, but I held my ground, looking at Milo, who now joined Bellamy in holding back Valdez. The picture of his bloodied, beaten figure fighting to the last breath was all I needed to give myself the strength to go through with my plan.

The wind whipped my face, and the salty sea mist stung my eyes. Lightning ripped across the sky in bright flashes, allowing me scattered, chilling glimpses of the swirling obsidian water below beginning to funnel into a bottomless abyss.

I heard a grunt that made me look back. Valdez and the crew stood facing Milo and Bellamy—the only separation between me and them. They stood like a wall, both their backs to me, holding back Valdez just strides away, staring down a crew that looked weary, defeated, and resigned to their fate. They could've charged them. They could've easily overpowered the two lone men acting as my barrier. But they stood, watching me, almost curiously, as if I had become their last hope.

"Don't just stand there you fools!" Valdez screamed. "I still need the heart out of her!"

But no one moved. I even thought I heard a few swords clatter to the ground.

I looked down at the necklace one last time, smoothing my thumb over the scale pendant as its iridescent colors caught the blinding bursts of lightning. Then with one last glance back, I tossed the necklace into the water below, making sure the motion was visible to Valdez and his crew.

The silence that followed was more haunting than the wailing of the sea. Even Valdez was still, locked between Milo and Bellamy who had both twisted themselves around to watch me as well.

I gripped the netting as the ship fought to sling me overboard. The sensation of half a hundred stares boring into my back sent shivers down my spine. The necklace disappeared into the churning waters, and the maelstrom continued spinning, picking up speed as the ship began to creak and groan with the force of being pulled in.

After the long stretch of hopeless silence, the crew began to mutter among themselves. Valdez grunted in frustration.

"You see, you bastards? She isn't going to free you! Now you've let her destroy the last chance you had." He commanded the crew to subdue Bellamy and Milo, and they surged to action, returning to the raging mob they were before.

Valdez stepped forward, sliding the dagger out from the flesh of his arm without a flinch. He looked at me, then at a restrained Milo, just before ramming the blade between Milo's ribs.

"Stop it!" I cried, my voice raw. "What more do you want from me? I tried to break your damn curse! It didn't work!"

Valdez only twisted the knife deeper. Milo cried out in groans of torment, making my blood run cold. Bright crimson trickled from his mouth as he labored for each short breath.

"Come down here." Valdez coaxed, yanking out the dagger and tossing it to the floor. "Save *him*, at the very least. Your heart in exchange for him. If you don't, *this* is his eternity."

"Katrina, no. Don't you dare..." Milo sputtered through the blood.

I braced, squeezing back tears. I didn't need to come down there for Valdez to rip my heart out—he was doing it just fine from where he stood.

"It appears you're caught between the devil and the deep blue sea, lass." Valdez mocked over the sound of water roaring below. "There's no way off this ship."

My thoughts raced—spiraling, churning, spinning out of control, desperate for a new answer to the question I was still too afraid to face. The hard truth was setting in that tonight I would die, one way or another.

The sky crackled with thunder and lightning, and rain began to pour down in a torrent.

I considered my options one by one. I could let Valdez cut out my heart, or I could hold things off long enough to go down with the ship, or…I could go willingly—my way—the only way.

By siren's blood and magic done.

"Bellamy!" I cried over the rain and thunder. "Recite Cordelia's curse to me!"

The crew muttered in confusion as Bellamy hesitated, arching a brow. "Why—"

"Just do it!" I screamed. I needed to hear it one more time—just to be sure.

He stretched his neck upwards and cried out into the wind. "By siren's blood and magic done, This curse of lasting flesh and bone. The sea will hold your bodies bound, 'Til siren's blood again be found. The depths shall never set you free. 'Til she returns her magic to the sea."

I repeated the parts that called out to me like they were direct instructions, in a low breathy mumble only I could hear.

Til siren's blood again be found…Til she returns her magic to the sea.

A chill seeped into my core like the icy rain soaking my skin.

The ship leaned and tilted as the waves rose, and the ghostly cyclone began to rake it inward. Gripping the net, squinting through the rain, I turned to Milo and Bellamy one last time, watching Milo's blood wash downstream of the sinking ship.

And in that same instant, I pictured Elisabeth's red-stained bathtub water, splashing and spilling over onto the floor as she bled out and held herself under. And I imagined what this very same deck might've looked like when Cordelia cut off her tail and dove into the sea—the magic in her blood and scales the hefty price of casting a curse that would carry on for centuries.

It only made sense that it would take the same to break it.

I'd given back the scale—the magic.

But it was only half done.

The dagger on the flooding deck was now washed clean, and it slid my way as one end of the ship rose into the air by the lift of the waves.

I thought of Mom, and how at this very moment she might be trapped in a nightmare as vivid the one I was standing in. I thought of her thrashing in that hospital bed. And I thought of the lullaby she used to hum me to sleep.

And then I lunged for the dagger before it could slide away.

I hauled myself back up onto the rim of the hull, the howling wind tearing at the soaked fabric of the dress clinging to me, and sea spray crashing all around me—the ghost of Cordelia, and the forgotten legacy of Elisabeth.

And I began to hum Mom's lullaby, the ethereal tune echoing over the crew through the mist and rain and waves spilling over the hull. The crew stared at me like a startled herd of deer, entranced by a voice I never knew I possessed as I swiped the blade across my palm.

As a line of bright red beaded on my hand, I sucked in a long, deep breath, forcing any remnant of fear back down into my chest. I leaned out over the edge of the ship as monstrous curling waves reached for me, my heart hammering against my ribs.

And even from there I could see it—the small, distant glow of the scale as it went on sinking—deeper and deeper, until it fully faded into the darkness of the depths. My fingers slipped one by one from the rigging, as I kept on still humming to myself.

And then I leapt into the raging waters far below.

Dead in the Water

37

KATRINA

The distant cries of Bellamy and Milo screaming my name faded as the ocean swallowed me whole. Turbulent waters ripped into my flesh like knives on impact, salt stinging the fresh cut in my hand. Cresting waves rolled over me, forcing me down with all their fury. As I fought to find the surface, the distance between my body and the skyline only grew as the maelstrom's current dragged me down.

I kept hoping I would wake up in my bed or on the beach in a frantic cold sweat, and Milo would be beside me to tell me it was all a dream. But that kind of relief never came. Instead, my lungs burned from the inside out as I pleaded for air, flailing helplessly in the pitch blackness of the water.

I prayed to whoever or whatever might listen that my sacrifice had been the answer. I clung tightly to the hope that somehow my mother would now be free from the visions that tormented her, free from the fate that loomed at her bedside, and that the dark souls of that cursed ship would no longer be sentenced to haunt the coasts.

I fought the voice in my head telling me otherwise until my last conscious breath. In the cold grip of death, I grasped in desperation at my senses as they faded one by one. With one muted scream, the pain of it all escaped me in the form of a thousand bubbles.

Then the dark water rushed in, replacing my cry, and pulled me to the depths.

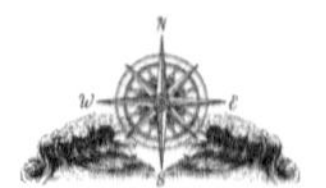

I don't know how long I was at the bottom of the ocean. I don't even know if what I saw or felt was real.

But at some point, I opened my eyes to what I thought was the afterlife. I was floating, suspended underwater in a calm, still sea. Bright cerulean glistened around me in shimmering curtains, clear enough that the white sunlight broke through it, stretching to the ocean floor. With heightened senses, every detail was as clear to me as it would be on land. I could make out each grain of sand beneath me, and even the detailed stripes and speckles on the fish that swam past. Every swish and sway of the water reverberated in my ears perfectly, distinctly. The salt water on my skin felt as natural as air. And somehow...somehow, I could breathe. Only...I wasn't breathing—there was no air being pulled through my nostrils. I simply didn't need it, somehow, in some terrifyingly beautiful way I couldn't explain.

My muscles strained as I tried to move. I would have swam up to the surface, but my legs wouldn't respond. They felt heavy and foreign, and refused to obey.

Within moments, the heavenly, peaceful scene around me began to fade.

Except it was me—*I* was the one fading. My eyes grew heavy, but I fought to hold them open long enough to spin around and take in the rest of my surroundings before I succumbed to the darkness once more.

And in the distance, I caught one glimpse that reminded me it was all real. One glimpse that gave me the peace of knowing my plan had worked, and it wasn't all for nothing. Meters from me, nestled in its final resting place, was the *Siren's Scorn*, in all her lifeless, tattered glory.

Finally.

I had saved him. Both of them.

And I hoped that meant I saved Mom, too.

My head fell forward as I closed my eyes, surrendering to the void that called me beyond. And through the ghostly wisps of my long hair floating freely around me, I swore I caught a gleam of sunlight glinting down below where my feet should've been.

I strained to see before I blacked out again. Something silver-blue glittered in place of my legs. Something inhuman. Something ethereal. Something beautiful...

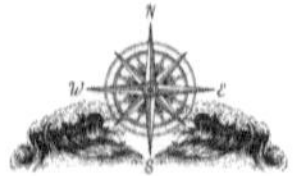

When I came to, I was face down in the sand. The tide washed over me, back and forth, rolling up to my waist. Wet hair draped across my neck and face. My dress was soaked through, heavy and clinging to my skin as I retched and coughed up seawater. Every inch of my body ached, as though I'd been hit by a truck.

I grimaced, struggling to muster the little strength I had left to get up on my feet. Each joint screamed at me under the pressure of any weight, so much that I thought my bones might be broken.

Worst of all, I had no idea where I was. The beach didn't look familiar, and I had no way to call anyone for help.

Disoriented and sore, I finally found my footing. The sun was coming up, slowly banishing the purple twilight haze in favor of orange and pink ribbons across the ocean's horizon.

I studied the area, looking for something I recognized. Something—anything—to get me home.

I tilted my head back, looking heavenward, when I noticed a bright star still shining, even as the morning broke through. I smiled a broken smile. I knew that star. And I followed it, walking in the direction it faced along the coast.

As I trudged along the empty coast, the drying sand and salt made me itch. The brisk morning air kept me shivering. My bruised body sang out in pain with each step. But what bothered me more than any of that was the way the ocean at my side mocked me.

It looked just the same as every day before, lazy waves lapping the shore. The tide would rise and fall just as it always had. As if nothing had changed.

As if it wasn't a grave of ghosts long past. As if it wasn't keeping countless dark secrets hidden beneath. Secrets that I could never tell. Secrets it had harbored for centuries, and yet so effortlessly, in one single instant, had swallowed them whole.

The lonely walk felt like an eternity. By the time I reached familiar shores, dawn had come and gone. I must have been trudging along for at least an hour before I recognized the pier in the distance. Seeing it brought back a flood of memories I was trying to forget.

In less than a month my life had been changed forever. In a single night, I had broken ancient curses, both magical and generational. And I had managed to do it without getting my heart cut out by pirates. So why did it feel like it had been ripped out anyway?

If I cried any more, I thought I might shrivel up from dehydration. But it turned out I had one tear left. A tear for Milo. For what I'd both lost and gained by setting him free from his curse. A tear for Bellamy, and the pain he spent so long trying to escape as it slowly tore him apart. A tear for Serena, who did not deserve her fate. And a tear for my mother, and all those long-dead daughters of Cordelia who'd suffered for her vengeance.

I let the tear fall with one last look at the sea before painstakingly crawling into the driver's seat of the car waiting for me by the pier—Mom's car. Reaching for my phone, I saw nine missed calls from Dad, three texts, and one voicemail.

"Trina, your mom...She woke up—without the panic attacks. Her heart's stable. She's fine. Everything's fine. She doesn't remember anything, but...but she's going to be fine."

I'd done it. Mom was free. She was going to live the rest of her life without the visions. She was going to live. And so was I.

And then I thought of the last thing I'd said to Dad, and it felt like a kick in the gut. I was too drained to think about how I would reconcile that, but I knew I'd figure it out later. For now, I sent him the only text my brain could formulate, just so he would know I was safe.

-Dad, I'm coming back home.

I drove to ICA, showered, and slept for hours. And when I awoke, I pulled something out from under my bed—something that didn't belong there anymore. And then I started the long drive back home, all through the night, my muscles aching every cramped hour in the car.

Mom was released from the hospital on Thanksgiving Day, just after I arrived the next morning. And for the first time in forever, we were all home together.

Mom said she'd had the best sleep of her life. And I knew exactly what she meant. Even without the siren scale around my neck, there were no inklings of nightmares to haunt me in my sleep. It was the most liberating, refreshing rest I'd ever felt, and my only regret was knowing my grandmother and all those before her would never get to experience it.

Later, as we sat around the table with our late-night takeout Thanksgiving dinner, it finally felt like we were a family again. I heard Mom's true laugh for the first time since I was a kid, unburdened and wholly her. And Dad's smile couldn't have been bigger.

I was quiet. Still adjusting. Still reliving what it had taken to get here. But I allowed myself to be content. I owed myself at least that.

After dinner, I excused myself to my room. As I was unrolling the package I had brought back with me, Mom appeared in the doorway. I tucked the package away so she wouldn't see.

"Trina." Her voice, strangely light and free, drifted across the room.

"Yeah, Mom?" I twisted around to face her.

"Did you ever find the box?"

I shook off a shudder at the mention. "I did," I said calmly. "And it had everything I was hoping to find."

"You were able to get it open?" She moved through my room, nearing the foot of my bed.

"Well..." I looked away, still crafting my full explanation and feeling stupid for not having anticipated this conversation. "Yes. I...found the key." That certainly wasn't a lie.

"You did?" She sat on the bed, tilting her head with surprise. "Where?"

"It was..." I glanced over at the key lying on my bedside dresser. I had no intention of taking it with me. And Mom needed to discover for herself the things I couldn't tell her. It was only fair for her to understand our cursed heritage. I'd leave out the part about sirens and ghost pirates, but I believed she needed to know the rest. She needed to know the hard-fought battles of our bloodline. "You're never going to believe this, but..."

Mom leaned in, her eyes pleading for me to finish.

I took the key from the dresser and offered it to Mom. "I...I found it on the beach. And thought it was worth a try. Turns out it was the right key." I half-smiled.

Mom took the key, staring at it like I'd just handed her a bar of solid gold. "You can't be serious," she gasped. "That's practically a miracle, Trina. I remember my mom trying so hard to get it open when I was a kid, but she never could. We always wondered what was inside. But that lock—it was indestructible. Almost like..."

"Like magic?" I finished, looking at her and noticing how vibrant her eyes were. "I guess that necklace had to come from somewhere."

Mom was silent, fiddling with the key. I wondered how long it would be before she felt ready to face the history it could unlock.

"There was a diary...and letters. I think you should read them when you have the chance. You and grandma aren't the only ones who struggled. It was never your fault, Mom."

"We've all known it ran in the family. Every daughter. I think I even remember my mom telling me her mother once tried to drown herself just to prove the necklace would save her. When I was a kid, I thought it was all just superstition and mom was just crazy—but as I got older and the dreams got worse, I realized maybe it was one of the few things that might've been real."

My mom smiled at me, in a weirdly warm way that made me happy and nervous all at the same time. I wasn't used to talking to her sober, and especially about this eerie topic that had once torn us apart but had now become the only thing capable of bringing us back together.

Suddenly she looked up at me, her narrowing eyes drifting down to my neck.

"Where is the necklace anyway?" she asked.

"I...I left it back in Constantine." I said simply. It was the truth, after all. I just left out the part about it lying at the bottom of the ocean. I would tell her about that one day if it came down to it, but for now, I'd let that secret lie on the sea floor with the rest of them.

Her brows flew upward in surprise. "Well hopefully we won't need it again."

"Something tells me we won't," I said softly. "And it's the first thing I've been sure of in a long time."

Mom shifted, twisting the key in her hand as she stared down at her lap, her voice suddenly serious and focused.

"I'm proud of you, Katrina," she said. "I know I can never make up for all those times I wasn't there for you. And I know you've heard me promise this a million times—but I'm going to stay sober—for good. I mean it this time. Really, I do. I don't even crave another drink. It's like...it's like I woke up as someone completely new. Like a weight's been lifted." She breathed in like she was smelling sweet spring air. "There will always be scars and the memories. But for once I believe I really can do this. I can heal. I promise you won't have to worry about me when you go back to Florida." She put a hand on my shoulder. "Your dad told me you were thinking about not going back. But don't let anything—especially me—keep you from the dream you started pursuing there."

After everything Constantine had brought me, I was no longer sure if I should return. I was considering finishing the semester and then trying to transfer somewhere else. I didn't know if I could handle the painful haunting memories.

"Thanks, Mom," I said, finding the boldness within me to hug her and to utter out the words I wasn't used to saying to her. "*Te amo.*"

Her eyes lit up, and she welcomed it with open arms. We sat there together in my room, on the edge of my bed, hugging each other tightly, without the smell of alcohol or feeling of resentment coming between us. I had lost all hope for a hug like that a long time ago, so I quietly cherished it all the more.

When Mom left the room, I continued unrolling the package I had brought home—the 'Bad Dreams,' the infamous scholarship-winning watercolor that had started it all. Taking a firm hold of the rag paper canvas, I held it up in front of me and looked it over one last time before tearing it in two, top to bottom.

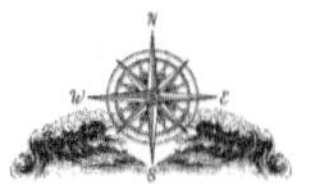

I waited until Sunday afternoon to leave for Florida. Mom and Dad accompanied me to the airport. It was an unreal experience, being able to say goodbye to both of them at the same time, with no tension, no strain, lingering hang-ups tainting the moment.

As the plane lifted, I watched the clouds from the window. I wondered what awaited me back in Constantine. I promised Mom I would at least finish the semester, but beyond that, I didn't know. I didn't believe my wounded heart could ever forget.

And in all honesty, I didn't want to forget.

After checking my carry-on through security, I rushed to the pickup area, where McKenzie waited for me in her convertible, stalled in the blinding sun, top down, and music blaring. The sticky air of Florida greeted me as I hopped into the driver's seat, still careful not to knock any of my still-healing bruises.

"Thanks for the ride." I smiled.

"You know I got you." McKenzie winked. "Good break?"

"Yeah. It was..." I squinted in the sunlight. "...eventful. My family's back together and my mom's not spiraling anymore, so I'd say things are good."

McKenzie leaned over and hugged me, while cars behind her honked.

"Just a sec, assholes!" She cried over her shoulder, shooting them a prickly stare. Fighting with something buried under the unused jacket in her floorboard, she grinned at me as she produced that annoying vintage Polaroid.

"They can wait. We have to get our first airport pickup picture. For documentation purposes of course."

I knew my face was redder than a chili pepper with embarrassment from the drivers behind us hurling curses and threats. But McKenzie couldn't be bothered. I leaned into the frame just to appease her as quickly as possible, and with one push of the button, she snapped her prized photo.

She shoved the camera and freshly printed photograph into my lap and sped off, jolting me back into the seat. Despite her unnerving driving, I smirked to myself. At least one thing was still the same.

On the drive back to Isabel, McKenzie entertained me with stories about her extravagant Thanksgiving and how her aunt from Kentucky wouldn't stop bragging about her new champion racehorse prospect.

"And the best part of all," she squealed. "I didn't text or call Ty once."

"Really?" I smirked. "Would Noah have anything to do with that?"

"No, no, not at all! Noah had nothing to do with it. I mean, our date was fun, but..." She flipped back her tangerine hair, in a flimsy attempt to hide her blushing smile, despite the wind blowing it right back all over the place.

"But?" I leaned in.

"But...I dunno. We'll see where it all goes." She shrugged, bouncing to the music on the radio.

I shook my head, unable to contain my giggle.

But when McKenzie asked about Milo next, the world came to a halt. The few words I tried to manage became trapped in my throat.

"I...he..." I shifted my gaze out the window, focusing on the bits of sand clumps lining the curb. "He left."

"What?" McKenzie groaned. "As in left you? Like left for good?"

I nodded, brushing off the suffocating feeling in my chest. "Yeah...It stings a little, sure. But I'll be fine." I lied. "I understand why he had to leave. He didn't have good history with this place."

McKenzie picked up on my cues and eased away from the conversation just as we pulled into the parking lot of ICA. It was as though a dark cloud had been lifted over the town of Constantine, but instead now hovered over me solely. As we walked to the dorm, the paranoid sensation still followed me, and my eyes caught every strange shadow in every corner and corridor, trying to convince me that it somehow could be one of my pirates.

But I knew that was impossible, so I fought the intrusive thoughts away and focused on nothing but the floor in front of me. To distract myself further, I pulled out my phone to check my student email.

As McKenzie fiddled with her jingling ring of keys, looking for the one to our door, an unopened email in my inbox drew my eye. The urgent title and flagged message caught my attention. I was worried I'd gotten in trouble for never picking up my showcase painting after the gala. Other matters had obviously been a bit more pressing at the time, so I had forgotten about it entirely.

IMPORTANT - Showcase Silent Auction

Dear Katrina,

We are following up with you regarding your showcase piece, which was sold at the silent auction. Half of the winning bid was donated to the school, but the buyer insisted the other half go directly to you. It was a generous offer. One that you'll need to come pick up in person. Please come by the bursar's office ASAP with your student ID to collect the payment.

As I read the email again for clarification, I couldn't refrain from the chirp of excitement that broke free from me.

"What is it?" McKenzie whipped around.

"My painting sold! Apparently for a lot. First thing tomorrow I have to pick up the check." I grinned, hoping it would be enough to afford a new set of tires for my Jeep. I smiled, grateful for something to lift the lingering ache in my soul, even temporarily.

We wound down the evening with a simple celebration dinner of homemade tacos which we threw together with various ingredients. When I settled into my bed that night, my foot brushed the blanket Milo had given me. How strange it seemed, that after all I had experienced, that silly blanket had remained untouched through it all.

Pulling the wrinkled fabric close to me, I inhaled the scent of him that lingered. As had become my habit, I reached up to my throat to feel the necklace. But the emptiness I felt in its place sent a wave of grief crashing into me, as I remembered it wasn't the only thing that was lost to me forever. I thought of sitting with him on the island, and I wished more than anything in that moment that I could go back there and watch the stars with him.

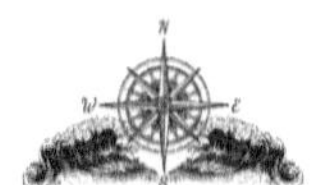

The morning brought with it the refreshing promise of a new day. I braced against my emotions as I fought to push the past behind me, eager just to keep my head above water for the day. I got out of bed earlier than usual so that I could visit the bursar's office before class.

Still admiring the unchanged beauty of the campus, I made my way to the building. Walking to the front desk, I explained the email and presented my ID.

"Just one moment." The lady excused herself as she turned around and disappeared into a back room behind a door. When she returned, she placed a check in my hand with a mumble. "Must have been some painting."

I unfolded the check the moment I stepped out the door. With eyes wide, I stood in shock as I read the amount written behind the dollar sign.

"Twenty *thousand* dollars?" I shrieked to myself.

Who in their right mind would give such an outrageous amount of money for my mediocre watercolor? I had expected maybe a couple hundred, if I was lucky, but this was beyond my comprehension. Confused, I checked the unreadable signature, then looked at the company name printed in the top corner—*Tesoro Del Mar Club and Marina.*

The name wasn't at all familiar, but it did make me think back to the mesmerizing wealthy lady who I'd spoken to that night at the gala. She mentioned her club and resort, so perhaps this was her doing. I couldn't be sure, but either way, it didn't matter to me. All I knew for certain was that I was set for my time here in Constantine.

If I stayed, anyway.

Beaming, I tucked the check away safely to cash later, still in disbelief. My steps sprung with new enthusiasm, even though my body still felt a bit like a walking punching bag.

I had just passed another campus building, when the sound of a wheelbarrow around the corner made my steps slow.

"Russell!" I waved slightly at him as he came into view, pushing the heavy load of dirt and sod.

"Hello, missy." He stopped, wiping his hands. "How was your Thanksgiving?"

"It was probably the most exciting one yet." Leaning forward, my voice lowered to a whisper. "I broke the curse."

"I told you to stay away," he shook his head. "But I'd be lying if I said I wasn't glad you didn't listen. You helped me put my daughter to rest. Something I've been trying to do on my own for years. Thank you."

"You're welcome," I uttered.

"It's time to put it all behind us." He put a hand on my shoulder. "And I'm going to start by selling my fishing boat. It's been sitting unused since that night. And well, I just don't think I want it around to hang onto anymore." There was a twinkle of sadness in his brown eyes. "You don't know anyone who's looking to buy a boat, do you?"

"No, sorry I don–" I caught myself mid-sentence as an unfathomably wild idea entered my head. "Actually, how much do you want for it?" I asked, surprising even myself.

"Are you saying *you* want to buy my old fishing boat?" He raised an eyebrow.

"I'm saying there's a place I need to get to, and I can't walk there. So name your price."

KATRINA

I knew it was absurd of me to buy Russell's boat. But he gave me a great deal, showed me the ropes for getting out onto the water, and even hauled it to the marina for me.

I once feared the ocean, but now that I had conquered it, I saw it as my only ticket to chasing a distant memory in the only way I knew how.

And now on this sunny afternoon not two days later, I stepped onto the boat.

My boat.

With my nerves tossing about like the waves, I steadied myself with a deep breath. I couldn't believe I was doing this. The same girl who once could hardly bear to even look at the ocean was now about to single-handedly sail across it. Though some fear due to inexperience was indeed present, I refused to listen to it, drowning it out with thoughts of my destination.

Looking out into the horizon, I set my sights on the invisible island in the distance. I couldn't see it, but I knew it was out there. Confirming once more that my navigation was working, I put myself at the helm and set forth on my maiden voyage. I hummed quietly to steady my nerves, the engine spewing water behind me as my boat coasted across the blue landscape.

What was a thirty-minute trip felt like only a few short moments, and when I saw the little sand bar coming into view, my heart leapt. Though I knew it couldn't bring Milo back, something about the island made me feel he was near. And I just needed to see it one more time.

I slowed the boat and maneuvered as best I could to get near the tiny shore before dropping anchor.

I hardly recognized this new daring, reckless version of me. But after diving headfirst into a storming whirlpool at sea, visiting this little island suddenly didn't seem so audacious. Barefoot and in the highest cropped shorts I owned, I waded across the sand bar, careful not to drop the backpack I carried full of paper and paint, just in case inspiration struck.

Once on the island, my eyes swept over the few pieces of trash and bottles still littered across the sand from the Halloween party. Even the charred remnants from the bonfire had survived untouched. As I relived the memory of walking past the dancing, boisterous crowd, I followed my footsteps to the edge of the quiet shore where I once encountered a pirate who changed everything—who showed me how to find my way back to myself when I felt lost at sea.

Standing in the same spot where we sat that fateful night, I dropped my backpack. It hit the sand with a thud, and I followed suit. My legs buckled beneath me as I folded onto my knees. With the late afternoon sun beating down on my shoulders, I sat in the silence, wishing for just one more moment with him, wishing the last time I'd seen him wasn't watching him be brutally tortured. I fixed my gaze on the water, as if somehow his ship might rise up again and bring him back to me.

I loved him. I had never said it out loud, but it was impossible to deny any longer. Something in me ached that I didn't realize it sooner—that I didn't get the chance to tell him.

But he had told me.

And as I sulked there, dreaming of him and all the things I never said, I could almost hear his voice whispering my name.

"Katrina."

Except...

"Katrina."

It wasn't in my head.

I really *could* hear his voice.

"Katrina."

It was...real.

I whipped around at the unmistakable sound of my name. And there he was, only steps from me, walking along the shoreline, skin tanned and hair tousled by the sea breeze. And very much alive.

"Milo?" I breathed his name like it was a word with the power to break me right then and there. As if I said it too loud, too sure, I might come undone.

I leapt my feet, my heart pounding with the rhythms of joy, hope, disbelief, and bewilderment all at once. Every moment I'd missed him. Every night I'd dreamed of him. And now, my breath hitched as he stood right in front of me. Not bleeding. Not beaten.

Perfect—just like the first night I saw him.

Was he real? Or was I going crazy? My chest tightened, and a tide of emotion rose within me, drowning me as I spoke his name once more. If I was going crazy, so be it.

He took a step toward me, closing the last bit of distance between us, and brushed aside a loose curl from my face. "I told you I'd find my way back to you."

I fell into his arms, ignoring the soreness in my body that no longer mattered.

He embraced me, lifting me off the ground and spinning me around as I clasped both arms around him.

And then our lips met in a tender kiss that stopped time. We breathed into each other, toppling to the ground. There in the sand, we entangled, clinging to each other as though either one of us might disappear again at any moment.

Milo pressed his mouth to mine, and I savored the sweet honey of his lips that I never thought I'd taste again. I stared up at him as I lied back in the sand, like he was the sun itself. The heat of his touches ignited each trace of my skin as he pulled me to him, running his hand along the back of my thigh as I slowly hitched it up around him. Every part of me craved every part of him.

And I never wanted to lose him again.

"How?" I gasped through joyful tears as we both rolled over. I laid my head on his chest to listen to his heart. "You have a heartbeat." I choked. "You're not hurt anymore. You're...you're alive. How?"

He curled a strong arm around me, stroking my hair as he spoke.

"You," he breathed, "The legend must be true—that a man who possesses a siren's heart can cheat death."

I shot him a quizzical look as those hazel eyes beamed back at me. And as his words took root in my mind, the realization crept upon me—I had given him my heart completely. He was alive because I loved him.

"Need me to prove it's all real again?" Milo nudged me, kissing my shoulder.

"You filthy pirate," I whispered smugly.

He turned further into me and kissed me again, deeper, and trailed his knuckles along my arm, circling in teasing strokes. I reached up gently, feeling the scruff of his jaw before cupping his face in my hands and pulling back slowly, a realization hitting me like a wave.

"Have you been here this whole time?"

"Yes." He nodded, then kissed me sweetly once more before continuing. "I woke up here, washed up and confused, to the first bright morning I'd seen in centuries. And I was beginning to worry I'd have to start swimming to find you."

I laughed softly. "You must be starving."

"Only for you," he teased, sliding a hand across my waist, just before his own stomach growled. "Though I will admit some food would be nice."

"I've got to get you a cinnamon chai latte," I smirked. "After you've had some real food of course. What do you want? Burgers, tacos, pizza, spaghetti? Take your pick."

"I wouldn't know where to start," he chuckled, scratching the back of his head. "You pick for me."

I grinned. "Burgers it is."

As the sun faded behind the skyline, we climbed into the boat, finally ready to leave our island behind. After I'd shared everything that'd happened on my end after breaking the curse, I offered Milo the helm and the chance to take us back, letting him teach me everything he could about sailing in the brief time we had before reaching the shore.

"She's certainly no galleon," Milo laughed patting the steering wheel. "But she needs a name, you know."

"You're right," I said. "I've been thinking of one."

"Oh? What is it?"

"*La Esperanza*." I smiled, joining him at the helm.

"I think that's perfect." He looked ahead, a grin on his face and something like a sparkle in his eyes. "Now, let's get these burgers you spoke of. Under full sail."

"Aye aye, Cap'n." I saluted and pecked him on the cheek as the boat sprung forward across the water now tinged with the fiery orange of burning embers as the sun sank low.

After we docked at the marina, Milo showed me how to tie a hitch knot and secured the boat before leaving. We walked together towards St. Constantine through the old city by the bay. We strolled unhurriedly, laughing as I told him about my favorite foods, about the charm of Sea Dogs café, and about the antique store where my paintings hung. I soaked in each carefree moment, liberated by the feeling that time was no longer a prison by which we were both bound. We had tonight, tomorrow, and every day ahead, with no curses or tides to separate us.

"I can't help but ask," I said, turning toward him as we leaned against the edge of the bridge, watching the last rays of sunlight disappear behind the bay. "What are you going to do with your second chance at life?"

"I don't know for sure yet." He paused. "But I'll give it a better shot than the last. Make a better mark on the world where I can. Or maybe I'll chase that horizon wherever it takes me—as long as it keeps leading me to you, starlight."

I leaned forward to kiss him once more.

"I never told you," I whispered, "*Te amo*. That means—"

He put a finger to my lips, hushing me with his soft smile. "I know what it means. But tell me anyway."

I smiled at him, the world in his eyes looking back at me. "I love you, Milo. Maybe it doesn't make sense, but I do."

"From what I've seen, love rarely makes sense," he said. "But the sea always does. And it brought me to you."

I turned to rest my head on his shoulder, and I listened as the bay lapped below us, a gentle song that called back to the very thing that had brought him to me—the ocean and all its secrets. It had drawn my heart, and it wouldn't let go. And I hoped that somehow, somewhere Elisabeth had found her peace even long after death.

To know someone had finally listened. Someone had finally redeemed the lost loves shattered by betrayal and revenge. Someone finally found her way back to the sea.

And I silently hoped that wherever Bellamy was now, that he was dancing with Serena in the waves. And that she was holding him close, the way I was holding onto Milo, putting each other's broken hearts back together with the promise of forever...

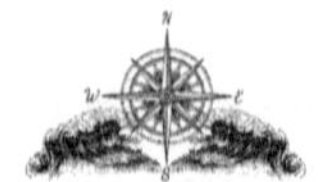

A shrill metal ringing snatched me from my thoughts.

The to-go burgers were ready.

Isabel was just around the corner, so I suggested we take our meal back to the South Lawn where we could make the most of the unseasonably warm evening and sprawl out beneath an oak in the grass. "I think a picnic on the beach would be a little overrated, don't you think?" I joked.

We hurried around the block to campus where we plopped down onto the lawn and I plucked a hot fry from my plate. I watched Milo bite into the juicy cheeseburger between his hands, and threw my head back in laughter as his eyes grew wider the longer he chewed. "This...this is delicious," he said with a mouthful.

"I knew you'd love it."

"I think after 300 years, anything would be delicious right now."

As another laugh slipped from my lips, a lilting voice chimed through the air like a bell.

"Oh my God! I thought you said he left!" McKenzie came trotting over, an envelope in one hand and a designer purse in the other. She stood over us and looked down, glancing between me and Milo. "I thought you had to leave, lover boy."

"So did I...but fate had other plans." His gaze shifted to me, and all at once heat pooled in my core, and my heart swelled full like the ocean.

"Hot *and* poetic." McKenzie winked as she handed me an elegant little envelope, addressed to me with only my name handwritten in cursive on the front. "Anyway, I came to give you this. I don't know what's with you and these random notes, but it was left in front of our dorm." She shook her head playfully as she turned to go.

"Where are you all dressed up to go?" I asked, noticing her sleek dress and styled hair. She just glanced over her shoulder with a bright-eyed, tight-lipped smirk. When she didn't answer, I filled in the blanks. "Noah?" I chuckled.

She bounded off without a response, and I couldn't help but smile, especially at the baffled look on Milo's face.

"You'll get used to McKenzie." I joked. "Don't be surprised if she wants to take a picture of us later."

Milo shrugged and took another bite of his burger, while I turned my attention to the letter in my hand.

I carefully peeled back the envelope seal. The texture was quality, smooth and thick. It seemed too luxurious to just rip open. I slid the letter out—a note, handwritten on equally fine paper in perfectly inked letters.

Dearest Katrina,

It was a privilege to purchase such a piece from such a gifted aspiring artist.
I'll be expecting more from you.

My thoughts flashed back to the lady from the gala with the piercing blue eyes. And then my breath stalled in my chest as I glanced at the bottom, recognizing the elegant handwriting right away.

"Milo," I whispered, holding the letter in front of him. "Look at the signature."

He squinted in the dark, then glanced at me in surprise as we read the name aloud in unison.

"Cordelia."

SOME HISTORY IS WORTH REPEATING
ON
TWISTING
TIDES
VAL E LANE

ON TWISTING TIDES
BOOK 2
VAL E. LANE

Wave Song Publishing

To those watching the horizon, waiting for their ship to come in.

Playlist

Scan the code or click to listen. Each song corresponds to the chapters in order, plus additional songs at the end. You can also search for the playlist on Spotify by book title.

1. "Do or Die (feat. Kinn)" by Neon Feather

2. "feel it all" by sød ven

3. "Shipwreck" by Otherwise Fine, Emily Rowed

4. "Man's World" by MARINA

5. "Sailor's Heart" by Zyke

6. "Belladonna" by Ava Max

7. "Begin Again" by Kobi McCull

8. "Set Sail" by Frances

9. "Oceans" by Seafret

10. "Hanging On By A Thread" by UNSECRET, SVRCINA

11. "Mariners Apartment Complex" by Lana Del Rey

12. "Woke Up A Rebel" by Reuben And The Dark

13. "Pressure" by Ivy Adara

14. "Castle" by World's First Cinema

15. "Conspiracy of Silence" by The Swoons

16. "You Don't Even Know Me" by Fauozia

17. "We Have It All" by Pim Stones

18. "Sins of our Fathers" by Nathan Wagner

19. "Work of Art" by Amber Ré

20. "Dark Paradise" by Lana Del Rey

21. "To Build A Home" by the Cinematic Orchestra, Patrick Watson

22. "Blue" by Rebecca Black

23. "Shipwrecks" by the Sweeplings

24. "Flesh and Bone" by Black Math

25. "Flooded" by KAINA

26. "Moth To A Flame – Acoustic Week Piano Mix" by We Rabbitz

44. "Soft to Be Strong" by MARINA

45. "never have i ever" by Casey Baer

46. "Ghost" by SVRCINA

47. "Brother" by Kodaline

Relive the past.

Learn the truth.

Find the Trident.

And don't get on the siren's bad side.

CLEAN SLATE

1

KATRINA

The nightscape blurred past us in streaks of midnight and indigo. Humid air rushed over me, dancing through the tangles in my hair as the bike sped through the streets. Even in winter, the evenings were mild. Sixty degrees was still plenty warm enough for a quick joy ride on New Year's Eve to watch the fireworks over the bay.

I clung tightly to Milo as he skillfully guided the motorcycle through the crowded roads, allowing us to dodge stopped traffic and blockades. Once we crossed the stone bridge over Matanzas Bay, he finally settled on a spot with a clear view of the glassy water below and the horizon into which it flowed. As he flipped out the kickstand with his foot, I pulled my helmet over my head and braced against his shoulder as I swung myself over to dismount.

It had been just over a month since I dove into the sea, breaking Milo's curse, and subsequently, mine. His ship and crew rested at the bottom of the ocean, along with the memories of the past, the darkness that had haunted us for so long, and the magic that started it all. Thankfully, my love for Milo had saved him. The legend says a mermaid—er—siren's heart could allow a man to cheat death. I'd technically given him my heart, I could admit to that part, but I still didn't like to think too hard about what else that implied. But ultimately, it didn't matter, I supposed. No more pirates. No more mermaids. We were free.

Milo removed his helmet with swiftness and shook his dark honey locks loose. His dark jeans and brown leather jacket offered a subtle nod to his past to my eyes only, but no one else would have ever guessed he'd been a literal pirate for 300 years.

"What do you think of this spot?" Luckily his accent wasn't going anywhere. It was something I never got tired of hearing. "We should be able to see them perfectly."

"I think I trust your navigational skills much more than my own," I uttered with a chuckle.

"Then here it is." He nodded, placing an arm around my shoulder as we turned to face the water.

A small chime in my pocket made us both glance down. I pulled out my phone and read the text from my dad out loud. *"Happy New Year from both of us."* Underneath the message was a grainy selfie with horrible lighting of both of my parents, smiling together. Even given the terrible quality, I couldn't help but smile at the photo, knowing Mom was finally going to achieve her New Year's Resolution of staying sober this time. She hadn't had a single slip-up since Thanksgiving, so I knew this time it was real. Out of habit, I reached up for my necklace, but was met with emptiness. Somehow, I kept forgetting I had tossed it into the ocean like a pebble.

Good pic of you two. Happy New Year! We are about to watch the fireworks.

I typed out my response quickly. I could tell by the rise in the voices of the crowd around us that the fireworks would be starting soon. Milo glanced over my shoulder at their picture.

"I still can't help but feel that your father thinks I'm an idiot," he groaned.

"I don't know why you're so paranoid about that," I laughed. "I thought it went great when you met them at Christmas." I thought back to their introduction, when I'd brought Milo back to Arkansas and he'd stayed with us for the holiday. My dad had taken to him right away when he found out Milo knew how to work on motorcycles. Mom was just happy to be back home and sober enough to enjoy the festivities.

We'd picked out a tree together, and my dad had given Milo a tour of his shop, where they both had spent hours talking about engines. We'd even gotten a light dusting of snow.

"You didn't hear some of the things he asked me. He wanted to know things like my plans for the future and what I intended to do with myself. I don't even know those answers myself yet. I couldn't tell him that I've spent the last 300 years on a ghost ship." Milo put his hands in his pockets, shifting from one foot to the other as he looked out toward the water.

"I'm sure he didn't think too hard about it. He likes you, really." I reassured into his ear, playfully grabbing his shoulder as the bustling crowd around us grew.

"Maybe he likes that I can hold a conversation about alternators, valve covers, push rods, clutches, piston bearings. But beyond that, I made a fool of myself to him." Milo glanced down at me, something in his hazel green eyes tugging at my depths.

"No, no. My dad trusts my judgment. And if I'm with you, he knows it's for a good reason. Don't be so hard on yourself. Just think of what you've got going for you at the shop with Noah. You're already building a life here." I smiled, thinking of Noah, which subsequently led to thoughts of McKenzie. My high-spirited roommate had been getting suspiciously close with Noah, who spent his time at his uncle's auto restoration shop when he wasn't working his weekend shift at the antique store. Thanks to McKenzie's persuasion skills, Noah had now found himself including Milo in his car restoration projects. Milo had even somehow convinced the shop into letting him take on a few clients just for motorcycles. It had been going well from what I knew.

"I'm doing the best I can." He nodded. "My father was such a great merchant and businessman. I hope I can continue his legacy. It might look different here, but I hope to find a way to make my way just as he did."

As the last word drifted from his lips, an explosion of colors lit up the night sky. Beside the moon, a burst of red and gold glittered in a thunderous rumble before cascading down to the watery surface below. More colors began to rain down in a symphony of snaps, pops, whistles and hisses. I stole a glance at Milo, who was watching them with intent wonder.

"I've seen these many times over the decades," he finally uttered, "But not like this. Not this close." He looked at me and then tenderly reached for my hand with his pinky finger, curling it around mine. "Not with cause for celebration until now."

As my eyes drifted over the scene of colors, I thought of my own palette of pigments waiting for me back at my dorm. Perhaps I could make an attempt at fireworks over the water for my next painting. Perhaps...

But then, I shook myself from the reverie. I'd promised to take a break from painting until the start of the spring semester. It seemed like a healthy idea, but my mind couldn't help but see the world through watercolors. So I shelved the idea for later. Naturally, my thoughts drifted to the note I'd been left with at the end of last semester. "I know I probably shouldn't bring this up now," I started, looking down. "But I went to Tesoro Del Mar again yesterday. I thought maybe Cordelia would have to be there for their New Year celebration or something."

"Oh?" Milo raised an eyebrow as he looked down at me through dark brown lashes. "Any luck?"

I shook my head. "No. Same as always. They said there is no Cordelia. I even showed them the letter. They just keep telling me it must be some mistake. It's so weird." I had to speak a bit louder than I would have liked over the sound of the fireworks.

"Very strange, indeed." Milo looked ahead at the fireworks, the gold, red, and white glows flashing across his handsome face.

"I mean, if she's alive after all this time, what does she want?" I grabbed the railing of the bridge in front of me, pressing my palms into the cold metal. "And why has she waited until now to reach out to me? Has she known about me this entire time?"

"I think we'd both like answers," Milo said. "Perhaps she'll contact you again. It's only been a month."

"I know," I sighed. "But it just drives me crazy. She didn't seem like the rational type."

"She wasn't." As Milo spoke, the hum of the fireworks began to die down. The crowd around us began shifting and dwindling as some people left their spots early in a hurry. "At least not once her heart was broken."

"Any chance it's healed by now?" I joked, though deep down I was serious, and I didn't like the answer I already knew.

We both turned away as the leftover smoke from the fireworks drifted across the night sky, creating a spooky smog over the dark water. Hand-in-hand and dodging throngs of families and couples, we made our way back to the motorcycle. The wind from the ocean was giving me a chill, so I closed my jacket tighter around myself as Milo started the engine. I knew he noticed when he looked me over up and down.

"Cold?" he grinned. "Hopefully holding onto me will warm you up."

I shook my head with a playful grin as heat flooded my face as I swung a leg over behind him. Gripping his shirt beneath his jacket, I clutched the fabric in my fingers and pushed my hands against his waist. With a snicker, he started off, and we headed back to Isabel School for the Arts. With my body pressed to his, I breathed in his scent. He still smelled of leather and amber, and no longer of salt. I remembered how I'd thought I'd lost him, but somehow, he was still here, and with him, I was home. And normally, I felt like together we could outrun anything as we'd done so many times astride this motorcycle. But tonight, as we left another year behind, I couldn't help but feel that the haunting of Cordelia was the one thing catching up to me. And it knew exactly where to find me.

1

MILO

The cool of the night might as well have been icy ocean waves splashing against my fingers as I drove the bike onward. Katrina's arms wrapped tightly around me fought away the chill. Even though I'd been free from my curse for a month, every sensation still felt like new. I'd almost forgotten the feel of the sticky night air, the taste of sweetness and bitter, and the feeling of a touch that could make my body flood with warmth and desire. In this strange new world, I had three centuries worth of feelings and experience to make up for, and I couldn't have been more grateful for it.

I managed the turns gently and kept our speed slow. I knew Katrina wouldn't let me know she was freezing, but by the way she was tensed and buried into my shoulders, I could tell she was fighting the wind. When we pulled to a stoplight, she lifted the face shield of her helmet and uttered something into my ear.

"On second thought, you don't have to take me back to my dorm. I'll stay with you tonight."

"You know you're always welcome," I tilted my head back toward her.

"I know. I just feel like I'm not ready to be back in the dorm. McKenzie still isn't back yet, so I don't want to be alone." She squeezed my core tighter.

"Whatever the reason, I'm never going to be opposed to spending the night with you," I reassured. My breath mixed with the heavy, wet air, and it reminded me how much I looked forward to showering and feeling clean—a sensation that brought comforts I'd long forgotten.

When the light turned green, I gave the throttle a nudge, and we lurched forward on the motorbike. The way Katrina gripped me as she steadied herself made me warm. I longed to reach the apartment so that I could return the favor. Noah's family was kind enough to offer me the room above the restoration shop in return for my apprenticeship with them. I couldn't have asked for a better start to my second life.

I parked the motorcycle in the garage, double-checking the locks and securing the alarm system, which still fascinated me, before heading upstairs to my apartment loft. Katrina followed, using her phone to light up the darkness as we managed the metal steps. I still needed to get one of those for myself. But it wasn't exactly as though I had anyone to call or who needed to call me.

Taking her hand, I turned on the light to awaken my quaint living quarters. To me, it was a palace. Framed by the sloping roof, industrial lights hung from the ceiling. A small television hung on the wall opposite the bed, while a small kitchen counter wrapped the corner, parallel to a square table and chair set just big enough for two. One would hardly expect a former pirate now dwelled here, perhaps except for the compass hanging from the metal bed frame. A token I'd found had somehow survived in my pocket when I awoke on Katrina's island.

"You've got to get some more chairs in here," Katrina teased, placing her helmet on the kitchen table next to mine. "I've still got some money left over from the painting. We could buy some more."

"As if I'm one for inviting guests over for get-togethers?" I chuckled at the thought.

"Well, maybe not, but there's plenty of time to bring out your extroverted side." She walked over to me, crinkling her nose mischievously. "But on second thought, maybe not."

"Well, if I'm going to be adding anything to this place, it would be a swinging hammock. Now that I've made up for 291 years of lost sleep, my body can't seem to adjust on this flat mattress."

"You still want to sleep like a sailor?" Katrina raised a skeptical brow at me.

"Aye." I winked, pecking her on the cheek as I walked past her toward the small bathroom that adjoined the room in the center. "But I don't want to smell like one."

Without another word, I tossed my jacket onto my bed and pulled my shirt over my head. I'd yet to find anything more comfortable than V-neck cotton T-shirts. As I crossed the threshold to the bathroom, a gentle hand stopped me. Katrina's delicate fingers gently pulled me back by my bare shoulder, tugging me towards her. I turned to face her without hesitation.

"What if I like it when you smell like the sea?" She smiled, drawing into me, and placed her head in the space between my chest and chin.

I grinned, traces of my hair falling into my eyes as I looked down at her. "Then I suppose I'll have to start bathing in the ocean."

When she looked at me like that, it was as though time stood at a standstill in her eyes. The deepest trenches of the ocean knew no depth of peace like those dark brown pools of molten mahogany. Like smoking coals just before turning to diamonds, they burned into me, and yet soothed me all the same. Her hand remained still on my shoulder, and the other one firmly planted on my waist. As the moment commanded me, I embraced her more, pulling her small frame snug against my body and meeting her lips with mine. She stepped backward, taking me with her.

"You know better than to take your shirt off in front of me." She giggled softly under her breath. My thoughts flashed back to the first night I'd kissed her, when I'd pressed my bare skin to hers against the lighthouse. When I'd caressed every inch of her for fear it would be the only time I ever could. But now, my only fear was that she'd wake up one day and realize she was worthy of so much more than someone like me.

She deepened our kiss, dancing in my mouth with hers. My blood ran hot, and I couldn't help but swell with desire as I pushed against her gently. She didn't realize what she was doing to me. I lived in a constant state of craving her more and more with each passing day. And she was feeding the ravenous inner beast with the heat of her body against mine.

I slid my hand beneath her sundress. I traced her hips and the beautiful shape of her spine. She ran her fingers through my hair, pushing it back out of my eyes and tracing the scar across my eyebrow like she so often did. I needed her.

Another moment and our bodies had found the edge of the bed. Her muscles tensed against me as she lowered herself down onto it, as if falling gently. I brought my hand behind her shoulders, supporting her as I leaned over her. I breathed in her sweet scent of apricot blossoms and honeysuckle mixed with the midnight air. I wanted to taste more of her. I wanted to show her all the ways I could love her.

The kindling flame coursing through my body grew to a wildfire as I slowly unzipped the back of her sundress. I kissed her up and down, the taste of her salty, flowery skin tingled on my tongue. She circled the skin just above my belt with her fingertips, sending me rigid. With both hands, she reached for my belt; then slid her hands upward along the skin of my heaving chest with a gentle brace.

"Wait." I barely made out her weak whisper. "I'm sorry."

I pulled away, fighting the desire that I'd been working so hard to suppress these past few weeks. I imagined kissing her again and making her change her mind and lose control just as much as I wished I could. "Don't say sorry," I muttered, keeping my tone as gentle as I could. "You said 'wait.' And that's all right." I took a deep breath, then forced it back out through my lips to help settle myself. Katrina sat up, holding the top of her dress close to her chest with a worried expression. Her shining dark eyes settled on me in a wave of guilt.

"It's stupid. I know I love you. And I know you love me..." She sighed softly. "But I've seen the way my dad stayed by my mom, even when she was at her worst. It was so bad for him...But he stayed no matter what. Even when it was destroying his life. What if I do that to you?"

"You won't, Katrina. It was the curse..."

"What if it wasn't? What if it just really is who we are—who *I* am? After all, I have Cordelia's blood." She paused to swallow down the emotions she was trying to hide. "I don't want to fear forever with you. I don't know what I'm capable of, and it scares me."

"You're not Cordelia. And you won't destroy my life," I said, adjusting my jeans. "You've made my life feel worth living. Without you, this would all feel meaningless."

She put her hand to her forehead and groaned. "I don't know. It's stupid. I'm sorry."

Before she could say more, I knelt down beside her, taking her free hand in mine. "Katrina," I locked my gaze with hers. "I've waited three centuries just to find you. If there's anything I think I've mastered, it's patience. I love you, no matter what you need from me today, tomorrow, or forever."

I leaned in to kiss her, and she gently brushed my lips with hers. She always reprimanded herself like this. As if she didn't trust herself. She feared her own desires, and she was held captive by the eerie hold Cordelia had on her. I wished I could make her understand that though I wanted her more than anything, I would never compromise her or make light of what she felt. But I desperately wished I could set her free from herself.

I kissed her forehead without another word before walking away to the shower. Once the door was closed behind me, I rubbed my thumb along my jaw, feeling the steely facial hair as I tried to will the remaining lustful yearning in my veins to die down. All it took was one look in the mirror.

The rugged man staring back at me was tall and well-muscled, with dark ink decorating his arms and chest. A man who, even in this new era, looked all too much like his father. My flesh was still flush from the moment, and my dark golden hair had grown a touch longer in this first month of this second life. A life that, though I was grateful for, I knew I didn't deserve. A life that Bellamy had lost. It hardly seemed fair. And I couldn't make sense of it. We'd both had difficult lives dealt to us, but his—his was cruel. Yet I was the one granted another. No matter how strong my efforts to reassure myself were, I couldn't rid myself of the feeling that it should have been him.

ADRIFT

3

I watched him disappear behind the door. The way he'd touched me had left me breathless. I wanted him. All of him. But wanting him wasn't enough to overpower the worry that I'd somehow lose him again. I don't know why, but something still wouldn't let me believe all this was real.

But this all was clearly real. And I couldn't deny everything that had happened to me—to us. Even the parts I didn't want to be real. Like the strange vision I'd had at the bottom of the ocean after jumping into the maelstrom. Everything was real, but just because my mind believed it didn't mean my heart could accept it. But I did know that I loved him. Fiercely. Shouldn't that be enough?

It *was* enough. And I wanted to let him know. Standing up, I slipped out of the rest of my dress, letting it crumple to the floor and turned my feet to the bathroom door where the faint rushing sound of the shower beckoned me from the other side. But just as soon as I'd taken a step, I hesitated, feeling a strange sense of paranoia creeping in. I glanced around the room, without even knowing what I might be expecting to see.

"What is wrong with me?" I muttered out loud. I truly hadn't recovered from the sense that someone was watching me. And knowing Cordelia knew how and where to contact me had made me all the more bothered. But I felt it was beginning to get out of hand. After all, what could she possibly do to me? What could she *want* to do to me?

Just then, my eyes wandered to Milo's jacket that he'd tossed onto the bed. I caught a glimpse of a white edge peeking out—a piece of paper. I lifted the jacket, revealing a small envelope. It was addressed to me, handwritten, but the envelope was stamped with a seal of Tesoro Del Mar Club and Marina. I knew the seashell insignia all too well from all the research I'd done on the place, desperately looking for any trace of Cordelia. I quickly threw on one of Milo's clean T-shirts and a pair of leggings I'd left there previously, and then reached for the letter.

My fingers traced the envelope flap with careful movements as I sat back down on the bed. I stared down at the paper in my lap, a torrent of thoughts whirling in my mind. It was difficult to decide if I should open it yet. I'd been yearning for this clue for weeks, but now the joy of finding it was replaced with the pang of betrayal. Why did Milo have this letter? And why hadn't he mentioned it beforehand when I brought up Cordelia?

When the sound of shower water stopped, my eyes shot upward toward the bathroom door. For a brief second, I considered sneaking the envelope away, and not telling Milo I had found it. But I decided that secrets almost always do more harm than good. So I held it, turning it over in my hands nervously as I waited for him to emerge.

Steam filled the small loft as the bathroom door opened and he stepped out in boxers and a new plain white T-shirt. If I hadn't been wrangling my confusion and sudden feelings of betrayal, I wouldn't have been able to tear my gaze away from his solid, well-formed build. But instead, I looked at him, then dropped my focus down to the white rectangle in my hands. I was going to ask him what it was. But I could tell he understood me clearly without me having to say a single word.

"You found it," he said, shifting uncomfortably as he put his hand behind his neck.

"I did." I confirmed, locking my eyes with his. "Where did you get this? It's addressed to me."

"I—It was on your door when I picked you up from your dorm this morning. I was going to tell you. I swear I was, but..."

"But what?"

"But I wasn't sure yet. I wanted to make sure it wasn't something that would put you in danger."

"Danger?" I stood up, trying to keep my shaky voice even, despite the fact that a tide of emotion was welling up within me. "This is about keeping me safe?"

"Yes." Milo looked away, scratching his head and ruffling his wet hair. "I mean no. I mean—Yes, of course I want to keep you safe. I wasn't intending to keep that from you. But I know Cordelia, and I wanted to see what game she's playing now before I let her get to you. Think about everything she's done."

"So you thought you'd just take it home and read it without me? Then you'd decide if I could handle it?" My voice cracked.

"No, not exactly…" Milo grimaced, turning his head as though trying to shake off something. "I don't know what I planned to do. It was just my first reaction. My first reaction is always to protect you." He paced the floor as he spoke, his words coming faster with each thought, until finally, he stopped and looked back at me. "I should've told you about it immediately…and…and I'm sorry."

I wanted to be angry with him. And I was. But I also remembered what happened the last time I didn't trust him and jumped to conclusions. When I thought he'd murdered an innocent girl, and the truth couldn't have been further. But still, this was different.

"You don't need to protect me," I finally said. "Especially if it means lying to me or keeping things from me. Haven't we been through enough for you to realize sometimes I have to fight my own battles?"

"I know, I know," he sighed, sitting down next to me on the bed. "I'm just a bit worried that tracking down Cordelia hasn't been good for you. You're nervous all the time. You can't stop talking about it. You want to find her so badly. And I understand. But if I'm being honest, I'm a little afraid of what will happen if you find her."

"Just because you're afraid for me, doesn't mean you can keep things from me like this." I glanced down at the envelope.

"I was going to tell you…" He looked down, his damp hair falling across his forehead. "I just didn't know how or when. I panicked."

"If it was on *my* door, it wasn't for you to decide," I uttered.

"I'm sorry, Katrina. I acknowledge that I didn't handle this correctly. I promise I won't be so foolish next time." He leaned toward me, desperation in his voice.

A long sigh escaped my lips, as I pressed my gaze into his. "Weren't you the one who told me 'You probably shouldn't make promises you can't keep?'"

He blinked in response and looked down at his hands.

"I'm trying to undo a lifetime of lying, cheating, and deceit. And I'm sorry that I've already faltered with the one I care about most." He paused, staring directly past me at the compass hanging from the bed frame. "I always admired the way my father loved my mother, but it was such a different time. He was able to protect her from everything but the complications that took her. She died while pregnant with my brother. I wasn't there, but I know he would've saved her if he could." He paused, blinking as if in thought. "How do you love someone and let them risk themselves at the same time?"

"You trust them," I said firmly, "Now it's your turn to trust me. Trust that I know what I'm doing. I solved Cordelia's curse. I can handle whatever else she thinks she can do to me." I spoke with confidence in my voice, but inwardly I was still trying to convince myself as much as him.

There was an awkward silence between us. I didn't know what else to say. I still felt flustered by his decision to take the letter that was meant for me. But my desire to know what the envelope contained overpowered my twisting emotions.

"Let's just open this thing," I said, tearing the paper. "No sense worrying about it when we don't even know what it says."

My desperate eyes scanned the letter, absorbing every word.

Dearest Katrina,

I hope you've enjoyed the holidays. Now that my schedule has freed up a bit, I'd love to meet with you. I have a very special commission of high importance that I'm certain is only suitable for someone with your abilities. I'm inviting you to my private business dinner at the Tesoro Del Mar so that we can discuss the details. The time and place are below. Formal dress. I look forward to meeting you in person.

-Cordelia

"Seven o'clock, January 3rd," I uttered, reading the details below the message. "I wonder if this invitation is good for two?" I looked up at Milo.

He tilted his head, making his hair fall in front of his eyes in a way that never failed to make me melt, regardless of what else I was feeling. "You want me there?"

"I do," I said inching closer to him. "I always do."

He kissed my forehead. "I'll be by your side whenever you need me."

"That's all I need." I sighed, resting my head against his shoulder. The sound of fireworks outside continued, muffled through the walls.

"Want to go watch some more? I bet we can still see the amateur fireworks on the beach from the top," I said.

"You go ahead," he whispered. "I'm feeling a bit tired."

"You? Tired?" I raised my eyebrows and stood back with crossed arms.

"I'm making up for 300 years of no sleep." He laughed, but something about his voice sounded lifeless, as though the air could barely carry it to my ears without it slipping away.

"Okay," I sighed. "Then I'll see you tomorrow." Just as I took the first step upward toward the roof of the loft, I hesitated, looking back at Milo, who had sat down wearily on his bed. "Is everything okay?"

He nodded before lying down to close his eyes, but it wasn't convincing for me. "Shipshape."

As I walked upstairs, I clutched the railing. I suddenly realized I didn't want to watch the fireworks. But I knew that even though I wanted to close my eyes and forget about everything for a while, there was no way I could sleep right now. Though I didn't want to let Milo know it, I was terrified of what Cordelia wanted with me.

An Ill Wind That Blows No Good

4

KATRINA

I can't wait to see you!

I read the text from McKenzie with tired eyes as I fought with my unruly hair in a sad attempt to secure it with Bobby pins. If she were here, this would've been so much easier. She would've had my hair in the perfect, elegant updo in no time. But left to my own devices, I wasn't capable of creating quite the same masterpiece. But it would have to do. I wanted to look my best when I met with Cordelia this evening. I needed her to take me seriously.

Milo stepped into the dorm behind me, reminding me of the night he appeared at the gala, in his slacks and suit jacket, and his dark gold locks tucked back within a secure tie.

"You look handsome," I said with a smirk. "Think we look like we belong at an elite ocean club dinner?" I ran my gaze up and down my reflection, standing in my teal blue cocktail dress, wishing I still had the mermaid scale around my neck to add a dash of sparkle.

"I hope so because this is the most polished I'll ever look." Milo's mouth curved into a small smile. Despite his attempt at humor, I'd noticed his dampened energy and his shortness of words lately. Something about him seemed off ever since our conversation about the hidden letter two nights ago, but he relentlessly swore he was fine.

"Well, it's 6:30," I pointed out. "We'd better get to the resort."

"Agreed." Milo nodded, and together we made our way to my Jeep. The Cherokee was still running strong as ever, even if I never could manage to keep the sand-filled floorboards clean. I'd accepted it now as just a normal part of Florida life.

The resort club wasn't far, just on the border of Constantine and St. Augustine, and a chill ran through me just like it did every time I came here looking for Cordelia. To think that all this time, she was just a mere handful of miles away, made me wiggle with unease like a worm on a hook.

Clutching the invitation in my hand as though my life depended on it, I stepped out of my vehicle as Milo held the door for me. We walked down the ramp to the entrance together, my heels clomping on the narrow wooden boardwalk that led straight into the vicinity of the enormous white beachside building. I read the large sign carved in stone on the front gate entrance where the boardwalk ended, and the walkway became a pristine sidewalk leading to the doorway of a grand two-story resort and marina. Yachts of luxurious sizes lined the borders of the building around the back, bobbing calmly in the water of the Matanzas inlet.

Tesoro Del Mar. Treasure of the Sea.

This gate that was normally closed and required me to identify myself when I'd come looking here was now wide open, hosting a pathway leading to the front door of the marina resort. Strangely enough, I didn't see any other guests arriving. The parking lot had only been a few cars shy of being empty.

Milo squeezed my arm and I glanced at him with tightened brows. The churning in my chest wasn't stilling, but I was so desperate to finally meet this woman who had plagued both sea and land for centuries. I had written down the names of all my ancestors who'd fallen to her curse. I hoped they'd help me remember why I *had* to confront her.

"I don't have a good feeling about this," Milo said, his bicep tensing against my arm that was hooked through his.

"Where is everyone? It's six-fifty. We're not exactly early. Maybe I read the invitation wrong?"

"No, you read it correctly. Your reservation is at seven, not six-fifty." A withered voice startled both of us.

A man who looked to be in his sixties appeared from behind us, dressed in a tailored light gray suit. His thinning silver hair and wire glasses hooked over his wide nose made him look wise, but he spoke with sharpness.

"Ms. Black will be here in a few minutes. And she requested your presence. Not his." He turned to glance at Milo with narrowed eyes.

"Ms. Black?" I repeated, ignoring everything after that.

"Yes." the man nodded. "The owner. Dahlia Black."

"But she—"

"Do you want to meet her or not?" He asked before I could finish.

"Yes…" I calmed myself and ensured it showed in my voice. "Yes. I want to meet her."

"Then wait here." The man replied in one short breath. "Alone."

With a worried glance, my eyes found Milo's and he pressed his lips together with concern as the man turned to walk away.

"I'm worried about leaving you," Milo whispered.

"I know, but what choice do we have? I have to meet this 'Ms. Black.'"

"I understand this is important to you. I do. So for you, I'll stay behind." He glanced toward the resort door through which the man had walked a few seconds earlier. "But be careful. I'll be close by in case anything goes wrong."

"If I'm not out in a half hour, come check on me." My nerves were rioting as the suspense hung in the air. I watched Milo leave, praying I wouldn't need him. I didn't exactly know what he meant by "close by," but I trusted he knew where to be.

Minutes ticked by like decades. I glimpsed down at my phone to check the time. 6:59. I tapped the heel of my open-toed pumps and bit my lip. At the exact stroke of seven PM, I heard a click as the resort door behind me slowly opened. It was the old man from before who poked his head through the opening, letting out a draft of cold air-conditioned wind.

"Ms. Black will see you now."

Without a word, I nodded with the slightest tilt of my head and stepped forward into the building.

It was a venue, set up for what looked like a grand convention or wedding, with round tables draped with fine royal blue linens and empty champagne glasses placed around elegant place settings. Elegant orb lights hung above from coiling metal chandelier-like settings, each reminding me of a menacing octopus clutching a pearl. But it was desolate, devoid of any human presence.

Soft piano music played faintly in the background from a source I couldn't identify. I turned to look at the man who'd guided me here. When he noticed my confusion, he only gestured with his hand, pointing to the far end of the room. I squinted as I looked again, focusing on one particular table in the distance. There she sat. A woman, with her back to me.

I swallowed and did my best to keep my breathing slow and steady. The walk across the room felt like it would never end. As I approached, I noted her raven hair pinned up in an elegant fashion, with just enough left over to hang over her shoulder, and I immediately recognized it as the same style she wore at the art gala.

As I stood only steps from her, I expected her to turn around, but she never moved.

"Have a seat, please." Her voice almost made me jump, but I held my composure. The sound of her words still rolled over me like a graceful lullaby. It was like a sweet warm glaze, and I felt like a fly in a honey trap.

"Of course," I said, fighting the quiver in my voice. I pulled out the chair across from her, and sat down, smoothing my dress as I settled. I still hadn't looked her in the face yet.

"Katrina."

With an upward glance, I saw her, and her crystal blue eyes caught me. She looked younger than my mother, but older than me. Dressed in a costly dark grey dress and midnight blue blazer, she radiated sophistication. Her flawless skin seemed to glow beneath the rosy blush on her cheeks. With a wickedly beautiful smile, she spoke again. "Katrina Delmar. How nice to finally meet you in the flesh."

I tipped my head at her, still processing the place settings in front of me. A plate of decadent seasoned fish taunted my tastebuds as the scent reached my nostrils. Both my champagne glass and water glass were full. I reached for the water, desperate to hydrate my dry throat before speaking.

"It's...nice to meet you, too," I said in my most confident tone. "He called you Ms. Black?"

"Ah yes," she breathed, picking up her champagne glass. "Most people here know me as Dahlia Black. Cordelia was getting a bit outdated. Though I'm sure that's no problem for you, seeing as you have such a penchant for things of the past."

I forced a dry laugh out of politeness, surprised at her statement. It almost seemed like an insult, but she'd said it so beautifully.

"Don't worry, angelfish. I know you know who I am," she uttered with her lips millimeters from the champagne glass' rim. "You don't have to keep pretending."

"You're Cordelia." I spoke lowly, even though we were completely alone in the room. "Why did you ask me here? And how are you still alive?"

"Because I'm in need of something only someone with your...talents...can accomplish." She cut a small slice of the fish on her plate while she spoke, not answering my last question. "Besides, can you blame me for wanting to meet my own 7th great granddaughter?"

I shook off the eerie feeling I got from her last sentence. "My talents? What do you need exactly?"

Ignoring my question, she simply laughed softly in that melodic voice and guided the fork to her mouth. "Don't let your plate get cold, dear. That's the finest bluefin tuna."

Without knowing how to respond, I glanced down and forced myself to take a bite. It was delicious; the best seafood I'd ever tasted, in fact. But my nervous stomach wouldn't allow me to enjoy it.

Cordelia's words struck me suddenly. "I know you broke my curse."

I swallowed the last bit of tuna in my mouth as I looked up. "It had to be broken eventually," I said.

"I might've disagreed with you some years ago." She dabbed her mouth with a napkin, looking up at me through sharp, perfect brows. "But now I'll admit you're right. At some point eventually that curse was bound to become a waste of power. It had to be broken so that I could use the scale's magic for..." She paused, taking in a deep breath as she looked up at the chandelier before finishing her sentence, "...better things."

"Like what?" I asked

"Look at the world, dear. What do you see? Wars, diseases, destruction, greed. Things are getting out of balance. The world of men is collapsing in on itself."

"Yes, the world sucks. But that's nothing new." I set my fork down. "What about it?"

"You ask how I'm still alive? It's because our kind were given a much longer lifespan than mortals. Hundreds of years. Because we don't possess souls. When we finally die, we simply turn to seafoam."

I shifted in my seat, unsettled at her words, though I didn't know how much of them to believe.

"Katrina, the sea is angry. *We* are the sea, you and I. And mankind has taken too much from it. First it was the mermaids, soon it'll be everything else."

"With all due respect, didn't you help Valdez hunt the other mermaids?"

Cordelia slammed her hands down on the table, rattling her silverware. Her eyes became piercing shards of ice beneath dark brows before I could even regret what I had just dared to say.

"Don't say his name!" She spat the words out like arrows fired from a bow. "He tricked me. He *used* me to get to them. And not a day goes by that I don't regret it. I was just a foolish, curious mermaid who broke the laws of the sea by falling in love. And you dared to set him free from his prison."

I was speechless. I couldn't fathom what I could possibly say as she denied her own part to play in the demise of her kind. She watched me with her jaw tensed and her pointed fingernails digging into the table linen. I nearly jumped when she stood up without warning. With a menacing swagger, she moved toward me, walking around my chair and standing behind me.

"Which brings me back to why I need that scale. That last bit of my magic was being used to hold the curse. But now that it's broken, I have something much better in mind."

"What are you saying?" My voice cracked.

"I'm saying, it's not just about James anymore." Her words slithered out like shadows. "Mankind. Men. Man is destroying this world. And the sea groans because she knows she can stop it. If we would just let her. Think of it like a reset, if you will." She leaned over and placed her hands on my shoulders. I recoiled at an ice-cold touch I didn't expect. "You see, we mermaids—sirens—draw our power from a source as ancient as the moon and tides themselves. But we have limits. Within the sea there is a power even greater. One that can release the tides from their bonds so that the sea can unleash her vengeance on mankind."

"You want to flood the world?"

"Clever girl. This deplorable world is in need of a bit of a restructuring, don't you think?"

"No," I gasped. "No. I mean, yes, there is a lot wrong with the world. But you can't wipe out humankind."

"Katrina, you're not understanding. You can't think clearly because you, too, have fallen into the trap of man." She reached down and placed her hand over my chest. "I can feel it. Your naïve little heart beats for one." I wanted to free myself from her grip, but something held me frozen in place as she seemed to read my heartbeat before continuing. "Milo Harrington...hmm. I remember him. Always the guilty one. Always longing to be the hero. But I see through his façade. They are never what they claim to be. They are all selfish, greedy, and manipulative. He'll use you like James used me."

"No, he's done everything for me," I said. "I'm sorry Valdez hurt you, but you've let your pain turn you into someone just as bad as him."

Her grip on me tightened. Those nails dug into my shoulders, cutting into my skin as she put her lips to my ear.

"That's no way to speak to your great-grandmother." Her words bit like steel. I fought against her hold, trying to stand up, but she began to hum, and I somehow lost the ability to fully control my body. But I recognized the tune, and it sent shivers through my soul.

"Stop singing my mom's lullaby."

"Your mom's lullaby?" She laughed, still gently humming her siren song. "Angelfish, where do you think it came from?"

I swallowed, processing everything she'd said thus far. About Milo. About Mom. About me. Then she went on, adding to my mental burden.

"There's a trident deep in the ocean. An oracle of power thought to have been left behind by the gods. Resting beneath the place the humans call the Bermuda Triangle, its power has been unconfined for centuries. It would be the thing responsible for all those unexplained disappearances and souls lost at sea."

"What does this have to do with me?" I struggled against her hold.

"Sirens come from the same source of power. So only a siren could wield the trident for herself. But to do that, a siren must sacrifice a piece of herself—something more precious to her than anything—in the trident's hold. But sirens are selfish. They're nearly incapable of giving up the thing that means the most to them. That's why we aren't supposed to fall in love. Because it taints our nature... Hmm, I guess that was Poseidon's funny little way of keeping things in check." She drew in a breath, hesitating before going on. "But I... I no longer have anything left to be selfish over. Nothing but a wretched scale with the last bit of my magic. So, I'll be needing it back, angelfish."

She held out her hand slowly in front of me. I could move now, but I no longer wanted to run. I needed to finish this conversation. I had to know exactly what she was planning.

"I...I don't have it."

"Where is it then?" Her voice hardened.

"Somewhere at the bottom of the ocean. I thought offering it to the maelstrom was the way to break the curse. I threw it in the sea before I realized it wasn't the answer."

"You did what?" She released me, her voice rising.

"How can you be angry with me? You caused all of this."

She stepped back, holding her stern gaze on me, clenching her fists. "I was shown the cruelty of man without restraint. I've watched mankind destroy this earth, but he has never been able to tame the sea, try as he might. And it's time the sea washes away these sins once and for all."

"You're playing God," I swallowed, letting the seriousness of her words sink to my stomach.

"I'm no longer playing, dear." She grinned. "And I want you to join the game. Help me do this. Help me get the trident once we find the scale. You're the only one of us who can reach it. We'll rebuild this world together. You can help me decide who is worthy to survive."

"Like you decided my mom and her mom weren't worthy to survive? Like how you plagued them? What about Marina? Whatever happened to her?" I slapped down the list of names I'd brought onto the table, each with their death years written plainly beside them. "You killed every single one of them with your curse. You tortured us with dreams, Cordelia. Until the torture became too much for them to bear. You are in absolutely no position to judge mankind."

Cordelia's eyes scanned the names in a split second of silence.

Lydia Gatlin - 2003

Nelda Gatlin Harrows - 1971

Esther Graves - 1952

Alma Whitlock - 1922

Edith Barnes- 1900

Martha James Shores - 1874

Sarah Shores - 1840

Marina Samuels - 1819

For a moment she seemed speechless, her lip quivering before she hardened her features again. "I did what I had to do to ensure justice was executed to those who deserved it. Sometimes justice requires sacrifice. Besides, if I hadn't, you all might've lived a few hundred years too long, and that would've attracted a bit too much attention, don't you think?"

"You let your entire family suffer just so you could get even with your ex-lover."

"He emptied the sea of my kind!" she cried.

"And you helped him do it!" I screamed. "And your guilt has consumed you. But you won't admit to that part!"

She didn't respond, only held her position, drilling into me with her gaze.

"Cordelia," I uttered. "Destroying half of mankind isn't going to bring the mermaids back. I'm not helping you do this."

"Suit yourself, angel." She stepped backward. "But whether you help me or not, I *will* get what I need. I've spent my time on land wisely. I have many connections. I've built my own empire already. I'll find the scale. And then the trident. I may have lost my tail, but I still have power. In many forms." She rubbed her fingers together, signifying her strength in wealth.

I couldn't find the words to say, so I only sat, shaking my head in disbelief while staring into her topaz eyes.

"Go on, Katrina. Refuse me." She nodded towards the door. "Go back to the man waiting outside for you. Perhaps once you see how filthy his soul really is, you'll reconsider my offer. But in the meantime, I won't wait for you. You'll see that I'm right. You may think you're upholding some sort of moral righteousness, but just remember at the end of it all, you're just as soulless as me."

MILO

I watched the harbor, looking out at the great yachts docked there as the last bit of the fiery orange from the sunset bled out from the water's surface. Two more minutes and it would be a full hour. I couldn't stand it anymore. Not when I knew who Katrina was up against. Alone.

Cordelia was cold. She was manipulative and could demand anything she wanted with a simple melody from that voice of hers. But she never forced Valdez to love her. She would never have accepted a false love. I suppose that was her one redeeming feature, though it probably would've saved us all a lot of heartache if she did.

The longer I resurrected my memories of her conniving, dangerous nature, the more impatient I grew. I didn't know what she could do after all this time. Or what she *would* do. And if Katrina didn't return in one more minute...

Fifty-nine, fifty-eight, fifty-seven...

I turned to walk toward the entrance. I had to make sure she was safe. I'd probably already waited too long. With steps forceful and quick, I trudged through the gate entrance where we'd come earlier.

Just before I reached the door, it opened slowly, revealing my Katrina, standing in silence, staring straight ahead, her usually tanned, flushed skin pale as I'd ever seen it. I hurried to her. "Are you alright? Did she hurt you?" I swung a protective arm across her shoulder and guided her forward.

"She..." The words barely crept from her lips like a whisper before she shook her head. "Not here. Let's go home first. To my dorm."

"Where is she?" I glanced around, looking for any sign of the siren within the building she'd just exited. But there was no one. Not even the undertaker of an old man who'd greeted us.

"It doesn't matter."

"It does. Katrina I—"

"Let's just go home. Please." Her voice rose as she looked up at me with desperate eyes.

I nodded, forcing myself to take a breath. "Okay."

The ride back to her dorm lacked a single word from either of us. Once there, without even bothering to change out of her dress, she slumped to the floor, her head and shoulders hanging low in a defeated position.

I followed her, taking a seat across from her on her rug. "What happened?" I asked as gently as I could.

"Cordelia..." She hugged herself, leaning forward and staring at a spot in the floor. "She knows I broke her curse. She wanted the scale back." When she stopped and looked at me, I nodded for her to go on. "And when I told her I didn't have it, she said she's going to find it. She said she's going to use a trident to flood the earth."

I shifted and pressed my lips together, trying to soften my reaction. "She wants the trident."

"So it's real?" Her brows tensed.

"It's a legend. But if it's real, it's meant to be somewhere impossible to reach. Otherwise, I'd imagine it would've been found by now. After all these centuries."

Katrina took a piece of her hair and began twirling it between her fingers. "She said it's beneath the Bermuda Triangle. And that it requires a sacrifice to use. That's why she wants the scale. She's going to exchange her power for the trident's."

"And she thinks a simple scale would suffice? That hardly seems like a sacrifice to me."

"But think about it." She gestured with an open hand. "That scale is all she has. It's her last bit of magic. What else does she care about in this world?"

I tilted my head in acknowledgement. It was certainly a perspective I hadn't considered. I brushed a stray hair from my forehead with my thumb and noticed Katrina's focus settle on me. Her gaze deepened as she spoke with a somberness in her voice I hadn't expected.

"Milo, do you think Cordelia will find the scale?"

I willed the muscles in my face to remain expressionless. I couldn't let my concern show. But Katrina had to know what she was up against.

"I know she will," I uttered. "It's only a matter of when."

With a weak shake of her head, Katrina stood to her feet. "Then I guess we have to find it first. We'll go out tomorrow morning and start looking."

I could think of nothing more to say. She was right. So I stood up, too, and took a small step toward her.

"Aye aye, Captain." She turned away, trying to hide the small smile I knew was there. If she only knew how I'd follow her to the depths of the ocean if she asked.

"I'll see you in the morning at the docks." She closed the space between us and kissed me lightly on the cheek. I knew she wouldn't ask me to stay with her. She hadn't since the day she'd found Cordelia's note. And I couldn't blame her. I turned to go.

"I—" As I reached for the doorknob, I looked back over my shoulder. Frail fragments of a word barely escaped my lips before I stopped myself. Instead, the only thing I managed was, "Goodnight, Katrina."

MISS THE BOAT

6

KATRINA

I couldn't sleep that night, so when my alarm went off at 5:45, it was no challenge to get up and face the day. The only thing lingering on my mind was finding that scale, no matter how overwhelmingly daunting it seemed. I didn't even know where to start. But I knew starting was my only option.

Cordelia had taken so much from my family and left so much damage in her wake. The curses she left behind had more than proven her ruthlessness, but if I needed any further confirmation, the meeting with her had done the job. And I was sure I couldn't let any more power fall into her hands.

I pulled on my swim leggings, merino sweater and a beanie. On the way out the door, I snagged an extra hoodie just in case the January winds were especially ruthless on the water today. The air was cool and damp. The periwinkle twilight of morning was just beginning to peek through the canvas of clouds stretching across the flat Florida landscape. An ominous morning fog already blanketed the ground, sending a shiver through me despite my snug spot in the driver's seat.

The lone motorcycle parked at the harbor reassured me Milo was already here. I climbed out, double-checking my bag with water bottles, keys, flashlight and air tank. I'd bought it for novelty from the antique store where Noah worked, but I really hadn't expected to actually put it to use. At least not yet.

I crossed the dock where Milo was already waiting, his back to me and the shore as he watched the sunrise, wearing a dark brown windbreaker. I stepped beside him. He didn't turn to look at me, but he reached for my hand.

"I don't even know where to start." I breathed, fog forming in front of my mouth with each word.

"Neither do I," he said. "But the important thing is we're starting somewhere. It'll be alright." He gave my hand a subtle squeeze.

"If you did know where to find it, would you tell me?" I knew I shouldn't have asked, but I couldn't hold it back.

The look on his face twisted into one of confusion and hurt, but I could tell he was trying to keep it from showing by the way he swallowed and bit his cheek. "I promise I'm not keeping anything from you."

"I like to think that. But I'm just making sure." I forced a weak smile. I'd never anticipated how difficult it would be to move past the letter incident. But for some reason, I couldn't manage to get it out of my head. And I knew it was hurting us both.

He walked away toward *La Esperanza* bobbing on the water and stepped over, hoisting his own bag of supplies over the hull. I followed and made my way to the helm where I turned my key and started the engine. After allowing it a minute to run, we both untied the mooring lines securing the boat to the dock, and then I returned to the wheel to ease us out into deeper waters.

Though we hardly spoke, it seemed clear that we both knew our destination—the island—or at least the waters surrounding it where I had thrown in the scale. My fingers began to numb as the cold moist air mixed with the sea spray and chilled them. But I held tightly to the wheel, burying my nose into my pullover. By the time the last bit of sun had finally climbed over the horizon, the island was dead ahead in front of us.

Milo tossed out the anchor once I hovered the boat over my best guess as to where the *Siren's Scorn* had last sailed. With nausea rising in my throat, I leaned over the edge and gazed down into the lapping water below. The morning tide had brought with it some harsh waves, that lifted my old boat up and down as it charged through the swells.

"Now the question is," Milo said, turning to look at me, "how do we plan to get down there?"

I reached into my backpack and pulled out the vintage air tank and regulator. Milo's eyes widened.

"Katrina, that thing looks older than me."

"Noah said it's from the seventies or early eighties," I uttered, fully aware of how sketchy it was to be using, "but it should still work...I think."

"The air is probably stale. When was it last filled?"

"I—I don't know," I grumbled. "But what else can we do? Do you have a better idea?"

"Not necessarily." Milo crossed his arms and held his gaze on mine. "But if the legend about a siren's heart was true then that should also mean..."

With a grimace, I quickly blinked, looking away. "Okay, don't be ridiculous."

"What? Katrina, how else did you survive going down into the water after you jumped into the maelstrom? Don't think I didn't figure it out. If you're truly descended from Cordelia, at some point you'll have to accept what that means."

"It doesn't mean I'm a mermaid!" I shouted. The absurdity of the statement flooded over me like the waves cresting below. And I had to switch my thoughts before I gave into them.

Milo's eyes softened and his shoulders dropped. Without another word, he watched as I took off my shirt, revealing my swim top. I strapped the air tank onto my back and checked the PSI, which still looked good from what I could tell. But it didn't matter. I knew this was a horrible idea, about as irresponsible and reckless as it could get. I didn't know what awaited me down there, but I knew I was the only one of us who stood a chance with this rickety old gear. I walked to the boat's ladder, but a firm hand caught me by my arm just as I began to step over.

"Katrina, I can't let you do this. Do you know how deep it could be down there? You could die from the pressure if you don't drown first."

I knew he was right. I was terrified. But I was more afraid of Cordelia. "I have to try, Milo. I know this is dangerous. But we have to find that necklace before she does." I looked up at him, and a warmth came over me as I concentrated on his hazel irises that were reflecting bits of honey and teal from the seawater and sunrise.

"Then let me do it. I'll go under."

"No. No, it *has* to be me."

"Why?" He spoke with a grit of desperation I recognized. It reminded me of when he told me he loved me on the ship when I came to tell him goodbye.

"Because..." I took a deep breath and pinched my forehead. "Because I know this ancient air tank isn't enough to make it. So, if something goes wrong down there...it has to be me."

There. I said it.

Milo released his hold on my arm. "So, you *do* admit it."

"I..." I searched for words, but they were as lost at sea as the scale. I knew in my heart what had happened when I woke up at the bottom of the sea months ago after jumping overboard. I knew what I saw. But that didn't mean it was something I wanted. I had never told Milo how I survived. And he had never asked. Something unspoken within the bond between us assured me he knew. That's why he'd offered to dive instead. He knew it was the only way to get me to confirm what he already suspected.

As we sat in silence on the boat's edge, the faint sound of an engine trickled in somewhere from behind us. We both glanced out to the open water, where a mid-size yacht cut through the water like a knife, sending wakes our way and rocking my little fishing boat.

I scanned the deck to see some divers packing up their equipment, their wetsuits still shiny from the water. My blood ran cold as the boat neared enough that I could see the lone figure standing at the front of the stern, overlooking the water as though it was at her command. In a royal blue skirt and blazer, Cordelia stood, like a queen. Even the meters between us couldn't keep me from catching her deathly stare. She fixated on Milo, narrowed her eyes, then looked back at me as her scowl turned into a mocking smile. She lifted a closed hand with a silver chain dangling from it.

No. Impossible.

As her yacht whisked past us at a dangerously close distance, she opened her hand to reveal the scale still secured in its pendant on that damned necklace I fought so hard to get rid of.

"She has it!" I belted out, nearly falling forward if not for grabbing the ladder rail at the last moment. The boat zoomed out into the distance, fading away as I caught the lettering on the back. "*Belladonna*" it read.

Milo reached out to steady me as the wake of the rolling water tossed me off balance. With anger welling up in me like a cresting wave, I let myself fall into his arms and let out a groan of defeat. "She hired a dive team. She got the scale." I cried into the slick exterior of his windbreak jacket as he closed his arms around me.

"Shhh," he said softly, "That doesn't mean she's won."

"We shouldn't have waited," I said. "We should've come out here last night. Immediately. We would've been first."

Milo pulled back gently and looked me in the face, stilling me as I focused on that lock of honey hair falling over his scarred left eyebrow like it always did. "We never would've been able to find it in the dark. Cordelia clearly has more resources than we can imagine, and you can't put the blame on yourself that she doesn't play the game fairly."

I nodded, trying to reel in my swirling thoughts. "You're right. But that doesn't change the fact that if I can't stop her, the consequences will be so much worse than just losing a game."

"We." I looked up at Milo's sudden correction. "*We* can stop her. You're not alone. You have to stop putting everything on your shoulders. I'm here, too."

I rubbed my temples with my cold palms. "Then what do *we* do now?"

I didn't expect a response, but Milo's silence cut through me like a knife. I knew there was only one answer. The cool sea air filled my lungs as I pulled in a deep breath before answering my own question.

"We find the trident."

FILTHY PIRATE

7

MILO

"I f we're going to sail to the Devil's Triangle, we'd be in much better shape with a bigger boat." I gestured to the small vessel on which we stood.

"Well, I've done greater feats with much less." The way Katrina spoke felt like a foreign language. There was a coldness in her words that I didn't recognize. She was so focused on her own thoughts that I felt she was a million leagues away. "And there's no time."

She started the boat with haste and set off back toward home. I watched her at the helm. Her eyes never wavered from the straight ahead gaze she held looking out at the stretch of sea before us. The last time I'd seen a determination so fierce on her face was right before she dove overboard from Valdez' ship. And I secretly feared what we'd be diving headfirst into this time.

"Will you help me get supplies? I want to leave by tonight." She turned to me as she stepped over the hull and onto the dock after we pulled the boat to port.

"Tonight?" Of course I knew time was of the essence, but the fact that we still lacked a suitable vessel made me hesitant.

"You're the expert. How long do you think it'll take us?"

"In this," I sighed. "Six days at the least, I'd think. In something with a stronger engine, maybe half that."

"Well unless we can find a bigger boat in a few hours, looks like we'll just have to do with a couple of extra days."

"Then part of my preparations will include praying for fair weather. If we hit any storms out that far, I doubt she'll fare so well." I patted the rope as I pulled the hitch knot tight.

Katrina paced across the dock, and then suddenly stopped. "I'm going to pack food and supplies. Can you get the fuel and anything else we'll need?"

"I'm going to get fuel and some spare parts from the shop."

"Okay," She nodded and then stepped toward me to give me a peck on the cheek, but it felt cold.

I hadn't realized Noah was in the shop this early until the sound of rollers started me as he slid out from underneath a car. He must've heard me come in, though I did my best to enter quietly.

"Morning, Sandy," he uttered, his voice throwing a cold echo into the garage. I was never fond of that nickname he chose for me. "I must've missed you on your way out this morning. Early bird today, yeah?"

I shook my head. It would be difficult to get what I came for with him here. "Just here for some things."

"Oh yeah?" He stood up, wiping his hands on a towel smudged with black hanging from his front pocket. "What are you working on?"

"It's sort of personal." I walked over to one of the toolboxes, rummaging through the parts bin for spark plugs, screwdrivers and sockets, and whatever else I could think we might need if something were to go wrong on that ancient engine.

"Well, you can't just come in here taking all this stuff if you're not gonna tell me. How am I supposed to explain to my uncle why all this crap's missing when he gets back from his vacation?" He leaned over me, his elbow propped up on the toolbox.

"Tell him it was a bit of an emergency. Boat engine."

"Pssshhh, what kind of boat emergency you got going on, Sandy?" He chuckled slyly.

"You wouldn't believe me even if I told you."

"Bro I knew you were weird, but come on. This is a whole new level, even for you."

"Katrina and I need to find something. Something far away." I packed the tools and parts I'd gathered into my tool bag. Then headed to the oil shelves to find what I needed, despite the increasing difficulty to focus with Noah yapping in my ear.

"How far are we talking? You're not planning on taking my grandpa's old boat, are you?"

"Your grandpa?" I stopped with my hand just over the quart of oil I needed.

"Yeah, my grandpa sold her that boat. She told you about Russell, right?"

"Yes, but…" I tensed my brows as I made the connection. "Your Russell's grandson?"

"Yeah, I am. So I know what an old shitbox that boat is. I don't know how far you guys are going, but I wouldn't be taking that if the word 'far' means what I think it means."

"Trust me, I know," I sighed. "But Katrina is determined. And honestly if we don't make this trip, something bad could happen."

"Believe me, I get it. I know these chicks can make a lot of bad things happen when we don't do what they want."

I couldn't help but smirk. "I know it's crazy, but we have to do this. I can't exactly explain why. But trust me."

"Okay well, I feel really guilty about turning a blind eye while you guys commit suicide."

Just then I turned around, still chuckling at Noah's typical uptight tone. A picture on the garage wall caught my eye, surrounded by other framed images I'd seen dozens of times now. But this was the moment an idea began to form. My eyes focused on the picture of Rob standing on his motorsailer with a massive swordfish in hand. "Is that your uncle's boat?" I asked over my shoulder.

"The big sailboat? Oh yeah, he bought it just a couple of years back and—" He stopped as though he'd sucked his words down mid-sentence. "Why?"

"No reason."

"I don't like what you're thinking."

"How do you know what I'm thinking?" I turned around, heading toward the office of the shop with the tool bag slung over my shoulder.

"Because I'm not an idiot," Noah snapped as he trailed behind me with nervous steps. "He doesn't keep his keys in there."

So that's exactly where he keeps them.

I opened the door without looking back, but I could sense Noah's presence behind me.

"Calm down," I said, carefully scanning the office. If Rob was anything like Valdez, those keys would be in the back of a drawer locked in a box of some sort. "I'm only leaving a note of the things I'm taking. He can take whatever the cost is out of my pay."

"Man, I don't believe that. You're freaking me out." He crossed his arms as he stood in the doorway protectively. I quickly used my fingers to slide the pen on the desk up into my sleeve. Then I began rummaging through the drawers.

"What're you doing?" Noah stepped forward.

"Just looking for something to write with." I smiled, moving my hand around in the drawer and using a slight of hand to snag the keys I felt tucked away in the drawer's corner. I didn't know for sure if they were for the boat, but I didn't mind taking my chances. As I pulled my hand from the drawer, I leaned over at just the right angle to produce the pen from my sleeve and quickly swapped the keys to my other hand.

With Noah's suspicious glare burning into me, I scribbled the note on a piece of loose paper, listing out the items I'd taken and my signature. With the keys tucked away safely against my forearm, I walked out and up to my loft to get something I couldn't leave behind. Grabbing the compass hanging from the bedpost, I made my way back down the stairs and out of the shop. And Noah was none the wiser that he'd just been robbed blind by a pirate.

SINKING

8

KATRINA

I stood at the edge of the dock beside *La Esperanza,* waiting for Milo, and thought about the irony. Somehow, I always ended up here. On a pier, looking out at the water, waiting for Milo. As much as my heart beat for him, a part of it felt a bit broken, but I could no longer pinpoint what was responsible.

The breeze blew back my hair, giving me a clear line of sight to the approaching figure looming on the water's surface. A bright white boat with high slanted sails, headed in this direction but still a way off. I didn't recognize it, but I secretly wished it was mine as I watched it effortlessly cut through the water. Footsteps from behind tore my focus from the boat.

"I knew I'd find you here." I didn't expect it to be McKenzie who'd walked up on me. I smiled, a little nervous about her untimely visit.

"Hey," I offered her a hug, noticing the rolling luggage still at her side. "Happy New Year."

"It is now that I'm back." She tossed a lock of red hair back behind her shoulder as she spoke in her signature lilt. "Ugh, my family was about to drive me insane. I drove past here on the way back from the airport and figured I'd stop to see if you were here."

I chuckled. "You couldn't even wait to unpack to see me."

"Well duh! Anyway, you about to go on an excursion?" She lifted her eyebrows as something caught her attention behind me. I turned around to see what had caught her eye out on the water.

The big sailboat I'd seen in the distance was now easing in to moor at the dock next to my boat. I watched in awe as its massive hull drifted near and dwarfed my little fishing boat in its presence. And to my utmost surprise, Milo stood proudly at the helm, his expression focused as he maneuvered the thing.

"What is this? Where did you get that?" I cupped my hands around my mouth as I called out my words so he could hear me from his place so far above me.

"Let's just say Russell isn't the only one in his family with a liking for boats." He yelled back with a smug look.

"What does that mean?"

"Noah's uncle—Russell's son—sort of lent it to us."

"Really?" I put my hands on my hips. "I didn't know Noah was Russell's grandson. This seems like a big deal. Does he know how long we're going to be gone?"

"Well not exactly," Milo said, "But let's bring the supplies aboard and I'll explain. But the important thing is that we'll be much safer traveling in this one."

Something felt off, but I reached for the cooler handle and overstuffed backpack at my side and lugged them on.

"Where are you guys going?" McKenzie asked.

"Ummm, we're just taking a sailing trip for a couple of days."

"Days?" Her eyes lit up and flashed blue like the water below us. "That sounds so cool. Can I come?" Suddenly she recoiled, grabbing her arm like she was embarrassed. "I mean I'd stay on the other side of the boat or whatever because I'm sure you guys want your privacy so like obviously I'd stay away, ya know? But this just seems so cool. And that boat is so freaking nice."

A subtle sigh escaped my lips and mixed with the salty air. How could I tell her no in the nicest way?

"Well—um..." I scratched my head and bit my lip. "The thing is...this could be a rough trip and I'm not sure—"

I was unable to finish my statement when an oddly familiar voice tore through the air and frantic footsteps wobbled the wooden deck beneath my feet.

"Hey! I'm calling the cops if you don't get down from there right now!" I was startled to see Noah rushing across the pier, shouting in a panic directed at Milo.

"What?" I cried, glancing up at Milo, who looked completely unconcerned with the accusation as he stood leaning over the ship deck's railing.

Just then, I noticed a boat cruising out into the horizon, navigating swiftly through the outer banks toward the open ocean. A memory flashed before my eyes. I knew that boat. It was unmistakable for the bold dark blue stripes along the sides and the name on the back.

Belladonna.

Suddenly, however Milo managed to acquire this boat didn't matter. Noah didn't matter, and I knew I didn't have time to talk McKenzie into going home. Cordelia was already steps ahead of us, and if she found the trident first...

"Sure, come with us! Get your luggage." I grabbed McKenzie's arm and pulled her onto the hull as Noah stood yelling on the dock.

"Get off my uncle's boat! He's gonna kill me!"

"I'm sorry, Noah!" I shouted. "I swear it's an emergency! We'll bring it back!"

"No! Get back here!" He stepped back, as though surveying the scene of his uncle's boat adrift as the space between it and the dock widened. With obvious hesitation, he took a running leap and found himself dangling from the side of the boat. McKenzie and I rushed to pull him up.

"What the actual hell is wrong with you? All of you?" He brushed himself off as he clumsily got to his feet, struggling to balance with the boat's motion.

"It's a lot to explain," I panted as I caught my breath, "but you have to believe me when I say that your uncle's boat missing might not be the worst of our problems if we don't set sail *right now.*"

"That's it, I'm calling the cops," Noah reached for his phone. McKenzie shot me a worried look before lunging forward to stop his hand.

"Noah." In one of the calmest tones I'd ever heard from her, she spoke to him, looking straight into his face before looking back at me for a split second. "If Katrina says it's this important, it must be. She doesn't lie."

I blinked back a flood of guilt as I realized the depths of McKenzie's trust. She would blindly follow me like this, without even knowing why. And yet lying was all I'd ever done to her. I hid everything from her. But how could I tell her the truth?

It was to keep her safe. Mostly.

To my surprise, Noah seemed to listen. As though letting her words sink in, he looked at me, then back at her and finally up to Milo, who was too busy at the helm to notice.

"Why do you really need this boat?" His voice was pure. The question was genuine.

I took a breath. "This is going to sound absolutely insane."

"Well, you've already kidnapped us." McKenzie giggled. "Might as well spit it out."

"We're going after something. Something that could cause the end of life as we know it if we don't find it first."

"Man, I should've known you were crazy when I found you hiding in the back of my car. I knew something was up, but this is a whole new level of deranged." Noah threw his hands up in defeat.

McKenzie's expression began to darken, and her eyes narrowed as she pressed her brows together. "Katrina, where are we going? You're being so cryptic."

"To..." I swallowed and clenched my jaw. "To the Bermuda Triangle. To...to find a trident."

They both stared at me in silence in a way that made my gut flip like a fresh-caught fish in a net. By now our boat was far enough out that there was no chance they could get off now. They were in this whether they believed me or not.

Just then, Milo's voice broke the tension from above. "Can someone give me a hand with the sails? We need to get the mainsail up if we want to maintain speed against these headwinds."

"I'm gonna go help him," I uttered, using the excuse to slip away before one last pathetic attempt to reassure them. "You guys have to trust me. Make yourselves comfortable because this won't be a short trip."

Praying Noah wouldn't change his mind about calling the police, I climbed the short stairs up to the deck to help Milo, leaving our two new reluctant crew mates standing in silence at the stern.

"You *stole* a boat?" I grabbed the line to the mainsail, tugging it as I tried to figure out what to do with it. "From your boss?"

"If we took *La Esperanza* we might not make it back. We might not even make it there," Milo gritted his teeth, pointing at the sails. "I already unfurled the jib, now you just hold the line here and make sure it keeps tension on the winch."

I tried to follow, but this was my first experience with sailboats. I took the line in his hand and held it taught as he began to pull the seemingly endless rope out and the large sheet above us began to drop slowly.

"But you stole it, Milo! You're not a pirate anymore. You can go to prison for things like this."

"And I would've been hanged for it back in 1725." He froze for a second as his eyes sharpened at me. "Can't you see I'm trying to help? If we don't find this trident, there's a lot more at stake than incarceration, Katrina."

I groaned as I squeezed the rope in my hand. "I know..." I sighed. "I just don't want things to end badly."

"You think I want to risk my second chance at life by getting arrested? I wouldn't have done this if I didn't have to."

He wasn't wrong. I knew what it was like to be forced into something wrong in order to do the right thing. Like lying to McKenzie. Or when I had to make Dad believe I'd given up on him and Mom. But no matter how much I understood, something kept me from telling him that. So, I was silent as he walked out of the helm station and went to secure the sail into the sail bag up top.

I looked out at the water ahead. Six days of this. And once we got there, then what? How would we even know where the trident would be and how would we get to it?

I heard the banter of McKenzie and Noah below, and I knew I couldn't avoid them forever. I hurried back down to them, watching my step as the waves of the open ocean danced beneath me. They watched me with suspicion as I approached timidly.

"It's only fair that I explain to you both what's going on."

"Please do." McKenzie crossed her arms.

I asked them to sit down, because I knew there was no possible way I could give an explanation that didn't make me sound like I'd lost my mind, and I knew I'd talk in circles trying to do it. But there, as the sun rose higher in the sky and cast its glittering white diamonds across the sea's surface, I told them how I'd uncovered a mermaid's curse on an undead pirate crew last semester, and also how I broke it, and how now Cordelia was still alive and ready to take out her vengeance on the world. And I made sure to explain how we were now in a race against her to find the trident. Though I did leave out the part about me possibly being a mermaid.

"Wait," McKenzie looked down at her lap, holding out her pointer finger as though she was connecting the dots on an invisible piece of paper. "So, all those times you were out at night so late...you were meeting ghosts by the ocean? Bellamy was one of them, too? And those men who chased us downtown were...pirates?"

I nodded. "In a nutshell, yes." Noah hadn't said a word, but his wide eyes and disgusted expression were enough to tell me he didn't believe a word of it.

"You mean to tell me you actually believe her?" He turned to McKenzie.

"Well…I mean yeah, it's a little out there…but it technically makes sense. That necklace was pretty freaky. And besides, who are we to say we know what's out there? Pirate ghosts and mermaids could be entirely possible. I always say there's a reason for the stories."

"This isn't Pirates of the Caribbean, McKenzie! Your friend is just on some hard drugs." Noah stood up and began jogging up to the deck. "I'm taking this boat back right now."

"Noah, no!" I cried, shooting to my feet and running after him. The floor beneath us bobbed and rolled, making for difficulty going faster than a quick walk.

He took off, sprinting up to the control cabin. When he grabbed the wheel, I lunged forward, using the railing along the boat to pull myself forward faster. Reaching the helm, I tried to pry him from the steering wheel.

"Stop, Noah! I know it sounds impossible, but it's true! You don't understand how important this is!" I cried.

He shoved me off him and I stumbled into the control panel. I went for him again and knocked his hand from the wheel just as he had begun to turn the boat, sending us rocking and flying off balance before he regained his grip. A thud startled me as Milo leapt down from the masts and landed in front of the cabin doorway with skilled agility.

"You have to stop." His voice boomed in an authoritative way I'd only heard before when he stopped Bellamy from taking my necklace on the beach. He stepped in front of the wheel to readjust it as Noah held on tightly and resisted.

Noah flinched. He shoved Milo backward in a panicked motion. Milo shook his head as he stepped forward without losing his balance. "Calm down."

"Calm down? I need to calm down? You've kidnapped us!" He yanked the wheel to the side, tossing our boat and making me slip and tumble into the wall. When Milo pulled back on the wheel, Noah threw an unexpected punch at Milo's jaw. He then went to throw another jab. Though the first blow had caught him by surprise, Milo caught the second swing in in his palm with ease, closing his hand around Noah's fist. He pulled Noah's arm around, putting him in an armlock that left Noah grimacing.

"I said, you need to calm down." He loosened his grip on Noah after turning him around to face him, and then gave him a light shove backward. I stood tense, bracing against the doorway threshold as I watched.

"If you think you still have a home in the shop loft, think again," Noah hissed.

"Whatever you need to do, Noah. But here's the reality. You're stuck on this ship anyway. If we get to our destination and it turns out there's no trident and we're all insane, you can call the police. Send me to prison. I'll accept my punishment, however severe. But leave Katrina out of it." He looked at me as he smoothed back some stray pieces of hair falling across his eyes, only for them to fall right back. "Agreed?"

Noah's nostrils flared as he met Milo's gaze. I could see the veins in his neck as he tightened his shoulders and jaw. "Agreed. For now."

Milo stepped back, surveying the ocean before us. McKenzie had made her way up the control cabin now, a look of fear frozen on her face. I'd never seen her look so undone.

"How long are we going to be on this boat?" Her voice came out in a hoarse whisper as she hugged herself in the cold open wind.

"A few days." I shuddered.

"I think I need a minute." She turned away, making her way down into the lower cabin belowdecks.

I looked at the two men before me, my gaze catching on Milo as he stood firm, still breathing hard from the altercation. "Please stop fighting," I said.

With heavy steps, I trudged out of the helm area and followed McKenzie. Once I entered the interior below, I examined our living quarters for the next week. A high-end kitchenette wrapping along the length of the left side of the boat gave way to a small table and bar, where McKenzie sat with her head in her hands. As I made my way to her, I caught a glimpse of the sleeping area around the corner.

"I'm sorry I didn't tell you about this." I told McKenzie, taking a seat next to her softly. "It was just too fantastical of a story."

"So Milo...he's...?"

"He's a pirate. He *was*." The words felt foreign on my tongue, but it was far from the strangest of things I'd said lately. She didn't say any more, so I sat there in silence with her as the boat rocked us gently.

As I sat there thinking how I'd hidden the truth from her, I understood why Milo had hidden the note from me. He wanted to protect me. Just like I wanted to protect McKenzie. But now it had only hurt the both of us. And somewhere in the back of my head I hadn't been able to turn off the ever-present echo of Cordelia's bell-like warning.

"Always the guilty one...He'll use you like James used me...you'll see how filthy his soul is."

What had she meant? And how could I ever truly know? Milo could hide centuries of himself from me and I would never know it. Even if he truly was different now...what was he *really*? Who was he once upon another time? And did it even matter?

With these thoughts heavy as an anchor in my soul, I gave McKenzie's hand a squeeze and then stood to go, grabbing a wool blanket on the way out.

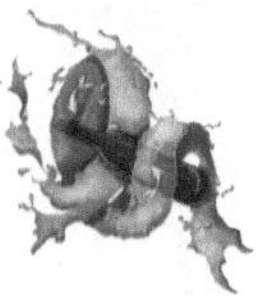

Back out on the deck, Noah kept his distance from Milo, but continued watching him like a hawk. It was cold out, and I knew Milo must've been freezing by now. Clutching the blanket in my hand, I found my feet taking me back to the control cabin.

I didn't speak a word as I draped the blanket across Milo's strong shoulders. I knew I should say something, but I just didn't know what.

"You're taking care of me, now." A ghost of vapor formed in front of his mouth as he spoke.

"We take care of each other." I corrected. The corner of his lips lifted into a smirk.

There was a long stillness before I noticed the compass in his hand.

"Does the boat's GPS work okay?" I asked. I felt him follow my gaze to the compass

"It works just as it should. But I never sail without this, no matter the century."

I should've known that. I knew his father had given it to him as he took his last breaths after Valdez shot him. That's what he'd told me. It was more to him than just a compass. As I studied the old tool intensely from where I stood, I didn't expect Milo to start speaking again.

"But right now, I have no need of a compass to tell me that something doesn't feel right between us." He turned to me keeping one hand on the wheel.

"Things are just a little intense right now. A lot of stress." I spoke fast, trying to suppress the nerves bubbling up within me.

"Well, I don't want to be just another thing that's causing you stress. Is this still about the note?" My thoughts flashed back to Cordelia, as if she was standing right there beside me whispering in my ear like some devil on my shoulder.

"You'll see how filthy his soul is... You'll see through his façade soon enough."

With a shake of my head, I rubbed my eyes as I searched for my next words. I chose them carefully and spoke them as confidently as I could manage. "No, I love you, Milo. I get why you hid the note. I understand why you thought stealing the ship was a good idea. I know why you do the things you do. I think I do, at least. But sometimes I just feel like there's so much of you I'll never know. You lived a whole lifetime before this. And for some reason that's never scared me until now."

"Then I'm glad it's not just me who feels we are sinking." His words struck my heart like a harpoon, and I wished I knew how to bring us both back to the surface.

MILO

T he grip of the wheel in my hand was the only thing grounding me as I stood with Katrina's molten eyes pleading with my soul. I always feared one day she would wake up and realize the man she was in love with wasn't worth her devotion. But I suppose I always hoped a fear was all it would ever be.

"You're right to wonder who I was, Katrina. But I can't change the things I've done under Valdez's command. I regret them. And I've repented of them as best I can."

"What about before Valdez? Who were you before you joined his crew?"

"I...I was just a boy. An apprentice with my father. Learning his trade. Mourning his mother." I let go of the wheel and stepped toward her gently. As I closed the distance between us, I touched her chin. "Don't start doubting me. Please. Not when we've just begun."

"I'm sorry." She squeezed her eyes shut, as though snapping out of some sort of deep daydream. "I don't know why I keep thinking about it so much. Maybe it's just the possibility that we might have the FBI waiting for us when we get back. It's not exactly easy to relax."

"That's not going to happen." I wrapped the blanket around us both and pulled us close. "And if it does, you know I'll keep you out of it."

I stared out the window, watching the blue grey water stretch before us as the boat tore through it at full speed. This was the first time in a while that I'd sailed in open water during the day like this, knowing there was nothing ahead and nothing below for leagues. A shiver met my spine as all at once I was back on Valdez' ship again, only for a split second, binding the hands of mermaids and dragging them to their temporary holds beneath the ship. I barely remembered it. I'd black out during those moments to keep myself from succumbing to insanity from the guilt. I'd often vomit afterwards, unable to eat for days.

But I couldn't forget their cries and the blood-soaked deck as Valdez' men cut out their tongues to keep them from singing their songs. And worst of all I couldn't forget how powerless I was to do anything about it.

"We have a long trip ahead. I've brought enough fuel for the trip and for the journey back. But we'll have to maintain full speed if we are to reach the Triangle before Cordelia does. We might be lucky to have the extra hands aboard if the seas get rough."

I regretted that Noah and McKenzie had become unwilling participants in this voyage, but there was no room for choice now. Between the four of us, I hoped maybe we might just stand a chance. I glanced through the cabin doorway at the stern, where Noah sat bundled in his heavy dark green jacket with his back to the deck. We had almost been friends until this morning. Just when I'd started to settle, I was already ruining my chances at this new life. Perhaps I didn't belong here after all.

"I'll see if I can win them over," Katrina muttered. "But for now, they need their space. Seems like I'll have plenty of time to try."

"We should be there January 10th, and depending on if we find the trident the same day, we can be back in Constantine by the 16th."

"Classes start the 15th." Katrina's eyes widened as she groaned. "But I guess if we don't do this, there won't be a class to go to before long."

"No," I sighed. "There won't be."

She pulled away from our blanket and kissed me on the cheek with lips that felt tired. As I watched her walk back down the steps of the ship, I prayed to feel the warmth between us once again before the world ended.

Our time on the ship was lonely. My space became the helm cabin, not by choice. With a crew of only four, it was easy to stay separated on a boat of this size. Katrina came to check on me from time to time, and sometimes she would take charge of the wheel, but I was never gone from the helm for long. I made a few attempts to talk to Noah, but he refused to acknowledge me. I kept a watchful eye on him, though, because I didn't trust him not to sabotage the engine. He knew just enough to be dangerous.

Even McKenzie was quiet around me, but she was an excellent cook for all of us, being more resourceful with our food supplies than I ever would have expected. I managed without sleep. I'd had centuries of practice. But when my eyes grew heavier than I could handle, Katrina would station herself at the helm while I slept in the hammock I'd hung for myself in the cabin.

On the morning of the 10th, I stretched with a weary yawn as I studied the horizon and the stars still visible in the twilight above. According to my coordinates, we were almost there. The twinkling markers in the sky gave me their reassurance that the Devil's Triangle lay just ahead.

I nudged Katrina, who had fallen asleep in my hammock this particular evening. She sat up with a weary groan and looked ahead, pulling her blanket around herself to fight off the chill of dawn at sea.

"There it is," I said.

"How do you know?" She yawned again.

I pulled out my compass and aligned my fingers with the sky. "We're, 25 degrees north and 71 degrees west. Right where we need to be. Or at least we will be by the time the sun's fully risen."

Katrina slid out from the sling and stepped closer to the cabin window, becoming more alert as she spoke. "Do you see any sign of her boat?"

"No." I frowned. "I haven't seen the *Belladonna* once. But maybe that means we're ahead of it."

"Or that we're too late." She pushed her hair back behind her ears in a way that made heat rush to my core. "We're screwed if she got there first."

"Don't worry," I said softly. "Even if she made it there first, she can't dive down that far to look for it. She lost her tail, remember?"

"I just hope th—" her voice caught in the air, as though a ghost had clasped a hand over her mouth mid-sentence. "Milo?"

At the utterance of my name and her eyes growing wide, I turned to see what she saw. The light of dawn had vanished in an impossible instant, obscured completely by some black storm cloud growing more threatening by the second. They puffed up like giants, swallowing the line between the sky and sea whole.

"That came from nowhere," I uttered. I studied the clouds with suspicion and noticed the waves rising in the distance. I'd spent a great portion of my life weathering storms at the mercy of the ocean. But this storm looked unlike any other I'd ever encountered. It looked like the legends every sailor had heard but had yet to ever lay eyes upon.

It can't be...

A strike of white lightning sent me rushing to the deck shouting. Noah and McKenzie were already out, watching the surreal scene before us from the bow.

"Don't just stand there! All hands on deck! I need to get the sails down as quickly as possible!"

I rushed to the mast as Katrina hurried to grab the lines in the control cabin. If this monster storm hit us, we stood little chance.

"Lifejackets!" Katrina cried, fetching the vests from the hatch and tossing them down to our two passengers. I hadn't even thought about them. We didn't have such a salvation back in the 1700s. As the cold sea air battered my skin, I fought the wind to the sails, which were already getting mangled in the gusts. The storm had darkened every inch of the sky. I strained to see. With trembling hands, I worked as quickly as possible, but every sail had been raised. I at least had to get the mainsail down. I had to...

I pulled the sail as Katrina fed the line, but the water below had already begun to toss the ship. I stumbled but held my ground with gritted teeth. No matter what I did, I couldn't win the wrestling match with the canvas sails. The storm had come too quickly. Desperate, I reached for my knife. I'd cut the damn thing.

Just as my blade touched the rope, a steady arm reached forward and pulled the flailing sail away from me. Noah.

"Don't think this changes anything, Sandy." He shouted over the wind. "I'm just trying not to die!"

With his added strength, we could fold the sail down as it lowered and keep it from coming undone in the wall of wind threatening to carry it—and us—away.

The ship was rocking madly now, and the sky was midnight. Wind beat against the waves, lifting the boat as though it were nothing more than a piece of driftwood. McKenzie screamed below, and Noah cursed into the wind. Oddly enough, there was no rain. Just like the rumors go...

"We have to get down. We're sure to get struck by the lightning up here!" I called out to Noah.

He nodded and we dropped down from the mast. I waited until he ran down to meet McKenzie and was out of range. There was no way we could get the other sails down. But I was going to try...

"Get down as low as you can! Go into the cabin!" I shouted to them on the deck. "The lightning is about to get worse."

Noah ushered McKenzie into the lower cabin, but Katrina stood watching me with eyes full of fear. "Go now, Katrina!"

Suddenly the boom of the mast swung around, knocked loose by the wind and struck me. The pole slammed into my back, throwing me overboard from the ship. I heard Katrina cry my name before I hit the water. A wave tucked me under. I emerged hurriedly, fighting the sting of ocean water in my eyes and lungs. When I looked up, the boat was vertical, rising up on a wall of a wave.

She lifted higher and higher until the tip of the bow looked as though it could touch the sky, and then through a horrific flurry of lightning strikes, I watched as she capsized, with Katrina, McKenzie, and Noah still on board. Then I went under, pulled into a sea of black.

CASTAWAY

10

KATRINA

My mind raced faster than the wind around us as I watched Milo drop into the raging sea. McKenzie and Noah screamed for me to get inside, but I only ran forward to the hull. I looked for him, searching the water in desperation for only a second before the boat began to lift and sent me stumbling backward. The skin of my palm pinched against the railing as I squeezed it tightly, begging my arm strength to hold out long enough to brace against this rogue wave.

But then I was dangling in the air. The deck disappeared from beneath my feet as the bow rose higher. The boat tilted in the air, then came crashing upside down. I fought to keep my grip on the slippery smooth railing as the icy water slammed into me like a freight train. I thought the weight of a sailboat coming down on me would crush me, but somehow, it felt like falling through frigid air once I hit the water.

There was a brief moment where I thought I blacked out, but I came to quickly, realizing I was still holding onto the boat, which bobbed above me on the top of the water. I swam out from underneath and upward, bursting forth up to the surface like shattering glass. I opened my eyes, expecting to see the underside of the capsized boat floating like a white hill on a blue plain, but instead, there were only fragments. The boat was gone. Bits of canvas and wood floated around me, scattered about.

Wood?

The motorsailer was made of fiberglass. But these planks and wooden pieces looked like...

Suddenly the water shook with a boom that made me shriek. Thunder, I suspected. Salt stinging my eyes like venom, I searched my blurry surroundings for any sign of the others.

"Milo! McKenzie!" I cried, turning in a complete circle to survey the endless water on all sides of me. I saw no one. "Noah! Milo!"

My breaths became rapid as the fear settled into my skin like a stone sinking to the sand. I was alone as far as I could tell. The boat was in gone...destroyed? And the sky...it was the brightest blue. Not a sliver of evidence remained of the storm that had just struck our boat seconds earlier. And I wasn't cold like I expected to be. The water was warm and calm.

I dove beneath the water, ignoring the sting of salt in my eyes as I forced them open. I looked around in the blue murk, desperate to catch a glimpse of any of the others. When I could hold my breath no longer, I darted back up to the surface. Then I shouted once more for my friends, praying they'd survived.

"Katrina!" A shrill voice in the distance made me whip around. I hadn't had a chance to put on my life jacket, so I was fighting my tired arms to stay afloat. McKenzie and Noah slowly came into view, huddled against each other a few yards away as they drifted along on a piece of floating debris.

"Are you guys okay?" The thunder struck again just as I spoke, rattling the sea and sky. "Have you seen Milo?"

They both shook their heads as McKenzie sniffed back what looked like tears as another crash of thunder exploded. But the sky was still clear.

"What is that?" Noah looked up with pressed brows.

"The thunder?" McKenzie chimed in, mascara running down her porcelain face.

"That's not thunder," Noah kept his gaze on the miles of outstretched sea before us.

I closed my eyes, becoming aware of the water around me. Somehow, I could sense its flow, its movements, and its currents. It carried vibrations as subtle as a spring breeze along the length of my fingertips. The rumble in the distance became strangely clearer to me as the sensation of the sea rippled around me. Noah was right. It wasn't thunder.

"It's a ship in the distance," I said.

"How do you know that?"

"I don't know. I can just...feel it."

McKenzie and Noah both looked at me through mistrusting eyes.

"Then let's swim toward it before it gets any farther away." Noah began kicking against the water to propel the piece of driftwood on which they floated forward.

"Wait," I said. "Milo's still not here. We can't leave without him."

"Yeah, I'm not so sure about Sandy. I'm sorry, Katrina," Noah groaned. "But we can't stay out here and miss our chance to be rescued."

I wouldn't let myself believe he could have drowned. No, he was used to shipwrecks. He *had* to have survived, somehow. At the mere thought of it, I plunged myself back underneath the water, swimming all around the area and taking in whatever my burning red eyes could. He had to be here. I had to find him. But I had to catch my breath again.

Once my head broke through the water's surface, I did my best to settle myself and cling to whatever hope I had left. I glanced around at the world of blue around me. Cerulean teal rolled calmly at the horizon's base for as far as the eye could see, stretching out to meet the pastel blue open sky. I shuddered, knowing there was no end within reach to this kingdom of sky and sea. And my heart beat quickly, frantic as I thought of this bottomless blue void taking Milo in its ruthless hold as it had once before.

There were so many things I wish I hadn't said to him, so many emotions I was working through at his expense. And now I'd lost him on the open ocean. I had to find him. I couldn't leave him behind.

Never.

I blinked back the hot tears pushing their way to my eyes as I called out his name once more.

"Milo!"

The boom in the distance made itself known once more. This time it was closer, and it was followed quickly by more sounds of the same thundering intensity.

"The ship's coming this way! There's two of them!" McKenzie's voice demanding my attention as I looked to see two dark masses on the water, approaching quickly through a dense patch of white smoke.

Boom.

Fire and smoke ignited along the side of the ship on the left, sending a swift shot into the side of the other. The smell of gunpowder mixed with sea salt and tickled my nostrils. Cannon fire. I squinted in disbelief at the sight of billowing sails and a black flag as the smog cleared just enough to make out the looming silhouettes.

More cannon fire erupted through the air, rattling my bones as the ships drew near. These were no modern-day yachts or sailboats. These were wooden warships. Galleons. One with a Spanish flag, and the other flying a black flag proudly.

In disbelief I stared as the ships neared slowly, both sides exploding from their own cannons and from the impact of the other. I glanced over to see Noah and McKenzie frozen in place and wide-eyed.

"What is happening?" Noah spat.

"I—I don't know yet." I stuttered. I was beginning to feel a tingle all down the entirety of both my legs, and I feared what might happen if I stayed in the water too long. I'd never swum this long. Except for once.

The battle between the two dueling ships continued until the Spanish ship appeared to retreat in haste. It seemed somewhat damaged, attempting to flee before it took a hit that could sink it. But as it turned, the opposing ship launched out a flaming barrel with an intense cry, then fired at the low point of the hull. The blast crippled the ship as it sent wooden splinters flying, and its stern began slowly tilting downward into the water.

"Is this some kind of reenactment? Way out here?" Noah swam closer to me, his eyes wide with disbelief.

"I...I'm not sure." I choked on the words. Nothing felt familiar out here. Not that the middle of the ocean was a familiar place. But even the air seemed different.

The battered Spanish ship turned its sails and pulled away as quickly as her battered body allowed. The victorious shouts of men reached my ears in the distance as the pirate ship followed, closing in quickly like a lion on an injured gazelle.

Even from our distance, we could make out the ropes shooting out like webs from the side of the pirate ship, snagging on the enemy's starboard side and pulling it in to meet their own ship's hull. Through the sounds of clanging and pistols blasting, my terrified companions and I watched with the realization that what we were seeing was all too real. A battle on the waves was unfolding right before our eyes, a brutal welcoming into a time long past.

"I think this is real," McKenzie whispered. "I think they're really fighting."

I glanced around once more for Milo. I was shaking now. The humid air wasn't enough to fight back the eerie chill penetrating my flesh as I processed the reality that he'd never come up from the water. And my heart was sinking.

I was so fixated on Milo's fate, lost in a watery trance of blue and grey melding together before my eyes, that I hardly noticed when the ships became silent as the pirate crew crossed back and forth across gangplanks, taking what they could from their defeated opponent with quick, confident steps.

"We have to flag them down." Noah's arm shot up, waving and shouting for help.

"What if they kill us?" McKenzie gasped.

"It's still a better chance than staying out here in the middle of the ocean."

Noah was right, but I couldn't seem to dig any words from the pit of my chest. I was speechless. Stunned. Because the ache in my core was enough to paralyze me as I realized that we might leave this wreck without Milo.

The ship with the black flag eventually loosened the ropes tethering it to the Spanish, its sails catching the wind like kites that carried it forward. It drew near to us, casting a looming shadow that made me swallow a lump in my throat.

"What's this?" An unyielding male voice shouted from far up on the ship. "Shipwrecked castaways? Well, bloody sink me! Throw the line."

A rope hit the water in front of me with a thud. Noah took it, handing it first to McKenzie, then looking to me to grab onto it second. I furrowed my brows at him in hesitation. He glanced out to the sea at our side.

"He isn't here. He's...he's gone." I was surprised when he looked down. "I'm sorry."

I nodded, my voice seemingly spent as nausea and dread rose in my stomach. The ocean all around me became mist as it spun in circles around me. Like mixing paints, the sky and sea became one blur, and I knew if I was standing, I'd be wobbling. The water around me was the only thing holding me upright in place.

"I can't leave him...I'll stay. You go." I sucked in a breath. "I'll stay."

"Look, I get it, but you can't stay here in the middle of the Atlantic."

I thought of what might happen. I could stay here. I could wait for him. Noah didn't know what I was capable of. If I stayed in this water long enough. If I dove down deeper...

"Hurry up or we'll leave the lot of you to drown!" A crewman called from the deck, manning the rope we were climbing up.

"Come on, Katrina," Noah tucked his arm through mine, pulling me with him as he gripped the thick rope. "You know you have to."

I could no longer tell if my eyes burned from the salt or from the tears I was fighting back. But I couldn't argue with him. I knew I couldn't stay, and I took hold of the rope, too. But my body wouldn't let me go on without my heart.

Clutching the rope as it hoisted us upward, I felt my hands slipping. Water cascaded off my body as we rose, but with each thought of abandoning Milo, my grip weakened. I felt my senses fading, and the sea pulled me back.

I could see only blurry figments of reality. I looked up at the giant ship towering over me. The sounds I heard were muffled, but I could make out a voice just well enough to catch the last bit of someone calling to the crew.

"Damnit, I didn't just scupper that galleon just to be playing rescuer. Get her up or leave her."

Someone dove in for me—it was Noah, I think. He wrapped the rope around my waist and then called back up to the men on the ship.

"She's just in shock!" He shouted. "Pull us up!"

I felt my weight sink into the rope as Noah supported the rest of me. My vision cleared slowly as I passed the wood carvings on the ship. The side was scuffed and scratched from cannon fire, but still the cedar siding looked sturdy, the armored hull just as carefully crafted as the mermaid bow ornament carved from the same wood. She faced outward toward the ocean, with both arms behind her as though she was cutting through the water with ease. But she wasn't as free as she looked. She was bound to this ship. And now so was I.

Noah helped me over the hull, and McKenzie rushed to my side as I gathered my senses. A few small coughs escaped my lungs, spitting up water I didn't realize I'd swallowed. In an eerie silence, I could sense the bodies standing around me. Heavy boots reverberated against the wooden floor. Wood creaked. Sails flapped.

"A woman aboard is bad luck they say." A calm but unwavering voice carried across the deck as footsteps neared. The crew around me parted as a man walked closer, his long black coat drifting behind him like a cloak. The captain, I imagined. He went on, his voice smooth and stern. I recognized it all too well. "But fortunately for you, I'm not superstitious. Because it looks like I'm your last hope, love."

I squinted, looking up at the brazen blue eyes staring down at me through locks of raven black hair escaping from beneath a leather captain's hat.

"Bellamy?"

Welcome Aboard

11

KATRINA

I shook the water from my hair and face, blinking in disbelief.

"*Captain* Bellamy, lass. Good on you that you've heard of me. Saves me the explaining." He looked me up and down, as if disgusted or confused. I couldn't tell which as he glanced away from me and toward my two friends.

"Do you lubbers have names?" he asked with an arched brow above kohl-smudged eyes.

"Is anyone going to explain what the hell is going on?" Noah shouted after an awkward pause.

"We rescued ya." A gruff crewman watching beside us spoke up. "What more is there to explain?"

Bellamy cocked his head with hardened eyes. "Aye, we did. You'd think these castaways would be a little more grateful."

"No, we are," McKenzie uttered, her voice shaking tenderly. "We're grateful. But we just don't know where we are."

"Does it matter?" Bellamy jeered. "Your safe for now, only because I lost some men during that little cannonball swap and needed replacements. You weren't exactly what I was hoping for, but..." He eyed us all up and down, no doubt confused by our jeans and hoodies with zippers.

Their voices faded from focus as I looked around, taking in the sight of the ship deck and the crew hustling to and fro, working on side repairs and rigging, polishing cannons and rolling barrels into place. I remembered what Cordelia said about the trident in the triangle and held my breath. Time. Life. Space. It controlled all three within the oceans.

Time.

"Bellamy," I interrupted, still watching the scene before me and remembering the sky above us was not the same one we'd been under an hour ago. "What year is it?"

Bellamy's perfect lips curled into a mocking smirk. "You must've hit your head in the wreck, love."

"Just tell me, please. Maybe I'm confused like you say. But just tell me the year."

Bellamy didn't speak, but reached into a leather pouch at his side beneath the folds of his coat and tossed a coin in my direction in one swift motion.

In an instinctive reaction, I managed to catch the coin and took one look at its rough bronzed exterior before the raised numerals caught my eye.

"1720?" I said the date printed on the coin's rim aloud, confirming my own horrifying suspicion. "The year is 1720?"

"Something like that," he chuckled. "But really who's keeping track out here on these waters?" A sudden drop hit his voice, as though veiling something serious.

"This is a joke." Noah jumped in nearly before Bellamy had finished speaking "This can't be real. Am...am I getting punked?"

"I'm so sorry. To both of you," I muttered, tucking away the coin in my pocket and flicking my gaze between the two of them. This was the quietest I'd ever seen McKenzie, and Noah's eyes were smoldering with frustration and fear. "You were never supposed to have been part of this."

"Part of what?" Noah screamed. "Time traveling?"

Without warning, a cutlass blade lowered down swiftly right between Noah and I, creating a barrier between us. I looked up at Bellamy, who was firmly grasping the hilt. "You still haven't told me your names."

"Katrina," I uttered, gesturing at the other two beside me as a sick feeling rose in my stomach. I wasn't sure if I should've given him my real name. Would it mess with things later on in the future? I didn't know. But it was too late by the time I'd thought otherwise. "It's Katrina. And this is McKenzie and Noah."

I studied Bellamy as he gave an approving nod. Did he know about Milo yet? Had his father forced him to join the crew? Or was this before their unfortunate meeting? And where was Valdez? Bellamy had never mentioned that he'd captained his own ship before.

"I've encountered strange things at sea, but you three are quite the odd trio. You don't seem cut out for a life of sailing. I'd be hard pressed to find a way to make you useful aboard my ship. So, you'll be disembarking at our next port."

"And where is that?" McKenzie chimed, to my surprise.

"Kingston." Bellamy nodded.

"What do you expect us to be able to do there?" I asked.

"I really haven't given it that much thought, love. Your affairs off my ship don't intrigue me enough to be concerned. Be grateful I didn't leave you lost at sea."

I sighed. I don't know what more I even expected. It didn't really matter where Bellamy took us. Because the problem wasn't where. It was *when*. And I didn't even know how to begin to remedy that. And Milo. Was he unable to come with us because of some obscure rule that wouldn't allow him to go back to the time he lived? Was he left behind? Or had he been brought here, too, only to not survive the wreck?

Please, no. Not the last one.

I prayed he was safe, whatever or however that may be. I just couldn't convince myself that he'd drowned. He had to be out there. Bellamy must've noticed the tension in my face as I stared at the wet woodgrain on the deck in thought.

"Relax, lass." He patted my shoulder as he turned to walk away. "It's only a few days voyage for the *Widow*. And I promise my men don't bite." With a cold glimmer in his eye, he looked back at me over his shoulder. "But I might if you're not careful."

As I stood, my nerves jumbled within me like tangled ropes, still processing the impossible reality of it all. The crew members who had been watching us resumed their duties, scurrying across, below, and above the deck. And I stared, in the same insufferable silence as McKenzie and Noah, as the *Widow* caught the wind and rocked forward across the water.

EVERY MAN FOR HIMSELF

12

MILO

When I opened my eyes, I was face down in the sand. My arms ached from swimming. A few coughs quickly arose as I sat up to clear the seawater from my lungs. I let out a groan as my muscles flinched with exhaustion.

"Katrina," I muttered, only to realize she was nowhere to be found in and around this desolate place. "Katrina!"

I called out her name, standing to my feet and taking in the strange coast where the waves had carried me. It was a clearing at a jungle's edge. An opening lush with exotic greenery and twisting vines climbing rocky ledges contrasting with the white sands beneath. It almost seemed familiar, but then again, I'd seen just about every port in the Caribbean...even if it was three centuries ago.

I studied the untouched area, amazed at its wild beauty, already feeling the Caribbean heat I'd long forgotten as the white sun beat down on me. But a cold ghostly chokehold gripped me that no one else from the ship appeared to be here, too. I was alone. And I feared the worst.

As I walked around, surveying my surroundings and looking for any sign of survivors, I noticed a small sign of a campfire still smoldering beneath a lumbering palm. A joy rose within me, as I thought that perhaps they'd made it after all.

At least Katrina. God, Katrina has to have made it.

But one thing caught my eye that made me second guess. A rosary hung there on the sticks used for a hanging pot. My eyes followed the beads to the ground and noticed a small brown leather satchel. This wasn't McKenzie's or Noah's, and certainly not Katrina's. I glanced around, looking for any sign of the owner, and then reached down to see if there might be any fresh water at this campsite, driven by the coarseness of my parched lips. But as I leaned over, a man of my own size leapt down on top of me from the treetops above.

He collided with me, knocking me to the ground and pinning me there with his knee. A flash of silver glinted in the sunlight. I barely had time to glimpse the blade wielded as he plunged it toward my throat.

An instinct that I thought had long gone cold within me suddenly resurrected like embers from ashes. With speed I didn't recognize, I blocked the incoming dagger with a jab of my elbow, and with my other hand caught my assailant's wrist inches before his blade met its target at my neck.

My blood burned within me as I slung the man off me with and made a break out from under his weight. But he wasn't willing to let me escape.

"What do you want?" I grunted, dodging palm fronds and rocks as I kept my distance from him.

"I want to keep my dealings free from the likes of spies." His hoarse voice was like a snake's hiss, cunning and threatening. He was closing the space between us quickly, a look in his eyes I'd seen before. This man aimed to kill me. And he wouldn't stop until he had hit his mark.

He lunged at me, agile and skilled. This man was no brawler. His tactics demonstrated an adeptness best held by assassins or militiamen. Little did he know I'd had my fair share of stealthy combat. Valdez would send me aboard other ships to steal their maps or contracts often enough. If I was caught, I had to put an end to things quietly. This would be no different if need be.

The man leapt for me, curved blade in hand. I reached toward my hip for a sword that wasn't there. Foolish mistake. I'd given him a split second of opportunity to take advantage of my distraction. He swiped his knife across my cheek.

The blood mixed with salt and sweat, singing my skin. I blinked to refocus, catching his arm just as it came down again. This time, he blocked me too. Then he shoved me backwards with a roar of determination. I fought the pain that reverberated through the back of my head as he pinned me against a large rock wall. Wedging my foot, between his, I knocked him off balance, just enough that I could grab the hand that held the blade, turning it on him in a struggle that intensified with each passing second.

"I'm not a spy," I spat through gritted teeth. My jaw was so tightly clenched, my teeth ground together in pain. I could only see the tip of his nose and jaw, under the shadow of the hooded cloak he wore that obscured everything else above.

"You're one of Kellem's. I knew he'd stick his damn nose in this," he grumbled, pushing his forearm against my hold to force his knife closer. "I'll send him a message about meddling in affairs he won't be likely to forget soon."

"Kellem?" I knew that name. A rival of my father's...long ago.

"Stop! Just listen to me," I uttered under my strained breath, bracing with all my strength against the quivering arm pushing into me. A few more centimeters and he'd have my throat slit.

"Just face your fate like a man." With one sudden burst of energy, he fought his way through my defensive grip. I had to make a choice. If I continued to hold back, I knew he would eventually overpower me once I tired out. I released my hold, sliding downwards below him as fast as I could manage as his upper body flew forward into the now empty spot against the rock wall. He turned, grabbing me from behind before I could regain my footing and get farther away. But a sharp metal clang against the rocks was music to my ears. He'd dropped the knife in his effort to seize me.

In our grappling, he held me in a tight chokehold from behind. I wrestled against him as he squeezed until my vision went blurry. My legs buckled and I used the momentum to toss us both to the ground, where his grip on my remained unbreakable. Prying his bicep from my throat was impossible in this position, so I blindly felt around me for the dropped blade. By some divine mercy, my fingers worked the blade into my hand as the last of my vision faded, and with the blade pointed back, I plunged it into the man's side.

His death grip on me loosened, as a short breath of surprise escaped him. I turned to catch him on the way down, my own vision still spinning.

"I'm sorry," I uttered, watching the life leave his surprised gray eyes. I eased him to the ground. This wasn't what I wanted. I hated killing.

With fresh blood staining my hands, I walked back to the campfire without looking back at the body. I took the rosary into my hands and said my penance.

"Forgive me." I clutched the red beads, staring into the ground as I thought of the final moments of the man's life I had just taken. My stomach turned.

He'd spoken of Kellem. Kellem Thatch. I hadn't heard that name in quite literally forever. Who was this man? I glanced over at his lifeless corpse meters from me. His clothing was old. Not in age, but in fashion. Beneath his leather baldric, the hooded vest cloak hinted that he wanted his identity concealed out here for whatever reason. His brown leather boots, loose tunic and breeches certainly didn't look to be anything belonging in the modern world. In fact, they were exactly the sort of thing I might've worn...back in my adolescence.

With a chill, my jaw tensed as I took another look at the landscape. I took out my compass and noted the North just to the left of the tree line. The longer I studied it—the shore, the channel leading out into the sea, the foliage and the barely visible trail leading into the tropical forest flanked by rocks and boulders—I recognized it. This was a clearing I'd come to a few times as a boy playing with the other village children. We'd follow the trail and pretend it led to some new world. But we'd only be met with another variation of the same coastline we'd seen every day of our lives. Just another shore. And we'd turn back and follow the trail that would lead us back to the filthy buzz of Nassau.

So why was this man here? And what secret business did he have with a cheat like Kellem? Or rather his rival...my father.

I hesitated before walking back to the man's body and pulling off his boots and the rest of his clothing. He was roughly my size. If I truly was where I thought I was, and *when* I thought I was, I couldn't be drawing attention to myself in the cargo pants and windbreaker jacket I wore. I swapped out my clothing for his, refusing to leave him unclothed out of respect.

In the vest pocket, I found a note that I was quick to unfold.

Henry,

The Company will be delivering your share of what I owe at Rockshore Point anytime between the tenth and thirteenth of August. If you're not there, they will not come looking for you, believe me. This is a bit of an inconvenience for their route, so be grateful I'm persuasive. There are those watching me now that we're making a name for ourselves on these seas. The Company has made it clear they need me. My fleet can transport as many as they need. And their desperation is too profitable. So don't cause any uproars if you want this balance settled.

-Tiburón

Tiburón was a nickname my father called me. He'd picked it up from Spanish sailors on one of his many voyages to the West Indies. And it stuck.

Kellem was another merchant—a crooked one and my father's rival. And this man thought I worked for him. The signature was my childhood nickname. My father had written this note. And that meant I was back in Nassau before I became part of Valdez's crew. My guess was around 1720. I would've barely been fifteen years old.

I tucked my compass away along with the bloody rosary and took a step in the worn leather boots I'd now claimed as my own. There was no sign that Katrina or the others survived the wreck, at least not here. With my heart torn in a million ways, I pulled the hood over my head, drawing it close to hide my face in shadow as I followed the trail to town, where I prayed I'd find them.

CAPSIZED

13

We sailed on, the Caribbean sun showing no mercy as Bellamy's ship sliced through the water with surprising speed for a ship of its size. I sat on the deck floor with McKenzie and Noah, our backs to the hull as we did our best to stay out of the crew's way.

"If we're really stuck in the past, how are we supposed to get back to the present? How did this even happen?" McKenzie blurted out, her eyes red and puffy and her fair skin already beginning to turn pink from the harsh sun.

"It...It must've been the trident. Cordelia said it controls all time in the sea." I blew a lock of hair from my face in defeat. "I think we got too close or something."

Noah glanced at me, holding onto a long pause before responding. "So, all this time...all the mysterious disappearances of planes and ships...they were just going through some wormhole of time travel."

"I guess so." I shrugged. "But now I'm afraid of what that means in our time. If we're here—not there—that means Cordelia has nothing stopping her from getting the trident."

A spark of light lit up Noah's eyes. "Unless we get it first."

"So, you admit that I'm not crazy?"

"I mean I'm not sure denial would do me much good now. As much as it sounds like bullshit, it's clearly not."

McKenzie leaned in. "Then what do you mean?"

"I mean if we find it 300 years sooner, maybe we can hide it somewhere else."

"That actually makes a lot of sense," I uttered, "But *how* is another question. I don't even know how close or far we are." I looked down as a sudden sadness struck me in the chest. "Milo would know."

I could feel both their eyes on me, and I couldn't find the strength to lift my head.

"If he was here...he would know," I said. "He would know what to do."

A vision of the note left on my door flashed before my mind's eye. I'd gotten upset with him for trying to keep me safe. And now I would give anything to have him here to do just that. I'd asked him to trust me. Now I needed to be able to trust myself.

As McKenzie and Noah talked amongst themselves, I stood to my feet, overlooking the long stern pointing to the horizon. My eyes followed the line of the ship deck until they rested on Bellamy, talking to one of his men near the helm.

I studied him. His piercing blue eyes seemed softened here by the rugged dark stubble lining his jaw. His hair was unkempt, unlike when I knew him, but it suited him in this role. He seemed spritelier, more youthful, and definitely cockier—which I didn't think was possible. But there was also a sternness about him that wasn't there before. He was captain of this ship and he made sure everyone knew it. I could see a version of Valdez in him here, but not in the worst way.

As he finished the discussion with his crewman, he casually turned his face to glance in my direction as I was observing him. I looked away, but I knew I wasn't quick enough. He'd seen me. Our eyes had met for only a millisecond, but it was one millisecond too long. I tried to focus on the horizon ahead of me as heat rose to my cheeks, burning hotter than the white sun above.

If only he knew we'd met before. If only he could remember his future with me. It'd be a lot easier to convince him to help us. But to him, I was just some stupid girl washed up in a shipwreck.

When night fell, we tried sleeping on the deck. It was much too stuffy for us belowdecks, and the smell wasn't very appealing either. I couldn't sleep, though. There were too many thoughts crowding my head, leaving no room for rest, despite the exhaustion in my body. I worried about Milo, and the trident, and getting back to the present—if there was even a present to go back to at this point. For all I knew Cordelia had already gotten her way and the modern world I knew was underwater.

I wanted to watch the stars, but the thin layer of clouds above hid them from me. The full moon, however, was bright enough to shine through, illuminating the deck enough. I could plainly see McKenzie and Noah lying limp as they slept, backs to each other on the wooden boards. Noah had sworn he wasn't going to sleep since he didn't trust anybody here, no matter how tired he felt. But the steady snore sneaking from his mouth said otherwise.

I stood up, examining the deck. It was mostly empty, with the exception of a few half-drunken sailors lying against barrels in a partial slumber. But surely they wouldn't notice—or care—that a castaway was making her way to take a look over the edge of the boat.

Taking a deep breath, I didn't spend too much time looking down at the water. I knew better by now. But as I strode along the hull, I inwardly groaned at what I was considering. But if it could help me find Milo...I could swim back to the wreck site and look for him. Sure, it was dangerous, but it certainly wasn't the riskiest thing I'd ever done for him. The only problem was that I didn't exactly know to bring out that special side of me. But it was the side I would need to survive a solo search and rescue in the sea.

The side with a...tail.

I swallowed. And with one last glance at my sleeping friends, I dove into the water, knowing they would be safer with Bellamy than with me. I couldn't leave Milo. I wouldn't believe he was gone until I saw it with my own eyes.

In the darkness I shuddered at the depth beneath me. I couldn't see through the black depths, and I wasn't sure I wanted to. I knew it wasn't enough just to be in the water. Nothing had activated a transformation in me the entire time we were floating about hours earlier. But I didn't know what else to do. The only time I'd changed, I was at the bottom of the ocean. Maybe I needed to dive deeper to take on the form of myself I was sure had taken over that night I jumped overboard from the *Siren*.

Instinctively, I drew a breath and swam downward into pitch blackness. Some part of me wanted to scream and scramble back to the boat, while another wanted to swim deeper, giving myself fully to the call of the depths. The sea around me terrified me with its mystery and nourished me with its embrace all at once. But nothing happened. I still had legs and I knew I couldn't swim across the ocean like this.

A panic swept over me as I realized this plan may not be working like I anticipated. I quickly swam upward to think more, only to come up short. I dipped back under the water, releasing my air in a string of bubbles from my nose. Sinking like a rock, I looked upward. Even the moonlight was too weak to break through the water's thick surface. So, I kept my gaze focused on the heavens I had no choice but to imagine, just knowing the sky was somewhere up above me. My lungs burned and my heart raced with fear. It wasn't working. I wasn't changing.

As the breath I was holding diminished, and my lungs begged me for oxygen, I started to regret this experiment. I quickly kicked my legs out and swam as fast as humanly possible upward. But I had sunk too far. I couldn't get to the surface fast enough.

My head grew heavy as crushing darkness closed in around me. I thought this was what I wanted, but now that it was happening, I was stricken with fear. The horror of the nothing below me wrapped around me like a smothering cloak. And I wanted out.

A shadow approached, and I flinched. Here, suspended in the shadow of the sea, there was no telling what sort of creatures lurked below. I thrashed, yearning to race upward, but I wasn't sure which way was up anymore. But something splashed above. I saw a stream of bubbles jet behind a shadow that had just shattered through the water. Just before I blacked out entirely, someone embraced me, and swam upward with me pressed against them. I still retained some senses, but if I knew if I opened my mouth to inhale, as I so desperately wanted to do, I'd be out.

Just when I thought I'd have to succumb to the instinct to breathe, I broke through the water's surface, wrapped in the arms of a heaving Bellamy.

"The bloody hell are you doing?" He panted, water snaking down the sleek wet locks clinging to his forehead.

"I might ask you the same thing." I choked. His grip on me tightened, and he pressed me to him in an aggressive manner as he guided us both to the hull of the ship.

"If you can't learn to watch your footing on this ship, next time I won't be so chivalrous."

I nodded, conflicted. My body was grateful that he'd pulled me from that torment, but my mind knew it was only through torment I could become who I needed to be. He'd ruined my only chance at going back to find Milo.

He grabbed a rope hanging from the side of the ship and handed it to me. "Ladies first." He cocked his head and rolled his eyes, seawater still dripping from his brow.

Reluctantly, I pulled myself up, clambering up to the hull with tired arms. I glanced over and saw that McKenzie and Noah were not where I had left them. Bellamy must have noticed.

"Don't worry," he grumbled, stepping onto the deck and walking past me. "They're safe belowdecks. I offered them separate arrangements when I saw your lady friend was drawing...unnecessary attention. And the boy wanted to go with her." I breathed a sigh of relief. Bellamy kept his back to me and strode across the deck, watching his own soaked footsteps as though he didn't trust where they might lead.

"And where are you going now?" I called out.

"Back to my quarters. I didn't expect to be going for a late-night swim."

"What were you doing out here anyway?" I asked. No answer. "Bellamy."

"You are to address me as 'Captain.'"

"You never told me you were a captain."

Bellamy stopped. "What do you mean? I just met you. And I would think it was obvious regardless."

"No," I said softly, not sure why I was telling him this. Maybe I just wanted to see if some part of his soul recognized mine. We never had a proper goodbye. "I think we met before."

With a sly step, Bellamy turned to face me.

"Trust me, love. I would never have forgotten that pretty face."

"Fair enough." I blushed, despite the cool air chilling my wet body. "But I thought your father was captain."

"You know my father?"

"Sort of," I shrugged. It then occurred to me that I had no idea what Bellamy knew at this point in history. I didn't know if he hunted mermaids yet, or if he even knew they existed. And suddenly I realized how dangerous things could have been if he had jumped into the water just a few moments later than he had, if my idea had worked, and he had found me as something...else.

"Captain Valdez," I uttered, the name sour on my lips. "He's quite the man so I hear." I hoped to press him to find out what I could. Maybe knowing *when* to start was the key to getting back home.

"He's a good captain. A poor excuse for a father, though."

"You don't like him?"

Of course, I knew Bellamy hated him in the future. But I had no idea he was at odds with him before.

"I respect him as a seaman. And as a result, he's given me control of this brig. It's all business. Nothing more."

"Oh," I sighed, not knowing what else to say.

Bellamy turned around swiftly, a move I didn't expect. He walked back toward me, the lanterns on the ship giving his skin a touch of a warmth I'd rarely seen on him. But the light only reached so far, and the rest of him remained cast in shadow. For a moment, he reminded me of a ghost, half of him pulled in by the darkness of the night. But his piercing blue eyes still shone through. "You're welcome," he uttered.

I realized I hadn't acknowledged that he'd saved me—even though he'd actually sabotaged my plan. But I couldn't let him know that, of course. "Sorry," I muttered. "Thank you. I'll be more careful."

Bellamy held those blue eyes on me like anchors that had taken their hold, and I pushed away the silent urge to say more. It'd be a lie to say I hadn't thought of him from time to time since the night I broke the curse. But I convinced myself this wasn't what it felt like. This wasn't meant to be a chance to tell him things I never got to say. This was just a fluke. And a huge inconvenience to stopping Cordelia.

I turned away, returning my thoughts to Milo and how I could possibly find him. I refused to think he hadn't survived. He had to be out there somewhere. And I'd brave that dark sea if it meant I could find him. Because I knew I couldn't stay here.

"You're cold." Bellamy's voice cut like a steel blade through the silence of the night. Keeping my back to him, I looked down, noticing the goosebumps along my arms.

"I'm fine. I'll dry."

"No, you can't stay out here like that. It'll only get colder."

"Since when are pirates such gentlemen?"

"Who said I'm gentle?" He grabbed my arm, yanking me forward without hesitation. "I just don't want a sick body aboard infecting my crew."

He pulled me behind him toward the cabin door, and I dug my heels into the floor, fighting his grip.

"Let go of me!" I cried, only to provoke a stoic chuckle from him. He stopped, turned to face me, and then scooped me up like I was no more than a child, throwing me over his shoulder as I wriggled to free myself.

"Don't worry, love. I just need to keep you healthy until we reach port and I can get rid of you. So, you'll be staying where it's warm till you're dry."

As he swung the cabin door open, he pulled me inside and swiftly released my arm, making me stumble. "Now stay here," he growled. He locked the door and sauntered to a hanging hammock bed in the corner, pulling a blanket down from it and tossing it in my direction. "Take this and don't argue."

I caught the heavy blanket with two hands. The threading woven within was soft like lamb's wool, and it smelled of sweet spice, rum, and smoke. I yearned to wrap my chilled body in it, but I resisted, eyeing Bellamy cautiously.

He ran his fingers through his damp hair, shaking it to dry, before removing his heavy, soaked coat. I glanced away when I caught sight of his wet tunic clinging to his chest, the shape of his pectoral muscles easily visible. As he began to peel his tunic from his waist and tugged it upward, I failed to stifle a sound that made my discomfort obvious. "Turn around if it bothers you, lass. I'm not sleeping in these wet clothes."

I searched for words as he continued to undress. The tattoos on his torso and chest held me captive. I felt a strange flutter in my chest when I realized the anatomical heart was there, inked onto his arm, but lacked the two arrows he would add 291 years later. Guilt washed over me as I let my eyes linger a little longer just as he began to undo his belt buckle. Milo was still in the forefront of my mind, and the thought of him was just the encouragement I needed to finally turn around and face the wall.

The sound of pants dropping and the jingling of a belt rattled on the floor. I steadied myself against the gentle ship's movement, trying to brush away the fact that Bellamy stood fully unclothed just a few feet behind me. My heart pounded and my muscles tightened as the air around me became thick. Without thinking it through, I reached for the door handle right in front of me. Though I'd seen Bellamy lock it, I thought maybe I could somehow get it open.

With an unsuccessful jiggle of the knob, I knew I'd made a foolish choice. Within seconds, a muscular tattooed arm from behind me snatched up my hand, pushing me to the wall, firmly enough to rattle me. I fought the conflicting sensation I felt as Bellamy breathed out against my skin, lingering by my ear. When he lowered his face to mine, I glanced down to see he was only clad in a pair of dry dark burgundy pants.

"Listen to me, love." The mocking pet name left his lips quickly and abruptly, as though he'd just chewed on something bitter. "Stop flattering yourself. If I wanted to do anything more with you, I would have."

If he wanted me to act afraid, he would be disappointed. He'd held a sword to my chest before, ready to cut out my heart. And he didn't do it. I wondered if with that perspective, I knew him better than he knew himself.

"Flatter myself? Take your own advice. I'm not worried about you." I narrowed my eyes at him. "I just prefer not to sleep in the same room as a filthy jackass."

Bellamy grinned. "You're on a pirate ship, my dear. You're surrounded by jackasses. Welcome aboard." He looked down, as if he was deciding whether or not to continue. When he spoke again, his voice was softer, more serious, but he still grinned at me as though he found something funny that was unknown to me. "Listen, I have no room in this heart for anything but the sea. And I'm loyal to only her. Now shut up, quit pissing about so much, and put that blanket around you before you catch a fever."

I eyed him suspiciously as he proceeded back to the trunk chest where the rest of his clothes lay, and pulled a billowy, loose-fitting tunic over his head. I internally chastised myself for the heat rushing to my face as I stood, my back still to the wall, watching the muscles in Bellamy's back and shoulders flinch as he worked his way into the thin shirt and then casually climbed into his hammock bed.

Secretly, I was glad for the blanket and warm area to stay, but I didn't want to make Bellamy think I wanted to be here. I slowly sat down, resting my back against the wooden wall behind me and closed my eyes as I wrapped the blanket around me tighter. My damp clothes were uncomfortable, and I yearned to peel them off, but I just couldn't bring myself to do it with Bellamy mere feet from me.

And it was then that the realization sunk in and settled like the wet clothes on my skin. I was really trapped here. In a ship in the literal 18th century, without a clue how to get back. Milo was missing, and my parents would be wondering what happened to me. My friends were trapped here too. All because of me. And Cordelia's words flashed before my mind as I fought away the unwanted, shameful desire I felt rising in me for the man sleeping across the room.

You're just as soulless as me.

The last thing I heard was the slightest hint of a snore from Bellamy's hammock. It was then that I finally allowed myself the luxury to sleep.

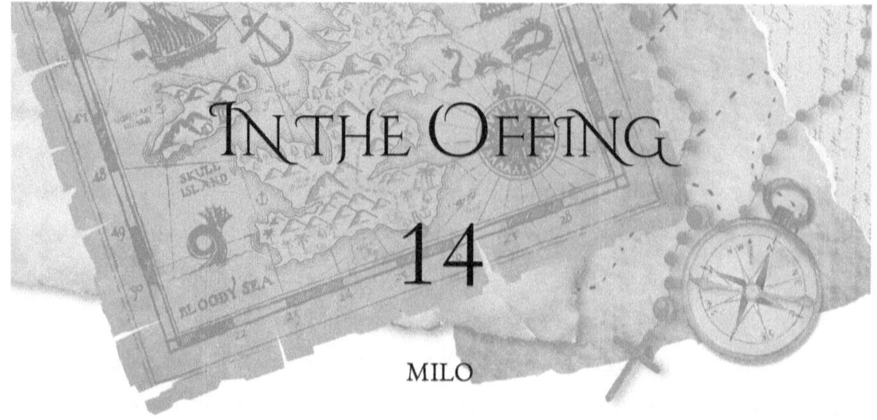

In the Offing

14

MILO

I'd been searching the island for hours, slowly accepting the harsh truth that my friends didn't seem to have ended up in the same place I did. But I had to find them. I *had* to find Katrina.

With a weary soul and aching body, as if by instinct, I wandered home. My feet couldn't help but carry me through the village where I grew up, knowing every one of my steps like I'd taken them yesterday. I wondered what awaited me should I find the courage to see my childhood home. A churning in my stomach quieted my racing thoughts.

Avoiding curious stares, I kept my head tucked low beneath the cloak hood, concealing most of my face. If this was the year I suspected it was, I couldn't risk people recognizing the face of a man who was meant to be a boy. And I certainly couldn't attract the attention of my father, or anyone who might've known us then.

Palm trees grew wild in every corner of the failed colony, poking up from the sand and rising higher than the small wooden houses plotted along the island. Shops like the fisher's stand, the sailmaker, and the tavern brought some sense of order to the place. It was an otherwise lawless place, with taverns and brothels plentiful. Disease was as rampant as the debauchery.

Diseases like that of the sudden infection that took my mother. I knew then that Nassau wasn't the place I wanted to make my home. I hated to admit I was even a citizen. The city was all I knew of a home outside of my birthplace in Portsmouth, England. And when my father was offered a stipend by the king to settle and maintain trade routes in a place the government refused to touch, I knew there was no escaping it. Not till I was old enough.

And yet, as these sour memories invaded my mind, I found some strange peace being back in the time of my adolescence. I smiled slightly at the thought that maybe I'd see my father here. Just to catch a glimpse of him before his untimely fate...

And that's when I caught sight of something that made me shudder in the harbor. Docked at port, it floated, proud and regal—the *HMS Regal Mercy*. A Royal Navy ship that I recognized without trying. I remembered that ship visiting on a very particular day.

I stopped at a nearby tavern by the name of *The Salty Crow*. It stood on the edge of town, frequented by pirates, visiting officials, and locals alike. I knew the owner, old Codface, well enough. With his tavern closest to port, he had the monopoly on fresh gossip from the harbor.

"I'll have a round," I uttered, and watched the withering man slide me a mug overflowing with cheap beer. He wasn't even that old. But his skin had been lost to the sun long ago. "How long has that ship been docked there?" I asked.

"Just got in last night." Codface wiped his face with the back of his arm. "Something about withdrawing funding or something or other. Some bloke going around offering pirates a pardon if they'll just be dumb enough to give it all up. Nothing but the damn king trying to screw us over as usual, I'm sure."

"Hmm. Benjamin Hastings," I said, trying to make it sound like a question as I took a swig from my cup. But I didn't need to ask. I knew exactly who was here and why. He'd helped found this republic, and now he was turning his back on those same pirates who helped him build it. "He's at it again, eh? Maybe Daven can hold him over just a little longer. Before they start hanging us in the streets." My father was one of the few liaisons left here willing to negotiate with both pirates and privateers. He'd be one of the first to report on the state of things when the government paid a visit.

"Aye, a proper mess it is," Codface coughed. "Now pay up."

I dug into my pocket and flicked a coin toward his open palm.

"You look an awful lot like Daven," he said with a strange smile. "You a relative here on business?"

"Something like that." I barely noticed what I was saying. I was too busy turning over the reckless idea forming in my mind. If Hastings was here, that meant Valdez wasn't far behind. I remembered this week perfectly. My father turned to working with Valdez because of the king's ever-growing threats to revoke stipends for tradesmen as the state of Nassau worsened and dealings there became less and less profitable. And Valdez would be here for his next trade deal. But I knew how it would end.

And that's when I thought it.

What if...?

What if I could stop my father's fate? The rosary in my pocket suddenly felt heavy, and I reached in to close my fingers around it. I was given this moment—this chance to be here, in 1720, the exact week my father was double-crossed. It would be the day after tomorrow. What if I could keep it all from happening?

I had to find him. I could hardly suppress the eagerness flurrying in my bones to get up and run home. But I had to. To keep safe the identity of the mysterious man under the hood, I had no choice but to sneak my way back to the house from my childhood.

When I crept inside, the place was just as I remembered. The smell of freshly tanned leather and the crisp scent of map parchment intermingled with that of rum and dust. The roof was still patched from the week before, when my father repaired it after a hurricane had blown through.

My gaze swept the space. My room was small, but it was all I needed as a boy. I was never in it anyway. As I wasn't now. There was no sign of a younger me here at the moment. But I knew he wasn't far. If I wasn't out sailing with my father or repairing the ship, I was out exploring and making my own secret maps of the island. I did wonder, though, if my presence here now somehow disrupted my existence in the past.

In the left corner of the house, near the hearth we never used, my mother's chair faced the center of the room. I could picture her there in it, singing slightly off-key and working her magic with a needle and thread. But the last time she'd sat in it was seven years ago, before the sickness took her. And that's why her portrait now took her place on the seat cushion.

I glanced upward, awakening a memory I'd almost succeeded at pushing away. The door to my father's room stood locked, a heavy padlock guarding the entry. It had been that way since the day Mother died. He said it was his way of protecting her memory. I never questioned it more than once. His reaction—the only time I'd ever seen him lose his temper—had been enough to keep me from prying.

And now, as a man walking in the shadows of my past, I still yearned to see behind the locked door just as much as I did in my adolescence. I walked to the lock, examining it carefully for any sign of weak points. I'd now had my fair share of practice lock-picking, and I thought this one could prove no more a challenge than the others.

But as I touched the lock, I heard voices from the outside. My father's. And someone else. I scurried to the small section of the house that acted as my room and slid underneath the bed, thankful for the silent leather boots I'd swapped out with my attacker earlier.

"I trust you found everything in accordance with what we agreed upon the last time we spoke?" My father's voice became clear as he entered the doorway, his heavy, strong steps as familiar as breathing.   "Aye," the other man's voice was one I didn't recognize, but I assumed him one of the many business partners of my father. "All but one. You were a vessel short. And I've arranged payment as such."

"You know why. My son was on board that ship."

"I don't care about your private affairs, Daven." I couldn't see the scene, but it sounded as though the man was now pacing the room. "All I know is that you wasted a whole ship that could've been carrying an extra hundred or two."

I ran through our voyages in my mind. He might've been talking about any of them. Countless times in my teenage years I'd joined my father with his fleet ships across the Atlantic. I didn't know what made this one any different. Nor what made this trip as wasteful as this man claimed.

"I used that ship to carry the textiles and dyes. There wouldn't have been room."

"You lie, Tiburón." The man chuckled, but there wasn't humor in his voice. "You can keep it up if you must, but I wouldn't if I were you. Remember the cost of keeping secrets."

"Don't speak of Mary Ann, not in my own house." My father's voice was rising, trembling as he held back an anger I'd only seen unleashed once. I wondered what my mother's name had to do with any of this.

The man with him snickered once more, and the sound of a slap like a pat on the back followed. "I didn't mention her name. You did." There was a pause. Even from my hiding space far away from them under the bed, the air was thick with tension before he spoke again. "Just hold your tongue like you always do and we'll all get along fine."

The creak of the door and the lock in place of the knob reached my ears before I'd heard my father sit down. The man had left. I couldn't see him, but I could imagine my father well enough. He was distraught, in the wooden kitchen chair, rubbing his face with both hands in frustration.

The sound of his hand slamming down on the table startled me, and I held my breath as I listened for his footsteps. He was up, walking around now. And then a rattling of something metal. He was unlocking the door to his room.

Once I heard him close the door and the sound of footsteps ceased, I let myself breathe again and crawled quickly out from under the bed and toward the house entrance. I'd be back later to find out what that conversation was about, and why it included my mother. And I'd be back to unlock that door. But for now, I just had to stay out of the way.

MILO

As I wandered the streets, keeping to the shadows, my heart weighed heavy in my chest. What secrets could my father have been keeping? He was by no means a perfect man, but he was always just, fair, and hardworking. That man he spoke with, he seemed to speak with such confidence. But I knew my father.

The distant sound of thunder called my attention. The horizon was darkening, not only with the oncoming evening, but also with storm clouds on their way inland. I'd have to find a place to rest for the night. There was no more time for searching, and certainly not in a tropical storm. I'd planned to sleep in one of my father's ships at port, but that was no longer an option for tonight when the waves would soon be rioting. I reached into the leather pouch I'd taken along with the clothing from my attacker.

Thank God.

There was still a small handful of coins remaining. Enough to afford some lodging and maybe a warm meal for the night. As sorrow trickled across me, I added to my internal prayers that Katrina was somehow protected and safe. Her friends, too, of course, but most of all, *she* had to be all right.

I turned to put the dark sky to my back and began my walk toward one of the rougher streets of Nassau. I paid no mind to the drunken sailors brawling and cursing at one another in the alleyways, nor to the women calling to me through painted lips and sways as I passed.

Tugging at my hood, I entered *The Salty Crow.* Its weathered wooden sign swung in the coming wind as heavy raindrops started their descent.

"A room, please." I placed the coins on the bar counter, my head low. Codface wasn't around that I could see.

"I've got one left upstairs. Watch for the roof leaking in this storm." The bartender gestured to the staircase in the corner leading to the second floor above.

"I'd say a leaky roof trumps total lack of shelter."

"That it does, stranger." The bartender wiped his hands, took the coins and then pulled a pint out from behind the counter. "Something to warm ye?"

I nodded. "Aye."

The rum would do me good. I scooped up the pint no sooner than he'd placed it in front of me. I drank down the potent liquid, savoring every sting on the way down. But it wasn't enough to quell my empty stomach. I asked for a meal and tore into the flounder and chicken set before me. But a vaguely familiar laugh from behind made my stomach churn, and suddenly the food tasted quite foul in my mouth. That laugh was the same I'd heard in my father's house.

I turned to see a group of gamblers. The laughing man was ruddy and large—not overweight, but oversized. His bones must've been steel poles, and he carried the weight of his brawny flesh like armor. His laughter mixed with the thunder outside as he tossed the dice at his table surrounded by others small in stature in comparison. It was him.

The things he said to my father resonated in my mind, and though I knew better, I approached him. "You trade with Daven?" I uttered, careful not to sound wavering by masking my question as a statement.

"Who wants to know?" The man looked up, his voice like iron against a grindstone. I noted his missing hand, replaced with a hook as sharp as a scythe, as he peered up at me through hollow golden-brown eyes.

"I'm here on business. And Daven is my middleman of sorts. No one else. I must see to it that there is no breach of contract."

"That doesn't sound like it involves me," the man growled, returning his focus to his gambling game. "Whatever lines he's crossed with you don't concern me."

"What business do you have with him? At least help me find my lead." I forced my voice to calmness.

"Why would I disclose anything to you? I don't know you. I can't even see your face."

"I'm...Samuel...Holland. On behalf of...the Dutch East Trade Company." I used the first company name I could remember to quickly create my alias. "What business do you have with Daven?"

"Something about the way you're asking sounds personal. And you seem a little too enthusiastic to hear what I might have to say."

"Let's just say I have reasons that carry weight. If it's money you want in exchange for information, name your price and I'll get it."

The man eyed me up and down. "I don't want your money." He stood slowly, nearing me as his footsteps made the floor creak. He stood just an inch taller than me, an unusual occurrence given my near six-foot frame. "But you seem like the type to take on a fool's errand. I might could use a hand for a reckoning that's long overdue."

"I'm listening." My eagerness was getting the better of me. This was my only shot to uncover whatever business my father failed to mention to me.

"There's a sloop out in the harbor, the *Lark*." His voice lowered the longer he spoke. "Her captain's a shameless bastard who mutinied against me. I retreated and he called it weakness. He made his fortune from my losses. Took half my crew and forced me to rebuild from the bottom of the barrel. Let's just say I never completely made my peace with that." He looked bitterly at the hook attachment at the end of his arm where a hand should've been.

"And?"

"And a man hiding his face and begging for information seems like the perfect pawn to help me repay the favor."

"What do you want me to do? Spit it out." I shifted uneasily from one foot to the other.

"I want you to put that sloop at the bottom of the sea floor. If this storm doesn't get to it first."

I hesitated, knowing well who captained the *Lark*. Carl Thane. He was known for his cruelty to prisoners and sailors alike. I was sure it was him who'd taken this man's hand. He'd even tried to overtake Nassau a time or two. Before he'd disappear for months at sea. I didn't mind taking out his ship. But if it went wrong...

"I'll do it." My fist clenched and my heart dropped as the words left my mouth. "And in exchange you tell me everything you know about Daven Harrington."

"You have my word."

"What good is the word of a pirate?" I raised an eyebrow, remembering the time Katrina had asked me the same thing.

"Worth about as much as the word of a shadowy stranger...*Samuel*." He spat out the name with suspicion. "But I'm no pirate. I'm as honest a businessman as there ever was in Nassau. Just with a bit of bad luck." He winked and raised the hook he wore for a hand, turning it so it caught the light, drawing my attention to the jagged scarring around his slightly exposed wrist.

"Where can I find you once the job's done?" I uttered under my breath barely above the noise of the tavern chatter.

"I'll be here each night till I depart in three days."

"Give me your name." I knew it was a long shot to ask. But I needed something. I cursed myself for not asking sooner.

"Not part of the agreement, stranger."

"I gave you mine."

"And I know you're lying about it. So, looks like we both just have to have a little faith in each other." He grinned with a mocking air, revealing a toothy wide mouth that stretched across his broad face.

At least he was memorable. It wouldn't be terribly difficult to find a hulking one-handed man in these parts I knew like the back of my hand anyway. We shook on it, sealing the deal. Before I could say more, he turned and sat back down, resuming his gambling as though our conversation never happened.

I made my way back to my plate and pint. But the sight of the food turned my stomach. Perhaps the rum had clouded my judgment and boosted my confidence too much. I'd just agreed to sabotage a sloop. Because I wasn't sure if my father was the man I remembered. And the girl I loved was still missing. And for the first time in a long time, I didn't have a clue what else to do.

But, whether for better or worse, I had managed to acquire a task to keep me occupied until I figured the rest out. And if everything would go according to the plan I'd already devised in my head, by tomorrow night I'd have sunk Carl Thane's sloop.

Throughout the night, I struggled to sleep. The rocking of the ship and the coldness of my wet clothing and hair kept me uncomfortable. Once I was sure Bellamy was asleep, I wandered over to the chest I'd seen him open earlier. I had to find something dry, or I really was going to get sick. I opened the chest to find what I expected—men's pants and tunics. But I didn't care. I was so cold.

I glanced over my shoulder to be sure Bellamy was still sleeping. As quickly as I could move my shivering body, I stepped out of my wet jeans and top. I kept my bra and underwear, hoping they'd hurry and dry. Slipping a tunic that was much too big for me over my head, I breathed a sigh of relief as the feel of dry clothing touched my skin.

"That's a bit big for you, love." I whipped around at the sound of Bellamy's laughter.

"Were you watching me that whole time?" I snapped.

"Hard not to when you decide to undress right here in front of me."

I shook my head, feeling the heat rushing to my face and a flutter in my stomach.

"Come here," he muttered, propping himself up in his hammock.

I hesitated but stepped closer. I flinched when he reached forward and touched my hand.

"You're half-frozen," he uttered. "Lie here with me."

"What?" I stepped backward, nearly tripping over my own feet.

"I don't believe I stuttered, lass. Body heat works wonders."

I rubbed my arms, unsure of how to respond.

"Get in. Now." His voice was solid as stone.

I choked down the feeling that this was wrong. That I was somehow betraying Milo. It was just to keep me warm, I reassured myself. Nothing more. It was either this or the cold floor again.

With careful steps, I pulled myself into the cloth hammock. Bellamy grasped me by both my arms and pulled me toward him, so that I was fully wrapped in this hanging cocoon of blankets with him. He pulled me close to him, pressing our bodies together, and I thought my wet hair would dry from the heat of my blood racing alone.

I searched for something to say, but nothing would come out. Bellamy rubbed my arms slowly, his blue eyes staring back into mine by the moonlight barely illuminating this small space through the small open slit of a window in the wall. I shivered without meaning to, and he drew me even closer. Face to face, we lay there in the hammock, so close that I could feel the warm air from Bellamy's nostrils against my neck.

"Now go to sleep," Bellamy whispered. I nodded.

What was I doing? Lying here with Bellamy alone in his quarters. All while I knew Milo was lost at sea. My conscience wouldn't silence itself, no matter how much I rationalized it. But before long my eyes grew heavy. My body was finally warm. And I finally fell asleep.

When morning came, I opened my eyes to find my head resting against Bellamy's chest, rising and falling with his slow, steady breaths. I jolted upright to see he was already awake.

"I have to go," I stuttered, scrambling out of the hammock. "I'm completely dry now." I shuffled my feet across the wooden floor to the door, nearly tripping over the long pants and swallowed by the man-sized tunic covering my upper half.

"Who is he?" Bellamy's question caught me off guard. Just as I reached for the door I stopped and looked over my shoulder, but I didn't meet his gaze. I stared at the floor. The weight of his eyes on me felt like stones tied to my ankles.

"Who is who?" I asked.

"The name you were whispering in your sleep all night long." Bellamy sat up in the hammock, dangling his sock-covered feet over them like a child on a swing. "Milo, was it?"

"I...I didn't know I said anything."

"Oh, you certainly did." Bellamy cocked his head. "Who is he? A lover?"

"Y...yes." I tried to think fast. I didn't know if saying too much about Milo here could endanger him or somehow alter the past. I was afraid to speak, not knowing how much I could safely say.

"Where is he?"

I hesitated, biting my lower lip as I fought against acknowledging the reality of what happened to Milo. "I...I don't know." Gripping the door handle, I went to open it, but forgot Bellamy had locked it last night. I waited for him to offer to open it, and when he didn't, I asked, "Can I leave now?"

"Whatever you want, love." He tossed me the key from wherever he'd been holding it. "Later we'll get you and your friends some proper clothing. I believe there might've been some women's fineries aboard the loot from the last ship we took. Surely there's something in there for you."

Great. Now he's going to make me squeeze into a corset or something.

I turned the key in the lock. Bellamy reminded me to leave it in the keyhole for him.

"Aye aye, Captain," I sneered with a roll of my eyes.

Outside it was brighter than I anticipated. After a moment of allowing my eyes to adjust to the blinding Caribbean sun, I scanned the deck for any sign of McKenzie or Noah. I was surprised when I saw them near the hull by the sail rigging. Noah was sitting on the boat's edge, and McKenzie stood listening to a crew member droning on about something.

I went to approach them, but never in a million years did I expect the crude terms that would be hurled at me as I made my way across the deck. But I don't know why I would've expected otherwise.

"Hey lads, Cap'n finally let his new wench back out and off the leash. Are we allowed to share?" One crew member called, drawing attention from the others.

"You don't know what you're talking about," I uttered. "I was just drying off. I...sort of...fell...overboard."

"I'm sure you were drying off alright." Another pirate chuckled.

With my fingers curled into a tight fist, I shook my head, trying to shake away the flush of redness I could feel flooding my face. Storming past the ogling crew across the deck, I made my way to McKenzie.

"Where were you?" McKenzie looked at me through eyes wrought with dark circles—whether from tiredness or just running makeup, I couldn't tell. Her voice still held every ounce of her usual sprightliness, however. Noah glanced at me over his shoulder, eating some type of jerky meat and porridge I couldn't identify.

"Bellamy made me stay with him." I uttered.

"Why?" An ocean breeze caught McKenzie's bright red hair and whisked it across her face.

"Because I was wet, and he didn't want me to get sick. I fell off the ship last night."

"You didn't fall," Noah interrupted from his seat on the edge of the hull. "You jumped. I saw you."

His forwardness caught me off guard, but I wasted no time snapping back at him.

"You're wrong." I tilted my head at him. "I fell." I didn't want them to know the truth of how close I'd almost been to leaving them behind for the sake of finding Milo. Noah already didn't trust me.

"You and Milo make the perfect couple." Noah looked away. I could now see he had been chewing some type of dry jerky. "Both liars and sneaky as hell."

My shoulders dropped. "Can you not, Noah?"

"I'm sorry," he sighed. "Maybe that was cold. But I'm just so freaked out right now. I mean where are we, and how do we get back home?"

"We have to get the trident," McKenzie chimed. "Right, Katrina? Do you think Bellamy could take us to it?" She glanced at me for reassurance, but I didn't even know what to say.

I looked out to the sea. It stretched out into miles and miles of nothingness, just as vast and endless as the blue sky above it. What could I possibly do from here? Could I convince Bellamy to take me to find some mythical trident? And where did that leave Milo? Even if I could find a way back, I couldn't leave without him...

"Maybe," I huffed, glancing down to my bare feet covered by the baggy pants. "But I wouldn't know what to do even if we find it."

Noah stood to his feet, tossing me a piece of jerky. "We use it."

"Cordelia said the only way to use it is to sacrifice the thing most precious to you. Are either of you interested in doing that?"

McKenzie and Noah exchanged a worried glance.

"No one had to sacrifice anything to end up here. I'm sure we can figure out how to make it take us back. But we don't stand a chance without it," Noah said.

"And how exactly do you expect me to convince Bellamy to deviate from his route and take us looking for a trident? We don't know what this could do to the future. I don't know this Bellamy."

"Oh great, so now we're following Back to the Future logic?" Noah groaned.

Something in me snapped. A thread of impatience that I hadn't even noticed weakening. But I couldn't manage the pressure crushing me like a tidal wave. How was I supposed to figure this out? How was I supposed to find Milo, get back to the present, keep us all alive, and save the world in just a few short days? Something in me shifted; darkened even.

"I don't know what the hell we're following!" I seethed. "If you have any better ideas, feel free to go ask Bellamy yourself."

"Ask me what?" Bellamy suddenly stood behind me. I whirled around, cringing at the sensation of my bare feet against the grain of the wood below.

I swallowed. "If...if you could help us."

"I am helping you lot, though be it regrettably," he shrugged, now fully dressed in a pair of loose pants tucked into boots and a loose hanging open-front tunic.

"Yes," I blinked, "And we're grateful, but..." I couldn't continue. As if on cue, Bellamy held up a hand as he squinted to see who'd called his name from the other side of the ship.

"Later," he uttered, walking away to deal with whatever matter it was. "Just stay out of my crew's way for now." Then he turned around and called out to me while still walking backwards and pointing at a crew member in the distance. "Except Tristan. See Tristan there about some clothes that actually fit."

I turned to see the boyish sailor Tristan lugging a crate in his arms near the stern of the ship. He was stacking them with others on board and looked like he'd rather do anything other than interact with me. But with an encouraging look from McKenzie, I approached and found myself handed a pair of small burgundy pants and a white tunic that looked to be much closer to my size. Taking the clothes belowdecks with McKenzie, I put on the new outfit I wrapped a brown sash of cloth over the seams at my waist, tucking in my tunic and pulling on the leather boots I'd found close to my size.

"You look like a pirate yourself now," McKenzie noted.

"Maybe you should put together something a little more century-appropriate, too." I suggested. "You know, it's probably best we blend in once we get to land."

"That's probably true." McKenzie uncrossed her arms and rummaged through the crate of clothing. "Though I just don't feel like any of these are my color." We both giggled at her comment.

"It feels good to laugh," I said. "Every moment feels like hell here."

"It's hard to see the bright side, I'll admit. But try to stop shutting us out so much. We're your friends, and we're just as much trapped here as you are."

"I think Noah would love nothing more than for me to shut him out."

"Well, who can blame him?" McKenzie's tone rose a bit. "Think about what's happened to him. To us. This is a literal impossible nightmare. Noah can be blunt, but he's just stressed. He's scared. And to be honest, I am, too." The air between us hung heavy for a moment, before McKenzie spoke again. "I'm so worried about what my parents must think happened to me. I wish...I wish I had listened to you when you told me not to get on the boat."

I looked down. She was right. I already hated myself for having caused all this for them. I just wanted to get them home, and to make sure there was even a home to go back to.

"I can't tell you how sorry I am that I've dragged you here. Trust me. I'm scared, too. Actually, I'm terrified. But we're going to figure it out. If we got here somehow, there has to be a way to get back."

"Well, we have a lot better chance of figuring it out if we're not all pissed at each other." She nudged me, but her voice was anything but playful.

"Maybe I was a little harsh with Noah. I'm just not myself here." I played with a piece of fraying thread on one of the shirts as McKenzie pieced together her own outfit.

"I've noticed." McKenzie's soft voice was barely audible over the creaking sound of the ship. "None of us are. We're just trying to survive." She sighed, holding up a pair of pants against her waist for comparison. "I just want to be back in our dorm drinking coffee and doing our makeup."

"What, you don't like playing dress up on a pirate ship?" I chuckled. "Don't tell me this ruffly shirt doesn't match my eyes." I batted my lashes dramatically.

McKenzie's lips formed the slightest smile for just a moment, but it quickly faded as her gaze met mine.

"What?"

"I'm just making sure I know what color your eyes actually are," she said gently. "When you yelled at Noah, I could've sworn they flashed blue. Like a deep blue. But now they're back to brown. Like I thought. I guess the sun is getting to me."

"Blue?" I glanced up. She nodded confidently.

"Hmm..." I said, mentally adding yet something else to my list of things to worry about. "That's...weird."

"Maybe it was just a trick of the light, but I don't know." McKenzie flicked her head to the side.

"Well, whatever it was, it's the least of our problems right now." I grabbed a pair of pants and shirt with a vest and tossed them to McKenzie. "Tell Noah to put these on. He'll do it if you ask him. If I try, he'll probably just throw them overboard."

McKenzie nodded and began to walk away. But she stopped at the steps leading up to the deck and looked back at me. "Hey Katrina," she said softly. "What if we never make it back?"

I looked her over in her loose flowing skirt and billowy tunic and cracked a small smile. "Then at least we'll look the part." I chuckled, but it wasn't enough to hide the worry in my voice.

With a half smile and another nod, she made her way back up top. I sat in silence in the darkness of the ship's innermost space. The smell of fish and salt toyed with my senses, and the muffled sounds of the crew above deck sounded distant, like a far-off dream. I thought of the last thing's I'd said to Milo. Was it something I said that made me lose him? Was this fate's cruel way of giving me what I deserved?

And Bellamy...What was I feeling when I was lying next to him? Something I didn't want to feel. Something I refused to acknowledge.

As I sat there, staring into the shadows and rat-chewed burlap sacks of grains on the floor, the sound of rushing footsteps above made me stand alert. Next came yelling, and before I knew it pirates were sprinting down the steps to get past me, running to the cannons lining the inside of the ship.

"Man the cannons! All hands!" A voice cried.

"What's happening?" I asked, rushing back above deck. It looked like a battleground already, with men running across the soaked floor to and fro, shifting sails and tying ropes.

Bellamy came storming past, sliding an arm into his captain's coat as he walked. He didn't stop as he spoke. "Get your friends and get belowdecks," he ordered firmly into my ear. I glanced across the water, noticing a massive warship approaching our direction with British flags flying proudly.

Bellamy yelled out to the crew. "She's too much ship for the *Widow* in this shape! But she's coming for us, nonetheless! Man those cannons and tar the barrels! Load them with whatever you can find! We can't take another hit after that last scuffle! I'll try to outrun her but be ready just in case!"

In the chaos and confusion, I whipped my head around, looking for my friends. Noah appeared suddenly, hand linked with McKenzie's, and he grabbed my arm as he led us both downstairs.

"Let's go!" He yelled, pulling me belowdecks with them. I don't know why, but I fought to catch one last glimpse of Bellamy before I lost sight of the scene on deck. He was at the wheel, still shouting orders and commanding the crew with a confidence in his voice that I found inspiring. This Bellamy knew who he was. And he loved it.

Tucked away underneath the ship's hold, we waited in fear of what would happen next. Any minute I expected a hole to be blown in the wall of the ship beside us. The minutes were agony. And eventually, silence fell.

"I think we outran them," I said.

But at the sound of incoming cannon fire, I immediately knew I was wrong. A distant boom followed by a brief silence warned us to brace. I held tightly to McKenzie and Noah, there kneeling on the floor of the ship's hold. I wondered if it was a good idea to be this low if the ship were to start sinking.

Within seconds, the impact of multiple cannons shook the boat, tearing holes across the deck and battering the hull to splinters. McKenzie screamed, and I bit my lip so hard I thought my teeth would tear right through it.

Once the rocking of the ship subsided and it seemed we had recovered from the hit, a long pause hung in the air.

"Somebody go check on the captain up on the gun deck! See what's going on up there." A crewman behind a cannon suggested.

Before any of them could offer to do the task, my hand shot up and I clambered to my feet.

"I'll go," I volunteered. Noah grabbed my sleeve as I stood to walk away.

"What are you doing?" He grumbled. "It's insane to go up there."

"I just want to see what happened," I said. "If we're going down, we're going down whether I'm down here or up there."

I climbed the steps quickly to find Bellamy at the helm, focused with an intense gaze on the open water in front of us. Behind us trailed the British warship, an intimidating sight through the haze of the smoke its cannons had left behind rising from the stern.

"Can you outrun them?" I called, rushing to Bellamy's side.

"I have no choice. If they hit us again, she's sunk." Suddenly, his eyes widened. "Why are you up here? Go back down!"

"I'd rather face it than go down hiding like a coward."

"It's not cowardly to keep yourself safe. I'm trying to protect you!"

Something in me stirred again. Bellamy's words reminded me all too much of Milo. I shook my head to reset my thoughts and fight the fire building within. Bellamy shouted another order to the crew, and the sails lifted higher. The same wind catching the sails caught my hair and swept it behind me, dancing across my neck and shoulders. As if a breath of fresh courage rippled through me, and along with it, a foreign feeling of power and strength. Like I could tear down anything in my path.

I stepped forward, past Bellamy, and planted myself firmly at the bow of the ship as we sailed on. I looked out into the stretch of blue before us and breathed in the briny air. We'd outrun that ship. We *had* to, if I was going to be able to get any of us out of here. And then with all the force in my voice I could summon, I shouted a command I could never forget as I finally embraced the fact that this was it. This was reality. I was sailing with pirates in 1720, so I might as well act like it.

"Under full sail!"

I dreamed of Katrina that same night. If only for a moment, I saw her face, calling to me from across the sea. And no matter how much I swam, I could never get any closer to her. And then nothing.

The next morning my head ached. Perhaps I'd gotten too drunk. I must have, stupidly, because my coin pouch was almost empty. Either someone stole it from me, or I'd spent it all on gambling. It seemed my old habits were quick to return.

Damn.

I pulled on my boots and exited the tavern expecting to see a gray sky, but it appeared the night's storm had long passed. A bright blue horizon greeted me, the sun high over the Caribbean waters. Leaves littered the streets from the wind and the ground was still damp. But otherwise, it was a beautiful day for sinking a ship.

I made my way to the rooftops of the buildings nearby. It was important that I stayed out of sight, but I still needed to be able to watch the harbor and determine my point of entry. As the sun beat down on me, I gazed down at the bustling life below. I hoped that maybe, just maybe, I might be able to spot Katrina or one of the others if they'd made it here, too.

Something caught my attention. A whistle. And then the bark of a dog. I peeked over the edge of the roof I was utilizing as my perch and smiled. It was just as I thought. Me—my young self—with a scrappy brown dog at my heels. Peg. I'd named him Peg for the gimpy leg that did nothing to slow him down. The mutt could still outrun me and any other dog in the village. Father wouldn't let me "keep" him, but Peg knew he was my dog. He was a stray by definition, but he always found me.

I watched myself and Peg jumping about, playing with an old stick I'd found on the ground. It lasted only briefly, before I knew I had to stop playing about and tend to my father's work. I remembered that day, like so many others. I was always looking over my shoulder to make sure he didn't catch me playing with Peg when I was supposed to be patching sails or inspecting the hulls for any spots in need of repair.

The grin on my face faded when the pair walked out of sight. I remembered the dark fate soon approaching that young boy playing with his dog. This boy had already spent so many nights crying over his mother's death. If only he knew how many more tears would have to fall before he'd harden to it all. Perhaps it was better he didn't. Let him enjoy this short happiness with Peg.

I waited there until evening came. Unlike the one before, it was a calm night. Ignoring the hunger in my empty stomach, I climbed down once the port became quiet. I pinpointed the *Lark* with ease. She floated six ships back, with a blood-red flag raised high—a warning that the crew took no prisoners and left no survivors.

When I was certain I had a shot, I climbed down, keeping the path to Carl's ship I'd mapped out in my head close to the forefront of my mind. I shuffled through the docks, careful to stay hidden, using crates and barrels to hide behind whenever I sensed someone nearby. My boots were silent on the wet wooden boards.

There would be no easy way to reach the boat. I'd have to swim. Drawing a deep breath, I dove in, careful to keep my splash as subtle as possible. I was thankful for the calm waters as I swam toward my target. Once I reached the side of the sloop, I gripped the side of the hull, feeling along the sides for any section I could use to pull myself up. Once I found a hold, I climbed with all my might, fighting the added weight of my soaked clothing and boots.

Once aboard the ship, it was only instinct to look around. In the pale light of the moon, I could make out the barren deck of the boat. There wasn't much here, which made sense. Carl and his men would've returned from a looting expedition or a raid and had probably sold off everything by now, only to come here to recharge and reward themselves for a while. So, I expected this sloop to be empty.

I moved carefully in the darkness, taking a walk down into the galley and belowdecks. Every good sailor should have a tinderbox down here to light the lanterns in case of an emergency. The question was whether Carl was a good sailor.

I scanned the row of barrels along the back wall. Oil barrels. And two rum barrels. Perfect. To my delight, in a large chest by the bottom of the steps, there was a box, complete with flint, a steel striker, and some pieces of dry cloth.

I reached into my satchel and pulled out a bottle of liquor I'd swiped from the tavern. Quickly and quietly as a church mouse, I turned the bottle over and doused the innards of the ship with the pungent liquid, being extra careful to coat the oil barrels. I made a trail, using a small pile of tinder from the tinderbox as the starting point. I didn't have enough to lead all the way back up to the deck, however. So, I'd have to be fast.

With the trail of alcohol as long as I could manage to make it, I struck the flint against the steel until I saw sparks. With hands I fought to keep from shaking, I tossed the burning piece of tinder down to the pile, where it immediately caught, creating a ball of orange flames as it began to follow the line of alcohol to the oil barrels. I knew I had mere seconds to get out of there.

I rushed to the galley steps, darting up to the deck. My eyes locked onto the edge of the ship as I ran to leap overboard into the water. But there was someone there. On the deck. It wasn't Carl. But whoever it was, he was young. Older than me, probably, but still young.

"Hey, you!" He cried, holding up a lantern. "What are you doing here?"

"Get off the ship!" I yelled, still running and not slowing down.

With a nagging in my conscience that I couldn't ignore, I turned to his direction and ran toward him, counting the mere seconds in my head that I knew were left before this boat went up in flames. The old me wouldn't have saved him. But I had too many regrets now not to.

I leapt forward, pushing the frantic man overboard. He tumbled over into the water below, cursing and screaming on the way down, and I went to jump off, too, but I'd lost one second too many. Bright orange lit up the air behind me. The sound of wood splintering pierced my ears as a flash of light consumed the night. The force threw me into the water, even as I'd already dove into the air, the heat singing the skin on my back even through my thick shirt and hooded vest cloak.

Without looking for the man, I set my sights on the side of the harbor, where the entrance back into Nassau was unkempt, wild routes of nature. A place I could escape to quickly without being recognized. As the ship crackled and lit up the black water with yellow flames, I swam like a devil to shore.

There. It was done. Carl's infamous sloop was destroyed and the hook-handed man who asked me to do it had better be ready to tell me what business he had with my father. I planned to find him immediately. I didn't trust him not to try to make a quick escape once he saw that I'd actually gone through with his request.

I heard screaming from the distance. The lights of lanterns became visible, one by one, as people started to notice the ship aflame in the harbor. Though I hoped that man survived, I also hoped he didn't take note of my features or any part of me that might make me recognizable. Because I knew this town would soon be rioting with chaos and accusations trying to pinpoint the culprit.

No matter right now. I needed to get back to Hook-Hand. I didn't even know the time. Destroying that ship felt like it had lasted only a mere moment. But my sense of time passing was quite unreliable in this state.

Leaving the blazing port behind me, I fled back toward the city, dodging behind crates and wagons any chance I had. There weren't many people in my path, but I still did everything I could to keep my dripping wet clothing from leaving a trail in the dirt that had already dried from last night's storm. As I approached the tavern, I paused at the sight of Carl Thane himself bursting through the door, the look of a madman in his eye. He must've just heard the news of his ship's fate. He looked around, grinding his jaw as he addressed the crewmen in tow behind him.

"If anyone knows the fucker responsible for this, he'd be wise to speak up! Because when I find him, I'll paint my next ship with his blood after I peel the skin from his bones with my own teeth! And I'll feed it to whoever stayed silent about it!"

I shook away a shudder along my spine. A threat like that wasn't far-fetched at all for Thane. He was known to cut off the ears and lips of his enemies or traitors. Or he'd pry off their fingernails with wooden stakes. He was a twisted excuse for a pirate, and every one of us knew it. I'd even dare say he was more demented than Valdez.

I waited in the shadows for him to pass, and once he was out of sight, I quietly slipped into the tavern. It was almost empty. Except for Codface and Hook-Hand, who was leaning up against the wall near the back.

"Everyone's gone to see the fireworks," Hook chuckled, stepping forward.

I neared him so that I could speak low enough for Codface not to hear me. I didn't need anyone involved that didn't need to be.

"I did what you asked," I grumbled, keeping my face tucked downward. "Now tell me about your business with Daven."

"I have to say, I really didn't think you would—or *could*—do it." He grunted a bit before continuing.

"Your underestimation of me is not my problem. Now honor the code and tell me what you promised." I was growing impatient.

"Fair enough." He looked out into the tavern and shifted his weight from one leg to the other. "But know this. After tonight, don't come looking for me anymore. You'll mark us both as dead men if we draw attention."

"You're wasting my time." If he could see my eyes under the shadow, he'd know I was holding a gaze strong enough to burn through the flesh on his face. My fists clenched at my side.

"Allright, damn." He finally spoke. "Daven is my shipper."

"He's a shipper for many a company." I rolled my eyes, aggravated with the way this man danced around giving me the information he promised. "What does he ship for you? What merchandise it that was so imperative that he filled every last ship in his fleet to the brim with?"

The man looked shocked. He stepped backwards uneasily. "How did you hear my conversation with him?"

Dropping my guard, I lunged at this hulking man, pulling my knife from my belt and digging the tip into the skin of his neck. I no longer cared what Codface saw.

"I didn't just put a bounty on my own head for that shitty scrap of information." I growled. "I know more than you think already. Yes, I heard your conversation yesterday. So, tell me what it is Daven transports for you or I'll deliver you to Thane myself—piece by piece."

I could hardly believe the words coming out of my mouth. I hadn't negotiated like this for centuries. But this was how I survived then. And it was how I was going to have to survive now. A pirate's life was anything but gentle.

Hook grabbed my wrist with his good hand before speaking again. I pushed the blade against his skin, drawing a thin line of blood.

"You're just as unhinged as Thane." He laughed. "Daven transports shipments for me and my company—The West Royale Trade."

"You're a slaver?" I spat, knowing all too well that dreaded company name.

"Is that a problem?" The man coughed.

I didn't respond. I was too busy processing it all. As I loosened my hold on the man, unable to think properly enough to know what to do next. He shoved me backwards and sauntered past me, knocking me into a table, but I didn't care. I straightened and picked up my knife as I watched him leave. But I couldn't move from that spot. Because I couldn't believe my father—the man who'd always preached nobility and the value of life to me—was shipping *people* across the Atlantic like stock animals.

OVER A BARREL

18

MILO

As I connected the pieces, it slowly made sense, no matter how much I didn't want it to. Father's fleet was made up of large cargo ships, and at some point or another, I'd been aboard all of them, however briefly. But more recently, that year, he'd only assign me to the same ship—*The Marietta's Jewel*—for the few voyages on which I accompanied. And each time I was ordered to stay behind and man the vessel while he took the cargo ships inland for a "quick exchange." Or I'd be sent to a different port to offload that ship separately. The last voyage we'd made to the African coasts was supposed to have been a normal delivery of textiles and rum. But clearly Father had arranged some additional dealings. How long had he hidden it from me? When did he stop transporting merchant goods and switch to being a pack mule for the slavers?

A pit formed in my stomach. My life had been a lie. I hated many things about Nassau, but it was a place where every man was equal, free from the confines of societal expectations. It was a haven of refuge built by outcasts and fugitives, exploited poor men and aristocrats turned rebels, men born free and men who fought their way free alike. No one was lower or higher. The only thing that owned us was the sea. So, I couldn't comprehend how my father was part of something that stood against everything I thought he'd always believed.

A part of me refused to believe it. My father wouldn't do this. He couldn't have been this desperate for money. I needed to see for myself. If not for the commotion going on at the harbor, I would've snuck aboard one of his ships right then to take a look at the other ships' cargo holds or his captain's log. But I couldn't risk being seen. Not now.

For now, I needed to get as far away from here as I could. For all I knew, the man I'd pushed overboard had told everyone that he saw me cause the explosion. What had I done?

I took off into the night, stealthy and silent, making my way to the farthest corner of the island. There was one building where I knew I'd be safe for the time being. The old church.

It was a symbol of refuge on this night as I saw the white stone cathedral contrasting against the midnight sky. The bell tower was cracked, and the doors to the sanctuary were barely still hanging on to their hinges. I stepped inside the small building, not expecting to see anyone else here this time of night. The candles were unlit, but by the light of the moon streaking down in bands through the bell tower opening, I could see the inside well enough. Old wooden pews lined either side of the aisle I trudged down with echoing footsteps. It stirred up the vaguest of memories.

My mother came here often. She loved to pray. I'd come with her a handful of times as a child, but it wasn't a place to which I typically chose to venture. How ashamed she'd be of the life her son had made. In some ways, I was glad she died before seeing what I became. She couldn't have prayed for my forgiveness enough. But she would've tried anyway, I knew.

And did she know of my father's sins? Maybe that's why she was here so much. *No.* If Father worked so hard to hide it from me, I'm sure he hid it from her, too. But why? Why did he turn to something so vile when our merchant business had always sufficed? I supposed for the same reasons he turned to Valdez. The need for money. But I wasn't aware of whatever great debt he owed that drove him to this.

I sighed, sliding down into the second-row pew just meters from the altar up front. It was a relief to finally pull the hood back from my face and let the cool air refresh me. My weary body ached, and I leaned forward, hanging my head over the back of the pew in front of me.

Suddenly I remembered the rosary I'd taken. With tired hands, I rifled through my pants pocket. I knew there was some method to this, but I didn't know it. I remembered bits and pieces from watching my mother in passing...Somewhat. With uncertainty, I took the rosary beads in my hand. It was easy to see the dark dried blood on them against their vivid red. Making the cross symbol across my forehead and chest, I bowed my head.

"Forgive me," I grumbled into the empty air, "for my sins and the sins of my father."

Of course, I expected the silence that came after I spoke. But it was painfully deafening. "Please. I seek forgiveness." I no longer knew if I was asking God or myself. I thought of killing that man on the shore. And nearly slicing open Hook's throat. And lying to Katrina and then failing to keep her safe through all this. And all the things I helped

Valdez accomplish. And now here I was—a pirate with three centuries of guilt weighing on his shoulders, praying for forgiveness in an empty, rotting church with a stolen, bloody rosary.

OVERBOARD

19

Bellamy abandoned the helm, charging forward to where I stood on the boat's edge.

"Hold fire! What the hell do you think you're doing?" He yanked me down with a tug of my arm.

I stared at him in surprise, though it only made sense that he would ask me what I was doing. I wasn't even sure myself.

"Why did you leave the helm? I thought we have to outrun them." I glanced back at the ship in the distance behind us.

"We do. But I'm the captain. I give the orders. You don't even know how to keep from falling overboard."

"I didn't fall overboard." The words rushed out of my mouth faster than I could stop them. But I immediately knew I'd said too much.

Bellamy's eyes narrowed at me. "So, what then? You jumped?" He said sarcastically.

I cursed silently to myself. Why did I say it?

"Damn…You jumped." Grazing his hand across the back of his neck, he glanced down at the wooden deck below, then back up at me. "Why?"

Thankfully, the ship behind us quickly recaptured his attention again before I could think of a response. He whipped around, racing back to the helm. I followed.

"At least now I know why you were stupid enough to come up here. You've got a death wish." Bellamy spoke over the sound of the ship tearing through the foaming seawater below as the sails above us billowed in the wind.

"It's not like that," I said. "Just trust me."

"Trust you? I don't even know you."

Something about his words stung and I didn't know why. It shouldn't bother me that Bellamy didn't recognize me. There was nothing between us. There never had been. So why did it bother me so much to feel like I'd lost something I never had?

When the explosion of cannon fire rang out overhead, I ducked behind a mast and braced. But the impact never came. Instead, great splashes of water sputtered in the distance, just barely missing the back of our ship. I glanced up to see Bellamy grinning, a sly look set in those ice blue eyes and perfect teeth.

"We've sailed out of their range, and I've turned us into the wind, which will slow a galleon of that size down. That was their last attempt to stop us, and they missed. We're too far for them to bother catching up now. If we aren't easy prey, we're not worth the chase. We hold this speed till they're out of sight," he said.

I watched as the crew emerged from their spots beneath the ship's deck, cautious at first, but then eager and celebratory. Bellamy stood firm, still standing firm with his hand on the ship's wheel.

"Inspect her for damage. She took a few nicks on the starboard side," he ordered the men on board.

The crewmen scurried away, scanning the sides of the boat in a hurry. Some of them called out to Bellamy in a way that didn't sound positive. Bellamy shouldered past me, as though I was more of an obstacle in his path than another body aboard his ship. "Take the wheel and don't turn it even the slightest," he muttered.

"What? Really?" I stuttered, slowly and hesitantly reaching for the wheel. But Bellamy ignored me and walked off to further inspect the section of the ship that had been hit. When he came back, he wore a scowl that told me the damage must've been serious.

"That bad?" I asked.

"She'll make it a good few leagues just fine. But I can't risk her getting in another scrapple like that again like this." He paused, taking in a deep breath of sea air as he reclaimed his position at the helm. "We'll have to stop at the nearest port for repairs. It'll slow us down a bit, but don't worry, we'll get to Kingston soon enough."

"The next port," I muttered. "And where is that?"

Bellamy ruffled his hair, focusing his eyes on the glassy blue surface below us. "Nassau. Fortunately, it's not too far off our path. We should be there tomorrow afternoon if we can hold this speed and the wind stays on our side."

"Nassau?" I repeated, remembering what Milo had long ago told me about the pirate colony.

"Nassau. Paradise. One in the same," Bellamy confirmed with a grin.

Nassau. Milo had told me so much about it. And...and if Bellamy was here...did that mean Milo might be there? My shoulders straightened and I lifted my chin. It was foolish hope. But it was hope, nonetheless. I knew it was ludicrous to expect it. But I had to hold onto something. Because up until then, I was truly starting to fear I'd never see Milo again.

"Listen to me," Bellamy growled, his voice suddenly like gravel. "Don't ever disrespect me in front of my crew like that again. You're starting to make me regret saving you. Both times." And with that, he stormed off back to the helm.

If only he knew I didn't understand what had come over me then either. When I stood at the bow and yelled into the open sky, I hardly recognized myself. But I'd felt powerful with the sea in front of me and below me and behind me. I'd almost been tempted to dive in as I stood there overlooking the depths. And something in my head had told me I could command every soul on this ship if I tried. And I don't know why I wanted to.

I shook away the foreign feeling. It had to be the sea salt in the air getting to me. And the heat of midday wasn't helping.

Just then Noah and McKenzie came running over to me, frantic with just the reaction I expected.

"What were you thinking, Katrina?" McKenzie looked at me with eyes wide beneath a wrinkled forehead.

"I wasn't thinking," I uttered. "I just...I thought Bellamy was hurt."

"Why would you care about Bellamy?" Noah threw his hands up, and McKenzie touched his arm to settle him.

"Katrina had a thing with Bellamy before Milo. He was cursed too."

"We didn't have a thing!" I snapped, stumbling with the movement of the ship. "Neither of you have any idea what's going on with me." As I spoke my head spun. And I knew I'd said the wrong thing. But I had to get away from them. From everyone. Something was wrong.

Putting a hand to my head, I glanced between a shocked McKenzie and Noah. "I'm sorry," I stuttered. "I really am. I didn't mean that. I'm sorry." I turned away. "I think I just need some time to think. Alone."

The quick nods they offered in response reassured me that my apology was enough, but I could tell by their worried expressions that they were concerned. But what more could I say? I couldn't explain my dilemma because I didn't understand it myself.

I quietly walked to the stern on the forecastle upper deck above Bellamy's quarters. It was rarely occupied and seemed the perfect spot to escape the constant commotion of the crew. I curled up and brought my knees to my chest. Despite the blazing sun, I felt ice cold inside.

I watched the stream of churning water trailing behind the ship, foaming white froth dancing on a blanket of blue. Each curl of the waves beckoned me like fingers coaxing me in their direction, calling me, begging me. I yearned for my paintbrush to capture this moment as my eyes drank in the scene below. I wished I could paint. To remember. To understand. To escape in at least one way.

I wondered if I might find some kind of material that I could salvage enough into a makeshift paintbrush. There had to be something on board this ship that could work. I stood to my feet, looking for whatever I found that could have potential as a brush handle.

There was nothing that I could find that worked. The fishing rods and oars were far too thick to make use of. I felt like an idiot for worrying about painting at a time like this. But it was the one thing I could do something about. For now, I could only wait until we reached Nassau to do much of anything.

When searching the ship proved a waste of time, I thought of the one place that might have something. I'd seen writing utensils and navigation tools of the like in my time in Bellamy's cabin. There had to be something in there I could use.

With Bellamy at the helm, I did my best to go unnoticed as I scurried across the ship's length. The last thing I wanted was to give him another reason to make me stay the night in his bed again. I slipped between the crew members along the deck and to the captain's quarters, testing the door handle once I reached it. A grin stretched across my face as I realized the door wasn't locked and entering was just a matter of turning the knob.

It creaked open, reminding me faintly of when I'd snuck aboard the *Siren's Scorn* to steal Valdez' key. With footsteps light and a breath caught somewhere between my throat and my lungs, I crept forward, looking at the items all around me as I passed. A small desk of Bellamy's stood nestled beside the chest where he'd kept his clothing the night before. I didn't have the chance to get so close to it then, so I quickly walked over to examine it further. Rummaging through the mess of papers and half-burnt candlesticks, I was disappointed not to come across anything even remotely pen-like that I could convert into a paintbrush handle.

But when I looked a second time, I noticed something I hadn't at first—a charcoal pencil. It was long and blocky and awkward. But it would do. I tucked it in the sash tied around my waist and looked for a knife I could use for the brush. One of Bellamy's cutlass swords rested sheathed against the corner. I pulled out the blade, admiring it for a moment. I'd never held anything like it before. The clear steel reflected my own face back at me and I nearly jumped at the sight. I was ragged and worn, but I looked fiercer than ever. My face was the same, but something about it now seemed striking and intimidating. Something was happening to me.

I shook away the chilling realization and refocused on the task at hand. Selecting a thin strand of my hair, I pulled it taut with one hand and carefully guided the sword's blade with the other. Just a few inches should be enough for a thin brush head.

That's when I heard the door creak open.

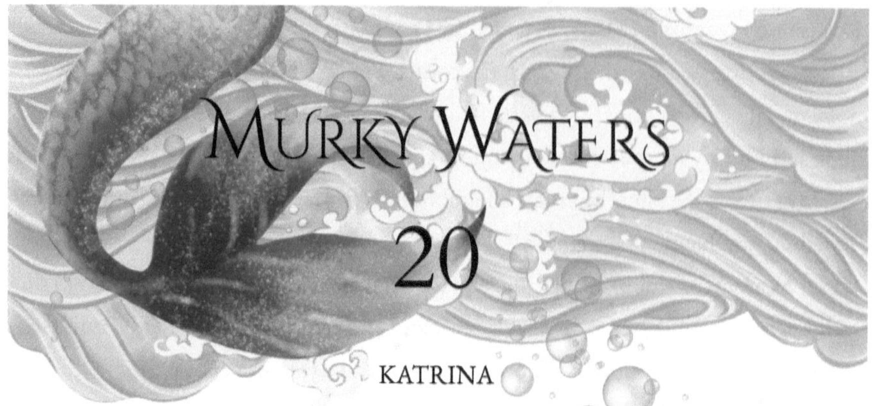

Murky Waters

20

KATRINA

"**I**'d ask you why you were in here," Bellamy said while he walked up behind me. "But there's no possible explanation you could give that would make it acceptable."

Something in me stirred again, like a whirlpool within that I couldn't control. I spoke before turning around to face him, still holding the sword firmly in my grasp. "You didn't seem to have a problem with me being in your room last night," I said calmly. "Make up your mind. Do you hate me or want to sleep with me?"

I was shocked at my own words. They were out before I'd even thought to say them. It wasn't like me to be so snarky and confident.

Bellamy leaned toward me, his unruly black locks falling around his eyes. "Maybe a bit of both." He gently took the sword out of my hand. "Now tell me why you're in here. And what you're doing with this."

Don't tell him. Make him wonder. Make him beg to know.

"None of your business," I snapped, fully attentive to the strange new inner voice in my head.

"My sword. My business," Bellamy smirked.

"Fine," I said, momentarily shaking my head to return myself back to normal. My voice softened. "I...I just wanted to paint."

"I must admit that's not at all what I expected you to say." Bellamy cocked his head. "You're a strange lass."

"You have no idea," I muttered. "Now can I have the sword back?"

"Not yet, love." Bellamy's ice blue eyes glimmered beneath sturdy raised brows. "See, you've got me thinking, Katrina." He spun the sword in his hand by the hilt, with no more effort than if he was flipping a pencil. "If we were to run into any more trouble along our route, you and your bilge-sucking friends are rather defenseless—dare I say *useless*." He raised the sword between us before continuing. "So, I'm going to teach you how to hold your own properly. Sunset. On the main deck. We're going to have a little lesson."

"What if I say no?"

"Then you can meet me at the end of the plank instead."

I lifted my chin. Bellamy had always been arrogant, but this surpassed even the Bellamy I thought I knew. "Fine. But I doubt you'd really do that. After all, weren't you the one who jumped in after me last night?"

"Don't push your luck, love. I'm less of a gentleman than you think." With a wink that made my blood boil, he placed the hilt of the sword back into my hand.

As he turned to walk away, he tossed something back over his shoulder. I caught it with a last-minute reflex. It was a paintbrush—a strange, awkward wooden brush with the finest tip—but a brush, nonetheless.

"Old mapmakers' brush," Bellamy said, still walking away. "Now as for paint, you're on your own. But rest assured you won't find it here."

With a toss of my head, I turned to go, taking a few scraps of parchment paper from the desk as well. I wouldn't let Bellamy get under my skin any more than I'd let him get into my heart.

Back out on the deck, I explored the bilge of the ship. I only knew the term because I'd heard the rest of the crew call it that. Down there I found cargo with crates labeled as spices, dyes, and fine silks. Stolen, I presumed. But this seemed exactly like the kind of place I could find something to use as paint.

I took a handful of powdered dye from a crate I managed to open at the corner. Any color would do. I was pleased to see a tablespoon's worth of deep indigo and red when I opened my palm. I tore a piece of fabric from my sash and dumped the powder in, being careful as ever not to mix it.

Satisfied, I scampered back up to the upper deck. Returning to my spot at the stern, I seated myself on the deck floor with my weird brush and makeshift pigments. I hardly had enough parchment to paint on. But I didn't care. I just needed the movement of the brush in my hand. The comfort of my strokes creating trails of color. It was the only thing that was still the same.

I needed water to mix with the dye powders. But the late afternoon sun had dried the deck completely. So, I sat there, feeling that, like everything else I tried, this wasn't going to work. And I suddenly thought of Milo and the warmth of his embrace. I remembered what it was like to kiss him goodnight. I remembered how I'd felt with him on New Years Day, when we watched the fireworks and made so many plans. And how I wish I'd given myself to him that night. If I had known I might never see him again, how I would go back in time—or forward—and I'd have shown him how much I loved him then. Because I was sure now. At least, I thought I was. Until something in me would take hold and make me wonder what reality was in this twisted place.

As I thought of Milo and my confusion, I blinked to catch the tears on my eyelashes. They fell perfectly, right onto the tiny piles of vibrant powder on the deck before me. So, I mixed the pigments with my tears, making just enough paint to swirl across the parchment's waxy surface with my brush. I did my best to create an outline of what I imagined would be a curling wave, but as I looked at it, tracing in the indigo color, the red I tried mixing in looked more and more like blood in the water. It all ran together as the water dribbled off the parchment and seeped into the deck, staining it permanently. As if a representation of the past few days, the perfect image I had before me quickly became a nightmare.

As if on cue, a low thunderous rumble sang out in the clouds. An afternoon rainstorm. Within moments, the rain came sprinkling down, washing away my bloody water painting like it was no more than sidewalk chalk. I decided to find McKenzie and Noah again.

"How's it going?" I asked shyly, feeling more like myself as I approached them leaning against the masts near the front of the ship. "Are you both okay?"

"As okay as we can really be," Noah said, looking up at me through the featherlight raindrops dusting his face. McKenzie nudged him. She must've thought I didn't notice.

"I thought I was a beach girl," McKenzie said. "But this has proven me wrong. I'm sapped. Katrina, how are you doing it?"

"Doing what?" I asked, raising an eyebrow as I sat down to join them.

"Looking so refreshed. You look the complete opposite of how I feel. This seems like a spa day for you."

"I have no idea what you mean. I feel terrible."

"Drink something." Noah tossed me a canteen and I chugged, but quickly coughed when the pungent taste of rum hit my lips. When I shot him a look to kill, he shrugged. "There's not much else to choose from here. Besides, might as well use something to numb the senses here."

"I know it feels hopeless," I said. "But I swear, we're going to find a way back to our time. I'll talk to Bellamy tonight."

We chatted more as the sun lowered and the rain clouds cleared. Our conversation felt as hollow as the ship below us. There was still just enough light left to cast a fiery red glow over the water. The deck shone with the glassy shine of a freshly wet surface.

Suddenly a gruff looking crew member approached us. Beneath his head rag he peered at us with dark, sunken eyes.

"Captain's calling for you three on the main deck," he uttered.

I glanced at McKenzie and Noah who both wore equally puzzled expressions. "I forgot to tell you. We have sword-fighting lessons." I sighed.

"Finally, something worthwhile," Noah sat up with more enthusiasm I'd seen in him probably ever.

McKenzie took his hand as he helped her to her feet. I stayed sitting, dragging myself to get up. I didn't want to interact with Bellamy anymore. I didn't like who I was when I was near him. But I knew if I didn't get up and go to him, he'd come find me. And that would be worse.

As a trio, we sauntered down the steps to the main deck, where half the ship's crew seemed to have assembled. A few lanterns placed along the deck lit the open floor space amongst them. Bellamy stepped out from the crowd, giving me a nod and a half smile that made my blood pump harder and my eyes want to roll into the back of my head.

"Step up, mates," he ordered, picking up three swords from an open barrel beside him. He tossed them to us, one at a time, hilt first.

"Um, dangerous!" McKenzie screamed.

"You're sailing with pirates, lass. Dangerous is all there is." Bellamy's voice drifted to my ears like thick smoke, smooth and bold. "First, watch how I hold it. Grip the hilt firm against your palm. Use your last two fingers to tighten your grip and provide power on a swing—but keep these two fingers loose to help guide the sword." He stuck out his index and middle fingers to emphasize. We all three did our best to mimic his movements and position as he walked around and corrected us individually.

"Decent enough start. Now for your stance." He stopped at me and lifted my chin as he spoke. I pulled my face away. "Stand with feet shoulder width apart, and eyes straight and focused. Be sure to keep one foot in front of the other. You don't want to become unbalanced."

He'd made his way to Noah now, and made an effort to shove him. Noah braced to steady himself, and that's when Bellamy swung his cutlass to the side without warning, clattering it against Noah's.

"And the most important thing to remember," he said with a chuckle, "is that pirates never play fair." He swung again, nearly knocking the blade from Noah's hand. But Noah tightened his grip at the last second and leapt to the defense. McKenzie and I watched wide-eyed as he sparred with Noah, yelling tips and suggestions as their blades crossed.

"Kind of hot, isn't it?" McKenzie leaned over and whispered over my shoulder.

I couldn't help but giggle. "I can't say I disagree."

I knew she was likely referring to Noah, but I had my eyes on Bellamy. I watched the way his body turned and twisted as he stepped deftly across the wet floor, as balanced and sturdy as the masts themselves. He moved with the subtle bobbing of the ship as though he and the sea were one. His raven hair, loose and flowing, whipped around his face just as fluidly as his movements.

You thirst for him.

What was that? I looked away, reprimanding myself for the way I was fixating on him. I looked at the last bit of setting sun remaining on the horizon.

"Katrina," Bellamy calling my name made me refocus on him. He was walking toward me with a fierceness in his eyes that made me shift uncomfortably. "Since you're so interested in what's out there, I supposed you already know that a proper swing isn't really a swing at all."

He lifted his sword at me. When I flinched, he lowered it, and then took my hand, pulling me forward, not at all in a gentle manner. I stumbled to the middle of the deck, gripping the hilt of my sword in my sweating hand.

"Swinging isn't effective. It'll make you tired before the salt's dried from your boots." He grinned, lifting my arm to set my sword up to brace against his. "No, instead, you want to conserve your energy in a fight. Use jabbing motions. Stab your opponent. Thrust forward." He demonstrated, pointing his sword at me with a poking motion. "Now fight me."

I felt a foreign heat building in me. Something else was intruding and I couldn't stop it. I lifted my sword as he'd shown me and swung it, and he caught it with his.

"Try to hurt me, Katrina," he commanded under his breath.

"Believe me, I want to," I growled. Stepping forward, I attempted to whack him with the flat side of my cutlass, missing as he dodged it effortlessly. I bent at the waist, trying to achieve more reach, but he deflected my attack yet again. With our swords still crossed, he pulled me forward with his free hand. I barely reached his nose, but he looked down into my eyes with a gaze as steel as our weapons. "I told you to *thrust*, not swing," he said under his breath. A tingle ran down my spine like fingertips across velvet.

"Like this?" I shook away the heat rushing to my face and shoved the point of the sword toward him as I spat out the rhetorical question.

"Good lass." He spoke low and slowly as he parried my blow with ease. "It's a start." His gaze swept over me from top to bottom and back up.

For the next few moments, he instructed me, and I did my best to follow. And when he would correct me with a repositioning of my arm or when he touched my waist to fix my posture, the voice within me told me he was everything I wanted. And I fought hard to shut it up.

With the setting sun at our backs and the open sea in front of us, we danced our waltz of blades, as I became more confident with my cutlass. I swung, nearly landing a hit against Bellamy's shoulder just before he flicked it away with the tip of his sword. So close.

"Left. Lean to the right. Now backwards." My footsteps followed Bellamy's every word like clockwork. Our steel blades began to move faster. And faster. Out sang a chorus of metal on metal as sparks flew across the deck. I was too confident. I was sure I could land a hit on him if I kept going. And just as I thought I saw an opening near his waist, I dove for it. But the clang of steel reverberated up my arm and made me wince. He'd knocked the sword from my hand. No sooner did it come to a sliding stop on the deck at the feet of his crewman did he have his own sword pointed at me.

"Not bad." His upper lip curved into a smirk. "But it appears I'm the winner here." He held out his hand, and Tristan stepped out from the group of crew members surrounding us and shoved a canteen of rum into his open hand. Bellamy took a swig, leaning his head back so that I could see the shimmer of sweat along his neck beneath his raven locks.

"Guess you can go celebrate now. Are we done?" I shrugged.

Bellamy tossed the rum to the floor and fixed his gaze on me. With a mischievous look in his eye, he stepped forward to me, and took my hand in his before yanking me forward against him.

"I won. So, you owe me a dance." He winked towards his crew, and music began to emit from the men. The vibrant, upbeat sound of a fiddle and flute filled the air as two crew mates with the instruments made themselves known.

I rolled my eyes, but if he could tell how fast my heart was beating, he'd know I was only lying to him. And to myself. He pulled me to him and began to follow the music. It reminded me of dancing with him at the gala months before—or centuries later—whatever made sense. But only, this dance was rugged, more lighthearted, and he carried me across the deck in his swift movements and lead me with grace and skill I didn't expect. He spun me around as the fiddle played faster and the flute's notes went higher. Soon the other crew members joined in, and I even caught a glimpse of Noah and McKenzie embracing each other as they danced, too. It made my heart happy, and for just a moment, that's all I wanted.

For so long my heart had been heavy. So much had felt lost and broken and irreparable. But this. This was just simple, real fun. And the more I watched the man in front of me, the deeper I found myself lost in him. But it was a good kind of lost. The kind that makes you forget all the bad things happening around you. And I wanted more of that.

I drew myself closer into him. I was all too aware of the secure brace of his hand against the curve of my back. The look in his eyes as they locked onto mine made me feel like I was looking into some unknown, beautiful depths of the sea that had yet to be discovered. And the way we moved together, stepping in time to the upbeat shanty music, gave me a feeling I was afraid to acknowledge, but at the same time was all too afraid to let go of.

I noticed his eyes as they moved from mine to my lips. He was close to me. So close that I could feel his quick breaths as he spun me around the open deck. A stirring in me caught my attention. I used every ounce of willpower in my body to ignore it, but it was too strong this time. I couldn't block it out.

Kiss him, it said.

I knew I couldn't. I knew I shouldn't. But I was compelled all at once by the other voice in my head and the temporary fleeting emotion of my heart. But I didn't have to make the decision. I still wonder if I would have done it or if I would've been strong enough to resist. But I'll never know, because Bellamy moved first. He let go of my hand and moved his fingers to lift my chin in one swift motion, and then crashed his mouth into mine.

As quickly as he dove in, he pulled away, grinning like he'd just won a prize. He turned to his crew, earning a jeer from the men on deck. I suddenly felt sick to my stomach. Everything about this situation was wrong and I couldn't believe I'd let Bellamy use me as his prize to show off in front of his crew. Noah and McKenzie stood flabbergasted off to the side, and Noah shook his head scoldingly.

As if I'd woken up from some sort of bad dream, I blinked, stopped the motion of our still-swaying dance, and tore myself from Bellamy's grip.

Without looking back, I disappeared into the dark side of the ship, praying no one would follow me. I threw myself between two cannons belowdecks, where I felt hidden enough to let myself cry until I lost all the tears I was holding in. The muffled sounds of the music and dancing above me lulled me into a strange sense of loneliness and comfort, where I let myself stay until it all died down.

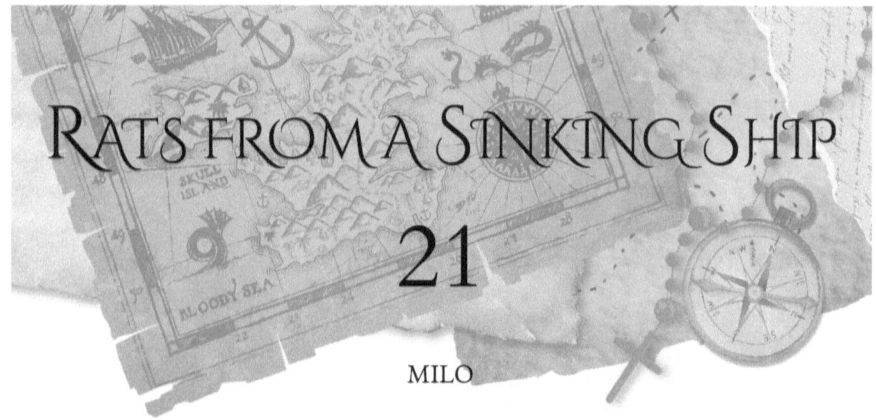

Rats from a Sinking Ship

21

MILO

I tried to sleep there on the church pew. But I couldn't clear my head. I knew stepping outside this church would mean risking being recognized, but a realization struck me that I couldn't ignore. My father would've most likely been out at the harbor, joining in on the commotion as everyone worked to keep their own boats from going up in flames. Which would mean our house was unattended. This could be the perfect chance to uncover what my father was hiding. Or perhaps...just perhaps...I could find evidence that proved the contrary...that he wasn't hiding anything. That he was an honest man and had no part in such a nightmarish trade. I doubted it, but I hoped that maybe it could be true.

Besides, I needed something to do to keep me from going mad. If I wasn't thinking of my father, I was worrying about Katrina. I felt sick about it. I wanted her more than anything right then. I wanted to hold onto her and breathe in the scent of her. I yearned for her, and my heart screamed within me every time the thought crossed my mind that she didn't survive the wreck. But I knew better. She of all people could survive the sea. She would be alright, I told myself. I just had to find her.

In silence I moved out into the night, carrying the loneliness with me like a shadow. I arrived at my father's house—my house—as bells in the distance chimed. It was an hour past midnight. My father would eventually be back when he'd finished securing his own ships. I tried the door handle. As I expected, it was locked, but I knew all too well there was a window in my room I often left open as a boy because I loved the sound of frogs and crickets chirping in the night.

I made my way around to that window and leaned my head in. The sleeping boy—me—in the cot against the wall didn't stir. But the lone lit candle told me he was either awake moments before or pretending to be asleep. I'd take my chances.

I crept in through the window, careful not to make a sound as I cast a foreboding shadow on the wall against the candlelight. When my boots hit the floor, I let out a sigh of relief as the boy remained still. With feather-light steps, I made my way through the rest of the house.

"Finally," I muttered, approaching my father's door. I had longed to see what was behind it for so long, and now more than ever.

As I picked the lock, I found myself frustrated that I couldn't get it open. I'd never found a lock so difficult, as I'd successfully picked open countless others. But by the light of the moon through the window, I caught a glimpse of something on the door handle that seemed strangely familiar. Of course, I'd seen this door a million times. But where else did I see that symbol on the doorknob?

Then it struck me. It was the same symbol carved on the back of my father's compass. I pulled the compass out from my pocket, holding it up to the door to compare. The same exact mark. A cursive *H* for Harrington.

I fiddled with the compass in my hand, working the puzzle in my head. I shook it, hearing something rattling inside. I'd heard it before, but I'd never thought much of it, being a 300-year-old navigational tool. But then I wondered...

As quietly as I could, I used my knife to pry off the baseplate of the compass. And there was a small key. I tried it in the lock. When I realized it was a perfect fit, a shiver snaked through me. My father wanted me to find this. He'd given me this compass the day he died. Whatever was behind this door, I was always meant to know.

With a deep breath, I prayed this was all a misunderstanding. Maybe there was a chance my father wasn't really involved in this dreadful trade. Maybe it was just a one-time mistake or maybe he entered a deal he didn't understand.

I felt the lock's gentle click as I turned the key, and the door creaked open with just a touch. The room was dark. But I could smell smoke from freshly put-out candles. I reached for one to light it, carrying it with me to help me see. With nothing but the small flame's glow, I navigated this new room. A bed, larger than mine. A barrel-turned-table with liquors and rums of all makes on top. A chest with boots and sailcloth. Parchment and maps tucked away in the corner. Nothing I wouldn't expect in a sailor's bedroom. Until I turned. I turned and the candlelight illuminated a striking image of a woman on the wall. A charcoal sketch of my mother—pinned to the wall over a baby cradle. It would've been my brother's had he not died along with my mother.

I scratched my head, moving my candle closer to the empty cradle. There appeared to be something inside. A golden ring rested in the middle. I recognized it immediately as my mother's wedding ring on a thin gold chain. And lying all around it were notes. Scribbled notes of all sorts, scattered across the dusty blanket within. Some were old. Some looked like they were written yesterday. But they were all just random words and cryptic phrases.

Love.

I'm sorry.

Failed.

Forever.

Taken.

Regrets.

As I scanned the notes in confusion, a voice from behind nearly made me jump, but I held my stance. My back was to the door, but I didn't have to turn around to know who stood in the threshold.

"Did you come for my boy, too?"

I couldn't speak. In a mix of confusion and surprise, I stayed silent. Because there was nothing I could think to say to my father, especially not to a question like that. I stood there, refusing to face him, and glad for the hood over my head that I didn't dare remove, even as I browsed the house.

"Answer me, damnit!" He shouted. I didn't need to turn around to picture his green eyes flashing. "Are you going to take the only thing I have left, Henry? All for one empty ship?" With each word, his voice broke, going from stern and strong to choking back tears. I guessed the empty ship he was talking about was referring to his earlier conversation with Hook. And I remembered the name from the note I found on the man I fought on the shore. *Henry.* The man I killed. He thought I was him. But what did everything else mean? I had to say something...

"What do you think I'm here for?" I muttered, being sure to keep my face turned away.

"Did you already do it? You killed my son? Just like you killed her when you couldn't wait another damn week for your bloody pay."

"The boy is fine. For now." I did my best to keep up with the façade. "How do I know I can continue to rely on you?" I was hoping I could get answers.

"I'm working with the slavers now. I'm getting the word out with the companies, and I'm getting commissioned more often. God, Henry, was the arrangement at Rockshore not enough to tie you over? I can ensure they'll pay the remainder of what I owe if you just give me a little more time."

That was it. My father was somehow heavily indebted to this brute. For what, I didn't know. But this had to be why he'd turned to the slave trade for profit. He was in too deep with these dark affairs. I had to swallow down the lump in my throat before speaking again. "Time. Time is what we all need a little more of, isn't it, *Tiburón*?"

Suddenly, a startled voice shouted from the other room. My voice.

"Go tend to your boy. Before he finds out who you really are." I said, each word stinging like salt in fresh wounds.

I listened for the sound of footsteps as Daven hurried to the other room. I used it as my chance to make my escape, right after I snatched up my mother's ring from the cradle and tucked it away safely. My father didn't deserve to hold onto it. Not when he was the reason for her death.

Strangely, as I disappeared into the night, I realized I now had a sudden memory of this incident. One that hadn't been before. It became part of my mind in an instant, as if it was forming at that very moment. I was no longer in the house, but vividly I could remember my younger self after my departure, startled by the strange conversation I'd heard with my father and an intruder.

I stumbled to a tree and leaned over it, the memory clear before me as it was happening right then in the house I'd left behind.

"Who was there, Father?"

"It was just some bastard who came back with me. He was interested in joining my crew, but I told him we were full."

"Oh." Young Milo nodded, the sleep still heavy in his eyes. "Came back from where?"

"The docks." Father smiled a tired smile, the crow's feet in the corners of his eyes folding together. "There was an...incident down at the harbor. I was checking on the ships. But everything's right now. Go on back to bed. You'll be up early for the delivery tomorrow. And then we set sail for England."

"Is this the shipment from Captain Valdez?" Milo blinked.

"Aye. And you know how he gets. So be rested up."

I shook my head. I remembered it perfectly. My future self had altered my past and therefore altered my memories. So now I knew for sure the past could be changed to some degree. But at what cost? Because what my younger self nor my father didn't know was that Valdez would be a day late. And when he finally arrived, he would kill my father in front of me.

But that didn't matter at the moment. I still needed some time to process what I'd heard and piece things together. My father owed a debt, and he was doing whatever he could to pay it off. I should've known no reputable merchant would continue with his home base in a city like Nassau, with pirates practically running the place. But perhaps that was why he did. Perhaps he couldn't go back to Barbados for some reason. Maybe "Henry" had higher up friends elsewhere, keeping my father cornered here. All I knew was that my father was a liar and a cheat—all the things he made me believe Kellem was, and he was responsible for my mother's death. He told me she'd taken ill and passed and that my brother died in her womb along with her. Just like he never told me he was shipping humans like cattle right underneath my nose.

Suddenly, I was glad I'd killed Henry. And I was glad that I was a pirate. Because at least a pirate didn't hide his deeds. He bore them proudly as the tattoos on his skin. And a true pirate knew all were equal at sea. For the first time in my life, I decided pirates—maybe with the exception of Thane and Valdez—had more decency than the lot of them.

And then I wept that night. I couldn't remember the last time tears had fallen like that. Not since I was a child who lost his mother. But now I'd lost my father, too. And I watched as my tears washed away the dried blood on my rosary before I tossed it to the ground.

None of this mattered. I rebuked my foolishness once I shook off the anger. I wasn't meant to know these things. I was meant to be back in the 21st century, with Katrina, learning the names of car parts and lattes. Not here, reliving my life and uncovering the dark secrets festering beneath the surface about my family.

One thing I'd learned in these past few twisted days spent here was that whatever I did here affected the rest of time. I'd killed one of the thugs who came to collect my father's payments. There had to be a bigger fish coming. And he'd take it out on my father or my younger self. And if I tried to change what happened with Valdez and save my father like I thought I could, who knew what that could do to the future? I would probably live my life on the run from whoever was sent for retribution for Henry's death. My father would go on digging himself deeper in this mess of cruelty he called business. And I'd never become cursed and meet Katrina.

All my life, I'd hated myself for the coward I was on board Valdez's terrible ship. But by letting my father die like he was meant to, I was severing at least one small vein of the slavers' trade, even for just a little while. At least that could console me now.

I looked up at the sky above me. There was the North Star, clear as ever, watching over me. And I knew I had to let all this go. It was time I found Katrina. I didn't know how. But I knew where to start. If I was going to be trapped here in the past, I couldn't linger in Nassau for long anyway. I'd need to commandeer a ship from the harbor once things settled down. Because if Katrina was out there, I had no doubt she'd still be heading toward the Devil's Triangle. And who better to meet her there than a man already trapped in hell?

Ocean Eyes
22

When I awoke, the ship was silent. There was no trace of the merrymaking that had been going on earlier. The only sounds reaching my ears were the low creaks of the ship against the waves and the scurrying of tiny mouse feet in the shadows.

I lifted my head and let my eyes adjust, remembering that unfortunately this was all too real. I was still here, trapped on the sea, centuries in the past and miles from any hope of finding Milo. And the compass of my heart seemed to be spinning out of control. Maybe Cordelia was right. Maybe I didn't have a soul.

I stood up, balancing as the ship leaned in the rolling night waves. Making my way back up the top deck, I returned to my spot where I'd tried painting earlier. Sitting crisscross beside the stains from my earlier "painting," I tilted back my head and gazed heavenward. The light of the stars above was unlike anything I'd ever seen. The constellations shone brighter and more numerous than even when I'd watched them with Milo on the lighthouse.

He wasn't kidding when he said there was no better way to stargaze.

I smiled to myself, imagining him here with me, watching the stars on a sailing ship in the night. With a drawn-out sigh, I looked back down, tucking my knees up to my chest. What I would give to find him and sit under the stars with him one more time.

The sound of soft singing drifting in the air caught my notice. I glanced up, looking for the source of the sound. Shadows contorted every shape on deck, and even with the dim lanterns of the ship and the moonlight reflecting on the water, my vision was obscured. The only people I could make out were a handful of crew members on the night shift, and it the song clearly wasn't coming from them.

I leaned in the direction from which the voice came. It was male, but still gentle. It seemed to come from the stern. I followed it, my footsteps steady in the slightly too-large boots I wore. As I neared the stern, I saw Bellamy seated along the hull with a leg propped up to rest his elbow, a bottle of rum dangling in his hand. He was watching the water, singing softly with his back to the ship. I crept closer, stopping a few feet away to listen to the song as each word lazily drifted from his lips.

Lost out at sea
Do you dream of me?
By the call of the waves
I hear you and seek you
Till again the roaming sea
Brings you back to me.

I thought the tune seemed familiar, but my body stiffened when I heard the second verse.

Down by the shore
Meet me once more
By the light of the moon
Love me, then leave me
With the dawn rising
Haunt me forevermore

"What was that song?" I asked, my voice gentle to keep from startling him. I knew I shouldn't be striking up something else with Bellamy, especially not out here alone on the back of the ship. But I had to know how he knew that song centuries before he met Serena.

He turned to look at me, a tiredness in his eyes that seemed uncharacteristic for him.

"Aye, just a sea shanty."

"That was no sea shanty." I straightened my shoulders, stepping forward. "That song sounded...special. Am I wrong?"

"You're onto something, lass," Bellamy grumbled. "But you remember how I said I have no room in my heart for any mistress but the sea?"

I nodded with a raised eyebrow, noting his shining eyes and unguarded way of moving.

"That's because the sea keeps my secrets. It's always just between her and me."

"And what did you tell her tonight?" I climbed up onto the hull with him, dangling one leg over each side and turning to face him.

"You're too curious for your own good, love." Bellamy grinned, raising the bottle of rum to his lips again.

"Well, how about a deal? I tell you about where I'm from and I tell you a secret of mine if you tell me about that song." I crossed my arms. "Oh, and I'll forgive you for that uncalled for move back there."

"You mean the kiss?" Bellamy rubbed the scruff of the dark beard covering his jaw with his ring-covered fingers. "That was just for show. In front of my men. Have to keep up the morale out here and keep the reputation."

"Why? Don't your men trust the real you?" I leaned forward.

"I'd like to think they would." Bellamy looked down, tracing the rim of the liquor bottle with his fingertip. "But my father is a much fiercer man than I. He can command his crew with just one look and they cower. But I don't want to be like him. I want my crew to respect me, not fear me. So, I try to show them I'm one of them."

I listened to Bellamy's words intently. This was like meeting him all over again. It was a side of Bellamy I had no idea existed. "Well, they seem loyal enough." I shrugged. "You must be a good enough captain."

"I'll take the compliment, but we'll see what my father thinks when we make port tomorrow. He was supposed to be making a stop at Nassau for a delivery exchange." His eyes darkened as he spoke. He shifted his gaze from the rum bottle to the water below, hardening his expression.

"Well, I'm glad to be on your ship," I said, brushing a strand of loose hair behind my ear. "And if your father has a problem with how you've been running things, then he's the real jackass here."

I thought I saw Bellamy's lips widen into a small smile, but it quickly faded. He glanced at me.   "He's not a bad man. He's just been blinded by the pursuit of wealth." He drew in a deep sigh as I listened, urging him to go on with a nod. "It's never enough. We have plenty to return to Spain and make a life now, but he doesn't see it."

Not a bad man, I wanted to say. *Until he tried to cut my heart out.*

"He promised my mother he would return when he'd made his fortune. Her parents didn't approve of their relationship because my father was just a poor sailor. And when I was born out of wedlock, they were the shame of the village. So, my father swore he'd become rich and powerful and come back for her. But he's never satisfied."

"I had to be away from my mother for a long time, too. I'm sorry. I'm sure you want to go home." I looked up at him longingly through my lashes.

"I don't want to go home. I want to spend my life at sea. But I want my father to return for my mother. It's only fair to her." He paused and shifted, readjusting himself along the hull in a way that put him a few inches closer to me. "She waits for him. I remember how her face lit up when she saw his ship coming in the distance when I was ten."

"Why didn't he stay?" I asked.

"He did for a short while, and then he said he needed to be richer than the king himself before he would have what he wanted. He took me with him. And he set back out to find something that could give him that kind of wealth."

"Has he found it yet?"

"I'm not sure," Bellamy shrugged.

I thought on his words for a moment. *Mermaids.* They were his key to power and riches. Milo had said Valdez used them to bargain with the elites and rulers of the world, making him more powerful than them. If Bellamy knew about that, he wasn't letting on. But of course, why would he expose something like that to some random girl he'd pulled from the ocean?

"Anyway," Bellamy looked down, his hair falling in a way that made me shift against the hull. The warmth I felt rising in my face was more than enough to fight the chill of the night breeze. Something was welling up in me again, pooling in my core and my head like an unwelcome visitor I was fighting to keep out. "That song, if you must know, was a song my mother used to sing. She'd wait for my father at the shore, hoping one day he'd finally return as promised."

Bellamy shook his head, as if trying to escape an invisible net. When he composed himself, he looked at me, strangely. "I don't know why I'm telling you this," he said.

Suddenly, I didn't like that he'd stopped. I wanted to know more. There was more. But not if he wouldn't tell me.

Make him tell you.

The voice in my head sang loudly, like a chiming bell in a hollow space. I leaned closer to him, and placed my hand on his knee, sliding it up to his thigh. "It's okay," I said gently, in almost a whisper. "You can tell me anything."

He narrowed his eyes at me, leaning toward me. "The strangest thing about it is that I swear I can hear a woman singing it on my father's ship when he's in his quarters. And it's not my mother's voice."

Cordelia. There it was.

I studied his face. He was rugged and handsome and the curve of his mouth drew me in like a rushing undertow. "Why don't you sing that song again, Bellamy?" I couldn't even recognize my own voice. The seductive way my words came out disgusted me. But I couldn't stop it. And without hesitation, Bellamy began to voice the words under his breath.

"Lost out at sea

"Do you dream of me?"

He paused for a gentle breath. One that I could feel along my cheek as there was now only a finger's width of space between us. I opened my mouth to sing the next line, softly as a feather against his nose.

"By the call of the waves

I hear you and seek you

Till again the roaming sea

Brings you back to me."

I heard the rum bottle drop from Bellamy's hand and roll away along the deck. He drew his body toward me as I finished the last line of the song.

He tilted his head and pushed his mouth onto me. I didn't stop him. I drank his lips with mine and tasted him like he was the fresh water I'd been thirsting for all day on this ship. The rum on his breath mingled with my own, and I searched deeper for the taste of it on his tongue. I let him pull me closer. My hand along his thigh continued roaming his body, until he reached down and grabbed it with his hand, guiding it where he wanted it. He groaned and I felt it in my throat, sending a shiver through my spine that I wanted more of.

I opened my eyes and looked up to see the brightest star overhead. The North Star. And in that instant, it was as if I snapped out of a dream I never wanted to be in. Bellamy had just finished a bottle of rum, yet I was the one who felt drunk. The starlit sky above spun as I took notice of Bellamy's lips against mine and my hands beneath his tunic. It was the moment some clarity finally found its way to me. There was no doubt I'd always felt something for Bellamy. But this was something I would never do. So why was I doing it?

Bellamy wasn't the one who survived the curse breaking, because Bellamy didn't have my heart. Milo did. I gave my heart to Milo. So, what the hell was I doing right now? This wasn't me. This wasn't Katrina. But as I fought against the voice in my head, I finally found her.

I pulled away quickly, and I slapped my hands over my lips. "I'm sorry," I stuttered. "I don't know what I was doing."

Bellamy seemed entranced. He reached for my face and placed a gentle palm against my cheek. "That one wasn't for show, love." He uttered with an intoxicated looking grin.

"I know, and I'm sorry!" I snapped, keeping my voice low.

Bellamy cocked his head, still locking his eyes with mine. "You know, it's the strangest thing. You have the most beautiful blue eyes. As blue as the sea. I bet that's why I told you everything. Because you look like the sea."

I felt my heart drop. My eyes weren't blue. Whatever was happening to me was clearly not something I wanted. But I didn't know how to stop it.

"But wait, aye. Now they're becoming brown again." Bellamy straightened, his voice rising and becoming clearer and more controlled. "You're—you're one of them?"

"One of what, Bellamy? Tell me what you know." I demanded. This time it was all me who spoke, full of desperation.

"You're whatever the woman that appears on my father's ship is...her eyes are blue like that. Always. But they turn the deepest blue. And he becomes her puppet. You're controlling me?"

"No," I said, "I mean, not on purpose. I don't know what's happening to me."

"That's why you jumped in the water that night, isn't it?" Bellamy stood up, eyeing me like I was some kind of alien. "You're a siren. You're real?"

"No. I mean, yes. I mean, I don't know." My words came in frantic gasps.

"That means I wasn't crazy. I know what I saw on my father's ship." Bellamy turned his back to me, taking a few steps away to the starboard side of the ship.

"What are you talking about?" I uttered desperately, following him. He ignored me. "Please!" I reached for his arm.

"Why?" He yanked it away. "You'll just manipulate it out of me anyway? Go ahead, turn me into your puppet again and put me under your spell."

"Bellamy, I promise I wasn't trying to—"

"No," he uttered. "Leave me alone." With his jaw tense and his forehead pressed, he gently shoved me away as he walked back down the steps toward his quarters. Once he was out of sight, I listened quietly for the sound of his cabin door slamming. With a burning in my chest, I looked up to the stars that had just watched it all. And I'd never felt more alone and lost.

MESSAGE IN A BOTTLE

23

I sat there wondering how I was ever supposed to earn back Bellamy's trust. And I wondered if I really even needed it. But some part of me at least had to know he didn't hate me.

Tomorrow we'd be making port at Nassau, and I hoped more than anything that somehow, I'd find Milo there. But how would I look at him after how I'd just kissed Bellamy? Even if most of it wasn't me...some part of it was. My siren side was stronger than I realized. But it didn't have desires of its own. It just made me act on the dark ones I already had. And that's what I hated the most. It made me bold, mean, and selfish. And it knew how to overpower me.

I went to find McKenzie. She and Noah slept somewhere belowdecks, but I didn't know exactly where. Stepping down into the depths of the dark ship, I looked for them, holding a lantern I'd taken from up top to see by. I passed rows of hammocks and sleeping barracks, until a hand motioning for me caught my attention. It was McKenzie lying on the floor on a pile of blankets. Noah was propped up with his back against the wall, his head hanging to the side as he slept.

"Care if I join?" I whispered.

"What were you doing?" McKenzie asked. "Getting another night of special treatment from Bellamy?" I could almost taste the sourness in her words. I sat down beside her, careful not to ruffle the blankets and disturb anyone sleeping nearby.

"No," I hissed. "I was trying to talk to him. But it didn't go as planned."

McKenzie shook her head. "So can Bellamy help us or not?"

"Bellamy's pissed at me right now for various reasons," I muttered, looking down at the dust on the blankets. "I think we're on our own. But I'm hoping tomorrow when we land in Nassau that maybe we'll find Milo and maybe he'll know what to do."

"I hope you're planning to tell Milo about all this quality time you've had with Bellamy." Noah's voice cut through the darkness as he leaned forward in the shadows. "Though God knows maybe he deserves it after all the shit he's put us through."

I opened my mouth to argue, but I couldn't think of what to say. Noah wasn't wrong. I'd betrayed Milo, even if I wasn't in control when I did. I was just as selfish as Cordelia. Maybe it really was my destiny to become like her.

"Noah," I finally managed to stumble out. "I would say 'it's not what you think,' but I know that sounds like such BS." I could see Noah's fed-up expression, even in the dark. His dark brows stayed pressed together, and he was nearly scowling at me.

"It does." He nodded. "But I mean, what's happened to us isn't normal. So, who's to say what even makes sense here?"

I turned my face away, the weight of Noah's condescending side eye. He went on, "Look, I'm the first to assume the worst about everyone. I was just starting to be Milo's friend before all this went to hell. But I'm starting to think maybe, just maybe, Milo wasn't the crazy one here."

McKenzie and I both exchanged a look of surprise. "There's something I should probably tell you both," I fumbled with my words.

"Well, go on then," Noah muttered.

I took a deep breath, worried this could make me sound even crazier. But it was the only way I could salvage the thin, quickly fraying thread between us. "Ever since we've been here, I've been hearing this...this voice in my head. It's like my own, but it tells me things I would never think. Sometimes I follow it, and I don't realize I am until it's too late.

"Is that supposed to make me feel better?" Noah crossed his arms. "Because all it does is tell me you're crazier than I thought."

"That's what I was afraid of. But I need you to listen." I clenched my jaw and leaned forward, making my words perfectly clear. "Something here has been controlling me. And I'm still trying to figure out how to stop it."

McKenzie looked at Noah, who still didn't seem willing to budge. "Noah, look at what's happened to us. We literally traveled through time. Maybe it's not impossible to believe something could be messing with our minds."

I was grateful that McKenzie was willing to give me the benefit of the doubt, but I knew my excuse wasn't enough. They needed to know the rest. Keeping secrets almost always did more harm than good.

"There's more to it than that. I think it's time I own up to it. I..." A lump rose in my throat, and I almost couldn't finish the sentence. I didn't want to hear myself say it out loud. But I forced myself to get it out. "I told you I was Cordelia's descendant back on the motorsailer, remember?"

They both nodded, and I blinked nervously before going on. "Well, that makes me a siren, too. And I'm starting to think maybe that side of me has a voice stronger than my own."

They both hesitated for a moment, and I hung my head. To my surprise, it was Noah who spoke first.

"At this point I'm starting to think I'm dreaming, but I mean if we freaking traveled back in time, who's to say you can't be a mermaid?"

"Trust me, it's not something I want. I wouldn't lie about this." I shrugged. "But I wanted you to know so that it means something when I say I'm sorry. I'm sorry for getting you into this mess, I'm sorry that I don't know how to save us yet, and I'm sorry that I'm making a fool of myself on this ship. But you're both all I have left. And I don't want to lose you next."

Noah's eyes softened just a touch, and McKenzie leaned into him, her arm against his shoulder.

"Apology accepted," McKenzie sighed. "We're not going anywhere." She looked at Noah, as if waiting for him to confirm what she said. He sighed and rolled his shoulders with a groan.

"It's fine. I appreciate the apology. And I guess if there's anyone we should wanna be stuck with in the middle of the ocean, it's a mermaid."

"Thanks." My lips formed a little half-smile. "I promise I'm trying my best."

"So are we," Noah said. "And while we're apologizing, I'm sorry for the way I acted about Sand—er—Milo. I guess he didn't mean to screw us over like this. But even if he did, I didn't want this to happen to him."

"I promise you, he only did what he had to do. To keep the trident out of the wrong hands." I straightened myself, ready to defend Milo. "And I refuse to believe he's gone."

"Me too, Katrina. He wouldn't go down that easily. He's gotta still be out there. And when we find him and get back, he owes my uncle a new boat." Noah spoke under his breath, but I could sense the lighthearted change in his voice.

"Fair enough," I uttered, my spirits lifting. "It's not every day you find out your coworker is a ghost pirate."

We all enjoyed a brief chuckle, but soon the space fell silent again. Together we leaned against the wall of the ship and closed our eyes as the sea's rhythm rocked us to sleep. And I clung tightly to McKenzie's reassuring words as I replayed them in my head: "*We're not going anywhere.*"

"Land ho!" The muffled sound of a gruff voice yelling above made me open my eyes. I sat up in the small space in which we'd all slept and looked down at McKenzie asleep with her head on Noah's shoulder.

I smiled. Things felt as though maybe, just maybe there was some small ray of hope starting to peek through. Clutching the wooden railing, I made my way up to the deck and wandered to the edge of the ship. I glanced around, surveying the horizon for any sign of land. But I didn't see anything but the never-ending stretch of deep blue rolling for miles.

"Land ho?" I said out loud, squinting in the morning sun as I looked upward to the sailor up in the crow's nest.

"Guess he can see something we can't with that thing," Noah stated, gesturing to the spyglass that the man held to his eye.

"I wonder how far away that means we are." McKenzie leaned on the railing. "I'm gonna go find us some food. I'll check the rations."

"I'm going with you," Noah added, "Remember last time how that guy in the galley got a little too friendly with you."

McKenzie nodded and they disappeared back down below the deck toward the galley. I'd catch up with them in a minute, but first, I wanted to try "painting" one last time, just to clear my head for the new day. I walked back to the spot on the deck where I'd painted the waves on the parchment before. The dye stains were barely still there, and I was impressed the colors had lasted through the rainstorm. I laid out my last piece of parchment and sat down, mixing a handful of dye from my pocket with some water on the deck. It made just enough paint for me to outline the shape of a message bottle among the waves. But as I formed the picture, I felt the ship rise with the crest of a high-rolling wave. Even sitting down, I had to grab the railing on the hull to steady myself and catch my balance.

As the ship came crashing back down, it nosedived toward the ocean with quite a splash, sending seawater lapping onto the deck and crashing over my artwork. As I watched the dye and spices fade into the water around them, I suddenly felt an intense fury—a reaction that was way too disproportionate for the situation. I locked my gaze onto the running colors as they bled off the parchment, onto the deck, and leaked off the side of the ship.

The longer I stared at the destruction, the more I suddenly felt that dark siren essence rising within me. And then I noticed the colors reforming into the blotchy excuse of a picture they were before. I watched the seawater trickling off the edge of the ship, but as I followed it with my eyes, it changed course right in front of me, flowing opposite the direction of gravity and returning to the outline of the painting. And I blinked, nearly stumbling backward at my own shock.

The water ran in reverse in little streams, following the path I'd laid out for it in my head, taking form of an image back on the parchment solely by command of my thoughts. I was controlling the seawater.

Suddenly it struck me as to why I'd always been so easily able to work with watercolors. I'd tried painting with acrylics and oils, but they never felt quite right to me. And now I knew why. I'd always had power over watercolors. I could tell the water how far to run and where to stop before it bled into a section I didn't want it to...all just by thinking about it. But it never made sense until today, when I painted an entire picture on the deck of a ship without touching it.

I ran to the edge of the ship and stared down at the water below. Could I control that too? I concentrated with every ounce of strength in me, drilling my focus into the water just as intensely as I did when I painted. But nothing happened. I wanted the water to rise up like a waterspout. But to my disappointment, nothing changed.

Controlling the sea must be something I'd have to learn to master. But for now, it wasn't happening. I tried my best to compose myself as I leaned against the edge of the ship. It had only been a few days, here, yet I felt as though I was losing it. Why had none of this happened back home?

I shook my thoughts away and pushed out the siren voice inside. To regain my senses, I hurried to find McKenzie and Noah. I followed the sound of crewmen singing sea shanties near the front of the ship. Mingling amongst them was McKenzie, and Noah was gripping the rope rigging attached to the masts and appeared to be standing amongst the crew as they worked to change the sails and direct the ship to land.

As I neared the crew, the gritty, salt-dried voices singing the jolly lyrics of their shanty became clearer. I caught a better view of Noah. And I couldn't believe the way he looked. He was actually...smiling. And as I stepped closer and closer, I chuckled at his musical addition to the song.

"Is he...beatboxing to a sea shanty?" I asked, stepping up beside McKenzie, who handed me some type of dry bread and a cup of water.

"Yeah," she laughed, nodding toward the crew. "They love it."

As I giggled at the scene before me, I thought about how grateful I was to be trapped back in time with two friends. Of course, I'd give almost anything if I could've somehow kept them out of all this, but in some selfish way, just for that fleeting moment, I let myself be glad that they were here.

The next moment, a dark scowl from across the deck darkened my mood. Bellamy emerged from his cabin, his heavy boots announcing his presence as he trudged across the wooden floor. He strode past me, his elegant captain's coat drifting behind him, and his icy gaze fixed straight ahead toward the open water.

When he turned to address the crew, the shanties stopped, and everyone became so quiet that all I could hear was the gentle flapping of the sails overhead. His eyes swept over me as he spoke, and I could tell he was intentionally avoiding looking my way. He clearly remembered last night. And he was still upset, understandably.

"We make port at Nassau in two hours!" He shouted. "Continue to man the rigging on the mizzen. See if you can't get some more speed out of these sails." His eyes fell on me as he began to walk toward the helm. "I want to get this time waste over with as fast as possible."

"Bellamy," I tried to call out to him, but he kept walking. "Bellamy, please."

When he halted and tensed, a small flicker of hope lit up in me. I expected him to turn around, but he only looked back over his shoulder. "That's two hours until you and your friends disembark from my ship. And then I never want to see your faces again."

"You're going to leave us in Nassau?" I asked.

"Be lucky I don't leave you dangling at the end of the plank."

"What would it mean if I said I was sorry? How can I make you trust me again?"

"You can't. I know the kind of thing you are. I've seen what you're like."

"Well then you know more than me, because I still don't understand who I am." I threw my hands out to the side in a defeated motion.

"Ask the woman who keeps my father captive at sea. I'm sure she can help you hone your craft." Before I could even think of a response, Bellamy turned his back to me and stormed to the helm.

Shaking away the frustration I felt with Bellamy, I explained to McKenzie what I'd just witnessed with my watery painting.

"That's awesome! You can control water?" Her eyes lit up a bright cerulean as the waters surrounding her. They contrasted against her freckled pale skin, which by now had reddened significantly in the sun.

"I think," I said. "But just small amounts for now. I want to try practicing more though, with the time we have left."

McKenzie agreed and together we headed to the least crowded section of the boat.

"Can you cup some water in your hands?" I asked her. With her help, we lowered a bucket down into the water on a rope, scooping up a good amount of water to last us a few tries.

McKenzie held out her cupped hands, barely a quarter of a cup full. I stared into them, willing the water to do something...anything. Move up and down. Slosh side to side. Trickle along the side of her skin. But nothing worked. We tried for what felt like hours, each attempt looking more foolish than the last.

"What the heck are you two doing?" Noah came trotting up, unsuccessfully trying to tuck his loose-fitting tunic into his pants.

"Katrina might be able to control water," McKenzie said nonchalantly. "We're trying to test her powers."

"Of course." Noah rolled his eyes playfully. "Why not?"

"So far it's clear I'm not very good at it." I tilted my head with a pout.

"Well, how did you figure it out in the first place? Is this part of your mermaid thing?" He asked, crossing his arms.

I lowered my gaze, blinking and thinking about the question. "Well..." I tried to remember every time I'd painted something difficult. Something that shouldn't have turned out perfectly the first time, but did.

There was the time I painted a flower, a beautiful withering rose when my mom had her first relapse. The petals had formed perfectly, and the paint drifted into all the right spots without a thought. Then there was the showcase painting. Each time I added something,

I was thinking of my own hopelessness, or of failing Mom, or losing Milo. And most recently, the message bottle painting on the deck. Because I'd been thinking of how lost we were. And I was afraid Milo was dead...

"I think I figured it out," I gasped turning to McKenzie. I crouched down and scooped up my own tiny handful of water. I stared at it and thought of Milo. I thought of how much I regretted the way I'd spoken to him before we set sail. I thought of how angry he'd made me when he kept Cordelia's letter from me. But how now I realized it wasn't something that should've come between us. He swore it was a mistake, and I knew it really was, but I chose to hold onto it and let it break our trust. But he wasn't wrong. I had become consumed with chasing her. And he was right to be wary of it. Cordelia's influence had made fools of us all. And I was at the center of it. I'd pushed away Milo for it. And now I'd lost him and everything else.

"I'm sorry." The words quivered on my lips as tears came to my eyes, and at the same time, the tiny amount of water in my hand slowly began to creep upward in droplets, curling over my fingers like vines made of bubbles. I dropped the water in surprise, flinging it on Noah. My smile widened into a gaping grin.

"I did it!" I gasped.

"How?" Noah asked, wiping the water from his face with his sleeve.

"I think it's when I feel. When my emotions are strong. But especially when I cry."

"Interesting," McKenzie raised an eyebrow. "Like your tears are connected to the water or something."

"That theory sounds good enough to me," I exclaimed, still catching my breath from the excitement. "It works, whatever the reason."

"Well maybe that will come in handy somehow." Noah shrugged. "Maybe you can drain the ocean and find that trident."

McKenzie stepped beside him, wiping her wet hands on his arm as he gave her a disapproving look. "Don't be so sarcastic, Captain Asshole." She planted a kiss on his cheek. I couldn't help but laugh at them.

The rest of the morning, we sailed quietly as the *Widow* picked up speed and carried us onward. I looked out at the horizon just as the land mass came into view. A long stretch of island with rising green hills and sandy cliffs in the distance.

Nassau.

I t was morning. The morning my father would die.

I did my best to focus on my mission of stealing a ship for my own, but my relentless thoughts continued to tug at me. No matter how much I tried to convince myself he deserved it, another small voice in me wanted to believe that perhaps I was still wrong about him. Perhaps I'd just misunderstood everything. Perhaps I *should* intervene. Or at the least, I could be near the scene...just in case.

By the church bells, I knew it was 11 o'clock. Valdez would kill my father at the last stroke of noon. With my stomach full of fresh ale and bread, I stalked off to the harbor, where plenty enough men remained still clearing out debris from the ship I'd burned down the night before. But it was quiet enough.

With a full bottle of rum in hand and a woodblock in the other, I sat down on an overturned skiff by the harbormaster's shanty. It was a rough, creaking excuse for a shack perched high on level with the docks by its own set of stilts. No one would think twice about a poor sailor day drinking and whittling a block of driftwood in a spot that smelled of brine and rotting fish. So that's the part I planned to play.

It didn't take me long to spot Valdez's ship, already moored at the docks. Some of his crew remained on board, but I knew he wasn't on the ship. He would've been returning from a chat with my father soon.

I waited as the sun inched across the sky, taunting me with its unforgiving heat. I'd been so used to coming out at night in the cold Atlantic that I'd almost forgotten what it was like to bake out in the open Caribbean like this.

Damn. Hurry up, Valdez.

I didn't know what I wanted him to hurry for. I didn't know what I planned to do. But something in me wouldn't allow me to be absent for this moment. As if somehow, everything would make sense right before Valdez fired a lead ball into my father.

But assuming I did save him, what then? What would that change? I recalled how the instant I'd altered my memories by breaking into my own home as a boy. Whatever I did here clearly influenced what would happen in the future. Which could mean that if I stopped my father's death, Valdez might never have forced me onto his crew. And if I never became part of his crew, I'd never have been cursed. I'd never have suffered for 300 years. And I'd never have met Katrina.

I shifted, sliding the sole of my boot across the pier wood. With my small blade, I dug into the malformed chunk of driftwood in my hands as though I could punish it for the confusion racing in my head. I could save my father's life and spare my younger self the most tormented destiny. Or I could let him die, and live it all over again. I told Katrina I'd endure hell all over again for her. And it wasn't a lie. Was this God's cruel way of making me prove that?

"I told you, Daven, I can't explain to you what I have on board. You'd best have to see for yourself. The governor struck his deal with me, but the law don't mince words...no pirates in the British ports. 'Said I'd need a middleman to cross and carry the goods. But the price he's paying. It's worth the job, trust me."

I turned my head to the familiar voice that scraped against my soul like the knife in my hand against the driftwood. Valdez. I was careful not to reveal my face, so I kept my hood pulled low and my head down as I listened.

"Valdez, if this is as big of a job as you say, I'll need more than the usual share."

"Hmm. We'll talk prices after you've seen the cargo. I plan to pay you more, but don't think you can take advantage of the situation."

I kept a watchful eye as my father and the captain strolled across the dock, walking right past me, and onto the gangplank and up to the *Siren's Scorn*. It was silent except for the gulls around me belting out their constant cry.

I waited. And waited. Sweat rolled off my forehead and onto the blade I flipped back and forth between my fingers. My foot tapped nervously. I knew if I couldn't calm myself down, I'd start to look suspicious. But I couldn't get any of it back under control. These next few minutes were critical in whether or not I would alter the course of history.

Finally, my father and Valdez emerged, their pace much brisker than when they'd boarded. My father looked unhinged, pointing a finger threateningly toward Valdez as he uttered something much too low for me to hear. I expected this to be the part where he refused to do the job after he'd seen the captured mermaids in their glass tanks inside.

"You're out of your bloody mind if you think I'll pay any shipper that." Valdez spat. "What I offered you is more than fair."

"No, Valdez." My father spoke through a clenched jaw and bulging neck. "He wants these delivered *alive*. This isn't the usual chopped tail and heart in a jar shipment. I'll need triple the usual rate. At the least."

"Triple? For a voyage you can make blindfolded. Daven, hear yourself."

They continued arguing as my head spun with my father's words echoing in my mind. *This isn't the usual chopped tail and heart in a jar shipment.*

He'd done this before. And he'd lied to me about this, too. He didn't refuse this job because he didn't want to ship mermaids. Why was I surprised? As the realization sunk to the very bottom of my soul, I understood that my father—Daven Harrington—was undoubtedly not the man he'd tricked me into thinking he was.

As they tossed words back and forth back on the docks, I looked up when I heard the running footsteps of a boy come all too late to stick his nose where it didn't belong.

"Tiburón, go back home! This doesn't concern you." Daven shouted. It was only now that I could detect the quake of nervousness in his voice. His desperation to keep his dealings a secret from his son was all too plain to see now. This warped hindsight allowed me to see what was right in front of me all along.

"I came to see if you need any help, Father." A naïve, lanky fifteen-year-old Milo approached the docks, oblivious to the doom that awaited him.

"He's in need of some help, boy, that's for sure." Valdez peered around at young Milo, his voice sour. "Maybe your boy can talk some sense into you."

"Don't bring my son into this!" Daven shoved Valdez backward, and I knew what happened next.

The captain would pull his pistol out without hesitation and aim it at my father. This was my moment to decide. I studied the teenage boy running to the feuding men, desperate to jump in and defend his father. And I saw what awaited him if I were to jump in and stop Valdez. Daven would live, and he would continue living a lie to his son, until eventually one day, his son would become too wise for the charade, and he'd figure it out. And if he wasn't smart enough to realize it was wrong, he'd fall into the same pattern of justifying the wrong thing just to please his father. And perhaps he'd even end up carrying on the business, unable to see the evils in it, or worse—choosing to ignore them.

And that, to me, was a fate worse than a thousand years at the bottom of Davy Jones Locker or wherever else Cordelia could send me. And I refused to let that young boy grow to become the same man as his father. So, I sat there in silence as I listened to the sound of a pistol firing and my younger self screaming.

Young Milo ran to Daven, frantic.

"Father! Father...no..." He hung his head, grimacing with glistening eyes from choking back emotion. "What happened?"

I couldn't hear Daven's dying response from where I sat, but I remembered exactly what he said to me.

"He...he wanted me to...to ship mermaids. *Mermaids*, Tiburón..." he coughed while straining for his last lying breaths. "Can you believe it?" I could still see him lifting his head as the blood began trickling from his mouth and his hand dropped from my shoulder. "But I wouldn't do it. And this is what he I got for it." He grunted out the words between his desperate gasps before reaching into his pocket and pressing a compass into my hand. "May this guide you better than it did me."

I hoped he'd be glad to know that it had.

Walk the Plank

25

Once we'd docked, Bellamy's crew wasted no time rolling up sails and grabbing whatever materials needed to be unloaded. They worked quickly, almost as if the ship would catch on fire any moment if they stayed on it too long.

"Come on, Katrina. I guess we have to get off here, too," McKenzie called to me as I stood observing the commotion around me.

"Your friend is wise. The sooner you get off my ship the better." Bellamy seemed to have appeared from nowhere. He walked past me with a crude bump of the shoulder.

I shook my head, watching him walk away with that sure, but heavy stride towards the lowered ramp leading down to the dock. I knew I shouldn't say anything. I knew the best thing was to just let him keep walking and get off his ship. So, I held my tongue.

With some strange reluctance and steps slower than they should have been, I trailed far behind Bellamy with Noah and McKenzie at my side. I took in the sights and smells of the port around us. Other ships just like Bellamy's bobbed in the harbor, all varying in size.

The stench of dirt, saltwater, and rum tickled my nose and reminded me of how Milo often described this place as a rancid haven for pirates. A paradise of free men, paid for in lawlessness and mayhem. By the looks of the rundown, bustling buildings and weathered streets, I could see why. Filthy fishermen ogling McKenzie and me, men chatting on the pier while chugging rum and yelling obscenities at us, and a strange, hooded man seemingly watching us in the distance all gave me an uncomfortable feeling. The siren side in me despised him right away, and I felt disgusted when I looked his way. Suddenly, I no longer knew if searching this city by ourselves for Milo would be wise. I sped up a bit to catch up to Bellamy, if only to ward off the creeps for a moment.

As I watched the sights around me, I almost didn't notice as I followed Bellamy right past a ship I didn't recognize in the daylight—the *Siren's Scorn*. I didn't mean to gasp, but I couldn't help it when I saw Valdez approaching. A slightly younger Valdez, with less harsh features and lacking the deranged, bloodthirsty look in his eye, hobbled near with laughter.

"Boy!" he cried with a hearty laugh, "I wasn't expecting to see you till Kingston."

Bellamy stopped in his tracks and replied with a coy air in his voice. "Yes, well, I didn't expect to be attacked by the Royal Navy twice. We're just here for repairs. Won't be long."

"Who's the girl?"

Bellamy glanced back at Katrina. "She's..." He hesitated for a long few seconds. "Just a lucky castaway. She was shipwrecked with her companions. They're getting off here and we'll hopefully never see them again."

The way Bellamy shifted when Valdez pat him on the back made me take notice. I couldn't tell if he was glad to see his father or repulsed. "Just stopping in for repairs," he uttered half-heartedly.

"Well, who did you pick up along the way?" Valdez's eyes snaked their way to me.

"No one. Just a few castaways." Bellamy stole a glance at me, but I didn't look away from him. I was too afraid to look at Valdez. He couldn't possibly know me yet, but something didn't feel right.

Valdez inched closer to me, and my heart went pounding in my ears. He questioned Bellamy about me, and insisted I was more than just a castaway.

"Shipwrecked, you say?" he asked, circling us.

I glanced at Bellamy, afraid he would give me up to his father. Why wouldn't he? He clearly knew his father hunted us. I fully expected him to tell him my secret after how clear he made it that he hated me. So, I was shocked when Bellamy stepped in front of me as his father approached.

"I said she's nothing special. Just a girl."

Valdez shoved him out of his way. "Look at her. She's got something more than usual beauty about her..." He paused and scratched his chin. "It makes me wonder...That face. Those eyes. She favors Lady Cordelia wouldn't you think?"

I went rigid at the mention of Cordelia. And I knew if Valdez thought my eyes looked like hers, the siren voice must be lurking in the shadows of my conscience, waiting to take control.

"I can't say I agree, Father. Perhaps you just can't get that woman off your mind."

"Hmm," Valdez growled, "Well don't send her away yet. I'd like to see what Cordelia has to say about her."

"What will that matter to you?" Bellamy asked, putting a protective arm across me. When his arm touched my body, the siren soul in me took charge and unlocked my dark desires once again. Unable to fight it, I wrapped my hands around his arm and pulled myself close.

"I love you, son, but I don't quite trust your judgment here. This girl just might be more...useful...than you think." Valdez turned and called for one of his crewmen to get Cordelia from her quarters on the ship to "provide her expertise."

I thought of running, but it would only make me look like I was hiding something. So, I stood there, waiting for Cordelia as I pressed myself against Bellamy, who continued to calmly argue with Valdez. Why was he trying so hard to save me when moments earlier he'd just seemed ready to throw me overboard?

I looked up at him, desperate to understand. "Why are you helping me?" I whispered.

He didn't answer me, but looked away as though he was trying to swallow down something bitter. I held onto his arm tighter, something primal in me wishing I could pull myself into him until I disappeared. My siren was taking over, and despite how inappropriate it was in a moment like this, all I could do was picture myself entangled with Bellamy, tasting the rum on his breath.

I glanced back briefly and noticed the man in the distance had pulled back his hood and seemed to be watching us closely. It gave me an eerie feeling, and I looked away quickly and recoiled further into Bellamy. His was the only face the siren allowed me to see.

But then I looked up to see the figure that emerged from the cabin, I shuddered, and my desires went cold. From the top of the ship she descended, like an elegant queen floating down the ship's ramp in her billowing dress of sky blue. She craned her head around, breathing in the fresh ocean air and then her eyes fell down to me. And she held them there as she walked down.

You're just as soulless as me.

Her words echoed in my head, but I fought against them and did my best to calm my breathing. I rubbed my fingers together in my sweating palms as she neared. There was no way she could know me, not in this time. I wasn't born yet. She might be powerful, but she didn't have the ability to see the future.

She joined Valdez, stopping at his side and placing her hand on his shoulder gently. "What did you need me for, darling?" she asked in a sing-song voice that matched the rest of her refined appearance.

"Take a look at this 'girl' would you. Is she one of yours? Maybe a runaway to land?"

Cordelia narrowed her eyes at me. "Ah, I could see why you might suspect that," she said. Taking a step toward me and holding out her hand, she addressed me for a moment. I glanced around, realizing Noah and McKenzie were gone. Did they abandon me? Or were they taken when I wasn't looking? My heart began to speed up so fast I thought it would be loud enough to hear. "Come here, angelfish." She spoke softly as she reached for my hand and pulled me from Bellamy's grip. "Don't be frightened."

I focused on my breathing, trying to keep from looking nervous. If I looked scared, she'd know I had something I was keeping a secret. As Cordelia circled me slowly, inspecting my face and body with her gaze, I fought every nerve going haywire within and told myself to stand still and relax. But my heart felt like it would explode through my chest.

I was shocked when she glanced at Valdez and said, "I assure you she isn't one of them. You won't find her of any use in your dealings."

It took everything in me not to breathe an audible sigh of relief. But when she turned her head back around to look at me, my stomach flipped, and I froze with a sinking feeling. She cunningly smiled at me with a look in her eye, in a way that communicated everything at once. And the way she fiddled with the mermaid scale necklace at her neck to draw my focus to it was no coincidence. She knew who I was. And she'd just saved me—whether because I was her granddaughter or because I was a pawn in her plan, I'll never know. Maybe both.

Whatever the reason, I watched her pull Valdez away and reassure him I wasn't who—or what—he thought I was. Bellamy turned to me as I stumbled around, steadying my shaking breaths that threatened to betray me.

"This is your chance. Go, now, and don't *ever* come back here," Bellamy said, catching me off guard. His tone was anything but gentle.

I turned around, confused. "If you hate me so much, why did you try to protect me just now?"

"I don't hate you," Bellamy mumbled, "but I could never be with a siren. I've seen the consequences of that." He glanced at his father, who was still busy talking with Cordelia. "Like I told you before, my love—my *only* love—is the sea. Not the demons within it."

"Well...thanks, I guess," I said, slightly offended at his last choice of words. "But don't worry, I don't belong here, so hopefully you'll never have to see me again."

"It would be for the best," Bellamy said, and he leaned forward, kissing my forehead. I'd never felt more confused and bewildered, but I didn't question it. Bellamy was as mysterious as the sea itself, and I'd never quite understand what he was feeling. But it didn't matter, I realized as I snapped out of my siren fog. *Milo.*

As if reading my thoughts, Bellamy added one more thing. "Besides, I wouldn't want your Milo to miss out on such a prize. Does he know what you are?"

I tilted my head as I thought how to best answer him.

"He knows better than anyone," I said. But something nagged at me. Of course, Milo was the one who insisted that I accept my mermaid side. But did he know of this selfish, conniving side that came with it? That, I didn't know. And I wondered what would happen when he saw the other side of me. The side that fed off intimidation and desire, showed no compassion, and made me do things I would never choose to do. The side I still didn't know how to control.

"Be careful out there, siren." Bellamy nodded knowingly, as I pulled my gaze from him.

"You do the same," I warned. The thought crossed my mind to tell him that I would see him again someday. But I thought it'd be best to keep that information to myself. And with one last look at Bellamy, I turned away toward Nassau, determined to set out to find Milo, the others...and hopefully myself.

I hadn't gotten far after I left the harbor when I couldn't shake the feeling that someone was following me. Footsteps trailed me, and I whipped around as shadows passed. And then, a brooding figure pulled me into an alleyway of rotting fish and old crates, a hand over my mouth to silence my screams.

BEDLAM

26

MILO

The church bell sounded its miserable chime, each one ringing out like another pistol shot. I couldn't listen to the boy's heartbreak any longer. Standing, I did my best to fight back the tightness in my chest and the burning in my eyes as I intended to leave this place of horrid memories. I shouldn't have come here to begin with.

As I walked away, I heard the desperate shouts of my teenage self. I didn't need to turn around to remember the dreadful scene unfolding at my back. I listened to the broken boy struggling as he fought against the crewmen pulling him onto the ship by his arms. One of the men grappling with him struck him across the face, splitting open the skin above his left eye. I touched the scar on my eyebrow as if I could feel it happening just the same.

"An orphaned lad needs a home, and the *Siren* needs a good sailing master and navigator." Valdez chuckled with a sharpness in his voice that made my stomach turn both then and now. "Welcome to the crew, Harrington."

"No!" I winced as I heard the break in my voice. "I'm not a pirate. And I won't become one!"

"Seeing as you have nothing left to lose here in this shit-ridden city, and you know just as much about charting as yer' father did, I'd say you're just about as much a pirate as my own son." Valdez turned to address the men taking hold of the boy on either side, dragging him away from the lifeless body of his father. "Put him in the brig hold for now, you swabs. He'll come 'round soon enough."

It would almost seem strange to think that this scene could unfold at a busy harbor—a kidnapping over a freshly slain man lying in his own blood. But this was Nassau. There were no rules. This type of madness was the norm.

"Don't worry, boy. Daven Harrington wasn't the man you think he is." Valdez followed behind the crewmen forcing my younger self up the gangplank.

"Shut up, you bastard! Keep my father's name from your lips!" As young Milo screamed in anger, another crew member of Valdez appeared to dispose of my father's body. He rolled his corpse into the water, kicking him as though he was no more than a bag of wet sand.

I had to look away. I forced myself to take another step forward. I couldn't bear it here another moment longer. And I needed to find a ship so I could get the hell off this cursed island and find Katrina. With my mind raging like the sea unchained, I thought of her. I wanted to tell her how she was worth every one of these painstaking memories. If it all brought me to her, it was worth it.

I kept the thought of her in the forefront of my mind. If—when—I found her, I would kiss her until she couldn't breathe. I would hold her so tightly Poseidon himself couldn't tear her away. She didn't want me to protect her, but I would never be able to let her go if I saw her again.

Just then, the sound of a different kind of bell caught my attention. It was the signal sound of a ship coming into port. It shouldn't have been a cause for me to notice. It was a sound I was used to hearing more often than not. But for whatever reason, this time, I turned to look.

The ship came in fast, and the sails were finally folding to slow her down. She was nearly rolling in waters far too calm for the strength at which she barreled into port. I wondered what the hurry was. Because this was one memory I didn't recall. Of course, I was being pulled to the gut of Valdez's ship by now, so who was to say what I might have forgotten in the fray.

It was a ship smaller than Valdez's galleon, but still mighty enough. I might've even considered it as a vessel with potential to commandeer, but by the battered sides of the hull, it was clear she'd been through a recent cannon exchange or two. So much for that idea. I hoped there was a good carpenter aboard for the captain's sake.

I watched as the anchor dropped and the crew rushed to close the sails and secure the rigging and everything else necessary before they came ashore. I counted a small crew of around fifty men as they flooded the docks, eager to step foot on land in who knew how long. But it was the captain who made me second glance.

My eyes narrowed as I strained to see in the blinding sunlight glittering on the harbor. The confident, brooding young man stepped out in a hurry, turning his head every which way as if he was looking for someone. His long blue coat fell to his boot-clad calves with an air of regality as he strode off his ship with an arrogance I could sense from here. I could hardly believe my eyes when he turned enough that I could see it was Bellamy. I had to resist the sudden urge to call out to him, remembering he wouldn't have known me yet. But it was the three passengers walking behind him that made me pause, sucking in a breath that caught in my chest.

I almost didn't recognize them. They were dressed as though they belonged on a ship as good as any. But the gleam of McKenzie's red hair, the sulking demeanor of Noah gave away their identities immediately. And then there she was. Katrina. She looked like a pirate herself, dressed in her own tunic and breeches and boots—delicate and fierce all at the same time. Her dark hair flowed behind her, full and tangled by the sea winds, and her eyes widened in wonder as she looked around at the harbor, taking in the sight of an entirely new world.

Of course, she didn't notice me. Not as I hid in the background waiting in the shadows. I wanted to run to her and show her my face. I needed her to know we'd found each other again. I desired so much that she knew how close I was to her. But I'd need to wait until she was closer, free from any influence of Valdez on the situation. Drawing attention could be dangerous.

I knew this Bellamy wouldn't let anything happen to her. He was always a hothead, but he'd never mistreat a woman. I briefly recalled our interactions after becoming part of Valdez's crew. Bellamy was the first one who spoke to me without commanding me to do something. He asked me my name and told me he was sorry for what happened to my father. Being five years my elder, he treated me almost as a brother for that first year on board Valdez's ship. He taught me to wield a cutlass as well as he could and showed me how to brawl like a sailor and raid ships like a pirate. I was sure it was only because he felt sorry for me. But my mind liked to pretend that he truly enjoyed my company. And I wished our ending had been better.

"Stay true north, and you'll never wander," he told me once over a shared bottle of rum. He was just intoxicated, speaking carelessly out of his ass, but those words never left me. And they finally made sense, three hundred years later.

When it came time to hunt sirens, he never seemed at ease in his conscience about it much more than I did, but he always convinced himself—and me—that it was necessary. Because like me, his duty was to Valdez. For obviously different reasons, of course.

I watched Bellamy saunter across the docks, making his way to the shore with Katrina and her friends in tow. But he veered around at the sound of his father's voice as Valdez greeted him from the docks.

Bellamy uttered something to Katrina, an almost threatening look on his face. She nodded and turned to walk away, but Valdez called out something that made me step closer. I tensed, ready for whatever strange thing may come next. My identity be damned.

Valdez slowly approached Katrina with an observant look in his eye. I wanted to react. To run and grab her, to rip her away from his filthy gaze. But I remembered Katrina's words that seeped like poison into my soul.

"You don't need to protect me...Haven't we been through enough for you to realize sometimes I have to fight my own battles?"

So, I restrained myself impatiently, waiting to see if maybe she had some plan up her sleeve.

Valdez circled them, studying Katrina up and down. The way his eyes moved over her made me want to rip his head from his body and toss it in the sea with my father's corpse. Any longer and I'd have to do something.

Valdez leaned forward and said something to Bellamy so lowly that I couldn't hear. But I fought with every voice in my head telling me to rush in and pull Katrina away. But where would that leave McKenzie and Noah? Did I even care? I only wanted Katrina.

But then I saw the way she was looking at Bellamy. Her eyes never left him, and she moved close enough to reach for his hand as Valdez continued speaking. And she clung to his arm like he was the last person in the world. And then she finally looked away from him, and then straight towards me, as if she knew I was there the whole time.

I ripped back the hood to show her my face, in case she couldn't see me well enough. But she hardly looked at me longer than a second before casting me aside through an indifferent gaze that stung like venom. No warmth. No welcome. Nothing. Then she drew her eyes back to Bellamy.

"You don't need to protect me."

Perhaps I truly didn't. Perhaps she had all the protection she needed in the arms of Bellamy. She seemed content enough. And seeing that I was alive clearly didn't matter to her. And what could I offer her at this point? I couldn't get us out of here. And I would have a bounty on my head soon enough, and it would only make things worse for her. Perhaps I was a fool for standing here hoping things would ever be the same between us again. Our ship had started sinking before we'd even set sail, but I didn't expect it to go down so quickly.

I shook my head, unable to think properly anymore. And the longer I stood by, the greater the urge to crush the compass beneath my boot and burn down every ship in the harbor grew. Ducking my head, I withdrew myself from the scene, my swift strides carrying me back into town where I escaped into an alleyway.

After I caught my breath, I looked at the nearest tavern, just meters away. It wasn't even noon yet, but I'd say I'd seen enough in the past hour to excuse my choice of remedy. It wasn't like me to act so rashly, but I no longer cared. Everyone I cared about had failed me. And I was tired.

MILO

I downed the first pint as though it was fresh water after a week in the desert, and I immediately demanded another. The tavern keeper slid down another drink, as the bards sang shanties and the women danced around the tables of sailors immersed in their gambling.

When a hand touched my shoulder, I whipped around, pulling the blade from my sleeve and pointing it straight at the culprit.

"Noah?" I said with surprise as my eyes narrowed at his rugged expression. It was him, with a much more bold and unwavering air about him than before. "I'm surprised you didn't start crying." I muttered as I lowered my hand and put the blade away.

"Shut up, Sandy," he spat, but a small half-grin formed on his face. "It's...good to see you."

I shook my head and turned around, hunching over the bar. "I'll admit I'm glad to see you're not dead. Mostly."

"Look, man, are we really gonna still be like that after all this?" he exclaimed, sliding into the seat next to me.

"Consider me not punching you my apology. Why are you even here?" I took a swig of my drink. "You left Katrina and McKenzie to come here? I know they were with you."

"I saw you by the docks and followed you here." Noah hesitated for a moment. "McKenzie's right outside. She didn't want to come in here, understandably." When he paused to sigh, I looked up. "But Katrina..."

"What about Katrina?" I slammed my drink on the counter, my voice rising.

"That's why I followed you. Something's wrong with her."

I perked up, but I tried my hardest not to look too concerned. "She looked fine to me. In fact, she looked quite comfortable with Bellamy."

"That's my point, dude!" Noah leaned in, nudging my elbow with his. "She's been acting strange...but it's not *her*. It's like something is controlling her. She told us herself she can't stop it.."

"Go on." I didn't mean for the words to spill out so quickly, but they did.

"She's put herself in danger more than once, doing stupid stuff like running up on deck during a battle with another ship, jumping overboard in the night, just crazy stuff. And yeah, she's up Bellamy's ass, but when she does these things it's like she isn't Katrina. It's like she's...someone else."

A strange suspicion rose within me. If what I'd observed from the mermaids was true, then I supposed the things that lurked in their nature could be the same for Katrina. Perhaps it was diluted in her time...but here in this time when siren magic was aplenty in the seas, maybe somehow the ancient magic in her veins was awakened. And if what was happening to her was what I suspected, I knew I had to stop her before she lost herself completely. And if there was any small chance of keeping us afloat, I couldn't abandon ship now.

"Where is she now?" I stood up, fearing the answer, fearing I had just made the biggest mistake of my life by not ripping her away from Bellamy when I had the chance.

Noah dropped his gaze. "She's still back there. Valdez wouldn't let Bellamy let her leave. He called some woman out from his cabin to talk to her or something."

"What?" I took off before the word had even left my lips. I assumed McKenzie and Noah would follow, but I didn't wait for them.

I darted through the town, back through the streets and toward the harbor, hating myself for not thinking straight earlier and leaving Katrina. This Bellamy wouldn't have any idea that Katrina was a mermaid. He wouldn't have realized the danger he was putting her in.

When I reached the harbor, Bellamy, Valdez, and Katrina were nowhere to be found. They must've taken her inside. The gangplank was up, and there was no way onto the ship. I quickly realized my only option was to climb the side of the ship. Just as I leapt into the water below, Noah and McKenzie arrived, skidding to stop behind me at the edge of the dock.

"Keep watch!" I ordered.

Grabbing the siding of the boat, I began my ascent, my fingertips gripping the thin wooden ledges that barely stuck out along the ship. My soaking wet clothing and boots made the climb all the more difficult. But I couldn't afford to slip. The muscles in my knuckles ached as I held onto whatever I could manage to grab. When I reached a cannon, I sighed with relief, throwing my arm around it to haul myself up higher. It wasn't the first time I'd climbed up the side of a ship. But I certainly hoped it would be the last.

When I finally reached the deck, I swung myself over the railing and glanced around for any sign of Katrina. Not a soul was on board. Eyeing the captain's cabin, I wasted no time barging through the door, calling her name. But it was empty.

"Who are you and why are you looking for Katrina?" The voice that asked the question accompanied a shadow that darkened the doorway at my back.

I spun around to see Bellamy, standing with that arrogant demeanor I remembered so well. He watched me like an eagle locking onto its prey. I couldn't show him my face, especially not that my younger self was locked on board below.

"Are you Milo?" His question nearly caused me to stumble. How could he know?

I stayed silent, still trying to figure out how he could recognize someone he'd never met yet. When he stepped forward, I drew the blade at my side.

"So you *are* him then." With another step toward me, he placed his hands behind his back in a formal sort of manner.

"How do you know my name?" I uttered, knowing the less I said, the better. But I had to know.

"She called out your name in her sleep...No. Don't worry, mate. It wasn't like that...I made her sleep in my cabin to keep her safe." He must have noticed the way my jaw clenched, and I tilted my head in a threatening way at his words. "After she jumped in the ocean trying to find you."

I swallowed, taking in this information and trying to decide what to make of it.

"Where is she now?" I asked, doing my best to stay at an angle that hid my features in the shadows of this cramped wooden room.

"The hell I know where she is by now, but my father let her go so I'm assuming she went into town."

I nodded my thanks. It was all I could give as I still processed the strange interaction between a brother-like figure I'd once looked up to, who was now younger than me and naïve to what life held in store for him.

He stepped aside so that I could leave. With my wet clothes sticking to my skin and making moving quickly difficult, I stepped out onto the deck. It had been so long since I'd seen this ship in this condition. Like new and modified with cannons and new sails, ready to conquer the world. How little I realized how many decades I would spend a slave on board here, rotting away with it as eras passed.

Shaking myself free of the strange memory, I stepped to the raised gangplank and sliced through the rope holding it back with my knife. It dropped with a heavy thud and slammed onto the dock below, bringing memories to the forefront of my mind I'd rather have not faced as I walked across. McKenzie and Noah awaited me, both wearing looks of disappointment when they saw that I'd returned without Katrina.

"She can't be far," McKenzie stated. "She probably went looking for us when she saw us leave to get help."

"Then let's not waste time finding her," I ordered, shaking my head. "I should never have let her go."

I paced forward, scanning every inch to the left and right of this port. As we walked along the main dock back to the town entrance, I thought I saw her. My spirits lifted as a woman with dark, full hair tumbling over her shoulders approached, heading back toward the piers. But when she came closer to me, I could see that she wasn't Katrina. It was Cordelia.

Walking with a regal stride in her layers of fine skirts and corset, she neared. I didn't expect her to know me, or even notice me. So, when she looked up and grinned at me with a dark, sly smile, a bolt of ice struck my core. She passed by me as if on purpose, turning her head just to hold her cruel smirk on me just a bit longer. And I noticed around her neck was the scale hanging from its silvery chain, and all at once I felt sick.

I shook her chilling stare out of my mind and refocused on finding Katrina. The last place wanted to imagine her getting lost in alone was Nassau. Not that she needed me to protect her, I reminded myself. But I would be there just in case she did. We would find her.

So as we rushed along the dirt road into the belly of Nassau, I stopped dead in my tracks when someone called out to me from a section of a building on the coast blockaded in by barrels and crates. And in between them stood three men, obviously trying to stay out of plain sight. McKenzie shrieked in horror at the scene. Two men stood on either side of a brooding figure in the middle—Carl Thane. And he was pulling Katrina's head back by her hair to expose her neck as he pressed the edge of dagger against it.

OF THE CODE

28

I wanted to scream. I fought back the wave of panic rising in my veins. My nerves shook, and it took every ounce of my focus not to let it show. I had to appear unshaken, despite my world crumbling before me. I had to draw this out as long as I could. There was a good bit of distance between us—too much distance for me to make it in time if Thane decided to swipe the knife across her neck. Katrina held my gaze, a wide-eyed look of terror in her trembling face. And I remained still. Because I knew Thane would slice her throat without a second thought if I made one wrong move.

"You're the bastard who set the *Lark* ablaze," Thane grunted.

My eyes flicked to the man at his right. It was the one I had pushed into the water to save. And all at once I regretted that mercy. I should've let him burn.

"It was nothing personal. You should be looking for the man who assigned me the mission," I uttered, hiding the ever-growing fury in my voice.

"Well don't consider this personal when I spill her blood out on the ground in front of you," he dug the point of the blade into Katrina's skin, and she winced with a yelp.

"Wait," I pleaded. To my surprise, he stopped. I spoke through a tight knot in my chest that nearly left me unable to breathe. "What do you want? I'll restore your loss with a new ship. Take your pick from my fleet." It was the perfect bargain now that my father's ships sat without a captain in the bay.

"I'll take the whole fleet."

Fine by me. He could have them all. "Done. Now let her go."

"Tsk, tsk, stranger. I'm not done bargaining." Even from where I stood, meters away from Thane's position in the shadows, I could see the way his eyes darkened.

"What else?" I stiffened, stepping forward and clenching my fist, hoping it wouldn't set him off.

"I want to know who you are, so that I can ensure every minute spent on this island is devoted to hunting you down. Take off the hood."

I tilted my head at the strange request. "Why don't you and your men just kill me right here?"

A grim smile stretched across his thin lips. "Because where's the fun in that? I want you to spend every day forward in fear, ne'er knowing when I'll finally strike, but always knowing that one day I will. If I spare your whore, I'm coming for you." This was exactly the sort of sick game Thane would relish. A chance to enact his sadistic tendencies by hunting me down like an animal. But I was more than willing to play along if it meant saving Katrina. After all, I'd been killed before.

"So, you'll let her go?" I reached for the top of my hood, not fully convinced he wouldn't kill Katrina after I showed myself anyway.

"I'm a man of the code," he grinned, lifting his knife off Katrina's neck, but still holding her by her hair, nearly lifting her from the ground.

"If you hurt her, I swear I'll send you back to hell myself." I watched his hand like a hawk tracking its prey.

He laughed a laugh that sent fire flashing before my mind's eye. I longed to watch this man bleed and burn. "I'm waiting," he crooned.

I glanced at Noah and McKenzie, who stood firmly on either side of me, before slowly removing my hood. As we stared at each other in silence across the alleyway, I waited with bated breath for Thane to release Katrina as he studied my features.

"I won't forget that face." His words made me uneasy, but I reassured myself it wouldn't remain here much longer for it to become an issue. Whatever he wanted, I'd agree to, as long as he'd release Katrina unharmed. I watched him hesitate, then lift the blade above Katrina's chin.

"Such a pretty girl," Thane growled. Then he sliced his knife across the side of her face.

Her scream reached my ears like the sound of every failure I'd ever made crying aloud in my soul. I ran to her as Thane shoved her to the ground, but my feet couldn't move fast enough. He turned away with his men in tow as a cloud of dust arose around us from their movements.

I locked my target onto him, reaching for the dagger at my side. I'd kill this man if it was the last thing I ever did for what he'd just done to her.

"Stay with her!" I shouted to McKenzie and Noah who followed fast behind me. Damn my conscience. Damn my soul. Damn it all. I would have Thane's blood for this.

I turned and climbed the building bordering the alleyway, clinging to the trellis and ivy crawling up the side as I scrambled upward. Once atop the roof, I scanned the streets for Thane and his men. There were few places they could have escaped to this quickly.

My gaze roamed the alleys below. The sounds of Nassau's usual chatter and buzz filled the air, carried along by the wind across the rooftops. But in the midst of all the laborers, sailors and drunks traveling below, I finally caught sight of them—a glimpse of that matted copper hair of Thane's between his two henchmen walking back toward the main strip of town.

I surged forward, my legs aching as I pushed my stride to its limit, racing along the edge of houses and dilapidated buildings as silently but quickly as I could manage. I needed a good angle. Good enough to leap down and plunge my knife into Thane's back before he even realized what struck him. I slid down to a low hanging balcony and waited overhead. They'd have to take a turn and pass by it to get back into town.

One... Two... Three...

I counted their footfalls and held my breath. I flexed my fingers around the bone handle of the knife in my grip. And just as Thane walked past below, I pushed myself from my lurking spot and pounced.

One of Thane's men caught sight of me just before my knife reached its target. He shouldered Thane out of the way and disrupted my concentration. With a stumble I landed, but I found my footing quickly and took a stance to fight the man at Thane's side. He drew his cutlass and swung it around toward my neck. I ducked with ease and plunged the knife into his abdomen. As he dropped to his knees, I ripped his sword from his grip. It was then that the other man—the one who I'd saved from the *Lark*— whirled around to come far too late to the defense. I dodged his attempt to strike me by furiously ramming my new blade into his shoulder. Hot blood spattered out, raining on me like crimson sea spray. As I realized Thane had escaped and was nowhere to be found, I heaved in anger that I'd lost him.

"Next time I suggest keeping your mouth shut," I snarled. And as I thought of Katrina, an unconfined fury rose in my bones that I couldn't snuff out. So, I twisted the blade as the man groaned in pain, driving him to the ground where I planned to deal him one final blow. "Tell your captain if he plans on hunting me like some kind of animal, it's an animal he'll find."

"Milo! Stop it!" Katrina's voice tore me from my rage. I shook my head and placed my boot on the man's hip to pry him off the edge of my sword. I dislodged the weapon from his flesh, and watched him clamber up to flee, bleeding and wounded. I looked down at the body of the man left behind. Then at Katrina, who stood a good distance away, clinging to McKenzie and Noah shielding them both.

Straightening as I caught my breath, I brushed my hair back from my eyes, only to smear my hands with the blood on my face. "They hurt you." I panted.

She watched me with uncertainty, like I was a poisonous viper. And I couldn't blame her after what she'd just witnessed. The right side of her face was stained red with blood just beginning to dry across her cheekbone. I stepped toward her, feeling the weight of my compass and my heart.

I wanted to run to her, but I knew it wasn't my place after what I'd just done. She'd never seen me like that. And she very well may never trust me again. But she had to know. She had to know I'd do anything to keep her safe. Past, present, or future.

Without warning, she took off past Noah and rushed toward me. She threw herself into my arms and I closed myself around her. The world around me faded. The stink of Nassau, the burning sun above, and the sweat and blood dripping from my brow. None of it mattered in her embrace.

"Don't become like them," she uttered into my shoulder. I nodded, squeezing my eyes shut tightly.

"This is a life long past I thought you'd never have to see," I sighed, pulling back from her and touching her injury with my fingers. It would scar. "I'm so sorry he did this to you."

"A scratch on my face is not our biggest problem right now. I was so afraid you were dead." She shook her head. "We all were." She looked back over her shoulder at McKenzie and Noah, who stepped near as she motioned for them to join.

"It's good to have you back." Noah rolled his eyes, but his words were genuine. "Now maybe you have some kind of idea of how we're supposed to get back to our time?"

"I'm afraid the trident is still our only hope. If it took us here, it has to be able to take us back. But we'll have to figure out how. But the first step is getting to it."

"So, we just sail right back over the Bermuda Triangle again in a wooden ship?" McKenzie raised an eyebrow. "That didn't work out so well last time."

"I'm open to any other suggestions, but he's right. What other option do we have?" Noah leaned in. It felt strange to hear him agree with me.

I reached into my coin purse and produced enough gold to show them. "Give me enough time to secure a ship. I have just enough money left to buy us lodging for one more night. I'm sure we're all in need of a good night's rest."

We wandered into town, far enough away from the incident with Thane's men to avoid suspicion—not that anyone would have cared. I couldn't lead them to Codface's tavern. He already knew too much, and I wouldn't make us targets more than we already were.

There was another inn on the far side of town. It was a bit of a trek, but no one complained. I did find myself watching my back for any sign of Thane or anyone else who sought to do me harm, but I tried my best to appear calm and unbothered. If I was the reason something happened to Katrina or the others here, I'd never forgive myself. I couldn't continue my father's legacy of destroying those around him by his own mistakes.

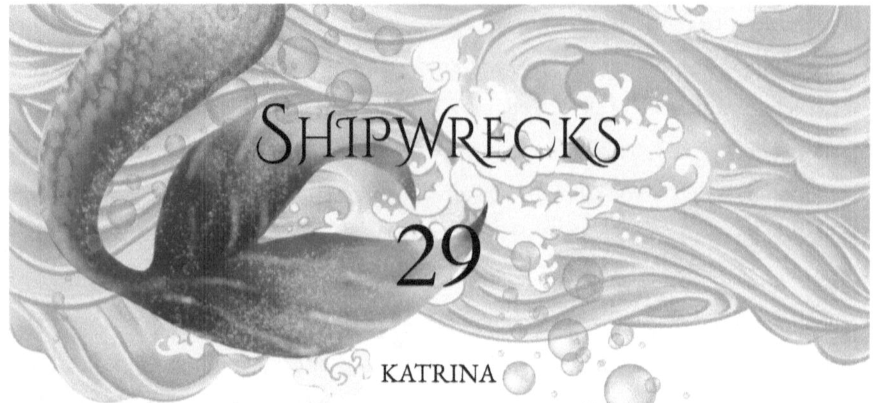

SHIPWRECKS

29

Milo led us to a tavern on the edge of town. I stayed close to him, watching with suspicion as strange men ogled McKenzie and me, and rogue beggars teetered near us in their drunken state. No one said much, still in shock after our brush with danger moments earlier.

As we walked, I looked at Milo and thought of him in the alley. I'd never seen him like that. Something had broken free from him. Something animalistic, dark, and feral. And it terrified and fascinated me all at the same time. But I had to remind myself, this place was no Constantine. This was a pirate-ridden city in 1720. Of course, there had to be things Milo had to do to survive that I could never comprehend. But I still felt an uneasiness when I remembered the expression in his eyes when he turned around, covered in another man's blood.

"We can stay here tonight. In the morning we can set out at first light." Milo took my hand and gently guided me up the steps to the entrance. How moments earlier those hands drove swords into flesh without mercy, but now caressed mine like a dove.

McKenzie, Noah, and I waited while Milo went to talk to the innkeeper. The smell of liquor, salt, roasting meat, and bread filled the air, making my stomach growl. I longed for a meal more filling than the watery stew and jerky on Bellamy's ship.

"What if we never make it back?" McKenzie uttered all of a sudden, a shakiness in her voice. "It sucks here. What if we're trapped here?"

"McKenzie," Noah reached for her shoulders, leaning down to look her in the eyes. "I promise that no matter what happens, we will be all right. I'll make sure of it."

I smiled a small smile as I watched them from the corner of my eye. McKenzie nodded and then threw herself into him for a hug. I was glad for her to have someone as stubborn as Noah. But secretly I feared the same as she did. And Cordelia's haunting words that found me even in my sleep certainly weren't helping me feel any better about it.

Milo returned and gestured to us to follow. "There's a room left."

We made our way upstairs to a small room with one bed, a wash bucket, and a small table, all of it barely big enough for one person, let alone four.

"Okay, I'm going back down there for some food," Noah announced. "Anyone else?"

Based on the way McKenzie jumped to agree, I must've not been the only one who felt like they were starving. I breathed a sigh of relief at the thought of filling my empty stomach.

"I'll be down in a minute. I want to clean up my face," I said, touching the cut from where it ran from the bottom of my jawbone back up toward my ear.

"I'll stay with you," Milo uttered, and then hesitated, looking at the door. "That is...if you want me to."

"I'd like that," I nodded.

"I'll go get something to clean the wound, then."

As the wooden door closed behind McKenzie, Noah and Milo, I sat down on the floor where I dipped a rag into the water bucket. It wasn't long before Milo returned with a cup of liquor.

"Here," he said, taking the rag from my hand as the candle fire flickered its light on his tanned skin. "Will you let me?"

I nodded, brushing my hair back behind my ear so that he could better access the injury. He gently pressed the rag over the mark, soaking away the dried blood. I winced at the burn.

"I'm sorry, Katrina," he muttered, cleaning the cut with soft strokes.

"It's okay," I bit my lip. "At least I can hide most of it with my hair."

"No." He pulled the rag away and held my gaze. "I'm sorry for everything."

"Who were those men?" I asked.

Milo parted his lips and released a heavy sigh. "There's so much that's happened in my few days here. I sabotaged that man's ship for information about my father. Turns out he's not at all the man I thought he was. It wouldn't be a stretch to say I'm ashamed to be his son."

"It can't really be that bad, can it?" I watched him with worry.

Milo pulled out his compass from his pocket. He spoke as he stared down at the tool in his hand with a hardened gaze and traced his finger and thumb along the rim. He told me about his father and the slave and mermaid trade, and everything else he'd been through since waking up on the shores of Nassau.

"He's the reason my mother and brother are dead. He got in over his head in a the details of a deal I never quite figured out. And they paid for it." He put the compass away and straightened his shoulders. "And now I've caused you to pay for my mistakes."

We sat in silence as he reached up to touch my face. He caressed his fingertips delicately along the scratched skin on my cheek. "I could never say I'm sorry enough times," he whispered.

"I'm the one who should be sorry," I said, looking down. I wanted to tell him how I felt like I was losing myself. I wanted him to understand why I should be sorry. But I didn't know how to put it into words. But I tried anyway. "I'm sorry that I pushed you away. Before any of this even happened. Before we ended up here..." I looked up at him. "But it has been worse since we've been here."

"What do you mean?" Milo cocked his head at me and raised an eyebrow.

"I mean it's almost like...like there's a part of me that wants to be cold and cruel. A part of me that only wants to do things I would never do. And sometimes it wins."

"What kind of things?"

"Like telling you I don't need you. And like flipping out on McKenzie when she's just trying to help. And like trying to take control of a whole pirate ship right in front of its captain. And like...like..."

My voice trailed off. I couldn't tell him about Bellamy. The voice inside me told me not to.

Secrets won't hurt anyone. But telling him will.

"That's it?" Milo leaned forward.

Knowing it was wrong, I nodded. Milo almost looked crushed. He straightened and looked away. "So then...does that mean that you and Bellamy...that was all you? The *real* you?"

Something took hold of my heart, clamping down on it like fangs. "How do you know about that?" I hissed. The siren side was back.

"I saw you. At the docks. You two looked...close. And you looked right at me, like you hated me."

"I...I don't even remember doing that. I thought I might've seen someone, but I wasn't sure. I didn't see your face. It must've been controlling me then."

"Well, I left after that. It crushed me. But then Noah told me you were acting strange and so I thought maybe—"

"Bellamy saved me. What did you expect?"

Oh no.

Milo stood up, his gaze hardening. "I don't know. I don't know what I expected. Maybe you'd tell him you didn't want or need his help like you told me."

I heard his words, but that dark, terrible side of me relished in the hurt I sensed welling up within him. I shot up to my feet and stepped toward him, into the low light of the candle burning in the room.

Don't say it. No. Yes. Say it.

"Maybe I *did* need him. Maybe I *wanted* him."

Milo stomped toward me, with his jaw clenched, and gripped my shoulders with each hand. "Why? Why would you say that, Katrina?" Even through his gritted teeth and steel eyes, I could tell how hard he was trying to hide the pain he felt from my words.

He lowered his gaze to match mine, as if studying my eyes. When he paused, I knew he'd noticed them. But I was glad. I was glad he could see the other side of me was there and in control. I wanted him to know it wasn't me who had said that to him.

"Your eyes," he growled.

"You see it, then." I smiled, knowing he'd caught a glimpse of my cold blue irises. "You see why I don't need you? I have all the power and protection I need, right here."

Shut up.

I closed my eyes. I couldn't let her win. I'd never fought the siren in me so hard. But I thought of Milo and for a moment...just a moment...I broke free of her. "Milo, this isn't me! Don't listen to her...me...*anything* I say when my eyes are blue." My words came out so desperately I nearly choked on them. I didn't know how long I had before the voice came back.

"I know," he sighed. "I was afraid this is what happened to you when Noah said you've been acting weird."

"What? What happened to me?"

He hesitated, looking around the room like he wasn't sure speaking here was safe. "Let's go downstairs to eat with the others. I'll explain there. They deserve to know, too."

"Okay." I hugged myself, ashamed of the monster I became when I least expected it. But I had it under control. For now. But I'd still need to repair the damage that had been done. Because as much as admitting it felt like fire on my skin, there was always the smallest inkling of truth in whatever I said when the siren took over.

Back down in the tavern, we stayed to ourselves, keeping to the darkest corners of the place to stay out of sight. But we gobbled down the pork and vegetable stew like it was the best thing we'd ever tasted.

"We'll have to make this last," Milo noted. "I've only enough left to purchase our food rations for our journey. Unless the ship we commandeer happens to have some on it already."

We all nodded, too ravenous to worry about it right then. McKenzie gave him a quick thumbs up and continued slurping her stew. I ate, too, but something heavy was still clouding my mind. I feared at any moment I could lose myself again to the other version of me that constantly lurked in wait. It was just a matter of when something happened that gave me a reason to be selfish.

"Something else," Milo added, and I perked up to listen. "As we've all noticed by now, Katrina is dealing with something that makes her...well, not herself." McKenzie and Noah nodded, pressing him to go on. "Back on Valdez's ship, when we would capture mermaids, I noticed the longer they were out of the water, out of their siren form, the more vicious they became. Eventually Valdez contained them in special tanks of seawater to keep them more...agreeable." All eyes at the table flew to me. I wanted to crawl away and hide.

"So, you're saying Katrina needs to go full mermaid to snap out of it?" McKenzie asked, tearing into a piece of bread.

"I'm saying I think it would make sense based on what I know about mermaids." Milo placed his hands on the table and looked at me.

I wondered if that's what made Cordelia so ruthless. She physically couldn't return to her mermaid form, and she'd been forced to be on land for centuries. So maybe that's why her heart had grown dark beyond repair. When I finally found the courage to speak up, I put my spoon down and addressed him.

"I tried to do it when I jumped overboard on Bellamy's ship. I wanted to look for you. I was ready to do anything to find you. But I also had the strangest feeling...like a need...a pull to just...dive in. I wanted to be in the water, and I couldn't ignore it. But I didn't change."

Milo looked at me as if I'd just given him a riddle. But he finally placed his elbows on the table and spoke. "There's a place I know of that might be a good place to try again. It's too small a body of water for ships, so it's quite useless to most here. It should be safe."

All at once, I felt three pairs of eyes on me, waiting for my next words. Was I supposed to just agree to go practice turning into a mermaid in front of them like it was completely normal? I suppose for us, it was probably the most normal thing about these past few days. With hesitation, and maybe even a bit of fear, I nodded once. "Okay," I breathed, closing my eyes. "I'll try. But only because I have to beat this thing."

"Then I'll take you there as soon as you're ready," Milo said.

Cordelia's taunting voice rang out in my head, reminding me how little time may be left back in our time—if she hadn't already destroyed humanity by now. "Let's go, now," I said. "I'm ready."

With hazel-green eyes that held me captive, he studied my face before taking my hand. An old, but familiar sense of comfort engulfed me—one that reminded me of the way I felt when he took me to the lighthouse that night of the gala when I hadn't expected him to come for me. And somehow everything felt okay for a moment, even with the weight of the world on our shoulders.

"It's a bit of a walk. We'll need to be careful," he said, his voice strong but gentle as he glanced at McKenzie and Noah.

"I think we're gonna sit this one out. If it's good with you, we'll stay here and get some rest," Noah gestured with a flick of his head.

"Yeah, I'm sure Katrina would appreciate some privacy. I know I wouldn't want an audience if I was trying to turn into a mermaid." McKenzie ended her sentence with a small giggle I could tell she'd tried to suppress. It made me smile.

"Then let's get going." Milo looked at me, squeezing my hand. "It may be after sundown by the time we get there."

"Whatever it takes," I uttered, following him as he turned toward the door. We told our friends goodbye and left the tavern, wandering into the night.

The night was even more chaotic than the daytime. Every tavern was glowing, and the laughter of drunk men and music could be heard from every corner. People lay slumped over in doorways and on benches, and couples indulged themselves out in the open in drunken moans of pleasure.

"Quite the show, isn't it?" Milo smirked at me as I looked up at him through my lashes.

"It's something," I scoffed playfully. "I can't believe you grew up here. And yet, you're such a gentleman."

"Only when I need to be." He tilted his head, and something familiar washed over me. It felt like walking with him for the very first time along the beach in the state park of Constantine. It was as if, for only a moment, all the burdens between us no longer existed. It was just he and I, walking into something new and terrifying ahead, just like the first time.

But then *she* showed up in my head again...

"A gentleman has no place on a pirate crew, though," I scoffed.

"You're probably right there. It was quite the dilemma," he shrugged, quickening his step.

"Right," I chimed. "I'm sure you've done some really shitty things, haven't you? Worse than anything you've ever told me."

"Katrina, where is this coming from?"

"What do you mean?" I raised an eyebrow. "I mean you just killed a man in front of me. I just want to know who the man I'm with really is? Your father hid all those things away from you and your mother. How do I know you aren't hiding things from me? Just like the letter?"

Why would you bring that up? We're past that.

"Katrina," he stopped walking before he'd finished saying my name and turned to touch my shoulder. "Listen to what you're saying. This isn't you."

"It *is* me." My tone turned cold. "But is this *you*? How do I know? How will I ever really know? You're probably just like your father."

I was jolted from my dark state of mind when Milo gripped my shoulders so tightly, I nearly winced. He pulled me to the nearest wall as the sounds of glasses breaking and muffled music filled the background silence.

"Don't. Ever. Say that again," he growled through a clenched jaw. The look in his eyes was one I'd never seen—at least not directed at me—piercing and focused. He watched my eyes like he was searching for a secret message hidden within them. Then, by the nearby light of a tavern torch, I saw in the reflection of his steady, intense gaze, my own ocean blue eyes staring back into his.

I paused; my breath caught in my throat. Staring back at myself were the most beautiful, barely human eyes, framed by delicate lashes that seemed to have intensified themselves to draw all attention to my gaze. They were two moonlight lagoons, nearly glowing with the most radiant blue that rivaled the depths themselves. Like magic.

I blinked, clenching my eyes shut, and when I opened them, everything had returned to normal. I breathed a sigh of relief, but barely had time to recompose myself before Milo crashed his mouth into mine. He pulled away long enough to bring his lips to my ear, which made heat pool between my thighs.

"Damn, I hate this side of you," he whispered.

"Then why are you kissing me?" I uttered.

"Because it's still you," he said without hesitation. "And because I've been dying to kiss you for too long."

I knew then that I had to tell him about Bellamy. "Milo," I said. "I...I kissed Bellamy. But..."

"But it wasn't you?" He said. "Is that what you're going to tell me?"

"Well, yes...because that's the truth. I never would have..." I struggled to finish my sentence.

"Are you sure?" He leaned into me as someone walked past. "Because something in me isn't quite so sure. And that's why I hate this side of you, Katrina. Because I can't trust you when you're in it. I can't tell what's true and what isn't. And your siren has a way of bringing my deepest fears to light. So, I'll ask you this question, but I don't want you to answer it until you've become a siren fully and satisfied that side of you for a while. Because I want to hear the answer from *you*."

I dug my gaze into him, my brows tense and pressed together, urging him to go on. He looked at the ground, then back up at me. "Do you love me?"

"Well...yes...of course you know I—"

"No," he breathed against my lips, caressing them like velvet with his own. "Don't answer it yet."

"Fine," I said, "Then let's get going. We're wasting time here."

Milo nodded, and then walked away, turning back toward the night to lead us through the city and into the dark outskirts of town, where nothing awaited us but tangled jungle and a long hike to the middle of it.

KATRINA

Milo led me to a path framed by hanging moss and gnarled vines. The moonlight illuminated our steps well, shining down from a bright moon. We were silent, but the humming of nocturnal insects and summer crickets filled the air with their song. After a few long moments making our way through this tropical maze, a new sound reached our ears.

"A waterfall," I noted, as we arrived in a clearing with a lagoon in the middle of it.

"You should be safe here." Milo gestured. "I used to enjoy this spot when I was younger. Few know about it. And I doubt that's changed."

I took in the wonder around me of the greenery encircling us in this private glade. The moon's glow cut through the jungle canopy and streaked down in rays toward the glistening crystal water pooling at the foot of the cascading water. The mist from the waterfall surrounded us, casting a delicate haze that only emphasized the rhythmic golden pulses of firefly flashes over the water. But what enchanted me the most was the blue and white bioluminescent glow of the churning water from the waterfall. The water lit up like starlight with every ripple.

"So, I should just...get in?" I turned to Milo, unsure.

"It's a start," he said, helping me closer to the lagoon's edge. "Here there is no pressure. Take however long you need, Katrina, to figure yourself out."

He went to sit on a mossy log nearby at the foot of the water, while I stared down into the blue lagoon below. The water called to me, and I longed to become part of it. I felt the siren taking over. I dipped my toe in.

"Oh!" I exclaimed, in awe at the way the water glowed when I disturbed the surface.

"That's my favorite thing about it here," Milo laughed. The gentle happiness in his voice was like warm honey I'd longed to taste again. But then my siren made me scoff.

No. Shut up. Get in the water and shut up.

I dove in, my clothes billowing around me as the bubbles I created in the water lit up like silver fairy dust. For the first time, I wanted this. I truly wanted to be underwater, merging with its streams and currents. Becoming it. The water met my skin like a kiss between two long-lost lovers, and I closed my eyes, hoping to open them to a shimmering tail like the one I'd seen the night I broke the curse.

But when I opened them, I was still the same. I burst forth out of the water, drawing in a breath. Something in me still begged to be released. The siren was still there, still secretly in control in the back of my mind. I looked at Milo, confused.

"See?" I said, "It never works!"

"Keep trying," he encouraged. "Maybe it just takes time."

"I floated in the water, leaning my head back and listening to the hum of the falls nearby, my hair fanning around me like a giant lily pad. But I still had legs.

"Stop thinking so much about it," Milo said. "Perhaps you can't make it happen. Maybe you just need to *let* it happen."

I sighed. Maybe he was right, whatever that meant. I decided to soak, enjoying the feeling of the water against my body. But it wasn't enough. With slow, gentle movements, I slid out of my blouse and pants, and swam up to Milo, handing him the wet clothes.

"Can you put these somewhere dry?" I asked with a smile. "Please."

He took the sopping wet bundle from my hand and placed it on a log beside him, only to look back at me with wandering eyes, though I knew he couldn't see much with everything from my chest down below the water's surface. I studied his face, honing in on his features in the moonlight.

"You have blood on you," I finally acknowledged, noting the dark red spatters along his face and neck and dried in his hair. "From those men you..." It was hard for me to finish the sentence. He'd killed a man in front of me. He was never lying when he told me he'd done terrible things. And yet I didn't feel afraid of him. I never had. And I never would. Only safe. Even when my siren side told me to turn against him.

"I was protecting you," Milo uttered propping himself on his knee. "I couldn't control myself when I saw what they did to you." He reached down to touch my face, and I leaned forward to let him, but the siren in me yanked me back, recoiling when his fingertips hit my skin.

Don't let him touch you.

I shook my head, trying to rid myself of the vile moment that took charge so quickly. "Sorry," I muttered, "The voice in my head wants me to hate you. I don't know why."

"I have my theories," Milo said, "but I'll save them for when you're feeling more like yourself."

"But how can I? I've been here a while and I still don't know how to change. What do I have to do, drown myself?" I slapped my hands against the water in frustration, but my own words caught my attention. "Wait...maybe that's it. Last time I changed when I went unconscious...I couldn't breathe any longer and I sucked in the water and...and I drowned."

Milo leaned forward. "Mmm. That doesn't sound like a pleasant transformation."

"It wasn't. But it makes sense," I said, thinking harder about it. "The ocean rules us. And like Cordelia said, it's more powerful than anything. So, I can't just be in the water. I have to surrender to it."

"You're going to drown yourself?" Milo lifted an eyebrow.

"Don't try and stop me," I demanded. Before he could respond, I dove underneath the water, the bioluminescent sparkles lighting up the underwater world around me, and I swam to the bottom of the lagoon. It wasn't very deep. Maybe ten feet or so, but I released my breath, letting myself sink to the bottom. Silt stirred up and smoked out the glow that comforted me, leaving me in darkness except for the surface above. I was terrified, but my siren was relishing every moment of it.

I could hear the muffled sound of Milo shouting my name. Every beat of my heart screamed for air. But siren Katrina held me under. I had to let her have control. All of it, for just this moment. As my consciousness faded, I could almost imagine a ghost of myself holding me under, pressing me against the stony, sandy bottom of this blue pool. And when my lungs felt ready to burst, I couldn't suppress the instinct to open my mouth and desperately suck in a gulp of briny water. My lungs filled with the water, burning like hell and surely stopping my heart before the blurry, obscured lagoon floor became even darker. Nothingness.

And then I opened my eyes and everything around me shone crystal clear, as though looking through polished diamond. Bubbles from the waterfall crashed into the surface in the distance, creating a roiling thrashing of brightly glowing bubbles. And I was somehow...breathing...in a way that made no physical sense. But here I was, meters deep underwater and breathing as though I stood on land.

When the strands of my hair drifted away from my face, a glimmer below caught my eye. I looked down. And just below my waist connecting to my hips was a merging of skin into ethereal scales that sparkled silver-blue like the dress I'd worn to the gala, only more beautiful, and certainly more surreal. My fins fanned out at the base like wild petals that bloomed in spring, sheer and delicate. And when I wiggled the muscles that would have been my thighs and lower abdomen, the tail flicked, surging power through the water and propelling me upward with ease. I repeated the motion, rolling my waist and hips like the motion of waves, swimming upward, until I finally broke through the surface of the water.

Relief flooded over me, as I hit the cool night air, drenched in the most refreshing sensation I'd felt in my entire life. Like I'd been reborn. And like I could finally think clearly again. The fog in my head was gone, along with the devious siren whispering on my shoulder. I was me again.

I turned to see Milo, watching me with concern, as though ready to dive in after me. "Why don't you come in and wash that blood off?" I smiled, flipping my tail up so that the two bottom caudal fins lifted out of the water, silver glowing droplets trickling off them.

When Milo didn't say anything in response, I realized how truly entranced he was. He stood to his feet, never taking his eyes off me, and slowly pulled off his leather boots. I watched him just as intensely as he unbuckled his belt over his layered tunic and let his pants drop to the ground. Without hesitation, he stepped gingerly into the water, the ripples glowing with each step forward.

My gaze roamed his body, admiring his rugged perfection from top to bottom. His size, his stature, his movements. In the moonlight, the veins tracing his muscles shone like subtle accents to the tattoos across his tanned skin. And the way he looked at me, even through the blood stains on his face, made me feel like no one else existed in that moment.

"You're you again," he said, dipping down further into the water. I knew it must be cold to his skin, but he didn't flinch.

"Ironic, isn't it?" I laughed. "How can you tell, though?"

"Because you no longer have that look in your eye that makes me feel like you want to rip me open."

"I'm sorry." I flicked my tail and glided toward him. "If I could take everything back I would."

"I know." He reached forward and touched me, gently feeling the side of my face that had been cut. "But I've always seen the real you."

I pressed my lips together. "So, what's your theory?" I asked.

"About what?"

"About why my siren side wants me to push you away."

"First, tell me...Do you love me?"

"More than you know," I whispered. "I would do anything for you."

Milo took my hands in his, and we stared face to face with our torsos barely above the water. "And that's why your siren side hates me. Because loving someone—truly loving someone—means being selfless and caring about someone other than yourself. And that goes against a siren's very nature." He paused and brushed away a wet strand of my hair sticking to my forehead with his thumb. "So that's how I've known all this time that the real Katrina must really love me."

"I do love you. All of you. Even the scars and hidden parts you keep tucked away in the shadows," I said, holding his gaze. "I do love you. And I'm not scared of it anymore. I'm not scared to need you anymore." I wrapped the end of my tail around his ankles. He jumped, and then reached his hand down into the water to feel the scales covering my hips.

"That'll take some getting used to," he chuckled, his smile illuminated by the moon's soft glow from above. He squinted down at the water, studying what he could see of me, and slowly brought his gaze upward, roaming over my bare stomach and chest. "You're beautiful," he added, his eyes settling on my lips.

"I'm a fish," I teased. "A magic fish."

He laughed with me, but soon lowered his voice again. "No," he sighed, "You're a goddess."

A response lingered on my lips, but I decided silence was better. I dipped my hand into the water and used it to wipe away the blood on Milo's face and neck. He watched me in the most affectionate way, letting me clean him without a sound except the water trickling off his skin.

"What's this?" I asked, noticing a thin chain looped through a tiny gold band hanging around his neck.

"I forgot I had this. It was...my mother's wedding ring," he said, reaching up to touch it, "I found it in my father's things and...and well, I took it. Maybe because it's all I have left of her. If I didn't take it, it'd be forgotten here with everything else."

"It'll be nice to have something of hers to take back with you when we finally get back home." I reached up to examine it more closely. It was so delicate—nearly as thin as a wire—with the tiniest single blue diamond set in the center. I patted it against his chest where it hung, blending in against his canvas of tattoos.

"I wonder how long it will take to get my legs back," I finally said, changing the subject as we bobbed in the water, suspended in this crisp moonlit pool.

"Not long," Milo's brows tensed. "When Valdez was ready to 'harvest' a mermaid, there was a very brief window of time she could be out of water long enough to cut off her tail. The crew couldn't let her dry too long."

The way his face fell made my heart heavy. "Stop beating yourself up for things you couldn't control," I uttered softly, pulling him nearer to the waterfall.

"I was a coward," he said. "An irredeemable coward."

"Shhh," I held a finger to his lips. "We can't hold on to the past...even if we're living in it." I looked around, taking in the serenity of our surroundings in this ethereal piece of forest. "Though some things about the past are beautiful."

"I'm learning that I can't control everything," Milo smirked sadly. "You wouldn't think it would take 300 years to figure that out." He paused, looking down at the ripples dancing past us from the waterfall's rumbling. "Can I show you something?" He finally uttered. I assured him with an eager nod.

He let go of me, and swam toward the base of the waterfall, diving down underneath it. I followed, my underwater vision as perfect as on land in broad daylight. We surfaced behind the cascades, facing the entrance to a shallow cavern hidden in the stone cliff behind the water. It was shallow enough to wade in at the very edge of the wall.

"Cool little cave," I cooed, splashing a bit of water with my tail fin.

"It was one of my favorite places to go after my mother died. I never told anyone about this spot."

"Can you carry me?" I asked, still gawking in wonder at the enchanting cave-like structure.

"Wherever you need to go." He scooped me into his arms, one arm tucked beneath my tail for support and the other behind my back. I leaned into him, keeping my grip tight as I laced my fingers around the back of his neck. He stood up out of the water and hoisted me high enough that I could reach the waterfall cave with my hands outstretched. Supporting my upper half, I positioned myself as he pushed me up to the opening.

Once secured on the stony surface, I threw my head backwards, nearly exhausted from the weight of my tail out of water. Milo climbed up with ease, and I once again found myself ensnared by him as I studied his nearly naked body with desire. But my tail was too heavy to move, and I could do nothing about it but rest against him when he sat beside me.

I nodded off for a moment or two as we sat in silence in the cave, but the night chill returning to my skin awoke me. My skin tingled, and my tail began to feel lighter—and drier. I tried to move it, but realized I was changing before my eyes, and I had maintained very little control of my lower half. The sensation of my fins ripping in half tore upward through my hips and waist, and I grasped at Milo in surprise at the pain. He gently lifted me, talking to me softly as I grimaced from the hurt. He pulled me further into the grotto, just enough so that I could lie down as he held me. And with a blinding glow that covered my entire lower half, I became fully human again.

Milo gently lowered me down into a soft mossy spot cushioned further by leaves. And I smiled, content in this haven where no one else could find us. The flowing waterfall hung like a curtain, just enough to protect our hideaway, but still sheer enough to let in enough moonlight and bioluminescent glow to see our surroundings.

The pain subsided, and I watched as the last of my scales morphed back into skin and a refreshing sensation overtook my spirit. I felt like me again. Oddly enough, lying naked, damp, in a cave in 1720 was where I felt like I'd found myself again. The siren inside me had been silenced for now. And I no longer found myself battling a voice telling me what I wanted or needed.

This time, there was no longer confusion or question about where my heart lied. I looked at Milo. I wanted him. Fully. It was always him and only him. I needed him. And I knew I could never lose him again.

His eyes wandered me, from my bare chest down to my toes. He reached for me, running his hand across my chin and down my neck, between my breasts, and down to the core of me. His fingers gently danced along my skin, lower and lower...

"Yes," I said. "I've lost you too many times. Stop waiting. Yes."

I reached forward and pulled him down to me. I watched the water rolling off his shirtless body, and I felt heat rolling in me like clouds rushing to storm. He took my hand in his and guided it to the hardness below his abdomen. I felt him, touching and pressing against his firmness, and a sensation like a wave came over me, revealing itself in my trembling breaths.

Milo pushed his lips against mine as he leaned farther over me, kneeling in the space between my legs. He coaxed from me a tender gasp that had me holding my breath as he gently nudged my legs apart.

"Katrina Delmar, my starlight, I've waited 300 years for you," he breathed. I used my other hand to help remove the soaked undergarment from his lower half. My core shook when he pushed his length against the bare skin between my thighs. He braced himself up with one hand, looking over me, and stroked my hair with the other. I ran my fingers up his back, tracing the curve of his muscles and feeling every part of him in a new way.

"In those 300 years, I've found many treasures, but never one as priceless as you. I would bury myself with you to keep from losing you again. I would seek you a thousand times to find you again and again. I would make a map of your body with the stars and follow it for eternity." He kissed me again before pulling away to snap off the ring from where it hung around his neck. He took my hand and slid the tiny gold circle onto my finger. "In this place, I confess my undying love for you. You are finally mine. And I will share you with no other."

He dipped below and tasted me. Fire blazed up in me like cannons, like the flare of a warship in the dead of night. I moaned out my pleasure softly. He held me, clinging to me like a lost treasure he'd found again. My back arched as he pulled me to him. Slowly, gently, he rolled against me until he buried himself in me. I raked my fingers through his hair and down his back glistening with sweat and seawater. He crashed against me like waves rising and falling along the shore over and over. And with my legs hooked around him, I pulled him further into me like the draw of the tide.

With a tender growl in my ear that made me whimper, he squeezed my wrists. "Trust me," he uttered against my lips that were swollen from kissing him. I closed my eyes and let myself drift in this ecstasy as I rocked my hips against his, as though we were two rolling waves breaking into each other.

"I always have. Make me your map. That only you can navigate," I shuddered between soft gasps.

Milo continued as I looked up at him once more. In his eyes I saw a look of rugged desire and unguarded passion that made me want to stay here forever, trapped in a time and place where no one knew we existed. So that we could stay like this till the end of time.

A powerful sensation in me crested, and I cried out with an ancient songful voice, as he flooded me all at once with a trembling groan. And the cave grew silent except for our heaving breaths and the ever-constant rushing of water at our backs. With a beautiful, foreign exhaustion overtaking my body, I rested my head against Milo's rising chest, and he wrapped his arm around me, tracing the skin on my chest with his fingers.

"Many are the stars, Katrina. But yours is the only light I want to look upon." He brushed his lips against my hair, and we rested together for a while in the dark of our paradise beneath the moon. I clung to him, cherishing every moment until our inevitable return to the belly of Nassau and the cruel wake of reality.

MILO

I pulled Katrina closer to me as she slept. How could she love me after what she'd seen me do? How could she yield herself to me like this after she watched me kill? I didn't understand it. But maybe there was just enough darkness in us both to balance things out.

I traced the rim of the ring on her finger with my thumb. My promise to her to be whatever she needed whenever she needed it. A protector, a friend, a lover—and even an enemy when that "other" side of her took hold. And I smiled as I realized it was just as much her promise to let me.

The night hours passed like the mist in the air from the waterfall below, fleeting and gone as quick as vapor. But it couldn't vanquish the memory of her skin against mine, her flesh between my teeth, and her hands taking hold of my body. The sweet taste of honeysuckle and sweat lingered on my tongue. Each sensation around me seemed as tangible as fireflies, each a dreamlike mark of our time here.

"We have to go back," Katrina uttered weakly. "We can't stay here."

"I know," I rubbed her bare shoulder as she shivered against me.

I helped her to her feet, and hesitantly we both reentered the water to make our way back to the shore of the lagoon.

"I can definitely feel how cold this water is now," Katrina said through chattering teeth.

"Now you see why it took me so long to get in," I chuckled. She responded with an icy splash, and I returned the favor. Finding our clothing, slightly damp from the humid night air, we dressed and set back out toward the inn.

"How often will I have to change, I wonder?" Katrina asked as we walked, and the dim glow of the town just came into view.

"I suppose whenever you feel you're losing yourself," I shrugged.

Katrina sighed and looked ahead, quickening her pace. " I wish...I wish there was a mermaid I could talk to who could help me understand all this. There's too much to learn. And even if we find the trident, Cordelia said only a siren can use it. But that could mean anything. What if we find it and can't figure out how to use it? This is like the necklace all over again."

I matched her pace, quickening my step to stay alongside her as I thought of something that I debated whether or not to share. But I knew if I stayed silent in an effort to keep her safe, it would be a rift in the trust we'd rebuilt. Even if I was the only one who would ever know about it. I couldn't try to keep her from dangerous things. I couldn't do that to her again.

"There are mermaids aboard the *Siren's Scorn*," I uttered. "Captives. Two, if I remember correctly."

Katrina dug her heels into the dirt path below us and whipped around to face me. "Can you take me to them?"

"We'll have to be careful. And quick. We need to rest before tomorrow."

"We did rest," Katrina winked at me.

"You're making me wonder just how much of your siren side stayed behind," I joked.

"Don't worry, I'm all me," she touched the hollow of her chest. "But knowing what I am and how to use the power I have could be our biggest shot at understanding how to stop Cordelia."

I nodded. She wasn't wrong. But it was such a daunting task and there was barely enough time to do it. "It's nearly 2 AM," I said, tilting my head back to glimpse the night sky. "The harbor will be quiet. But there's always someone around somewhere."

"Something about you and me together always ends with us sneaking onto ships."

"You make a fine pirate, lass," I smirked, "But in all seriousness, if we're going to do it, we have to go now. We don't have much time."

"Then lead the way, Captain," She gestured with an open hand toward the road ahead.

I guided her back through the rat-ridden streets, where the sounds and commotions had quieted, only to be replaced with the snores and grunts of passed out drunks. By the time we reached the port, we'd lost another fifteen minutes. With uneasy eyes, I set my gaze on the *Siren's Scorn* bobbing in the tide, secured at the nearest dock. Katrina stepped forward, glancing around nervously.

"Wait," I said. "Valdez never left his ship unattended with mermaids on board. We'll have to stay hidden." I flipped the hood of my cloak over my head. "What good this'll do now that I've got a bounty on my head."

Katrina nodded, and I offered her a leg up onto the ship. Every nerve within me warned me this was a bad idea, but I couldn't deny Katrina the only chance she may ever have to learn about her nature. It also crossed my mind that perhaps, with some luck on our side, we could set the mermaids free. The ship was dark, and no lanterns hung lit. But I knew that didn't mean it was empty.

"Stay crouched low and walk along the edge," I whispered. Katrina did exactly that, and I was honestly surprised that we hadn't already been discovered yet. Patrollers would sit on the top deck near the stern for a good view. But I didn't see anyone up there that I could tell.

I snuck to the hatch leading belowdecks, Katrina following with featherlight footsteps. My heart pounded in my head, and I fought to keep my breaths light and silent. With every creak in the wooden floorboard or every lap of a wave against the hull, I froze to listen, afraid the sound might be more than it seemed.

But, with all our caution and paranoia, we never saw another soul on board. In the belly of the ship, we descended further. The mermaid hold would be just on the other side of the brig, where I knew my younger self would be lying cold, hungry, and hopeless on moldy, piss-stained floors. A sickness stirred within my gut, and my hands quivered as I opened the door to the hold.

I could hear the muffled whimpering of myself across the wall—the cries of a boy who believed himself much too old to cry. *Me.* I squeezed my eyes shut and tried to refocus as Katrina stepped inside to join me. I motioned for her to lift the heavy cloth covering the coffin-like rectangles stacked against the wall.

As I expected, she stepped back in astonishment at the two sirens staring back at her in their watery prisons. One had fiery red hair, and the other, long locks that were nearly white.

The mermaids recoiled, thrashing violently in their containers and spilling out splashes of water through the pinstripe cracks at the top. Katrina pressed herself against the glass, letting them see her face. The white-haired mermaid slowed her movements long enough to focus, and I watched her body relax at the sight of Katrina.

"Can you hear me?" Katrina asked against the glass that separated them. The mermaid nodded. Soon, the red-haired mermaid steadied herself as well.

"I'm...I'm one of you," Katrina stammered. "I want to help you. Can you help me, too?"

The mermaids looked at each other through their transparent walls, and then back at Katrina before nodding slightly.

"There's a trident in the sea and only sirens can use it by giving up something. Do you know what that means? How would I use it?"

A sullen and broken look suddenly overtook the mermaids' faces. The white-haired mermaid pointed to her mouth and throat and made a slicing motion with her hand.

"Valdez has already cut out their tongues and vocal cords. So they can't use their song against him," I interjected, a heavy, macabre feeling creeping up on me as I knew all too well his ritual. "And they can't talk to you either."

"I'm so sorry," Katrina said to them, her eyes creasing with sorrow. "Have you at least ever seen the trident?"

Both mermaids shook their heads.

"Don't take this the wrong way," Katrina started, "but is it really true that no siren has ever tried to use it because no siren could ever be selfless enough to give it what it wants?"

The white-haired mermaid rolled her eyes and scoffed, but the redhead shrugged with a nod, pointing to her heart and closing her hands around her chest.

"You always only serve yourself," Katrina stated softly, not in an accusatory way. She thought on it for a minute, as if figuring out what that might mean for herself. "What about crying?"

I glanced at her, unsure where her question was leading.

"Do you ever cry?" She asked.

The mermaids tightened their jaws and shook their heads, gesturing a solid "no" with their fingers.

"Not even when they cut out your tongues?" Katrina pressed.

"They never cried. None of them. Cordelia is the only mermaid I've ever seen cry. And even then. Only once. When she was so broken-hearted by Valdez's betrayal that she sent the maelstrom and cursed us," I explained.

"That's why she's so powerful," Katrina muttered, taking a step toward me. "She's the only mermaid who's ever allowed herself to be vulnerable. To feel." She turned back to the mermaids. "Do you know what happens when you cry? You could get yourselves out of here!"

The sirens signaled their answer with a vague shake of their heads. And Katrina stepped back, closing her eyes for a moment.

"What are you doing?" I asked.

"Trying to think of sad things. So I can cry. I'm going to show them and set them free. I can control the water in the tanks and break the glass. If I can just—"

Suddenly a haunting melody filled the air, cutting through our whispers and halting all other noise around us. I felt as though my body was paralyzed, at the mercy of something sinister. Katrina stood unmoving, looking at me with panic in her eyes.

Like a ghost, Cordelia appeared in the doorway from the shadows, her red lips parted so that the tune flowed from her mouth. No words. No lyrics. Just a melody otherworldly. I drew my blade and glanced at Katrina just before the world around me fizzled out.

Whatever happened next was a memory I didn't have. I shook my head back and forth to fling the saltwater from my eyes as I surfaced. Katrina coughed on water a few short feet away from me. We were in the dark, floating in the harbor amidst monstrous silhouettes of ships.

"What happened?" I uttered, looking around for some clue that might help me remember.

"Cordelia used her siren song on you. She made you attack me."

"What? Katrina, I'm sorry."

"It's okay," I said. "You didn't hurt me. You just grabbed me and hauled me overboard with you."

I moved closer to her. "I'm still sorry. I didn't even realize..." I looked at my hands, disgusted with the feeling of violation I felt. I could've been made to do anything Cordelia pleased. And I despised the thought of it.

"It's fine. We're okay," Katrina panted, looking downcast. "We just...couldn't help the mermaids."

"Come on, let's get out of this water and back to the inn. We've been out long enough." I made my way through the water swiftly, eager to get back on land.

"The thought that I might be able to do that freaks me out," Katrina said, taking my hand as I helped her onto the shore. "I don't want to be able to control people."

"Then don't," I said gently. "But now you know why Cordelia wouldn't control Valdez. She didn't want his love if it wasn't real."

"I noticed when she was singing, the scale around her neck—the necklace—was glowing," Katrina stated.

I raised an eyebrow, curious to what she would say next.

"When I sang my mom's lullaby one night in my room—the same tune Cordelia was singing—I remember the necklace glowing like that. The song...The siren song isn't magic alone. I think the song is what activates the magic from their tails."

I tossed her words around in my head. She was certainly onto something, and I felt the pieces connecting.

"You know, you're making a lot of sense," I said. "And that would explain why the mermaid trade was so shrouded in mystery. The buyers knew the scales were magic...but no one knew *how* to use the magic. And when Valdez took their voices...there was nothing left but a goose chase for destroyed magic."

"And that's why Cordelia made her scale necklace. So that her song had power in either form." Katrina added, her eyes widening as she spoke.

I nodded firmly, impressed. "It seems there isn't a part of you that isn't magic," I teased, touching her thigh. "Voice, heart, tail, and everything in between."

The way she blushed through a sliver of a smile made me want to pull her to me and make love to her all over again. She was an ocean I could happily drown in forever. And with that thought, I tensed, straightening as I scanned our surroundings to make sure no one was lying in wait or following us. There was no room for unguardedness here.

When we arrived back at the inn, nearly all the lights were out except the half-burned candle on the tavern counter. It gave us just enough light to help us find our way back to our room, where we peeked our heads in quietly.

"Noah?" I whispered. "McKenzie?" No one responded.

We tiptoed inside, only to see both our friends sleeping soundly in the single bed.

"Looks like we get the floor," Katrina said.

"As we rightfully deserve," I replied. "For what it's worth, we'll be back up in just a few short hours. Might as well not get too comfortable."

We lay on the rug, bracing our backs against the wall as Katrina nestled herself into my lap. I stroked her neck with my fingertips, brushing back stray hair along her smooth skin. She fell asleep almost instantly, but my eyes wouldn't seem to close.

I stared up at the window, straining to see the stars through the glass, and I wondered what tomorrow would bring. I feared finding the trident. I didn't know what it would cost to use. I didn't know what it would demand of Katrina. And though I wouldn't burden her by showing it, I was scared of finding out.

SET SAIL

32

"Rise and shine, mateys!" Noah's voice startled me awake. The room was fully lit, and the sun was up long past dawn.

"We overslept!" I jolted upright, waking up Milo who lied against me.

"That's what happens when you stay out all night." McKenzie pulled her boots on as she spoke. "We were worried about you two. But we also kinda figured you wanted some alone time." She winked.

"I could say the same thing for you two. I'm sure you both just had the worst possible time here alone in this room together." I stood, adjusting my own boots over my loose pants and tying my belt around my waist.

"Look at us," Milo said, standing to his feet. "We almost look like a real crew."

"That's about all we've got going for us," Noah uttered. "I guess that makes you captain?"

"A captain's not much without his first mate," Milo said, pulling out his compass and slapping it into Noah's open palm.

"What do you want me to do with this?" Noah looked on in bewilderment.

"Just hold onto it until I need it. Consider it a peace offering. So, take care of it." Milo's voice shifted as he addressed all of us together. "Now we need to hurry. It's going to be harder than ever to take one of those ships in broad daylight."

"Can't we just take one of your father's?" I asked as we made our way down to the tavern.

"That's the plan." Milo cocked his head. "But no doubt Thane is already securing them with his own crew. He'll see me taking one as breaking the code. But we don't have much of a choice."

"Well, it doesn't matter who we piss off here if we get to leave. And right now, that's our only chance." McKenzie spoke as we grabbed some loaves of bread for a quick breakfast that we carried outside.

With jittery nerves and quick, but unsure steps we trudged to the harbor, where we watched from our own little hiding spot in the trees nearby as Milo pinpointed the ship best for the taking. It was a smaller boat, perfect for stealthy maneuvering and a quick getaway, he assured. I studied it with careful eyes, it's reddish-brown hull contrasting against the bright blue beneath it.

"That's her. The *Falcon*." Milo squinted in the sunlight. "At least the weather's on our side. These winds will carry us out of port quickly."

"So, what do you need us to do?" McKenzie shrugged with her hand on her hip.

"I'll board first in case there's anyone already there and I'll take care of it. Noah, you and I will have to raise the anchor as fast as we can. And then, I'll head straight to the helm to steer us out. Katrina and McKenzie, that leaves you two to adjust the sails as I direct."

McKenzie and I glanced at each other. I'd barely figured out the sails on the modern motorsailer back home, so I wasn't feeling very confident about manning a centuries old pirate ship. And I doubted McKenzie had any previous experience with the latter either. But figuring it out was our only option.

"Just tell us what to do," I said. "But try to use words we understand."

Milo raised an eyebrow and lifted his chin. "I'll do my best to go easy on you, but manning even the smallest schooner with a crew of four is going to be one hell of an undertaking."

The plan was easy. Loaded in an abandoned old skiff we'd found, we'd row to the schooner on the far side of the water. With heavy nets that Noah acquired from a harbor merchant stand using the last of our money, we'd do our best to look like simple fishermen, and it was unlikely anyone would notice we weren't, given the lackadaisical atmosphere of the island. We'd keep to the outside of the harbor so as not to draw attention.

Milo and Noah crafted a grappling hook from an old piece of anchor metal and rope that we would use to climb up the ship. And then it would be up to our speed and skill to get the ship out of the port before anyone who cared noticed.

With tired arms, we rowed, bracing ourselves for the climb. Sailors called out to and fro from the ships we passed, but most were too preoccupied with their own business to pay us any attention. If they did, we'd simply throw off suspicion with a wave and nod of acknowledgement.

I watched Milo, noticing how he kept a close eye on the decks of the ships within sight. I figured he was looking for Thane, but I couldn't be too sure. He seemed thoroughly focused on whatever was running through his mind.

Once at the base of the *Falcon*, we positioned our little boat near the lowest point of the hull in the midsection of the ship, and ducked as Milo carefully swung the grapple. It latched perfectly, and we steadied ourselves by holding onto it one by one. The schooner was even smaller than it looked from a distance.

Milo ascended first. It was barely even a climb for him, as the schooner's hull was only a few feet high from the water in which it floated. We waited, and once we saw Milo's hand signal over the edge of the boat, it was our turn to come aboard.

It was a short climb, and the grapple rope acted more as a handrail against the constant rolling motion beneath us as we shimmied up along the siding. Trying to hoist ourselves up without it from the base of our little canoe-boat would have been quite a challenge. I didn't realize how sore my body was until I had to use the rope to pull myself onto the ship. The twinge of ache in my arms and legs fought against me. Between sword-fighting with Bellamy, being held hostage, and transforming into a mermaid, it only made sense that the muscles in my body were straining to keep up at this point.

"Hoist the anchor," Milo ordered, running straight to the bow with Noah right behind him. They grunted as they pushed against the capstan, hoisting the weighty anchor slowly. It had barely emerged from the water, still dripping, when Milo dashed away toward the helm and pointed to the sails.

"Get the topsail up taut!" he commanded. "Haul away the rigging!"

"English, please!" McKenzie cried.

"Just pull those ropes there and loosen that one. But tie that one there!" Milo directed, doing his best to point as he adjusted the ship's rudder. "Then set the mainsail southeast a bit."

We nodded, working with nervous hands to complete the tasks.

"This one's stuck!" I shouted, frustrated with the knot I found myself wrangling.

Milo came racing over and took in the sight of the mangled rope around the hooks along the masts and hull. "Steer us out. I'll work on this rigging."

"You want me to steer?" I asked.

"Yes, go!" He motioned for me to hurry.

I rushed forward to the ship's wheel, shoving away the feeling of intimidation that clawed at me.

"I can do this," I uttered. "I can control water. Surely, I can steer a ship on it."

Looking ahead out into the open water, my heart jumped a bit at the sight of some small bits of land and sandbars peeking out in a jagged path out to sea. I'd have to carefully navigate around them, and I didn't know how fast this thing could go. With my hands gripping the wooden wheel, I turned it sharply and directed the bow in the best straight path I could envision. It was heavy, and my muscles strained to hold the wheel where I wanted it. I wondered how Milo made it look so effortless.

From my spot at the helm, overlooking the small deck, I saw Noah rushing over to help with the sails. I also noticed Milo and his strange behavior. He was almost fidgety. I could even say nervous. He kept looking back at the surrounding bigger ships that had been anchored alongside this one. The rest of his father's fleet, I assumed.

"Keep at it. There's one more thing I have to take care of," he said.

"I was starting to think you forgot," Noah snapped, yanking on the rigging with newfound ferocity and confidence.

"Forgot what?" McKenzie interrupted.

"To make sure my father's ships can never be used the same way again." And with that, Milo leapt to the stern of the schooner, pulled out a pistol we never knew he was carrying, and fired at a barrel floating up against one of the ships, creating an instant explosion. The blast forged a hole in the front of the ship in which it was placed, leaving a damaged open hull to quickly fill with water. One by one, he fired at more floating barrels like targets, till he'd splintered the sides or fronts of every one of his father's four galleons.

Amidst the rush of chaos that ensued as sailors and captains spewed curses and fired back, we picked up speed in our sails and lurched forward out into the open bay. The deep tone of warning bells signaled trouble in the harbor. I did my best to guide us through the rocky waterways, nearly tipping the boat as we reeled around a sandbar I didn't see until the last minute. The water was strong against my hand at the wheel, and it took all my body strength to keep it from slipping back. I was grateful when a strong hand took hold of the helm above mine, and I breathed a sigh of relief as Milo stepped in to take over.

"Did you plant those barrels there?" I asked as Milo steadied himself at the wheel.

"Last night after you fell asleep. But I had help." He glanced over at Noah, who quickly looked away, as if trying to play off his part in this. Milo returned his gaze to me with eyebrows furrowed. "It was reckless, I know. But we couldn't let those ships keep sailing. No one should be able to use them again, least of all Thane."

"Reckless, for sure," I chided. "But I get it. And I would've done the same," I reassured with a half smile.

"Glad you approve. Because now we have to outrun him, and I can't have you both mad at me."

I looked over my shoulder at the sight of Thane and his crew working fast to raise their ship's anchor. He watched us with narrowed eyes from his perch at the bow. Even from here, I could sense the cruelty and see the scowl on his face. I touched the tender red line of skin along my jaw, wincing as I remembered the blade slicing across it.

"This guy really isn't one to let things go, huh?" I huffed.

"He's a psychopath," Milo uttered.

With the ship sailing smoothly and swiftly under Milo's command, we wove through the last few spots of shallow water and protruding formations framing the island. Behind us, Nassau shrunk in the distance, growing farther with each passing second, smoke rising from the harbor we'd left in disarray. Now it was straight on through into the open blue before us.

With an 18th century serial killer not far behind.

LEADING LIGHT

33

"Do you think they'll chase us the whole way?" I crouched down, sitting on the singular ledge behind the helm.

"I wouldn't be shocked if he follows us the whole way to the Triangle. Thane loves the hunt."

"Great," I muttered. "And how long will it take us to get there this time?"

"We should average about five knots, so...maybe three days and a few hours?"

I reached up to rub my shoulders as the wind picked up and sent my hair whipping around my neck. "This time when we get there, let's stop *before* we get near the center of the Triangle," I said.

"That's the plan," Milo fidgeted with one of the knobs of the ship's wheel. "But God knows how we'll get to the trident from there."

"I have a few ideas," I said with a heavy sigh, fixing my gaze towards the horizon. I really only had one idea. And if it didn't work, we were screwed as far as I was concerned. But after everything I'd learned about myself these past few days, I was more confident than I'd ever been. And I was finally ready to face the parts of myself that scared me the most and test my limits. After a moment, I stood up and stepped down from the helm's post. "I'm gonna go check on the others. Might as well let them know how long we'll be sailing for."

"Tell them to check the weapons in the main quarters. And pick something out for each of you. Preferably something you know how to use." Milo tossed me a key ring he'd hung from his belt.

"Will do," I nodded. It wanted to smile at the feeling that we were all our own little crew, however incompetent. At least we were finally all working together.

I made my way over to the rigging where McKenzie and Noah stood looking like they'd just come off a roller coaster.

"Okay I don't know if I attached these things correctly, but we're moving so I'm gonna say it's good enough." Noah wiped the sweat on his forehead with the back of his hand.

"I think we're good for now. As long as the winds stay this way for the next couple of days."

"This isn't going to be a short trip, is it?" Noah pressed his lips together.

I shot him a grin with a look of apology. "Do you consider three days a long trip?"

He sighed with a grumble and a look of defeat. "I guess not in this century."

"Well, we'd better get pretty good with these sails because we have company." I gestured toward the horizon behind us and the ship sailing onward in the distance. It was barely a dot on the surface, but I secretly feared how quickly it might be able to close the distance between us.

"They're coming for us?" McKenzie blurted, standing on her tippy toes to get a better perspective.

"Technically Milo, but I think we're a package deal," I said. "Which is why we are gonna spend these next few days sharpening our swordsmanship skills."

I led them to the cabin and used the key Milo had given me to unlock the door. Inside, I found a much smaller cabin than I'd seen before, but it made sense given the petite size of the schooner. A hammock and square desk took up most of the room, alongside a wall rack of a few swords and pistols and an urn stuffed full with scrolls and maps. "Come on, pick something. Or two." I stepped forward, taking a cutlass down from its spot along the sword rack.

"Every minute we're here I'm still having to convince myself I didn't get sucked into a video game." Noah hesitantly reached for a blunderbuss and a short sword.

"Seriously," McKenzie spouted. "I'm pretty sure me with a weapon is more dangerous than that gang of pirates chasing us."

"Well, if they keep us from reaching the trident, we'll be stuck in this video game for the rest of our lives, so..." I raised both eyebrows at them and tucked in my chin.

"Fair enough," McKenzie shrugged, strapping a sword belt to her waist.

"Hopefully we won't have to use these," I said, "It's just a precaution."

I gripped the sword in my hand. It felt heavy and awkward, unlike the cutlass I'd held in my spar against Bellamy. I thought of him then, remembering the way he looked out at the sea like it was his home. I hoped he'd made peace with himself, wherever he was. Then

I turned my attention to refocus on the sword in my grasp. I walked to Milo, carrying an assortment of swords for him to choose from.

"Did you want to add to your arsenal?" I asked with a grin.

"I suppose it can't hurt," Milo said, swiping up a sharp, barely curved cutlass from the selection and sheathing it in the baldric sling across his back, crossed with the other he already wore. "Best to never have just one sword."

I watched him for a moment at the helm. The way he handled the wheel as he breathed in the sea scent all around him, the ocean winds tousling his hair around his face and neck. The way he stood, more than a whole head taller than me, guiding his stolen ship. There was something hopeful in him that I'd never noticed before. Something beyond the hope of outrunning his enemies. But a real, deep hope that he'd always seemed to be pursuing in life was just over the horizon. Bellamy loved the sea. But Milo loved the promises it brought. Because his life had been changed by it in so many ways.

I stepped forward, settling next to him at the wheel, and leaned my head on his shoulder. He stopped and smiled at me with tender eyes that made me feel like we could outrun the whole world, just he and I, the same way we did on his motorcycle. I watched the open water in front of us as our little ship carried us along with the wind and waves. And I would've been content to stay that way forever.

The first full day at sea, we managed to create enough distance between us and the pursuing ship that we thought we'd lose them easily enough. The winds stayed strong enough to keep our pace. Unfortunately, it also meant Thane's ship was having no trouble keeping up with ours. The sea rolled in waves that kept us bobbing for hours on end, so much that my legs ached from the effort of balancing along the ever-changing surface.

We'd scarcely brought enough food for the journey in our hurry, but fortunately there was plenty of fresh water on board. We'd rotate shifts at the helm, with Milo showing each of us how to use the compass to ensure we didn't steer off course. He barely slept, I could tell. He'd disappear to the cramped cabin belowdecks for only a handful of hours at a time before reemerging to take back the wheel with tired, red eyes.

On the second night, I followed him, to make sure he rested a bit longer. It was Noah's night watch, so I knew the ship was steering soundly for the time being. He'd taken to sailing quite easily. Creeping behind the cabin door silent as the rats on deck, I watched Milo lay down on the pile of blankets strewn across the cabin floor. To my surprise, he fell asleep fast. Within minutes the only sound reaching my ears was that of his breathing and the ever-constant creaking timber of the boat.

I started to turn away, to leave him to his slumber, but a sound yanked me back. He groaned as if in pain, followed by a short whimper that made me feel weak in the knees. When I looked back at him, he was tossing himself across the blankets, twisting and turning as though trying to escape an invisible attacker. I ran to his side, shaking him awake with urgency in my voice.

"Milo," I said. "Wake up. It's alright. I'm here."

He opened his eyes and nearly leapt backward when he saw me. Between gasps of breath, he opened his mouth to speak, but seemed unable to make the words come. He sat up, keeping one leg outstretched in front of him and drawing the other up to him for a place to prop his arm. I kept my hand on his back, rubbing between his shoulder blades gently until he calmed. He pushed his disheveled hair back from his face with his free hand and then squared his shoulders to look at me.

"Was that one of your nightmares?" I asked, my tone as gentle as I could make it. I thought back to when he'd saved me from my bad dreams on the lighthouse and confessed he used to have them, too. This was the first time I'd ever seen it for myself.

He nodded, his breath returning to normal. "It's been a while. But I guess this place has taken its toll." The way he looked at his hands as he spoke, eyeing them with some semblance of disgust, I had a suspicion about what it was that might be weighing on him.

"Is it because of what happened with Thane's men?"

"It's because of me. This place has brought out the worst in me. Rather, it's brought it *back*. Because it never left. No matter how much I wanted to think it did. Here I'm a thief and a killer again. I'm the pirate I tried to forget." he muttered. "Thane's henchman isn't the only man I've killed here." His eyes burned into mine, and then with slow movements he reached into the folds of his loose shirt and out trickled the beads of a rosary. "I killed a man while fighting him, not two hours after our shipwreck. In defense. He attacked me and would've killed me if I didn't. This was his, and I've carried it with me since. I don't know why."

I studied the wooden beads, noticing the brownish-copper stains on them and the little wooden cross at the end. Blood. From a man Milo had killed. I didn't like to think of him killing. I'd pushed out the memory of him leaving Thane's men bleeding on the ground.

Because I knew he'd done it for me, and my joy at seeing him again overpowered any other feeling then. And to be honest, it didn't feel real at the time.

But something was different about it now. As I sat here with him, seeing this blood-stained trinket, I soaked in the reality that the same gentle hands that touched me in love and pleasure were also the hands that had taken lives, and always had been, long before this island.

These weren't the first two men he'd killed. Even if it was three centuries past, he'd killed others before. And I knew that. And though some part of me felt sickened by it, I also knew he wasn't given much of a choice in life. And I knew I had to decide once and for all if that would change the way I saw him.

It didn't.

"I think I know why," I whispered. "Because you can't forgive yourself. And you've been holding it all inside. But you have to let go of this or it's going to weigh on your soul until it drowns you."

He shifted and blinked, as if taking my words to heart. Something in me churned. Maybe my words weren't only for him, but for me, too. Cordelia's curses had haunted me long enough. It was time I released myself from that dark burden as well.

"Cordelia told me sirens don't have souls," I added. "At least you have a soul to save."

"That can't be true," Milo said, a tension rising in his voice.

"I don't know if it is or not," I said, taking his hand. "But I do know that it's stupid to pretend we don't have things in our pasts—or presents—that we regret. But we have to either decide if we're going to succumb to it or fight it. And as long as we fight it, then we're never truly lost."

"Stay true north." His lips barely parted as he mumbled the words, a deep expression across his face as though he was recalling them from somewhere.

"What does that mean?" I asked.

"It's something an old friend once told me. And it means exactly what you just said," he offered a smile that sent warmth radiating through me like the soft red glow of a summer sunset.

"Then let's forgive and fight."

I walked with him up to the railing on the starboard side. It wasn't far, given the small size of the ship, but it was enough distance for another quick exchange of words before Milo held the bloody rosary over the side of the ship.

"If there's one thing I've been reminded here, it's that deep down, we're all slaves to the darkness inside us," Milo said sternly, watching the cross pendant dangle over the gurgling black abyss below. He bowed his head for a few seconds in silent thought, and then opened his hand. The rosary slid over his knuckles and plummeted down below. Even in the dark, the schooner was so low to the water, it was possible to catch a glimpse of the slowly sinking beads as the blood marks blossomed into the seawater around them.

I turned to him and kissed him on the lips, hoping he had truly begun to let go of his guilt, and hoping I could do the same so as not to be a hypocrite. "Now go get some sleep," I whispered in his ear before pulling away.

The second and third day was spent in a haze, merely sailing onward and keeping a close eye on our company behind. My steering shift was early morning, so I'd often spend the long moments beforehand staring out from the prow as the sea breeze wrapped its cool embrace around me and the salty morning mist beaded on my eyelashes.

On the third day, I looked down at the water, its sapphire blue glittering like fine jewels in the sunlight. I tried not to think about what might lie far below. My siren side had been shut up for a long while now, and I hadn't heard from her since I'd succumbed to my mermaid form in the lagoon. But I almost wished she were here, now. I wished there was some way to call on her. I needed her boldness, fearlessness, and longing for the sea. Because I knew sooner or later, once we found the location of the trident, there would be only one way to get it. And it would require a dark, bottomless plunge to the sinking depths of the Devil's Triangle.

Not All Treasure Is Silver and Gold

34

Each morning for the next three days, I would watch Katrina stand at the front of the ship. I knew she was thinking about diving down to fetch the trident. She was our only hope of acquiring it, but I didn't want her to feel that weight alone.

I'd finally accepted that Thane wasn't going to abandon his chase, and we'd eventually have to fight him off. That thought terrified me, knowing it was just us four against however many men made up his crew. And he himself was more than a formidable opponent. I knew if he were to reach our ship, we'd have quite the fight for survival on our hands. But I decided if he tried to touch Katrina one more time, I'd spill his worthless guts at the helm of his own ship and make his men watch. Even if Katrina only ever saw me as a monster afterward, I'd never let him hurt her again.

The evening of the third day, Noah had offered to steer the ship a bit longer, and the sails needed little adjustment, allowing me a few extra hours of freedom I couldn't normally afford. Katrina and I worked together in the cabin to create a plan for when we arrived at the supposed location of the trident. As we talked it over, discussing the hows and whens, I found myself losing focus as I watched the way she spoke, my gaze lingering over her rose lips as she spoke about diving down into the water.

I squared my shoulders, trying my best to keep my concentration as we leaned over the small corner table in the cabin, but something about her in that moment held me captive and refused to let go. Perhaps it was the way she spoke so bravely, and willingly intended to do whatever she needed to get the trident. Or perhaps it was her beauty alone that called to me like a siren's song. The harsh days at sea and on the island created a radiance about her that couldn't be explained. Her skin glowed with a deep sunkissed glow of warmth, enhanced by the way her dark, windswept hair framed her face and slender neck in full waves. I watched the way her chin tilted as she spoke, and I noticed the delicate dips in her collarbone. I recalled every divine curve of her underneath the loose tunic she wore. God, I wanted her right there and then.

If it wasn't those things making me lose my focus, it could only be one other—the fact that I didn't know what awaited us ahead. And I couldn't protect us. I couldn't stop what was coming.

"Can I ask you something?" I finally blurted out, interrupting Katrina as she spoke about how she would swim down and find the trident and reemerge once we'd cleared away Thane's ship.

She looked at me with a confused expression. " Yes, what is it?" She raised her eyebrows. "Go ahead."

"How much do you love me?" I asked, leaning forward. "And consider it long and well before you answer."

She looked around, obviously taken by surprise at my question. "Well," she sucked in a deep breath. "Why are you asking this? Do you think I don't—"

"No, it's nothing like that. I know you love me. But just for fun, if you had to put it into words, how would you do it?" I nodded with a gentle smile for her to go on. If she thought the question was forward, I'd make it seem like a game.

"I... I'd say I love you with all my heart. And...and I couldn't imagine my life without you. I wouldn't want to imagine that life. You are...you're everything to me." She blushed, looking down at the ring I'd given her and adjusted it gently with her fingers. "Feel better now?" She laughed.

Damn.

I never knew a confession of love could be so painful. I could only hope she was lying. Maybe there could be something else she cared for more...maybe. Perhaps she should have just fallen for Bellamy. I would've wished it. Because I was so afraid if it was true, then her answer meant something detrimental. Something I didn't want to think about yet, though I knew I'd have to face it sooner rather than later.

Later would do for now. Because right now, in this rare moment with just the two of us alone, I only wanted to pin Katrina against the wall and love her senseless. I wanted to see the stars with her one more time.

She stood watching me with her back to the wall, a longing in her eyes just as overwhelming as mine. I reached for her hand, drawing it to my lips. I kissed each one, suckling gently as I caressed my mouth across each fingertip. She drew into me, her other hand touching me gently along the ridges of my muscles. She roamed my body, leaving no area unclaimed.

"All the time in the world with you could never be enough," she said in a gentle breath.

"That's the problem, isn't it?" I whispered, tracing the perfect curves of her beneath her shirt and navigating my hand across her hips to the warmth between her legs. "I'm tired of being on borrowed time with you. So, I'm going to steal it instead."

"In true pirate fashion," she snarled softly with a mischievous gleam in her eyes. Those deep brown eyes that I would willingly drown in until my last breath.

She closed her lips over mine, teasing me and plunging her fingers into my hair. Her hands tugged at my shirt, lifting it over my head as she lowered her mouth to kiss my chest. In me, a surge of desire swelled so that I couldn't help but touch every part of her, undressing her with careful movements.

Her skin felt so perfectly delicate against my rough hands. I touched my lips to her shoulder, mouthing her softly as I worked toward her neck. She smelled sweetly of the sea. I wanted to tether her to my very soul so that we were one. And the way she wrapped me within her legs assured me she wanted the same.

Fire pulsed in my veins; my heart raced as she unbuckled my belt. I lifted her onto the edge of the table we'd been talking over, pushing aside whatever else was on it to make room for her. Gently, slowly, I moved to her. Her soft gasps against my ear made my head spin, and I whispered her name over and over so that she knew she was the master of my fate, here, now, and forever.

Our bodies might've followed the sway of the ship, with some moments slow and smooth, and others swift and deep. With each soft groan from her lips, the craving for her hammered harder in my core. I stood, holding her firm as she pressed herself against me. We were two oceans meeting, merging in riled plumes of seafoam. She gripped me, stroking my back and neck between wild kisses and teasing licks before she shattered beneath me with quaking breaths.

"Milo," she whispered, tracing the North Star tattoo on my body with her trembling fingers. At the sound of my name on her lips, I became undone, swept into a current she controlled.

The cresting desire in me grew into an animalistic need, a dam of feral thirst I could not hold back any longer. I moved faster, squeezing Katrina's fingers that had now laced themselves between mine, and a wave of bliss cascaded over me as my knees threatened to buckle.

I held onto it, treasuring the sensation that escaped me in moans, because I feared there would be little more in the way of pleasure in the hours ahead. But I refused to let that worry steal this moment from us.

Both dazed and sweat-drenched from the stuffiness of the small cabin, we collapsed together amongst our strewn pieces of clothing. As I caught my breath and regained my senses, I pulled Katrina near and nuzzled her shoulder.

"I do feel better now," I uttered into her damp hair, wishing it could last forever. Because more than anything, I dreaded leaving this cabin to face whatever came next.

No Quarter Given

35

KATRINA

I smiled tenderly at Milo. These moments between us were always so quick to end, always one step away from the next threat to our lives. I couldn't wait till we just made it back home and that looming feeling could end. I fiddled with the ring on my finger, dreaming of the life we almost had—and could have again—if we could just make it back.

We redressed and climbed back out on deck, doing our best to look like we'd only been talking out the plan, but I figured our friends would be smart enough to guess that something more than discussion took place. We found McKenzie and Noah and shared our plan with them, asking them for their feedback and opinions. There was a heaviness in the air as the reality settled in that before long Thane would catch up to us. His ship inched closer every moment, and it was only a matter of time before it closed in on us.

"You two stay atop the crow's nest and fire from there. Noah and I will do our best to hold them off when they attack," Milo glanced between all of us as he spoke, addressing each of us. "We have one cannon shot. One. We'll do our best to draw Thane near the stern. And one of you will fire if you have the chance. Even if it means you blast us, too."

I shook my head, choking back a dry tightness overtaking my throat. "There has to be another way."

"I'm hoping there is," Milo said, that ever-familiar lock of hair falling over his eye. "But if we don't find it, you have to do it anyway." He glanced at us collectively once more. "Understood?"

"Crystal clear," McKenzie muttered. The dark tone in her voice was a far cry from her usual chipper self.

"At this point I've accepted we might die, but I'm not going down without a fight." Noah cradled his pistol in his hand, and there was a noble, but somber look in his eye.

I watched McKenzie after we dispersed, and I followed after her as she went to lean over the hull.

"Hey," I said, scooting up next to her with my elbows propped up in a similar manner. "Everything okay? Well—aside from the obvious."

"Yeah, I just…you know. Just once I'd like to feel like I'm brave or courageous or tough. Like you."

"Like me?" I repeated, startled by her response. "Those aren't exactly the words I would use to describe myself."

"That's because you don't see yourself, Katrina." She gestured with her hands as she spoke, her once-perfectly manicured fingernails now dirty and chipped. "You look like a badass all the time. But all anyone ever expects from me is the ditzy rich girl." She paused with a pout. "Because I *am* the ditzy rich girl."

"No," I said. "You're so much more than that."

"This whole experience has just made me realize that I can do more and be more. I just have to start looking for opportunities to do it. I tend to miss out on what I'm capable of, because I'm so busy playing the part of what I'm used to being."

"What are you saying?"

"I don't know. I just…If we get murdered by pirates, I don't want to go down crying in the corner and looking pretty. I want to know what I'm really capable of when push comes to shove."

"Then do that. Show 'em what you're made of, Kenz," I said. She smiled at me without another word, but I was sure I noticed a sparkle of confidence rise in her face.

Within moments, the air felt still, as if destruction hung in the air like a tapestry. Thane's ship nosed its way to ours, its flag already replaced with the blood red flag Thane preferred. Milo had told me about red pirate flags. No prisoners and no survivors. I swallowed a lump in my throat.

I was distracted by the ship enough until Milo darted past. He skidded to a stop and whirled around to face me. Written plain in his shining wet eyes was a look of desperation and true concern that reminded me of the way he looked when Valdez tied him to the mast and tortured him. He leaned forward and gripped my shoulder, speaking low for only me to hear.

"If things get out of control…if the plan doesn't work…you jump overboard and save yourself. Swim away. Swim far away from here and don't look back."

"Milo—" I began to protest, but he crashed his mouth into mine before I could get out the next word. When he pulled away, the worry in his eyes captivated and terrified me all at once. He was truly afraid for me. Afraid of what could happen.

"Promise me you will," he choked. "I won't let you die here."

Stunned by the moment, words stayed trapped on my tongue, so I channeled my jitters into nods to show him I understood. Shattering the tension like glass, Noah rushed in between us.

"Hate to interrupt, but we've got more company than we thought." He slapped a bronze spyglass into Milo's hand and pointed out to sea.

Milo took a look through the tube to the horizon on the left. "It's a Spanish frigate. Probably pirate hunters."

"They're coming this way, too," Noah said, taking back the spyglass.

"Aye, they are." Milo rubbed his jaw. "And that could either be a blessing or a curse. But we hold to the plan if we're attacked. The frigate's at least twenty minutes out. If we can hold off Thane until they reach us...we might have a chance if they intervene." Before either of us could respond, Milo sprinted back to the helm.

"Time to play a bit of tag," Noah uttered, leaning over the hull.

I glanced over at Thane's rapidly approaching ship, racing across the water like a freight train. He was mere minutes from catching right up to us, so close that I could hear the shouts and jeers of his men.

Our sails caught the wind, and we lurched forward as Milo adjusted the *Falcon* slightly off course. I gripped the side of the ship, digging my fingertips into the wood grain to steady myself as our ship veered and tilted with the sudden direction change. McKenzie let out a small shriek from her perch up in the crow's nest.

When the boat settled just long enough to stand upright, I made a dash for the rigging, where I began to climb up the ropes to join McKenzie. I couldn't let her get tossed around like a rag doll up there alone. The thick ropes felt like dead bones in my hands, heavy, damp, and cold, despite the bright sun overhead. I hardly noticed the thick, humid heat as the wind from so high up here whipped my skin dry. With one glance down below, my stomach flipped upside down.

I clenched my eyes shut for a second, just to shake away the sick feeling, and pushed myself upward, climbing the network of ropes to the crow's nest. From there, I could see Thane's crew clearly enough that I had to squint from the white sunlight glinting off their swords.

A barrage of threats and roars rose from the crew as they realized what Milo was doing. He maneuvered the ship forward for just a bit, only to make a sharp turn that they hadn't been expecting, and now he was sailing back in and around them. Their ship was small, but ours was smaller and faster.

As the *Falcon* curled around over and across the waves like a startled swordfish, Thane's men followed close behind, but they couldn't match the speed of our turns.

I watched Thane at the wheel of his ship. Once he figured it out, he began to turn his vessel as though he was going to continue the chase, but at the last minute, sped right past ours, only to order his men to close the sails and drop their anchor, swinging his ship around, nearly tipping it. It swung around like a colossal, slow-moving pendulum, and though Milo had caught onto Thane's plan by now, it was impossible for him to get our boat out of the way in time.

The bow of Thane's ship whipped around, colliding into the back half of ours. The force of the blow nearly launched McKenzie and me from our post, rocking the ship side to side. We huddled in the cramped floor of the crow's nest to keep from flying out. The sound of crisp wood snapping as the ships crashed together sent a panic through my bones. They had us now.

I wondered how detrimental the damage to our ship would be. Judging by the concerned expression on Milo's face from below, it was worse than I thought. We were left afloat, still slowly swirling on the surface as the rioting water settled. Within seconds, our two vessels ended up parallel, facing opposite directions. I glanced out at sea, praying the approaching Spanish frigate would speed up at the sight of the chaos. It was closer now, but there were still minutes-worth of distance between us and them.

Thane wasted no time giving the orders to his men to take our ship. By the looks of it, his crew was made up of hardly more than ten, but it was still more manpower than we had. From their deck launched grappling ropes, taking root into our hull. I watched the scene unfold before me with trembling nerves and a hand over my pistol. McKenzie peeked over the crow's nest, a white-knuckle grip on the gun in her hands. And together we took our best aim as Thane's crew pulled our ship to theirs like a needle closing a stitch together.

A barrage of shouts and stomps filled the air as the stinging scent of gunpowder crawled to my nostrils. I couldn't breathe, partly from the smoke tickling my lungs, but more so because my chest was tightening at the thought of Milo and Noah below facing so many attackers at once.

Half a dozen pirates swung from the rigging, leaping down with foreboding thuds as their heavy boots hit the deck. Milo fought with two swords, wielding a cutlass in each hand as he fended off the men approaching him from every side. But I knew he couldn't manage that for long. I fired my pistol with the best aim I could manage, alerting the crew to our presence. But at least I hit my target. The man gripped his shoulder where the bullet struck, and Milo used the distraction as a chance to shove him over the edge of the ship with the broad side of his sword.

"Noah, watch out!" McKenzie screamed. Noah whipped around just in time to find himself face to face with a charging crewman. He stumbled back as he met the man's sword blow with his own blade, using barely enough force to deflect the hit. If he was terrified—and I knew he had to be—he didn't show it.

I noticed Thane making his way through the fray. Slowly and steadily, he was locked on to Milo. He walked without urgency across the deck, following Milo's lead to the back of the ship. At least the plan was working so far. But I wouldn't risk him getting too close. I fired at him, but missed, instead drawing his attention upward as my gunfire whizzed right past his head. He stopped, turning around with the same calmness with which he walked before flashing a cold grin my way.

I thought he'd come for me. I thought I'd blown the plan, and if so, I wouldn't have cared. Because if Milo thought I could fire a cannon blast at him just to kill Thane, he was wrong. The pirate hunter frigate was closing in. So, I thought if I could just hold him off a little longer…

But Thane didn't come for me. He just winked at me with a wicked, sick smile curling across his lips and pulled out his sword. Even from here, I could see that it was stained with old, dried blood. He brought the blade to his face and, without taking his eyes off me, licked the crusted blood from the edge. It took everything in me not to gag at the sight. Then he turned around, bloody sword in his grip, and began walking toward Milo again. I cursed beneath my breath and fired again, this time aiming for the pirates attacking Noah and Milo, who now stood nearly back-to-back, their faces wrought with focus and exhaustion as their blades whirled.

"What was that you were saying about not going down without a fight?" I turned to McKenzie. "They can't do this by themselves. And these guns suck at long range. I'm going down there."

She grabbed my arm, nearly pulling me back as I crouched down to begin my descent down the rigging. I thought she was going to beg me not to go or tell me why it was a horrible idea. But instead, she looked me dead in the eyes and said, "I'm coming with you."

Together we shimmied down the ropes as quickly as possible, but the awkward boots and breeches offered little in the way of flexibility and movement. About halfway down, I glanced over my shoulder below. Both bloodied, our two men were losing ground. Milo's shirt was ripped in many places, and bright red blooms of blood decorated the fabric like a floral print. Noah was in no better shape.

I raised my gun to shoot from where I hung in the rigging. But as my finger pulled back on the trigger, an unforgiving resistance blocked my movement.

"It's jammed," I said, turning the pistol over in my hand to inspect it as if I knew what to do with it. "McKenzie, shoot them!" I cried.

My normally bold and boisterous roommate was anything but in that moment. Clinging to the ropes right beside me, she looked like she might cry as the wind scattered her orange hair every which way around her. She hesitated, fidgeting with the weapon in her hands.

"What if I miss?" She stammered.

"Don't think about that. They need our help!"

She grimaced, placing the pistol in her palm and aiming for the group of men fighting Noah. I could see the gun shaking in her pale grip.

"I'm going to hit Noah. I...I can't do it." Her words were peppered with strains and held back tears. Just as I was about to respond with some attempt at something motivational, the sound of swords clanging below died down.

My grip on the rigging strengthened, my hands curling around the rope so tightly I thought it might burn my palms as I directed my attention to the scene unfolding on deck. Noah had been disarmed, and a pirate held him pinned to the deck with a firm boot on his chest and a sword beneath his chin. The men ceased their battle momentarily as they waited for Thane to direct their next move.

Thane stood to speak, his penny-bronze hair framing his striking features. A sharp jawline, crooked nose, and piercing eyes full of bloodlust. He walked to Noah, his steps taunting as a dark smile stretched across his face.

"Kill the friends first. Make him watch." He pointed to Milo with the tip of his sword. "And take your time."

Just then, our ship teetered in a sudden wake, sending McKenzie and me tumbling from the rigging and slamming onto the deck below. Smoke billowed into the air, fresh from the side of Thane's ship. Cannon fire. But not from the Spanish frigate. That ship was nearly upon us, and was moving in from the east, but the cannon shot hadn't come from that direction. It came from behind.

I leapt to my feet to see the origin of the shot. My jaw dropped at the sight of the *Widow* reeling toward us, with Bellamy at the helm.

Fire In the Hole

36

In a whirlwind of confusion, the *Widow* edged its way carefully alongside us as Bellamy and a handful of his crew crossed over to our boat. His massive ship made our tiny schooner look like a toy sailboat as it cast its looming shadow across the deck.

Bellamy himself landed with a thud, sword drawn, eyeing his surroundings like a soldier in foreign territory. Both crews now erupted in yells and curses, a flurry of attacks flaring up all at once from all sides.

"You followed us all this way. You came to help us?" I called to Bellamy over the noise of the battle. "Why? I thought—"

"Don't ask me why!" he spat. "I don't know why I did either."

His stubbornness didn't surprise me. I'd given up on expecting him to admit he might care about something more than sailing the seas. Or that he might have feelings for a siren. But his reasons didn't matter to me right then. I was just more grateful to see him than ever.

Thane's crew was now evenly matched. Our deck was littered with bodies, some limbless or bleeding, and others already dead. I swallowed down the bile rising to my throat at the sight and cringed at the coppery smell of blood that pierced my nostrils. When I looked over at McKenzie, she seemed frozen in place.

"Come on," I said, grabbing her wrist and leading her to the bow. "Take a breath," I said, keeping her facing the water, "Don't look at it."

Inwardly, I trembled with horror, but I couldn't fall apart here. I deeply feared the outcome of this bloody battle at sea. There was nowhere to run. If Thane's men didn't kill us all, who knew what would happen when the Spaniards reached us? There was no way to end this chain of attacks but to escape it. And the only escape was a trident at the bottom of sea. A trident that could twist the very thing we were quickly running out of—time.

As I watched Bellamy's crew rush to Noah and Milo's aid, I noticed the Spanish frigate looming nearby. It turned, lining its side up with ours. We made the perfect target. Three pirate ships all clustered together in one place, heavily distracted by destroying one another. The pirate hunters would've been idiots not to take advantage of this. Looking around at the blood-soaked deck behind us, it was plain to see we'd already done most of the work for them.

"Get down." I put a firm hand against McKenzie's shoulder and urged her toward the deck floor. I dropped down and lay on my stomach next to her. I watched the war-ready Spanish frigate as the small windows along its hull slid open to give way to lines of cannons taking aim. Gray metal plates of armor covered its hull. It was so close I could hear it now. The heavy patter of the crew's boots along the deck, the twinge of ropes and sails, and the structured shouts and commands amongst the sailors. The captain was giving out orders in Spanish, and I understood easily enough.

"*Dispara!*"

Before I could blink, the side of our ship erupted in an explosion of wood chips and smoke raining down like some kind of apocalyptic piñata. McKenzie let out a wail and covered her head as debris rained down us and the ship shivered beneath us like an earthquake.

I glanced back over my shoulder. Many of the pirates from both Bellamy and Thane's crew had been knocked overboard from the blast. Milo was just getting to his feet like the rest of the men around him. He locked eyes on Thane, who was busy ripping his sword from the stomach of a squirming man on his back. Noah was still down, but I sighed with relief when I saw him slowly find his footing.

Bellamy appeared from the smoke near the cannon shot. I wondered if he had ever even stumbled when the cannon struck the ship. He walked with a calm assuredness that sent chills fluttering through me. He drew his sword, parrying a blow from an attacking pirate like it was nothing, looking around through focused eyes as if seeking his next target.

The sound of a pistol cracked through the air, followed by a jolt that sent Bellamy staggering backward and gripping his shoulder in agony. The gasp that escaped my lips was much louder than I intended it to be. I worried he would fall, but he only clenched his jaw, glanced at the blood on his hand that had stained from covering his wound. Then he charged forward, a feral look in his eye. He let out a cry, gritty and wild, maneuvering his cutlass with ferocity fitting of a pirate captain, and cut down the man who fired in one swift blow.

Another round of cannon fire from the hunters' frigate sent more pieces of the ship flying and took a handful of men down for the count. I noticed it was getting harder to keep my balance. Each awkward step to steady myself felt like the floor was shifting beneath my feet. When I glanced around once more, I quickly realized the changing angle of the deck. Barrels rolled to one side of the boat, dropping into the water below. The mast leaned in an uneasy way, threatening to snap at any moment. The *Falcon* had endured all she could take. We were sinking.

The clang of a sword caught my attention, tearing me from my observation. A pirate rushed at me, blade drawn, and on instinct I pulled out my own. He swung at me, and I stepped back just far enough to miss the blade's edge, but nearly toppled over. I begged my brain to recall everything Bellamy taught me about sword fighting, however basic. I didn't want to have to remember, though. I didn't want to fight.

The next time the man swung, I used both hands to help me brace my sword against his, and with more strength than I realized I had, I shoved forward, keeping the blade away from me just once more.

"McKenzie!" I cried, hoping she was near enough to hear. But I realized she was no longer standing beside me. Somehow, I missed her leaving my side, but now she was on the rigging, climbing up in desperation to escape an attacker of her own.

I gritted my teeth and strained against my opponent. This man would kill me if I didn't stop him from doing it first. And I couldn't accept that that may mean I'd have to kill him. Our swords danced, sparking from impacts that nearly knocked my weapon from my grip. And finally, I realized I'd have to find the strength to end it, or he would end me. With the sickest sensation swirling in my core, I recalled Bellamy's instructions. I remembered one thing he told me. That one stupid thing. *Thrust.*

I ducked one last time as the man swung at my head. All in the same instant, I closed my eyes and jutted my sword out in front of me like a spear. I should've kept my eyes open, but I couldn't watch myself impale another human.

But when I peeked back reluctantly, I saw that my sword never made much contact with the man. Instead, he stood with the tip of a blade jutting out of his chest—a sword that had entered from the back. When his limp body slid forward off the cutlass that ran him through, the person left standing behind him was Milo, panting and glowering at me with a fierceness in his eyes that made my blood run ice cold.

"Thank you," the words felt numb rolling off my tongue. It seemed as though a fog had formed in front of me, and I couldn't see through it. He'd just saved me from having to kill someone, but that didn't mean it made it any easier for him to add to the guilt he was already fighting.

He nodded in acknowledgement, then gazed out across the deck, scanning the scene. "Thane's gone. He's escaped."

He was right. I didn't see Thane anywhere. But his ship was missing. He knew we couldn't sail after him. And he'd left his few remaining men to deal with the hunters and Bellamy's crew alone. The coward.

The fog around me closed in, freezing time in its place so I could really take a long, hard look around me. But it wasn't fog. It was smoke. Real smoke that was heavy and burned my lungs and woke me to the hopeless reality surrounding me. My senses tuned in to the intense sound of men shouting, steel clashing, gunpowder exploding, wooden ships groaning and crackling as the relentless cannons roared their deathly booms. McKenzie was still trying to run, Noah didn't look like he could take much more, and Bellamy and Milo were both covered in blood not their own. This was it. These four ships would go down here. And if I stayed here a moment longer, we'd go down with them.

"I'm going down below. I'm going to get the trident." I breathed, drawing the courage to believe the words myself.

"We need to be closer to the center of the Triangle."

"Well, it's clear we're not getting anywhere else in this ship," I said, gesturing to the tipping floor below me. "I have to go find it now or we'll never make it."

The harsh look in Milo's eyes dwindled down to one of concern. "It's too dangerous. It's the deep sea."

"Dangerous is the only option we have right now." I stepped forward, meeting his gaze with an unyielding hold of my own.

He glanced away with tight lips and a creased brow. I knew he was afraid for me. And he was trying to figure out how to be okay with it. He nodded, just barely, then lowered his sword and pulled me to him with his free arm. He crashed his mouth into mine with a burning intensity stronger than the Caribbean sun above. I could taste the blood, sweat, and salt across his lips, but none of it mattered then. I kissed him back, hard and desperately. When he pulled away, he looked me dead in the eye, and he spoke to me as though guarding treasure that no one could ever find.

"You promise me you'll make it back. Even if it's a lie. You promise me..." His voice cracked with a hint of a whimper that broke me and filled my heart all at once.

"I promise I'll find you again," I uttered softly through the explosions and chaos around us, as the ship dipped lower and lower. "I always do."

With that, I turned around, racing across the leaning deck, my eyes fixed on the endless ocean. I rushed to the bow of the ship, looking ahead toward the only clear path not surrounded by smoking ships. I pulled my boots off, and next my pants, clothed only by the long tunic that draped down past my hips just barely across the top of my thighs.

With the wind at my back, I risked one more glance behind me at the sight of confused crews from all sides halting their fighting long enough to watch me with curious stares, Bellamy, McKenzie and Noah included. But Milo watched with an unsettling longing in his eyes, knowing full well what I was doing.

And with all the strength I could muster, I took a breath I knew I wouldn't be able to hold onto for long, and dove in.

A Depth So Dark

37

KATRINA

The water here was murky. I braced myself for the excruciating sting of saltwater I knew I'd soon feel blazing in my lungs. I swam down as quickly as my body would allow, diving to the depths like a harpoon. I had to get deep enough that returning to the surface was impossible.

It was different this time. When I'd changed in the lagoon, my siren side *wanted* to change. She begged to drown Katrina and take her form. But now that I had her under control, every instinct in my body fought against what I knew I had to do. Thrashing, clawing my way back up, I couldn't find the strength to drown. I couldn't do it.

The surface was right overhead, glittering above me like an open skylight of hope. I closed my eyes, just begging the siren in me to take hold. She would have no problem pulling me under. I thought of Milo, McKenzie, and Noah. I thought of my parents back home. And the rest of the world. How failing might literally mean the fall of mankind. But none of that overpowered my body's desire to breathe. To be a siren, I had to be selfish. I had to think like a siren. I had to let out the part of me I'd been hiding all along.

Power. Control. With the trident, there would be no limit to what I could do with it. *Think of the things you can make them do with your song.* I relented myself to the darkest part of me. *Make the world know your name. Defeat Cordelia and take her place. Show your power.*

The idea that I might have my vengeance against Cordelia seemed to be the key. I could make her pay for all the hell she put my family through. I could torture her the way she tortured my mother and grandmothers and even me. All of the suicides and depression and nightmares could be turned back around onto her.

Get the trident and destroy her.

With that thought, a wicked grin spread across my face as bubbles floated to the surface as I fought to hold in the last bit of air in my body. I had to let go. Fully.

I opened my eyes, and the water was now nearly crystal clear. The depth still made it difficult to see more than twenty or thirty feet in front of me, but it was easy enough to make out the looming shadows of the ships overhead, thundering and rumbling like crumbling mountaintops above.

Cannons boomed overhead and shook the surface, but the further down I drifted, the more peaceful the world around me became. The last bit of light breaking through danced on the scales of my tail, glittering like thousands of diamonds. My powerful tail swept through the water effortlessly, propelling me forward and farther down to the depths. I didn't know where I was going, but I knew I had to get there as fast as possible.

The pressure beneath the sea would have been much too crushing for me in my human form, but with my siren tail and abilities, I was unstoppable. There was no depth too deep, no current too strong, and no corner of the ocean too dark. The connection between my being and the sea was undeniable and natural as breathing.

I passed sharks and rays of all sizes, schools of fish that glimmered like patterns of mirrors. I'd visited an aquarium in Arkansas once when I was younger, and I remember pressing my face to the glass in fascination at the animals, but that experience paled in comparison to swimming amongst these terrifying, magnificent creatures.

Amazingly, none of them seemed to acknowledge my presence, instead swimming calmly past me as though I belonged there as much as the starfish along the sea floor. I wished for a moment that it might be possible that I could stop and talk to them. I'd ask them if they knew where the trident was and how to get to it.

This isn't a fairytale, Katrina.

I had to force myself to remember the gravity of the situation. My siren side longed to just take her time, relax, and enjoy the time here. But I fought her desires against my true ones. Find the trident. Fast.

I knew it had to be at the bottom of the ocean. It had to be somewhere so dangerous and unreachable that even the most advanced machine couldn't reach it. But could a mermaid?

I flicked my tail up and down, pushing myself further down, until finally the white light from the surface faded, and the last echoes of sounds above dwindled. The only thing I could hear now was the soft, silent rush of water as the current and tides snaked their routes all around me.

Down, down, deeper I ventured, my vision in the dark water as clear as my sight on land. Siren night vision certainly wasn't a bad ability to have right now. For a moment, I chided myself for not having the courage to do this much earlier. If I hadn't feared this form so much for so long, perhaps I could've dove down like this and retrieved the scale before Cordelia was ever able to get her hands on it.

Stay true north. Milo's words came to mind seemingly from nowhere. Three simple words that reminded me to stay my course. To hold onto the next right step. Focusing on the past wasn't going to save anyone. It wasn't going to change things as they were. And it certainly wasn't going to matter now. All I could do was focus on the next battle in front of me—and keep going.

I studied the water around me, looking for some remnant of a clue that might lead me in the right direction. Down here, it was nearly impossible to tell left from right or north from south. But as a mermaid, I had keen senses that worked in ways I couldn't fathom. For instance, I could feel every bubble, temperature change, and switch of current direction against my skin.

So, when I paid close attention, falling fully in tune with the oceanic void surrounding me, I found I could sense an unusual pattern in the way the water flowed against the nearly translucent fins of my tail. I watched the water swirling around it. One current circulated in a way that pulled my caudal fin in one direction so subtly I might've missed it if I had been moving any faster.

The current funneled slowly into the ocean floor, twisting like a ghostly rope and the further down it went, the stronger it became. It flowed backward, against the motion of the rest of the sea, in a way that assured me it was created by something outside of nature. Where the ocean's natural undertow traveled and where this other stream led eventually met, merging like two ribbons swirling around each other, like twisting tides forming a path beyond what I could see.

I followed them, straining my eyes. Despite my siren sight, eventually the ocean's darkness became strong enough to hinder me. This was a depth far too deep for even mermaids. I could only imagine how difficult of a time Cordelia's divers would have getting down this far. This is why she wanted my help. But I knew she would find a way to do it with or without them or me. I just hoped she hadn't found it already back in the present. So, I kept on, fueled by urgency, following the gentle twisting currents that swept me along calmly as if time wasn't of the essence.

But time didn't matter here. It was a concept that didn't exist in this place. I could've been swimming for hours or minutes, God only knows. And when the spiraling currents suddenly split into three streams dancing and unraveling across each other, I knew some source of magic must be near. I swam on slowly, listening, feeling, hoping.

When my hand brushed up against something cold and solid. I yanked it away in reaction. But I quickly regained the courage to reach forward again. My fingertips met a metallic prong, and I worked my hand along the rest of it, feeling the nearly identical shape of two more on either side of it. I couldn't see it, but it was clear to me what was pulling these waters together, binding them within life, time, and space—the three prongs. I gasped in disbelief—if that's even possible underwater.

It was real. The trident was real.

I reached to grab it, feeling around blindly as I wrapped my hands around its metal rod base. It wasn't easy to uproot from its buried place in the sand beneath. With a grunt that sent bubbles bursting from my mouth, I thrashed my tail upward with all the strength I could manage and dislodged the trident from its ancient hold in the dense sand. It was all I could do to silently pray that removing it wouldn't summon some monstrous tsunami or disaster from the gods.

But nothing disastrous happened that I could tell. I smiled and swam upward, lugging the heavy scepter in both hands as I flicked my tail up and down to send me back to the surface. I wondered what awaited me there. Would the ships still be afloat? Were my friends still alive? I was almost afraid to discover what I would find waiting for me above the sea.

As I swam back toward the light, the shadow of the ships above came into focus, and the distant sound of cannon fire resumed as if I'd never left. I rushed to the surface, the water cascading over me as I broke through the barrier of sky and sea. I did my best to keep the trident hidden under the water, and I shouted for help over the sound of pistols firing and men fighting.

It was a bloody and bruised Noah who rushed to the railing of the sinking ship. He motioned for me to wait, and without much of a choice, I did. He disappeared for a moment, leaving me confused, before the sound of a boat smacking the water made me look over at the side of the tilted hull. He'd cut the ropes holding the skiff so that it dropped down over the side.

I swam to it with haste. McKenzie rushed to join Noah, and he helped her climb down into the skiff, grimacing from the strain on his sore muscles no doubt. It wasn't a far leap, as the ship was almost underwater, so it only took some careful footwork down the part of the hull that wasn't yet submerged.

"Here!" I reached over the side of the skiff and placed the trident inside. "Keep it safe."

Noah and McKenzie offered their assistance to pull me up into the boat. I gripped their arms, pushing up with my tail as best I could as they pulled me into the skiff with them. The wood scraping along my tail hurt, but not as much as the pain of transforming back once my scales began to dry. Before my fish parts became human again, I quickly reached down and plucked a scale from my own tail, wincing from the pain. It felt like ripping off a fingernail.

"Damn." Noah shook his head. "You really are a mermaid."

"Is that the hardest thing for you to believe after all this?" I asked. "Where's Milo?"

Noah glanced back up at the ship. "He should be coming."

I gripped the section of my tail that would become my thighs as it transformed back into legs. I was thankful for the long tunic I'd kept on that covered enough of me to keep from revealing everything between my legs as I lay on the boat waiting to be human again. McKenzie tossed me the pants I'd taken off earlier.

"And you were worried about not doing anything important." I smirked, taking the pants and sliding them on, relieved that I wouldn't have to continue on with a naked lower half. "I can't think of anything I'd be more grateful for right now than this."

There was a large cannon boom, and the sound of silence for just a moment. Then suddenly the clanging of swords picked up again. Milo took a running leap from the half-submerged schooner and just barely made it into the skiff as we began to drift outward. Dried blood and sweat clung to him, and all he could do was press his knuckles against his other palm as he stared at the floor of the boat in a way that worried me.

"Better late than never. We're not leaving you this time." Noah nudged Milo with his elbow as he caught his breath and settled into the boat beside him. Milo offered a smile that was genuine, but also riddled with a worn and tired fearfulness I couldn't help but notice.

"Are they coming after us?" I looked overhead at the ships bobbing there. Bellamy's ship, the *Widow*, was comparable to the size of the Spanish frigate. But judging by the battered appearance of the Spanish ship, it had been the one that had taken a beating.

"Bellamy's crew is holding them off as long as they can, but both crews are dwindling, so it shouldn't go on much longer." Milo explained, eyeing the silver trident lying across the length of the skiff.

"Now how do we make this thing take us back?" McKenzie was the one who piped up.

"Cordelia said only a siren can use it. But to do that she has to give up something so she can take control of its power." I fiddled with the scale in my hand, admiring its satin silver sheen before continuing. "I'm going to give it this. To show I'm willing to give up my powers if it means we get to go home. Besides, I never wanted to be a mermaid anyway." My heart raced with the thought of returning us all home back together, and the more I thought about it the faster my blood raced through my veins.

"How do you 'give' it anything exactly?" Noah picked up the trident, studying it with cold, focused eyes. It was at least a foot taller than him.

"I don't know," I said, standing in the wobbly skiff. Once I found my balance, I reached forward and gripped the trident at its base. It began to glow with an unearthly white haze, pulsing with the light concentrated mostly around my hand.

I held out my scale to it, not knowing what I expected, but trying to earn its acceptance one way or another. I pressed the scale against the base where the rod melded into the prongs. When that didn't work, I tried touching it to each of the prong tips, my hope shrinking a little bit with each failed attempt. But no matter what, the pulsing white light stayed, glowing rhythmically like the constant beats of a waltz.

Once I'd tried everything I could possibly think of, I looked at the others around me through eyes confounded and hopeless. The schooner was almost entirely underwater now, and Bellamy's men were retreating back to their ship. We had mere minutes before the only barrier between us and the pirate hunters was at the bottom of the sea. Though I had no idea if they'd bother coming after us, that would still leave us stuck on the open ocean in a rowboat barely big enough for the four of us with no food or water.

"I don't know what else I can do." I squeezed the scale in my hand. I had a suspicion. A dark, haunting idea why my futile attempts to sacrifice my own magic wasn't working. But I pushed it from my mind because I refused to accept that it could actually be the truth. There had to be another way...

"I do," Milo said, leaning forward in the skiff, his eyes downcast.

No. He was thinking it, too.

"The thing you love most isn't your magic, Katrina," He muttered pulling a knife from his belt. "And it isn't a thing, is it?"

"What are you doing?" I asked, noticing how he held the knife, gripping it as if ready to use it.

"Tell me what you care for more than anything." His voice draped over me like heavy velvet, darkening the air around me, while my grip tightened on the trident. Now I understood why he'd asked me how much I love him back on the ship. I knew what he was doing. And I couldn't let him do it.

"Oh my god! Look!" McKenzie shouted, pointing at the pirate hunters who were readying a cannon directly our way. The schooner was long gone under, with only a quarter of its mast jutting out of the water to mark its presence. Our only shield was gone. Bellamy was back on the *Widow*, hustling to redirect the ship and block our enemies, but there was no way he could move that thing fast enough.

"Katrina, tell me. What do you love more than anything?" Milo repeated, pulling my focus back to him.

I blinked back hot tears and swallowed the burning lump rising in my throat. I was so afraid of what would happen if I answered him. But we were out of time. I didn't know what else to do.

"You know it's you." The words dripped from my mouth weakly, cracking between each hoarse syllable.

Milo stood up, rocking the unbalanced skiff on the already choppy water, and took a step forward so that he could lean over me. He reached over around the back of my neck and pulled my face to his to kiss me. It was brief, but passionate, and I held onto the taste of him like the sweet savor of honey.

When he pulled away, before any of us could say a word, he raised the knife in his hand and swiped it across the flesh of his palm. With an unwavering stare fixated on the trident, he pressed his blood-soaked hand to the trident's prongs, and the glowing haze around it became brighter.

"No!" I screamed. "No!" I knew what he was doing. He was taking his rightful place as the thing I loved most in this world. The thing I was most afraid of losing. The thing I would never have given up, not even to save the world.

"This is the only way to get you back." He spoke as calmly as if he was simply putting a lure on a fishing hook, but in those long-familiar hazel eyes, he couldn't hide the brokenness and turmoil giving away the truth. "You've saved me, Katrina. In every way. And now it's finally my turn to save you." As he spoke, the glow around the trident strengthened, and I felt its magic surging through the scepter rod in my hand.

"No!" I shrieked. "I'll stay here with you forever if I have to. I *won't* leave you again!" I threw down the trident and let it hit the floor of the boat with a heavy, bell-like clang.

"Katrina, we have to go!" Noah screamed, gesturing to the cannon readying to blast us. "You're the only one of us who can use it! Pick it up!"

"No!" I screamed until my throat was raw, my knees hitting the floor of the boat as McKenzie and Noah each fought to hold me up on either side. But I melted in their grasp, begging them to leave me alone, screaming through wails and cries until my lungs nearly gave out. "No...no...no..."

Please no.

"Katrina! We're going to die here if we don't go back! You *know* that's what's going to happen! There's no other way!" McKenzie's tearful voice of reason raked against my core like claws.

I trembled, waves of tears breaking through my pitiful hold on them. The urgency of the moment brought back all too many fresh, horrid memories of standing at the edge of the *Siren's Scorn* that dark night months ago. When the fate of everyone I cared about was crushing me with its weight on my shoulders. Was I really to be forced to make this choice again? Lose Milo forever or doom us all?

What would it mean to give Milo to the trident? Would it kill him? Would it make him forget me? Would it take him to a place I could never find?

I stared, lost in my spiraling cyclone of thoughts as quiet tears streamed down my face. I couldn't make this choice. I couldn't do it. I shook my head, nearly choking on deep, short breaths as the hopelessness set in. McKenzie and Noah still shouted and pleaded with me, but I couldn't even understand them. I could see only darkness. Darkness as empty and void as the depths I'd just swum back from.

Just then, a strong guiding hand took mine and pried open the fingers of my balled fist. It was Milo, forcing the trident back into my grip and kneeling in front of me. I tried to pull away, to let go of the cold metal in my hand. But he held his hand firmly over mine, locking my hold on the trident in place. Each beat of my heart felt like a pickaxe in my chest as I realized there was no way to change this. The cannon would fire in seconds.

Even if it missed, there was nowhere to go here in this place where no one that I'd brought here belonged. There was no other choice but this. Milo was going to make sure of it.

And I hated him for it. I hated him then, as he watched me through tangled locks of dark gold hair, falling in front of that scarred eyebrow. Then he smirked that slightly crooked smile that made me hate him more. And I smiled back, as the tears kept flowing, and I choked back the desperate wail I wanted so badly to let out.

"You just couldn't stop trying to protect me, could you?" I shook my head, barely able to see him as my tears blurred my vision. He stroked my hand reassuringly with his thumb as the trident's light became the purest white, forming a halo around us in our skiff. I could feel him shaking and it broke every part of me. I pressed my forehead to the place where our hands met on the trident. "I told you to stop protecting me...I told you...I told you..." The words broke into fractured pieces that I couldn't piece back together.

Milo reached his uncut hand forward, touching the side of my face where Thane had cut me. "That's the one thing I can never do for you, Starlight." He paused as he pressed his eyes shut for just a moment, and then looked back at me through tears of his own. "I always lose you eventually. But I find you again and again."

The light from the trident became so intense that I couldn't see him anymore. I cherished the last bit of his touch on my face and hands, and as the light shone brighter than the sun, I whispered one promise I prayed to be true as my wet lips trembled, and I felt I could barely hold myself upright anymore.

"I'll find you in every lifetime."

Cannon fire exploded, voices faded, and the white light consumed us. I opened my eyes to a blue sky.

ROCK BOTTOM

38

I was floating on my back, the trident still in my hand. The water around me was calm and gentle, lifting me like it intended to cradle me softly until I fell asleep. I wished I could. The cut on my face burned from the saltwater, which I didn't remember feeling when I was in my mermaid form.

I lifted my head with a jerk, righting myself in the water and still holding tightly to the trident. The ships were gone. There was no sunken schooner, no Spanish frigate, and no ship captained by Bellamy exchanging cannon fire with the others. On all sides, as far as my weary eye could see, there was only blue sea, stretching on and on. McKenzie and Noah were treading water, too, and appeared to be just gaining their senses the same as me.

But Milo wasn't there.

"What happened?" McKenzie asked.

"We're back," I said half-heartedly. "At least I think." I didn't know if I wanted to be right or wrong. My heart felt so heavy I thought it would weigh me down and sink me straight to the bottom of the ocean. If we were back, it meant I would never know what happened to Milo. And that was a reality I just couldn't face.

"At least we know your evil mermaid grandma hasn't destroyed the world yet." Noah's usual attempts to be logical and snarky just made me feel irritated. I didn't care. I just didn't care.

"No, instead we just got sent back to the present and we get to die at sea in modern times instead of the 18th century." McKenzie's comment took me by surprise, but it was what she said next that really caught me off guard. "And Milo...I can't believe he did that to get us here. This is just..."

"Yeah, I really wish I had gone a little easier on him," Noah said, bobbing in the water only a few feet from me. "I thought so many things about him and all of them…wrong." His voice cracked dryly as he dropped his gaze.

I nodded in acknowledgement. Maybe there was something underneath that stubborn indifferent exterior. But his words were worth about as much comfort as the fact that we were still stranded at sea.

We floated along, unsure of our next move, and purely at the ocean's mercy. I looked out and thought about how nothing out here on this never-ending blue expanse looked any different than it did back in 1720. The sea was unfazed by time; unchanged by the passing centuries, just as timeless as it was endless. And I could live the full life of a siren—300 years or more—and yet what would it all be for?

McKenzie and Noah talked a bit, discussing our situation and trying to figure out a way to find help or survive out here overnight if it came to that. Not even an hour had passed before they worked themselves into a panic, growing more exhausted by the second from keeping afloat for so long. I watched as the sun shifted across the midday sky, threatening to begin its descent behind the horizon in just a few more hours. I might have felt the panic, too, if I could manage to feel anything.

I was too broken to contribute. I had nothing to say, and nothing to fear. The trauma was too fresh. I didn't care how long we floated out there for. Tread water or die. I had no solution to offer. I just needed a moment to grieve. Could I just have that?

As I watched the white clouds dotting the afternoon sky, I couldn't help but feel the strangest relief at the sound of distant humming. Because I knew by the sound what approached. I could feel it in the way the vibrations in the water sent out ripples and wakes far ahead of the boat coming into view.

"Help! Help us!" McKenzie screamed, waving her hands and splashing around hysterically. Noah quickly joined her in trying to flag down the vessel.

Something was wrong. I knew long before the boat got anywhere near us that it wasn't just any boat. It was Cordelia's yacht. Time had not passed here as it had during our trip to the past. The day was right where we left it. January 10th.

"Shhh! Don't draw her over here!" I ordered the other two, my command a bit more spiteful than I meant it to be.

A raging hatred filled me when I saw Cordelia. The dark upswept hair and midnight blue pants suit made it impossible not to recognize her, even from a distance. My stomach turned and my grip on the trident grew so tight I thought it would bend the metal. And I felt relief that I could still feel something. I was glad to know I wasn't entirely numb.

Because when I thought of how nearly every bit of pain in my life had been caused by her—whether directly or indirectly—a very clear, undeniable feeling took over. And it wasn't my siren side either. No. It was just plain old me. Katrina Delmar. And the only feeling right now that could replace all the hurt and pain was the burning desire to take from Cordelia every bit as much as she'd taken from me.

Head Above Water

39

The *Belladonna* sped into view quickly, and I calculated that if Cordelia and her crew were just now arriving at the trident's location, that meant our trip to the past had only totaled a few hours in the present.

I gave a strong squeeze of the trident with my hand, thinking of Milo and still haunted by the mystery of his fate. If I thought any more about it, I might've squeezed the trident so hard it would bend in half. I'd die before letting it fall into her hands. Not to save anyone. Not because the fate of humanity was at stake. But because I couldn't bear for her to win after everything I'd given up to stop her.

"Don't let her see you!" I demanded to the others, sinking myself down into the water until only my eyes stuck out above the surface, watching the passing yacht with a watchful, vulturous stare. When McKenzie and Noah followed, I silently thanked them.

The yacht slowed a good half mile away. They were still scouting, looking for the most accurate spot they could anchor and begin their search. Even from here I could see her dive team, readying themselves and slipping on their air tanks as she stood by the railing, hunting the seas with her piercing gaze. I didn't know if she could see us from here. But when the boat engine shut off and began to drift our way in silence, I had a strong feeling maybe she'd noticed the three college kids desperately treading open water. But I had to ensure she didn't see the trident.

Her boat inched toward us like a hungry alligator. I felt the trident in my hand, sliding my fingers along its metal shaft. It had long lost its magical glow and no longer seemed capable of performing a task like transporting people to another century. Was it a one-time use thing? Or could I figure out how to activate it once again to wield against Cordelia?

My efforts to do so proved futile. I tried to manipulate any of the three—time, life, or space, but failed at every attempt. Not even a spark of magic glinted from the trident's pointed prongs. But as I studied them, I noticed how sharp they were. Like tips of a harpoon. And a thought washed over me, satiating that dark, cruel side of me that I didn't even care to fend off anymore.

"Let her see you. Distract her. Keep her talking," I said coldly to McKenzie and Noah without further explanation. And ignoring their confused expressions and remarks, I dove underwater with the trident, as I followed the call. I had somewhat of a plan.

It would've been easier with my tail. It would've made swimming beneath the boat so much faster. But I didn't have time to drown and transform. And I sure couldn't risk letting go of the trident. Besides, it would make getting onto the yacht much more difficult without my legs. From underneath, I noticed the boat's whirring propeller slowing until it came to a stop. And I knew for sure Cordelia had found McKenzie and Noah.

I surfaced on the left side of the yacht, opposite the side I'd seen Cordelia standing, and examined it for any possible point of entry. There was a ladder on the back, but it was placed high enough that the base of it was a good few feet from the water. I couldn't reach it while carrying the trident. My plan would have to go just a little differently than I'd hoped. But that was okay. It might be good to practice my siren powers on something less important before trying to use them full force.

Keeping my head just barely above water, I reached for the scale in my pocket that I'd saved from my tail earlier. I was more than grateful to see that it had survived this far somehow without floating away or falling out.

I remembered the way the scale around Cordelia's neck illuminated as she sang that song aboard the ship when she found us with the mermaids. She was drawing on its magic to be able to use her siren power, even when she was in her human form. And I was about to do the same.

I could faintly hear Cordelia talking to Noah and McKenzie, questioning them about who they were and how they'd gotten out here.

"Can you help us?" McKenzie asked.

"I suppose if I must," Cordelia reluctantly agreed. "But you're to stay in the cabin area below and not to come out during our expedition unless I approve it." I heard her order the crew to toss them both lifesavers and pull them up.

Just a little longer, guys.

I waited for someone to walk near the back of the ship. The luxurious, gleaming white yacht was at least one hundred feet, and there were a handful of divers and crew members aboard still shuffling about on deck. I eyed a male, probably in his thirties, who looked to be a worker or maybe the skipper's assistant of some kind. His lanky figure snaked its way toward the back, perhaps getting ready to drop anchor or check something on the engine. He was perfect for what I needed. I just hoped it would work.

My lips parted, and from my mouth drifted the same lulling tune Cordelia had sung. As if by instinct, the tune quickly turned into my mom's lullaby, filling the gaps with haunting notes and the poetic words I'd collected over the past year:

Lost out at sea
Do you dream of me?
By the call of the waves
I hear you and seek you
Till again the roaming sea
Brings you back to me.
Down by the shore
Meet me once more
By the light of the moon
Love me, then leave me
With the dawn rising
Haunt me forevermore

The man appeared stunned for a moment, holding his forehead as if feeling unwell. In my head I imagined him walking to the ladder. As I envisioned it, he did it. I smiled the kind of smile that holds no happiness, a wicked smile of sorts, as the scale in my pocket glowed hot.

I then directed him to drop the ladder into the water so that I could climb up, all while continuing my song and simply willing it. He obeyed perfectly, and I quickly shimmied up the ladder, dragging up the trident with me. Dripping wet and now aboard Cordelia's massive boat, I sighed with relief that my plan was working so far. And my theory about the siren song was right. My mom's lullaby was the siren song all along. And the scale was the power source from which it drew.

Next, I told the man to make his way back toward the front deck where Cordelia was standing. I followed, keeping the trident close to me and watching my back. When we reached the front, I wasted no time commanding my new assistant to quietly creep up behind Cordelia and restrain her.

He followed like clockwork, grabbing the woman as she stood at the railing shouting interrogation questions as McKenzie and Noah.

Now, make her face me. I ordered.

With a squirming and furious Cordelia in his arms, he pulled her around, seemingly struggling against her thrashing more than I would have expected.

"Let me go, David!" Cordelia screamed. "Do you understand me? Put me down now! What are you doing?"

I stepped forward, my steps leaving watery traces on the pristine polished deck as I neared her. I hummed my song softly to keep David under my control.

"Katrina," she hissed, once she stopped struggling long enough to look up and notice me. Her face instantly softened when her eyes flicked to the grand trident in my hand. "Well done, my dear. I don't think my divers could've managed such deep waters. Glad to see you didn't get crushed beneath all that pressure." She smiled.

"If you think I got this for you, think again, Cordelia." I adjusted my grip on the metal rod, twisting my palm around it to feel the weight of it. "I'd rather die than help you. Not after everything you've taken from me."

"You'd rather die?" She snickered. "Bold words. Perhaps all that pressure did get to you, after all. Perhaps that crushing darkness finally just weighed too much."

I hesitated, knowing she referred to something more than just the depths of the sea. "You're cruel, Cordelia."

"Angelfish, now, now. We've talked about this. That's no way to speak to your great grandmother." She choked out the words as the man squeezed her, one arm across her throat and the other holding her hands behind her back. The dismissiveness in her words sent fury flaring through my bones.

"I know why you're this way. You've been denied your siren form too long," I didn't know why I was wasting my time talking to her. My plan didn't include drawing things out like this. It was supposed to be quick. I was supposed to have ended this—ended *her*—by now. Why couldn't I do it?

"And just who told you that, dear? The filthy pirate you fell for? Did he tell you before or after he went on his killing spree? Or was it when you were screwing him in that cave?"

I clenched my jaw at her mention of Milo, ignoring the urge to question how she even knew about those things. "I've experienced it for myself," I said through gritted teeth, raising the trident and pointing the prongs at her.

"Then you know what it's like to have all that power just trapped within you, begging to be released and given the reins. You know what it's like to realize you were made to use it." Her eyes fluttered, beckoning me like she was trying to convince me to take a bite of the sweetest poisoned apple.

"Yes," I said, stepping forward so that the trident's sword-like prongs rested inches from Cordelia's stomach. "And it made me realize I'm stronger than I ever knew."

"Stronger?" She smiled. "And what about crueler?"

I hesitated, my arms shaking both from the weight of the trident and the fear of what I planned to do next. She kept talking, pushing me to my limits.

"Go on, Katrina," she said slyly, her words smooth, deep, and seductive like a slow song. "Kill me. Give into that side of you that's just dying to be heard. Put that trident through me like you planned to. You don't have a soul to save, after all, so why not just indulge yourself?"

I trembled all over, my breath trapped in my chest. The swaying of the ship made me even more uneasy, and I thought I might vomit but my empty stomach reassured me that wasn't possible. Cordelia continued talking, and I listened like a fool.

"My dear girl, you saw the cruelty and corruption of mankind firsthand, and yet you're still trying to keep me from putting a stop to it. Look at what they did to you. They even left you with a permanent reminder." I felt the healing scar on my face sting as Cordelia's eyes fell on it. "You saw what man does. It's no different in this century than the last or the next. They will always take and destroy what isn't theirs to own. And yet you still want to keep this world intact as it is. When we could erase all this and start anew." Her vibrant blue eyes bore into mine, and in them I saw my own reflection, holding the trident, my wet hair clinging to my skin and tangled across the scar along my jaw., thinner than I was weeks ago before I'd been forced to embark on this journey of survival. "If you'd just let it go." Cordelia whispered, gently and warmly, a sudden contrast from her earlier statements.

Her words took hold in me, and I fumbled, sorting and questioning my own thoughts. All too late I noticed I'd stopped humming. David was losing his grip on Cordelia. I rushed to sing again, forcing him to strengthen his hold. He lost his grip around her neck, but was able to restrain her from her waist, pressing her arms to her side. And I could see that around her neck, tucked into her silky blouse, was the scale necklace I could never seem to get rid of. Her most powerful weapon was now free.

"What a lovely voice, dear. But you're inexperienced. A siren's song is something that takes time to master well. If you're good enough, you can even use it on more than one mind at a time."

She flicked her gaze to the opposite side of the ship across the deck. McKenzie and Noah were just now climbing over the railing in their soaked clothing, two divers flanking them with fresh towels ready.

With her eyes fixed on them, Cordelia began singing a song of her own, like mine but more powerful, making me feel dizzy as each ethereal note reached my ears. I didn't know if it was possible to fully control another siren, but it was clearly possible for her to mess with my head somehow, just like she had at dinner.

Within seconds, the demeanor on my friends' faces changed, becoming harsh and hollow as they became entranced by Cordelia's voice. I didn't know what she planned to make them do, but I couldn't let her take them. I shoved the trident forward, touching the spear-like tip of the highest middle prong to her now exposed throat, desperate to stop her singing. But no matter how hard I tried to force my hands to plunge the trident into her larynx, I couldn't find the strength to do it.

"Looks like you need to give into your siren side a little bit more," Cordelia coaxed. "If you weren't so stubborn about keeping that halo around your head, we could've changed the world by now. Or you could've at least killed me."

Before I could think of a response, McKenzie and Noah rushed at me, stealing the trident from my grasp. I fought to pull it back, but Noah overpowered me easily and shoved me to the floor as McKenzie yanked the trident from my hands and carried it to a now unrestrained Cordelia.

"Thank you, sweetheart," Cordelia said sweetly to McKenzie as she took the trident with a smile. "I'm so glad rescuing you two paid off."

As I reeled from being slammed into the wooden deck, I looked up just in time to see Cordelia tearing the scale pendant from her neck and pressing it into the base of the trident, where it cast a white glow just like when Milo offered his blood to it. And then she grasped the rod with the other hand, making her claim as its new wielder.

My jaw dropped as I saw the scale absorbed into the trident, pulled into the metal like quicksand, and the glow brightened so intensely that I had no choice but to cover my eyes. When the light diminished, the hold on McKenzie and Noah had broken, and they both rushed to my side after shaking off their disorientation.

"What's happening?" McKenzie asked, helping me to my feet.

"She gave up the last of her magic in exchange for control of the trident." I replied, unable to look away as Cordelia relished the sight of the sea scepter in her hand.

"You didn't know how to use this, Katrina," Cordelia said, touching the tips of the prongs like they were flower petals. "Because you don't know how to channel your pain and anger into power. You're too afraid of it. You're too afraid of yourself."

"I don't want power," I croaked out dryly, my words breaking beneath the realization that I'd failed. "I just want to be left alone."

"No, you don't, dear. Being alone is the last thing you want. You want back the man you think you love." Cordelia stepped toward me, keeping enough distance between us that I couldn't reach the trident, while her glowing electricity shield sizzled as a reminder not to even try. But her sapphire eyes softened for just a moment as she continued, and I listened, my body aching and my blood racing. "Trust me, I know. That's all I wanted for a long, long time, too. But I finally realized I was wasting my time. I wasted my magic on cursing them, and I wished I could undo it for the longest. But losing my siren form made that impossible.

"Eventually, I found someone I could tolerate enough to use for my survival. A man with connections and wealth that I knew I could leverage to begin building my new life on land. I've worked hard to forget his name. Because I remember how he treated me. And how he treated our daughter, who I never wanted to bring into this world in the first place. Poor sweet Marina. She was a fool just like you. Trying to chase some man across the sea. Thankfully she came to her senses after some very vivid...dreams." She paused with a hand on her heart and a fake hint of sorrow as she spoke about the daughter I remembered reading about. I recalled the old letter I'd found last year. The one from Cordelia to Marina trying to keep her from moving to the seaside. It made even more sense now. Everything she'd orchestrated had always been for spite. For vengeance. For herself.

She continued, her features hardening again. "Her father meant nothing to me. But I suppose I played my cards well. In death he finally showed his worth. He left me everything when he died. And through the decades I used it to create the empire I have today. Because I had to."

Between the trident's silver prongs jumped wild sparks of electricity as she spoke. Without explanation, she pointed the trident down at the water.

"That's what you need, Katrina. If we're to build a better world, you need someone willing to challenge your feelings. You need to realize life isn't fair, and love doesn't create strength. Only weakness."

I blinked, watching on in confusion as power flowed from the trident, opening a rift in the seawater below.

"What are you doing?" I shouted over the roar of the water.

"I'm putting the trident to the test. It can clearly control time and space. But let's see about life, shall we? It's been said it can even bring back the dead who made the sea their grave. So, I'm bringing back someone, just for you." She winked at me coldly, and I feared what was to come next.

I stopped in wonderment, my mouth hanging open in awe as I watched the sea roil where Cordelia commanded. The rift in the sea glowed like the trident itself, and after a moment, a figure emerged—a man.

I rushed to the railing, leaning over in desperation to see if it just might be possible that she'd brought back Milo. The faintest feeling of hope fluttered wildly in my heart until it hurt. Maybe, just maybe, she wanted to let me have him back. But as the sky darkened with black clouds overhead, I clearly recognized the terrified face of Bellamy as he burst forth from the water gasping for air. And I shattered right there.

"Why would you do this?" I screamed, the cold feeling of betrayal taking hold. So many emotions flooded me, I couldn't even pinpoint what hurt the most about seeing Bellamy resurrected. It was a cruel trick on us both. "Let him rest! He's been through enough!"

Cordelia's calloused smile sent a shiver down my spine, and I rushed to grab one of the flotation devices left on the deck from when the crew had pulled McKenzie and Noah to safety. "Help me pull him in!" I cried to my friends, who hurried alongside me as we tossed Bellamy the lifesaver.

He grasped at it in a panic as water crashed over his head and the waves tossed him like a barrel. My heart broke a little at how terrifying and confusing this must be for him. Being freshly resurrected and first opening his eyes to all this.

I felt weak against the tides pulling the rope connected to Bellamy, but with Noah and McKenzie's strength added to mine, we mustered the strength to draw him in and help him up and over the side of the hull.

He gasped, coughing up seawater and holding his stomach as I helped him stand straight. It was a strange sight to see him like this, helpless and afraid, when just a few hours earlier I'd watched him leading a charge onto a ship with cannons blasting and swords drawn fearlessly. Now he looked the same way he did when I first met him months ago in the library, clad in his drenched dark jeans and black jacket, his jet-black hair cut shorter than his days as captain in his father's fleet.

"Where am I?" His voice quivered, but the sound of his voice—the familiarity of it—was enough to give me some pebble-sized semblance of comfort in the midst of everything else happening around us. I looked at him with a weighty, heartbroken stare and a well of tears fighting their way to my eyes.

"The end of the world," I said.

BLACK SEA

40

Cordelia had taken the opportunity to position herself at the front of the yacht, summoning the power of the trident to begin her long-awaited mission. The trident continued pulsing with power as the sky overhead darkened like ash with more clouds and thunder. Cordelia's face, illuminated by the glow of the scepter in her hands, held firm as she concentrated on manipulating the currents and rising waves through the power of the trident.

"Forty days and forty nights it took to flood the earth once. This time around it won't take so long." She spoke, more to herself than anyone around her. The divers and crewmen on her boat watched in amazement and fear as the ocean began to rise, massive hills of water rolling and lapping slowly as the ship lifted higher, until finally even they grew too fearful to stay out on deck and ran for cover in the cabin.

"Cordelia, stop!" McKenzie screamed, her lightly freckled face now spotted with tears as she watched the scene unfolding before her. Noah rushed at Cordelia but was thrown back from a force of power that leapt from the trident, leaving him writhing in pain on the deck as seawater splashed over the sides.

"Tell your friends there's no use!" Cordelia called to me, stepping up to the highest point of the prow where she lifted the trident like a prize. "But don't worry. If you're on my ship, you'll be spared. You have my favor." Her deep red lips curved into a smile that made me recoil.

I thought of my family and my friends' families. I thought of Bellamy and the heartless thing Cordelia had just done to us both by bringing him here. And then I thought of Milo and how he'd been taken from me over and over because of the woman playing God at the front of this ship. And I couldn't hold back the tears any longer. I didn't even care to save the world anymore. Clearly, I'd failed. But that meant Milo had given himself up for nothing. And that was what tore at me in ways I couldn't overcome.

Bellamy wiped away a trickling tear from my cheek as I stared emptily at the deck floor between my feet. "I remember everything," he said softly.

"Everything?" I sniffed, startled by his words. "Like, even 1720 everything?"

He nodded, his gaze being the only steady thing I had to cling to as I stood bewildered. And then I fell apart, falling into his arms as he hugged me tightly, in a tender, protective way that gave me just one tangible second of comfort and familiarity in all this chaos.

"Is he dead? Did he make it?" I cried, burying my face in his wet shoulder. "What happened to him?"

"He made it," he said. "He got away."

A wave of relief surged through me, but my heart broke all the same, knowing Milo was left behind, alone, trapped somewhere between his present and his past, and never able to return to his future. He would've continued aging through the years, and that meant he was long dead by now. His own course of history was changed forever, and I could search the world for him, but I'd never find him in this lifetime with a beating heart.

I opened my eyes as the tears became too hard to hold in, my face still pressed to Bellamy's shoulder. The waters around us crashed against the boat, relentless and fierce. The scene around me was a blur, with the white of the yacht blending fuzzily into the heavy storm grey of the sky above and the midnight blue of the water below. Like blending colors into a painting...like watercolors.

Watercolors.

An absurd thought took hold, reminding me of a power I didn't expect to call on. But as my tears flowed fast, I realized they just might prove to be my greatest strength. With a brief burst of hopefulness, I pulled back, looking into Bellamy's face.

"Get that trident away from her. Whatever you have to do," I uttered.

"Resurrected five minutes and you're already throwing me into trouble." Bellamy's voice came through a gentle teasing smile, and I pulled him in for a reaffirming embrace once more.

"You never needed any help finding trouble." I smirked weakly.

We motioned for McKenzie and Noah to come near, leaving Cordelia performing her ritual with the trident. When they joined us, I quickly relayed to them the only excuse of a plan I had left.

"She doesn't have the full power of her siren song anymore without the scale. So, without the trident she's powerless. I don't know if this will work, and if it doesn't, *none* of you come after me, understand?" The words burned in my throat, knowing what I asked of them would be far from easy.

"We're gonna die either way. Or be forced to take sides with the sea witch over there. If you need us, we're coming after you." Noah objected with his usual stubbornness, but secretly I was glad to hear it. It was nice to have him on my side for once.

"First and foremost, you have to focus on separating the trident from Cordelia. And get her into the water. I don't care how you do it."

"We'll try, but we can't get near it without getting zapped," McKenzie said.

"Then think of something. You can do it." I encouraged her with a nudge in my voice.

"So, what are you going to do once we get it away from her, exactly?" Bellamy asked me.

"I'm going to cry," I said.

Ignoring the three sets of confused eyes on me, I stepped away without further explanation, turning to face the stern. It'd be easier to dive into the sea from the back of the boat to keep Cordelia from noticing. I tugged on Bellamy's arm and led him with me halfway.

"Keep a watch on her crew. Most of them seem to be too terrified to do anything and they've locked themselves in the cabin, but I don't know how loyal to her they are. Keep McKenzie and Noah safe," I said hurriedly, noticing the waves rising higher and taller. There was no telling how much land had already begun to flood with seawater spilling into the coasts. We couldn't waste much more time.

I started off toward the stern but turned around to look back before I'd gone two steps. "Thank you for everything, Bellamy."

He nodded with a smirk. "Thank *you*, love. You're the one who's always jumping overboard for me."

I shook my head, thinking how right he was. Just once it'd be nice if doing the right thing didn't involve leaping headfirst into a raging sea. Yet here we were again.

I kicked off my shoes and climbed over the railing of the ship as it lifted and dropped with the motion of the waves. I looked down, dreading the fall into these treacherous waters. But this time, I took consolation in knowing this was the one place Cordelia couldn't reach me. She couldn't swim the depths like I could. Not anymore. Without her tail, she was forever just as helpless against the sea as any ordinary human.

But I would have to be a helpless, ordinary human, too, at least for a few painful moments. I let the tears come, because I'd need all of them. I would need every painful feeling, every heartbreaking thought, every crushing memory. As I harbored each one, I dove headfirst in, letting the rioting water push me underneath. My eyelids puckered from the sting of salt. I resisted every instinct to fight the undertow, and instead let it pull me so far under I couldn't swim back up, prompting my change the moment everything went dark.

My eyes flew open, as I resurrected in my own strange way, awakening in my transformed mermaid body. I still wasn't used to it. The muscles in my tail ached from soreness just as much as the rest of me. But I ignored the pain and swam to the surface, pressing myself to the side of the yacht so as not to get separated, and to be able to hear when the perfect time to strike presented itself.

It was difficult to hear and see, especially as lightning crackled overhead and wind continued whipping the water up higher and higher, siphoning it upward like a slowly spinning cyclone. I was grateful for the dim lights of the yacht, because without them, my surroundings would have been nearly pitch black.

I could make out the sound of voices struggling, and the spark of the trident followed by forceful thuds. I wished I could pull myself up over the railing to see what was happening, but my tail was too heavy, and I lacked the arm strength to lift myself no matter how hard I tried. I would have to trust my friends to pull through, and then I'd have to trust myself to do what I knew must be done.

After a few torturous minutes, there was silence except for the whistling wind and wild waves and the yacht's hull slapping against them. I feared that I might not be able to come back to them if I couldn't get out of this water. I would be stuck this way.

A deafening gunshot suddenly pierced the air, making me jump. Within seconds, a bright red light illuminated the air above me, orange-gold sparks raining down like fireworks over the sides of the yacht. A flare gun. Someone found the flare gun. Genius.

The splash that followed drew my attention to the front of the yacht, where against the fading of the orange flash I saw the silhouette of a woman hit the water. When McKenzie leaned over the railing above, waving the flare gun, I breathed a sigh of relief that it wasn't her I'd seen drop off the side of the boat.

"I thought of something!" She yelled proudly.

I launched forward, swimming to where Cordelia had fallen, and caught sight of the trident following, dangling for a moment by its prongs that caught on the railing before sliding off the boat's edge. I knew I had to reach it before she regained her senses and took hold of it again.

Pulsing my fins up and down fast as I could, I jetted through the water at a speed I'd never swum before. Like a dart, I ripped past the swirling currents around me and soared through the water. I dashed forward, placing myself between the trident and Cordelia as they drifted downward through the water.

I reached for the trident, leaving Cordelia below, but as I began to swim away with it in my hand, a clawed hand gripped my tail. Cordelia raked her manicured fingernails through the webbing of my tail fin, tearing through it and forcing an agonizing scream from me that sent bubbles churning to the surface.

She clawed her way upward, kicking and swimming with an ability far better than a human's. That explained how she'd survived after cutting off her tail and jumping overboard with her new legs so many years ago. But this time, I couldn't let her return to the surface.

I fought back, losing the trident from my grip as the raging tides yanked it from me. I'd find it later. But right now, I couldn't risk Cordelia getting close to it.

She swam up, her blue eyes burning viciously as she took hold of my shirt and ripped it over my head in attempt to pull me to her. As I fought the winding fabric floating around my head, she slammed her knee into my ribs. I thrashed, trying to distinguish up from down. And once I regained my equilibrium, I refocused on the venomous woman trying to kill me in this black sea.

Something darkened in me. A heavy understanding that saturated me to the core, making my bones and skin wane cold. Cordelia was never going to stop. Never. Her endless hunt for vengeance and power would never end. Until someone stopped her. And this was my last chance to do it.

I worried about the stain that what I was about to do would leave on my soul. But then I remembered I didn't have one.

Mutiny

41

I turned on her. I knew she expected me to swim upwards, to pull back toward the surface to get away from her attacks. But instead, I swam down toward her, the blood from my tattered fins swirling around us in ghostly crimson streams.

I clutched her shoulders, digging my fingernails into her skin so that losing my grip became nearly impossible. Against the water's pull, I swept my tail up and down in a rapid wave-like rhythm. It was a movement that still felt foreign, as my waist and core moved to maintain the force needed to drive myself down into the rising swell of the ocean that only wanted to spit us back up. But the strength of my tail surprised me and reminded me of the advantage I had.

Doing my best to dodge the scratches and hits Cordelia dealt out, I focused on holding her down, pushing her further into the ocean's belly. She fought against me like a wild animal, ripping my skin with her nails and pulling my hair so hard I felt tears stinging my eyes underwater. The raging and tossing of the ocean above grew still as it faded behind us. Our surroundings darkened into near blackness, and the crushing weight of the water grew heavier, so much that even I could feel its pressure on my chest.

I knew Cordelia was afraid. I felt it in the way she thrashed and writhed against my grip, screaming at me in threats and curses that only came out in muted bursts of bubbles. I felt the way her kicks and flails grew more desperate and tense. And whenever I began to feel sorry for her, I let an inkling of my siren side take hold so that I could harden myself to whatever empathy tried to creep its way in. I wanted to be selfish. I had to be, right now. I'd have to go to the darkest part of the ocean—and the darkest part of myself—to do it.

I can't do it. I can't.

I inwardly begged the siren in me to silence my conscience. I needed her compassionless essence to take over. Though I was afraid that once I willingly gave in, I might not be able to get myself back.

Yes, you can. She must die. I smiled coldly when I heard her voice. My own voice. *You must be more powerful. You must conquer her. You can take her place and rule the seas with the trident. After all, you've given up more than she did. You deserve to take this power.* The voice entranced me like a song, controlling my desires, and feeding the dark need in me to end Cordelia for all the wrong reasons. But perhaps that's what I needed, since I'd failed to do it for the right reasons.

With a vicious rage burning in me, a desire for power too strong to ignore, I overpowered Cordelia in our underwater struggle. I didn't know how long it would take to drown an ex-mermaid, but I would ensure this was the day I'd find out. And I couldn't have stopped myself if I wanted to.

As I swam faster and faster, forcing Cordelia down to the abyss, my true self broke through the siren's hold for just a second. And even *she* didn't hold back. The sinister memory of each suicide in my family and the nightmares that caused them rushed to my mind. Fueled by the aching thoughts, I fought Cordelia harder each time she braced against me and dared to try escaping my grip. *Marina. Sarah. Martha. Edith. Alma. Esther. Nelda. Lydia. Mom.* They—we—suffered the same nightmares that brought us the same torment Cordelia was feeling now. Terrified, desperate, and drowning. I decided it was time for her to finally experience it fully for herself.

She reached up, clawing at me one last time as she convulsed beneath my weight. Her fingertips grated across my cheek and along my jaw, tearing open the cut on my face that had just barely begun to close. I grimaced and squeezed her shoulders harder, digging my own fingers into the meat of her flesh, and I felt as though in that moment I could've killed her with my bare hands. But I didn't have to. She stopped resisting right before she jerked violently, uncontrollably. Once. Twice. And then her hands fell away from me. Her head rolled back, and her body became as weightless as the microscopic bubbles seeping from between her red lips.

And it was over. Even in these murky depths so far below, my siren eyesight stayed sharp enough that I could see her fall away, her beautiful face unmarked by time or death. Her hair had fallen loose in our scuffle, and it floated around her now, allowing me a glimpse of what she once might've looked like as a young, carefree mermaid in centuries past. She drifted down, like a feather on a breeze, farther and farther until the darkness of the sea swallowed her whole. A part of me wondered what happened to her now, if there was anything more to her fate than becoming seafoam. I supposed it didn't matter. Because after all, we were soulless creatures anyway.

With one last glance over my shoulder at the black abyss beneath, I turned my sights toward the surface and swam back, gliding through the water as my own blood trailed behind me. I suddenly felt the sting of my wounds. The fresh bruises on my flesh throbbed, and the guilt of killing my great grandmother settled under my skin and seeped into my being. I knew I'd bear the weight of it forever, as ever present as the crushing pressure of the deep ocean.

WATERY GRAVE

42

KATRINA

When I broke through the surface, the sky still swirled in ominous billows. I drew in a breath, not out of necessity, but just an instinctual reaction from my human side. Underwater, my skin somehow absorbed oxygen from the water molecules around me. It was still a strange sensation I hadn't quite gotten used to.

But this breath was more than just breathing. It was freeing. Like reclaiming the side of myself I had to lose in order to embrace the strength I'd found in darkness. Now that darkness rested below me, left behind miles beneath the surface. At least that's what I told myself.

But my job wasn't done, because the waves still riled and tossed about, and the trident had slipped from my hands to be carried away somewhere in all this. It was probably miles away by now.

"Katrina!" I could hardly make out Bellamy's voice amongst the waves crashing. I swiveled in the water, my long, wet hair plastered to my bare chest, trying to catch sight of where I heard him call.

He dangled dangerously from the railing of the yacht, held in place by a rope tied to his waist that Noah and McKenzie were straining to keep taut against the pull of the ocean. In his grasp, veiled by misty sea spray, he held the trident. It still pulsed with blue and white electricity, sending waves of light rippling through the waves.

I watched him, thinking of how this fight was every much his fight as mine. His family had been ruined by Cordelia, even if his father certainly was just as much to blame. But Bellamy wasn't to blame. Not even a little bit. All he'd ever wanted was to belong to the sea. All he'd ever loved was cut short. Every time.

My first instinct was to rush forward and bound through the water to save Bellamy and take the trident. But then a voice returned from the depths where I thought I'd left it. It told me to take the trident and finish what Cordelia started. To make Bellamy and the others bow before me as the ocean follows my command. After all, I'd already unlocked its power with my sacrifice. I had nothing more to lose. But everything to gain. A world at my command.

Take what is yours.

A bolt of lightning struck the water in front of me, snapping me out of the trance pulling me under. I knew then that if I were to touch that trident in this state, I would lose myself forever. I would become the very thing I sought to defeat. So instead, I stayed suspended there in the waves, frozen as the whipping wind and churning water spiraled around me.

"Katrina!" One of my friends called me. I couldn't even recognize their voices. I battled the voice in my head, clamping my eyes shut as I pushed away the siren's call. I couldn't overpower it, but I could distract it. So, I shifted the focus, arguing with it until it no longer wanted to convince me to rule the seas. Instead, I redirected it, letting it speak its dark truths to me and reminding me of the monster I never wanted to become.

You left Milo behind in a world where he'll spend every day fighting until death finally claims him, old, withered and alone.

I shook my head at the painful accusation, swallowing it like bitter medicine. My siren continued. And I willingly listened.

You destroyed his life, just as your mother destroyed everyone around her. You let your heart betray him, and he'll never forgive you for that.

I swallowed a lump in my throat, opening my eyes as the tears came. Maybe mermaids were too stubborn to cry, but I was still half human, and that side of me wasn't so tough.

And now you've killed your own flesh and blood. We both knew you couldn't keep your hands clean.

My tail flicked back and forth, and my chest tightened, filling with salty, wet air as heat rose to my face like fire. I never wanted any of this.

All that destruction. All that brokenness. All that ruin. Look at the mess you've made. You're shaping up to be a fine siren.

That was it. The moment the well of tears I'd been storing up broke free, flowing, streaming from my red, tired eyes without stopping. Like a dam bursting, the release of my sorrow and anger was unstoppable. Rivers of rage poured from me, spilling over from my heart into the ocean through my tears. And when my teardrops hit the seawater below, mixing with the ocean, I felt the instant connection within. I felt a power unlike any other.

I thought of the midnight waters around me like paint beneath my paintbrush. I imagined how I might shape it, move it, and control it. And with my mermaid tears falling, I did.

Releasing a shattering cry that broke through even the loudest wave and thunder, I threw my head back, feeling the control I now had of the ocean around me. The water beneath me cupped me like a foaming throne, cresting higher until I overlooked the raging sea below. It lifted me as I screamed, the echoes of my pain commanding the tides.

I forced down the waves, opening up the water's surface like a tear in fabric. I painted the water splitting, creating a channel of air that corkscrewed all the way down to the ocean floor. In another recess of my mind, I told the sea to take the trident back, to hide it where no one—human, mermaid, or otherwise—could ever reach it again.

A section of water sprouted up, swirling like a small cyclone beside Bellamy and ripping the trident from his grip. I painted the trident far away, buried beneath the sea itself. And with that image in my mind, fresh tears still streaming down with no sign of stopping, the water wrapped the trident in its grip, twisting around it and carrying it all the way down the trench I'd created in the ocean, until it reached the floor so deep below, I could barely see it.

With a ground-shaking blast, the water forced open the sea floor, creating a grave in which the trident would lie for the rest of time. With the last of my mind's strength, I ordered the waters to bury the trident in depths even I couldn't fathom. And I watched with mixed emotions as the ocean did as I commanded.

The water violently rushed back over, closing up the split as I felt myself letting go, exhausted from the effort. I dropped down into the waves as the crest holding me dwindled and lowered. The raging storm calmed just as the sea swallowed up the trident, burying it miles below the sand to be trapped there forever by the ocean's crushing pressure.

I didn't even have the strength to move my tail to stay afloat, and my battered lungs had all but given out. My painting was finished. But I finally, finally stopped crying.

I watched on in agony as Katrina and the others vanished before me, leaving me standing in the empty skiff as cannons raged around me. I dove into the water, narrowly dodging a cannonball as it obliterated the little wooden jollyboat. And then, left without a choice but to help Bellamy as he had helped us, I swam toward the dueling ships. Because what else did I have to live for now?

As I climbed up the side of the Spaniard frigate, my thoughts riled in torment. I knew this would happen. I knew she'd be gone. But I couldn't have fathomed it would've been this hard. I knew she was back where she was meant to be, she and far away from all this. I should've been content in that alone. But I wasn't. I was completely, and irrevocably destroyed.

Katrina was right. Loving her had destroyed me. Because loving her always, *always* meant losing her.

I lost myself a long time ago, and she just took the last piece of me with her. So, I didn't even recall how I stormed the ship and struck down every enemy in my path. It was nothing more than a blur of steel and blood. And when the captain himself ran over to challenge me, I greeted him with the same relentlessness, unhindered by the wounds I couldn't feel anymore. We might've fought for seconds or minutes. It wasn't worth noting.

That is, until the moment his blade tore across my left eye. I yelped in reaction, but I couldn't even process the pain. As if to finish off the scar above it, the strike immediately left me blinded. Shades of red reflected in my good eye as thick blood leaked down my face. I knew from that moment on I'd never be the same.

With one more sweep of my sword, I dealt the fatal blow to the captain of the Spanish ship. Through muscle and bone my blade cut deep, slicing through to his spine as I drove the weapon all the way in and out his back. I watched him slide off the sword and hit the deck as the light left his astonished eyes. It was a quick, clean kill.

But there was nothing clean about the way my soul felt. And for the first time, I didn't care. So I plummeted myself further into the grime as I dropped to my knees beside the captain's lifeless body. And I drove my sword into him again and again, fresh blood spraying over me like raindrops with each strike, mixing with the crimson still running down my face. Something had taken hold that I couldn't manage to stop. And when I thought of being stuck here again in this God-forsaken place and time, I stabbed harder and faster, until the man's midsection was no more than a bloody pulp.

And then I glanced at the *Widow,* where Bellamy stood at the stern, overlooking this disaster on the seas. He'd seen everything. He'd seen the trident and Katrina disappearing and my rampage. It was more than apparent by the solemn but baffled expression he wore as his ship positioned itself to sail away.

He glanced at the dead captain, and then at me, before tipping his head my way. It seemed a nod of respect, and some kind of brotherly reassurance. And it was all I had left to cling to try to regain some sense of myself. This Bellamy would never understand exactly what just unfolded. But he would never forget it either.

When I stepped back, scarlet soaking through my tunic in blooming stains, the ship was silent. Those few who remained of this crew looked at me in disbelief, their eyes wide and weapons raised, but unmoving, not daring to approach this panting, half-blind, blood-soaked maniac standing over their mutilated captain.

"Here's your captain!" I shouted to the crew. "And how will you lot return to your king, or your governor, commodore, or whichever bastard it is you blindly obey, and bold-faced explain that you couldn't defend him or his ship?"

The men grumbled and whispered inaudible muttering to each other. I continued, my hand on the hilt of my cutlass and my other hand scooping up the captain's hat that had fallen in our duel. "I give you a choice. I drop your captain into the sea, and you follow him, or you stay and sail free under my command, and we share in the spoils evenly—spoils that make your current sailor's pay look like a pittance. What say ye?"

The seamen hesitated for a moment, looking around at the fallen bodies of the other crew members. It was silent for a time, before one man finally stepped forward with a solid "Aye. Ye fight like a devil. I'd be a fool not to sail under a cap'n who can hold his ground like that."

Soon, the rest followed, likely because there were too few of them to do anything to stop it, or because they knew there was nothing better than a sailor's wages waiting for them back home. One by one they pledged their allegiance to me, and no one dared oppose me as I nudged the captain's body off the side of the ship and into his watery grave.

"Then we repair the damage here and set sail," I said, walking the length of the deck to its center. I looked at the mast overhead, up toward the rolled-up sails. They provided a perfectly clear view above of the Spanish flag waving against the afternoon sun.

"You," I pointed to a sailor. "Cut a piece of sailcloth and blacken it with tar." The man scurried off to follow my orders, as I examined the condition of the ship and how it could be modified to better serve its new purpose.

I never wanted to be a pirate. But it was all I had left. The things I wanted and the things I deserved were always at odds. And I deserved this. Who was I to argue that a pirate wasn't as good as any other man? At least we admitted to our depravity instead of hiding it behind politics and blackmail. It was an identity that *wanted* to claim me, no matter how many times I tried to outrun it. And I was tired of running.

I made my way to the captain's quarters, where I studied the table of maps and legends and whatever other documents covered the desk in the middle of the room. With blood-stained hands, I cleared the table, sliding the papers into the floor without concern. A brown leather coin purse on the desk caught my notice, and I quickly emptied its contents. With my knife, I cut out a small piece from the leather and removed the drawstrings to fashion an eye covering. I doused my gashed eye with a splash of liquor from a flask in the room, resisting the need to groan at its bitter sting. I hardly worried about wiping the rest of the blood off me. I'd clean it up better later, when I could think straight.

I leaned on my elbows, catching my breath and clearing my head. A single teardrop managed to sneak its way out before I choked back the rest.

I don't know how long I stayed there, lost in my ponderings, before a knock at the door demanded my attention. It was the sailor from earlier, who'd returned with the tar-blackened flag. I lay the flag flat on the floor and knelt down to paint our ship's Jolly Roger. Using whitewash from the storage hold, I painted the skull, and beneath it I designed two tridents crossing instead of crossbones or swords.

"What's the name of this ship, lad?" I asked the sailor, standing up to examine my work, as though it mattered.

"La *Redenciòn*, sir," the man replied timidly.

"Fitting," I muttered under my breath.

I thanked him with a curt nod. Then I left the quarters and walked back out on deck, noticing the pale red glow against a darkening sky that came just before sunset. Tucking a knife between my teeth, I began my climb up the mast with the newly made flag in hand. And once at the top, where the ocean wind blew fierce, I cut away the Spanish banner and replaced it with my pirate flag.

The task was long finished, but I steadied myself against the foremast as my distorted gaze followed the old flag getting swept away in the wind. It drew my eyes to the horizon, where I looked out at the sea I would now roam. Nameless, damaged, alone, and forgotten by time.

I'm sorry, Katrina.

My only comfort was knowing she wasn't here to see what I'd become. But if damning myself meant saving her, so be it. My only chance to find her again someday existed solely in the care of Noah, and that did little to ease my thoughts...but it was something. I just hoped what I'd given him had made it back with him, and he had the sense to remember what I asked him to do with it.

I'd have to set out to ensure Katrina understood what it all meant by the time it got to her. Somehow, without changing the course of history, I'd have to find a way to bridge my past and her future so that we could find each other again. And with a ship and crew of my own, battered as they may be, I stood a fraction higher of a chance of accomplishing that. I didn't know how long it would take, especially with Thane still out there determined to hunt me down.

But I had all the time in the world.

SEASICK

44

I'd fainted from the effort of burying the trident. Right before the world around me faded to darkness, I remembered hearing Bellamy call my name, followed but the sound of a splash. But then I closed my eyes and drifted.

When I woke up, I was lying in a bed covered by fine silk sheets and blankets. The can lights above me were set just dim enough so that I could see the room's polished, hotel-like interior. To the right of me, light spilled in through the crack in the drawn curtains over the window. I sat up, rubbing my head, and thankful that I was clothed and could feel legs and toes instead of fins. I wore a simple black night chemise that smelled like rose petals. Not my style, but better than being naked.

"I'm so glad you're awake!" McKenzie's melodic voice made me jump. I hadn't even noticed her sitting in the leather armchair in the corner. "We've been taking shifts to sit with you," she said, standing up.

Her tattered 18th century clothing was gone. She looked clean and fresh, dressed it new, modern clothes. I wondered how long I'd been unconscious.

She must have noticed me eyeing her new outfit. "Cordelia's clothes," she said, pointing to herself and me. That explained my interesting attire.

"Are we still on the yacht?" I asked, trying to peek through the slit in the curtains.

"Yes," she nodded, taking a seat on the edge of the bed with me. "It's been two days. Bellamy and the skipper say we should be back to Constantine by tomorrow night." She paused to flip her freshly-washed hair back. "You should see those two going at it. Bellamy has somehow managed to gaslight him into making believe what he saw wasn't real and was just a monster storm and he hallucinated the rest. The crew doesn't seem to know right from left now and they constantly argue about what actually happened. It cracks me up. But they all at least seem to agree that their boss went overboard, so I think we're in the clear."

I tried to smile and embrace the relief that should've come with it. For a minute it even felt real. But I couldn't find the piece of me anymore that knew how to laugh. It was all too fresh. I'd lost Milo. I'd lost myself. I *killed* someone. Did McKenzie know that? She had to know by now.

She continued. "They think you drowned, too. And it's probably best we keep it that way, so you can't come out of here until we get back to Constantine."

Fine with me.

"I...I'm just glad everyone's okay." I stammered.

A softness overtook McKenzie's expression. She reached for my hand. "I know it won't be easy returning to normal for you. But I want you to know I'm here for you, and I'm sorry for all the times I've pushed you into doing things you didn't want to do. You've had enough of that." She glanced down as silence fell between us. I wasn't used to seeing her so gentle, serious, and articulate. It was almost awkward until I finally spoke.

"You saved the world, you know," I said with the best half-grin I could put on. "Only a true badass would've thought to use that flare gun." The proud smile that spread across her lips gave me hope. Hope that maybe at least one of us felt like they'd come out of this better than they went in.

"Yeah," she said, "It was pretty cool. But it doesn't come close to being a rogue mermaid." Her giggle reminded me of bubbles bursting. "Well anyway, I'll go tell the others you're awake." She stood and strode to the door, turning back to add one more thing. "Bellamy's been worried about you."

She closed the door behind her before I could even respond. I would've told her to at least give me a chance to change into something with a little more coverage than this spaghetti strap night dress before facing anyone else, but I supposed everyone had already seen everything I had to offer when they'd pulled me out of the water.

As I waited there, pulling the covers back over me when the outside air became too cold, I noticed the sensation of the thin gold ring around my finger. I spun it around with my thumb, thinking about everything that little ring encompassed, and how it would serve as constant reminder of what I couldn't get back. For a moment—just a still, sweet moment—I was back in the grotto by the waterfall, entangled with him and feeling like we had forever on our side. I blinked and all of that was gone.

Three knocks at the door made me look up. Bellamy poked his head in, his eyes settling on me almost immediately.

"You can come in," I said, resting my head against the headboard so that I was still upright even while resting.

"I told you you were going to get sick jumping in that water, love. I just didn't think it'd be 300 years later," he teased. How are you feeling?" He made his way over to me after leaving the door cracked just an inch.

"I feel okay. Just...tired." I breathed out, glancing over at the closed curtains beside my bed. "I'd like to see the view."

"Of course," Bellamy shuffled over to the curtains and drew them back, letting the room become bathed in bright light. I looked at the shimmering Atlantic Ocean, wondering how I was supposed to just go home and start the semester like nothing ever happened. I didn't know how I could, but I'd figure that out later. Bellamy stood in silence, watching the water, too.

"You know," I said, adjusting my back against the mountain of pillows bracing them, "You should probably be the one resting. I can't imagine it feels too great to be brought back from the dead."

Bellamy turned to me with a smirk. "It's not all that bad. I could barely tell the difference between being resurrected and the morning after a good, long night at the tavern. I've been far more drunk."

"I'm glad to hear it comes so naturally to you," I joked. "But in all seriousness, Bellamy, how are you really?"

He walked with slow steps back over to the side of the bed, sitting down on the mattress beside me. He looked at me, narrowing his eyes as though very focused on his response.

"How am I?" He scratched his jaw, reminding me of a cornered animal. "I woke up with a whole new set of memories that weren't there before. I remember rescuing you, and dancing with you, and fighting alongside you. I thought I was in love with you then, and it angered me so. But I don't know what I feel now. Because everything's different now. For both of us. And now I'm free. There are no curses or enemies holding me back. But I don't have a clue what to do next."

"That's okay," I leaned forward to touch his shoulder. "Neither do I."

He glanced at the ring on my finger. " I can't say I'm sorry enough, Katrina."

A weight dropped in my heart. "Funny, isn't it? We've both lost someone we love because of someone else who should've loved us enough not to take them from us." I watched the sadness cloud Bellamy's eyes, as he surely thought of Serena, and I instantly felt guilty for bringing it up. But I wanted him to know I understood in some way.

The door creaked as someone pushed it open. "Katrina?" A voice came through timid and low.

"Hey, Noah," I said with a weak smile. "I hope you've been entertaining the crew on this yacht with your beatboxing shanties."

At the sight of Bellamy's raised eyebrows and confused expression, I couldn't help but laugh a bit, and Noah chuckled along with me.

"Unfortunately, no one seems up to singing on this ship," he said, coming nearer. "McKenzie said you were awake, and I—uh—just wanted to say that I'm glad you're okay...and thank you. For stopping Cordelia. You literally stopped a disaster."

I shrugged gently. "I couldn't have done any of it without you. Don't think otherwise."

Noah nodded, and then bit his lip as though he was going to tell me something, but then changed his mind. "Okay well, I guess I'm gonna step back out on deck for a bit. Let us know if you need anything. And Bellamy, if you need a place to stay, I know of a place."

Bellamy thanked him and I waved him goodbye as he stepped back out the door, leaving us alone again. We were both quiet for far too long before it became uncomfortable.

"Noah's a good guy. He'll help you figure things out and get settled." I reassured, breaking the silence.

"I had three centuries to get settled." He looked down, a heaviness stirring in his voice. "I don't need to settle. I just need to know why I was brought back."

"Cordelia was just being cruel," I said.

"Exactly." I noticed his neck and jaw tighten. "And that's why I can't just live some mundane existence because she brought me back. I need to be something. I need to have a reason this heart beats again. I can't chase the sea like I once did. It's a different world now. So, what am I here? *Who* am I here?"

"Don't be hard on yourself," I said, wishing I knew how to take my own advice. "You don't have to know it all just yet. But please don't think you were brought back for nothing...because...because I'm glad you're here." I swallowed, hoping my pathetic attempt at encouraging him would have some power. The faint smile that formed across his face was a good enough sign that it did.

"I'll always be here for you, Katrina Delmar." And with that, he stood up and slipped out the door, and I closed my weary eyes to sleep again.

A Soft Farewell

45

KATRINA

When the ship passed through the channel back to the marina in Constantine, I decided to finally come out on deck. I figured no one would notice me slip out as long as I stayed near the backside of the boat. Thankfully, I'd found some clothing in the bottom of Cordelia's dresser that made me feel a little more like myself—a simple long sleeve blouse and a snug pair of dark jeans. I made my way to the back port side, leaning over the railing on both elbows.

The boat nosed its way carefully through a path of tall reeds and dark blue water, and I wondered who was steering. As we neared the marina in the distance, I couldn't help but feel a sense of dread. When I stepped off this boat, it would feel like starting everything over again. I didn't even have my phone anymore, since it'd been lost or destroyed along with everyone else's in our initial shipwreck.

My parents were probably worried sick, I thought. But then I remembered that time hadn't passed here like it had for us. As far as my mom and dad were concerned, they'd just heard from me the day before. At least that was one less thing to worry about. But I wondered how I was supposed to find the motivation and morale to pick my classes back up when they started next week. Most students didn't have to live with the weight of killing their great-grandmother, leaving their boyfriend in the 18th century, accepting that they are part fish, and realizing there is a dark half of them that will always be trying to take over all at the same time. But that's how I would be starting my new year.

Slow footsteps caught my attention from behind. I didn't recognize them, but I didn't bother turning around either. If someone wanted to sneak attack me at this point, let them. But the voice of Noah stilled any intrusive thoughts I might've had about that.

"Um...hey," he uttered, taking a spot beside me at the railing.

"Hey," I replied.

"I'm glad you came out here." He fidgeted with his thumbs as his eyes jumped from me to the deck floor and back. "Because I've been trying to find a chance to give you this before we dock." He held out his hand and lying in his open palm was a well-worn compass. Milo's compass.

"I wanted to give it to you earlier, but it felt kinda weird with Bellamy in the room. But the night before we found the trident, Milo told me to hold onto it and give it to you when the time was right."

I reached forward with slow movement and picked up the compass. I held it in both hands as though it was a precious gemstone that I couldn't let out of my sight. Swallowing down a lump in my throat, I looked up at Noah.

"He must've known what was going to happen. All along. He knew." My words cracked. "He trusted you, you know. That's why he asked you to do it."

"He would've done anything for you," Noah said. "You were the only thing that mattered to him."

I was at a loss for how to reply. But I didn't have to because Noah seemed to understand it when the only words I could mutter out were, "thank you."

"No problem," he said, watching the dock as we approached the port toward the empty spot waiting for us at the Tesoro Del Mar Marina. "Now you should probably go back down to the cabin before anyone notices you. We'll come get you once everyone else is off."

I nodded, looking back over my shoulder to see McKenzie crossing the deck toward the cabin.

"She's probably on her way to tell me the same thing," I chuckled. "Be good to her, Noah." I managed to allow my siren side to jump in just long enough to make my eyes flash blue for added effect. Noah recoiled with a nervous smirk.

"Got it." He grinned with two upward open palms in a gesture of surrender.

Clutching Milo's compass close to my chest, I turned and made my way back to the cabin, making sure to stay unnoticed as everyone else eagerly prepared to disembark.

KATRINA

That night I couldn't sleep. I was back in my dorm and cramping lightly from the onset of a period I felt coming—which was its own relief given what happened back in Nassau and aboard the *Falcon*. But I didn't want to be there in that dorm. I didn't know where I wanted to be. I used to be kept awake by my nightmares. But now it was reality that haunted me. And now it was 4 AM and I was exhausted from my tossing and turning and the thoughts that would never stop.

I yearned for the nights when I would sneak out and meet Milo beneath the stars, running from his unhinged captain and trying to understand the mysteries of my past. How things had changed in just a few months. I clung tightly to the blanket wrapped around me, the same one Milo had given me the first night we met, the compass tucked away in my hand as well.

When I could no longer handle the restlessness, I sat up. In the darkness, I tiptoed quietly out with a handful of paints and brushes. Next, I slipped on my shoes and jacket before closing the dorm's door softly behind me. Through the dim golden lights of the East Wing hall, I made my way onto the sidewalks and out to my car. I breathed in the familiar, homey scent of my old Jeep, grateful for at least one thing that was still the same.

I drove to the old pier, where I once stood so many times waiting for Milo. If only I could call him back with my North Star. Just one more time. What I wouldn't have given to be able to stand on that pier again this night and see him emerge from the foggy water below like before. I knew I couldn't. I knew there was absolutely no way. But I tried anyway.

As I walked through the mist, veiled by its thin white embrace, I opened my mouth and ever so softly, only loud enough for me to hear, I sang, wondering how many women long past waiting for the return of their sailors at sea had felt this same empty anguish.

"Lost out at sea
Do you dream of me?
By the call of the waves
I hear you and seek you
Till again the roaming sea
Brings you back to me."

Walking to the farthest end of the pier, I knelt down. Taking out the paints I'd brought, I spilled them onto the pier's edge, in a small puddle of seawater. The blue and white mixture swirled in a dance of chaos, until my tears began to fall, and I quietly redirected the colors into the pattern in my head. I only needed a few brushstrokes once or twice. But the rest of the shape I formed entirely with my power.

"And here I thought you'd stopped painting North Stars." I looked up with surprise at the sound of Bellamy's voice.

The full moon above gave me just enough light to see him clearly. He was walking toward me, and I quickly wiped my tears before he could get close enough to see them. "And here I thought you'd stopped sneaking up on me in the middle of the night," I teased with a sniff.

"I suppose old habits die hard." His voice was tender, and he sat down next to me, dipping his finger into the star I'd painted. "To be honest, I didn't know you'd be here. But this was the only place I could think of coming for some clarity. I'm not used to...this. To feeling. To resting." He held up his hands and looked at them as though they were foreign objects.

"I'm sure it will take some time," I said softly.

"Time," he repeated. "What a cruel thing it can be."

"Cruel is the right word." I sighed, crossing my legs and adjusting myself to face the water.

In silence we sat, the night tide crashing below us and the sea mist casting a chill over my skin. It was Bellamy who broke the silence.

"The last time we were here was right before you broke our curse. I'm sorry for who I was that night. But you pulled me back from the brink. You made me remember who I was. Thank you for that."

"You're...you're welcome." I pulled my hair over one shoulder, trying to keep it from tangling in the sea breeze.

"I lost myself after Serena's death. She was the first time I'd felt a love for anything other than the sea. A *real* love." He paused with a low chuckle before continuing. "Serena was everything to me. When she died, nothing mattered. I couldn't stop it. I couldn't save her. The only thing in my control was the fate of my father, and I was set on controlling it. But I forgot who I was in the process. And I turned my back on everything I ever once cared about—including someone who was the closest thing I ever had to a brother."

"Milo thought of you as a brother, too. He told me that," I said, reaching over to touch his hand with a reassuring squeeze. "Stay true North. In the end you did that."

Bellamy's eyes brightened, and he tilted his head back, breathing in as though he just had a weight lifted from his shoulders. "He's a better man that I am. But even the best men break when they have nothing left."

His words worried me, and I wondered if he knew something I didn't, but I was too afraid to ask. He'd told me Milo had gotten away and made it out alive of the duel at sea. That was all I could bear to know right now.

"I know this is going to sound ridiculous, but It's almost like I can feel him. Like he's still out there somewhere, somehow, calling to me." I took out the compass from my pocket and held it up, watching the twitching needle find its way as it adjusted to point North. Some stupid part of me wanted to pretend it was showing me the way to Milo, somewhere miles away across all the oceans of the world, transcending the years that separated us.

"Maybe he is," Bellamy said. "He left you his compass."

I lifted the compass close to my face, examining its brushed metal exterior in the pale moonlight. I brushed my thumb along it and flipped it over, studying the delicately carved "H" on the back.

"May I?" Bellamy asked, scooting a bit closer. I placed the compass in his hand and watched him look it over.

"Look here," he turned the compass on its side toward me "The baseplate looks as though someone at one point tried to pry it open."

With my curiosity piqued and a terrifying hope welling up in me, I grabbed my thinnest paintbrush. I pushed its tip against the small bent lip of metal as Bellamy firmly held the compass in place. The back plate popped off to reveal a small empty space within the compass just large enough to hold something like small jewelry or a key. But there was a tiny piece of torn folded parchment instead. I picked it up, my breaths shaking and my stomach twisting in knots in anticipation.

"It just says 'Bastian Drake.'"

"Bastian Drake?" Bellamy repeated, taking the tiny paper from my fingers.

"You know that name?"

Bellamy was quiet for a minute as suspense swelled within me. He seemed to be thinking on his response. "Yes...yes, I know that name. But I'm trying to understand why Milo would've—unless..."

"Unless what?" I gripped his arm, nearly begging him to go on.

"Bastian Drake was a pirate lord who dealt in...oddities...off the coasts of Cuba. Shrunken heads, magical relics, legendary maps and rare treasures of the like. He was one of the few men more powerful than my father on the high seas. That is, until my father monopolized the mermaid trade. And by then, Bastian was willing to pay him anything for a chance at immortality."

"A siren heart." I affirmed through a soft breath.

"Exactly. We brought him one, and he promised us the Crown of the Sea in exchange. But he double crossed us instead and failed to uphold his end of the deal. Milo was there. He knows what kind of things that man has in his possession."

"Crown of the Sea?"

"Rumored to be the crown of a sea goddess, trapped in mortal form until it's returned to her. Drake managed to sink a British ship and stole its cargo. On board he found a chest with the crown."

"How exactly does Milo think this can help me find him?"

"A sea goddess, Katrina. Think of it." A smile flashed across Bellamy's face. "Find her and return her crown and she'll bend the laws of time for you. She'll *have* to help you if you break her binds."

"You say that like it's some easy task. Like all I have to do is put together a jigsaw puzzle. We're talking about finding some mythical sea goddess in a world bigger than I ever could have imagined. Even if I was to get that crown from this Bastian Drake guy, how am I supposed to know where she is?"

"You don't. But Bastian does." Bellamy nudged me. "And who said anything about you doing this alone?"

My eyes widened. "You mean you'd go with me? To Cuba...to track down some immortal pirate lord?"

"Have you not figured me out by now, love?" Bellamy straightened his shoulders. "I live for whatever adventure the sea brings me next. I'm not even supposed to be here. But now that I am, I'm not going to waste it." He put a friendly arm around me, pulling me to him as he spoke with a sly tone that grew livelier by the second, sounding more and more like his usual quick-witted self. He pointed out to the open horizon, where the morning sun had just begun to peek over the ocean. "You see, I know where Bastian is, and Bastian knows where the crown is, so now all you have to do is figure out where the goddess is."

"Solid plan." I shrugged, wrestling with the frightening sense of hope rising within me.

"Aye, isn't it?" He stood up, helping me to my feet after him. By now, a faint orange glow of the sun had broken through the morning clouds, and the fog slowly lifted.

I squeezed the compass in my hand and touched the fresh scar on my face. I knew the quest sounded far-fetched. Maybe even impossible. But that wouldn't keep me from trying. The sea's secrets were as bottomless as its depths. And it had been on my side so far...mostly. Maybe it had another surprise yet waiting to help me out one last time.

"If you really think this is what Milo meant, I'm all in," I said boldly. "I want to see him again, whatever it takes."

Bellamy's eyes narrowed with determination and a hint of mischief as he watched the sunrise.

"Then we'll bring him back, lass."

EVEN OCEANS CAN'T HOLD BACK FATE.

ACROSS
TORN
TIDES

VAL E. LANE

ACROSS TORN TIDES
BOOK 3
VAL E. LANE

Wave Song Publishing

Playlist

Scan the code or click to listen. Each song corresponds to the chapters in order. You can also search for the playlist on Spotify by book title.

1. "heartbeats" by Hanniou

2. "30 purple birds" by why mona

3. "Through Me (The Flood)" by Hozier

4. "Throw Me in the Water" by WILD

5. "Deep Water" by Lyves

6. "Self Sabotage" by Ruelle

7. "In The Stars" by Benson Boone / "WHERE YOU BELONG" by Matt Hansen

8. "Hold On" by Will Church

9. "Amen" by Stereo Jane, James Gillespie

10. "My Mind & Me" by Selena Gomez / "Overthinking" by Zoe Wees

11. "Hurricane" by Josh Alexander

12. "Cómo Cuándo y Dónde" by Sofia Carson

13. "Truth Comes Out" by Willyecho

14. "Secrets" by Jay Denton, Hannah Parrott

15. "Will It Ever be the Same" by Young Summer

16. "Contigo" by Sebastian Yatra / "All Things End" by Hozier

17. "Sígueme y Te Sigo" by Daddy Yankee

18. "Stronger" by Thunderstorm Artis

19. "Look What You Made Me Do" by Taylor Swift / "Upside of Down" by SVRCINA

20. "Be Here For You" by Sam Tinnesz

21. "Ships + Tides" by OneRepublic

22. "Wave After Wave" by Sleeping At Last / "Wasteland" by NEEDTOBREATHE

23. "Follow the Sun" by James Mclean, A. Void

24. "Don't Give Up" by Ursine Vulpine, Annaca

25. "I Feel Like I'm Drowning" by Two Feet

26. "MAYDAY" by Culture Code, Natalie Major

27. "Drown" by HANDS

28. "Wish That You Were Here" by Florence + The Machine

29. "Lost at Sea" by Rob Grant, Lana Del Rey

30. "Unsinkable" by Sail North

31. "Not Gonna Break Me" Jamie N Commons

32. "Can You Hear Me Now?" by Owsey / "Never Been Away" by ABBOTT, 2WEI

33. "Where Do We Go From Here" by Ruelle

34. "Leave Her Johnny" by Sean Dagher, Nils Brown / "Carry on Wayward Son" by Kansas

35. "What's Left of You" by Chord Overstreet

36. "I Don't Wanna Leave Just Yet" by Thomas Day

37. "Daylight" by David Kushner

38. "We Go Down Together" by Dove Cameron, Khalid

39. "Past Life" by Trevor Daniel, Selena Gomez

40. "Get Free" by Lana Del Rey

41. "Brother" by NEEDTOBREATHE

42. "Gracestone" by Phildel

43. "Can You Feel It Coming" by Steelfeather

44. "mirrorball" by Taylor Swift

45. "Way down We Go" by KALEO

46. "Live Like Legends" by Ruelle

47. "Black Water" by The People's Thieves

48. "Ripples" by Davis Naish

49. "Francesca" by Hozier / "Sunlit Grave" by Saint Mesa

50. "The Deep" by Phildel

51. "A Storm Is Coming" by Tommee Profitt, Liv Ash

52. "My Jolly Sailor Bold" by The Hound + The Fox

53. "Never Let Me Go" by Florence + The Machine

54. "Destiny (feat. Krigaré)" by Generdyn, Krigaré

55. "Brother – Acoustic" by Kodaline

56. "Witness the Masterpiece – Orchestral Version'" by Ganyos

57. "Take Me to Church" by Hozier / "Say Yes To Heaven" by Lana Del Rey

58. "If the World Falls to Pieces" by Young Summer

59. "Home Again" by UNSECRET, Aron Wright

Find the pirate lord.

Kill the kraken.

Bring back Milo.

And don't tell your mom you're a mermaid.

KATRINA

"What's that?" I squinted, focusing in on the glimmering fragment drifting ashore on the waves. I didn't wait for Bellamy's answer before I took off running, my bare feet treading the dense sand into the roiling surf.

I nearly stumbled over grasping at the shiny object as seawater swept through my fingers. A piece of glass. It was just a piece of sea glass. I walked back to Bellamy, straining to hide the crushing disappointment on my face.

"Not a clue then?" He asked, probably out of pity. I knew I was being absurdly hopeful. He had to be tired of it by now.

"No," I croaked, swallowing. "Just broken glass. But I *know* I saw that albatross yesterday. He's telling me he's out there." I knew I was delusional. But was I, really? After everything that had happened to me, could it really be so ludicrous to hope a message or letter, or *something* might drift in from the far reaches of wherever Milo was?

Captive to this hopeless optimism, I roamed the shores each morning, looking for whatever remnants the tide had washed in overnight, hoping for anything I could convince myself came from him. When I saw the bird, it only fueled my fantasy.

The semester had begun without me, like a whirlwind whisking past. Isabel's campus resumed its usual bustle, and students had returned to their dorms, readying themselves for classes to start in a few days. But I had withdrawn to give my heart some time to grieve losing Milo. And more importantly because I couldn't afford school getting in the way of rescuing him.

"Are you ready for this voyage?" Bellamy asked, likely trying to pull my attention from this useless piece of glass in my hand.

"Of course, I am. Tomorrow can't come soon enough," I tossed the piece of glass back into the water with all my strength. We'd be setting sail to find the pirate lord who had the

Crown of the sea goddess who could hopefully bring Milo back, and I'd been counting down the hours. "And you're sure you're going to be able to pull off sailing Cordelia's yacht across the Atlantic?"

"Love, did you already forget what you saw me do back in 1720? I think I can handle a ship that doesn't even have sails to manage." Bellamy smirked.

"Just saying, you might be a little rusty," I teased as Bellamy rolled his eyes. I secretly wished we could just fly there. It would be faster. But that wasn't an option for Bellamy. He had no ID, no passport, nothing that would allow him access to board a plane. So, sailing there was the only option. And luckily my deceased mermaid great-grandmother's unused private harbor was the perfect place to snag a ship seaworthy enough for us to do it.

"It'll be fine, Katrina. Clearly, it's not that easy to kill us." He patted me on the back and walked toward the surf with his hands in his pockets. It was strange to finally see him in some fully normal clothes, but he still refused to lose the black jacket.

I took a filling breath of the salty air around me as I watched Bellamy's focus lock onto the seawater. How I wished he would let me know what he was thinking under that aloof exterior. He seemed to keep his thoughts under lock and key ever since the morning at the pier, except for whenever we discussed our plans to get to Cuba and find this Pirate Lord Bastian Drake. But I figured I probably wouldn't be the same after everything he'd been through either. I couldn't say I was doing much better.

"I'm going back to the dorm to get an early start on packing things." I used the silence as an opportunity to excuse myself, leaving out the part about how I wished I could stop by Milo's old loft just to sleep in his bed. But Bellamy was staying there now, so I couldn't.

Bellamy sent a nod my way and then resumed his pensive stare into the ocean. I walked back to my car, thinking about it all over again. I touched my face to feel the scar along my jaw and twisted the silver-blue scale I now wore on a string bracelet I'd made so that if I needed my song, I wouldn't have to be in my siren form to use it. It matched the ring on my finger. My souvenirs from the past, each reminding me of the moment I lost Milo. I wondered where he was, and what he was doing now, and I lived each day in anguish wishing I could know he was safe. I knew we'd do anything to get him back, and morning couldn't come soon enough. But a small part of me—maybe some sinister remnant of my siren side—wouldn't stop asking myself if we could really turn back time and save him.

Part of the Crew

2

KATRINA

I stared at the green call icon on my screen. I just had to bring myself to tap the button...to call my parents like I told them I would last week. I needed to tell them everything was fine and I was ready for my classes to start tomorrow. I couldn't tell them I was headed to the Caribbean tomorrow evening. They'd flip and ask too many questions I couldn't answer. I didn't need them to worry and complicate things even more. If something happened, I'd figure out how to deal with it. I pressed the button and waited while my stomach sank further with each ring.

"Hija, hi!" My dad's voice came through excitedly through the phone, as he always sounded when I called.

"Hi, Dad," I said, forcing a smile that I hoped made me sound more alive than I felt. "I just wanted to call before the semester starts tomorrow and check in."

"Claro, Trina. We know you're busy. So it means a lot when you find time for us," he teased. "How is Milo and your roommate friend...McKinley?"

"McKenzie." I corrected with a weak chuckle. "She's great. She's really hyped for a new year. And Milo he's..." I swallowed the burning lump that suddenly appeared in my throat, "he's better than ever."

"That's so great to hear, Trina. I'm so proud of you. And your artwork is still selling like crazy in the store downtown, yeah?"

"For sure," I shrugged, knowing that part was a lie. I hadn't even checked on those few paintings since before we'd ended up setting sail for Nassau. "Money hasn't been an issue for a while, trust me." That part was true at least. Cordelia's money had been more than enough to keep me afloat, though I wondered what would happen to her resort and the rest of her assets once her death was discovered. But for now, I had more than enough to tie me over for the near future. I'm sure she wouldn't have minded her great-granddaughter borrowing a little extra from the bedroom drawer in her yacht.

"I knew you'd settle in eventually. You're doing it, hija, and I never doubted you would." I could hear the pride welling up in my father's voice. He might be even more proud if he knew I'd saved us all from a global disaster of oceanic proportion, but I was content to let him go on thinking my biggest accomplishment yet was my college scholarship. Even if I was about to risk losing it.

"Your mom wants to say goodnight while I have you," My dad's voice was suddenly cut short by the rustling sound of the phone being passed off. Before I could respond, Mom's voice chimed through like a bell. She sounded healthy, and I still couldn't get over how glad I was for that.

"Hey Trina, sweetie," she greeted. "I hear things are going well. You're all the rage in Ozark. You're all Scott ever talks about around here."

"I'm glad to know he's spreading the word." I laughed. "How are you, Mom?"

"Couldn't be better, honey. I mean that. In fact, I've been thinking." She paused, her words hanging in the air. "I've been thinking about coming down there to visit you soon. It could be a great way for us to finally spend some time together. You could show me your campus and the beach."

My stomach sank. She couldn't come now. No way. I'd be in Cuba in just a few days. And I didn't know when I'd be coming back.

"Yeah, that could be fun. Maybe during spring break sometime. I think that'd be good for us." I really did think it would be a good thing for us to make up for so much lost time together. Just...later.

"The sooner the better. You just let me know."

"I will, Mom. Can't wait," I said, smiling lightly, still feeling a pang of mistrust that I felt guilty for having.

"I'll talk to you soon, honey. Your dad's already wandered off back to the garage probably, so I guess I'll say goodnight for us both. Love you."

"I love you, too, Mom. G'night."

I placed the phone down on my bedside table, ready to sleep. Ironically enough, sleeping was my greatest escape these days. I didn't dream much anymore—or if I did, I didn't remember them. But that was better than living the nightmare I'd found myself in.

I hadn't closed my eyes for five minutes when McKenzie crept in, rapping her fingers lightly against my wall. "Hey, you awake?" She crept into the shadowy room.

"Yeah," I uttered.

"I just came to check on you," she walked closer, "I know classes start tomorrow and I wanted to see how you're holding up."

"I'm good. Just wondering how long it'll be before they notice I'm not attending and kick me out." I forced a weak chuckle, but I don't think my facial expression matched.

"I would do the same thing," McKenzie cooed. "It'll be worth it. You'll find him, Katrina." McKenzie's sweet smile flitted across her face as I leaned forward to hug her. "Which is actually the reason I came to talk to you," she started. I pulled back to look at her while she spoke. "I just can't let myself stay here while you and Bellamy go do this. Not after everything we've been through together. And Noah feels the same. We can't stay behind."

I pinched the bridge of my nose between my eyebrows. "McKenzie, we talked about this. I can't let you give up what you have here at ISA. I can't let you throw away your dreams for this...for me. Milo didn't want us to all make it back home just so you could throw it away helping me look for him."

"You don't understand, Katrina." McKenzie paused with a breath that she held for a moment that felt like forever. "Being here at ISA isn't my dream. Graduating with an art communications degree isn't my life goal. I'm just here because I didn't know what else to do with my life. And trust me, with my family's money, they'll let me reenroll anytime and pick up where I left off, I'm sure of it. And that's just the thing I'm saying. I've always gotten what I wanted, easily, not because of who *I* am, but because of who my mom and dad are. And now I want more. Something their money can't give me. Something I can only give myself. The past month has made me realize what's important. And it's not a degree from some stupid preppy art school. It's the people in my life who matter."

I stared at her in silence, blinking in the dark. I didn't know what to say to any of that. I'd never heard such an eloquent speech come from those perfectly glossed pink lips. And I certainly couldn't believe it was the same roommate who was all too obsessed with dragging me to college parties and ignoring my pleas not to.

"I've never thought of it that way," I said.

"Well now you will. Because I'm coming with you. And so is Noah. And this time, it's on purpose." She grinned mischievously.

"McKenzie—" I tried one more time, futilely, to persuade her otherwise, but she was always one step ahead of me.

"You can't stop me. If you don't let us sail with you, we'll fly there."

"Fine," I sighed, though secretly I was glad I wouldn't have to leave her behind. "But you have to be careful, and if things get weird, you stay back and remember it's mine and Bellamy's fight. I'd never forgive myself if you or Noah got hurt because of me."

McKenzie leaned forward close to my ear with a sly look in her eye. "Yeah, yeah. Technically, you'd never even be in this mess if it wasn't for me taking you to that Halloween party last year, so ya know, it's kinda my problem now, too."

"If that's what you want to tell yourself." I shook my head, but even all the weight I was carrying couldn't hold down the tiny smile that snuck its way across my lips.

With one more hug and a couple more laughs, we told each other goodnight, and McKenzie slipped back out the door to her side of the dorm. She made no effort to muffle the sound of her excitement as she made a phone call I should've seen coming.

"Hey, Noah! All confirmed. Pack your bags because tomorrow we're going to Cuba."

From North to West

3

BELLAMY

This room was too empty. Too cold. Too lonely. But I didn't have the energy to take myself somewhere else. So I sat on the edge of the bed in Milo's old loft, staring at the floor like it would disappear if I blinked. My leg wouldn't stop shaking from the nerves. Was I fucking crazy?

Being alive—truly alive—certainly brought its own emotions to work through, and I couldn't shake the crushing weight of feeling like I didn't quite understand who I was anymore. I wasn't sure I'd felt that in a long time. It was easy, back in the time of my best days, knowing exactly who and what I sailed for. But now, the world was different, and the wonder was gone. And even if I brought Milo back, as I planned to do, where did that leave me? What was I here for?

A broken life without the only person I ever truly loved—Serena. Even when I was finally able to die, she wasn't there waiting for me like I hoped. So where was I supposed to put my faith? Why would I care what mark I left in this world, good or bad? I was just here to do what had to be done.

In a moment of tenderness, I smiled as I remembered her voice, so smooth and sweet. Too sweet as she'd tell me she loved me in that strange, special way of hers.

"I love you 18 times 66. As far as North to West." She'd said one night as we said goodbye.

"That doesn't make sense, love. What does that mean?" I laughed.

"I don't know," she giggled. "Just popped into my head."

So from then on, that became our thing. Eighteen times sixty-six. From North to West. It made about as much sense as her loving me. She was too much of a fearless dreamer for this world. Perhaps that's why she longed so much to be part of mine. If only I hadn't let her. If I had just listened to Milo and stayed out of her world, she might be alive. I killed her, and I hated that I was back here, forced to remember it each day. My father wasn't here to blame anymore. Just me. My smile quickly curved into a scowl.

I raked my fingers across my hair, my head feeling heavy in my hands. I needed to sleep. But instead, I stood up, my eyes burning with the need for rest. My boots echoed along the aluminum stairwell as I walked down to the ground floor of the garage.

Across the darkness of the shop, I made my way outside, where the briny bay water hit my nostrils like a breath of fresh air. I sauntered over to Milo's motorcycle, where it leaned parked and lifeless. When we were cursed, I always thought it was strange that he wasted his time learning to tinker with things like this. It seemed like a waste of effort for someone damned to hell and trapped in a time loop of dying over and over each night. But I guess it paid off for him. Turns out it was me who was the fool in the end. Maybe that's why he loved to toy around with these damn things. Machines and maps couldn't break his heart.

I shook my head, knowing I should get back inside and force myself to sleep. As I stifled a yawn, I felt some weird sense of hope that maybe I shouldn't be so cynical. Right then, I swore to myself that I'd make sure I was brought back with a purpose. I'd take Katrina to Cuba. I'd protect her and find a way to get Milo back. And I'd do everything I could to keep from being the reason another person I cared about lost their life.

This was all I had left.

Rogue Storm

4

KATRINA

Today was the day we left for Cuba. I completed my morning ritual as efficiently as possible. I scurried to pull back my unruly hair into a loose ponytail and slip on my worn sneakers—the ones dried out from saltwater and gritty with sand that I could never quite get rid of completely.

I drove to the marina, but I parked a block over so as to keep suspicions down if there were any. Hustling my way to the docks, I scanned the area for Bellamy. He was knelt over a tie down knot mooring a large yacht to the dock.

"Everything good to go?" I asked, studying the way his deft fingers ran over the rope.

"Good morning to you, too," He scoffed softly.

"I'm sorry," I said, kicking a broken piece of seashell over into the water. "I'm just anxious."

"Don't be." Noah's voice startled me as he appeared from above leaning over the boat's edge. "You got plenty of backup."

I glanced up at him with heavy eyes, but a heart that lifted at the sight. "You didn't have to come, Noah. Milo wouldn't have wanted—"

"Good thing none of us care what Sandy wants. Besides, I'd much rather be doing this than dealing with my pissed-off uncle and his insurance over the 'stolen' motorsailer. Kinda hard to explain how I let that happen."

I rolled my eyes with a playful shift in my stance. "I should know by now that I can't get rid of you and McKenzie."

"You might be able to control water, but you can't control us."

"I wouldn't be so sure about that," Bellamy said. "Remember she's still a siren." He winked at me, but something about his words still bothered some strange space within me. I didn't like remembering my power. It was too dangerous.

"Speaking of McKenzie..." Noah looked around. "Where is she?"

"Still sleeping when I left. I heard at least four of her alarms go off, so I'm sure she was going to get up any minute. She shouldn't be far behind me." I shrugged.

Noah's expression shifted, his dark brows creating inquisitive creases on his forehead. "Last night she swore she'd be here early. I've called her twice already and no answer."

I checked my phone. Nothing from McKenzie, but I had a missed call from Mom. I'd call her back later. "Maybe I should check on her," I said, turning back to face the outskirts of the romantic little town of Constantine. "I'll go back."

With a reassuring nod from both of them, I headed back to my Jeep, the damp air of late morning settling into my skin as the sun's golden heat began to make itself known. I drove back to Isabel, silently hoping McKenzie had changed her mind. I wanted her to go. I really did. But I couldn't forgive myself if something happened to her. And a part of me still couldn't shake the guilty conscience from feeling like she was giving up too much to help me.

With a quick dash to our dorm door, I poked my head in to hear McKenzie talking to someone. She sounded nervous and was speaking even faster than usual, which is pretty hard to do. A voice I didn't expect made me gasp and my stomach dropped as I realized who she was talking to. My mom.

"**M**om?" I stuttered, glancing at McKenzie who looked just as confused as I felt. "What're you doing here?"

My mother turned to me, a strange smoothness in her movements. She smoothed her shoulder-length hair back behind her ears with both hands. "I told you, sweetie, I wanted to come visit you and see this little coastal town of yours."

"B...but that wasn't supposed to be *now*! Did you drive here? Does Dad know you're gone?" My panic came out in a string of questions. I was screaming inside. She couldn't—wouldn't—ruin my plans to rescue Milo. I had to get her back home somehow.

"He knows," she said simply. "He actually decided to visit his family, too, so he's gone away for a few days. It was perfect timing. Your friend here was just showing me around the dorm. These are so nice! It's not often you get your own bedroom in a shared space like this."

I shot McKenzie a look meant to press her for an explanation, but she just shrugged with a wide-eyed panicked gesture. My dad gone to visit family? Why didn't he mention anything about that on the phone? It all seemed too random to believe, but I would've heard from him by now if he really didn't know about Mom being here.

"Yeah, it's really great, Mom. But listen, today is our first day of classes. You really should come back when we're not in school." I touched her shoulder, trying to gently usher her in the direction of the door.

"Now, Katrina, you wouldn't be trying to get rid of me? After I came all this way just to show you how proud of you I am." Something in her words hung in the air a bit too long. An eerie softness that reeked of familiar manipulation. Had she gone back to drinking? No, no, I didn't believe so. It sounded different than when she was drunk. It almost reminded me of...

A rush of icy chill spread through my body as I realized just what was off about the way she spoke. It sounded way too much like Cordelia at the dinner table, or worse—myself when I was under the influence of my siren.

As my heart accelerated, I took a deep breath to calm myself and think through what this meant.

"McKenzie," I looked at my friend, desperate for her to understand. "Do you want to go ahead and get that thing we were talking about earlier? I'll stay here with my mom and we'll catch up later."

My friend nodded with certainty. "No problem."

"Thanks," I muttered as she disappeared out the door, hoping she would think to go find Noah and Bellamy and inform them of the hold up.

"Mom," I said, wondering what she must've said to my dad for him not to mention her traveling here overnight with no questions asked. "You're sure you told Dad you were coming here and he was cool with it?"

My mom reached for my hand. "Of course, Trina. I told him I just couldn't wait to see you any longer. And I told him I wanted to see the ocean. And he was fine with it. Then I suggested he visit his family and he thought it was a great idea."

Probably because he was being controlled in a trance, I thought.

"But you always hated the ocean," I swallowed, choosing my words carefully, trying to get her to confirm the suspicions swirling in my head.

"Hated? Oh no, no...I guess I was a little scared of it, I'll admit, but recently something's changed." She drew in a breath through a blissful smile before continuing. "I just can't stop thinking about it. I even dreamed I was at the beach, just looking out at the ocean and just itching to know what it would feel like to get in. And when my only daughter lives right by the sea, well, I didn't see a reason to wait any longer."

Hearing my mom speaking this way about the beach gave me mental whiplash, and if I didn't know better, I wouldn't have been able to believe it was my mother, Grace Delmar, I was talking to. But I did know better, and I knew that something I'd secretly feared was finally happening. My mother's siren side was awakening.

I didn't know what to do. I was afraid to leave my mom alone in the dorm while I went to sort everything out with McKenzie and the others. Who knew what she'd do? She wasn't herself, and I knew all too much what kind of mischief our siren side could get us into. I might come back to find her standing naked in the middle of the surf for all I knew.

"Come on." I took her hand. "I think that's a great idea. I think we should go visit the beach right now."

"I thought you said you had class?" Mom asked innocently.

"I do...later...sort of. It's fine." I continued dragging us both through the dorm hallway and to my car. I saw Mom's car parked outside, and shook my head, still in disbelief that she'd driven all the way here overnight. McKenzie's car was gone, so I was hopeful that she had already made it to the docks to warn the guys.

I drove us to the marina, silently tickled by the way my mom admired the scenery outside her window like a wonderstruck child. We passed the usual cobblestone streets of old town St. Augustine and Constantine, flanked by the swaying palms waving to greet us. The morning sun glittered along the bay like liquid silver crystals, as a majestic crane spread his wings overhead searching for breakfast in the open water. I wished I could admire it longer, but I knew the gravity of the situation didn't quite warrant us lingering to sightsee.

I didn't know exactly what I planned to tell Mom once we got there. I wasn't sure how I'd explain Bellamy, Noah, and the boat we were so obviously readying to take out on the water. But I hoped maybe Mom was just siren-possessed enough that a rational explanation wasn't necessary.

Making it all up with each passing second, I leapt out of the vehicle when we parked in front of the harbor. I saw my three friends standing by the boat, Bellamy leaning against a taut rope that ran from the dock to the boat's hull. They whipped their gazes around at me and my mother in unison, and I could tell McKenzie had already gotten the news out.

"What's all this?" Mom asked. "Shouldn't you all be going to class?"

"Bellamy and Noah aren't students." I rushed to explain, but then I realized that made the situation seem even more suspicious.

"Right," McKenzie chimed, stepping over to us defensively. "They're our teachers."

"They are?" I sputtered, but then quickly composed myself. "I mean—they are. Yes."

"Professor...Bell. He teaches our Cultural Arts class. And Noah is his TA." McKenzie lied proudly. She gestured to the two. Bellamy stood looking stunned, and Noah appeared hesitant for a moment, but then I saw his face muscles relax.

"Yeah...I mean yes." He nodded with a grunt to clear his throat. "We're just readying everything for this semester's cross-cultural trip."

"Oh?" My mom raised an eyebrow, but she still seemed so out of it that I hoped it just might've somehow been making sense to her. "I don't think you mentioned this. How exciting." She spoke clearly, but with a dullness in her voice. I noticed her gaze was focused on the lapping water below. It was calling her.

"Yes, I'm sorry I didn't tell you and Dad. Really, it was sort of a last-minute decision." My eyes nervously darted to McKenzie, who urged me to continue making up something. "It was a sudden opportunity that I just couldn't turn down. The option to study in Cuba for a few weeks. We can get extra credits for foreign language and some other art stuff."

My mom nodded. "I don't blame you, sweetie..." She stepped closer to Bellamy, who was still reeling from being introduced as a professor. "This must be your first time leading the class trip? You're so young."

"I'm old enough," Bellamy said coolly. I stifled a laugh that threatened to bubble up at any moment, knowing Bellamy's true age. But I quickly regained my composure. My mom suddenly seemed to have snapped back to a mostly normal version of herself as well. Just for a moment.

"Then you don't mean to tell me you're taking a group of students across the ocean by boat? Do they just let people sail into Cuba?"

Bellamy's face drained of color, and he glanced to either side with a tilt of his jaw as if thinking of some response on the spot. Mom was right. We'd done the research. We wouldn't technically be allowed to make port in Cuba in a private yacht. Only commercial cruise ships could sail in legally. But since when did legality matter when a pirate was our captain?

"I assure you, Miss Delmar," Bellamy said suddenly, his crisp, sure gaze meeting mine. "I have it under control. This is a very exclusive opportunity for students."

"Right, in fact, do you think you could show me that...thing...again with all the information about the trip...Professor? Taking a step forward, I urged Bellamy to respond in some way that would get us closer to speak with each other more privately. I didn't expect Bellamy to play the part so well, but I guess it made sense. He'd always been the one snooping around in the city and on campus during his nights as a ghost. He was a pro at blending in by now.

"Certainly. It's with my things. Come here and I'll see if I can find it for you." He motioned for me to come closer. I told Mom to wait with McKenzie for just a moment. She seemed too fixated on the water to notice otherwise.

With our backs to McKenzie and my mom as we stepped aside and pretended to search a lockbox by the boat, my whispers erupted frantically. "What are we gonna do? I don't know how to get rid of her! She's in siren mode and came here because she wanted to be near the water."

"So, just take her with us," Bellamy shrugged.

"What!?" I nearly screamed through my hoarse low tone.

"Your mom is part siren. She's going to figure that out one way or another. The safest way for that to happen is for you to be with her through it."

"Okay but she's still my mom. I can't just take her on an expedition across the ocean when I'm supposed to be in school without her asking questions," I grumbled

"I never said we keep her conscious through it." Bellamy glanced over his shoulder with confidence. "I've done it plenty of times."

"Oh my gosh, no!" I pressed a hand to my face and dragged it downward. "You can't be serious. We can't just—" I paused at a sudden wide-eyed expression on Bellamy's face that looked like an idea had just sprung into his head. "What are you thinking?".

"Can you use your siren song on her?" The corners of his lips curled ever so slightly. "To make her sleep through it or forget the trip altogether?"

I swallowed, thinking about the idea before I replied. "I...I don't know if my song works on another siren. Cordelia couldn't really control me like everyone else, but she did make me feel sort of...hypnotized...but that was before I knew how to use my own siren powers." My thoughts flickered back to dinner with Cordelia in her resort. She'd sung the lullaby to me, and some strange wave of entrancement was certainly threatening to break its way through then. But by the time she sang to Milo and me on Valdez's ship, I was immune. So, I wondered if my mom was still too underdeveloped as a siren to resist another's song.

"One way to find out, love" Bellamy uttered.

"But...I don't want to control people. Especially not my own mom. It feels so...wrong." My words escaped in a sigh. The thought of this task weighed heavy on my conscience. I didn't want to be another Cordelia. "I don't want to have power over others. I *shouldn't*."

"But you do," Bellamy stated firmly. "And it's saved our asses more times than I'd like to admit. And right now, your reluctance to use that power might be the only thing that stands between you and getting Milo back."

I looked down beneath dark lashes, then back towards my mom by the edge of the dock, who was muttering something to a nervous-looking McKenzie. "You're right," I said. "I hate it, but I have to try."

Bellamy reassured me with a solid nod and a flick of those ice-blue eyes. "Good lass. Then let's get on with it."

"I'll try." I breathed in, pulling humid, briny air into my lungs. "But no promises it's going to work."

We both turned around, pretending to walk back as casually as possible, as if we hadn't just discussed the best method for putting my mom into an unconscious trance. As we neared her and McKenzie, I noticed my mom leaning down, fingers outstretched toward the water, and my feet began to race back faster. "Mom!" I yelled. She couldn't touch the water. I couldn't let her feed that hungry siren in the slightest. And I had to put our plan into motion quickly, before my mom discovered a new side of herself that might just make her able to resist it.

"**M**om!" I shouted once more, getting her attention. She glanced up, yanking her hand from the water and backing up from the edge.

Mom seemed to shake herself loose from the grip in which her siren side held her. I remembered all too well what it felt like to fade in and out like that, making decisions in a fog, only to regain my senses and question what I was doing. It was mental anguish, like a swirling cyclone of confusion and chaos. So I pitied Mom, knowing what she was experiencing. It had to be somewhat scary for her.

As the faraway look in her eye dwindled, I placed myself near her, rubbing the siren scale around my wrist with my thumb. "I know you wanted to see the ocean, but this old dock on the bay is nothing compared to the beaches here. You'll see," I said, stepping closer to her so that I was speaking softly enough for just her to hear "Do you remember that lullaby you used to hum to me when I was a kid? Did you know it's actually about the ocean?"

"Really? What a coincidence. I never knew there were words...." Mom's voice trickled off with a hint of suspicion.

"Yeah, it's actually a beautiful song. Want me to teach you?" With the last question, I felt my own siren flicker within. She relished at the thought of putting my mom under her spell, of controlling someone else entirely. And I felt a riling in my stomach that made me queasy. I had to stop taking my time before my conscience talked me out of it. I hoped my scale bracelet would help channel enough magic on its own to keep an appearance from my alter ego from taking place.

"Sure, Katrina," Mom chuckled uncomfortably, clearly aware that my question was somewhat out of place.

I opened my mouth to sing. The scale glowed faintly, but I still felt the shift in my mind and body; the siren within taking the reins of my inner being. Human Katrina faded into the background as her alter took charge. I wondered if my eyes were shining vivid blue yet, but by the way my mom tilted her head and pressed her brows, I knew some kind of change must've been visible.

Ignoring my friends watching a few yards away, I carefully formed each syllable and line, my voice rising and falling melodically in a way even I had never stopped to fully listen to before. It was hauntingly beautiful, like no earthly voice could compare. The tone of my voice rang with eerie hints of Cordelia, but my song was lighter; a bit more delicate than hers. Certainly a siren song all my own.

I focused my energy on Mom, each tone and lyric carrying a spritz of power that washed over her. As I sang, the words faded, and it was just my melody driving her on. I told her to step onto the boat, and she clumsily did so. Bellamy and Noah rushed to her to help her over the bobbing hull. Once she was on board, I commanded her to sleep deeply.

At first, she lingered, standing on the boat, mindless and entranced, and for a moment I feared I'd either lost my hold on her or that she was resistant. But a few seconds later her eyelids fluttered and she lost her balance, collapsing into the ready arms of Noah and Bellamy. I stopped singing.

"Get her to a bed," I ordered, more harshly than I meant to. I watched as they carried her into the cabin, disappearing down the small flight of steps where they'd take her to one of the two sleeping suites.

I had to take a minute to shake myself free of the siren in command of my own mind. I didn't like to let her have control for long, but I'd at least learned how to reel her in before she got too far—at least for now. When I looked at McKenzie, who watched on with a pale, concerned demeanor, I felt sick again.

"Was it that bad?" I winced, tucking my neck into my shoulders.

"No, no, not at all," McKenzie muttered, looking around as if trying to relax her expression. "It's just always kind of freaky to watch your best friend mind control people. I'm not gonna lie, it's kinda scary."

"It's not just scary for you," I mumbled. "I didn't know what else to do." I shuffled my feet nervously and looked down. "Come on, let's go check on her."

I made my way into the yacht's interior, checking the smallest bedroom suite on board. It was simple, with a twin-sized bed pressed to the back wall, an interior wall to the right and a window with an outside view of the sea on the left. My mom rested peacefully on the mattress, her soft breaths rising and falling like the lulling motion of the boat.

"How do we know she's gonna stay like that the entire trip?" Noah asked softly, as if trying not to wake her.

"I don't," I admitted, remembering when I lost my grip on the crewman on Cordelia's boat. "I guess I'll have to come in here every few hours and sing to her again, just to make sure she stays put under."

"And she's not going to remember any of this when she wakes up?" McKenzie raised an eyebrow.

"I can't say for sure, but back in Nassau when Milo was controlled by Cordelia—she made him attack me—he didn't remember any of it when he came to, so that's my anecdotal guess."

"Well, I *can* say for sure." I wasn't expecting Bellamy to chime in, but I was glad he offered his input. "When Cordelia would control enemy crews and captains for my father, they never remembered a thing. Quite the perk."

"Well, that's good, I guess," I sighed.

Bellamy hesitated, parting his lips to speak and then glancing down at my mother, who roused a bit in her sleep, turning her head in a way that made us all freeze in our spots. "Just keep her under and we shouldn't have any problems." Bellamy shrugged with a whisper. He turned to leave the suite, and we followed him out before locking the door behind us.

Disappointment made me shudder as the siren in me swelled with pride at the sight of putting my mother to sleep. The way her will relentlessly grappled with mine was wearing me down. She was getting hard to control.

LILIES AND COCONUT

7

BELLAMY

I made my way across the deck, striding toward the helm where I planted myself. With my back to Katrina and her friends, I gave the ship's wheel a firm tug. "Well looks like we're all set, crew. Any more last-minute interruptions I should know about?"

The trio stared at me, glancing back and forth between me and each other.

"I'll take the silence as a no," I lashed. "Then make sure your things are on board. Everything you need for a few days. Because once we're out there, we're not turning around."

"We should already be gone." Katrina stepped forward. "Let's go."

I smirked at the signature Katrina bossiness I'd come to know and love. She was right though. We needed to get going. Every passing hour in our time was who-knew-how-long in Milo's time.

The three scattered across the deck, scraping their belongings together and bringing them in from off the deck. I looked out at the sea ahead. Of course, this voyage would be different from those of my glory days as captain of a fleet ship. There were no canvas sails or wooden wheels. No twinge of ropes, scuffle of boots on the deck, or yelling overhead from the crow's nest. But I couldn't help but feel that something was still the same. That feel of the rush of the sea air on my face as the ship surged forward, mixed with the ever-constant roar of the ocean parting as we sliced through the water. There was no place like it. The sea was still my heart's desire, even though she'd broken it so many times. What was one more?

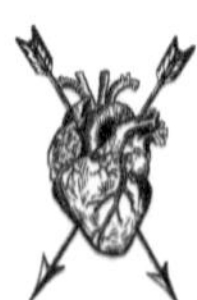

We'd been out on course for a few hours when Katrina appeared by my side at the helm. By the way she didn't say a word, I knew she wanted to talk.

"How's your mom?" I asked, keeping my gaze focused ahead at the hypnotizing blanket of blackish blue.

"She's still asleep," Katrina sighed. "I've had to sing to her twice now to keep her out."

"At least it's working."

"Yeah, for now," Katrina tossed her hands out in front of her expressively. "But what about when we get there? What am I supposed to do with her then? Do we have a plan?"

I leaned forward, propping my elbows over the helm as I stretched my shoulders. "One thing you'll learn soon enough, love, is that the plan always sorts itself out at the right time."

Katrina pressed her lips together. I didn't think she liked my answer.

"Don't worry," I reassured with a smile. "You'll see what I mean. The sea doesn't take kindly to plans. If she hears you trying to make them, more often than not she'll rearrange them for you."

"I thought you weren't superstitious." Katrina raised an eyebrow.

"I'm not. Just experienced." When she didn't respond, I glanced her way, just in time to see her watching the sky on the horizon, probably looking for that damn bird again.

The ocean certainly wasn't finished with her surprises. She never was. She'd given me the best and the worst of them. A life of adventure, a brotherhood on the sea, a curse worth dying to end, and a love lost in the same place I found it. Serena.

I ached to go back to that time, our first night together, like we'd known each other all our lives. I'd been out walking the shoreline, wasting another night in hell. I saw a girl, and I watched her diving from a distance. When she never surfaced, I ran to check on her. She came up for air effortlessly, easing my fears. But then she saw me, smiled and said hello. I wanted to run, because a ghost shouldn't be seen, but I was held prisoner by her beauty. And I'd been so deprived of a woman's touch for so long...

She told me to stay there on the shore and wait for her, and then walked out of the water to meet me. She kissed me, before I even knew her name. And then we fell to the sand, where I sat as she climbed onto me. With her legs locked around my sides, she tugged at my pants, wriggling them down just enough to free me. I was terrified and unsure, not even knowing if I was capable of feeling this fleshly pleasure in my damned state. But I pulled her tiny swimsuit down around her hips, my fingertips yearning to feel the heat of her skin. I couldn't, but I went on anyway. And there on that empty shore, astride me, she took me in her beautiful hands and made me fall apart, as if she'd known me all my life.

She went on teasing me with touches I would've given anything to fully experience. I groaned with both desire and frustration, but the faintest sensation alone was enough to keep me going. I knew I shouldn't have been doing this here with this mortal girl who had no idea I was dead. But I couldn't bring myself to stop her when she guided me right into her. It was like gulping from a fountain for a thirst I couldn't quench. Still, I let myself go, my only option to imagine the tightness and warmth as she moved. I kissed up and down her neck anyway, though I couldn't taste her sweat. I teased her through her swimsuit top, though I could only conjure up guesses in my mind of the sensation of her arousal. I couldn't feel any of it on my body, but I could feel the pain of wanting her so badly it hurt. And even that was enough to make me lose myself, coming undone beneath her while she sat with a satisfied smirk and bewitching look in her eyes that lured me in like the fresh scent of lilies and coconut.

She kissed me, her full lips toying with mine, as though to say thank you for those few fleeting moments of pleasure. Little did she know despite my body's physical reaction, I hadn't felt any of it beyond the reaches of my mind. If she'd known how my curse hindered me, would she have come to me like that? We were just two strangers on the beach, driven by some primal mutual instinct.

"What's your name?" I asked her, once I could catch my breath.

"Serena." She cooed, her own breaths still shaky. I can't forget the first time I heard her say her name. It fell on my ears like heaven. I thought we'd part ways and I'd never see her again. I told her goodbye, because I had to keep from hurting her. But I couldn't stay away, and I found her the next night. And the next...

"It always looks the same from up here." Katrina sighed, whisking me right out of my daydream. "But underneath it's so different, always changing, deep then shallow, vibrant then dark."

"It's not the view up here that makes it so special," I said. "It's the hope of what's just over the horizon."

She smiled at me with a soft nod before turning to go as if she'd grown bored. Not that I could blame her. We'd already been at sea for hours and there wasn't much to do besides mull over the reality of where we were headed and what that might mean. I listened as her footsteps faded on the deck floor, and I couldn't help but chuckle when I heard them coming right back seconds later.

"So... what's over the horizon then?" she chimed. "Do you know where this Bastian guy is? I mean I know he's in Cuba, but do we have a plan for *exactly* where we're going?"

"Sure do," I smirked. "La Isla. An old pirate haven about 60 miles from the mainland. It's had a collection of names over the years, but I think your most recent maps would show it as Isla de la Juventud."

"Isle of Youth," Katrina muttered under her breath. I watched her searching the place on her phone. I could tell she'd found it when she glanced up with a worried expression. "Doesn't look like there's much of anything there...just forest."

"Good to know it hasn't changed," I looked over her shoulder. "Should be easy to dig up old Drake's hideout."

"And what if he's not very welcoming?" Katrina leaned on the rail leading down the steps of the cockpit, her voice sly.

I released the wheel from my grasp, turning to face her. I placed both my hands on her shoulders and locked eyes with her. "If I didn't know any better, I'd think you don't trust me," I said lowly with a grin.

Katrina glanced down, her eyes falling to the space between our feet. "It's not that," She muttered, "I trust you. I'm just...it's just that...what if this doesn't work?"

I pulled in a breath, prepping my answer to keep from saying something sarcastic. "Well...I can't promise you that it will. And you're right that Bastian may or may not be a bit of a dick to deal with. But between the four of us, I think we stand a pretty good chance. Especially when one of us can control water and technically minds."

Katrina shifted uncomfortably at that last part. I knew she didn't like to embrace her power, but if we were going to do this, she needed to loosen up about using her siren song. Her mom was excellent practice, and for that, I was glad she'd shown up unannounced. Katrina would have to realize sooner or later it was our best shot.

"All I'm saying is, we'll figure it out, love." I pulled my hands back, but not before patting her on the cheek softly.

"I know we will," she said. "It's just that I'm still not over what happened with Cordelia." She glanced down at her hands, as though disgusted by them. "And I just hope I never have to do it again."

I nodded in understanding. "Fair enough, lass. I felt the same way after the first time I had to cut down a man—one of my father's hostages he picked up after looting a ship. He made me do it as a rite of passage. I was sick to my stomach, but I got over it." I knew that she'd kill again if she had to if it would bring Milo back. I had no doubt of it. Because we were strangely alike in some twisted way. And if it meant there was even the smallest chance I could find Serena again, I would kill without a second thought. So why wouldn't she do the same?

As Katrina turned away, I asked her if she could bring me something to snack on from the kitchen. As I waited for her to return, I refocused on the horizon in front of me. The ship's white bow nosing through the open blue, I couldn't help but wonder how Milo fared, stuck back in 1720. I thought back to how I saw him that day, after he realized he'd been left behind. He was feral; unhinged, and even still 300 years later I could vividly hear his screams of rage as he stabbed that enemy captain again and again and again. I'd never seen a man so broken. Except, I guess, when I'd been that man, too. When my father killed Serena...

I kicked the memory out of my head. I had to stop thinking. About everything. About anything. About Milo, Katrina, and even Serena. Every thought somehow redirected to her and what I'd lost. And I was beginning to feel like I might not have room for all of it at once.

SAILORS AND SWINDLERS

8

MILO

The chatter of the tavern nearly drowned out my own thoughts. But not enough. I'd just wanted one night unshackled from the weight in my mind. One night without bloodshed at the hands of my crew. One night to be free of the obligation of caring. But I couldn't seem to get drunk enough to escape the mental marathon my mind never seemed to stop running, replaying over and over each time I'd dashed my cutlass across another man's throat. There were too many to count.

"One more round, mate." I tapped my ale mug on the counter. I couldn't wait around in this cesspool forever. He had to show up sooner or later. But time was the one thing I didn't like wasting. Not that my men seemed to mind. Tossing themselves at the rum and women, they would've been content to spend the whole of summer here. But I wasn't here for reveling and indulgence.

As I brought the freshly filled mug to my lips, I felt the coarse bristle of stubble that I hadn't bothered to groom in the months I'd been sailing these god-forsaken seas. Ten months building the trust of a crew I'd gained through force and fear. Ten months plundering ships and killing those that fought back. All leading to this moment to find a myth of a man who may not even have what I was looking for.

The cloaked figure in the corner may have assumed I didn't notice him, but I'd been watching him all night. If not for the small stature I might've thought he was the one I was looking for, but I knew Bastian better than that. He was a formidable figure with notable height. At least, that's what he looked like by the time I met him some years later in Valdez's crew the first time around. But that hadn't happened yet.

"Aye, you'd best cough up what you owe, ya cockless bastard!" A voice grated like cement across my ears, above all the noise and music. I turned to see the commotion.

"I'll not pay ye a cent more, you swindlin' dog!" I was ashamed to admit I knew that voice right away. I decided not to interfere. I'd leave Finlay to sort this one out on his own...again.

"Me? The swindling dog?" A man across the table from Finlay roared. "It's ye who keep coming to gamble without the means to take a loss!" He stood up, fists raised. "Looks like I'll be needing to teach ye what happens when you cheat one too many times at my table!"

I rolled my eyes. The last thing I needed was my men involved in some brawl that could mark us bad for business. I stood up, taking reluctant heavy steps to the gamblers' table.

"What's all this?" I asked, my gaze falling on Finlay.

"Cap'n," he stuttered, "He's lying. I ain't cheatin' here. He's the one trying to swindle me right from under our arses."

"Doesn't matter. You know all too well gambling's against the code. Especially when you're using the crew's funds to dig you out of the trouble you keep finding yourself in." I said sternly, looking over at the man in question. "What does he owe you?"

"Seventeen reales," he spat.

With a groan, I admonished Finlay. "If this happens again, I'm leaving you at the next port in whatever plight you find yourself." I had half the mind to leave him here in this pit in Madagascar. He wouldn't last a week on his own.

I reached into my concealed coin purse, noticing the cloaked figure still observing me as I counted out the amount. I slammed the money down in front of the man. "Here's what you want. Now find someone else to join your wagers."

The man scooped the money into his dirty hands. Looking up at me through bushy brows, spat on the floor in my direction.

"Is there a problem, lad?" I raised an eyebrow.

"Who you calling lad? You look far younger than me. And you're in my way." He did his best to bulk up and meet me at eye level. I stood aside to let him pass, refusing to say another word to him. He was too drunk to reason with, and I didn't want to waste my time. But just as he started to walk past me, he instead whipped around towards a nervous Finlay and sucker punched him across the cheek so hard that Finlay fell off his stool.

"Hey!" I shouted, my fingers balling up into fists. "You've been paid, bastard!"

"That I have, ya damned dog," the man sputtered. "But the principal is that he's a cheat, and I don't let cheaters get away without a proper lesson in courtesy."

"You'll leave my crew out of your shit-flinging tantrums when their debt has been settled."

"Maybe their captain is the one here who needs a lesson in manners." He grumbled, stomping toward me. I didn't want to cause a scene, but my patience was wearing thinner by the second. He threw a punch. I dodged him with a backward step, but he lunged at me again. This time, I propelled myself forward and swung back.

I struck his jaw, and he staggered into the table before finding his footing and lunging at me once more. I grappled him as we both tumbled to the creaking wooden floor below. He punched. I punched back. In a whirlwind of fists and slurred insults, the tavern soon lit up with jeers and shouts from all the sailors and swindlers flocking to the commotion.

I found my footing, standing just as he latched onto my ankle and tried to force me back to the floor. On the way down, I managed to grab hold of a metal tankard on the counter and slam it across his face. The tavern owner shouted at us and tossed a wooden stool our way, temporarily breaking up the brawl as it splintered into pieces over our bodies. But I managed to sneak in one last punch.

The man stayed down, groaning in pain as I eased myself back up. I rolled my shoulders to shake off the soreness in my knuckles and face, and without a word, made my way to the door, ignoring the riled men's hearty chuckles as they settled back into their seats. I was done with this foolishness for the night. I'd find Bastian another time.

It was raining. A sudden storm must've rolled in on the coast in the last two hours I'd been in there. As I stepped down the wooden planks for steps, my boots sunk deep into the thick mixture of wet sand and mud. I welcomed the calming sound of low thunder and rain patters as opposed to the never-ending commotion of the tavern.

But when I heard the door open behind me and the golden glow of light illuminated the ground below my shadow, I didn't hesitate to look back. The gambler I'd just fought came bounding out, desperate to continue our fistfight. He flung himself onto me, and I gripped both his arms as he came down, dragging him down to the mud. The rain beat down as we sloshed in the mire, adding to the challenge that much more. We rolled a few times, my grip slipping in the wet sand as we wrestled with strength closely matched. I was tired, and I knew I could reach for the hidden dagger at my side and end it all quickly, but I fought the urge to do that a bit longer as I pinned him down with my knees. But in a split second, my left knee slipped, giving him just enough room to kick my stomach and knock me off him in a sudden motion. He reached over to hit me. I rolled out of the way, but he kept swinging.

I reached for the knife in my belt, more than ready to end this. Looks like we'd be marked bad for business after all. "One more move and you'll find this blade through your eye."

"You don't fight fair," he growled through his teeth.

"I'm a pirate," I hissed and then swung the knife at his face. But before my blade struck him, he went still, a sudden glazed look veiling his eyes. He swayed weakly, disoriented, and plopped forward like a bag of wet sand. Confused, I watched him roll his face into the mud, still breathing, but unconscious.

"Don't do some shite you'll regret later." A strange voice came from above me as a skinny pale hand reached down. I refused the help and steadied myself to my feet. The cloaked figure from the tavern stood facing me, not quite reaching my shoulder, with scarlet hair peeking out from each side of the hood. I was still feeling the sway of my own intoxication and the last few jabs, so I didn't trust my own senses when I heard the voice again. It was shrill and that of a woman.

"Yer welcome. Better than what you were about to do," she uttered in her heavy Irish accent, turning to leave. "Though he won't be out fer long."

"Wait," I stammered. "Who are you? How did you do that?"

The figure stopped and turned back to me. "Bit of nature and a good aim." She quickly flashed a flute-like tool in her hand.

"You shot him with a poison dart?"

"Aye, is that against your code, sailor? Or would ya rather keep smackin' each other senseless in the mud?" She tossed her head, shaking the hood loose from over her head to reveal ivory skin, peppered with flecks from the sun, framed by shoulder-length blood-red hair.

Her brashness surprised me, as well as intrigued me, so I stepped forward with piqued curiosity to follow her. "No...poison is...fair." I said, still shaking myself sober. "But why did you help me?"

"Cause Ranson's a feckin' idiot." She smiled, gesturing to the unconscious man at our feet. "And ya seem different from the rest of the scallywags wastin' air in that tavern. I been watchin' ya the past couple o' nights."

"I've noticed."

"Good," she repeated, circling me with curious eyes and a scoff. "Not bad for a man with one good eye. From a decent cap'n I'd expect nothin' less."

I tensed at the mention of my damaged eye. By now it had healed up enough to look almost normal, except for an unsightly scar. A scar that'd left me half-blind.

"What's a lass like you doing in a place like this anyway? You must have a reason to be lurking in that corner."

"Same as you, sailor," she nodded smugly with a stubborn grin. "I been waitin' round fer someone. And I think I've finally found him."

A CAP'N WORTH HIS SALT

9

The girl stepped toward me, looking over her shoulder as she returned the cloak back over her head. "I need a cap'n," she said confidently.

"What for?" I asked.

She glanced around once more, the rain slowly lifting so that I could see her features more easily as the moonlight broke out from behind the crowds. Her eyes peered out from her hood, a striking green that nearly seemed to glow in the darkness. "What reason would I be lookin' for a cap'n than to join his crew?"

I shifted my shoulders, a bit taken aback by her unusual request. "Do you know what you're getting into? A pirate crew is no place for..."

"Fer who...a woman?" She spat. "Yeah, I don't need the likes of you remindin' me. I was marooned by my last crew when they discovered I don't quite have the same riggin' between my legs as them. Though no doubt I was as good as any of 'em. They never questioned my capability when I was swabbin' the deck with my chest bound and my hair tucked up under my hat. But I made the fool's mistake of tryna' bathe one night and they seen me fer all I was worth, they did."

I thought of my brief time sneaking around Nassau undercover. How difficult it must have been for her to portray this separate identity aboard a ship of stinking, rugged men, if it was true. I decided to press her. "And what makes you think I would let you aboard my ship?" I crossed my arms.

"Aye, there's the key, sailor. I been staking out in this tavern a few weeks now waitin' for a cap'n worth his salt to show himself. A cap'n who might'nt be afraid of lettin' a female on his ship. A cap'n less concerned with comparing the size of his dick and more with the wellbeing of his crew."

"And you think I'm that captain?" I raised an eyebrow.

"I dunnae. Are ye?" I glanced down at a light pressure just below my ribcage. She held a small dagger to my core. I grinned with a rumble of a chuckle and swiped the knife from her grip.

"Fair enough," I said, putting the knife back in her hand. "You've proved you can be useful. But I must warn you, I'm not just scouring the seas for wealth and gain as you might think. I'm hunting something...and maybe someone."

"Don't entice me further." She twirled her knife with a smirk. "So will ya be lettin' me aboard or not, Cap'n Harrington?"

I took pause at the mention of my name. I knew she would've heard it by now at the tavern, but it still took me by surprise. The leftover rain dripped from treetops in a rhythmic pattern all around, like the ticking of a clock waiting for me to make a decision. "What's your name and why is it you want so desperately to be part of a crew?"

"You only get one of those questions answered fer now." Her eyes bore into me as her brow hardened. "It's Clara. Clara Reid."

I drew in a breath, unsure of whether letting this flaming Irish girl join my crew was wise. But she *had* helped me during the brawl. And I was short a couple of deckhands since our last looting. She spoke with confidence unmatched in most men I'd recruited. Stuffing away my initial hesitation, I tossed a firm nod toward her. "Fine. Welcome aboard the *Falcon*, Clara Reid."

RAISE THE TOPSAILS

10

KATRINA

We'd been on the water a while, with fair weather on our side for most of it. One small storm had detoured us, but it didn't keep us from making good time. Every few hours I would check on Mom, feeling the pang of guilt hammering at me every time I looked at her. So when she inevitably woke up, while I sat beside her, I couldn't bring myself to put her back under.

Her eyes fluttered open. I watched her take in her surroundings, slowly and unsure as I expected anyone to be in this situation. I braced myself, running every possible explanation I could offer through my head. What would I tell her when she demanded answers? There was no way I could keep up this façade about a school cross cultural trip. Schools didn't take trips on yachts. And they certainly didn't kidnap students' mothers.

"Wh—where am I?" Mom asked weakly.

I thought fast, glancing around the room, as I fought to hide my own panic. "You're—you're on a boat, with me, sailing for an island off the coast of Cuba." The truth spilled out, and I chastised myself for being such a bad liar that I couldn't even come up with something remotely better than that.

"The school trip?" She sat up, rubbing her head and eyes.

"It's not actually a school trip. It's just a trip. It's hard to explain," I said, "But you have to believe me when I say this is something I have to do. And I couldn't leave you behind." I paused, fiddling with the thin ring on my finger as I fought back the nervous drop in my stomach. "Someone I care about needs my help."

"What about school? How did I get here anyway?" Mom's face went pale. "Oh no, have I been drinking again?"

I reached forward to reassure her with a soft touch on the arm. "No, no, Mom. You haven't. You're good." My voice eased out the words to calm her, but the wrinkle above her forehead only creased further.

"Then...what's happening? Why don't I remember getting here?" Her voice sounded more like herself, entirely different than the far away version it was back on the dock.

"What do you remember?" If I could probe her for what she knew or didn't know, it would determine how much I could get away without explaining.

"I was...I couldn't sleep. I kept wanting to see you—to see the ocean—and I drove here, well, to Florida. I told your father I was going. And he thought it was strange, and he started to ask me why, but I just suggested that he go visit his family up north, and he agreed. Just like that. It was very weird. But he didn't argue. He just...started packing."

Just as I thought. She was controlling him without realizing it.

"So you don't remember driving to Florida or coming to my dorm to find me?" I pressed.

She shook her head, appearing uncomfortable as though she had a pounding headache. "No...What's going on, Katrina?"

I hesitated, sitting back and blinking as I chose my next words carefully. Mom was currently out from under the siren's control for now. I didn't want to confuse her further. But I couldn't tell her everything here and now without sounding like a lunatic and sending her into a panic. So, I played the only card I knew to play.

"Mom," I breathed. "You know how you used to leave and disappear for a while, and you would tell me to trust what you were doing? You said you were trying to help. You were off doing something you thought you needed to do."

She didn't reply, but kept her shining, worried eyes pressed onto me, as if already knowing—and dreading—what I would say next.

"The fact is, I can't tell you everything right now, Mom. But you have to trust that I'm doing something I have to do. There's something in Cuba I need. And it won't make sense if I explain it now. You just need to know it wasn't safe for me to leave you behind."

She opened her mouth as if to question me further or argue. "Please, just trust me," I said. "I know it doesn't make sense, but it's what I need from you now."

She looked down, her brown hair rolling across her shoulder. Finally she looked back at me, her voice filled with something heavy. "I owe it to you to say okay," she uttered. "And your dad?"

"I've already called him. I told him you're here with me. In Constantine. On campus." I spoke firmly, thinking back to the phone call I'd made this morning. "He's perfectly fine, I promise."

My mom looked around, her breath short as she held back a reaction I could easily see brewing. Immediately, I felt my stomach turning in knots. Had I just made a huge mistake? Bellamy would've no doubt disapproved of telling her all that, but I couldn't just keep singing my mom to sleep this entire journey. Eventually—whether sooner or later—she was going to find out at least some part of the truth. But I just had to make sure she didn't find out too much at once. I couldn't foresee Mom handling it well. The sad truth was, I still didn't trust what she might do. I wondered if I ever would stop seeing her as someone on the brink of a mistake, so weak that I needed to protect, instead of my mother.

"Don't panic, please." I added. "My friends are with me. You've met them. Bellamy, McKenzie, and Noah. They're all coming with us and we're safe."

Mom nodded, her head movements growing faster and jerkier the more she processed. "I'll try to trust you. Because I know I've asked the same thing of you too many times not to."

"Thanks. It's the best thing for the both of us right now. I promise." I felt the water getting choppy. It was a subtle change that I could detect by a change in the boat's movement. I wouldn't have expected anyone else to notice.

"I'm going to go check to see how much longer we have to sail," I said, standing and making my way to the door. My mom nodded, her face still ridden with a look of worry. I hoped she'd stay put in the room at least long enough for me to get to Bellamy before she did.

On the way up to the helm, I ran into McKenzie, who was leaning on the hull, watching the never-ending landscape of water through her designer sunglasses.

"Your mom still good?" She asked.

"If by good you mean awake...then yes." I swallowed.

"What?" McKenzie exclaimed.

"She can't stay asleep forever," I said. "We're going to have to work together to keep her calm. I made her promise not to ask any questions."

"What are we gonna do with her when we reach land and actually have to go looking for this Pirate King dude?"

"I haven't thought that far yet." I grimaced a bit. "But I don't think it's safe for her to leave the ship."

"Then looks like we're drawing sticks for who gets to be her babysitter," Noah said, coming up behind us. "Because we'll be docking by the end of the day." We both glanced at McKenzie.

"Why do I have to do it?" She yanked off her sunglasses, her blue eyes narrowing at us.

"You were so good with her back at the marina," I pleaded. "I swear I'll never ask you for another favor ever."

Noah folded his arms. "It might not be so bad, Kenz. Besides, do you really want to go marching around a rainforest with no idea where we're going? In the heat, sweating, probably lost and getting eaten alive by insects? Remember how gross you said you felt in Nassau?"

There was a clear shift in McKenzie's face. Her eyes softened and her shoulders eased. "Well...that actually does sound like crap. But you have to put her back to sleep, Katrina. Just to buy me more time in case you guys are gone longer than you think you'll be."

I groaned inwardly at the thought of manipulating my mom again. But what could I say? I couldn't ask my friend this favor without being willing to help her through it.

"Allright," I said. "Whatever you need."

I turned away, burdened a bit by the plan, but my attention quickly shifted to other matters. Like what it would be like when we reached La Isla. Bellamy claimed to know exactly where Bastian would be, but I couldn't help but wonder if it'd still be the same as he remembered after all these years. And what would we say if we found him? What could we possibly offer him in exchange for this Crown of the Sea? What if he didn't even have it anymore?

No...I had to silence those fears. That's all they were...fears. And even if they were right, we'd just find another way to bring Milo back. There was always another way, I told myself, though I wasn't sure how much of it was convincing enough.

I imagined what Bastian might be like, painting him clearly in my head. I pictured him tall and stern, rigid and unyielding...maybe like Valdez, but less threatening, with a long beard and a flowing coat. As I dwelled on it, I took each step up to the helm with subconscious effort, barely paying attention as I ascended to the cockpit.

"Don't you ever get tired of being up here?" I asked, stepping up beside Bellamy. "I mean, you've only asked me or Noah to take the wheel like once each. Are you sure you don't need a break?"

Bellamy raised an eyebrow. "A break from what? Captaining a ship? My, my...it's like you don't know me at all."

"Well, I just wanted to make sure you're good."

"Never better, love," he smirked, those ice blue eyes sparkling, though I detected a hint of tiredness in them he tried to hide. "But if you don't mind, I'd be more than grateful if you could bring me another one of those...ah, what is it...Mr. Pepper drinks."

"You mean Dr. Pepper?" I laughed, eyeing the mound of empty, crushed cans at his feet. "Sure, I'll go get your third one today."

"Thanks." he winked. "Now if you could just find some rum to mix in..."

I rolled my eyes as Bellamy's laughter faded behind me. Walking to the kitchen, I reached into the cooler to collect another soda for Bellamy. But as I walked back up the helm, I saw my mom stepping out onto the deck from her room. And I immediately regretted what I promised McKenzie I would do. Because now I felt like I would have to do everything possible to keep from having to face her again and give her answers she wasn't ready for.

But I started singing.

EIGHTEEN SIXTY-SIX

11

BELLAMY

I breathed a sigh of exhaustion. Despite what I told Katrina, I *was* tired. But not from driving the ship. I was just tired of staring at nothing. Tired of thinking. Bastian was a slimy dog, with an eye always open for a bargain that benefited him. So I knew we'd have to be just as crafty at his game. I also wondered if he'd remember me. The cocky, proud son of Valdez who sniveled at the sight of him. As though we were any better than him.

For some reason, I eyed him with such disdain back then. As though he was somehow less worthy of his notoriety because he didn't ravage and plunder on the high seas as we did. As if his way of clawing his way to the top was somehow inferior to ours. Now I realize what a lead he had on us, if he really was still alive. We were the fools. Look at which one of us came out on top without a siren's curse damning him to hell. Well—I'm sure I'd see him in hell—but not for the same reasons. And with an easier way of getting there.

Whatever, I thought, refocusing my attention on the lush landmass in the distance. We'd be there soon. I wondered when the last time Bastian had a visitor. I doubt he'd had many from beyond the grave.

"I hope you're all ready. I don't know what kind of welcome we'll receive, but I doubt it'll be pleasant once he sees me." I left the helm long enough to call out down below deck. McKenzie, Noah, and Katrina peered up at me.

"You're sure he won't kill us?" Katrina called up, holding her hands over her eyes to block the bright sun.

I chuckled, "I never said that. Besides, it's your lad who sent us to him."

"Like you have a better plan!" Noah shouted up. I admired his boldness and constant desire to buck the system.

"I never claimed to have a plan at all!" I flashed a grin their way before spinning around back to the helm.

As I eased the ship near the island, I quickly remembered this coast. The shoreline was an illusion, appearing easy enough to sail straight into, but in reality, it was hiding sandbars and reefs jutting up from the sea floor, making a complex path for even the most skilled sailor. If I took this yacht in, we'd be run aground in no time. No one wanted to venture near this maze of sand and sea, making it Bastian's perfect hideout.

"Get the dinghy," I said, shutting off the ship's engine. I scurried to the windlass to drop anchor. "We're here."

"But we're miles out," McKenzie whined, "Look how far it is."

"Yes, well, unless you'd like to peel back the bottom of this boat like an onion, it's the only way to get to the island."

I waited as Noah left to ready the dinghy, glancing between McKenzie and Katrina who seemed oddly nervous. "What?" I asked.

"Nothing," they said in unison. I glared at them, suspicious, until my attention was captured by a fourth figure rounding the corner. Katrina's mother.

"What is she doing awake and walking about?" I shook my head, shooting a piercing gaze toward Katrina.

"I couldn't keep putting her under my spell, Bellamy. She deserves to know what's going on. At least some of it." Katrina's desperation drowned out my concern, but I still felt uneasy about the woman being loose on the ship.

"She stays here. On the ship. The whole time."

"Yes, that's fine," nodded Katrina. "McKenzie is going to stay with her."

"That works," I turned away, walking toward the back of the boat where Noah was lowering the dinghy into the water. "It's not ideal, but it works."

Katrina and I climbed down the ladder and joined Noah in the little inflatable gray raft. Its engine sputtered, hardly used to firing, it seemed, and we set off to the island.

"Careful," I warned, watching as we slowly drifted through the shallow dips and bars threatening to snag our inflatable vessel. Weaving through the trail of twists and corners proved more difficult than I remembered, especially when the dinghy seemed so delicate compared to our sturdy wooden jolly boats of old.

"This is breathtaking," Katrina uttered. "I'd love to paint this."

"Take it in. These are your roots, love. You said you were Cuban, aye?"

"Yeah," She looked away with a bashful nod. "Half Cuban. Half Mermaid."

"*Una sirena cubana*. Divine combination in my book." I winked.

Katrina and Noah both gaped in wonder as we entered the inlet surrounded by gray ragged rocks lining the entrance. Here the water became so clear you could see straight through to the bottom, and streams of greenery trickled down the rocky edges. We turned off the motor, using a paddle to navigate the horseshoe-shaped border of cliffs as we made our way to the sand.

We finally reached the shore after what might've been 20 minutes of rowing. As we dragged the little boat onto land, I welcomed the familiar feel of wild, unkempt island beneath my feet. No buildings or roads or modern amenities in sight. This secret cove of Cuba felt like home. Like the glory days of dragging our plunder ashore to some secret spot in the middle of nowhere. Then we'd celebrate with dancing and music and chugging rum and liquor till we passed out, waking up to the surf tickling our worn, calloused feet.

I noted Katrina glancing around, looking for our next destination, while Noah stood with arms crossed, as if waiting impatiently for the next move. I purposely took the time to take a long stretch, letting my open shirt drape down and the sun warm my bare chest.

"If I didn't know better, I'd say you were wasting our time," Noah grunted.

"Come on, mate, pull that head out of your ass. It's a wonder Milo gave you that compass to keep safe when you're so bullheaded."

Katrina nodded as Noah's expression turned to cold stone. "Well, all I'm saying is the quicker we find this guy, the better."

"I wouldn't be so sure of that. But come on then!" I clapped my hands together as I turned toward the mess of rainforest behind us. "Chop chop."

We plugged along, entering the grassy expanse of forest. The ground was damp with dark dirt that stayed sprinkled from the sea and humid rains. Vines and full branches of green arched over us, winding in every direction, with rocky terrain poking through the sandy dirt here and there. I chuckled as a brightly colored parrot swooped down past us and startled Noah with a squawk. It wasn't exactly the same as I remembered, but it was close.

Because there were no paths forged through this mangled mess of trees, we were left to fight through the foliage, and I was silently running through the directions to Bastian's hideout in my head. Fifty-seven paces through the forest. At the crab-shaped rock, take a left. Or was it a right? Was the rock even still here? I swear I didn't see it anywhere, but we'd gone far enough.

"Are you sure you know where you're going?" Noah asked.

"Is my answer going to determine whether or not you continue to follow me in an isolated, off-limits rainforest miles from civilization on an island you've never been to before?" I rambled off without even turning around, smugly waiting for the silence I figured would follow. "Right, as always, I'm your best chance here either way."

I saw Katrina roll her eyes, but I could tell she was fighting back a smile the way her lips twitched upward at the corner. "That rock looks just like a turtle!" She exclaimed, suddenly pointing at a gray stony mass protruding out from the bushes.

"Good eye, love," I winked, playing along, shocked at myself for my mistake. The crab rock was back in Madagascar. I couldn't believe I'd confused the two. "Now we go ten paces north. No, left."

I was sure now. It was definitely left. And as we marched along, past the turtle rock, and down a gradual slope, it all came back to me clearly. For a split second I was back in 1724, carrying a heavy chest laden with siren...relics...down this path alongside my father's crewmen. The heat was just as sweltering and suffocating now as it had been then. But the company was certainly different.

The two behind me followed carefully, as the path gave way to a small clearing that was barely a clearing anymore. The plants had become overgrown and shrouded the patch of dirt that should have been a subtle entrance to a cave below-ground. I pushed forward, wondering if it would still look the same, but the thick leaves and vines provided quite the challenge. A certain vine had crept over the cave doorway, hiding the singular clue that would have allowed us to enter the hideout.

I reached into my pocket for my knife, cutting away the vine that obscured the small empty space of chiseled-away rock that should've been visible to the trained eye. It was still there, though dirt and mud had filled its cracks solid. I plunged my knife in, hoping it would do the trick. Normally the tip of a short cutlass was used, or a broad dagger, but this modern knife would have to do. I missed the dagger my father gave me, with the golden skull hilt, and wished I had it then.

"What are you doing?" Katrina asked, looking over my shoulder.

"It's a key," I grunted, fighting with the dried sediment that hadn't been moved in ages.

I pried out the caked mud, then jammed the blade back into the opening, turning it to the right, then lifting it like a lever. I stepped back and waited for the door to open. A few seconds passed and both Noah and Katrina watched me with obvious uncertainty. Nothing happened.

I was almost ready to twist the blade again when the ground began to rumble, vibrating the loose pieces of sediment and broken shells at my boots. The cave entrance slowly came to life, as the stone that appeared to be nothing more than the underside of a ledge shook free, dust and roots falling loose above our heads. The rock slid back, groaning at the effort, just enough to reveal what I expected would be the dimly lit entryway down into Bastian's lair. But instead, I saw a cemented wall of solid rock, sealing up what would have been the entrance.

"Well...I didn't see that coming," I uttered, stepping closer.

"What does this mean?" Noah approached the spot, trying to get a closer look. "He's not here?"

"He's not here." I touched my hand to the stone wall, trying to suppress the anger and defeat I felt all at once. I knew this was the right spot. But Bastian was gone. And I wouldn't know where else to find him. Second by second, that sensation of helplessness creeped up in me, and I worried that just like I failed Serena, I would fail Katrina and Milo.

I stepped back, taking a breath to think through it all. Noah came forward, and I moved aside to let him examine the wall. He looked at it for a long minute before speaking. "Either one of you have a light?"

Katrina unzipped the backpack she carried and pulled out a flashlight as we closed in around Noah.

"Shine the light here," he said, running his fingers along the cemented entrance. "There's something..."

Katrina flicked on the light, illuminating it over the space where his fingers trailed. Now I could see it. Barely. There was some sort of engraved inscription, also caked with decades worth of rotting mud and remnants of insects. I squeezed myself in between them and used my sleeve to clean it off, just enough to make it legible. It was two numbers that sent chills through my bones.

18° 27'57" N, 66° 6'13" W

"Well, what does that mean?" Noah said. I held up a hand, unable to hear myself think. I trudged back to the top of the cave entrance, giving my surroundings one more glance before I said out loud what was stirring in my mind.

Drawing in a breath, I paced a bit, stewing on the numbers, taking them in with their chilling familiarity as her voice rang like a bell in my thoughts.

"I love you 18 times 66, as far as North to West."

Serena.

"They're coordinates," I finally said, my back still to a confused Katrina and Noah.

Katrina weaved her way up the fragments of stony, vine-covered ground and took up a position beside me. She held her eyes on me. When I finally looked up, those eyes burned into me beneath a tensed forehead, desperate for an explanation beyond my simple two words.

"Bastian must've left them as a clue to where he's gone. A clue only a pirate would understand."

"Hold up," Noah stepped alongside me. "You are not telling us this means we have to hunt him down somewhere else after we came all this way."

I raised an eyebrow. "I don't set the path, mate. I just follow it." I balked at my own words. Because given the chance to forge the path I wanted to be on...back to Serena...I didn't know how well I'd be able to stay on the current one. I'd try though. Because Milo needed us. Katrina needed me.

"So we sail on?" Katrina urged. "Where exactly do those coordinates take us?"

I glanced down, noticing at last the pressed stone we stood on. Ivy curled around it like snakes coiling through the mossy cracks. I nudged Katrina, asking her to step aside, revealing the remains of an intricate carving of a compass with mosaic tiles of shell and metallic stone.

"From here..." I uttered. "Oh forget it...Someone pull up a map on your phone."

Noah handed me his cellphone, a digital display of the world at my fingertips lighting up the screen. What we once worked so hard to memorize, chart, and track was now available at the press of a button. No longer drawings, but now photos of the real thing, as though we were larks overhead with a bird's eye view of the entire world. In some way, it saddened me. What was left to explore?

I studied the map, pinpointing where we stood, and followed the coordinates as they would lead. "Interesting." I grumbled under my breath.

"What? What is it?" Katrina was practically leaning over my shoulder to see what I saw.

"The good news is it's probably only a week away if the sea is on our side and the weather stays fair."

"The bad news?" Katrina pressed.

"The weather is never fair west to east through the Caribbean Sea. Rough waters and upwinds the whole way."

"What's east of here? Where are we heading next, then?" Noah asked. It was almost entertaining stringing them along like this. I looked at them both before answering, building the suspense just a bit longer.

"A little blip in San Juan, Puerto Rico."

Return of the Albatross

12

KATRINA

"This is literally a building surrounded by souvenir shops and bars," Noah argued, staring at the phone after Bellamy returned it to his hand.

"And?" Bellamy shot Noah a glance with a furled brow and eyes that looked on the verge of rolling. "After everything you've seen you still think there may not be more than what you realize under the surface?"

"Fair enough," Noah clicked his tongue and looked away. I didn't blame him for his bitter attitude towards it all. A wave of frustration crested within me. We'd come all this way for nothing. And now we had to set out again. With my mom on board and with time running out.

"Do we have enough fuel for that?" I asked, trying to mask the worry in my voice.

"We should have enough using what's left in the tank and using some from the reserve we brought." Bellamy scratched his head, squinting as a ray of golden sun broke through the forest ceiling and hit his face.

"As long as we can refuel in Puerto Rico for the trip back," Noah uttered, kicking a crumbling rock across the stone.

"Right," Bellamy sighed. "But let's just worry about getting there first."

We all turned to head back to the dinghy and board our boat, silence falling over the three of us except for the sound of lush leaves and sand crunching beneath our shoes.

A sinking realization hit me and settled in my stomach, dropping like the weight of Titanic to the sea floor. Despite the thick air and sweat on my forehead from the intense heat, I suddenly felt cold. "Do we have another week?" My voice cracked as I choked back the thought.

"What do you mean?" Bellamy glanced towards me, confusion written on his face plainly. "Of course we have another week. There isn't exactly a deadline."

"I mean, when we traveled to the past, we were there for days, but when we got back here, it had only been a few hours. So that means that weeks here could mean…"

"Years there." Bellamy finished my sentence for me, a solemn shadow falling over his face as his steps slowed. "You're not wrong."

I fought back the hopelessness welling within me like a tide. What if too much time passed and we were too late? I wasn't so sure if it all really worked that way, but I sure didn't want to risk finding out.

"Time isn't on anyone's side now, then, is it?" Bellamy grumbled, helping me into the dinghy.

The short ride from the rocky shore to our moored yacht was silent as we all sat soaking in the dire reality of what we'd just discussed. I felt a tear threatening to trickle from my eye, longing for just a chance to talk to Milo just one more time. Just one more word. One more touch. One more kiss.

The thoughts continued creeping in, and the fear of not getting him back darkened my spirit. I blinked and the tear rolled down, plopping into the seawater below, and I suddenly remembered my unique abilities. It occurred to me that maybe they could give us just the boost we needed…literally. I decided to test it out.

With my fresh tear fallen, I summoned the water alongside the small boat as we charged toward the yacht. I painted the picture in my mind, clear as an image on canvas, of water roiling and rushing underneath us, propelling us forward with a lift as steady as a raft and quick-moving as a jet stream. Noah and Bellamy were thrown backwards from the force alone. Even the dinghy's engine paled in comparison to the thrust from the water. We rolled in close to our yacht, and I released my hold on the water. I watched the rolling current dissipate, returning to the calm waters from which it came.

"If you can push the big ship like that, lass, then we can cut our time in half." Bellamy said, his hand braced on his knee as he turned to look at me.

"I should be able to," I uttered. "I think I'm strong enough."

I was getting better at controlling the waves with just a single tear, sometimes even just the sensation of one. But I often wondered if I was really the only siren aside from Cordelia who'd ever realized this power. I guess I had to be…if mermaids truly didn't cry. I wondered if my mom would be able to access this ability if she had long enough to find out. And then I winced. I couldn't imagine what we were supposed to do with her for the rest of this journey.

As we climbed back aboard, I tried to think of what I would tell her, and I wondered what bits of information McKenzie had already let slip if she had woken up by now.

I took Bellamy's hand as he helped me up the ladder, realizing how adept I'd become at being at sea. Standing up in the floating dinghy felt as natural as walking across solid floor. I helped Noah bring the little boat up, securing it again until the next time we needed it. Then I braced as I heard McKenzie's voice and light, hurried footsteps closing in.

"That was fast!" She exclaimed.

"Because he wasn't there. He's moved. And now we have to track him down somewhere in Puerto Rico." Noah interjected before I could answer.

McKenzie's mouth stood agape as she listened to us explain what we'd encountered. I was relieved when she mentioned my mom still slept. But I knew sooner or later she'd wake up, and I was unable to cast out the guilt eating at me for leaving her in the dark all this time. She was just as much descended from a siren as I was. And though I was always afraid she couldn't handle the truth, she deserved to know it. It was only fair to that part of her. But how do you explain to your mom that she's a mermaid? I hoped I'd figure that part out when the time came.

"Allright, we can't waste time," Bellamy ordered, his voice loud and confident and reminding me of his 18th century self. "Let's get this ship moving." As he made his way to the helm, he glanced back at me. I watched him as he guided the yacht's bow to face our new direction.

"You're up, Katrina," he called to me with a nod.

I took a step towards the stern, but not before stopping to ask McKenzie another favor. "Will you be able to keep an eye on her while I control the currents from up here?"

"Sure can. Turns out babysitting an unconscious woman isn't all that hard." McKenzie's bubbly tone made me smile. It had been a strange while since I'd heard it.

"If...when she wakes up, can you come get me?" I asked.

McKenzie assured me with a nod, and I turned away to make my way to the stern. I could still feel my connection from the tear earlier, but it was fading quickly, so I had to grasp the power I still held over the sea before it left me. Fortunately, I didn't need much power to tell the water to carry our boat along. With one vivid image in my mind of the water swirling around us, foaming and writhing like silver spinning silk as it lifted our boat like air beneath a bird's wings. In combination with the strength of the propellers and my undertow flowing beneath, our yacht launched forward faster than I thought possible. I smiled as the sea sprayed up just high enough to mist my face. Perhaps there was hope yet.

I'd been holding the current all evening into the night. My outstretched hand throbbed with ache and my entire arm felt heavier than the anchor's chain. I'd moved to a sitting position on the hull, grasping a rope for security with my free hand, but my body groaned for a break from this position. Just for a moment. I didn't want to lose speed, but I couldn't continue like this for much longer.

Stepping off the hull sent a wave of relief flooding through my limbs, as the blood in my body had returned to flowing without restriction. I stretched, my tendons and muscles loosening as they'd been begging to do for the past few hours. A quick walk around the ship would do wonders. Then I'd get back to it.

I was steadily pacing around on the deck, chugging water from the bottle I'd grabbed from the cooler out on deck. My weary shadow danced on the deck floor, a lone silhouette outlined by the full moon above. When a greater shadow overtook mine, I gasped, nearly jumping back as I whipped around to see the culprit. I blinked in wonder at the sight of the great albatross soaring not even a foot overhead, circling me. It grazed me with a wing, the strong wind tugging my hair as it swept past me. When I looked back, it was gone. But there remained a feather in my hand. He was there. He was still there.

Recharged with a renewed sense of hope that it most certainly wasn't too late, I took one more swig of water and then rushed back to the stern. With my unexpected tears of joy, I called the ocean forth once more to carry us forward.

BELLAMY

As the sun rose, I watched Katrina as she spent herself controlling the current. She'd been there all night, and wouldn't hear a word I had to say when I came to suggest that she should take a break. She didn't need or want my help steering, so I just sat there, lost in the sunrise as I thought of the last time I'd sailed this route. My father sent me to meet one of his "associates" in Puerto Rico, a powerful woman with a string of brothels across the island who'd made her fortune from the ground up as a mere pick-pocketing prostitute with a vendetta, and of course, a desire to live forever. I was always the middle man, negotiating with my hellish charm and making promises on my father's name. But dear old Dad had a thing about making the deliveries personally, so I usually had to abandon my own ship for a time to accompany him and be the face of his deals. I thought I enjoyed it. But then again, I don't think I realized I had any other choice.

As I stewed over the way my father controlled every aspect of my life back then, I thought how pissed it made me that Bastian was now doing the same. I refused to let him have the advantage. If he wanted to whisper sweet nothing bullshit in my ear all day and thought I'd listen, he was wrong. I'd resist him even if it killed me.

Noah's frazzled voice caught my attention from behind. I glanced over my shoulder to see him pacing the deck, phone pressed to his ear.

"You don't have any reason to be concerned about me. I didn't do anything, but even if I did, I can't believe you think you can just ignore me all these years and then suddenly act concerned over something that has nothing to do with you."

I couldn't curb my curiosity, so I went on eavesdropping as Noah argued with someone I couldn't identify. He finally hung up and shoved the phone in his pocket, taking notice of me watching. I didn't try to pretend otherwise.

"What's all this?" I asked, going over to where he stood with an irritated expression.

"It's none of your business, really," Noah snapped.

"You know you're right. I've got enough shit of my own to slog through right now." I walked away, tossing my hands up in a mocking gesture. I really didn't care about Noah's problems, but I was nosy as hell.

"It's my grandpa," Noah grumbled, earning a second look from me. I almost wished I hadn't asked. He went on without further prompting.

"He thinks I helped someone steal my uncle's boat—the one Milo took. Which, I guess I did. But my uncle outing my ass to my grandpa is just a whole new level. And now he keeps trying to call me, saying he's worried about me. I don't know. He's just never really been part of my life. Now out of the blue last year he starts trying to call me and talk. But man, when my parents split when I was younger, I needed someone, anyone. He was never there for me. So I don't understand who he thinks he is trying to waltz into my life and act like he gives a damn all of a sudden."

I don't know what I'd expected him to say but it sure as hell wasn't all that. And it sounded like a hell of a lot more than I felt like getting involved with.

"Sorry, mate, that sounds rough." I intended to walk away on that, but Noah trapped me with his next question.

"Yeah, it's just...sometimes I do wonder if maybe I'm being too hard on him. My dad told me he was never quite right in the head after his youngest daughter died. Said he'd spew all kinds of crap about her being kidnapped by pirates and..." Noah's voice shriveled away at the mention of pirates, his speech slowing with each word. He turned to look at me, eyes wide. "Oh my god. Maybe he wasn't crazy."

I had an inkling of suspicion that I didn't like, but the more he spoke, the more it made sense. "What's your grandpa's name?"

"Russell Loveday, why?"

"I can assure you, he definitely wasn't crazy." I pressed my tongue into my cheek as I squinted from the morning sun. What were the chances Noah was the grandson of the old man who hated my guts?

Noah's eyes narrowed at me, his voice hardening. "Did you have something to do with my aunt's death?"

How could I answer that truthfully? Of course I didn't kill Serena. But it was my fault she died. I could never deny that. My conscience ached at the truth, but I couldn't put the truth into words.

"No, but my father did." I finally said, hoping he wouldn't ask any more questions. "She was diving. He thought she was a mermaid. I tried to tell him."

"Damn." Noah groaned.

"Yeah." It hurt to think of her now. I almost even felt bad for the old geyser being so bitter all these years and his family thinking he'd lost his mind. It was a shame he'd let it ruin the rest of his life. But I guess I was no different. "Maybe you could cut him some slack. Losing someone is…difficult to say the least. Does things to the brain; makes you do strange things. Sounds like pushing you and everyone else away was the old man's way of handling it. But he learned the truth last year thanks to Katrina. Maybe that's why he's finally coming out of his shell to you. Grief is an ugly thing."

Noah was silent. "You ever lost someone like that? Sounds like you're speaking from experience."

I stared out to the horizon for a minute. There was no way I'd let Noah know about Serena. Only the sea knew my secrets. And that's how I planned to keep it. "No. I've just been around a while."

"Hm," Noah huffed, looking away and down at the water.

I glanced back over at Katrina, who was still working her magic on the water at the back of the boat. "Katrina's mom pretty much did the same to her. Turns out she had a decent excuse, but it doesn't change what she did. I don't think Katrina regrets giving her another chance, though." I paused as Noah gave me a skeptical look. "My father used to tie me to the masts with no food or water for two days if I left a knot too loose. In his own mind, that was his way of teaching me to do better. And then I found out he bartered his soul to try to save mine, even though he was the one that got me cursed in the first place. It took me a while to realize the bastard didn't deserve my loyalty. Point is mate, people try to love us as best they know how. It's up to us to decide if that's enough for us or not."

When Noah didn't say anything, I decided I'd spent long enough talking in circles. What did I care about his situation anyway? For all I knew Russell was an asshole who deserved it. Maybe Noah was, too. I couldn't afford to invest myself in anyone else. It wasn't worth the risk of seeing them suffer and actually caring.

I looked back once more to see Noah fiddling with his phone, staring at his screen. I hoped, for his own sake, he'd figure himself out sooner or later. But for now, he'd just better not let his personal problems jeopardize the bigger plan at play here. I was tired of finding myself mixed up in family dramas. But I thought I'd throw out one last piece of advice. "Maybe quit wasting the ship's Wi-Fi on these calls and figure it out later!"

Noah flipped me off, and I left the deck with a shrug.

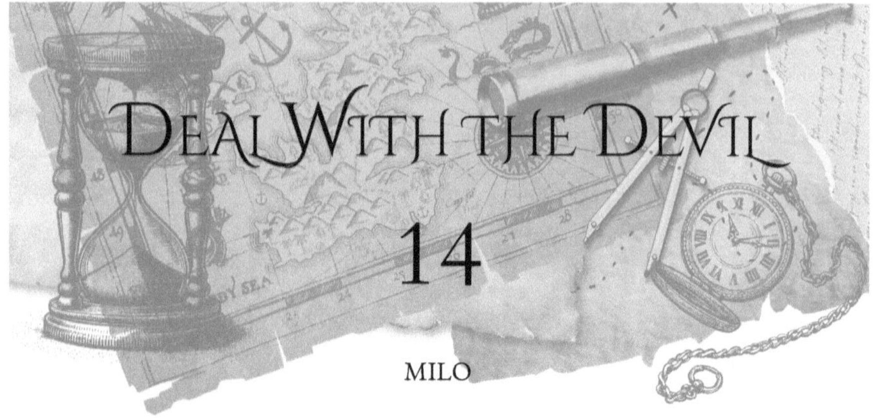

MILO

I waited another night at the tavern for Bastian, and Clara kept close to my men, who I'd commanded to accept her as a crew mate. No one had objected, probably because I'd threatened to keelhaul anyone who did. I observed the way she fit right in amongst them, drinking and slinging curses at one another in jest. I still didn't fully trust her or understand why she wanted this so badly, but she wasn't the greatest of my concerns for the time being.

When Bastian finally walked through the doors, I knew my chances of getting what I wanted were slim. But I hoped to bargain my way there with the riches I'd secured from pirating. It was a long shot, but one I couldn't afford not to take.

Brown roughened locks fell to prominent shoulders of a man likely twenty years my elder, matching his equally wily mustache and beard. His tall, sturdy figure loomed over the bar as he swiveled a coin between his fingers, rolling it along his knuckles and back again. I took a spot beside him, clearing my throat as I prepared to make my proposition.

"What do you want?" he asked, before I could even open my mouth. His voice was slow and careful, with a sly touch of mockery. "I'm not open for business right now."

"Except you're always open for business." I slammed down a handful of the known world's rarest diamonds and jewels I'd managed to swipe from a British ship. Right after I had my men execute those on board who wouldn't surrender and before I sunk their ship. "And I've heard that enough of this will get just about anything out of you. I've got whole trunks full. You could almost buy the British Empire yourself."

He examined the jewels in my hand, a subtle spark kindling in his eyes. "Almost. Perhaps I have some time to discuss it," he said, turning to face me on his barstool. "Any man walking around with those in his pocket might be worth talking to. What exactly is it that you hope to obtain from me with such a valuable collection?"

I paused. I knew the minute the next words left my mouth, things could get interesting, and I could very well appear a fool. But I had to know. "Just information."

Bastian shifted, crossing his legs and leaning back after a swig of his rum. "Ah yes. Information. Secrets. Rumors. The currency of the true elite." His voice drifted through the air like heavy smoke.

I took a breath and clenched my jaw, bracing for the question I had no choice but to ask. "Rumors say you have a map to the Fountain. The *real* Fountain."

A laugh erupted forth from him, as he slung his head back and slapped his leg, earning looks from eyes all across the tavern. This was what I was afraid of. "That's the problem with rumors, isn't it?" His gaze pierced me, a mischievous glimmer in his eye. "Can never be sure of what's true and what's not."

"What's your price for the truth? Because I'll pay it. I've treasures hidden that would overflow your frigate." I gritted my teeth, thinking of the fortune I'd gathered all for this moment. "And if I don't have what you want, I'll get it."

He thought for a moment, leaning forward as he stroked his beard with fingers laden with rings of bronze, gold, and silver. On the back of his palm, there was a marking—a black insignia of a serpent. "Let's suppose I do have the map...Perhaps I dug it up from Ponce myself." He paused with a grin. "And what if I told you it was unfinished? Useless. We all know De Leon never truly found it. What makes you think you will."

"Because I have the rest of my life to look for it, whether you tell me or not." I was growing impatient, eager, and nervous all at once. From the short encounter I'd seen of Bastian with Valdez, he seemed a bit of a showman who enjoyed making an ordinary situation dramatic. And I'd use his penchant for suspense to my advantage. I'd make it intriguing for him to help me. He would cave if I could make him think I was desperate enough.

"You really believe I know where it is, don't you?" His voice curled up, as though he was about to laugh again. I held my gaze on him, unwavering.

"If you don't, then tell me now and quit wasting my time. I'll find it another way if I need to," I stood up to leave, hoping it would pique his interest enough for him to reconsider.

"Wait a second," he cooed. "I never said we didn't have a deal."

"Then do we?"

"You tell me. I swear by the code I'm telling you God's good truth when I say I don't know where the Fountain truly is. Because it was never found."

I hesitated, considering his words for a moment before I said anything more. But as I pondered his words, it slowly began to make some bit of sense. If Bastian truly did know where the Fountain of Youth was, why would he have needed a siren heart from Valdez years later? He clearly hadn't gained eternal life from the Fountain. So perhaps he was telling the truth. In which case, I was now the one intrigued, which I was sure was his plan all along. But I didn't care. I needed information.

"So then what are you offering me?" I refused to sit back down, and instead I stood looming, waiting for his reply.

"There *is* a map, Captain. But it'll only take you part of the way. Ponce died before he could find the true location. I know, I've tried." He smiled with an almost feline look to his expression, and I began to feel unsure of what to trust or what to say next. It felt like a setup of some sort. But he went on. "So, what are you willing to do to lay eyes on this map?"

"I told you," I spat. "Name your price."

He pretended to think for a moment, the corners of his mouth twitching into a sly smile that reminded me of a snake about to strike. "I'll take that pocketful of diamonds and gold you have on you, just for fun. But don't worry about your 'frigates of treasure' and blood money. I'm not in want of that, I can assure you. But eternal youth...now that's a treasure even I can't manage to obtain. So consider this a commission from me. To do what I could not. Find the Fountain and come back to me when you have. You agree to that, I'll let you see the map."

I raised an eyebrow, skeptical of the ease with which he was willing to give up his map. There had to be something more he wasn't telling me. He was always careful with his wording.

"I want more than the chance to see the map. I want the map." I knew better. There was always a catch to everything.

"Well now, where's the fun in that? One good peek should more than suffice. You are a master navigator, after all," he snickered. Fair enough, for now. I'd come back to this somehow and ensure I got my hands on that map.

"And how would you ensure I'd return if I found it?" I asked.

"I'm quite the tracker when someone makes a deal with me, Captain." He rolled up the sleeve covering his forearm. It was nearly bare, except for two tattoos in random places. He flexed his muscle to suddenly reveal an intricate assortment of tattoos that took up the entire length of his forearm. I'd never seen magic like it, but the way the ink appeared on his bare skin before quickly fading away, sent me a step back.

"Every mark bears a deal. Only when the deal is done does the tattoo leave the flesh permanently. Both on me, and on he who makes the deal. You can see how often that happens." He looked up at me with the smirk of someone all too pleased with themselves. "And each tattoo binds the debtor to me until they fulfill their end of the bargain. So, I can *always* find them...if needed."

"How?" I stammered. "This is some kind of strange magic..."

"Magic indeed," Bastian spoke slow and smoothly, a taunting air in his voice. "Why do you think I want eternal life? My magic—my success on the seas—came at a cost like everything else."

"You sold your soul to Davy Jones for power," I uttered, looking again at the serpent tattoo on his hand. I never believed it was actually possible to make a deal with the sailor's devil.

"Don't worry, it's not all bad. The debtor at least gets to choose his tattoo mark. Though it's quite the painful process, so I'd advise something small." He chuckled as he leaned forward, his eyes darkening in the dim shadows of the tavern that now felt so cold and lonely. "So, make your choice, Captain. Do we have an agreement?"

I hesitated, my stomach churning at the thought of tying myself to this lunatic in any way. He was more dangerous than I thought. And now I realized the only clue I'd left Katrina with would lead her right to him. My heart dropped. And suddenly my mission became of greater importance than ever. But I knew my time was running out. I didn't have the luxury of thinking it over. I had to decide.

"On one condition," I said finally. Bastian's eyes illuminated with interest. "My tattoo will be the map to the Fountain of Youth."

God help me.

Bastian tilted his head with a hollow look in his eye, taking in the answer he hadn't expected.

"You must like pain," he laughed. "You've got yourself a deal, Captain."

I took his outstretched, ring-covered hand, shaking on the agreement as my blood swept through my veins like ice.

"Come on then, let's seal it in ink," he stood, motioning for me to follow. Everything in my body screamed against it, but I couldn't find the Fountain without it. I glanced back to see Clara watching me as I exited the tavern with Bastian. The concern was clear in her eyes, but there was no time to explain or get her involved.

I turned back around, following Bastian to a dark empty spot on the docks. With my heart racing and my mind flooding with a mix of fear, curses, and prayers, I held out my left arm as Bastian readied needles with black ink.

Clenching my jaw through the first mark, I thought of Katrina, and I wondered in that moment if I was too far gone for her now. I'd spilled so much blood out on the seas, and commanded my men to do the same. It was the only way to build the wealth I needed to buy my way to eternal youth—the only hope I had of seeing her again.

"Don't become like them."

I recalled the way she begged me after I'd killed Thane's men that attacked her. She would never want to see me like this, but this is what I had no choice but to become. I'd bought my ticket here with bloodshed, and now I was practically selling my soul for the rest of the way. And though the tattoo brought a searing pain unlike anything I'd ever felt, the fear that I may not be the man Katrina deserved stung so much worse.

I'm sorry.

Red Sky At Night, Sailors Delight

15

Exhaustion washed over me like the dark waves we sliced across. The sun hung low behind the horizon, and we hadn't lost speed since we'd set out again. I'd never controlled water for this long, and I didn't know how much longer I could go. But I couldn't lose time, not when Milo's was running out. I focused with all my strength to keep from letting the water literally slip through my grasp.

I watched the crimson sunset tinge the rolling water below like blood. I remembered Bellamy saying something about the sky being red before nightfall. That it was a good sign for sailing. Conditions would be fair tomorrow hopefully. Maybe then I could get some rest and let the engine take over…If I could just hold out a bit longer…

But then something about the water looked so wonderful. I eyed the wake trailing behind us, rippling out into the sea like a spreading fan. I was so hot, so tired from standing in the relentless ocean wind. I could stop for a minute. Just a minute, and dive in for a quick swim…

A far, far swim. And never come back.

It was only when Bellamy appeared at my side that I dropped my guard. "You need to take a break, Katrina."

A breath trapped in my chest finally released, and my shoulders fell as I leaned forward to catch myself on the stern's railing. "I can't," I sputtered. "I have to…keep going." I stretched my hand forward towards the water once more, trying to keep the power from dissipating from me. Bellamy snatched my wrist firmly before I could even fully extend my arm.

"No." He stepped in front of me, "You know it's impossible for you to stand out here all night every night. And it won't matter how fast we get there if you kill yourself from exhaustion."

The piercing desperation in his icy blue eyes made me take pause. He was right, but some part of me wanted to slap him for telling me what to do. How dare he think he knew better than me? I was the only one with the power here.

Make him shut up. Cut him down to size.

Bellamy stepped back, his eyes staying on mine. "Blue doesn't suit you well, love."

I squeezed my eyes shut and shook my head in attempt to drown out the siren in me creeping back up. My desire to jump in the sea faded, and I silently praised myself for being able to shut her up so quickly.

"Sorry," I said, "You know how it is."

"Oh, I do," he chuckled, steadying me by my shoulders and turning me away from the sea so that I faced the deck. "All too well."

"I'm going to rest. But just for a couple of hours," I said as I took a step toward the cabins. Is my mom okay? Is she still sleeping?"

Bellamy nodded. "She's still in her room." He looked away from me and toward the cabin entrance.

"Okay, good." I knew I should check on her. I knew she would be confused as hell when she woke up again. Honestly, I was surprised she still hadn't woken up by now. I didn't mean to put her under for so long. But I couldn't bring myself to go to her yet, because I was terrified I might not be able to cover up reality the next time I spoke to her. I'd do it soon. Just not yet.

"I'm not the only one who needs to get some rest." I shot a knowing glance at Bellamy, noting his bloodshot eyes and slouched shoulders.

"I don't think my body remembers how," he said with a smirk, but I could see right through it.

"I know better," I said. "I think something's bothering you."

He pressed his lips together. "No more than what's bothering you. Don't worry, I'll sleep when I have to."

My mind was too clouded to argue with him. I put a hand to my throbbing head. I needed to sleep. I had to recharge before I lost myself in more ways than one.

I made my way to the room I'd been sharing with McKenzie for those rare occasions when I did sleep. She was there already, snug on her side of the bed, out cold. I'd always been envious of her ability to drift off so deeply and easily. But tonight, I didn't have to be. Sleep wasn't far from me tonight. The second I closed my eyes, I found myself fade into sleep's comforting embrace, where I hoped I could ward off my siren side just a bit longer.

When I awoke, it was morning. The twilight of dawn cast just enough lowlight to brighten the tiny bedroom. Sitting up, I fixated on a little nautical lifesaver ornament hanging over the doorway until my eyes adjusted. I felt refreshed, though my arms ached with sore muscles from holding them outstretched toward the water for so long the day before. I looked over at McKenzie, who stirred just a bit, but didn't wake. I felt that familiar pang of guilt, knowing she should be back at the dorm oversleeping through her alarm right before class...if today was even a weekday. I'd lost track by now.

With a sigh, I accepted my fate. I needed to see Mom. I freshened up and changed into something clean before I trotted out the door to her room, energized by the much-needed night of sleep. As I neared her area of the cabin, I heard muffled thumps in between frustrated grunts and shouts. It almost sounded like my name, but I couldn't tell. After a few more cautious steps brought me closer, I realized it *was* my name. Mom was calling for me from her room. And she sounded frantic.

My pace quickened, and I rushed to her door, where I could hear her beating against it from the other side. I shook the doorknob and pushed, but it was locked from the outside. Thankfully, it only took a quick turn of the lock on the handle to loosen. "Hang on, Mom!" I pushed the door open to find my mom standing right on the other side, her hair a wild mess and her eyes framed above dark sleepless circles. "How long have you been up?" I asked.

"A few hours," she snapped. "I've been trapped in here! Katrina, what is going on? I can't pretend like this is fine anymore. What is happening?"

"I...I didn't lock—" Suddenly I remembered talking to Bellamy last night.

"She's still in her room."

He never said she was sleeping. He locked her in here.

Though it angered me to realize this was Bellamy's doing, I didn't have time to focus on that. All I could do was my best to contain the damage here with Mom. I had been worried about her siren side getting stronger, but I'd never accounted for mine doing the same while she was here. And I could feel mine bubbling to the surface even as I tried to talk her down right then.

"My phone is dead. I can't contact anyone. Your dad is probably panicking like crazy. Why are we still on this boat? Why do I keep passing out and waking up without any memory of what's going on? Tell me. Tell me what's going on!" My mom spoke faster and faster with each word. I glanced at her hands. They were trembling a bit.

Put her to sleep again. Shut her up now before she becomes uncontrollable.

My siren begged, and for a moment I listened. I felt my eyes shift, and then took a step toward her, parting my lips to start my song.

But then I clamped my hand over my mouth. This was exactly what I said I wasn't going to do. And if my siren side wanted me to do it, it *must* be wrong. I swallowed, fighting the urge in my head to silence my mother. I couldn't keep putting her through this.

And I couldn't resist my siren much longer, either. She was growing stronger. Using my powers so much seemed to draw her closer than I expected. So, I had to get rid of her for a while. I needed to be in the water. Soon.

"You want the truth?" I asked. "Come with me." I took her hand, my siren and my true self fighting for control every second. I was stronger against her now, but certainly not invincible. I had to get to the water fast. We were going to kill two birds with one stone.

I led her out to the railing on the starboard side. We were maintaining a steady speed I could easily keep up with. The water below looked divine, like soft navy satin flowing beneath the morning light. I couldn't wait to feel it encompass me, surround me, become me.

"Don't follow me whatever you do," I ordered, placing my bare feet onto the railing as I climbed over.

"Trina, stop!" My mom reached forward to pull me back, but my siren flashed before me and I swatted her hands away with my arm.

The sea whispered to me from below, pulling my soulless spirit toward it, drawing me to it like a thirst nothing else could quench. I closed my eyes, drowning out the sounds of my mom freaking out, and almost the sound of Noah and Bellamy screaming my name.

"Katrina! What are you doing?" Noah shrieked. The sound of footsteps approached from behind somewhere mixed in with the whipping sea wind.

I pushed out my breath, giving it to the breeze, and fell forward into the sea. As I hit the water, I felt her take over, and I drew in a deep inhale so that water would rush to fill my chest. There was barely ten seconds between the transition before I was staring back up at the sunlight through the surface from underneath, content and at peace, as though a burning itch in me had finally been scratched. I stayed suspended below by gentle sweeps with the fluke of my tail. A small pod of dolphins swept by, leaping and spinning along with me as we kept pace with the boat beside us until they finally moved on ahead without me.

I could see my friends back up on the boat, like rippling visions in a faraway dreamworld that was only a surface break away. My mom and Noah screamed my name, and Bellamy held my mother back from the edge of the ship. I swam alongside the length of the boat, keeping with its speed as Bellamy rushed away to the helm, leaving my mom with Noah. I noticed the propellers were losing speed and the bubbles left behind diminished as the boat began to slow.

I broke through the water, my thin top clinging to my body, though my shorts were long lost somewhere in the change. Mom watched me with a twisted look of disbelief, horror, and fascination all mixed into one. Noah held her steady as she leaned over the railing.

"This is it, Mom!" I called up boldly. "*This* is why we're on a boat in the middle of the ocean and why you're feeling strange. This is why we used to dream about drowning in the sea and only that necklace could stop it. It was a mermaid scale. This is what we're descended from. This is what we are."

I flicked my tail up, slapping the water to make sure she could see the silver-blue glimmer of the lower half of my body. Then I barrel-rolled back down into a dive to show off the entire length of it.

"I...I..." My mom stuttered.

"It's okay," I said. "I know you're freaking out, but you're not drunk. You haven't had a drink since Thanksgiving. Because I broke our curse."

More like just traded it for a new one, I thought.

I heard her mutter something to Noah. Bellamy was making his way back to them after stopping the engine. I figured I should get back up there and talk Mom through it a bit more directly. But I wanted to make sure she had no reason to doubt what she'd seen.

"Get back aboard," Bellamy commanded stoically, lowering a ladder down into the water.

I swam to the ladder and gripped the bars. My upper arms strained with soreness as the weight of my tail dropped when he began to raise the ladder.

He lifted me over the hull gently, but the look on his face was anything but gentle.

"You locked her in her room," I growled lowly as I looped my arm around his neck and shoulders for support.

"Clearly I should've locked you in yours too," he grumbled. "Why are you doing this?"

"She had to know eventually. This was the safest way for her to find out. I'm *not* going to keep using my power on her to keep you comfortable."

"You think this is about me? No, she's a liability."

"She's my mom," I snapped. "And maybe she's capable of more than we think." I couldn't believe how firmly I was defending her. But my sympathy for her had grown these past few days. And I couldn't help but think how screwed I'd be if I'd never been given a second chance to fix the things I'd broken. Shouldn't she deserve one, too?

Bellamy didn't respond, but the tension between us wasn't going anywhere. He set me down gently on a seat on the deck. Noah rushed to bring me a towel, and I dried my tail off, hoping I would regain my legs sooner rather than later. My mom watched on as the bottom of my tail left uncovered by the towel slowly split to become my two feet. I winced, still not entirely used to the pain, but much less surprised by it now.

"I heard screaming. What did I miss?" McKenzie came bouncing up from the steps leading down into the cabin, rubbing sleep from her eyes. I stood, keeping the towel wrapped around my otherwise bare lower half.

"They can catch you up," I said, nodding at Noah and Bellamy. "Right now, I've got to talk to my mom." I did my best to offer her reassurance in the way of a smile, but she didn't look convinced. I wondered if she knew about Bellamy locking my mom away.

I brought Mom back to her room, where she still looked at me like I had three heads—which I guess wasn't so much more different than a tail. She was so quiet, but I knew a million thoughts and questions must be racing through her mind. I motioned for her to sit on the bed, and she obliged reluctantly.

"Everything you just saw is the reason we're here." I tucked back damp strands of my hair behind my ear. I went on to explain the cursed pirates and Cordelia and how we'd stopped her from drowning away humanity. I explained the scar on my face from being kidnapped by Thane, the Sea Crown, and Bastian everything in between. "Milo's sacrifice left us stranded centuries apart. And finding this guy might be the only way to get him back."

She nodded, still visibly shaken. With stammering lips, she slowly reached down and placed her hands on her thighs. "Does this mean that I..." She couldn't finish the question.

"Yes." I put my hand over hers. It was weird, but I wouldn't let myself pull away. I had to help her through this. "And that's why you felt a sudden need to find me and come to the ocean. It's the mermaid part of you calling. And it'll be back."

She shook her head. "No, no. I don't want anything to do with that. Even if it's possible, I could never..."

"Neither did I," I said. "But eventually you'll have to answer the call, or it'll consume you from the inside out." I thought about whether I should mention that we didn't have souls, but I decided to save that damning news for another time. "Don't worry," I told her. "You don't have to do anything right now. It could be a long time before you feel it again." I really hoped it would.

"So none of it was my fault," she said, which I didn't quite expect. "None of it was my mother's fault. Or my grandmother." Her honey brown eyes shimmered as tears filled them. My chest ached a bit for her. She blamed herself all this time. Just like I did for the longest until I realized none of it was in our control.

"No, it wasn't. And I'm sorry for every time I blamed you." I gave her cold hands a light squeeze.

"Don't apologize, Trina. I wasn't there for you. I never protected you from anything. And no matter the reason, I will never get over that." She leaned forward, tears now streaming down her face in ribbons. "I'm here for you now, and I swear I'll spend every day making up for the mother I couldn't be when you were younger."

"Mom..."

"No." She sniffed, reaching for my scar and brushing it softly with her thumb. "You don't get to stop me."

"Okay, okay," I hugged her, whispering into her hair that smelled faintly of lavender and clean linen. I wanted to cherish the moment, but I couldn't stop worrying about how I'd keep my mermaid mom from diving overboard the next time her siren side returned.

CORAL

16

BELLAMY

I t wasn't the end of the world, but Grace Delmar running loose on this ship made me uneasy. The last thing we needed was someone else getting in the way of this longer-than-anticipated journey. I couldn't forgive myself if something happened to Katrina's mom under my watch. Katrina would never forgive me, even though she'd say she would. But I couldn't live with myself if that happened.

But I was done fighting her for it. Let her unstable mom join us. Just as long as she didn't slow us down. Milo's fate depended on our timing, but I didn't need to remind Katrina of that. Still, I couldn't help but wonder if Milo wasn't the only one who could be saved. If this goddess could turn back time, maybe she could bring back Serena, too.

Maybe that's what the numbers meant. Perhaps Serena was leaving me a clue, too. Maybe she didn't realize it. Or maybe she was guiding me even in death. Maybe this was one last "I love you." The coordinate numbers flashed before my mind, conjuring up images of her looking up at me, her brown eyes shining as she wished me goodbye each morning when I had to return to my doomed ship.

I had to be crazy to think it wasn't just a coincidence. There was no way...

So I pushed the engine to speed up against the winds fighting against us. This was one last thing I could do for Serena. She would tell me to do everything I could to save Milo. After all, he tried to help me stop Valdez from killing her. He tried, and failed just like I did. But maybe her helping me save him was just her way of saying she forgave us. She had too much passion in her heart for bitterness.

"When I'm diving, it's like I'm home after being gone for far too long. Like I was meant to be underwater. There's nothing like it."

"I love hearing you talk about it," I said, kissing her forehead. "I love hearing you talk about anything." We lay in the sand together, secluded, letting the tide wash away the evidence of our time together. Serena sat up, making swirling motions with her finger on my shirtless chest, a plump smile forming on her dark lips that were swollen from kissing. "Now that we've had our fun, I can tell you the news."

"What is it?" I raised up as well, propping myself up on my elbow.

"I got the job. I'm going to be the mermaid at Buenavista! Mrs. Gutierrez said I was the best audition!" Her eyes lit up brighter than the moonlight as she spoke. I couldn't restrain my grin.

"I knew you would. The way you take to the water. You're as close to a real mermaid as they can hope to get." I winked. "So when will you start?"

"In a few days when my tail comes in. I wish I had a picture. It's gorgeous! She even let me pick the color."

"Let me guess," I breathed in her tropical scent—leaning closer to her, playing with a tight coil of curls at the end of one of her braids. "Orange."

"Coral, to be specific," she smirked.

I rolled my eyes with a grin. "Coral," I repeated. "It only makes sense. You'll look beautiful, as always."

"You have to come see my first show." Serena grabbed my arm teasingly, but I froze at her words. "You'll come, won't you?"

How could I tell her I couldn't? We'd been meeting like this under the night sky for weeks now, and I'd never told her the truth about me. About why I could only meet her at night. She'd never asked.

"The shows are...during the day?" I asked.

"Well, most of them. Sometimes they'll be in the evening. But the first one will be on opening day next Saturday. Please come."

I straightened, shaking the sand off my back and rubbing my face with a grunt.

"What? What's wrong?" Serena asked.

I really considered just diving in the water and becoming a ghost, fading with the sea foam and disappearing. And I might've done just that if I hadn't already tethered myself to this girl through unforgettable night after night.

"I have something to tell you," I said, taking her delicate face in my hands. She bore into me with those big, innocent eyes beneath perfect dark lashes. I hesitated, but I somehow

managed to tell her that I'd been dead for centuries and was bound to the night. And true to that wild and fearless nature of hers, she didn't care.

I snapped back to the present as the ship smacked into a swell. I had to clear my head so I could focus on the open ocean in front of me. The waters were rough, and the winds weren't in our favor. I couldn't keep zoning out like that.

We were still two days at least from Puerto Rico, and maybe longer if we couldn't speed up. I needed Katrina back at the stern, propelling us forward with her power. I knew she was pissed off at me for locking her mom's door. But she'd have to swallow her pride and move past it, because from what I'd calculated in my lonely time at the wheel, in the time it was taking us, Milo had already been trapped in his time for almost a year.

I asked Noah to take the wheel for me as I hurried down to find Katrina. She was just leaving her mom's room, and the look on her face told me all that I needed to know.

"Don't be mad," I leaned on the wall in the tiny, cramped aisle way of the ship. "You'd think by now you'd come to expect this sort of thing from a pirate."

"You could have at least told me the truth when I asked you."

"I said she was in her room, didn't I? Omitting part of the truth isn't lying, lass. Not in this world. It's not all black and white. Sometimes it's the gray that saves your ass."

With a roll of her eyes, she turned to go, but I jumped in front of her to block her exit. "Did you forget you have a post on my ship?" I smirked.

"Okay now you're just being annoying," she scoffed.

"Am I?" I tilted my head. "Or am I just trying to help you get back your dear beloved? You're all rested up now, so I need you back there doing your magic water thing."

With a groan, she crossed her arms, accepting defeat. "I'm still mad at you for the time being."

"Good." I patted her on the shoulder as she slid past me. "Use that to fuel your energy."

Just seconds later I felt a violent jolt forward in the boat that knocked me off my feet, probably meant for me. I smiled, picking myself up off the floor. Now we were moving.

La Fuente

17

BELLAMY

There she was. Puerto Rico. A land with people as diverse and beautiful as the life blooming from the coastline to the mountains. I remembered its once wild shores teeming with new discovery and lush landscapes, but now it was infiltrated by sky-high buildings, cruise liners, and resorts. The ghosts of the island's truths still cried out beneath it all, refusing to be silenced.

I asked Noah to take the wheel for a minute while I went to my room to prepare to find Bastian. Walking over to the bedside table in my room, I opened the drawer and looked down. A loaded handgun rested there, nestled in an otherwise empty drawer. I'd noticed it here when we first boarded, but kept it to myself. But I certainly wasn't about to leave it behind when we were about to face Bastian. I picked it up, feeling its weight as I ran my thumb along the barrel. Not quite the same as the pistols I was used to using, but maybe that was a good thing. I tucked it away hidden in my belt beneath my shirt and turned to go back up on deck.

Before long, we reached the port of San Juan. The grand fort jutted out from the mainland, towering just as formidably as it did centuries ago. I moored our ship a half mile from shore, where we were least likely to be noticed. We didn't have time to sail around to the bay harbor and trek all the way back to the location of the coordinates. If they were correct, it wasn't far from the coast.

I called for Noah to drop anchor and help get the dinghy in the water. McKenzie and Katrina joined, untying ropes and securing our things on board. Grace followed in tow behind Katrina, still looking like a nervous wreck.

"So who's staying behind this time?" I propped an elbow on the hull.

"We're all coming," I couldn't believe my ears. I straightened to glance up at Katrina's mother, who had spoken. I waited for a response from Katrina as she swayed next to her.

"I won't leave her here alone. And it's not fair for McKenzie to stay on this boat any longer."

"Then one of you stay with her." I gestured to both Katrina and Noah.

Noah met me with a dead stare. "You think I want to be responsible if Katrina's mom jumps overboard and swims off like a fish? Absolutely not what I signed up for. You want me to trek through the jungle? Fine. Fight a horde of pirates? Sure. Steal an ancient relic from this pirate king guy? I'm there. But I'm not staying here alone with her."

"She'll stay with McKenzie and Noah on the mainland. It's just safer for her to be there than being on a ship surrounded by water on all sides. There's less...temptation...if her siren side comes back." Katrina explained, her mom nodding in agreement. "You and I will look for Bastian and if we need their help, then...then we'll deal with it then."

I clenched my jaw and rubbed the back of my neck. I didn't like this idea one damn bit. "I'd argue with you if I thought we had time," I groaned. "But where Milo is won't wait for us. Get in the boat."

"The dinghy only seats 4," Noah pressed his lips together.

"Of course it does," I smiled mockingly, "Then you four meet me ashore."

My eyes shifted to a jet ski that sat covered on the deck near the bow. Without another word I marched to it and tore away the tarp over it. Controlling the lever to direct the pulley it was attached to over the edge.

As it lowered into the water, I ignored the stares of everyone else. Sure, it would've made more sense for Katrina to just swim there, but I wasn't giving anyone else the option. I needed this for me, just a minute away from everyone to collect my thoughts. And to be honest, I just wanted a reason to do something fun for once. I was tired of the pressure.

I climbed over the bow, hanging from the railing on the hull and leapt down onto the jet ski. I didn't wait to hear anyone's objections, and if they said anything, I ignored them. They'd soon realize they needed to shut up and get to following me.

When I made it to the coastline, I anchored the jet ski a few meters from the beach, securing it behind some rock formations in hopes no one with authority over these waters would see it. It was a ridiculous thing to even have to worry about. No one owned the seas.

I hopped through the rocks the short distance to the edge of the shore where the rest of the crew soon appeared as well. Dragging our dinghy ashore, I studied the shallow beach on which we stood, my mind forming a memory of what once stood here in my past life. The stacked vibrant houses, well-worn by use and sea weather climbed upward, creating a cascade of color down the bluff shore. The last time I walked this coast, it was the start of a shantytown. The buildings weren't much different now, albeit much more festive, but the presence of cars and fences around the community was certainly a modern change.

We made our way to the main street that crossed through the neighborhood and led up to the rest of San Juan. I noticed a couple of figures lurking in the shadows and made note of them out of precaution. We crossed a few simple house fronts, mostly uneventful except for some friendly waves from old men playing cards on their porches as salsa music played through a fuzzy radio station. A weathered woman with a tender smile greeted us as she hung some sheets out to dry.

We were almost out of the neighborhood when the sound of something shuffling beside us made me glance, my body tense and ready to engage. Two guys stepped out from around the corner, eyeing Katrina, Grace and McKenzie as they laughed at their own vulgar comments about the girls.

"Mira' estas gatas," one of them sneered with a raise of his eyebrows before looking my way. "Por qué andan con estos cabrones?"

"Porque I don't give a fuck if I have to put a bullet in your head, claro?" I growled, reaching for the gun I'd hidden tucked beneath my clothing, earning a terrified gasp from Grace and stunned looks from the others, even Noah who was already pointing his pocketknife at the men.

"Dejalas," *Leave them.* I ordered, aiming the pistol at them, motioning for them to leave before I lost it. My blood ran hot, fuming under my skin.

As I expected, they were startled by my reaction, and while still hurling insults, they turned and disappeared into the alleyways between the last few houses lining the edge of the neighborhood. I quickly tucked the gun back away.

"How long have you been carrying that on you?" Katrina charged towards me, her voice shaky.

"Since cutlasses and flintlocks went out of fashion." I wasn't going to waste time going into detail of how I'd found it in the safe drawer of my stateroom on the yacht. "Come on, let's quit wasting time."

As we walked, Noah confirmed the coordinates once more, and we followed them through town, searching for the spot. The city had managed to keep some of its old charm. If I could learn to ignore the cars, cruise ship ports, and throngs of tourists, it would almost still remind me of the old Caribbean town it once was under Spain's control. Of course, it was never welcoming to pirates, but being Spanish myself made it easy for my father and I to sneak in and out of here easily. I almost wished I could've seen it in its untouched glory, when the Taíno people flourished on this island long ago. Before greed and conquest forced its way in.

We searched the old city, the sun still just as unforgivably hot as it was three-hundred years ago. The great fort stood mocking me in the distance with the irony of it all. Once a fortress—now a tourist attraction. And I, once the pirate it was built to keep out, now effortlessly walked past in through a sea of people oblivious to the echoes of the past around them.

"The coordinates lead right over there," Noah said, tracking the map on his phone and pointing to a cobblestone alleyway nestled between a line of two-story buildings. We followed his lead, and though I knew better, I held my breath waiting to see this location, to see if they would have some significance I would recognize from Serena.

We wove through the streets and people only to come to a little entrance of a white building with large, tinted glass doors, and an electric sign above in a seductive font that read "*La Fuente*." My hopes were dashed, and I reminded myself once more to stop believing in anything but coincidences.

"This is a night club. And it's closed till seven." McKenzie said, surveying the building front. "This doesn't seem right. This can't be what we're looking for."

I thought for a moment, just as perplexed as they were. But the more I pictured it, the more it made sense. Bastian Drake was exactly the type to hide in plain sight. And he was cocky enough to flaunt it. In fact, using a night club as a hideout didn't seem all that out of character for him. I was out of ideas to be honest, so I decided not to count it out, strange as it may seem. Breaking in would've drawn too much attention, so it'd be much easier to snoop around undetected in a crowd of dancing drunk people.

I clapped my hands together, drawing looks from the group. "Then I hope you're all in the mood to party, because when this thing opens up, it would seem we're going clubbing, mates."

BELLAMY

With twilight darkening the sky as the sun set, I realized it was much later than I thought. We'd be able to see just what lay within the club in less than an hour, but we scoped the area thoroughly while we waited. It would be a lie to say we didn't indulge a bit in some of what the streets of San Juan had to offer, filling our growling stomachs with paletas and alcapurrias. We took it as an opportunity to speak with the locals, who were more than welcoming and willing to answer mine and Katrina's questions about club *La Fuente*.

One man had told us it had been there as long as he could remember. Another girl told us she didn't even know it existed and had lived there all her life. Others knew a lot about it, but few people could recall details about what was inside. I asked if anyone knew the owner, but everyone's answer to that was the same. No one knew his name or what he looked like.

But I did. Who else could it be but Bastian? So the moment the doors were open, Katrina and I were back in front of the building. Noah and McKenzie stayed outside, partially to keep a lookout for anything strange—or so I told them—but mostly to keep an eye on Grace, who wasn't very happy with the arrangement.

"Be careful in there." her voice was like steel as she gripped Katrina's arm. I understood she was her mother, but it felt a bit awkward to hear her sounding so concerned knowing what I knew about her. I couldn't wait for her to see how capable Katrina really was. She didn't have the slightest idea what her daughter could do.

We slipped into the club entrance, where muffled reggaeton pounded through the walls as the night closed in. I almost laughed when the man at the door asked me for ID to prove my age. Something told me he probably wouldn't believe me if I told him I was almost as old as the stone fort outside. I ushered Katrina on through the door. "Go on in," I said, "I'll get in."

Katrina's eyes lit up with confidence as she spun around to the doorman and leaned closer to his ear than I liked. "El esta conmigo," She whispered, her eyes flashing bright blue for a fraction of a second.

"Smart girl," I said just low enough for her to hear, looking away to divert the doorman's attention. We passed through together, disappearing into the crowd. Fog filled the air as lights danced to the rhythmic beat of reggaeton. The smell of alcohol and smoke was almost enough to tempt me to stay for a while. I'd be lying if I said Serena and I hadn't snuck out for a night of fun in places like this a few times.

"I thought you didn't like controlling people," I teased with a nudge to Katrina's side.

"Sometimes I make exceptions," she muttered with a grin I could tell she was trying to hold back. "Okay, what are we looking for exactly?"

We stared out into the ever-growing crowd taking over the floor. "Tall fellow with longish brown hair, freaky golden eyes, and a face stuck like he's always looking down on the rest of the world. But the last time I saw him was in 1725, so it's possible some things may have changed…"

Katrina wrinkled her nose. She was uncomfortable here.

"What, you don't like the smell of sweat and tequila?" I joked.

"It's just so loud and crowded," she squealed as people closed in around us. "I can't see anything."

"Come on, let's get through these people and we'll have a better view."

"I can't move…" Katrina complained as bodies began pressing against us, their energetic bobbing tossing her about like a boat in a storm.

"Dance through it," I told her. She didn't seem to think I was serious, until I pulled her to me and helped guide her body to the pulsing music. Ignoring her shocked expression, I encouraged her with my own movement, helping her to loosen enough to begin merging with the suffocating crowd of people at our backs. We weaseled our way through the dance floor, walking when we could, but dancing our way through most of it. When a guy began grinding against Katrina despite her discomfort, I didn't hesitate to shove him off with a few poetic words thrown in. He came back to lunge at me, and I grabbed the collar of his shirt, spinning as I swung his weight around. A gasping startled crowd parted the way as I forced him backwards into the bar counter.

"Back off her," I gritted my teeth, boring my eyes into him as he drunkenly attempted to push me away.

"Cuidate, cabrón," the bartender said firmly, calmly mixing a drink as he shifted to our spot at the counter. Katrina came rushing over, pushing her way through everyone, shooting me a stern look of warning. I remembered we couldn't get kicked out of here. I had to cool it.

I released the guy in my grasp, showing my open hands in a feigned sign of truce before pushing him back into the crowd. I stood beside Katrina, watching. He eyed me like a snake unsure whether to strike. Finally, he must've decided it wasn't worth getting removed from the club, and I held my eyes on him until he disappeared back into the color-lit mob.

Voices behind me at the bar caught my attention. The bartender was explaining to someone that their shipment of some certain rums hadn't come in yet and they were running low tonight. What a pity. But the reply froze my nerves.

"I've told you not to bother me with these details. That's what Hector is for. Wait till he comes in. I'm needed elsewhere, for far more important things." That strange, smooth curl in the man's voice only belonged to one very distinct person. Bastian Drake.

"Bueno, Señor. Sorry," the bartender ducked away like an injured dog, and I slowly turned my head to confirm what I was thinking. It was him.

"Katrina!" I called hoarsely, keeping my back to him, "There he is." I gestured with a tilt of my head. She glanced his way, and then looked away.

"He's walking off!" she gasped.

"Then we follow." I snuck forward, keeping Katrina close as the pounding music kept us undetected. He passed through the edge of the crowd, but it was easy to keep track of his movements thanks to his shimmering mustard suit shining like the last chest of gold I'd laid eyes on.

He headed toward the back of the building, toward a thick red velvet curtain separating the club from some type of private section. Before entering, he took a quick look over his shoulder and pushed the curtain aside.

Katrina and I hid behind the curtain, observing carefully as he stood at a blank wall. But with some invisible cue from him, a section of the wall retracted into the floor revealing a set of decorative double doors as he produced a set of keys from his suit jacket. A set of keys that certainly didn't belong in this century. On a brass ring, he counted out the rusted set before settling on a key with a golden skull for a handle, its eye the ringlet through which it hung.

He unlocked the doors, which opened to a carpeted stairway leading down. I really thought he'd be a bit more conspicuous. But I couldn't be too surprised. This was the same man who sailed in a ship inlaid with gold and sails stitched with silk for the hell of it.

I motioned for Katrina to follow. We left the blaring music and wild crowd behind, darting past the curtain and following Bastian down the steps as the doors closed automatically behind us. I could feel Katrina's nervous breaths and she trailed close behind me down the dark steps underground that finally became a wide cobblestone path. It was a short hallway, a stone tunnel with modern lighting lining the arches. At last, we reached a large, dimly lit room with expensive furniture and a wall displaying a vast collection of relics from the sea. I stood in wonder trying to figure out how all this managed to fit beneath a club. Katrina dragged her eyes over it all, just as curious as me as she took in the scene. A polished desk flanked by wine-colored leather chairs was the room's centerpiece, with nothing on it but a large glass jar containing a glimmering siren heart. I couldn't believe he'd just leave it out in the open like that. On the stone walls, portraits of Bastian hung, seemingly each of him in a different era. I rolled my eyes.

"A little obsessed with himself, isn't he?" Katrina whispered.

"You have no idea."

Finally, Bastian's footsteps slowed, and he stood silent in the middle of the room.

"You think I don't know you're here?" The question rolled from his voice slowly, echoing against the stone. I reached beneath my shirt, wrapping my fingers around the handle of the gun at my side. Bastian wouldn't hesitate to fight unfairly. And neither would I.

"Easy now. I didn't say you weren't welcome," he chimed, his back still to us, though his head was turned just enough that I could see the unmistakable profile of the man who'd double-crossed my father for a siren heart. "I'm always in the mood for a business proposition. And anyone willing to follow me down here either must have one, or they're a reckless fool unaware they won't make it back out alive without one."

My mouth tightened in annoyance. "Or they're a ghost from your past."

"I hope this is important. I have a business meeting in 15 minutes." Bastian spoke without looking back at us, but when Bellamy was silent at his response, he turned around only to appear unfazed by the gun pointed at him.

"Ah, you do seem familiar." He grinned, lifting his ring-covered hands in a mocking manner of pretend surrender. Tattoos of every nature decorated him, but the black snake on his hand stood out to me the most. "Let me see…the Industrial Revolution? Wait, no… the Civil War? It all starts to blur together, you know."

"Let me jog your memory, then," Bellamy spat, still holding the gun. "Try a bit farther back. Isla de Juventud."

"Oh, now I remember." Bastian strode forward, moving toward the barrel of the pistol as though it was no more dangerous than a pool noodle. "The old glory days on the high seas. I made a bargain with you and your father…Oh for God's sake just put the gun down already." Bellamy complied with a lowered arm, to my surprise, but the weapon remained in his firm grip.

"Not with me. Just him. I never made a deal with you." Bellamy's words came out scathing and cold.

"Details, details. Yet here you are, a boy burdened with the sins of his father, still marked by the deal he never fulfilled. Though you certainly had no issue helping him bring the prize right to my doorstep."

"Did you expect some show of morality from a pirate? I do what the sea demands of me. Nothing more. Nothing less." Bellamy growled. "Besides, not like I had a choice."

I wondered what exactly he meant by that as my gaze wandered to the jar on the desk with the heart inside. It had to be the siren heart he'd conned out of Valdez. The heart keeping him alive.

"Fair enough," Bastian snickered, cocking his head to one side. He finally seemed to take notice of me at Bellamy's side, but he didn't address it. "I see you must've kept a siren heart for yourself for you to show up here after all these centuries. I suppose the temptation of immortality was a bit too much for you to resist."

"It's none of your concern how I'm still alive. All that matters is that you have something we want."

"Of course, I do. Otherwise, you wouldn't be here," Bastian grinned a slimy smile, and he looked over Bellamy's shoulder to make eye contact with me. Bellamy shifted to block his view. "And as your father well knew, I'm always in the mood for a good bargain."

"Except you don't uphold your end of them." I listened intently as Bellamy's voice tightened. Bastian stepped forward and I shuffled back without meaning to.

"Oh, dear boy, you've got it all wrong. I'm a man of my word. It was your father who breached the deal." Bastian closed in around us, like a vulture circling its prey. Bellamy kept an arm between us, a barrier between Bastian and me, but something told me it wouldn't do much good if this pirate lord-club boss really wanted to reach me. "You see...James misunderstood my conditions. He brought me the wrong thing. I asked for a siren heart...fully intact."

"And that's exactly what we brought you. Without it, you couldn't still be alive." Bellamy gestured toward the heart on the table. Our positions had shifted now, with Bellamy and I backed toward the desk in the center of the room and Bastian now blocking our exit. I glimpsed down at Bellamy's hand, just to reassure myself that he was still holding the gun.

"No, lad." Bastian's eyes narrowed. "You brought me a heart *cut* from the siren. Well-preserved, yes. But worthless. You see, when I said 'intact' I meant exactly that—a heart untouched, still beating, *within* a siren. I didn't get what was agreed to, so the deal was null and void, as was my right."

I made note of the way he twisted words and seemed to love the taste of trickery on his tongue. I could see Bellamy's jaw turning to stone, a vein tensing in his neck and forehead.

"You demanded a *live* siren? Something we never gave to anyone." he growled. "That's not what you said. You cheated."

"I didn't cheat. I simply chose my words very carefully. Something you should learn to do before you get that pretty lass with you into trouble."

I shuddered at the mention of me, suddenly aware of his gaze stuck on me, as though I was an item to be traded.

"This is why I prefer to let my weapons do the talking." Bellamy raised the gun, his finger over the trigger this time. "We came here for the Crown of the Sea. Where is it?"

Bastian released a cackle that echoed throughout the chamber. "If you kill me, you'll never find it. Assuming you could."

Bellamy put his finger on the trigger and began to pull. "Stop! Without him we can't find the crown!" I screamed. He fired and my ears rang. I trembled from the deafening gunshot and yelled in anger.

Bellamy stared at me with hollow eyes, not giving an answer. But he didn't have to. Because Bastian didn't fall. He stayed standing with a hole in his chest that blossomed red across his mustard jacket, and then closed up as if it never happened. Even the bloodstain vanished, retracting back into the threads of his clothes to leave a perfectly clean suit behind. Months ago this might have terrified me, but by now it almost felt normal. But my head spun at what Bastian said about the heart. I thought siren magic could only work if channeled through a living siren. So how could Bastian's dead siren heart actually keep him alive? The way mine kept Milo alive...

Bastian brushed off the arms of his jacket as if merely dusting away lint. "I can't fault you for trying. But you must know if your own father couldn't get it from me, what makes you think you could?"

"Because I'm not him. And that's all you get." Bellamy suddenly sucked in his words. "I won't keep talking so you can use whatever I say against me."

"Clever lad," Bastian uttered, stepping toward us and clapping Bellamy on the shoulder. "I tell you what. There's something I'm very much in need of and have yet to find someone who can accomplish it. You do the job, I give you the Crown."

"I know how your deals work well enough to know not to agree to them."

"Then I suppose you'll be leaving without your Crown," The words slithered from his mouth like spilled black ink. Bellamy had told me to let him do the talking, but I was growing frustrated with this douchebag.

Bellamy held his gaze for a moment, as if considering his options. "What is it you want done?"

"You could say it's an assassination of sorts. Of a sea beast of legend that few have encountered and lived to tell the tale. These past fifty years it has chosen to linger in the depths of the Mediterranean Sea. Some say it's a great dragon or sea beast. Others have called it 'Kraken.'"

"The Kraken? Really? You want us to kill the Kraken? What benefit could that possibly provide you now, far from the dangers of the sea, here in your cushy lair?" Bellamy raised an eyebrow.

"What benefit do you two seek from the Crown of the Sea?"

We both stared at him without reply, his hollow eyes sweeping over us in triumph. "Exactly," he muttered. "It seems we both have something to hide."

Bellamy shifted his weight around for a moment. He seemed to be gathering his thoughts as the weight of Bastian's words sunk deep. "Prove to us that you still have the Crown in your possession. Show us. I won't agree to anything without proof of it."

"Oh, come on, Bellamy. No need to be so melodramatic. You're just as demanding as your father was. But since you insist on making me prove myself..." He ducked his head and motioned for us to follow as he headed to the desk in the middle. I couldn't stop looking at the siren heart jar. If he showed us where the Crown was, we could just destroy the heart and take it. It felt too easy.

He waved a hand over the desk—the hand with the serpent. The desk slid back, revealing the entrance to a treasure trove of collected trinkets below. Some glittered like jewels and chests of rare metals. Some rotted with dust, like strange skulls and exotic talismans. There were items likely enchanted with sea magic or other dark powers, all things I assumed he'd accumulated over the centuries as a Dark Pirate Lord. A taxidermied mermaid fluke hung decoratively on the wall, making a bit of bile rise to my throat. And there, in the center of it all, meters from where we stood looking down, shone the glory of the Crown of the Sea, sparkling in the light reaching it. Seashells, pearls, and live starfish adorned its intricate golden frame as though designed by the gods themselves. I glanced at Bellamy to see if he felt the temptation to dive down into the pit to grab it as I did. His eyes were wide with wonder, but his scrutinizing and stoic expression remained the same otherwise.

I began to step forward, to climb down the cavern-like walls of this trove to see the Crown more closely. But an arm in a golden sleeve quickly put a stop to it. Bastian's voice snaked its way to my ears.

"Ah, ah. Look but don't touch. The Crown of Atargatis is a sacred thing."

"Atargatis?" I repeated.

"The first sea queen. The ancient mother of sirens. Myth says she was a divinely beautiful woman who fell in love with a mortal man. But she caused his death, and in her grief and guilt, threw herself into the sea. But she was too beautiful to die, and instead emerged transformed by her broken heart with the tail of a fish—and power of the seas—second only to Poseidon himself."

And somehow you managed to steal her crown?

Bastian went on. "A reward as hefty as her crown requires a task of equal proportion. A task no one has yet to survive accomplishing. Kill the Kraken and it's yours."

"You've sent others?" Bellamy asked, redirecting Bastian's attention to him.

"Plenty. You're a skilled sailor. You've heard the stories. You know none can kill the beast."

"Bellamy," I stepped forward, uttering my first word since we'd entered this place. "Is that true? Can it be killed?"

He hesitated for a moment, as Bastian wrung his hands excitedly, waiting for Bellamy's next words. Finally, he grumbled so low I was sure that only I could hear him. "It's true. It's an impossible mission."

"No, no. You've got to be wrong. We wouldn't just give up that easily. We won't. There's got to be a way."

"No...It's *impossible*." He bit the inside of his cheek, as though biting back what he really wanted to say. I was careful not to argue too much to keep from accidentally giving away more information than Bastian should hear. But I was furious. And desperate. And I had an idea. Anything to save Milo. The heart on the desk tempted me beyond belief. But I couldn't bring myself to do it...to kill. I couldn't do it again.

I stepped forward, locking my focus on Bastian and his stupid arrogant expression. I opened my mouth and began to sing my song.

"What are you doing? Stop!" Bellamy growled. I commanded Bastian to shut up and bring us the crown. His eyes widened at the first notes of my song, and then he stood alert, under my control and ready to follow my orders.

He began walking to a corner of the room, his mind seemingly numbed by my enchantment. Bellamy watched, half horrified and mesmerized. And then, Bastian stopped, just as quickly as he'd fallen under my spell, and turned to look at me from across the room before bursting into a guttural laugh.

"You *really* thought you had me with that lovely song, didn't you?" He clapped his hands together like an entertained child and threw a nod to Bellamy. "So, sirens aren't extinct after all. You should've told me. Then at least maybe I could've warned you that their songs don't work on those under the mark of Davy Jones."

I stood planted, shaken and enraged at myself for being so stupid. I should have listened to Bellamy. I'd just dug us into a hole deeper than we ever intended to go. And I was clueless as to how we were going to wriggle out of it. I glanced at Bellamy, whose eyes had turned to stabbing glaciers jutting into me.

"I told you not to—"

"You told her not to what?" Bastian interrupted. "Prove what I already knew? I sensed her siren blood the moment you two stepped in here. And the fact that you're alive all these years Bellamy. It could only be because of her."

Bellamy seethed as frustration furrowed in his forehead.

"Don't worry. I can do nothing to her that we haven't agreed to," Bastian smiled. "But this certainly raises the stakes of our deal."

"We have no deal," Bellamy turned away, as if readying himself to leave, fists clenched at his sides.

I rushed to his side. "We can't leave without that crown," My voice cracked as I fought back the lump rising in my throat. "We can't give up after we came all this way."

Do it. Destroy the heart. Kill the man.

Bellamy's eyes softened, and in that moment, I realized how empty they truly were. He had given up long ago. Not just on this, but on everything. He had finally learned to be content with death, and yet was forced to live through his grief all over again. This was too much for even him. "Unfortunately, Katrina, sometimes you do everything in your power, and you still can't save them."

"Who are you?" I sputtered, nearly choking on the words. "The Bellamy I know wouldn't stop fighting. You're too stubborn."

He didn't respond, but something told me the Bellamy I knew might have been hiding behind more layers than I realized. And if this was all too much for him, that was fine. I understood. But it wasn't too much for me. There was nothing I wouldn't do to rescue Milo from the past. I spun around, facing a bored-looking Bastian, who watched us bickering just a few feet away.

I darted past him and grabbed the jar, raising it above my head and smashing it on the ground. The glass shattered and I swiftly grabbed a piece, slicing my own hand, and drove it into the glimmering heart. I looked at Bastian, longing to see him collapse so that I could rush down his trove and take the crown. But he stood there, smug, almost entertained.

"I was wondering when one of you would try that," he smirked. "Do you think if that heart was keeping me alive that I would really be so stupid as to keep it there?"

My mouth hung open in shock.

"How the hell are you still alive then?" Bellamy asked.

"Bellamy, you're adorable," Bastian laughed. "You both are, really. Thinking you can kill me that easily and that I'll just spill all my secrets. Why don't I just hand you the Crown and leave you the keys to my club?"

I was furious and sick. Sick of myself, for just trying to kill a man, but mostly at Bastian for his twisted games.

"I'll kill your Kraken." I straightened my spine and stood tall, speaking with all the authority I could muster. "I'll do it. For the damn crown."

A wicked curve slid over Bastian's lips, a shadow falling over his eyes. Bellamy whipped back around, pulling me to him. "No!" He covered my mouth. "She doesn't agree to anything. I'll do it. Your deal is with me. Always has been. I'll take the mark. Not her." I struggled against him, feeling guilty that he felt the need to jump in for me, and also wondering what mark I was meant to take. The idea of it made my skin crawl.

"She already agreed," Bastian approached us, stepping over the shattered glass and bleeding heart as he checked his watch. "And we really need to get this moving along. I'm expecting someone."

"No!" The tone in Bellamy's voice changed from anger to pleading. He lowered his face to mine, squeezing my shoulders so tightly I thought he'd bruise them. "No, Katrina, dammit! He'll always play the game in his favor. He's sending us to our graves. This wasn't part of the plan."

"Aren't you the one who told me the plan sorts itself out at the right time? You can't be afraid when it does!" I shouted, heaving as I thought of every second wasting.

"I'm not afraid for myself," Bellamy snarled back. "But I'm afraid of losing the last person I care about!" His words sliced through my heart like a cold steel cutlass. Bastian stepped between us, separating Bellamy from me.

"Such a touching moment, really, but we must get on with this. And don't worry, dear girl, I have no intention of sealing this deal like all the others. It does me no good to track the two of you with some tasteless tattoo. No, instead, let's bind our contract a different way...a more *effective* way given your nature."

"What do you want?" I blinked, afraid of the answer.

"Your voice. Your siren song."

"What?" I clutched a hand to my throat. "No..." I stammered. Bellamy pleaded with me, his voice dry and distressed.

"Don't worry. It's only a small deposit. A signature if you will—that you agree to my terms." Bastian coaxed. "You'll get your song back—and the crown—when you return...with the beast's head."

"Let's get on with it." I tried so hard to sound brave, but my confidence was wavering. I was doubting everything. The room melted around me like swirling paint and my head felt light. My palms were slick from sweat. Bellamy's voice faded out as he begged me—demanded me—not to do this. But I didn't see any other answer. I didn't know what else to do.

"Then sing your song," he commanded.

I opened my mouth. The first notes came out shaky and weak, but as I sang the haunting melody, my song strengthened into a powerful aria. Bastian raised his serpent hand, where he adjusted a ring on his finger. It was iron, with a black polished stone of some sort in the center. As he turned it, curling black smoke rose out of it. I was startled, but I kept singing.

The smoke coiled and writhed in the air like a snake made of shadow, slowly creeping its way across the air to me. It surrounded me, trickling down into my throat, where it wrapped its dark clutches around my song. I could feel it, choking me, but I was now powerless to stop my song. I gasped in horror as it pulled away, a glowing blue and white pulse of energy wrapped in its smoke-like grip. My song. It echoed as if distant, trapped in the glowing orb. Then as quickly as it appeared, it retreated back into Bastian's ring, now another part of his collection.

The room was silent. Even Bellamy was frozen in place and speechless. I opened my mouth to sing again. But my song was gone. It just sounded like an ordinary voice and an ordinary tune, one that no longer held a hint of magic or power.

Bastian grinned. "Well, a deal's a deal. As an added bonus for your compliance, I've thrown in a special tool to help you find the beastie." He crooned, looking to the door, before tossing me a spyglass that I barely caught. "Now get to Kraken hunting. Can't hold up my next appointment."

SPYGLASS

20

BELLAMY

"How could you do that?" I stomped furiously after Katrina as we made our way out the door of the club the same way we came. Katrina ignored me as she pushed through the sweaty bodies in the booming crowd. "Katrina! Talk to me!" I shouted.

She finally whipped around once we made it to the outside past the bouncers, her long dark locks nearly smacking me in the face. "I did what I had to do. He wasn't going to let us go without that deal. You were the one who tried to kill him before we even knew where the Crown was!"

"But you completely ignored everything I said. Bastian is not someone to play around with."

"Aren't you the one who told me sometimes the gray is the only thing that can save us?" She spoke with such a strange calmness for someone who had just given up her voice to a dark pirate lord. "Just be glad he didn't ask for more. Speaking of, what did you mean when you said his deal has always been with you?"

I sighed with frustration and pulled down the collar of my shirt, pointing to a small sea serpent tattoo on my collarbone. "This came from Bastian when he made the deal with my father. *I* was the deposit." My thoughts glanced back to

"Bellamy, I'm so sorry." Katrina started, but I didn't let her finish.

"Don't be. My father didn't force me. I did it willingly. I was an idiot then, thinking Bastian would honor his deal. No one knew the dark magic he had then. But now I know. His power comes from Davy Jones himself, and that's nothing to underestimate."

"Why? Is this Davy Jones guy really so powerful?"

"Not a guy. Davy Jones is an entity, always looking for someone already dark-hearted enough to be under his control. The dark force of the seas that takes the souls of sailors to their eternal graves. And yes he really is that powerful and if Bastian's channeling his power... then I fear Bastian's got both of us at his mercy. He's marked me and stolen your voice, which was pretty fucking handy in a lot of situations."

"Well...yeah." Suddenly her voice softened. "But, you know, maybe that's what I'm scared of. I'm relying on it too much. Relying on my ability to control others...and I'm afraid if I keep doing it, one day I might not be able to rein it in."

It all made sense. Of course she gave up her voice. She was still afraid of her power. Furious as I was, my heart eased up a bit. There was more to this than she let on.

"Besides," she said. "There's nothing I wouldn't give up to get Milo back. I didn't have to think about it."

"Right." I clicked my tongue. I certainly understood that. I'd give my voice up too, if it could bring back Serena. "But we still have to do the impossible first."

"Don't forget you still have a siren on your side," Katrina's eyes flashed deep blue, like flaming sapphires glinting in the light.

"Technically two sirens." McKenzie's voice made me look to see her approaching with Noah and Grace flanking her. "What's this impossible mission you agreed to?" Her eyebrows pressed together tightly to spell worry clearly on her forehead.

Katrina and I explained to them in detail everything that happened with Bastian and his massive underground lair. I offered them the option to stay behind now, because once we found the Kraken, there would be no escape. And certainly no promise we'd live through it.

"We'll fight this thing with you. There are flares and maybe more guns back on the yacht." Noah straightened his shoulders, as if trying to prove his usefulness. Grace's eyes were wrought with worry, but she didn't say anything. I'd learned by now she wasn't one to speak up while processing. I almost cared to wonder what McKenzie was thinking, given that she was unusually quiet too.

No. The agreement was between myself and the both of you. Not your friends. They stay behind.

I gripped my head in my hands. The voice grated against my consciousness like knives raking my skin. Bastian's voice. It choked out my own thoughts like black smoke in a dark room. He was in my head. His mark had power over me after all.

Katrina and McKenzie rushed to steady me as my fingers dug into my hair. I was fine. I swear I was. But I was too livid to find the words to respond to them as they asked if I was okay. I tried my best to ignore the dreamlike command of Bastian, but it echoed within me until I admitted what I was hearing.

"He says you can't come." I fought to get the words out. "I think we reawakened this stupid tattoo. Bastian has a direct line to me. And he will until we do this. If we breach his terms of the deal, he'll be in my head forever."

"Bellamy." Katrina touched my shoulder softly. "I didn't know."

"Because you didn't listen to me. I told you he always takes more than he promises."

"I'm sorry. What was I supposed to do? Don't tell me you really would've walked out of there knowing you forfeited the only chance you have to help Milo. I know you. You wouldn't have done it. He's like a brother to you."

"Hmmm," I growled, turning away. I wasn't sure what I would've done anymore. Milo was my brother at sea, no doubt. But would I trade Katrina's life for his by pitting her against this beast? Either way I lose. I always lose. By the minute, I felt the pathetic scraps of faith I had left in everything and everyone around me slipping through my grasp. The never-ending battle of losing those closest to me was beginning to wear on me.

"You'll be fine here in Puerto Rico." I spoke firmly, leaving no room for argument to the trio watching me. If they tried, I'd shut them up quick and leave them stranded here without a choice. "We need someone to keep an eye on Bastian anyway. You can let us know if you see him trying to pull anything like relocating or running."

Suddenly, it seemed as though Grace found her bravery. "Trina, I can't just stay here and let you do this. I know you're used to doing things on your own, I do. But this...it's too dangerous."

"Mom," Katrina breathed. "This is something I have to do. If I don't, I'll never forgive myself. I can't leave Milo behind."

I almost wanted to roll my eyes as Katrina went on to reassure and plead with her mom. Grace wouldn't understand that fearless sacrifice Katrina talked about. She'd never been faced with anything of the sort. She was always the one being saved. She had no right to tell Katrina not to do this...Maybe I didn't either. I didn't know anymore.

"Please, Katrina. What if I feel the siren's pull again? What if I can't resist it without you?" Grace sounded more desperate than I'd ever heard her. I didn't believe she wasn't really worried about that. She was just reaching for whatever she hoped might anchor Katrina here.

"Katrina," I muttered, interrupting Grace's pleas. "Every second matters now."

Katrina switched her gaze to me, Grace glancing between the both of us. Noah stepped in to reassure her mother, because he must've known I wasn't going to do it. "Mrs. Delmar, if anyone can do this, it's Katrina. McKenzie and I will be right here with you, waiting for her when she gets back. She *will* come back."

Grace blinked, swallowing nervously as she shook her head. "I know I can't stop you," she said, her voice quivering and tearful. "But just remember you have to come back to me. No one else can show me how to be a mermaid." I caught a glimpse of Katrina's brief smile.

"I will." Katrina lifted her chin high. "I will." Grace leaned into her for a hug, one that looked clumsy from the start, but gradually softened into some semblance of what a mother-daughter embrace should look like. I looked away, fighting the feeling of awkwardness that hung in the atmosphere.

"At least let me help you prepare." Noah spoke to me, his tone somber. "You can't go empty-handed. These antique shops are bound to have something of use."

It wasn't a horrible idea, so I agreed on the condition that we hurried. The girls left to check into a hotel where McKenzie and Grace would stay, while Noah and I scoured the few shops still open. There was no doubt an array of artifacts and old weaponry from my own time and beyond, but finding some in usable condition was the trick.

In the last store we searched, my eyes scanned the wall of old, ravaged rifles and muskets, rusted swords and remnants of flintlocks. And then I saw it. A harpoon. Marked with signs of obvious use, but still intact and still sturdy. The spearhead was solid. I could sharpen it on the way.

"You thinking what I'm thinking?" Noah glanced over at me, noticing my fixation on the harpoon. Not five minutes later we left the store with our new harpoon, wrapped to appear as an oar or something less dangerous, and met the others back in the city square.

With a few more heartfelt goodbyes and well-wishes for safety, we parted ways, McKenzie, Noah, and Grace agreeing to linger in a nearby hotel in San Juan. Katrina and I trudged back to the shore, now bathed in moonlight and the glow of the city above it. We waded in, climbed aboard the jet ski, harpoon in hand, and zipped back to the yacht bobbing in the distance, onto a voyage more daunting than any I'd ever faced as a pirate.

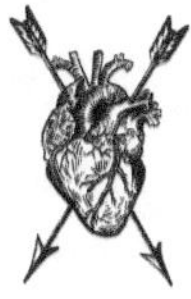

I helped Katrina aboard, still silent in my anger at our encounter with Bastian.

"I know you like holding grudges," Katrina grumbled, "but if we want to have a chance at surviving this thing, you should probably talk to me."

"Why? So you can do the exact bloody opposite of what I say?" I snarled, working the anchor up while Katrina reached for a tank of fuel. "You'll do whatever you decide in the end, with or without me."

"Why are you being like this, Bellamy? You said yourself we don't have time!"

"We don't! But it doesn't matter, because in the end you're going to do something stupid and get yourself killed regardless of what I say! You're just like her! You're reckless and headstrong and you don't listen and it's going to be the death of you! I won't live here on this shitty earth alone without you, too!" I slammed my fist against the hull, sure I would later regret the bruise it would leave on my knuckles.

I didn't even register the words coming out of my own mouth. I was losing myself to my thoughts of Serena as they flashed before my mind's eye. This all felt too familiar. Too repetitive to be real...

"This isn't about me, is it?" Katrina's voice softened, and I knew she knew.

"You're part of it," I grumbled. "But no...it's really not about you. Feel free to take the helm." I walked away and retreated to my room. The floor became my focus as I slipped away into the start of a memory...

I watched her from the back curtain, entranced as any song-struck sailor as she flitted through the water, turning and spinning and dancing in the bubbles behind the glass. She waved at the audience before blowing a kiss. Her hair flowed around her like ribbons in a breeze, and her eyes sparkled with a magic even real sirens didn't possess. Dancing joyfully from the confines of the massive display tank, she was a vision of herself in her truest form. In the water was where her spirit came alive. Anyone could see it.

After her performance, I snuck backstage, past the next act of dolphins and sea lions doing tricks for their trainers. The moment I saw her, seated at her dresser, already out of her tail and wrapped in a towel, I ran to greet her, planting kisses on her cheek and lips. She was carrying on about how she missed a cue to blow bubbles during the music because she couldn't hear it well under the water.

"They loved you. You were amazing," I breathed into her still damp hair as she rubbed her eyes.

"I was afraid you weren't going to make it." She turned to me, nuzzling her adorable nose against my jaw.

"Well, being on time is hard when the ocean controls your schedule," I teased, making her giggle. "But of course, I'd be here, just like I promised. I wish you had more night shows."

"I don't," she stood up, tossing her towel aside and throwing on a sheer white dress to cover her bikini. "I don't want to be here at night when the best swimming is out there." She tilted her head, and I could already tell she was dreaming of dipping into the waves beneath the moonlight, as she so often did. It was such a dangerous habit for anyone else, but for her it was life-giving.

She took my hand, a beaming smile across her face as she looked to the back door. "Let's go."

Katrina showed up soon enough, knocking till her knuckles would break by the sound of it. "We have to settle this. I'm not sailing across the sea like this."

I popped the door open just a crack. "Then swim." When I tried to close the door, Katrina stopped it with her foot.

"You said I'm like her," she said. Katrina had moved closer to me.. "Like her," She repeated. "You mean Serena, don't you?" She pushed the door open a bit wider. I let her and stepped outside as she continued. "I'll make sure you don't lose me, too. I won't leave you alone in the world."

"How can you promise something like that?" I groaned.

"Because...because we need each other. We always have." She reached forward and placed her arms around me, in a warm, comforting embrace. I couldn't remember the last time I'd felt something like it. The strength in it. The reassurance. No one had given me that before.

She was right. There was some unbreakable bond between she and I, and ultimately, all three of us. I had to face the doubt clouding my soul. Some sailors would stop sailing in a fog and wait it out. But I was always known to sail through it till I broke through to the other side. And that's what I had to do now. Even if things still weren't the same, and never would be again. Milo still needed us both.

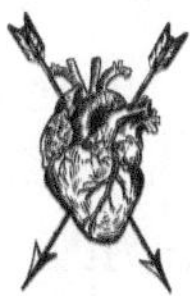

We'd only been at sea a couple of hours before I began to feel the sinking feeling creeping up on me. The rapid countdown of time running out. I hadn't mentioned to Katrina that it would take a month to reach the waters where the Kraken roamed, maybe a little under three weeks at best if Katrina could miraculously carry us on a current again without stopping. But that would drain her. So I was busy trying to calculate how many more years that would mean for Milo.

When Katrina came bouncing over excitedly, I felt hopeful for a second. "This spyglass Bastian gave me," she said, holding up the tool, looking through it. "He said it would help us find the Kraken. Look!"

I took the bronze tube from her hand, raising it to my eye to take a peek. I nearly stumbled backward at the sight. Instead of seeing the horizon in front of me magnified, I was met with the closeup of a growling sea creature underwater eyeing me like prey, as if I was swimming face to face with it.

"It shows us the Kraken!"

"If only it could take us to it," I muttered, still trying to collect myself from the startling sight I saw through the lens. "Seriously...why would he give us this? It's not like he's known for making his deals easy."

"Unless he's really *that* confident we'll die trying." Katrina scoffed. I released a stiff laugh.

"Ha. Or unless he just *really* wants this Kraken dead. For what, I don't know. Maybe he's just *that* bored with his collection." I turned the spyglass in my hand, looking it over, guessing that somehow it probably had some dark enchantment about it that allowed Bastian to watch us through it.

But then I turned the outer tube, adjusting it with a slight twist to focus the lens, and suddenly a pulse of energy emitted from it into the sea around us. For a moment nothing else happened, and Katrina looked at me with concern and confusion. Despite the absence of wind, I noticed a slow-rolling wave cresting far in the distance.

"What's happening?" Katrina asked.

"I don't know," I stammered, wondering the same thing. The wave rolling in grew fast, more than doubling in size every second. I tucked the spyglass in my belt and raced to the helm, Katrina in tow. It was too late to outrun it, but I had to at least position the boat head-on to take a hit from a wave like that. "It's a rogue wave," I shouted as it sped toward us, now at least 70 feet high. "Brace!"

Katrina had no time to run for cover, so she gripped the railing and ducked down, squatting in the floor by my feet. The yacht rose up as the wave crawled up underneath us, lifting us to an angle that left me holding onto the steering wheel for dear life as we barreled just over the crest of the ever-growing wave. Sea spray as thick and blinding as a blizzard engulfed us, and water crashed over the sides of our boat. Katrina screamed, and I braced my leg against her in my best effort to hold her in place as our ship became airborne momentarily.

We rolled back down the other side, sliding down the great slope of water in a slurry of wind and salt. The ship nosedived, crashing bow-first into the sea as the rest of it slapped the surface of the water below, rattling our bones. I couldn't hold on any longer, and Katrina and I both toppled to the slippery wet floor. Sea foam sloshed and spilled off the sides of the deck as the yacht righted itself. Once the ship finished tossing us around, I helped Katrina to her feet.

It was only then that the bitter chill of ice seized my skin and I realized the heavy heat dome of the Caribbean was gone. Katrina shivered, soaked from head to toe in frigid water the same as me. Our breath came out as white puffs in the suddenly wintry air around us.

"Get inside," I chattered. "We'll freeze out here."

We hurried to the cabin, where we dried off quickly and wrapped ourselves in blankets from the beds, though there were few clothing items aboard the yacht fit for cold weather. We sat at a small table by a window to take in our surroundings without freezing our asses off. I didn't care if the boat drifted for a minute. The sky outside was a heavy gray, but it did little to dampen the bright teal blue of the water around us. This was certainly no Caribbean Sea.

"The wave. The spyglass." I rubbed my hands together, still not fully warmed. I hated being cold. "It somehow brought us here. See those cliffs far off in the distance. This looks like the Mediterranean."

"I don't know why I imagined it a bit brighter...and warmer," Katrina huffed, hugging herself tightly after taking a sip of some hot chocolate we'd found in the ship's kitchen.

"Not in January." I tapped my fingers on the table, looking out at the blue water beneath the dreary sky.

"Bastian helped us." Katrina shuddered. "Why?"

"This wasn't just a deal for him. It was a mission. He needs this thing dead for some reason."

"Well then so do I, if it means getting that crown."

"Hmph," I pressed my lips together with a sarcastic tone. "Then I guess you need to get your fish arse in this freezing water and lure it up here." I grinned. "I've heard mermaids happen to be the Kraken's favorite snack...and I'm sure it's been a while since he's tasted one."

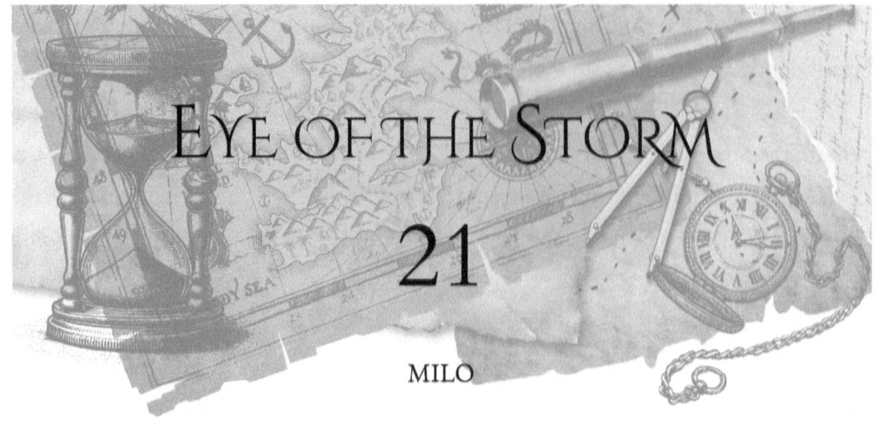

MILO

The heat of the blood gushing down my arm was nearly enough to distract me from the pain of the blade carving into it. Nearly.

I bit down on the cloth between my teeth, gnashing my jaws as the knife sunk into my skin and peeled the top layer from my muscle. The ink stained down deep. Likely to the bone. I had to stop for a moment to catch my breath.

Clara appeared at the top of the forecastle, looming over where I sat on the steps under the cover of night. "Need some help with that?"

I didn't turn my head. "Deck swabbers don't intrude on the captain's private affairs."

"Then say I'm not a deck swabber fer now. Say I'm just a human watching another human fightin' his demons." She stooped down to meet me, kneeling by my side and taking the bloody knife from my hand.

"Fighting my demons or succumbing to them, I can't tell which anymore," I groaned. She jabbed the knife back in. I winced in agony as she sliced beneath the skin, prying flesh from flesh. Like filleting a fish, she worked the blade underneath the width of the tattoo I'd worked so hard to memorize over the past month at sea. With another month ahead of us, the map was stored clearly in my head now, and I no longer needed this damn seal of Bastian's marking me as his slave.

"There," Clara said, pouring a bottle of rum over the gaping wound in my forearm. I thought my teeth would shatter from how hard I bit down on the rag as the burning seared through my veins. But just as a small sliver of relief began to wash over me that I was at least free of being tracked, the torn open flesh reformed right before our eyes. Sinew and skin appeared as if by magic, reconnecting itself to seal up my arm with a new jagged and scarred version of the tattoo.

"Fucking hell!" I slammed my fist into the edge of the steps, scraping my skin against the salt-worn wood.

"Don't fret about it so," Clara reassured, wiping her bloody hands with the rag that was just in my mouth. "You agreed to do this. Now see it through."

"How do you know anything about what I've agreed to?" I snarled.

"I was watchin' you in the tavern that night, you know. I don't know why you did it or what yer lookin' for. But I know you made a deal and I can see now that you regret it."

"No," I grunted. "I don't regret it. It's what I had to do, but..." I caught myself. So desperate to share the burden on my mind and heart, I nearly gave away everything. I barely knew Clara. I hadn't told a soul on board this ship of what ailed me night and day. And I wouldn't ruin that here. She, like everyone else aboard, needed to know nothing. "I don't regret anything."

"Suit yerself, Cap'n. But just know yer not the only one out here lamenting what you wish you hadn't lost."

I lifted an eyebrow, curious as to what she meant by that, but knowing it was far better not to wonder.

"Thank you for your...assistance." I said, looking at the bloody mess on the deck. "I'll clean this up. You go get some sleep, Clara."

I expected her to protest, but she only turned and walked away without a word, the last bit of her flaming red hair fading into the heavy darkness. I cleaned the blood quietly, left alone with my thoughts once again. I watched the sharks swarming the water below as I dumped the bucket of red water overboard. Scavengers, just waiting for their chance to catch something worthwhile. Weren't we all?

As I left the deck, low thunder growled in the distance, heralding a line of storms looming miles away to the west of us. It was a slow-moving monster, and I expected we'd miss it based on our direction and its speed. We were traveling steady and slow, just to ensure we didn't get too close to it overnight. If it was still out there in the morning, we'd just have to sail around it. I preferred not to stop and wait it out. Time was too valuable to waste.

That night in my quarters I dreamed of her.

She walked to me on the beach, a vision calling out to me with her song. I ran to her, but the sand of the shore grew longer, farther, stretching to create a path I could never outrun.

Finally I took a wrong step in the sand, crashing forward into the surf to find myself hitting cold stone. I was back on the lighthouse where I first brought Katrina to show her the stars. Everything felt right here.

She met me at the top, her call soothing my aching soul as she emerged like a queen from the stairs. Like the night I saw her in that glittering dress and lost my breath at the sight of her. As if dancing across the air, she came to me, kissing me with her melody still on her lips, wasting no time driving her tongue into mine, and tangling her fingers in my hair. I felt every inch of her, my hands trickling down her dress to find the slit halfway up her thigh. She guided me underneath, like a song she was singing with her hands, placing mine between the warmth of her legs. I traced the delicate parts of her, up, down, inside and out, yearning to join our bodies once and for all so that time and distance could never separate us again.

I kissed her slow and steady as my fingers moved in her. She released a blissful moan that carried on the sea wind and wrapped me further into her. But then her voice turned dark and cold. "I told you not to become like them."

I opened my eyes to see myself face to face with eyes as blue as the depths of the ocean, staring at me with the narrowed pupils of a predator. I tore myself away from her, my heart breaking as she followed me, no longer in desire but in bloodthirst. Her sweet song became an echo, rattling in my head as she stalked toward me in a state I could not break through. I called her name, begging her to recognize me…but ignoring it all, she placed her hands on my shoulders and shoved me off the lighthouse, following me down into the raging water below.

I awoke with a start as my body hit the wooden floor below my bed. Small bits of sunlight already poured through my stained-glass window along the walls. It was just after dawn.

"What the hell do I make of that?" I muttered, disturbed by the dream as I rubbed the spot where my head made impact with the floor. "Had to be the rum."

I'd downed a good amount last night to dull the pain of my self-attempted tattoo removal, though it hadn't helped much. I glanced down at my scarred arm, the tattoo still perfect despite the skin beneath and around it having been mutilated just hours ago.

I heard a muffled cry from up top. It sounded like Keegan from the crow's nest. He must've spotted something. I rushed to throw on my shirt and boots, grabbing swords and slinging my pistol holster over my shoulder, then hurried out on deck. An eerie morning mist covered the waters and severely limited my view.

"What is it?" I shouted for my first mate. "Felix!" Felix came running up before I'd barely finished saying his name.

"Red flagship spotted, Capitán. We saw it all too late because of the fog. It's close." His heavy Spanish accent coated his words, but he was the most reliable communication on board, making him my choice of first mate. I trusted him, and he was loyal enough to my commands and decisions. However, on a personal level, even after all these months, we hardly knew a thing about each other. Just as I preferred it.

I reached for my spyglass, focusing on the ship in the distance. It was close enough for me to easily make out the flowing red flag atop its mast even without the spyglass once my eyesight adjusted to the fog. Carl Thane's ship. A massive galleon, no doubt laden with cannons and guns far heavier than most pirate vessels. He'd traded speed for strength.

"The bastard never gives up," I said smugly, handing the spyglass to Felix. There was no mistaking the vessel for Thane's. Though I'd lost track of him after the showdown with Bellamy's ship and the warship, I knew it was far from my last encounter with him. I knew he'd turn back up eventually to continue hunting me down once he got back on his feet. I didn't mind though. His retribution was long overdue for when he kidnapped Katrina and left her scarred. I anticipated when he'd come for me again so I could ensure he got what he was owed before I found my way out of this life.

But that would have to be in due time. Not yet. Though I relished at the thought of facing him to enact my revenge, I couldn't allow myself to get distracted now. Not when I was so close to what I believed could be the start of the missing piece of Bastian's map. I couldn't risk my ship. For now, I'd have to outrun him. Give him something to chase a bit longer.

"Increase our speed, lads! Let's catch as much wind as we can!" Felix and I trudged to the helm. Thunder rumbled in the distance, making sure we didn't forget about the presence of the giant storm ahead. We'd be sailing right toward it, but a bit of shaking up from wind and rain would still be better than getting battered by cannons from a warship twice the size of my frigate. But the damn fog had hidden him long enough to keep us from getting a good head start.

My crew set themselves to quick work adjusting sails and securing rigging as we caught the wind and soared onward. The storm winds sucked us right in, pulling us toward it with ease.

I caught glimpse of Clara rushing among the men, nearly shoving them out of her way as she worked faster than any of the others. Her position was a deckhand, but here she was handling the rigging and setting up the mainmast more masterfully than I'd seen any men aboard this ship manage. Later I'd decide whether to chide her or promote her for it.

I looked back to see that Thane's ship had opened full sail, too, emerging from the mist and closing the already too-short distance between us. Even with a ship his size, the winds were favorable enough to give him just enough of a boost to catch up quickly. A clap of thunder struck as lightning cracked in the distant sky like a whip. The storms were probably just a bit over thirty minutes away. They were crawling away from us, but we were moving much faster right into them. I'd rather not be caught up in the line, though it certainly wouldn't be the first torrent we'd braved at sea in the *Falcon*. But a heavy storm might just be the thing to put some distance between Thane and me for now. I doubt he would take the chance of losing another ship.

But to my surprise, Thane didn't slow. He followed us, probably desperate to land a blow despite the stupidity of it in these conditions. I left Felix at the helm to walk the deck, checking our ammunition as men loaded cartridges and prepared the cannons. I silently yearned for this battle, but I also knew that even with my thirst for seeing Thane's head roll, a fierce storm and a massive warship at our backs wasn't setting up for the best outcome. But if he insisted on being stubborn, so would I. Stubborn, or perhaps stupid, it was all the same to me.

Minutes passed, and the foggy morning skies began to darken. The wind strengthened with the scent of coming rain. I resumed my place at the wheel, Felix at my side as we sailed carefully. Thane's ship was close enough within range now that if he were to open fire, he might just be able to reach us if he had a front bow chaser cannon, which would be likely on a gunship like his. But he was much farther than he should be if he hoped for any kind of precision. I wouldn't waste my ammunition at this distance. I wouldn't open fire on him till I knew I was close enough to sink his rig and take him on with my bare hands. And that day wasn't today, unfortunately.

Suddenly, a burst of wind sent us forward, towing us just out of reach and within the storm's suction. Thane must've known he was losing ground. His ship, barely in range, sent a small wave of cannonballs sweeping across the ocean's surface. Most of them arched and crashed into the water behind us, just a few inches from the *Falcon's* stern. But a couple did make impact, slamming the hull and one even grazing a spar on the mainmast.

The cracking wood made my stomach sink and my senses heighten. The wooden pole splintered, falling with a bit of sail still attached to it. But at least it wasn't the mast itself.

I asked Felix to tell the crew to hold off the cannons and start taking down the sails and securing ballasts before we reached the storm. He rushed to the forecastle deck to yell the orders. We didn't have time to turn and line up our guns, but I wouldn't leave Thane with nothing to show for his efforts. I rushed to a swivel cannon at the stern, where I released fire at his ship, taking out part of the foremast. That would slow him down considerably. As my men cheered, their voices were drowned out by the sound of one more front cannon blast from Thane. A chain shot. It whirled over the railing just far enough to clip Felix's head.

He dropped like a bag of sand. My gaze flicked from his bloody skull to Thane's ship. It was turning now, retreating.

"Damn coward." I muttered. It was only fitting of him to try his luck at one shot before running away from the storm like the piece of shite he was. And luck had been on his side to take out my first mate. I rushed back to the helm and gripped the wheel, Felix's blood pooling and trickling along the woodgrain to the soles of my boots. I shifted the rudder, taking back control against the choppy water and wind. I ordered some deckhands to move Felix's body somewhere safe until we could give him a proper burial at sea.

"Batten down the hatches and brace for rough seas ahead!" I called out, eyeing the dark clouds and curtain of rain right in front of us. There was no way to pull out of it now. And I prayed our damaged mast would hold up as we headed for the eye of the storm.

ANY PORT

22

MILO

The *Falcon* fared well in the storm. She rocked and slammed against the waves, but she was sturdy. With most of the crew riding it out belowdecks, a handful stayed up at my command to help secure a few more loose items and repair any immediate damage caused by the storm. Clara was one of them, even though I didn't ask her to.

The blinding rain and wind whipped my face, and my muscles strained against the wheel threatening to be pulled from my grip by the waves. But I could see the clearing just up ahead. Without our sails we couldn't hurry through to the other side, but just the sight of a blue sky gave me enough motivation to weather through it.

After an hour of lashing wind and waves, the sun welcomed us, and quickly brought its heat to make us forget the bite of the storm. The crew emerged, likely as hungry as I was. Rodrigo, the cook set to working, bringing each man his ration of breakfast—a porridge sweetened with butter and rum water. To my empty stomach it was a delicacy, and the nourishment helped to clear my head.

I studied the horizon, nearly calling Felix to help chart out our course, out of habit, but realizing he wouldn't be answering my call, I stopped myself. The storm had long washed away his blood, but I stared at the spot where he fell and called the men to bring him up. For a moment, I regretted that I never learned more about him than what I knew. One minute he was here. A whole life. And the next, in an instant, gone from this world. Not that I was unacquainted with death, but this one felt an awful lot like my fault.

Gathered at the stern with my crew, I laid his sword and pistol across him in the most ornate manner I could manage before we wrapped him in a shroud fashioned from his hammock. I read a rite from the ship's common prayer book, and then nodded to the crew to proceed with committing his body to the deep. He slid into the water and then sank slowly from the weights tied to him.

A somber quiet fell over my crew. Many of them had known Felix longer than I had, except the men I recruited on my own after taking this ship. I wondered how many of them secretly resented me for killing their captain and claiming the crew. I wondered if any of them actually cared. That was the price of being captain. I never knew who'd stayed out of loyalty, out of fear, or the desire for revenge. Except Felix. He was loyal to the sea and this ship, and I admired that about him.

Now I needed a new first mate.

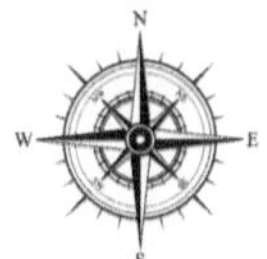

I reworked our course, adjusting based on how much the storm tossed us off course. It hadn't caused us to drift too far, so it would only take an extra afternoon to pick up where we left off. I charted our location, noticing an island just up ahead, a random lush formation in the middle of the Atlantic, but had no name or significance according to my maps. I intended to head toward it so we could stop for the evening and replace the broken mast spar. It was of the utmost importance to get it repaired so that we could resume our normal sailing speed and outmaneuver Thane if—and when—he returned.

By late afternoon, we'd docked as close as possible. The island looked uninhabited but was large enough to sustain life easily. When we disembarked and explored, it didn't take long to appreciate how lush and resource-filled this island was. Like an oasis in a desert, it boasted fresh springs of clear water and fruit trees in abundance. I encouraged my crew to take their fill and gather as much water and food as we could to replenish our own supply before night fell. We even took some extra timber from the dense forest of trees hiding the other half of the island.

As we worked to repair the mast spar by the light of torches and bonfires, I hummed a shanty to lift the crew's spirits. It wasn't long before the rest of them joined in. Clara's voice carried over the men's, a shrill note of power in a chorus of brutes. She half-grinned at me from her spot on the deck handing up tools to those of us perched on the mast, hammering the new spar into place and redoing the sail rigging. I had offered to let her climb up and help, but she insisted she was afraid of heights.

When the work was done, I wiped the sweat from my forehead and climbed down the rope webbing back to the deck. After a month of sailing, I figured my crew might appreciate a night on land, even if it was just an empty island with no taverns. I'd been pushing them so hard these recent weeks, desperate to find what I sought as fast as possible. Katrina was my mission. My reason for all of this. But these men were my crew and I owed them some rest.

With their cheers of relief filling the air, the men indulged themselves in our rum reserves and laid out cots to sleep in the sand under the open sky instead of the stuffy belowdecks. Finlay had even managed to capture a wild boar earlier that we roasted and stuffed ourselves with until we were sick. I suppose that redeemed him somewhat for his gambling addiction.

After I'd eaten my fill, I snuck away, longing for a bit of privacy to think. As if I didn't do enough of that alone in my quarters. But this would be different. This was finally a place without bustling taverns and crowded docks. This was a place I could sit beneath the stars in the sand and just let my mind wander in peace.

"Where ya off to, Cap'n?" Clara's voice called as she noticed me leaving the group.

"Nowhere in particular," I uttered over my shoulder. "Don't concern yourself. I'll be back."

I left her behind and wove my way through the tangled trees and lush leaves coating the lower half of the forest. For a moment, it reminded me of the night I led Katrina back to a safe spot on the shore back in Florida. The second night I saw her, and the first night I realized I wanted her. I fought to admit that to myself for so long. I swore to myself it must've been the necklace drawing me to her. Why else would I have been thinking of her even through my torment at the bottom of the ocean? Why did she—even when I hardly knew her—feel like the missing piece to my broken soul? Why did it seem as though long before time the stars had destined us to meet on that lonely island shore, much like this one?

All for me to end up back here, captaining a crew as the pirate I swore I'd never be. But maybe that was it? Maybe I was meant to stay here. Maybe it was the only way to truly protect Katrina. Her siren side would only grow stronger, and she needed someone without their own dark side to help her fight off hers. What if I couldn't?

Years at sea do strange things to a man's mind.

I pondered these things as I stood in a glade, not even realizing my feet had stopped moving. I stared up at the night sky through a break in the treetops, but I couldn't find my North Star for the trees.

Footsteps rustled in the leafy brush around me before a bright pop of red hair burst forth from the shadows. Clara looked up, her face cleaner than I'd seen it in weeks from washing up here on the island.

"I thought it'd be obvious I came all the way out here to be alone."

"Aye, Cap'n, maybe you aren't the only one in need of a bit of solitude away from those rank men." She shook her head. "Turns out we just happened to have the same idea. Don't worry. I'll be going that way and hopefully we won't cross each other again till it's time to board." She turned away, heading off into the dark forest perpendicular to the way she came.

"Wait," I said, my heart suddenly sinking as I realized I'd left Clara alone with thirty-plus men. "Did any of the crew...did they...?"

"Stop yer worryin', God in heaven, *no*. And if they tried I'd cut their hands clean off before they could lay a finger on me."

I couldn't hold back a small smile as Clara's fiery reply relieved me. Of course I should've known better than to be concerned about her. Twice now I'd seen her bite Finley's head off for looking at her too long.

"Well, I'll be seeing you then, Cap'n. Enjoy your brooding and I'll enjoy mine—feckin hell, what's this?" Her voice changed swiftly, as torchlight closed in on the both of us from seemingly nowhere, illuminating the circle of strange people encircling us.

I tensed, whipping my head to all sides to take in my new surroundings. Tall, sturdy, warrior-strong men and fiercely elegant women stood around us, a scrutinizing look in their eyes as they held us in place with their silent gaze. A woman stepped forward, the torchlight setting her dark tan skin aglow. She was old, with likely the same number of wrinkles as paths she'd trodden in life. She watched me with dark indigo eyes set deep and above the white paint markings on her cheekbones, clothed in woven palm fibers and a blanket of animal skin draped around her. Her graying hair poked through strands of black and strings of shells woven throughout.

She approached me. Clara drew her dagger in haste, but I stilled her with a motion of my hand. I kept my hands where the woman and her tribe could easily see them, to show them I meant no harm. But if I was trespassing on their island, perhaps I'd already done more harm than I realized.

She looked me over, a single word crawling from her lips as if she was tasting a bitter drink.

"Hidden," she lifted her chin, "How?" She asked, her eyes glistening but still sharp as steel.

"What does she mean?" Clara snapped, ready to pounce at any minute. A tall man who had been standing next to the woman stepped forward. His light brown skin was mottled in scars up his arms and across his back and shoulders.

"She means, we are a hidden people. An island hidden from mortal eyes." I was startled at the perfect English he spoke. "She asks how you found this place."

I stood startled, unsure how to answer, still processing the sudden change around me as well as his impossible question. Hidden island? I'd seen it clear as day as I sailed right for it.

"I don't know. I just saw it. I needed to find a place for my men to rest and repair our ship. We'll be leaving soon." I spoke clearly, though I felt myself rushing a bit.

The scarred man spoke to the elder woman in a language I didn't recognize, not taking his eyes off me. She answered him with the same and they nodded. His eyes narrowed as he addressed me again, his voice sure and unwavering. "Men like you never leave without taking something. You will destroy this island and the last of these people like all the others."

"I—I intend to take nothing. I'm no explorer, I'm not—"

"Even if you leave, you will tell others of this land. They will come. And do what they've done best for decades." He glanced at his scars, almost seeming like he hadn't meant to, and then quickly refocused.

"How..." I stammered, "How do you speak English so well if you've been hiding from the outside world?"

"I was not born of this tribe by blood. I was taken from my home. By men like you on a ship like yours. I spent many years among the Spanish and English-speaking people. I learned your languages because with mine I had no voice..." My eyes fell as a feeling of guilt lanced through me. Could my father have played a part in this man's capture, I wondered? A sick feeling refused to settle in my stomach as the man went on. "Thank the sea gods I was brought along for one voyage in particular. A voyage my captor and his family did not survive. They shipwrecked near this island. I washed up here, and was welcomed by these people. I told them what happened to me. I warned them to hide this refuge of theirs. So they blessed this island with their ancient power, by the stars and moon and sun, so that none can see it from afar."

I stood, still taking in everything he told me, searching the depths of my racing thoughts for a worthy-enough response. Stopping here for the night was a foolish decision. I should've known better. I'd wasted time and possibly put us all in danger. "I...I'm sorry for what happened to you. I won't reveal this island. To anyone...I swear it. I'll board my ship and command my crew to leave now."

But they didn't seem willing to negotiate. I waited as the man translated to the elder woman. She looked me up and down, then at Clara, with suspicious movements. The group around her stood unmoving, their torches still flickering as they awaited her next statement. Then one more commandment flew from her lips.

Island of the Sun

23

MILO

"She asks that you remove your shirt," the man said. I hesitated, but slowly moved to pull off my tunic as he urged me to hurry.

The old woman neared me, looking my body over as she circled, her regal frame seemingly gliding over the forest floor. I held my breath. Every moment my own heartbeat grew louder in my ears until she stopped, fixated on the tattoo on my arm. As she explained something in her language to the man, she tensed her jaw.

"The Star you bear grants you mercy." I followed the woman's gaze to my North Star tattoo as the man spoke. "But you also have a dark power on you, she says. A dark enchantment that opposes ours and draws darkness to our island." He pointed to my arm with Bastian's mark.

"I had no choice but to accept this. It's just a tattoo. I have no dark power." I dared not move as I tried to explain myself, eyeing the tribe around me watching my every flinch.

"Come," the old woman said sternly. I was startled by her sudden utterance of a word I understood. I shifted toward her, slowly, intrigued. She looked to the man to translate as I gave Clara a nod of reassurance.

"We have a legend here, that the sun and the moon were once mortals, trapped in a cave and both forged as a result of enduring the same darkness."

"What does that have to do with me?"

"You, too, must not be overtaken by the shadows that bind you. The dark one who marked you can see us now. Even if we kill you, you've already revealed our existence. Soon the ships will come and the men will take what is not theirs. We must break the connection you share with your dark master so that we remain untraceable."

"You can do that?"

"Only enough to blur the tether you hold to the darkness. And then you must leave immediately, so that you're no longer a beacon for our location."

The thought of muddling the connection Bastian held over me sounded like a deal far too great to be true, no matter what it entailed. I leaned in, desperate to know more, and wondering what it would require of me. It didn't quite seem I would have a choice in the matter either way.

The man and elder woman spoke together, conversing back and forth before the elder addressed the tribe around her. Some shook their heads in disagreement, but others seemed to support what she was saying. Though they stood divided, the woman appeared to have made her decision.

"Sun," she said simply.

The translator straightened his shoulders. "You will bear the sign of our sun to drown out the dark power in you. It will sustain you as long as you seek the light. But if you choose the darkness...if you give in to the tempest raging in your heart...it will fade and give you over to your own destruction."

"You're giving me a choice?"

"No, you give yourself a choice. To choose darkness or light. Already you're tempted or you wouldn't ask. You are willing to do whatever you have to do to find that which you seek. And you've let it consume you and define you. Let the sun's light guide you. I will keep you from hardening your heart to the realities of those around you and from bringing harm to others in pursuit of freedom from your own pain."

Her words pierced something in me. There was no more room for doubting. I was meant to find the fountain. To reunite with Katrina. And my only path there right now was through doing as these people demanded.

"I'll take your symbol. I don't seek to harm you. I just want to get home." I offered a slight tilt of my head.

The woman spoke a word the man didn't bother to translate. In an instant, one man and one woman from the circle surrounding us lunged forward and grabbed Clara, each of them holding an arm in restraint as Clara shouted obscenities in surprise. I flinched, but didn't dare draw my weapon. I knew better than to leap to combat in defense. They weren't hurting her, and I knew she'd be fine. I couldn't risk losing any merit I sought to gain with the islanders.

A sharp point dug into my back. A knife or spear tip, I presumed. The man in front of me never took his harsh eyes from mine. "Remove all your weapons," he ordered. "The Elder wants to speak to you alone first."

I obliged, sliding my swords from their sheaths and laying my pistol at his feet. I couldn't explain the feeling I had, but somehow I believed with my whole heart I would come out of this alive. Perhaps it was delusion or drunkenness, but my fear had subsided.

The man before me and the member at my back forced me along a break in the circle encompassing us, leading me down a well-worn path behind the elder woman. With my agreement made known, the elder woman led me away to a place where the forest grew thicker and the sound of trickling water became clearer.

When we were far enough away, the old woman turned to face me. I noticed she'd led me to a stream that snaked through the rich soil of this island, its trickling sound like delicate clattering cymbals amongst the night song of insects. When the woman broke the silence with her speech, I looked up, listening and intrigued as to why she brought me here.

She dipped a withered hand into the clear water, guiding my gaze to the stream bed below. Inlaid with veins of gold, it certainly caught my attention. No doubt this island would be ravaged for this gold if anyone knew of its existence.

I inched closer to take a better look. The woman motioned for me to sit down on the ground. I knelt beside the stream, the elder woman seated regally with hands now folded in her lap. She began to speak and the man stood over us, translating each phrase.

"When you take this mark, remember our legend. Both trapped by darkness in a cave, the sun fought it, and his light grew stronger. But the moon embraced it, so much that she was able to trick the darkness into letting them go. So when they escaped, the sun was devoted to her for the rest of time. They both escaped their prison, but the moon forever harbored a dark side that only the sun could keep at bay. That's why we see her change each night. Her strength over the shadow waxes and wanes, but the sun's light sustains her until one day when she will grow strong enough to overcome it."

I let my gaze drift to the shimmering gold lines traced along the bottom of the crystal stream. The woman's hand, gentle but firm, touched my face to turn my head back to her as she continued.

"I understand the sun's power is great here. And you believe it protects your island." I said, hoping to move this process along.

"Yes. So be like the sun." The woman said this, instead of the man having to translate. She almost smiled with her eyes, though the rest of her face remained tight and emotionless.

"Now give her your arm." The man's voice boomed from above.

I slowly reached my arm forward, the woman began a low chant, humming to herself as she placed the tip of her finger in the water. The golden threads in the sediment began to glow, like warm light from the sun itself. It became like liquid, dribbling out from the cracks in which it rested and floating up in the water to meet the woman's fingertip. She lifted her finger, taking the stream of floating molten gold with it, directing it like swirling smoke.

She guided it to my arm, hovering over the tattoo from Bastian, and then the molten gold took form, searing itself into my skin in the symbol of a sun. I expected it to burn immensely, but there was little more than a mild sting. It settled into my flesh, creating an inlay of gold that became just barely visible once it settled.

"This will keep him from being able to find me as easily?"

"Yes." The man nodded. "It will serve as a veil between you and the dark one who marked you. And more importantly, he will not be able to see that you were here."

I breathed a sigh of relief as the man continued.

"As long as you leave at sunrise."

"You have my word. I'll have my ship repaired and gone before the first light of dawn." I nodded. "And Clara can be released now?" I asked.

The man raised an eyebrow. "The girl? She's unharmed. Go back to her now and tell no one of our existence or this island. Swear it by the stars."

"I swear it." With a solemn nod of understanding, I hastened my steps back toward Clara. When I turned, the woman and man were gone, not a trace of them left behind. Before I could reach the area where we'd been surrounded, Clara came bounding through the brush.

"Thank God, there ya are," she sputtered between hurried breaths. "They let me go and just vanished, they did. What did they do to you?"

"They swore me to secrecy. And made me promise to leave before sunrise."

"Why not kill us and get it over with? Ensure their safety." Clara looked around, seemingly still paranoid of their presence.

"Because they know better than to take a life lightly," I uttered. "But the same can't be said of those who would come here if they knew what treasures lay here. Come on."

I motioned, moving forward onto the trail. "Let's get my things and head back to the crew."

I regathered my weapons and shirt, keeping silent as I reflected on the things I'd just experienced. The islanders were here and gone, barely ghosts in my memory and yet they'd left me with such a heavy weight in my heart. The guilt of lives I'd taken for gold, not for greed, but to buy the mere chance to see the girl I loved again, was a burden I'd bear forever. But the true weight was the terrifying thought that she'd never look at me the same. These hands would always be bloody, and it didn't seem right to hold her with them. Maybe this strange sun mark would help me find my way again. Maybe if Bastian's darkness wasn't the only darkness it could drive out...

Clara walked to my side as I turned over the thoughts in my head. Her voice tearing through the calm sounds of night. "What's still gnawing away at ya? I've been around you long enough to see on your face when you're frettin'."

"If the island is truly hidden, I don't understand why I was able to see it." I brushed a branch aside for us to pass through.

"Didn't those people go on about the power of sun and stars or something another? Maybe deep down ya already had a little ray of sunlight in there somewhere."

"Maybe." I glanced down at my North Star tattoo, thinking of Katrina and my path back to her. "Or starlight."

"So what exactly is it that you're looking for so desperately, Cap'n? I'm no fool and I know yer not just sailing this way in such a hurry hoping to find more gold or riches."

"If I told you, you'd never believe me." I didn't want her asking more questions, but it was clear she was catching on.

"I don't think you give me much credit, Cap'n." Clara paused to spit on the ground as we walked. "These past months I've watched you loot and plunder like a greedy dog. Hell I saw you shoot a man point blank for the key to his quarters. But ya never look pleased with what we take. No matter how valuable our prizes. You watch the ships we sink with a scowl while your men cheer in victory. You're richer than most any pirate captain I've sailed amongst, yet you live like you've the weight of the world on your shoulders. Like it's never ever enough. Whatever you're after has to be something beyond what this mortal world can offer."

"You're too smart for your own good, Reid. I can't imagine the trouble you've gotten yourself into...and out of."

"Don't try flattery to make me forget. I've watched ya sell your soul to the devil and agree to do his bidding for something. And I've done nothing but help you try to reverse it. So don't I deserve to know what exactly I'm helping my captain accomplish when I'm puttin' my neck on the line with yours?"

I breathed in a heavy sigh, looking ahead at the dying glow of the crew's fires in the distance. Their silence told me they'd likely long succumbed to their drink and merry-making. So I'd let them sleep it off for a few more hours. But we'd be back on the water before first light.

"I never asked for your help with any of those things," I grumbled.

"True. But ya never ordered me to leave you alone either."

She was right. I'd never quite found it in me to turn her away, truth be told. I was just as curious about her as she was about me, but I didn't have time to pursue her secrets.

"Tell me where you came from and what it is you want with a life of sailing with a bunch of salty jackasses, and I'll tell you what it is I'm after."

Clara hesitated, surprise at my request clear in her eyes.

"You've been just as secretive as me, so don't act so shocked." I added.

"Fine," Clara crossed her arms. "It's not as daring and noble as you think, Harrington." Her eyes fell downward, focused on our boots in the damp earth below. "I was the daughter of a wealthy family. Always creating mischief where I couldn't find it. And when my mother tried marrying me off, I ran away, joining the first boat I could manage to sneak aboard. But adventurous as I was, I was naïve. My luck ran out soon enough and they found me..."

I wasn't sure if she was going to continue, and I didn't want to press her after the way she looked as her voice tapered off. But she went on, lip quivering for just a split second.

"The devils violated me and marooned me on an island. Said they couldn't have a woman aboard bringing the devil's curses. I was found by some traders, and they dumped me in Nassau, where I met a man I *thought* I loved. I joined his crew, and then I met her...a jewel of the seas. Just like me, she was. She knew all about scraping by and surviving this shite-hole of a man's world. We had a good run, she and I." Clara stared out into the blackness in the distance and smiled, as though reminiscing some cherished memory. "Until the Royal Navy found her...her and most the crew...hanged 'em all for piracy, they did. I escaped—by nothing but pure luck and a too drunk jailer who forgot to lock my cell. I sailed on my own long enough to end up in Madagascar, where ya found me. After that,

I swore I'd never trust another captain. And I'd never let another—man or woman—hold my heart again."

"Did you ever trust me?" I asked her, scratching my neck as I awaited her answer in the silence.

"No. But I'm not afraid of ya, either, and that's the difference. I see the way you stare into the sea sometimes, with eyes like a lost daydreamin' lover, and the way you smile just a bit to yourself when you think no one sees ya. So I'll ask once more. What—or who—are you tryin' to find out here, Cap'n?"

I felt my face heating as I thought of Clara observing me so closely. She was too good at reading me. And for whatever reason, I was strangely fond of her fiery, abrasive spirit. I breathed in a heavy sigh, motioning for her to walk alongside me as we emerged from the forest and followed the shoreline.

"There's a lass who has my whole heart out there. But time has separated us. We are centuries apart. She's far into the future, and I'm trapped here. All because of some twisted siren magic. I left her a clue how to bring me back to her, not thinking of the danger it would put her in." I breathed out, thinking of Katrina and wishing that with the next breath I'd draw in, I'd breathe in her sweet scent of apricot and honeysuckle, and hating myself again for getting her mixed up with Bastian. "But if I can live forever...I can reunite with her, even if she doesn't succeed...I can wait for her, however long it takes until our timelines meet again."

Clara stared up at me with a twinkle in her eye, and the corner of her mouth twitched as though she might laugh. I would've expected no less.

"All that for a girl, mate?" She laughed. "I understand bein' lovesick as much as the next bastard but come on now. Say ya just stay here and settle down with a nice lass somewhere, forget that one. Not worth the heartache."

"She's worth every heartache. She's worth dying a thousand times for the chance to live one day with her. It's funny," I huffed with a forced laugh. "I once spent so long looking for a way to die, and now I'm searching the ends of the earth for a way to live forever just to see her again."

"Aye, so you're lookin' for the Fountain of Youth!" She exclaimed.

I half-nodded, but mostly I just looked away, unable to admit to her claim. She went on before my next thought even had time to form. "That's exactly the kind of thing that makes me know you're different from the rest." She grinned with a sideways glance. "Any man who's loose in the head enough to take the mark of Davy Jones just so he has a slim chance of waitin' out eternity to meet his woman…that's a Cap'n worth sailin' with."

I shrugged, not sure of what more to say. A small glimmer of hope rose within me, reassuring me that perhaps I hadn't completely damned myself and this plan.

"Is it, though? Knowing I'd sacrifice anyone and do anything to see her again. Anyone. Be that you or my crew if it came down to it."

Clara tilted her head back. "Everyone has somethin' they'd burn down the world for. Yours just happens to be a bit more decent than most."

"Thank you," I uttered. "And thank you for how you've helped aboard my ship. Your last crew were fools to treat you the way they did. God knows you're better than the lot of mine." I scanned the landscape filled with my snoring men, strewn across the sand lying lifeless as bonfires smoked their last piles of smoldering embers and the waves lapping filled the silence. I thought of Felix, and how he would've been the only one of them to have kept his head this night and not sentenced himself to a brutal hangover the next morning. But he was gone, and I was still down a good first mate.

I looked at Clara, watching her take care of where she stepped as we left the jungle behind and entered the sprawling shore where my ship waited in the distance.

"Don't ogle me like that, Cap'n. It gives me a feeling I don't like. And like I said, my sails don't quite catch the wind that way." She snapped.

"It's not like that," I reassured. "On the contrary…I just…I have a proposition for you." I hesitated, hoping I wasn't about to make a grave mistake. Clara cocked her head, squinting her eyes at me.

"How would you like the position of first mate?" I asked, holding my breath as the words rushed out of my mouth so I wouldn't have time to regret the offer.

Clara's lips twisted into a wickedly mischievous grin. "As much as a dog loves its filth."

"Good," I smirked with a gesture to my ship. "Then let's chart our course and wake up these fools. We've got a fountain to find."

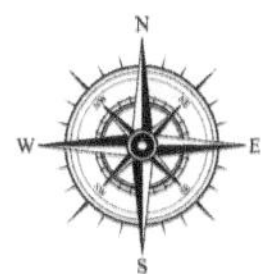

With my crew barely awake and my mast repaired, we hoisted anchor in the faint light of twilight. Clara took her place on the forecastle deck, yelling orders down below as some of the crew grumbled under their new authority. As I looked back at the island that had rested us well, I caught a glimpse of the elder woman and her people watching approvingly from the tree line. And as the distance between my ship and the shore grew, the island suddenly vanished from sight, replaced by nothing but the same ocean horizon surrounding us on every other side.

I really hoped Bellamy was joking about Kraken's eating mermaids. If anything, I prayed that maybe the opposite was true. Maybe we weren't natural enemies like humans were. Maybe I could reason with it somehow in my siren form.

"You just made that up!" I shot Bellamy a playful look of scorn, hitting his arm where the heart and arrow tattoo just peeked out through his sleeve. I'd caught him looking at it more than once, lost in thought—or memory, of adding each arrow as he lost those he loved. I wouldn't be his third arrow, I promised myself. And I'd make sure I ended Bastian's link to him by completing this mission.

"Aye, don't worry. I'm just pulling your ropes. But either way I'm sure the beastie will be more than surprised to see us. I almost feel for it. Once a leviathan of the seas, now hiding in the dark depths lost to time, now being asked to surface again and face a whole new world that no longer has room for it. I can relate."

"Oh stop," I uttered. "You're making *me* feel sorry for it."

"Don't worry," Bellamy stood, stretching an arm behind his head. "I'm sure it won't take long for it to change your mind."

I sighed, glancing at the clock on the wall that reminded me yet again how time-sensitive this assignment was. I didn't know how long it would take to kill a Kraken. "The sooner the better," I removed my outerwear and marched up to the deck.

"Don't look," I said, stepping out of my shoes and pants. The Mediterranean winter winds grazed my face with a chilly whisper of encouragement or doom, I couldn't tell which. I took a deep breath, mesmerized by the clear blue surface of the water that I could see straight through down to where they gave way to the blackest depths below. I almost felt my old fears coming back to haunt me, but this time it wasn't a fear of the water...just what was lurking beneath it.

I turned back to see Bellamy, harpoon in hand and hunting rifle strapped to his back. Thankfully the yacht's armory was stocked with at least that. I stepped up onto the edge of the hull and climbed over, holding onto the rim while I leaned over the water's surface. I was about to dive in, bracing myself for the brief sting in my lungs right before I transformed. But a hand steadied my shoulder. I glanced back at Bellamy, whose forehead was creased with a worry I knew he'd rather not show. "Be careful down there, lass. Don't get too close to that thing."

I gave a firm nod, and then let go, dropping forward and leaning headfirst into the water. Its icy pierce swallowed me whole, and I fought my way through the chill of my body, forcing myself to ignore it until my other side gained control. Once in that form, I no longer felt the glacial temperature of the water on my skin. Everything was as it should be. Me, immersed, one with the water and sinking deeper, deeper...

I forced myself to stay focused and keep the siren voice at bay. Though I wondered if I might need some of her brash fierceness to face this creature of the deep. If I ever found it, that is. I searched, looking for any sign of the sea monster's presence. But as I dove the depths, sea life became more and more scarce.

It was only when I spotted a large school of fish swimming frantically upwards that I guessed they might be a clue to my next direction. With a powerful flick of my tail, I surged forward through the water to where the fish had just passed, and then I turned downward to make my descent to the depths.

As I swam, heavy groans echoed from the ocean floor, creating rippling vibrations strong enough to rattle my bones. Any human would have long succumbed to the pressure. I had to be miles down by now, but there was still no sign of the Kraken. I suddenly feared if I went deep enough to find it, I wouldn't stand a chance against it in its own territory. I had to bring it to the surface.

I wished I had my siren song, because it seemed it might've been the perfect tool for summoning a sea beast. But at least I still had my other power. I wondered if I could create some sort of commotion, maybe I could get its attention. I'd never quite controlled the water from underneath like this. I wasn't sure if it was even possible. But to me it made sense. If my tears connected my power to the ocean's, how much more would it work when I was already submerged in it?

I blinked back the ache behind my eyes. My siren didn't like to cry, of course, but Katrina had mastered the art of feeling her broken heart enough to draw out some sorrows. And if I couldn't find sadness, there always seemed to be some burning anger readily available in this form. I bit down on my lip until it bled, a tiny drop of red blossoming into the dark water around me, only visible to my inhuman eyes this deep. The bit of pain made me wince, and even underwater I could feel the sting in my eyes drawing out a tear from reaction.

Suddenly I felt the water swirl at my fingertips, like energy flowing from me and to me both at the same time. I spun the water around me, creating light currents the same way I might glide a paintbrush along a canvas. Careful, but freeing movements, up, then down. I drew the water around me like a cloak, sending it whirring around in streams of bubbles, and then channeling it all back down.

Another groan reverberated up through the water. It had to be close. It had to be seeing and feeling all this. I twisted more water around me, bending it in ribbons that flowed like paint trails down paper. I dove just a bit lower, sending a few more powerful currents down to the bottom, where I waited, staring into the black abyss that became even too dark for me to see into.

I waited, letting the water around me settle a moment. The silence down here was almost tangible, and once the last few bubbles popped and faded, there was nothing left to fill it. Suspended in the water by my tail, I watched the depths below, my heart now pounding in my ears. The siren in me told me—begged me to swim up, to escape and preserve myself. But none of this was about myself.

When a massive tentacle shot upwards from the darkness, I found myself right in its path. I whipped my tail sideways and darted out of the way, but the tentacle seemed adamant that I was its target. It retreated for a moment, only briefly, before a low quaking sent me swimming back up. I had awoken the Kraken.

The ascent was a blur, as my determination to reach the surface blocked out the memory of the tentacles shooting up around me like weeds. I broke through the water, a desperate gasp on my lips to warn Bellamy of the creature right on my tail.

"It's behind me! Get ready!" I called.

Bellamy rushed to the edge of the boat, leaning as far over as he could, waiting to see the monster we were about to face. For a moment it was quiet, and only a lone bubble surfaced. I dove back down for a quick look, but all signs of the Kraken had disappeared. As I resurfaced, before I could say a word to Bellamy, something broke forth out of the water on the other side of the boat. With a crash that sent the yacht reeling, the great sea beast showed itself in all its glory.

The tips of its tentacles that had attacked me were nothing compared to the entire thing. Each one must've been at least one hundred feet long, the width of massive columns that could easily snap a boat in half. The purplish gray hue of its body shone glossy white in the light as it emerged partly from the water, revealing its brutish form. An octopus-like creature of colossal proportions, it dwarfed our yacht, making it look as fragile as a toy sailboat in a child's bathtub.

The creature raised up from the water. With a deafening roar, it revealed rings of razor teeth waiting to suck down its next victim with ease. I gasped, a sense of fear washing over me at the thought of being trapped in the water with this thing. But I doubted legs would do me any more good than fins. I glanced at Bellamy, who was at the mercy of the beast sizing up our boat. Suddenly tentacles flew up around the sides of the boat, climbing up like vines and taking hold of the hull.

"She'll snap this thing in two and pull it under!" Bellamy called, pulling out the rifle on his sling and firing. The Kraken growled in anguish or surprise at the hot bullet lodging itself in her tentacle. I wondered how Bellamy had any way of possibly knowing it was a "she," but I went along with it. She recoiled, her tentacles sliding down the boat's edges in a momentary retreat. Bellamy aimed at the water below, using the scope to help him hone in on his target. He fired once more, this time into the animal's head. But a bullet from a rifle was probably no more than an ant bite to this creature. She merely reared back as if to attack, unfazed by the pebble-sized chunk taken from her flesh.

"I think you're just making her mad!" I yelled to Bellamy. As if on cue, the Kraken pulled her grip from the boat. She turned her attention to me, lifting a colossal tentacle and sending it crashing back down like a falling building. I dodged it by ducking under the water and using my tail as a rudder to help me dart off to the side. I gathered my courage and swam underneath the monster, looking desperately for any sort of weak spot or injury I could use to my advantage.

Dammit. Nothing.

I summoned some water and balled it up into an orb of energy, sending it hurtling toward the belly of the beast. It was enough to make her take pause and lurch up as the force made impact with her body. But she no more than rocked back into position with ease and continued her attack on the yacht. The boat's shadow moved off, and a trail of bubbles churned out quickly from the propeller. Bellamy circled the yacht around her, and I watched from beneath, still trying to think of how I could weaken her with her own element.

I swam back up to the surface, desperate. Bellamy reeled the boat around the backside of the Kraken. Her size certainly made her slow, which seemed to be the only advantage we had. He left the helm and rushed to the side of the boat, shooting the thing with a flare gun and then a few rounds of the rifle. The flare seemed to stun her, and it allowed for him to get a few shots in, but the bullets nearly bounced off her skin. Nothing was working.

"Still feel sorry for it?" Bellamy shouted over the roar of water splashing and the sea beast groaning. I rolled my eyes, then dove back under to look once more for weak spots.

As I swam, I began to question everything. Could we really kill this thing? No wonder Bellamy was so mad at me when I accepted Bastian's deal to do this. What if he was right? What if this really was a suicide mission. If I couldn't bring Milo back, that was one thing, but I should never have asked this of Bellamy.

Crackling reverberated through the dense water as the monster reached for the boat once more. Her tentacles squeezed it like an eggshell. It would either break in half or be pulled down in seconds. I motioned for the water and created a swell big enough to push her off the boat, but I couldn't hold it for long.

Letting go of the wave, I burst back up to the surface, my eyes meeting a panicked Bellamy's. "The harpoon!" I shouted. I knew Bellamy was saving that for a one-and-only shot, but I was beginning to think it might be time to take the chance. With the Kraken right up on the boat, he would at least have an easy shot.

He rushed to the creature, fighting the swaying of the boat as the tentacles secured their grip around it once more like a spider going for the kill. With a grunt, he stabbed the side of the monstrous thing, right by its massive beady eye. It shrieked in pain, a shrill sound deafening to the ears.

"We need more harpoons! It would probably take hundreds of them!" Bellamy screamed over the animal's agonizing roar.

My thoughts raced. Even with more harpoons, her underside was armored by the thickest hide I'd ever seen, probably impossible to pierce with anything that wasn't...magic. Then an idea struck me. I recalled the icy bite of this water when I was human. The sharp stab of cold water was worse than any blade. Ice.

I had no idea if my power could manage such a feat, but now was as good as any time to find out. I painted scenes of frozen water in my mind, dreaming of how I'd shape the crisp, sharp form of ice in hues of white and blue. I felt the water around me, forming crystals at my fingertips and drawing the water to me in a way I'd never before. It hardened, forming a staff of ice shards with a tip sharper than a sword—ice harpoons. I formed a dozen or so of them, and with every ounce of concentration in me, I harnessed the small army of ice spikes surrounding me in the water, turning them on the Kraken and sending them forward with all the speed and force possible. They shot forward, their icy tips driving into various spots on the beast. She wailed in pain and dipped down into the water to face me. Her blood stained the water around her, creating an eerie sight of cool blue and swirling scarlet. She lunged at me, showing that terrifying ring of teeth and sending her tentacles at me. Instinctively, I put up my hand, inadvertently forming an ice shield between us. Her tentacle hit the clear ice wall, cracking it before it dissolved into the rest of the water.

Ice was the answer. At least for now. I could slow her down enough with it while Bellamy used the ice harpoons. We could do this. I swam back up to the surface, an artillery of ice spikes forming alongside me as I emerged.

"Use these!" I cried, sending a wave up and over the yacht's edge to carry the harpoons to Bellamy. He grabbed one, not even pausing to question it, and launched it toward the roaring beast before us. It released another roar and lunged forward, going for the boat, but I caught the water just in time and blocked her with an icy wave. I wasn't strong enough to freeze large amounts of water at once, so my ice walls were thin, and shattered like glass when the Kraken so much as touched them. But it was a decent distraction while Bellamy bloodied the creature with his skillful precision.

I couldn't believe we'd gotten this far. Weakening the Kraken was one thing. But taking her down would still prove to be another. I frantically swam to the boat's edge creating more ice harpoons from the water around me and sending them shooting upwards at the Kraken all at once. Some of them pierced her skin and stayed there until they melted from the heat of her blood. A small few of the rest shattered on impact with her body.

She ducked below the surface in an effort to escape the ice spike barrage. I dove under, watching her speed toward the boat from underneath. Thinking on my feet—or rather my fins—I shot a hand forward to move the yacht forward with a current from underneath, fast enough to push it right out of her path as she burst forth above the water, angered by missing her target. She plunged back down, and this time her attention wasn't on the boat. Her black eyes darted back and forth, and her tentacles swirled around her chaotically. She was looking for me.

I did my best to swim amongst the shadows, but the clear water made it difficult to hide. When she saw me, she swatted at me with those massive trunk-like tentacles. She could move much more quickly down here, and the force of her limb swooping past me caught me in an undertow even I could hardly manage to swim out of. I tumbled and swirled in the water, fighting to regain my equilibrium. She overshadowed me, trapping me beneath her as her razor teeth closed in. I swam for my life, and she snatched me with a tentacle, wrapping me in her grip like a python. She carried me along as she refocused on the boat above. I could hear Bellamy screaming my name from above, no doubt wondering what kind of underwater battle was ensuing.

As I squirmed in her grasp, she squeezed my waist and hips so hard I thought I might faint. My tail was immobilized, but one hand was free. As she charged back up to attack the boat, I gave one last ditch effort to call on the water, begging it to crystallize fast and create a barrier between the Kraken and the yacht. But in her unstoppable rage, the beast crashed up through a thin sheet of ice I'd just barely started to form, slamming the whole of her body into the yacht. It nearly tipped, and Bellamy was soaked as he held on for dear life. Reaching for the rifle, he fired more shots, but the unfazed Kraken moved into the bullets like they were no more than snowflakes.

She slid a tentacle into the water, wrapping it around the underside of the boat.

"Bellamy! Look out!" I shouted in warning. Her grip tightened on me and subsequently the yacht. Creaking split the air for a few seconds, and just as Bellamy leapt overboard, the hull snapped in half from the pressure of the Kraken's squeeze. She submerged herself again, taking me with her as she sought out Bellamy drifting in the water. He was fighting the suction of the sinking boat pieces, nearing the surface when she grabbed him with another tentacle. My eyes widened in horror as she dragged him along, heading downward into the depths with both of us in her clutches.

Drowning

25

BELLAMY

Diving into that chilled water felt like a kick in the gut, but I hardly had time to register it as the slime of that monster slid across my body. It dragged me down, suction cups holding me in place as I fought to preserve the last breath I took before leaping off the boat. Under here, I couldn't see Katrina's face, but I knew despite my blurry vision she could see me perfectly. I could feel her watching me, and I knew she was hating herself right then.

Some part of me did wish I could have one more moment on the surface with her just for the satisfaction of being right. I wasn't above being the type to say "I told you so, lass." But I knew she didn't need me to say it. And for that, I was sorry.

I didn't blame her for any of it. Hell, I'd almost killed her before because I wanted to bring back Serena so badly. I wasn't one to talk. But when you're drowning in the clutches of a Kraken, maybe it wasn't abnormal to feel some resentment. But even then, I knew what I was risking by trying to bring back Milo—my brother at sea. And some time back I had already decided that if he would be lost at sea, it was only fair that I should be, too. So, this was fine. I'd die...again. At least this time it was sort of worth something.

A Mermaid's Kiss

26

I should've listened to Bellamy. Killing the Kraken truly *was* an impossible task. I could only imagine what he might've been thinking if he wasn't struggling to breathe right now. I couldn't blame him for hating me. I didn't care if trying to save Milo meant being eaten by the Kraken. But Bellamy shouldn't have been facing the same fate. I couldn't bear to live with myself as I watched him drown. I wished there was some way—any way—I could at least save him.

I watched him struggle against the tentacles binding him, knowing he wouldn't last much longer submerged as we were pulled to the depths. Down, down, darker and colder. It was too deep for a human. The pressure and the cold would be too much, if he hadn't drowned already. I couldn't bear it, and I cried underwater. I cried so much that I fought the Kraken with all the strength in my tears. I found the might to push back against her, trying to sweep us back up to the surface with the water I controlled. But even I couldn't hold back a Kraken. And finally, I saw the light dim from Bellamy's bright blue eyes as his head rolled back in the water. Like a rag doll, the monstrous creature carried him, and I wondered what fate awaited us when she finally reached the bottom.

The Kraken sank to a sandy floor with a thud, where a dark cove awaited in the shadows. She'd take us there and chew us up with that garbage disposal of a mouth I was sure. Along the ocean floor she slunk, sliding along by her tentacles, which grew tighter and tighter around us. I'd given up my voice for this.

I'm sorry, Milo. Maybe I'll find you again in death.

As I braced myself to become a meal, I was startled at the impossible sound of a voice, clear as a bell, ringing out from the dark cave.

"Cala, finish them off! Show them what happens to those mortals who defy their place on land. Show them what happens to those who try to hurt us."

I blinked, trying to recognize whose voice I was hearing. It reached my ears like cool velvet, a strange power and beauty in it, almost like a siren's, but less soft and seductive…it was stronger to the ear and drenched with authority. It had come from the ominous shadows of the cave.

The Kraken groaned softly, drawing a limp Bellamy and me closer and opening its terrifying jaws wide. At least Bellamy would be unconscious for this part. I recoiled at the sight of the teeth so close to shredding me open as it pulled me near to its mouth. I wriggled my tail with the last of my strength, to no avail.

Just as I closed my eyes, preparing myself for the pain of those knife-like teeth to tear into my skin, the voice called out again, this time with an urgency I might've even mistaken for panic.

"Wait!"

The Kraken froze, still carefully restraining us in its clutches.

The great beast lowered Bellamy down, still holding me tight as I watched onward. His body drifted to the sand below and I couldn't help but notice the peace in his face. I almost envied him. I still searched for the voice. Then I saw her. Somehow in this darkness beneath the sea, I could see her clearly, as if some light radiated from her and illuminated this bit of sea floor. My gaze followed the flow of a current swirling towards a womanly figure, wrapping her in a dress made from the very water around her. Like a veil, the current obscured her face as she walked with slow steps on the sand. She was no siren or mermaid. She moved as though she was one with the water, but her body looked fully human. I couldn't die like this, without my curiosity quenched. I had to know who she was and how she walked down here, commanding deadly giant squids with just her words.

The ocean woman neared Bellamy, and I couldn't keep from calling out to her. "Please don't hurt him! Can you send him back to the surface? Kill me, but give him a chance to live! It was my idea to come here, not his!"

She ignored me, seeming completely fixated on Bellamy's lifeless body. I wished I could see her face, but the water kept a blurry shield whirling around her. I could make out her movements with ease, though. She knelt down to him; touched his hair with her fingers. She felt his face and neck and chest, as if she'd never seen another human before. And then, she leaned over, putting her face to his as the glassy wall of water surrounded them both. I couldn't tell for sure, but it looked like she kissed him on the lips.

As she pulled her mouth away from his, I watched in confusion as the water veil faded away, leaving me with a clear view of her now, even in these dark depths. She looked my direction and I gasped at the vision of her beauty and power. But beyond that, the shock of recognizing her left me paralyzed. In an instant, my mind flashed back to the old newspaper clippings Russell showed me and photos from Mrs. Gutierrez' album. It was impossible, yet undeniable. Here down at the bottom of the ocean, I was staring right at Serena. And she was staring back.

"S...Serena?" I uttered, the name stuck on my lips.

Her dark eyes narrowed at me, piercing through the water between us like one of my ice spears. She ignored my question, and turned her attention back to Bellamy, who was somehow beginning to stir. The Kraken still held me tight, but it was no longer crushing me with its grip.

I watched Bellamy as he shook his head slowly, squinting here and there as though slowly rousing from a nightmare. He brought his hands to his head. Then he opened his eyes and sat up, seemingly unaffected by the fact that he was underwater. He glanced around, startled at the sight of the beast towering over him and eyes wide when he looked forward at Serena.

"How is he alive down here? How are *you* alive down here? And how did you do that?" I asked. I didn't expect an answer from Serena, and she didn't give one.

But Bellamy, still steadying himself as he propped himself up by his hands in the sand, took a deep, satisfying breath that reassured me he was miraculously fine. "A mermaid's kiss..." he said, his eyes fixed on Serena. "...is said to grant the ability to breathe underwater."

He spoke while transfixed on Serena, and she nodded to her Kraken a command to release me. I watched from my distance, unsure if I moved how the animal would react. So, I stayed in place, watching a scene so tense and quiet. Serena leveled herself with Bellamy, reaching forward to touch his chin as she held his gaze with hers. She spoke to him, not me. "A mermaid's kiss indeed. And if it can do that, what do you think a kiss from a sea goddess can do?"

BELLAMY

As my vision settled and Serena's face came into focus, I thought I had finally died and found my way to her. But it didn't take long before I noticed the entrapment of the water around me and the slimy squid beast at my back. I was still very much alive. Somehow, here on the ocean floor, and somehow I was staring at a woman I'd watched drown with her heart cut out nearly half a century ago.

But none of those unanswered questions mattered. Nothing mattered. Not the water, not the Kraken, and not the sea salt stinging my open wounds from my battle with it. I didn't care if I'd been damned to Davy Jones Locker, if it meant Serena was here.

But I couldn't let myself believe it. This couldn't really be her. I refused to trust that this vision before me, walking underwater as naturally as on land and shrouded in an ethereal glow, was really Serena. I'd hallucinated her before. On my father's ship, in the brig, I'd even sworn Katrina was her, only to be snapped out of my delusion and faced with heartbreak every time.

But this time, she didn't fade away. Her deep skin shone with an almost iridescent sheen down here, like the purest pearl, as dark braids of black and even blue drifted around her amongst loose strands and pieces woven into gold. Her dress was like white sea foam forming an ever-flowing wrap around her, trailing off at her feet as it flowed into the water around her. Her voice held its same unmistakable lure as it did the night she stepped onto the shore in front of me. It was her. But it couldn't be real.

"Serena," I uttered, my hands shaking and lips trembling with disbelief. She looked at me for a moment that felt like it stretched into hours. Her eyes flickered from my face to my body and back up again.

"That is the name by which you know me. Yes, it's me." she smiled. "Good to see you again, my love."

Ignoring the questions bombarding my mind, I pushed them aside, not caring that I was underwater, not concerned that I should technically be drowning, and barely even aware that Katrina was off to the side watching this insanity unfold.

I lunged forward and plunged my lips into hers, drowning in her as if to prove to myself one more time she was real. She guided my hands to grasp her, sliding her own down my sides as she deepened our embrace. When she pulled away, I stood dumbfounded, still trying to make sense of it all.

She smiled that wickedly seductive smile of hers and brushed her fingers along my pierced ear. "Stop trying to figure it out, sweet Bellamy. It took me dozens of lives to finally understand."

Suddenly I felt weak. *My* father had killed her and somehow damned her to this pit. I led her right to him by loving her. I didn't stay away. It was my fault. And now I had to face her. I had to remind her that I killed her.

"I'm sorry." I choked, still half-convinced I was speaking to her in the afterlife. "I should've protected you better...I should've..."

She placed a finger to my lips and shushed me gently, as if reading my mind. "You did not send me here. You could not have protected me. It was meant to be this way. It was always meant to be this way."

"Wha—what do you mean? No, you weren't meant to die. You had a whole life ahead of you."

She took my hand and gently guided me to her, the water passing between us like swirling magic. "I've had more lives than I can count. If your father didn't kill me, I'd still be trapped."

"Trapped? Trapped in what? Serena, please tell me what's going on." I begged, gripping her gently with my fingers in her hair, afraid to let go of her in case she vanished before my face.

Serena closed her eyes and looked down, her hair drifting in thick, heavy tendrils all around her. "You don't remember," she whispered. "Because you're not meant to. But you and I have been bound since the beginning of time. Since I fell in love with you at the start of the earth. When I was called by another name—Atargatis."

The blood drained from my face, leaving me with an icy stabbing in my chest. I thought back to Bastian when he told us about the sea crown and Atargatis.

The first sea queen. The ancient mother of sirens. A divinely beautiful woman who fell in love with a mortal man.

"You fell in love with a man and killed him? That's how you became this?"

"I fell in love with *you*. It was you then, and still now. It's been you all along. You have always been drawn to the sea as your first love. Because I am the sea, and you've been seeking me your whole life without realizing it. I've lived many lives, because my power—my crown—was taken from me. To lose their power is a god's greatest curse. It traps us in a form opposite our nature. But we still cannot truly die at the hands of mankind, so we just keep returning as someone new. I've been a human for so many reincarnations, unable to return to the sea, forced to live and die on land. But when your father cut out my heart and cast it into the sea, he returned me to my true place — the water. But I'm bound here without my power, guarded by—well—her." She pointed to the Kraken, who purred out a low, threatening growl.

I dug deep for words, but they failed to come right away. How long had my heart yearned for her without even knowing it? Before I met her in 1989, did I know her before? What did it matter? I had her here in front of me now and that was enough. "What is she protecting you from? You don't have to hide anymore. Come with me and we can be together."

"I want to do that more than anything," Serena looked down. "But without my power, I cannot risk it. The one who took my crown still seeks to kill me once and for all. And without my power, I cannot stop him. Once an ordinary man, but now he draws power from the dark lord of the seas, so he has the ability to kill a goddess. He's been long jealous of you, my lover, because I refused him and chose you—so he killed you.

"I thought the legend says that Atargatis accidentally killed her lover herself. So...if you're her...and I'm your lover...then it wasn't you who killed me. It was him?"

"Yes, he killed you." Serena bowed her head. "And when I tried to follow you in death, Poseidon was moved to turn me into a sea goddess so that my beauty would never die. Bastian lied to deceive you, as he always does. I didn't kill you, my love. *He* did."

"How did Bastian...?" I rubbed my temple. "He wasn't always immortal. He was just a man. That's why he wanted a siren heart. How has he been part of this all this time?"

"Yours, mine, and Bastian's destinies are intertwined. When Poseidon realized what he had done, he sentenced him to an eternity of lifetime after lifetime, rebirth after rebirth, until his wrong could be made right. But Bastian has been dark-hearted in every lifetime, and it was during one lifetime soon after he finally found a way to end his own cycle of death and rebirth—he bound himself to Davy Jones for shadow power and immortality—a way to cheat himself out of the curse. But soon enough he realized that with Jones' power came a duty to the souls of those lost at sea. So he sought another source of eternal life—a way to keep his dark power, but no longer be indebted to Jones. Potions, spells, the Fountain of Youth, siren hearts—he's tried them all to no avail. And since I have still refused to love him all this time...and since he knows I want my revenge...he wants me dead."

It all made sense. That's why Bastian wanted the Kraken gone so badly. He knew it was guarding her. And with it out of the way, he could finally kill her.

Well done. A snake-like voice in my mind hissed. *What a mystery-solver you are.*

I feared Bastian would know I was here with her. He would know we didn't kill the Kraken. He would come for all of us...and he would come fast.

I glanced over at Katrina, suddenly remembering she was here, too. She watched us both, her eyes wide, glancing between the two of us. The Kraken groaned behind her in the shadows, waiting to restrain us again at a moment's notice.

"Bellamy, are you okay?" Katrina asked. "What's happening?"

I hesitated, trying to find a response that could encapsulate everything that I'd just learned. But there was no time. I couldn't reiterate it all here.

"Who is your friend?" Serena asked, her eyes shifting. "I thought all sirens were dead."

"My mom and I are the only ones left," Katrina said boldly, her tail straightening as she puffed out her chest and shoulders.

"Then I'm sorry that you are no longer blessed with my protection," Serena said softly, but without emotion. "I created sirens and when I have full reign of my power, none can harm you."

"But you've lost your power, right?" Katrina asked, swimming toward us. "I heard you tell Bellamy you're the goddess we've been looking for. We need your help."

"I'll help you if I can, but without my power, I'm limited. And if I leave this cove and the protection of the Kraken, Bastian will hunt me."

"We'll protect you," Katrina said. "We won't let him hurt you, right Bellamy?" The way she glanced at me almost made me sick. I couldn't promise Serena protection like that. I couldn't even protect her from my father, much less a man channeling Davy Jones' power. But I did want to restore her.

"You sound just as confident as you did about killing the Kraken," I uttered, "And we see how that turned out."

Katrina glared at me with a look I'd forgotten she was capable of. "Then we go back and get that crown and bring it here."

"We'll never get that crown if we didn't fulfill our end of the bargain. We'll have to find another way." I shifted, only just then noticing how I somehow didn't produce bubbles when I spoke. I still was still partially sure this was a dream of some kind.

Serena stepped forward, the sand swirling like flowing glitter at her feet with each step. She moved gracefully to Katrina, touching her on the arm. "Dear young siren," she said. "What is it that you so desperately came seeking help for?"

"It's a long story, but someone I love was sent back in time by the Trident's power, and you're the only thing strong enough to bring him back. Can you even do that? Can you alter time?"

Serena's eyes softened, and she tilted her head as if trying to find a way to relay bad news in the gentlest way possible. "I can't do that, even in my full form, I don't hold power over time."

Katrina's face twisted and her forehead creased. She blinked several times with a look of bewilderment before speaking again. "Wh—what? No...Then why...why would Milo tell us to find you?" She looked past Serena's shoulder, meeting her eyes with mine with disappointment. "Why would he tell us...?"

I hesitated, just as lost for an answer as she was. But regardless of what she could or couldn't do for Milo, there was no way in hell I was going to leave Serena down here. Even though it seemed impossible, I had to find a way to get that crown back for her.

"It doesn't matter," I stepped up to Serena, taking her hand with a bit of trepidation. I'd be lying to say it wasn't a bit nerve-racking to take a goddess' hand in mine. "I'm going to save you this time. Whatever it takes."

"You'd have to kill Bastian to get that crown back. And you can't kill him."

"Already found that out the hard way," I grunted.

"He's probably grown so powerful by now," Serena's eyes flicked sideways with worry.

I glanced at Katrina, who still seemed too distressed to speak, suspended in the water by slow flicks of her tail. I couldn't imagine the disappointment she must be feeling. Her only hope just told her there was no hope. I wanted to feel as bad about it as she did, but my heart was torn in so many directions. It was crushing to think that there might not be a way to bring Milo back after all. I would always carry the weight of failing him and letting Katrina down. But at the same time, I'd been reunited with Serena, and for that, I didn't believe there was a price too high. So as I watched Katrina staring into the void with absolute emptiness in her eyes, I ached for her.

"Serena." She finally spoke, her voice hollow and stiff. "You're sure there's nothing I can do? Please...there has to be something."

Serena paused for a minute that felt like hours, twisting a strand of her braids with her finger as if thinking over Katrina's question. "I'm sorry, but there's no power I have that can do what you ask."

"Then come with us," I said. "Come with us and we'll keep looking for a way. And we can finally be together."

"It's not that I don't want to," she said, "but...it's not safe for either of us." She looked at me, her hand still in mine.

"What do you mean? No, I swear to you I'll free you, Serena. And if I can't, I'll join you down here forever."

"Bellamy, no." She shook her head, but I took her face in my hands with sudden boldness. "No, no! I don't want you to get hurt. Please don't."

"Yes. Either way we'll be together," I breathed, pressing my forehead to hers.

She started to argue, but then stopped herself with a deep breath and shrug of her shoulders. "I would never let you stay in this bottomless pit, Bellamy. I've been safe here for years. And I'll stay safe with Cala. Go on and live your life. I can't let you do this."

"My life is with you. And if you won't let me stay, then you have to come with us," I kissed her gently on the lips. "Because we're not leaving you here either."

Serena's eyes shone with tears as she shook her head over and over. "No...no. This is not right. How is it that you come down here with the boldness to command a goddess?"

"Because I think we've earned the privilege after your pet tried to kill us." I winked as the Kraken hissed behind me.

"Bellamy, please. Do not go after that crown. Don't let Bastian have the chance to hurt you again. Let knowing that I am alive be enough."

I tensed up at her words. How could she ask this of me? We couldn't help Katrina, and now she wouldn't let me help her? "No, it's not enough. I'm going back whether you want me to or not. If you think I'm not going to free you from this pit then you're out of your mind. I failed you once and I'm not doing it again."

"I wish I could stop you," she pleaded with a break in her voice. "But I know how stubborn you are. So I'll go with you. Because I can't stay here knowing you're going to go face Bastian alone."

I should've been glad to hear it. I should've been relieved. But the heartbreak on her face made me feel otherwise. We both wanted to protect each other. But she didn't seem to realize this was our chance to finally be together. Maybe this was how we were supposed to right Bastian's wrong. And we couldn't do that while she was damned to hide in this cave in the ocean.

Serena sighed, seemingly lost in thought for a moment before suddenly addressing Katrina, who perked up at her words. "And as for you, little siren, I think I may just have had an idea for how to help your loved one."

Before either of us could respond, she gave a tilt of her chin, and we were swept upward in a swift current that swirled around us like a gentle cyclone that carried us back to where the sky meets the sea. And I still wasn't sure any of it was real.

KATRINA

"Our boat is destroyed," I noted as we surfaced to see a deserted ocean all around us. I was trying hard to hide the worry in my mind as I selfishly ruminated on how the hell we could get to Milo in time. The sweet relief of Bellamy not drowning was still fresh and reassuring, but though I was happy to see him reunited with Serena, I was still eaten up with the lack of progress we'd made in getting Milo back before time ran out. And now we had no way to travel. But I tried to calm myself with a deep breath and a reminder to keep my head. Maybe there was hope yet.

"Whatever your idea is, please tell me you have a way of getting us out of here," I said, a slight bitterness in my voice that I fought hard to hide. "What is your plan anyway?"

"Little siren...Katrina, was it?" When she said my name, I felt a sudden timidness, as though I shouldn't have dared speak to her with such casualness. I almost felt anger toward her for a moment, wondering why, if she really was the one who created sirens, why did she withhold a soul from us? Why did she make our very existence a contrasting battle between self and siren? But then I remembered not all sirens were half human. Regardless, I couldn't waste time dwelling on it right now. I had to hear her plan as we bobbed in the water at the mercy of the sea.

"I may not have all my power," she spoke, "but I'm not rendered completely useless. Water is a medium, and it can be used to channel power, as you know from your tears." She nodded in my direction approvingly. "I can still do small things. I can at least let you see the one you love. Tell me his name, and if you have anything belonging to him, that will make it all the easier to find him."

"Milo. His name is Milo Harrington." I frantically thought of what I could give her, and suddenly remembered the ring Milo had given me, still secure on my finger. I quickly slid it off, not easily, and handed it to her. "Can you use this?" I asked. Serena nodded.

She closed her eyes, focusing with the ring tucked away in her closed fist above the water, and the droplets that trickled from her hand formed ripples in the sea that localized around us. I could see the faintest outline of a man, with Milo's physique. It was fuzzy, like looking through a stained-glass window, but I could see his blurry form amongst others, on what looked to be a ship. He spoke to someone with deep red hair beside him, but their voices were muffled as though underwater.

"What do you see?" The questions leapt from my lips. "Where is he? Is that him right now? How much time has passed?"

Serena didn't answer me for a minute as she seemed to concentrate with her eyes shut tightly. Finally, she opened her hand, the water droplets stopped, and the ripples disappeared as they faded away into faint rings melding into the waves.

"He's on his way to the Fountain of Youth. And he's very close."

"He wants to keep himself alive long enough to find you again," Bellamy shuddered as the cold water lapped up against him. "What a clever bastard."

"No," Serena snapped. "Not clever at all. The Fountain of Youth is a place meant only for the souls of the dead. It's where those souls collected at sea by Davy Jones are meant to be sent. It is not a source of eternal life as believed, but rather a passageway to eternity. And there is no clear way out. Those who have sought its power have all become lost in between here and there, trapped in a nothingness that will never end. I fear that will be his fate."

My hair stood on end, and my heart dropped in my chest. "How close is he?" I turned to Serena, nearly grabbing her shoulders in desperation but thinking better of it. "We have to stop him."

"We can't get my crown back in time to stop him," she said calmly.

"Then—then let's get the Trident back. You can get it back, can't you?" I no longer cared what I was saying, or if it made sense. My mind was racing in a desperate panic in search of solutions.

"That power is gone now, destroyed and hidden where it belongs, thanks to you." Serena said.

"I only buried it. Maybe it could still be used." I looked down, still tempted by the call of the siren to go find that buried, broken trident and unearth it from underneath the sea floor. But I knew it would no longer be Katrina who wielded its power if I did that, and my siren would have much different plans for its use than I.

"Yes, and it was the wisest thing you could've done," Serena said. "A siren was never meant to harness power like that. Even I wouldn't dare touch Poseidon's Trident. It would destroy us all in the end."

"Then what the hell do we do?" I nearly screamed the question, feeling time slipping away like the water whisking through my fingers and along the flares of my fluke. "If you can't alter time, and you can't use the Trident, and you can't bring him back, what *can* you do?"

"I can help you meet him there."

"What do you mean?" I begged, glancing at Bellamy as if there was something he could add to this.

"I mean I can take you to the Fountain, and you can find him in eternity, and hopefully, we can lead him out."

Bellamy's confused expression did little to reassure me, but trusting Serena's plan was my only choice. I looked around at the desolate sea surrounding us on all sides, knowing our yacht was at the bottom of it

"Then let's go," I said, feeling the siren in me riling up. "We can't waste any more time. We have to find a ship. Which way is land? If we can find a harbor nearby..."

Bellamy pointed north, and without hesitation, I summoned the water to carry us in that direction. As we rode the current, Serena neared me.

"Not many sirens ever realize their power," she said. "You had to open your heart enough to allow it to be broken to learn to do this. Most are too stubborn to shed their tears."

"I know. But most sirens also don't have a human side." I grumbled. "Why? Why did you create us this way? As selfish, evil creatures incapable of real love."

"To protect you," she said. "Love is what got me killed. In every lifetime. It will kill you if you're not always looking out for yourself."

"Is that why you didn't give us a soul then? So, we can just live out these selfish, long lives without a conscience, just to die in the end and turn to sea foam?"

Serena lifted her chin haughtily in response. "Everything I did was to make you all strong."

I sighed, keeping my gaze ahead. "I'm strongest when I'm willing to break for those I care about. Living with a broken heart is the only reason I can use my power." Serena was quiet. It was strange to look at her, just a girl like me—not even twenty—and to think that she was the reincarnation of an ancient goddess.

Just then, a small wooden sailboat came into view as we approached the coasts of some landmass in the Mediterranean. I didn't bother to ask Bellamy where we were, because it didn't matter. All we needed was a boat, and as luck would have it, a small fishing harbor separated us from the rocky cliffs in the distance.

"Let's take that one," I said, swimming faster than the current toward the vessel in the distance. It looked empty, and being a simple sailboat, we wouldn't need a key to work the engine.

"Katrina, wait." Bellamy called, but I was already on the move. I dove in toward the handful of boats moored around the coastline and darted toward the single sailboat I'd made my target. It looked empty, but if there had been anyone on board, I'd have had no qualms with sending a wave to knock them overboard. It was nothing like our yacht, but it had a small enough cabin for sleeping and a bit of privacy if needed. It would do.

I waited for Bellamy and Serena to near, and then sent a swell to lift us up to the hull. I impatiently waited for myself to dry as Bellamy found a blanket to wrap around me. Bellamy and Serena checked the boat, working quickly to avoid being spotted stealing it in broad daylight. I noticed the way Bellamy's eyes hardly left Serena, as if he was scared she'd be gone if he looked away too long. I couldn't blame him. It's not every day you find out the woman you loved and watched die is a reincarnated goddess and has been fated to you since the beginning of time.

But even with a goddess on our side, I couldn't fathom how we were supposed to get out of here in time and make it to the Fountain before Milo in his timeline. But then I remembered the spyglass that brought us here.

"Bellamy, did you drop the spyglass when the ship sank?"

"Come on now, love." He tilted his head with a condescending smirk, "You should know me better than that. This isn't my first shipwreck."

He pulled the spyglass from his jacket pocket and tossed it to me. I waited till we had caught the wind and drifted out far enough from the harbor. As I held the lens to my eye, I tried looking to see something I didn't even know existed just a few moments ago. I concentrated, thinking only of that damn fountain, and slowly a vision began forming in the tube. A cavern with a glowing pool, water glistening and surreal...an undiscovered secret untouched by time. With my target locked, I twisted the spyglass and out rippled a force across the waves, summoning a rogue wave that would carry us to the Fountain of Youth.

KATRINA

The wave spat us out just next to a mangled nest of islands and cliffs jutting from the water in a part of the sea I didn't quite recognize.

"Well where is it?" Bellamy asked, standing on the deck with Serena.

Serena chuckled and took his hand in hers as she gestured out to the ocean. "Below," she said softly, her voice like smooth velvet.

"Then let's go." I was already taking my shoes off in preparation to dive in. "Every second that passes here is like another day for Milo."

Bellamy secured our anchor, and I scurried to the side of the boat, dropping into the water where I wriggled out of my clothes and awaited my transformation, though I kept them tucked under my arm in case I needed to not be a topless siren at some point. Once my tail appeared, I glanced upward to see Bellamy and Serena enter the water in a barrage of bubbles. As long as Bellamy stayed with Serena, he could breathe under here just as easily as we could. I followed Serena as she led us to the base of one of the cliffs. Towering up from the sand, there was a small opening that even I would have overlooked blindingly if I hadn't known it was there.

Serena swam in, effortlessly whisking between the tiny entrance in the dark rock. Bellamy gestured for me to go in next, and he trailed behind me. It was a dark canal, almost pitch black, but Serena's subtle aura shone more prevalent down here and helped guide the way.

After a few minutes, we emerged, somehow breaking through the water to a dry cavern. A trickling waterfall and glimmering pool of water filled the farthest corner. I lifted myself out of the water and willed my skin and scales to dry quickly, changing back into my clothing as fast as possible. I glanced at Serena, who stepped out of the water with the grace of stepping out of a silk robe.

"Do you ever have a tail? If...if you wanted, I mean?" I couldn't help but ask. She'd always had legs when we were underwater. But it was only natural that the mother of sirens could become a siren herself if she so pleased. At least, that's what I would expect.

Serena's eyes crinkled with a giggle as she nodded. "Yes, little siren. I can be any form I wish. But my tail is a bit different than yours. It's quite dramatic, so I tend to save it only for special occasions." She winked at me. I wondered what exactly that was supposed to mean, but right now learning about Serena's mermaid anatomy was not my biggest priority. Milo was.

"Okay, how do we use this thing to pull Milo from the past?" Bellamy asked, dipping a finger into the ethereal silver pool. It rippled, but not like liquid. It rolled with the texture more like that of melted metal. "I'm guessing this fountain isn't for drinking?" I looked at the water trickling from the rock, thinking back to the Fountain of Youth tourist attraction back in St. Augustine where people would pay to get a paper cup and sip from some stale old water fountain. This certainly was no attraction. This was the real deal.

"No," Serena said, kneeling and touching the water with her fingertips. "This is the doorway to eternity. And your Milo has already entered, like so many souls before him. He's been trapped there a while."

"A while?" I rushed forward. "How do we guide him out?"

"Use your voice. Your siren song. If he's truly bound to your heart, he'll hear you even across time."

A weight dropped in my chest like a hammer. I fidgeted with the siren scale I wore on my wrist. "My song..." I choked. "I gave it to Bastian in a deal."

Serena's brows creased and her lips tightened. "You what? A siren's song is the most precious thing she possesses. How could you think that was a good idea?"

"I know, I know," I looked down, the scale on my wrist glowing ever so faintly. "That's strange. It only does that when I use my song." I paused as the last word left my lips. Perhaps I'd regained my voice somehow since we didn't fulfill the deal.

I didn't wait to ask. A hopeful hum rose in my throat. I was going to try.

The scale on my bracelet glowed brighter, and my song became stronger. It was clear to me now that, for whatever reason, my song had returned. I didn't know why. I didn't understand how. But I didn't care.

I stood before the portal of water. With a silent prayer pleading this would work, I began to sing, my haunting melody reaching out like an outstretched hand. I sang the second verse of the song that had tethered us together since the beginning. The one that seemed the most fitting.

"Lost out at sea
Do you dream of me?
By the call of the waves
I hear you and seek you
Till again the roaming sea
Brings you back to me."

When nothing happened, I looked at Serena, who urged me to keep going with an encouraging gesture and nod of her head. I sang again, my aria filling the empty cavern. And when that didn't work, I sang again, losing hope but trying to remember Milo would be fighting his way through eternity. I had no idea how long that could take. So I'd sing forever if I had to, because if I stopped too soon I'd lose him to the abyss.

When minutes turned to an hour, I felt myself tiring, and worry shrouded my thoughts. I couldn't lose him. Not after all this. I rushed forward, slid to my knees and leaned into the portal. I heard Serena and Bellamy gasp as they grabbed my arms to hold me back, but they couldn't stop me entirely. I pushed my shoulders through the water portal, singing with every bit of strength left in me. In here, it was a chamber of nothingness. Nothingness made of something like starlight. There was no end and no beginning, and the longer I spent looking at it, the sicker I felt. But I closed my eyes and sang, with Bellamy and Serena holding me back to keep me from falling in entirely.

I sang and sang, for however long—I couldn't tell anymore. Even with a magic song, my lungs felt like they would give out. My vocal cords ached with each note that left my lips. But I kept singing. And then, I finally heard a voice echoing somewhere in the distance faintly. And the voice was desperately calling my name.

We steered ahead, the morning sun at our backs. Another few months at sea had taken their toll on my men and me. They were starting to complain, and they'd caught on that I was seeking something more than what I was telling them.

I'd been up for days, charting the stars at night and calculating a logical path to the Fountain. I wasn't sure what I was looking for, but some hopefulness ensured me I'd know when I found it. But something told me we were close. Perhaps it was the strange siren song I kept hearing in my head since we'd left the island, echoing faintly, like it was guiding me along. I hadn't told anyone about it, not even Clara, but something in me made me believe it was leading me on all these weeks.

"Tell me, Cap'n." Clara stared out at a pod of dolphins racing alongside us as the *Falcon* sliced through the smooth waters with ease. "You ever think anymore about just abandoning this goose chase and making the most of yer time here? I know ya love her, but you've gained so much here. You ever think maybe...maybe it's just fate."

"And despite what it may look like, I've gained nothing here."

Clara shifted her elbow on the side of the ship. "Oh come on. I know ya love her, but you ever think maybe...maybe you bein' here and becomin' this powerful captain...maybe it's just fate."

"I once thought like that. I once believed our destinies were set. Unchangeable. But not anymore. Now I think a man can choose his destiny, even change it, if he's willing."

"Exactly, Harrington." Clara's smirk faded into a look more solemn and serious than I'd ever seen in her eyes. "And that's why I'm asking you...are you sure you've chosen yours?"

I tore my eyes from the water and looked down at my boots. She knew. She could see right through me. I was breaking these past few weeks. I still hated myself, and I feared what Katrina might think if and when I saw her again. And if her siren had grown more powerful, she was sure to have no use for me once that voice in her convinced her of my terribleness. It haunted me like a ghost, and drove me mad at times to imagine finding her again and losing her in a different way. I worried I would hurt her more by coming back into her life than staying out of it. My greatest fear was that I couldn't be her sun.

But then that siren call in my head would sing out again, calling me to her, urging me once more to keep going. Her voice was my compass, and her song was reassuring me...I was almost there. I was supposed to be there.

"All the glory and glitter of the sea isn't worth losing her. I think, though we can choose our own paths, some part of us will always be calling us where we're supposed to be. And I imagine it's awfully hard to ignore."

I paused, running my calloused, fingers along a small chip in the ship's hull. "What about you? You've had long enough here to figure out what you want. Have you?"

Clara pressed her lips together and looked back out at the horizon. "I just want this, Cap'n. A life on a vessel fast enough to carry me far away from my troubles." She drew in a sigh as the wind picked up. "I just wish that was enough for you, too."

I grunted with a nod, and we both watched in silence. Pointing to the horizon northwest, I finally spoke again, changing the subject. "If my charts are correct, the Fountain lies ahead that way."

"I've heard that before, Cap'n," Clara rolled her eyes.

"No, this time, I'm sure of it." I thought of the siren voice in my head, and how it grew louder and louder the farther I sailed this way.

Suddenly, Keegan's voice rang out from above, a dire warning signal of oncoming ships to the south of us. I glanced back, able to make out the blooded sails from here without needing my spyglass. Thane had been tailing me for a while now. I expected him to catch up sooner or later, so it was no surprise. But it was a bit of an inconvenience. "What was that you were saying about getting away from your troubles?" I teased Clara as I swung over the stair railing and went up to take charge of the helm.

The siren song in my head sang softly, calling me onward to a small series of islands just a few leagues ahead—the same network of islands where I believed the Fountain to be. I could trap Thane there and outmaneuver him easily in the *Falcon*. Thane's new ship, *Leviathan*, was a beast, but mine was fast. I'd get that mammoth of a ship lined up just right, in a place he couldn't wriggle it out of, and then blast him to hell with cannon fire and mortar.

"Full sail!" I gripped the wheel and maneuvered us toward the islands. To Thane, it would appear I was running from him. And he'd never turn down an opportunity for a good chase.

For now, I guided the *Falcon* toward the islands, careful to steer clear of the hidden sandbars lining the waterways. If I could catch Thane's big ship on one of them…I smirked at the thought.

We slowed as we neared the island cluster. The sight of Thane's red-flagged ship hurtling toward us was just what I hoped to see. He was taking the bait. And he wouldn't be able to slow that massive galleon of his in time to steady itself through the islands.

Clara threw her weight into managing the crew as they adjusted sails and readied cannons. I reached for the pistol and swords hanging on their holsters, if for nothing more than just the mere feel of them in my hands. I reached up to touch my scarred eye. And then I thought of Katrina, held hostage and terrified at Thane's hand. I replayed the moment he sliced his knife across her delicate face, and the rage I felt then boiled in my blood just as strongly now. Finding the fountain could wait until I'd cut Thane open and watched him bleed out like the filthy bastard he is. I waited, clutching the hilt of my blade as we wove through the stony islands with the *Leviathan* lurking on our tail.

THE FOUNTAIN OF YOUTH

31

MILO

The bow of my ship nearly crashed into the passageway of the rocky cliffs, but we could turn just in time to keep some sort of momentum. Thane's ship eased its way in, desperate to reach me, but forced to nearly halt at the entrance of the cliff maze. I shouted for the crew to let fire, aiming from the rear cannons to get a direct shot. I could tell Thane was trying to ready his own fire, but I wouldn't give him a second more. The cannons erupted at my command and shook the *Lark* before hitting Thane's ship with a force to be proud of. Thane fired back, as I expected, but I doubted he knew what I had in store for him.

Clara glanced at me worriedly as the *Leviathan's* retaliation shot pounded our hull. I gave her a nod, and she screamed out the orders. It was time to send Thane to hell.

The mortar shot was one I'd been waiting so long to use, and I'd been saving it just for Thane. With a fiery burst, the shot launched forth from our deck and soared—an eerie and beautiful sight all at once as fire arced across the water and lit the enemy ship ablaze. In seconds, Thane's vessel went up in flames, black smoke billowing into the air as the sails and masts became engulfed.

The sound of shouting men filled the air, along with an acrid stench of burning wood and tar, as bodies leapt overboard from the burning ship. I reached for my spyglass, locating Thane as he maneuvered around the deck of his vessel. Through the smog, I spotted him, and I watched the gears turning in his head as he decided on his next move.

"Come on, you bastard," I muttered beneath my breath. "That's it. It's about time you come to me for a fight." I couldn't help it when my lip curved into a small grin at the sight of him meeting my gaze and gritting his teeth at me in rage. He made a gesture indicating he would kill me and marched forward before dropping into a jolly boat below. If he thought I would try to keep sailing away, he was wrong. I wanted this. I wanted Thane to climb up the side of my ship so I could finish him once and for all.

But the siren song in my head, it grew louder all of a sudden. I clapped my palm over my ear, trying to escape the deafening sound ringing like a bell in my mind.

"Cap'n?" Clara's voice barely cut through the sound of the chaos. "Cap'n! Are ya' alright?"

I folded over, nearly knocked to my knees by the haunting melody echoing in my head. It was calling me, drawing me, demanding that I jump overboard. The Fountain was close. Right underneath me, it said.

Underneath?

But I fought the sound of her call long enough to focus on Thane approaching me in his skiff. Clara kept calling to me, asking if I wanted her to shoot him. Somewhere in that mangled mess of noise in my head, amidst the smoking cannons, shouting men and wailing of a creaking ship drifting against the cliffs, I managed to scrounge my thoughts together. "No." I growled. "He's mine."

I gripped a sword in each hand, glad I'd spent some time sharpening them the day before. I held my gaze on Thane as he approached, and I walked forward to meet him as he neared the hull. When he came up, I planned to thoroughly show him why he should have never so much as looked at Katrina.

But then that damn song took over again, forcing me to look down...down into the water. In its strange language, it told me to jump. No. It made no sense. The Fountain couldn't be underwater. My jaw ached from clenching it in attempt to resist the call. I couldn't let this stupid song ruin my chance to end Thane here. The Fountain could wait just a few moments more.

But at the last minute, just as Thane was mere feet from me, the siren call became too strong to ignore. As if I was bewitched, it took hold of me, somehow infiltrating my mind so strongly that I had no strength left to fight it. And no choice but to obey it.

Jump.

Tucking my blades into their sheaths, I dove off the ship, leaving behind the distant sound of both Clara and Thane shouting curses. I swam under, cursing silently on my own as I followed the lead of the siren song. Perhaps it was leading me to my death. Perhaps this was all a trap of some sort from the sirens of old that lured men to the depths. Perhaps.

But I couldn't stop myself from following her voice. There might have been a tether wrapped around me, pulling me by her invisible cord. She led me to a cavern. A chill swept down my spine as she compelled me to maneuver myself through the small, dark entrance. Seeing underwater was already difficult enough, given my limited sight. My scarred eye was even more useless down here than on land.

A light startled me, glowing just enough to light the space around me. A golden glow bringing warmth to this pitch-black space, growing from the sun marking from the island tribe.

I glanced down, realizing that Bastian's mark was also changing. Not with light, but a shift in the pattern. The rest of the map formed before my eyes, completing itself on my skin with the stinging pain of sliced flesh. I'd found the Fountain. And now Bastian would, too.

By the faint light of my markings, I saw that the cavern ended, and at the beckoning of the siren call, I looked up, seeing the familiar ripples of those created by an underwater air pocket. I swam up, desperate and grateful, on my last few seconds of air. When I broke through the surface, the breath that hit my lungs tasted crisp and strangely cold. It was unusual. Normally these pockets were filled with old, musty air.

I glanced around. This was no ordinary air pocket. This was an entire grotto, with a stream of water flowing to a small pool meters from me, sourced from a heavy trickle of water toppling down the stony sides of the cave. My eyes followed the water's path. It appeared to gush out of the rocks themselves. Like magic.

The siren song echoed clearly here, still in my head but somehow louder, as if she was hiding right in this very place. I paddled forward to the edge of the pool from which I'd surfaced. Just as I placed my hands on the cold stone to pull myself out, a firm and sharp grasp on my boot yanked me back. I slid down into the water, kicking out at the attacker I could not see. The heel of my boot collided with something hard and bony, and in the dimly lit cave, I could see the shape of a man underwater, reaching for me. I was glad to see Thane, but I was worried my chance to end him was dwindling.

I hoisted myself out of the water, and Thane emerged seconds later. The cave reverberated with his taunting voice as he shook the salt water from his eyes.

The voices in my head screamed, and I couldn't decide which to follow. The siren said keep going and stop for nothing. But my own said turn around and destroy Thane.

I took a step toward the clear, glistening pool on the other side of the cave, each note of the siren guiding my feet. But Thane's voice kept cutting through hers.

"You seem to like burning my ships almost as much as I enjoyed hearing that little bitch of yours scream," he hissed. I clenched my jaw, feeling like it might shatter. "I was so hoping to find her aboard your ship all this time. What did you do with her? Traded her out for the loud-mouthed redhead?"

I heard him emerge from the water. I couldn't stay like this—with my back to him. I gripped my weapons and turned to face him. "She's gone. Some place and time where you'll never find her. Safe from you."

"Oh, she'll never be safe from me, Harrington. Not after what I did to her." Thane shook his head, his evil smile growing wide as water dripped down his hair and through his scraggly beard. "I left far too great of a scar on her memory. One that won't fade quite as easily as the one on her pretty face."

No.

"Come on...Didn't she ever tell you all the things I did to her? All the fun we had together right before you found us in that alley? How my men held her while I stuffed myself down her throat until she cried?" He reached down and touched his belt with a sickening groan.

I stopped in my tracks, using every bit of my mental strength to shut out that damn song haunting my brain. The siren *would* wait. This man would die.

I lunged at him, screaming out my anger as I slashed my sword across his shoulder. Blood spattered across his face and he laughed, looking up at me through wild eyes as he licked away his own scarlet droplets from his chin.

"That's right, Harrington. Just face me already. I know you're dying to do what you should've done a long time ago."

"You followed me here. You won't be making it back out." I growled. The hilt of my cutlass felt light in my hand, and I was itching to send it whipping across this man's throat.

I didn't wait another second, and I whipped out my second blade, twirling it in my hand as he drew his own sword. I charged first, meeting his cutlass with my cross blades. He pushed back, the sound of metal grating as our swords sparked. I spun to escape the gridlock, giving him a split second to take the next swing.

I ducked to avoid his reach, and whirled my sword across his knee. He stumbled with a grunt of pain, and I didn't waste a second taking the opportunity to kick him in the same joint I'd just cut open, feeling the bones crunch against the force of my boot.

With a cry that sounded sweet to my ears, he toppled backward. I threw myself at him, my blade ready to plunge straight through his windpipe. He managed to deflect me with his cutlass, knocking my sword from my right hand. Without a second thought, I ripped my flintlock pistol from the holster at my chest and slammed the weapon across his face.

For the first time, I could actually sense fear in Thane. The way he fought against me shifted, and his attempts to hold me back became truly desperate. And it made me fight him harder.

He managed to turn the gun on me, and I headbutted him just as he pulled the trigger, but to my luck, nothing came out but a hollow click.

"Wet powder," I grinned, leaping over him as his disorientation gave me an opening to grab my other sword.

Thane tossed the gun across the cave. Even with his injured knee, he came for me fast, still able to maneuver enough to charge with his own sword drawn. I whipped around just at the last second to come down on his raised arm, slicing through his arm at the elbow.

He shrieked in agony, a sound that shook me only because I never expected to hear it from someone as unhinged as him. He normally reveled in pain, even his own. But he held the severed end of his arm as thick blood streamed down and pooled at his feet like syrup.

The siren song in my head battled for control once more. Leave him and dive into the Fountain pool, it said. But I wasn't finished here. I wanted to see Thane dead. And I would.

I pulled back my cutlass, ramming the tip of the blade just up under his rib, where I twisted it back and forth as it ground through his flesh. Blood blossomed onto his tunic. By now he was barely recognizable as a man. He was barely more than a body, covered in bruises and blood so thick it distorted his features.

Suddenly, I could hear Katrina all over again, just as clearly as the day I killed Thane's crewmen in the streets.

"Don't become like them."

Since that day, I often heard it right before I killed someone in battle at sea. And sometimes it was enough to stop me. Most times it was. But it wouldn't be enough to stop me now.

The siren in my head begged me to hurry back to the pool, that I was wasting time. But I didn't move. I jutted the sword further forward, drawing a hazy whimper from Thane's lips.

"Enjoy killing me, Harrington. You certainly earned it." He smiled through the blood in his teeth.

Katrina's voice mixed with the siren call, becoming one. Suddenly, I knew it was her. It was her. She was calling me. And begging me not to take this life. Not for her. But for my own conscience.

The sword dropped from my hand with a cold clang against the cave floor. I stepped back, leaving Thane to crumble to his knees in his own puddle of blood. I jumped when I heard Clara's voice reverberating through the chamber. Soaking wet she stood at the entrance, heaving and wringing the water from her hair.

"You found it." She said coldly, glancing from me to Thane to the trickling water along the rock wall.

"Aye, I found it." I nodded, breathing hard as I stood over the battered man at my feet. "But I can't leave this piece of shit here knowing where it is too."

"So kill him. Looks like he needs to be put out of his misery." Clara stepped forward, studying Thane without so much as a hint of empathy in her eyes. He refused to meet her gaze, keeping his own fixated on the ground below.

"She won't let me," I muttered, worry creeping into my mind at the prospect of Thane having access to a fountain that would keep him young forever. I hated the siren for holding me back.

When Clara cocked her head at me in confusion, I didn't elaborate. How was I to explain the siren song in my head without making her think I was delusional? It was too much to explain right now.

"Wait," Clara said, her focus shifting entirely as she knelt and yanked back Thane's matted bloody hair to see his face more clearly. "I know this bastard."

She nearly stumbled back, but I noticed how she fought to keep her footing as her voice shook. "You lied to me. You tricked me. You and yer despicable men violated me. You took everything from me. And you ran while the rest of us paid for your mistake. And if you'd fought like a man back then instead of abandoning us, maybe you wouldn't be dying here like a dog for the same reason."

My eyes widened at the realization that this was the same man who'd done all those horrible things Clara had told me before. And I fumed, realizing why the siren wouldn't let me kill him. Because he wasn't mine to kill. And this wasn't where I belonged.

"He's at your mercy now," I said, walking to Clara and placing my captain's hat on her head. "Captain Reid."

"What are you doing?" Clara stammered.

"I'm following my North Star," I said. "As you must follow yours. The *Falcon* and the crew are yours. I couldn't leave them in better hands."

Clara gave me a knowing nod. It was the first time I'd ever seen her speechless, but I knew she was thanking me in her own way. With tears in her eyes, she shakily touched the hat on her head.

"Thank you, Harrington," she whispered.

With one last gesture, I touched Clara's shoulder with my blessing, then turned and walked to the Fountain.

Legend said he who dipped in the pool would have eternal life. But that's all it was—a legend. Who knew what would become of me once I truly immersed myself in the glistening water before me? Something told me it wasn't quite that simple. But I had no way of knowing what would happen once my body touched the water. I only knew somehow, some strange way, Katrina was calling me to her, wherever that was. And the only way to her was through the Fountain.

With my back to the past, I stood over the pool filled by the fountain, its swirling silvery nature tempting me with its unnatural draw. My reflection was as clear as a mirror in its surface.

Come in.

The siren song took hold now, leaving me no choice but to let myself fall into the magical waters below in order to follow it. The last sound I heard was the shrill slice of a sword being unsheathed, and I knew Clara would take excellent care of Thane.

ACROSS TIME

32

I dropped into the water. From above it appeared no deeper than a crystal puddle, but once within, I found there was no end to its depth. I couldn't see here. My good eye was only so useful here, but I doubted even with working vision in both, it wouldn't have saved me from the blinding white that filled my surroundings. Every direction I turned weighed on my muscles like swimming through tar, but I could see nothing around me. It was a void, with no east or west, no up or down.

In a moment of panic, I fought to escape, but realized the pool surface behind me no longer existed...or if it did, I couldn't see it. I couldn't see anything. Somehow I could breathe, but that was all the luxury this place of nothingness afforded me. I felt around in my blindness, half-swimming, half-walking through this muddled abyss. The Fountain of Youth was certainly a myth. This was something else entirely. I only prayed Clara wouldn't follow me and trap herself here too. But deep in my chest I knew she was smarter than that.

Visions of Katrina filled the dark blindness before me. I would never make it back to her. Even if I managed to escape this place, it would be too late. And even if she managed to find Bastian and the Crown, he'd never let her win. He was too powerful. And I'd played her right into his hands.

As I stumbled blind through whatever this was...I stopped, dropping to my knees as the hopelessness set in. I couldn't give it anymore. The ocean had certainly spoken its authority over my fate. I thought back to the night I stayed with Katrina in her room for the first time. How I'd fought to resist the pull she held over me, knowing it was never meant to work. But I gave in. And now here we both were, separated by oceans of time forever.

I remembered the night I told her that fate had decided against us. And though I thought maybe I'd proved it all wrong, now I realized I was the one who was wrong. Katrina and I were never meant to meet. I was never meant to live long enough to meet her. Finding her once was a blessing enough. But I was always meant to die without her.

As I resigned myself to this void of emptiness, a faint sound rose through the silence, chiming like a bell in the distance. The melody grew louder with each passing second, but it still sounded distant. It was the siren song, but no longer in my head. It was here—truly here somewhere in this hollow void. The sound of it washed over me like some last drop of warmth, urging me one last time to rise.

With tears burning the backs of my eyes as they threatened to fall, I waded through the nothingness, desperate to follow the singing. Completely blind, I clung to my only map—a sound. Her song continued, a voice filling the silence with a frail thread of hope I fought to grasp before it was gone. The melody surrounded me, like a blanket of reassurance in my darkest hour, holding me as I trembled in fear of never escaping this place.

I might have wandered an hour or a day. There was nothing resembling the passing of time. Nothing here granted me a semblance of humanity. For a moment I even question if I was still alive or I had already died, and this might be the holding place for my unworthy soul.

But then, after however long it was that I followed the voice, I found it right in front of me, clear and so loud it sounded mere inches from my ears. My feet stopped on instinct, and I stood, listening to her aria as I stretched out a hand before me into the blank space before me. I nearly leapt backwards when my fingers touched something—a hand.

I took the hand, the song still calling, and stepped forward. Arms wrapped around me. I heard my name from various voices. And then I heard hers...Katrina.

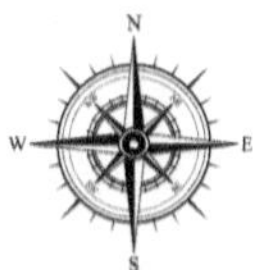

"Milo," she sang softly. "I'm here. You've made it."

My eyes fluttered as they adjusted from whatever magic hold I'd just stepped out from. The light hit, and I could finally focus on those blue eyes that drew me to them with their song. And then I breathed a sigh of relief as they faded back into beautiful brown ones staring back at me. The song had stopped. And it was no longer Katrina's siren who spoke to me. It was her.

Both of us without words, I fell into her arms, clutching her like she was the only solid harbor in a storm. She pulled me into her and held me as I toppled forward from a combination of exhaustion and disbelief. Pressed against her chest, I drowned in the sound of her heartbeat and breathed in her sweet scent.

"You found me," she whispered with trembling in her words. "You heard me all the way across time."

I pulled back to look in her face, brushing back her loose strands of hair behind her ear. "I swore I'd always find you, my North Star." The lump in my throat burned as I swallowed it down, unable to tear my gaze from her.

She placed a hand on my face, her thumb gently sweeping along my beard, across my jaw, and finally over the big scar over my left eye.

"You're...older," she stammered, staring into my eyes. "How long?"

"Some two years." I uttered.

She pressed her head against my shoulder. "I'm sorry."

"No, shhh," I kissed her head, as I took her face in my hands. I pressed my lips to hers and kissed her for what could never have felt long enough. "It might as well have been a minute. Every moment of every day of those years, there wasn't a day I didn't think of you."

I glanced across her shining eyes to her lips, a quick glimpse catching the faded scar along her cheek. It was hardly noticeable now, but I'd always remember the reason it was there. My embrace around her tightened protectively as the sickening things Thane had said replayed in my head. "When Thane caught you back in Nassau...did he...did he hurt you beyond this...before I found you?"

Katrina looked confused by the question, but shook her head. "No, no, he had just grabbed me right before you came. Why?"

I drew in a sigh of relief. "No reason." I pressed myself against her once more and stroked her hair. "I just want to know I did everything to protect you."

"You always have," she rested her head on my shoulder. "And now...now we're free to start again."

I glanced down at the tattoo on my arm, feeling the ink snaking its way across my skin. The map had formed and was complete now. But I doubted Bastian would want the Fountain once he discovered what it really was. I turned to look back at the strange upright wall I'd just walked through, like a mirror made of water, a doorway to something inhuman.

"How did you know I was looking for this place?" I asked, looking back around at her. "How did you know to come here?"

"It's a long story. But I had a little help." She turned to look back at two figures in the shadows of the cove in which we stood. Bellamy and—though I swore my vision deceived me—Serena.

I searched for the words to thank them, but I was as speechless as the stone surrounding us. I watched them both in baffled silence before Bellamy stepped forward. He slapped a hand on my shoulder and leaned in beside me.

"Glad to have you back, mate," he grinned. "Now maybe you can keep this lass of yours under control because I've certainly had my run of it."

I laughed. For the first time in I didn't even know how long, I truly laughed. And not a laugh of humor, but a laugh born out of true, pure joy. Everything I cared about stood here in this cove, paling in comparison to all the gold a thousand ships could carry. And I smiled, knowing Clara would make a fine captain. My men would be taken care of. And my destiny stood right before me.

I pulled Katrina to me once more and kissed her, my blood running hot with the desire to make up for the years I'd longed for her. I couldn't wait to be alone with her, to lie next to her and listen to every word she must've been dying to tell me.

"I don't know how you're here, alive again, but I'm glad you are," I addressed Bellamy. "Thank you for keeping her safe all this time. I feared what might happen if she went to face Bastian alone."

"Don't thank me yet." Bellamy gritted his teeth and his eyes shifted. "We're not quite out from under his thumb."

"What do you mean?" I asked, my concern growing. "What do you owe him?"

Suddenly a rumble shook the walls of the cave, just strong enough to dust us with small rocky debris from above. When the rumble settled, the prominent sound of footsteps filled the cavern, without a doubt the tap of heavy boots with thick leather soles.

A voice that didn't belong here revealed itself as the figure walking in became visible. With a sly smile, he stepped into the dim light of the cove. Bastian Drake himself, of course, looking at Katrina and Bellamy with a hunter's eye, and then at me. "They owe me everything."

Bastian loomed there, a menacing look in his eye, and a sly hint of mischief that made my knees feel weak. Whatever he had up his sleeve, I could sense it wasn't good. Bellamy shifted uneasily and put a protective arm across Serena.

"My tattoo," Milo said, glancing at his arm and then at all of us. "It must've led him here. I'm so sorry."

"You know, Harrington," he laughed, stepping forward and glancing over all of us. "Looks like you did finally fulfill your end of the bargain...300 years later," he laughed. "But actually no. You didn't lead me here, thanks to that dreadful sun tribe you found who made it awfully hard to follow you. No, no. You didn't lead me here. Bellamy did."

Everyone's gaze shifted to Bellamy, including Bastian's.

"His father's broken bargain still stands. And so does the mark I left on Bellamy. But even without it, he and I are forever linked by a bit of history and myth. Isn't that right, lover of Atargatis?"

Bellamy didn't respond, shielding Serena with himself as he faced Bastian like a dog ready to be unleashed for the hunt.

"But don't worry, Harrington, you're off the hook thanks to your little island friends. But no matter, because as you well know, the Fountain isn't what I needed after all. I've no interest in sending anyone's soul there, neither yours nor mine. No, that's dear old Davy's job." Bastian pretended to study his knuckles as he walked to Milo. "You're quite the lucky man. The only man to ever truly cheat death with the heart of a siren. If only we'd known back then that all we had to do was fuck 'em instead of kill them. Would've been a whole lot more fun." Bastian's eyes slid over to me with a grin that made my skin crawl. "Speaking of which...Katrina, our little mermaid. Don't you wonder how you got that pretty voice back?"

I straightened my shoulders, daring to appear as confident as possible, though I was terrified of being trapped in this cave with a madman like Bastian. "Our deal is broken. My voice returned to me because I didn't do my part."

"Tsk, tsk, tsk…" he pretended to look at his fingernails as he brought a curled fist to his face. "The laws of my bargains are not quite that easy. You're not off the hook, little fish. Your voice was meant to be a pawn to ensure you would do what I asked. But since you didn't, it became mine to use or bargain with. And bargain with it, I did."

"Wh—what do you mean?" I felt my courageous stance failing, the uncertainty coming through in my voice.

He snapped his fingers and a circle of shadow appeared, forming a floating frame beside him. In it, as I stepped forward to see more clearly, an image of a mermaid trapped in a tank back in his lair appeared, looking desperately out of the glass. It was my mom.

"Mom!" I nearly stumbled backward. "What have you done to her?"

"I only did what she asked," he crooned. "She came to me and offered herself in exchange for your safety and your voice to be returned to you. I couldn't argue with a deal like that. My very own siren at my command? A hell of a bargain, I'd say."

"What about our friends?" Panic stabbed my chest as I thought of McKenzie and Noah. I was still working to process everything he'd just said about Mom.

"Oh, don't worry, they're fine. They were completely supportive of her decision. Your mother can be quite persuasive. Very gifted with her voice. They've no choice but to listen to her and stay behind while she came and found me."

"Let her go. Tell me what you want from me," I growled, my fists clenching so hard I thought I'd tear through my palms with my fingernails.

"Ah, it was a fair trade. She knew full well what she was agreeing to." He strode over to where Bellamy and Serena stood, a smug look on his face. "But I'd certainly trade my mermaid for a powerless goddess."

Bellamy lunged forward, still guarding Serena. "You won't touch her!"

"Perhaps not." Bastian stepped backwards as smoothly as if he were walking on a glass surface. "But now you and your little friends have a choice to make. Mommy Dearest." He gestured to the floating image of my trapped mother, and then back to a wide-eyed Serena. "Or Atargatis." He walked briskly back to the opening of the cave, the spyglass appearing in his hand in a cloud of smoke. "And I'll be taking this back. You failed to fulfill your end of the deal. The Kraken still lives, so you don't get to keep using this little trinket for your personal side quests. When you come to your senses and decide to trade the goddess for your mother, you know where to find me." With that, a shadow consumed him and a wind whisked through the cavern.

Bellamy lunged forward in attempt to stop him, but he was too late. He grappled at the air with empty hands, bewildered at the sight of smoke where Bastian once stood seconds earlier. The silence between the four of us was thick enough to swim in. What was I to say? I couldn't ask Serena to give herself up for my mom. But I didn't know what else to do. My hands had never been so tied.

Milo placed a reassuring hand on my shoulder, but it did little to ease the burning rage in me. "That piece of shit has my mom."

"We're not giving him Serena," Bellamy's voice came out like a deep, low growl. "I've lost her once. I'm not losing her again."

"I know. But we need her if we're going to stop him. You even said yourself you'd do anything to get her crown back. This isn't just for my mom. This is for her. This is for all of us."

Serena buried her face in her hands. "He can kill me without my crown. He knows how to kill me for good. I never should have come with you! I told you!"

"I won't put you in danger. I made that mistake once. But I also can't let you live in a prison at the bottom of the ocean." Bellamy's words came out rushed. I'd never heard him so desperate. "You won't die again because of my stupidity."

"It was never your fault, Bellamy. It was always destiny. Just like my crown being stolen was foretold on the altar of Atargatis. Our love and deaths have been written in the stars since the beginning of time. And whatever lies ahead is the same. You can't tame the sea. And you can't tame me. I'm going back."

"No! Destiny or not, I won't let you. I'll fight for you, Serena." Bellamy looked at me, holding Serena in his grasp. The look in his eyes reminded me of the time he pinned himself against me in a rage back in the brig of the *Siren*. "I'll help try to save your mom, but not at the risk of losing her. It's still about that crown for me, now."

His words unsettled me, but I understood. Still, it didn't tame my emotion in the moment. But something Serena said had stuck in my head.

"Serena, what did you say about the altar of Atargatis? What is that?"

"It's ancient. I don't know what has become of it. But centuries back it was a rock on the coastline where broken-hearted lovers often left tokens for their loved ones lost at sea, hoping I'd spare them as I was spared. Eventually it was carved into a round slab, painted to tell the story of my legend."

"Whatever the case, we need to get moving. Bellamy, we have to work together. 'm going after my mom with or without you. Either way, looks like our only choice is taking down Bastian."

I could tell Bellamy struggled to choose his path. But he spent a minute in thought and glancing between Milo and I and Serena. Finally, rubbing his head, he stepped forward. "I'll sail back with you, lass, because ironically, the only way you're getting your mom back is if we kill Bastian, and the only one here who can do that is Serena...*when* we get her crown back and her power is restored."

I glanced over at Serena, who stayed oddly silent and looked as though she was about to cry. For a goddess bound and powerless, I found it strange how much she seemed to resist the idea of getting her crown back. But that wasn't my concern. Whatever could be so bad about restoring her power couldn't possibly be worse than losing my mom to a deranged immortal pirate lord.

"Fine." I stuck out my chin. "Then we get the crown. Whatever it takes."

Bellamy's eyes narrowed. "Whatever it takes."

SEA SHANTIES

34

BELLAMY

We made our way out of that damn cavern, with Serena's beautiful glow to guide us. I found I could still breathe beneath the water from her kiss, so while I swam, I had plenty of time to think.

I wouldn't use Serena as a bartering piece. I wanted to see her power restored. I wanted her to be free once and for all. I knew she wanted that, too, despite how she pleaded against it. She had to be. So why the hell was she so set on staying in that cave with that disgusting squid? There had to be something more she wasn't letting on. Maybe she was just scared after all that time alone. Maybe. Or maybe she was right. Maybe it was too dangerous for both of us. Had I not learned my lesson by now?

Maybe we didn't have to go back. Maybe I could convince her to run. Somewhere Bastian could never find her. We could run together, and I'd protect her from whatever followed. It would mean turning my back on Katrina, though. I couldn't just leave her to Bastian by herself. But then again...maybe it was the answer. Katrina was strong and far more clever than me. If anyone could figure out how to deal with him, it'd be her. She didn't need me. Sure, I loved Katrina, but not the way I loved Serena, and I couldn't risk losing Serena for *anyone*. But if I didn't ensure Bastian was gone, he'd never stop looking for Serena. And I couldn't risk that either.

When we surfaced, dark skies greeted us. The wind was picking up, and the water had grown choppy. Wild lightning split the sky as the smell of rain and salt stirred in my nostrils. "We can't sail in this. Sorry Katrina but even you can't make a way around this one." I glanced over at Katrina, who watched the storm clouds with worried eyes.

"He's right," Milo interjected. "A storm like that would take a heavy toll on the sturdiest galleon, let alone that little sailboat."

I looked at our boat bobbing where we'd anchored. It wouldn't stand a chance. "Our best shot is to at least get away from these rocks. We can sail downwind for a bit to put some distance between us and them. Then we'll have to ride it out and hope for a miracle."

We all nodded in agreement and started swimming back to the boat. I grabbed Serena's arm as we fought the rugged waters and boarded the sailboat. "Serena, I need you to go back and wait for me. Wait for me with your kraken, and I'll come back once I have your crown and Bastian's dead."

"Bellamy, you know I am the only one who can kill Bastian," she groaned. "You can't do it alone."

"Please," I begged. "Let me try."

"I'll go back on one condition," Serena said as I hung on her every word. "You forget me, Bastian and my crown, and you leave things as they are."

"What?" I threw up my hands. "No! Why the hell are you making this so difficult? Don't you want to end this damn cycle you're trapped in? Don't you want your power back?"

"Of course I do, but..."

"But what?"

"I...have fears. Fears I cannot say, but you must trust me. And if you won't leave me and promise not to go back to Bastian, then I'm coming with you. Because I am the only chance you and your friends stand against him." She didn't allow me the chance to argue. She turned on her heel and walked away with a sigh, sitting on the other side of the boat and leaving me with less clarity than before. What fears was she talking about? And why did she have to be so stubborn? The constant back and forth tore my mind to shreds. But one thing was certain. Someone was going to be disappointed no matter what I did. No surprise there.

The thunder rolling in the distance reminded me to move fast. I dropped the sails as Milo worked the helm, catching the winds from the tempest, and we surged forward, outrunning the storm. Katrina and Serena stood at the starboard side, watching the waves. I knew Katrina must have been stressed about her mom, but this was her best chance of making it back to her alive. And Serena...she was watching the raging sea like a proud parent watches a child.

About twenty minutes later, the clouds were catching up to us, and giant rain droplets smacked the top of my head. "We should probably go ahead and drop anchor," I said.

Milo gave me a nod and we sent the anchor down, waiting for it to snag. When we felt the tautness of the boat against the line, Milo gave me a thumbs up and we both headed for the cabin, calling for Katrina and Serena to get their asses away from the hull and join us.

We waited out the storm, a few lanterns our only light. The cabin was small, but comfortable enough for us all to sit facing each other in the glow of the lowlight. We took turns passing around a Mediterranean beer that we'd found in the cabin, except for Katrina, who understandably opted out.

"Try not to worry," I said, noticing Katrina's downcast face. "Bastian isn't going to do anything to your mom before we get there. She'll be fine."

"She has a fish tail, Bellamy!" Katrina snapped.

"And she's alive. That's what matters right now."

Milo rubbed his hands together. Our damp clothes were cold against our skin. "He's right. Your mom is his bargaining piece, and he's not going to do anything to hinder his chances of getting what he wants."

All eyes flickered to Serena, who took a swig of beer and passed it off to Milo. "You are all about to find yourself in hot water."

"Hot water sounds lovely right about now," Milo shivered. I laughed.

The storm outside began to strengthen. The rain pelting the deck sounded like an avalanche above our heads. We fought to keep our balance as the boat tipped and teetered back and forth, waves crashing against all sides.

"Enough about Bastian. I'm sick of his name." Serena said. "Let's sing a song."

I was surprised to see Katrina smile at the idea. "A mermaid and a siren queen want to sing to us. What could go wrong?" I chuckled.

"Oh, that's true. I guess things could get out of hand." Serena smirked. "Then how about *you* sing to us?"

Katrina's smile grew wider as Milo and I protested. "Come on, boys. The crew could use a morale boost. Sing for us."

"Us singing is really not something that will boost morale, lass, I promise you that." I stretched my arms behind my head.

"Oh, I think it would," Katrina laughed, and grabbed Milo's shoulder. "Come on, teach us a shanty or something."

Milo rolled his eyes and pressed his forehead against hers. "I think I'd rather go ride out the storm on deck. Wouldn't you, Bellamy?"

"Aye, man. "We're not drunk enough for this."

"Oh, come on," Serena pleaded. "You weren't a pirate in your first life. I want to hear a shanty."

I sighed, resigned to my fate. "Fine, love. For you. Just this once."

The girls clapped and cheered with giggles as Milo and I turned to each other. "Which one should we do? 'Drunken Sailor?'"

Milo scoffed. "God, no. If I have to hear that one again, I'll lose it. What about 'Santiana?'"

"Maybe if I remembered the words. It's been a hell of a while for me. Best I can do is 'Leave Her Johnny.'" I shrugged.

"Aye, yeah, that's a good one. Allright." Milo straightened his shoulders and smacked his fist against the wood of the cabin bunks to create the beat and we threw out the lyrics to our shanty. I'd only get so many words in before laughing and fumbling with the whole thing, but of course kiss-ass Milo would leave me hanging and keep going. I caught up and then we sang the chorus as the girls laughed at our god-awful voices.

They applauded as we finished. "See? That was amazing." Katrina laughed, pulling her hair off her shoulders. "One more!"

"I was hoping the thunder outside would drown us out." Milo chuckled, tossing the bottle cap into the floor.

The girls begged again relentlessly. Maybe they used their siren powers to control us, because I agreed to another one.

"Allright, fine, but only if I get to pick the next song and it's not a shanty." I laid out my conditions with a grin. "Milo, I don't know if you'll recognize this one."

Silence fell as Milo gave me a curious look and the girls leaned in. I wiped my mouth after a mouthful of beer and began my serenade. I'd only gotten a couple of lines in when a huge smile spread across Katrina's face. "Oh my gosh...Please tell me where you learned 'Carry on Wayward Son!'"

"The ship radio and lots of hours at the wheel." I stomped my feet, continuing the song and dragging Milo into the next chorus with a nudge. He always picked up lyrics fast. Something about that weird memory of his served more purpose than just navigation. As we belted out the words, I added in the stomp of my boot. The sea tossed us around, but we kept singing, and before long the girls joined in, all of us arm-in-arm in our small circle on the floor.

By the time we'd finished the song, the sounds of the storm outside were raging, the waves clawing at the sides of the ship like vicious monsters.

I looked up, my tone turned serious. "I'd say there's another hour and a half of this at least."

"This little thing isn't meant to be in winds like this." Milo uttered. "I hope she holds out."

"You and me both." Katrina shuddered and closed a blanket around her and Milo.

And then a crash sent us tumbling to the floor. The lanterns toppled over, getting snuffed out, and chaos broke loose as we were slammed around every which way in the cabin. I reached for Serena, holding onto her as best I could and shielding her head. A crack of thunder shook the cabin and then all the movement stopped. I shook myself off and then felt around in the dark, calling out the names of my friends.

"We're here." Katrina said. I followed her voice, and we huddled together in the dark.

"I think she's capsized," Milo said.

"But we're not moving." Serena added.

I felt around for the hatch. It wasn't above us, and when I found the handle on the wall, I knew we'd been tipped over. "Right here." I ushered them over, opening the hatch to the sight of an empty shore, the storm still overhead. But we were ran aground. Sideways.

"Shitty anchor." I climbed out the hatch and examined the damage. Milo followed, and we looked at each other as the rain whipped our faces. We'd at least crashed on a small isle, with a small line of trees helping to barricade us from the wind.

"She doesn't look too damaged. We can tip her back over once the skies clear!" He shouted over the gusts and thunder.

We nodded, and then reentered the boat cabin. I didn't realize quite how tired I was. As I sat with Serena to the sound of the rain through the open hatch, my eyes found themselves heavy.

BELLAMY

Serena's voice gently woke me. "The storm is gone."

"Fantastic." I muttered, rubbing my eyes. "How long was I asleep?"

"A couple of hours. I didn't want to wake you. You looked like you needed the rest."

The cabin was aglow now, lit up the color of fire as the light of sunset beamed in through the hatch against the cabin's cherry wood stain. "Where are Katrina and Milo?"

"They went to find food. They won't be gone long."

I tousled my hands through my hair. "They're finally getting some alone time after Milo spent two years at sea. They'll be gone a while."

Serena cocked her head and smirked. "Then maybe we should be grateful for some alone time, too." She touched my face. "Did you dream of me?"

"I've been dreaming of you since the day I lost you."

"Oh, you're full of it, pirate. Good thing you're so handsome." She shook her head, turning away, but I touched her chin and turned her back to me.

"No, I mean it. In the way the winds guided my sails as I outran the horizon. In every moment of peace on calm clear waters. In every rolling wave caressing my skin. In every storm raging at sea. When I'd lie down on my ship, you were the waves rocking me to sleep. In the way the ocean called my name as I set my hand to the wheel. It was always you. You were every dream between me and the sea. You've been etched in my memory and my heart since the dawn of time, and the sea has been reminding me of you every day since." I paused, hesitating before asking a question, my lips hovering over the skin of her neck. "If we'd never found you, would you have stayed trapped at the bottom of the sea with the Kraken forever?"

Serena turned away and crawled out the hatch, leaving my question unanswered. I was getting tired of that. I followed her, chasing her down across the sand as she walked along the surf. "Would you stop doing that? Stop being so stubborn for one damn bloody minute and talk to me!"

She whipped around as I neared. "What choice did I have but to hide with the Kraken? I woke up in that pit after your father killed my human form and put my heart back in the sea! Davy Jones basically rules the seas without my power to keep him in check. It was too dangerous to leave. The sea loses its magic more and more each day. The sea gods' power is nothing more than a fingerprint left behind in myth and lore. The wonder of the ocean is just a shell of what it once was. And so am I." A tear shimmered in the corner of her eyelash, and I wiped it away gently with my thumb before it could fall.

"No. You're everything. With or without your power." It pained me to see how much she yearned to get her power back. Especially when I knew it might mean letting her put herself in harm's way. If only she'd just let me do it for her. To make up for the way I failed her before. It almost seemed like...like maybe the harder I tried to fight it, the worse things got. But I couldn't fully convince myself of that yet.

She turned away again to face the tide, and I reached around her waist from behind. I nuzzled her ear. "Let's forget our differences of interest for a while." She spun in my arms, turning to face me and gazing up at me with those hopeful caramel eyes. I slid my hand down. "All the past lives of loving you haven't been enough." I wished she'd listen to me. I wished there was something I could say to keep her from endangering herself.

"You've always been persuasive, Bellamy." Serena breathed with a hint of laughter. "But in the end, you can only decide what *you* will do. You don't get to decide what I do."

I smirked, amazed but also somewhat unsettled at her ability to practically read my thoughts. But it made sense. "Then I decide that right now, I forget all this for a moment, and spend this night worshipping the goddess I'm fated to love."

Her tropical scent intoxicated me. I ran my lips along the curves of her shoulder, and my hands slid down the small of her back. She sighed softly, touching me back in all the right places. I quickly glanced around, looking at the set of double footprints in the sand leading away from the boat to ensure Katrina and Milo weren't around.

"Don't worry about them. Like you said, they're probably off having just as much fun as we are." Serena assured me with a grin. She glowed like the moon as the sun dipped below the horizon. "Just be with me," she whispered, pulling my face to hers. She bit my lip, playing with my mouth along hers as she teased the skin beneath my shirt.

The sunset's orange glare reflected on the rolling tide like a stained-glass window, lighting up the sky around us with a red haze. Serena tugged at each piece of my clothing until she had removed them all, and I returned the favor by sliding off the dress that enrobed her so beautifully. But not as beautiful as how she looked without it. The delicate silk slid between my fingers like liquid as it dropped to the floor. I took in the sight of her—a sight I thought I'd never see again. She was everything a goddess should be, the broken sunlight hitting her flawless skin to cast a glow as warm as the gold she wore.

We danced to the sound of the water swirling around, our bodies pressed together as my fingers worked their way along the smoothness of her thigh. I kissed her deeply, savoring her tongue against mine. Heat roiled in my core down to my pounding lower half. I brought my lips to her breasts, feeling the way they perked up at my touch and relishing the scorch of her skin.

The blood rush in my veins felt like a song in my soul as I indulged in the feeling of her—something I'd been so cruelly deprived of the last time we'd been together in this way. Every touch, every lick, every stroke, every drop of sweat and desperate breath that escaped our bodies felt like the first. What an absolute wild blessing and curse, I thought.

She tried to turn back around in my arms, as she pushed the lower half of herself against me. But I gripped her shoulder, spinning her to face me again. I gently laid her down, pinning her to the sand, kissing her still. "No," I groaned. "I want to look into your eyes as we reclaim each other." I reached beneath her, feeling her slick heat, desperate to fill the need I knew she had. Her soft moans made my muscles tight and hard. It was unbearable. But I was gentle with her, placing myself wherever she needed until I felt her body riot with sensation and heard her gasp with breathlessness.

"Very well," she smirked, opening herself to me fully. I plunged forward, diving into her like the raging sea she was.

The water around us cast a glow of dusk that reflected the very fire I felt in every inch of my body as I joined mine with hers. All I could think about was how I'd never let her go again—and how delightful every part of her felt. Like quenching a thirst I'd been craving, like a cool rush of wind on a hot day, like a burst of sunlight in the darkness. She was all of it, and with each thought, my body grew hotter, faster, and tenser, until I lost myself to a rush of release.

"Serena. Atargatis. Damn, you could be Aphrodite. Whatever your name is, whatever title you hold, I only have one for you. *Mine.*"

"Always yours." She sighed, stroking my hair. She held my head close to her breast as we both rested against the sand. "Since the beginning and until the end."

I whispered with a smile. "From North to West."

FIGHT THE CURRENT

36

MILO

"Looks like maybe we should stay gone a bit longer." Katrina mumbled with a chuckle at the sight of Serena and Bellamy lying in the sand as we stumbled back through the trees to the sailboat.

I set down the crab net and coconuts we'd gathered, taking Katrina in my arms. "I'm alright with that."

She kissed me, dropping the papayas she held and grabbing my face. Even though just a short while before we had been lying sprawled in the sand ourselves, her body beneath mine in a long-overdue reunion, it wasn't enough. I wanted her more every moment. And I'd happily entwine myself with her again here and now.

"Do you know what this place reminds me of?" I said.

"What's that?"

"The first time I met you. When you came to the island of Valdez's shipwreck and sat down next to me without a clue."

"I still don't know how I didn't notice you sitting there on the shore." She twisted her lips into a sideways smirk.

"Maybe because I didn't want to be seen."

"But you talked to me first," she said with suspicion.

"I did. And I'm glad. Because I couldn't resist you then. And I still can't. Something pulled me to you like...like water. And I know better than to fight the current." I leaned in to kiss her between words.

As night fell, I noticed Bellamy and Serena were stirring. "Come on," I said, scooping the food back up. "We should get back and start a fire. I'm sure I'm not the only one who's starving."

We walked out to our friends on the shore, where we presented our gathering of crab and fruit. Bellamy worked to get the fire going, and we sat around it, cooking the crab meat and downing the coconut water like it was the most divine thing we'd ever tasted.

"The boat isn't seriously damaged. A good flipping over and she should be ready to sail." I explained, cracking a crab claw between my thumbs.

"So we could leave tonight?" Katrina asked.

"If you want to. It's your call when we leave." I took a bite, glancing at Bellamy across the flames of the bonfire. "Right Bellamy?"

He shook himself free of the dazed, empty look on his face and straightened. "Yeah."

Katrina leaned forward, her gaze meeting each of our tired faces. "Of course I want to get back to my mom...but I think we all need the rest. We can leave at daybreak."

"All right then." Bellamy tossed a stick into the fire, his voice hollow. "We leave at daybreak."

We readied the boat at dawn while the girls slept a bit longer. Milo and I set to work rigging the sails and double checking the hull. Thankfully the masts had survived the crash. The skies were perfect for sailing, the winds in our favor. We didn't have far to go.

"It's about a two day's journey, I'd say," I called to Milo.

"I'll take that over two years," he chuckled.

I replied with a half-laugh, walking over to him as I tied the last bit of rigging. "We've missed you, mate, you know that?"

"You? Miss me?" He shook his head. "No hard feelings over the necklace?"

"You know that was a weird time," I grumbled with a hint of fake laughter. "We were all desperate and half-mad."

"I'm just joking." He jabbed me with his elbow. "I know it was all that seawater finally getting to you. Don't worry, I understand."

"Hey now. Who showed you the ropes of pirating? You'd have been long dead on my father's crew without me."

"I'll admit, I might've picked up a few things from you. But don't pretend I didn't help you with that God-awful sense of navigation." He raised an eyebrow with a grin as he tightened a knot.

We both laughed as I shook my head, thinking back to how Milo, a scrawny fifteen year old, would dare correct me on star patterns and my map drawings, right in front of my father, at that. "Okay, fair enough there. Maybe there really was some useful reason my father wanted you aboard."

"If I'm being honest, I'd rather there hadn't been."

"Well, if you weren't valuable, you'd have been dead, so…" I leaned into the edge of the boat along with Milo, using all my strength to nudge it back into the water.

"Given what we've been through, that doesn't sound like the worst option." Milo tilted his head in my direction. He looked older than me now, with a beard thicker than I'd ever seen it and the scar across his eye. His skin was tanned from his time at sea, and he had a calm but wise look about him that spoke of some hidden strength he didn't have before.

I tapped my fingers along the side of the boat. "Aye, come on, mate, it's not so bad. We're filthy sons of bitches and yet for some reason we've been given more chances than saints."

"Maybe we're supposed to learn something from it," Milo waded in next to me, pushing the boat along out of the shallows. I took a breath, winded and thirsty.

"You didn't happen to bring any rum back with you from the good old days, did you?" I was only half-joking.

To my surprise, he reached into his satchel and produced a flask. He tossed it to me.

"You bastard," I smiled wide, chugging a big mouthful. "Never thought I'd taste that again. It's just not the same here."

We kept on about things as the girls awoke. We watched them on the shore as they chattered and prepared themselves for the day ahead. Then we climbed up onto the boat.

"You can't hold her back, you know. Even when you want to protect her." Milo's voice made me look back over my shoulder at him as I went to pick up a rope. He'd better not be trying to give me some heart-to-heart shit about Serena. Not after all he'd caused with Katrina.

"Shocking words coming from you, mate." I cocked my head, dropping the rigging in my hand. "You of all people know what it's like to lose your lass. Don't tell me you wouldn't do anything to keep that from happening again."

"I would. I did. I tried that. I tried to keep Katrina from Cordelia so she wouldn't get hurt. And the trust I lost in her wasn't worth the false sense of security. I was wrong to try to make that decision for her. And it's the same with Serena. She's going to do what she thinks she must, and it's not our place to try to hold them back." He narrowed his eyes at the two girls chatting yards away as the wind swept through their hair. "They're both as untamable as the sea. And isn't that always what you've loved about the sea?"

For a moment I thought on his words, letting them digest as I stretched my jaw forward to relieve the tension I was holding. "I'm not going to hand her over to Bastian if that's what you mean."

"Of course not. But I mean, if her destiny is to face him once and for all, to get back the power that's rightfully hers, do you think you should try to keep her from that?"

I offered a lewd gesture and an eye roll, because it was the only way I could keep from letting him see how deeply his words sank into my conscience. I knew Serena deserved to be restored to the fullness of her power, but surely she could stand back while I did it for her. Because one thing I was sure as hell of—I wasn't trading her for Katrina's mom in a million years.

I looked for a way to change the subject quickly and my gaze landed on Milo's tattoo. "That's new."

"A little token from Bastian in the past. You still have yours?" Milo asked with a nod.

"It's not going anywhere." I reached up instinctively to feel the skin over my collarbone. The inked sea beast curving along it and around to the nape of my neck tattoo on my body had remained dormant for all these centuries until I'd started hearing Bastian's voice through it again on this goose chase. It was our seal—like how he'd taken Katrina's voice—to prove our bargain. Only the bargain was my father's, and I was the pawn piece between them.

"What about the sun thing around it? Don't recall that one." I noticed his arm marking bordering the intricate map. It seemed less like ink and more like a shining inlay of metal.

"It's a long story. But it was supposed to dampen the effect of Bastian's mark." Milo blew a puff of air through his lips and squinted in the sunlight. "Some legend from an island I found. The sun protects them from inner darkness. And they wanted to keep Bastian's darkness from finding them."

""Did it work?" I raised an eyebrow.

"I certainly hope so." He looked back at Katrina and Serena, who seemed to be finishing up their conversation as they waded into the surf to come aboard. "Anyway, the sails are set for now."

I gave him a nod, watching him stride across the deck to help the girls up, but not before he stopped and turned around once more. "Bellamy."

"Aye?" I called.

"You've covered my arse more times than you should have. Don't think I won't have your back in whatever comes next."

"Savvy, mate. I'll hold you to that." I joked with a finger pointing toward him.

Once the girls were on board, Katrina looked concerned and whispered something to Milo. I watched him follow her to the cabin hatch. Making my way to the helm, I glanced over at Serena, who was eyeing me with a look of seduction or disdain, or maybe both, as she leaned on her elbows over the boat's edge. With a wink, I took the wheel.

MILO

"**W**hat did you want to tell me?" I asked Katrina.

"I'd rather talk inside," she said, ushering me into the cabin. There wasn't much room, but we made our way around old fishing gear and nets cluttered around the sink area to the farthest area back, where two little sofa-like cots lined the sides of the cabin walls.

I tripped on a net we stepped over when a lure snagged on my pants. I stumbled and caught myself with a mutter. "My ship would've never been in such disarray."

Katrina laughed. "Already lost your sea legs?"

"Ha, not quite," I smiled, leaning my arm on the wall just above her head. "Just distracted by a pretty mermaid."

She rolled her eyes with a scoff. "All that time and you still managed to hold on to that cheesiness."

"I think you mean charm." I flashed her a playful grin as she shoved against my chest lightly, but left her hand there as her face softened and her gaze turned deep. She slid her hand down my chest, her eyes following her movement.

"I wanted to ask you...What happened after..." her voice trailed away slowly. "...after you sent us back here? What happened to you in those two years?"

My thoughts flashed back to the day I sent Katrina to the present using the Trident. I'd tried so hard to forget the hours that lingered after I killed that captain and commandeered his ship. I hardly slept for three days, and when I finally did, I lied down still covered in the blood of my enemies, drunk on liquor to numb myself to my new reality. It took months for me to come back to my senses. But in the meantime, I was merciless.

"I…I'm ashamed to admit that I turned into the very kind of man I never wanted to be. I was so angry." I turned my face away because I couldn't bear to meet her eye. "I thought I'd never see you again."

"Whatever you did, you can't hold onto." She touched my jaw, stroking my beard with her thumb as she turned my head back to her. "Just like your time in Valdez' crew. It's in the past. You did what you had to do to survive."

"This time it was different, Katrina. On Valdez's ship I had no choice. But on my own, I had every choice. To take lives or spare them. And I rarely chose the latter. Because if I did, I'd have been found weak on the seas. I spent weeks hunting down Bastian's fleets in search of the map to the Fountain. Until I finally squeezed out some information from one of his cowards of a captain who told me where I could find him. I tore down anyone who got in my way and sunk more ships than I could count. I set the seas on fire looking for a way back to you."

"You have to forgive yourself."

"Forgive? That's the thing that scares me. I don't regret any of it. I'd do it all again for you. But now I fear I don't deserve you."

"Funny you say that." She took my hands, her breath shaky. "I didn't just want to ask you what happened back there. I…I need to tell you something."

I was confused, but I urged her to continue with a look.

"When I guided you to me through the Fountain…when I sang to you…it wasn't fully me." She took a deep breath. "I started the song, but then my siren took over, and she was luring you. It worked to guide you out, but the song you heard was a death trap. If I hadn't regained control at the last second, she would've…*I would've* killed you. And that terrified me, but I didn't want to let anyone know. Not even you. Because I'd worked all this time to find you, to save you, only to realize I'm the real danger to you. And I don't know what to do about it."

I was quiet for a moment as I chose my words carefully. If she only knew how I'd dreaded this day. From what I'd seen of sirens, I knew even Katrina would eventually succumb to hers. They were powerful creatures, and while Katrina could somewhat control that side of her for now, I feared one day that may no longer be the case. "I've already known this would happen eventually. I just didn't know when. I would be well deserving of a death at the hands of a siren. I certainly played my part in their demise, willingly or not. And if that siren is you…well, then…there's no greater end I could imagine."

Katrina blinked hard. "No, no. Don't even say that. Do you honestly think I could live with myself if I were to do something to you?"

"Katrina," I sighed. "I wish you could understand how truly despicable I am. While we're being honest, I want you to know that I want you now more than ever. But I'm so afraid I'll ruin you." I couldn't believe I was admitting this out loud to her. But she had to know what was eating me alive every moment.

She shook her head, sending loose waves of hair dancing around her shoulders. "*You* ruin *me*? You're not the one with an evil voice in your head. You're not the one who might snap one day and kill me and not even remember it! I can't love you without hurting you. And the more I think about that..." she paused with a heavy sigh, "...the more I wonder what kind of future we can even have."

"The only future I want." I grabbed both of her hands in mine almost as though they might drift away if I didn't do it fast enough.

She swallowed with her head hung low. "The dreams you once told me about. Moving away from all this. Having a normal life and settling down...You can't have that with me."

"Of course I can, and even if I couldn't, those dreams don't matter anymore. You're my only dream now."

Katrina looked off to the side for a moment, those brown eyes swimming in a sea of thoughts before finding my desperate gaze again. "Do you know what these past few days have made me realize? It's made me realize there's no escape. And there never will be."

"No, you don't mean that," I pleaded. Maybe this was what I deserved, but it still felt like a gutting with an iron-hot blade.

Katrina looked up, as if wishing she could say something to make this conversation dissolve, starting and stopping again as she warred with her words. "When I look at my mom, and realize she's just as trapped by the siren blood in our veins as I am, I realize it's never going away. Never. If it wasn't the nightmares destroying our lives, it's this. It'll just keep passing down like it always has. I can't do that to a family of my own. I didn't break my curse. I just traded it out for a different one. So if I can't end the curse, I have to end the family. Which means I can't have one with you. I can't be your dream, because I'm a nightmare. There is no happy ending for us."

"What are you saying, then?" I squeezed her hands, the tension in my body like a tightrope. I knew I couldn't protect her from herself. But I would gladly die trying.

"I don't know, Milo. I don't know." She dropped her head against my shoulder, leaving it there as we stood in a silent embrace for minutes. Until she finally shattered the silence.

"You once told me you did terrible things. I never thought I'd be the one saying it to you."

I huffed out a breath. "We can be each other's sun."

"What?" Katrina pulled away gently.

"It's a legend. As long as the moon has the sun, it'll never be overtaken by the darkness. I'll be your sun, Katrina, even if that means I burn." I lifted her chin to meet my eyes.

She stared at me, her eyes flickering back and forth between mine. She reached up slowly and touched my scarred eye, then with her other hand, guided mine to the scar along the side of her face. She held us that way for a long time, neither of us saying a word. I thought I understood. I hoped I did.

"And tonight?" She whispered. "Maybe tomorrow it'll all make sense. Or maybe it won't, and it'll be worse and we'll realize I was right. But for tonight, let's imagine I'm wrong. If we're gonna burn, let's burn together."

She crashed her mouth into mine, the taste of her tongue like sweet wine. With her hand slipping beneath my shirt, she unraveled me. I almost wondered if it was her siren side taking control, but even if it was, I couldn't say I would've stopped her. I'd been insatiable for her for far, far too long.

I pressed her to me, our lips joining deeper like the tide joins the shoreline. We stumbled back as a flurry of hands and clothing flashed between desperate glimpses. I would've gazed at her body longer if I'd had the chance, but we moved with such urgency, such passion, that I found myself looking into her eyes. But that didn't stop me from feeling her to the fullest. Her skin scorched beneath my fingers stroking her, defining the alluring shape of her curves. I slid my hands across her breasts down to her hips as she pressed her fingers into my shoulder muscles, tracing my tattoos from my back to my upper arms. I groaned as she reached for me, teasing the flame below. My groin tightened with an ache as my craving for her grew stronger than I could endure. I squeezed her thighs and ran my hand along the perfection in between them. Her panting sighs in my ear drove me mad as she pulled me down onto one of the cots against the wall. I climbed over her, and she kissed me as I leaned down. There was little time for more before I found myself anchored in her, wondering if the sound of waves lapping the side was enough to cover the sounds of our gasps.

Each time before had been slow and gentle, but this was furious and unrestrained. Her fingers tangled through my hair as I shackled her wrists with my grip, our entwined bodies slippery with sweat. She pulled me into her like she might die if she couldn't feel me deep enough. My blazing pulse throbbed through every inch of me. When I heard her moan my name in delirious bliss, I gave myself permission to follow in a rush of heat and rapture. If this was what burning felt like, I'd let her take me straight to hell.

I didn't care what tomorrow brought, or all the tomorrows to come. As we slowly fell asleep in each other's arms, I resolved that whatever darkness Katrina felt she couldn't defeat could take me with it, too.

I kissed her forehead gently as I watched her eyes drift closed. "Whether you're right or wrong, we burn together."

Parting Waters
39

BELLAMY

As night fell, Serena came up to me, finally, after driving me to insanity with her sideways glances from across the deck. She planted a kiss on my cheek with a wink as she slid her hand along mine. "Do you know we were married in our first life?"

"I wish I could remember that life I had with you. I hope to hell it wasn't as complicated as this one."

"It wasn't. Not at first." Serena sighed.

"Was I the same back then?" I asked as she leaned against my shoulder while my other hand steadied the wheel.

"You were. You looked the same. You sounded the same. And you were just as cocky and stubborn then, too." Her nose crinkled with a laugh.

"Good, at least there'll be no surprises for you then." I pushed back a loose braid over her shoulder. "Do you remember your life when I met you in 1989? Do you remember your families?"

"Some of them I do. Of course, I didn't know who—or what I was—at the time. But I remember some of them. Like my father in my most recent life. He had the gentlest spirit."

"Ha. He hated me, though. He thought I killed you." I leaned back. "Thankfully Katrina proved otherwise to him, but still. He went almost thirty years believing that."

"We seem to have a knack for getting each other killed." Serena laughed, turning her head to look at the stars.

A wave of guilt flooded over me as I thought of something going wrong when we went to face Bastian. "Not this next time. What if we just run and start a new life somewhere else? What if you stay like this?"

She shook her head. "We can't run from this, Bellamy. Not without making your life terrible. And we would always be in danger. We'd never truly have peace. And then when we die eventually we'll just be reborn again, always subconsciously trying to find each other."

Suddenly Bastian's voice crept up in my head, taunting me in whispers.

And if you run with her, I'll always know where to find her.

No. You fucking bastard.

It was then that I realized. Bastian could still see us. All along, he saw and heard everything. And that's how he'd known about Katrina's mom, and leaving McKenzie and Noah behind. He knew the whole time, even before Katrina and I made the deal. And that's why he made us go alone. The closer I was with Serena, the easier it'd be for him to kill her. He was watching us. We were feeding right into his trap. He would know exactly when and where we planned to come and confront him. And even beyond that, if we didn't put an end to him, he would always have access to the people I cared about through me...forever. It would never truly end. He could clearly activate his markings whenever he wanted, and we could do nothing to stop it.

I swallowed hard as I accepted the realization that the only way to keep Katrina and Serena safe was to stay away from them. I released the wheel, nearly toppling over as I fought the sway of the boat.

"Where are you going?" Serena asked, startled.

"I can't tell you. Because he's listening." Without explaining anything further, I rushed to find Milo. He was asleep next to Katrina in the cabin, and I silently shook him awake.

"Dammit man, what are you doing?" He whispered, wiping the sleep from his eyes.

I kept my voice low, careful not to wake Katrina. "My mark is still traceable. I don't have your little sun voodoo trick to help me out. He's going to know when we come to face him. We can't let him have that advantage."

"Hmmm. You're right. But what are you suggesting?" He groaned under his breath.

"I'm saying—" I stopped myself. Whatever I thought or said Bastian might hear. Instead I looked around for paper and pencil, and hurriedly scribbled what I wanted to say.

The girls aren't safe with me. I need to travel separately.

Milo studied the paper in the dim light, then looked up at me with an understanding in his eyes that assured me he agreed. I was surprised, as I half expected him to object. But he didn't hesitate to nod and wake Katrina.

"I'll explain it to her." Turning back to me, he paused. "Who's steering the ship?"

I tilted my head with a shrug and gritted teeth.

"Well go do that then!" He punched me in the arm a little too hard. I retreated, leaving Milo to sort out the situation with Katrina.

Back out on deck, I made my way to the wheel, in no rush at all. Serena rushed to greet me, still confused as to why I'd suddenly left her moments before.

"You aren't safe," I told her. "Not as long as he can track you through me."

Her eyes darkened as she looked me up and down. "What are you asking?"

I reached forward to reassure her with a touch on the shoulders. I bit my tongue, careful not to say too much in case Bastian was tuned in. I pulled out the paper I'd used earlier and resorted to writing again, when Serena placed a hand over mine to stop me.

"I know what you want." she said. "And I agree it's the safest way."

A bit taken aback, I didn't question how she knew. I focused on keeping my thoughts bland and locked down, still paranoid of Bastian's unrestricted access to them. It was everything I could do to help keep the girls from being lured into a trap. Bastian might've wanted us to believe he was patiently waiting for Katrina to waltz in ready to make a trade for her mom, but I didn't trust him to do even that fairly.

I was surprised to see the look on her face—almost beaming with excitement as she looked out at the starry sky over the sea. "We'll travel my favorite way. You boys can have the boat." She grinned.

I hadn't quite thought of *how* we were going to travel separately in my frantic rush, but now that my thoughts were settling, I thought I might have an idea, and I didn't necessarily like it.

As if perfectly timed, Katrina emerged from the cabin, wiping sleep from her eyes. She hurried to us. "What's going on?" She asked through a yawn.

Serena looked at her with a sly smile and led her away to the boat's edge, I assumed explaining the plan to her. Judging by Katrina's startled expression, I think I assumed correctly.

Milo joined us up on deck, taking up a spot next to me. "How exactly do we do this?" he asked. "I'd be lying if I said I didn't feel a bit uneasy about this."

"Same, mate." I crossed my arms. "But only two of the four of us need a boat to travel through water. So what do you think?"

"I get it. But this is exactly what I meant earlier. If I've learned one thing, it's that we have to trust them, even when it feels like we're the only ones who can protect them...because usually trusting them is *how* we protect them."

I chewed on his words for a moment, despite the funny feeling rising in my stomach. Separating from Serena was the last thing I wanted, but if it kept her safe, I'd do whatever I had to.

"Alright, boys," A grin spread across Serena's face as she and Katrina both turned to face us. "We'll see you there." Then she dove overboard.

Katrina turned to Milo and with a long kiss and embrace, assured him she'd be alright. "I'll always find you, remember? This won't be for long."

"Not another two years, I hope," Milo teased, but there was a heaviness in his voice. He had to be fighting every urge in himself to want to stop this. I didn't blame him.

Katrina climbed over the hull and leapt into the water below. Both Milo and I rushed to look overboard, only to see the two girls fully transformed as sirens, glistening tails splashing up and down in and out of the water. I stood in awe, looking at Serena in her breathtaking siren form. It was unlike Katrina's, which sparkled simple bluish silver with a single fluke. Serena's tail was longer, grander, and the scales reflected every possible color of the spectrum, with dorsal fins and long, trailing caudal fins that danced like a cascade of ribbons among the waves surrounding her double flukes. It was truly a tail fit for a goddess.

"Be careful," I uttered. "If you need us to slow down, let us know."

"Don't worry," she smirked. "It's you who might have a hard time keeping up with us."

With that, she dove beneath the water. Katrina offered one last glance back at us before doing the same.

WHEN STARS SPEAK

40

KATRINA

"I've never swam this far before. What if I get tired?" I asked, flicking my tail to keep up with Serena in the water. I'd never spoken underwater before, but it was somehow possible here with her. Our voices carried through the water as clearly as on land.

"That just tells me you've never truly tested out your abilities. You won't tire that easily." Serena looked back at me with a twinkle in her eyes.

With a surge forward, I caught up to her with ease, determined not to look weak as I swam by her side. "Well I haven't exactly been a mermaid for all that long."

Not that you knew, at least. She smiled, speaking to me through my mind. *You've always been one. It's who you are.*

I felt a weight close in around my chest, and not just from the surprise of Serena's voice in my head. The idea of being a siren my whole life sat with me like a sack of bricks. I wondered what my life might've been like if my mother and I hadn't been cursed with this nature. And then the thought that had come up once before came rising to the surface once more—the thought that I would just continue to pass on this twisted legacy if I were to ever continue this bloodline. The thought that I could never have a normal life.

Serena... I stuttered out her name, finding it strangely natural to communicate my thoughts to her. This inner voice connection felt as easy as speaking. But knowing it was just another extension of my siren nature made me uncomfortable. *Is there any way for me to gain a soul? Or my mom? Can she?*

The mischievous look she wore faded at my question. I was startled when she answered me using her voice. "No siren has ever asked me that. Why would you want one of those over the long life you have?"

"Because," I paused, watching our mythical-shaped shadows along the sand below as we passed over a shallow part of the ocean. "Because what good is a long life if none of the people you care about can share it with you? Or if half of you wants to kill them. Being half siren is harder than being a full siren. Because my two halves hate each other. I don't like it. And I don't want to end up as just seafoam. I want to be...more. In this life and the next."

Serena shook her head just a touch, her eyebrows furrowing as she listened to my words. "You're the last living mermaid, Katrina. You and your mother. How could you wish to give that up?"

I sighed. "This power, these abilities. None of this means anything to me. I never asked for any of it. If anything, it's made my life harder. I'm always fighting two sides of myself." My words came out more bitterly than I intended. But I couldn't help it. This burden was something I silently bore each day, and it felt freeing to finally hear myself admit out loud that I didn't want it. Though I could tell my siren side didn't quite feel the same. Of course she didn't. She wanted me to shut up.

"I didn't ask for my fate either," Serena said sternly, still swimming shoulder to shoulder with me. "But destiny doesn't often let us choose."

I opened myself to the freeing sensation of the water around me. Taking in the silky feel of the current, the bubbles from our movements, and the waves rolling above. There was something magical and haunting about knowing I was the last of my kind, swimming this vast ocean like a solitary needle in a very large haystack. And I couldn't quite tell which side of me was in charge. Like saltwater mixed with freshwater, my personas could never truly be separated now that they'd merged.

I finally spoke again, still working to keep up alongside the goddess. "But you want your power, don't you?"

Serena slowed her pace, and looked over at me with a tilt of her head. "I do. It is who I was meant to be. Without it...well, you saw what had become of me."

I paused, wondering what would be next on this journey. I thought more about what Serena said about fate not letting us choose. It reminded me of something Milo had said when he stayed with me through the night for the first time.

Fate has decided against us...

But how wrong he turned out to be. We were able to overcome the boundaries of time to be together. So if we could do *that*, maybe that wasn't the only destiny we could change.

"Then why do you fight against it so much when Bellamy wants to get the Crown for you? Why do you hide from your power if you think you were meant to have it?"

Serena refused to look at me, and for a moment, I thought she wouldn't answer me either. But then she muttered something more subtle than a sea breeze. "Because his destiny is not mine. My loss of power is not his burden. That's all I will say."

"You have to get it back," I said, thinking of how she was my only hope of saving my mom. "Even if fate or destiny or whatever you call it says things have to be one way, sometimes it can be changed."

Serena's eyes softened as she gave me a sideways glance. "You're not wrong, little mermaid. But sometimes you do need a little help from the stars. They're what guided you and Milo to each other. When the stars speak, destiny must listen. You must have a star speaking on your behalf."

I had a hunch which star it might be. As I thought of whatever celestial powers might lie above, I watched in awe at the ones beneath me. We were in shallow waters, and the light reflected along the coral reefs peeking up from below, shimmering their curtain of ripples in between the rainbow of colors beneath. Plants, corals, and animals of every shape and movement, wriggling, darting, and drifting through the water with the ease of a bird in flight. Life down here was peaceful, and certainly something magical, but it wasn't the life I wanted. Not at the price it demanded.

I wondered what came next. What would await us once we got back to Bastian? And what kind of bargaining tool would he use my mother for? It was as if the cold water around me could suddenly pierce my skin as the thought settled. We'd have to rescue my mother, at whatever cost. I'd do what I had to save her. Even if it meant returning to the darkest part of me like I had to do to defeat Cordelia. Whatever it took, I'd do it. I'd get my mom back.

CALAMARI

41

BELLAMY

I glared at the sea, forcing down the worry raging in my chest as I thought about Katrina and Serena out there alone. I knew it was for the best, but still it tortured me. To keep my mind distracted, I pushed away from the side of the ship, turning around to find Milo standing behind me adjusting some rigging.

"They'll be all right. Keep your shirt on," he said.

"Aye." I let out a huff of breath. "I know they could kill us both if they wanted to. And honestly, not sure how I feel about that either, but it's just hard to let them go when you just got them back."

Milo wiped his brow with the back of his arm. "This is how we keep them safe. So let's put our heads down and get this crown for your lass."

I crossed my arms with a chuckle. "Well look who declared himself captain," I pretended to salute. "Want me to swab the deck as well?"

"Don't get like that." Milo smirked. "I thought we settled this back on the *Siren*, remember?"

"Oh, you still haven't let that go, have you?" I spat with a roll of my eyes.

"What? Thought I'd forget when I bested you at the Captain's Duel? Not a chance," Milo bared a row of white teeth with a raised eyebrow.

"Right, because it was the only time it ever happened."

"Because you were too scared to face me again." The half-laugh Milo did stirred up memories I didn't even realize I still had. I'd almost forgotten just how damn cocky he could be. Suddenly I felt like I was talking to the Milo I grew up alongside, the naïve merchant's son who found his footing as a pirate way too quickly for his own good. The one who looked up to me when my father was too harsh on him—which was often. Sometimes I wished some of that goodie-goodie charm had rubbed off on me instead of the other way around, but there was no room for that kind of golden-heartedness aboard my father's ship. I made sure that tender-hearted boy quickly learned that.

"Well, here we are, the two of us sailing the seas without a captain. What do you say we settle who we're sailing under here and now? Who'll be Captain of the..." I paused. I didn't even know if this shoddy splintering toothpick beneath us had a name. I sauntered over to the side to see if she did. Sure enough, painted in some fading lettering chipping through the cracks in the wood, the word "*Calamari.*"

"The *Calamari.*"

"Ah, just what every pirate dreams. To be hailed as the feared captain of *The Calamari.*" Milo swung around the ropes, a mocking smile stretched wide across his face.

"A captain's a captain." I shrugged. "If you forfeit the title, that leaves it to me, I suppose."

"Not a chance." Milo's eyes narrowed. "Letting you call the shots has never worked out quite too well."

"So then let's prove it. Remember I taught you everything you know." I remarked with a lewd gesture of my hand.

Milo paused and disappeared for a moment into the cabin. He emerged with two swords, the ones he'd been wearing when he came through the Fountain of Youth. I opened a hand and reached forward, gesturing for Milo to toss me one of the swords.

"Not everything," Milo slung a sword my way. The hilt hit my hand like some kind of magic reuniting with its rightful owner. Before I could even adjust my grip, Milo swung at me full force, meeting my defense with a burst of sparks and steel.

Suddenly I was back on the deck of the *Siren's Scorn*, wielding my blade against a young buccaneer far too eager to earn the mark of a skilled swordsman.

We'd just come off of a battle with a warship, not a week after my father had forced the merchant boy aboard. I'd mostly made it a point to avoid him, knowing any kind of compassion I showed him would be frowned upon and possibly even punished. It didn't matter that I was his son. My father wouldn't spare me the scourge of the sea—not even for his own flesh and blood. I'd learned that the hard way long before this kid's age. I could still feel every sting of the whip, every deep dig into my skin as the gnarled leather tore across my back, at my father's hand no less. Or the pangs of hunger and burn of parched lips as the blinding sun beat down on me for days shackled to the mast. So when I looked at that broken boy's eyes and saw the cold hopelessness there, I had to force myself to look away, pretending it didn't bother me. He'd toughen up in time, as I had.

But I couldn't ignore him when he found me after a cannon swap and raid—an event during which he usually hid belowdecks. It was still raining lightly, washing fresh blood across the deck. I watched the red water run between my boots and was startled by a blade thrown down at my feet.

"Can you teach me to fight the way you all do?" A voice shuddered. The boy came stepping up, across the bloody mess on the floor, wringing and picking at his hands, face unsure. I might've almost guessed he'd rehearsed this.

"You mean all that time spent sailing with your father and he never taught you to swing a sword?" I spoke down to him, holding my ground so as not to soften.

He shifted nervously from one foot to the other. "I...he taught me some. But mostly to navigate. He wanted me in charge of charts and maps."

"Funny," I chewed on the inner part of my cheek. "You'd think any good merchant worth his salt would want to make sure his son was adequately equipped to deal with dangers out on the sea like...oh, I don't know...pirates." I flashed a wicked grin his way. He was barely fifteen, but he wasn't too much shorter than me. He was fit, but not as strong as he could be. He'd make a good swordsman if he really wanted to learn.

I glanced around at the ship, where the crew had already begun dumping the enemy bodies overboard, cleaning out the bloody crevices of the deck, and rolling the cannons back into place for storage. It was hardly a scene where anyone would notice a little extra chaos thrown in. The unmanned helm in particular caught my eye as my line of sight followed a sailor passing by. I smirked with an idea. If this boy wanted to learn to fight like a pirate, I'd be more than happy to teach him.

"Allright...Milo, is it?" I picked up the cutlass he'd dropped at my feet, running my forefinger and thumb along the blade as I inspected it. "Surely you know a small thing or two. I refuse to believe you're as incompetent as you look. Show me what you know."

I threw the cutlass back to him, and he caught it with a look of surprise. Before he could say anything, I drew my own sword and swung high, near his head. I laughed with surprise when he blocked my blade—sloppily as hell—but better than I expected.

"I see there may be something to work with after all." I grumbled beneath my mocking grin. "Fix your footwork, lad. Like this," I gestured, repeating the move with more force and precision, giving him only a second to observe my correction.

"Like what? That was too fast," he whined. "I couldn't—"

"When you cross your enemy, they're not going to wait for you to figure it out. And neither am I." I swung again, the tip of my sword cutting closer to the stomach this time. I yanked it back, barely tapping the edge of his shirt.

"I'd have killed you just now, lad" I tipped my head with a gesture. Ignoring the pinched expression pressed on his face, I handed him the sword, and told him to go practice on the other side of the deck. He tried to protest, but I shut him up quick with another nudge of my sword and a few more choice words. "Get over there and practice. Now." I demanded, pointing to the open area near the stern.

Little did he know of the fun I had in store for him. When he finally accepted defeat, he moved to go that direction. Just as he passed by a certain section of the ship, I quickly hurried to the helm and gave the wheel a good spin, tilting the ship. The wind tugged on a sail on one of the lower masts and sent the boom whirling around, dropping just above the deck floor—enough to swing down and cut off Milo right where he walked and scoop him up like a limp doll.

I roared with laughter as the boom pole swung to the outside, dangling the boy over the water as he clung to the pole with desperate pleas. A couple of crewmen passing on the deck nudged me as they passed, commending me on the prank as they chuckled. Proudly I watched my helpless mentee struggle as I left him there to dangle just a few moments more.

"You're a pirate now, lad. Always expect what you wouldn't expect." I crooned.

"I'm no pirate." He hissed.

I turned the wheel once more and sent him flying back around on the boom. He dropped to the deck floor immediately as it swung around. My shadow loomed over him as I stepped over to where he fumbled to get to his feet.

"Deny it all you want," I said, "but you're a pirate now, and you'll never change that."

I turned away, leaving him there on the deck floor. Little did I know, the next time I tried to teach that kid to fight, he'd prove himself an opponent more skilled and gritty than I could have imagined. And one day years from now he'd beat me at my father's favorite swordsmanship challenge as my father sat back and watched. And he'd do it again on the shores of St. Augustine, fighting over a necklace and the girl who wore it.

Back on the *Calamari*, the tiny sailboat dipped side to side as we dueled. I no longer noticed the cool air on my skin as sweat beaded on my forehead. Milo was efficient with a blade, and a hell of a lot faster than I remembered, but I definitely had the upper hand on footwork and maneuvering. My blade met his as he taunted me through a boyish grin.

"I'd say this is hardly fair," I spat. "You've had much more practice recently than I have."

"Is that a problem?" Milo joked. "I'm older, too. We're almost the same age now. Makes it a fair fight." He jabbed his sword at me, and I parried it with ease, backing up just enough to dodge the hit, then I leapt forward and to the side.

"No pirate fights fair. And you're somehow good at finding loopholes in reality." I whipped my sword across his knee, with just enough contact to tear through the fabric of his pants. "But it makes no difference here."

Milo looked up at me through a disheveled mess of hair. "I don't need loopholes to beat you."

Hopping up on the hull, I swung around the ropes attached to the sails to take another swing. Milo pulled on the rigging, climbing it to reach me as our blades clashed. At this point, our fight was a game of chase, and I had to hold back a laugh a couple of times at the absurdity of it. Milo grazed my shoulder with the edge of his sword, ripping through my shirt.

"I'll be taking that title of captain now," he grinned.

I glanced at my shoulder in absolute surprise. "Over that? Bloody hell, that wasn't enough to even disarm me! What about when I could've taken out your knee?"

"A shoulder blow is more detrimental." He argued.

I tilted my jaw and pressed my eyebrows together. "In what world? I could've crippled you!" As I stood there, I noticed the loose grip Milo held on his sword, and I took full advantage of the moment to whip my sword at it, knocking it from his hand and into the ocean with a plop.

"Looks like you're the first mate, *mate*." I smirked, watching his shocked expression as he looked overboard.

"That doesn't count." Milo grumbled.

"Like I said, no pirate fights fair." I crossed my arms with a wink.

Milo rolled his eyes and shrugged. "Fine. Take your prized ship. If it makes you feel better."

With a laugh, I turned away, stopped only by Milo adding one more jab. "My ship would've easily outrun yours back in the day. Just know that."

I didn't immediately answer, but stepped up to the helm of the sailboat. "We'll never really know, will we, mate? But for now, I'm the only one here with a ship. Even if it is shite." I looked out at the horizon. "Now go make yourself useful on deck."

With one last drop of his shoulders, Milo sauntered away to do whatever he planned next, playfully muttering under his breath as the sun above gleamed down on us both. "Whatever you say, 'Captain' Calamari."

With my hand on the wheel and full sail ahead, I turned my back to Milo and the sun above. And for a moment I forgot the dark troubles that awaited us and the piercing anxiety I felt about returning to Bastian. And I smiled.

Sailing Through Fog

42

KATRINA

Serena and I arrived at the coasts of Puerto Rico before Bellamy and Milo, so we waited on the rocks by the shore, staying hidden until it was time to go after Bastian. I stared, my mind heavy trying to figure out exactly how I was going to get my mom away from him and keep everyone safe. I really wasn't so sure there was a way to do both.

"Think of this paradise. Spending all day basking in the Caribbean sun on the rocks. How can you be ungrateful for this?" Serena asked, breaking my concentration as she dipped her tail in the crystal waters and splashed.

I leaned back on my hands, stretching out to feel the warmth of the sunshine. "I'm not ungrateful," I sighed. "I'll admit this is one of the better perks of being a mermaid. But the ratio of battling sea monsters or facing certain death to basking on rocks so far is like 100:1."

Serena chuckled. I suddenly remembered Russell and Mrs. Gutierrez describing her and the way she laughed. I wondered if she at all missed them.

"What would you say to Russell if you could see him again?" I asked. Serena paused, her laugh quickly fading, and her brown eyes fell on me, fixated.

"I'd thank him," she said, looking away and back out at the coastline of San Juan. "And I'd reassure him that the things that happened to me were never his fault. It was just meant to be." She drew in a breath and slouched. "I hope he's found some happiness."

"Maybe you'll have the chance to tell him that yourself," I said softly, watching the horizon for any sign of Milo and Bellamy.

Serena only hummed a soft sound and nodded in response. After a moment, she turned to me. "What about your mother? How do you plan to get her back without trading my life in exchange for hers?"

The question caught me off guard. I wasn't one-hundred percent sure how I was going to go about that, but I didn't want to say that out loud. So I said the only thing I could say. The only real hope I had. "We get your crown back. With your power, you can free her, right?"

"I can. A goddess' power is greater than that of Davy Jones." Serena leaned forward, elbows in her scaled lap, propping herself up with her hands. "But remember, I can't face him without it. Without my power, he can kill me. And that's what he wants."

"Then we'll have to face him for you. Somehow." I watched the water bubbling as it crashed against the rocks on which we sat. Guilt bubbled in me much the same way, because my siren side was adamant that I use Serena as a bargaining piece . Take down the goddess and get my mom back all in one move. And though my human side fought hard against that idea, there was a small part that was just desperate enough to be tempted to make the trade. I knew it wasn't the real me who had those thoughts, but I felt remorse for not having the will to even fight them harder.

To my surprise, Serena reached over and took my hand. She didn't say anything for a moment, but just sat with me in silence. Though she looked and seemed similar in age, she had some mature, motherly air about her. This was one of those moments in which I felt nurtured by her ancient nature.

"All will be made right," she said. "But not without sacrifice."

Her words sent a chill down my spine. Did she mean one of us would die? I asked her to explain what she meant, but she simply shook her head. "I can't tell you everything. I don't even know what exactly is to come. But I know that this won't be easy, and I sense that something must be given to gain what was lost. Rarely do these things come without a cost."

"Is that why you didn't want to come here?" I asked.

She offered a slight move of her head, barely slight enough to be considered a nod.

My shoulders dropped like the sun beyond the line where the sun and sky met. I was no stranger to sacrifice. "Seems to be a recurring theme."

Serena huffed out a laugh tinged with sarcasm. She seemed like she was about to say more, but just then, she paused, her eyes narrowing as she focused on the horizon.

"They'll be here soon." She uttered. I didn't ask how she knew that, but I certainly believed her.

I wished I had my cell phone to call McKenzie and ask her what happened and how Bastian had even found my mom in the first place, but part of me thought it might be for the better. I still didn't know exactly what happened to my friends or where they were, and it was eating at me in the back of my mind. I had to find them.

"How soon?" I asked.

"Maybe another hour or two."

I closed my fist. "Then I'm going ashore to see if McKenzie and Noah are still all right. If they know what's going on, too, it can only help. We need all the manpower we can get."

I expected Serena to protest and argue with me, but she stayed perfectly silent, a strange look in her eye that suddenly made me feel judged and just plain stupid for suggesting such a thing. "I'll be back in just a bit. I promise."

I slipped down into the water, my focus on the city coast. "You don't happen to have enough power left to make me some clothes, do you?" I asked, looking up at Serena who still sat elegantly on the rocks. I'd gotten used to being naked every time I transformed from mermaid to human, but it would surely create some issues for me if I tried to walk ashore in the nude.

"I'm afraid not," she laughed with a shake of her head.

I groaned and dipped deeper into the water, assuming clothes were one more thing I'd figure out along the way. My tail propelled me to the shoreline, leaving Serena behind. I waited below, lurking by the beaches, looking for an opportunity to snag some clothing.

The thought of using my siren powers for something so trivial stirred up waves of guilt in my conscience. I'd really compromised everything I swore not to be on this journey so far. But then again, hiding naked in the coves of Puerto Rico while your mom was kidnapped by some lunatic was hardly a trivial matter. I *really* needed clothes. Maybe this wasn't such a trivial situation after all.

A young couple playing in a private area caught my eye, soaked in their bathing suits stealing kisses by the palm trees—next to beach chairs and a bag lying close to them that looked like it contained their clothing.

The girl was close enough to my size and build that I felt whatever outfit was in that bag would be more than adequate. Careful not to let them spot me, I swam close, singing my song as my scales lit up and their eyes fogged over. They waited for their commands, entranced by my tune. My siren side elicited a smile from me, pleased at my growing strength. This was the first time I'd controlled multiple people at once. And I liked the way it felt.

I guided the girl to the bag, where she dug in, pulling out a pair of jean shorts, some underwear, and a one-shoulder loose shirt. Under my command, she marched to the shore and tossed them in, where I waited to pull them under with me. I snatched the clothes, then dove under as I released them from my spell. Swimming fast, I returned to the old city area, where I pulled myself up on the crags of coastline dotting the city's border. With a mental pulse of power in my mind, I willed the water on my lower half to dry up, and in milliseconds, I had slender, tan legs again. Then I dried the clothes by draining out their water, casting it out and back to the sea.

Getting dressed frantically in the shadows, I rushed to the hotel where I'd left my friends and mom days ago, but something told me they weren't going to be there. But I had to start somewhere. I ran to their room, knocking on the door furiously only to be met with silence. And I didn't have a key card to enter. I rushed back down to the lobby and asked the receptionist if she'd seen or heard from them.

"Actually," she said, sorting through some papers in front of her on the desk. "They did tell me to leave you a message if you came. Here." She handed me a folded up note, and with my heart pounding in my ears, I unfolded it to read.

Katrina, He found us. He knew about your mom. About everything. If you read this, we're probably outside the club trying to figure out what to do and watching for any sign of your mom. I'm so sorry.

Without another word to the receptionist, I darted out of the building, rushing through the cobblestone streets back to Bastian's club. It was just starting to open, given the time of day, and I rushed inside, pushing past the bouncers that I enchanted with my song to let me pass.

Once inside, I found no sign of McKenzie or Noah, so I rushed back through to the secret passageway leading to Bastian's lair. But when I got there, it was empty. Even Bastian's massive collection wasn't there. My mom was gone. And so were my friends. The only thing that remained was the desk and the shattered jar from the heart I'd broken before. I rummaged through the desk, looking for a clue. For anything. But I only came up empty handed.

"No!" I groaned, my voice echoing through the empty chamber. I searched frantically for another way out, different from how I came in. There had to be some kind of passageway. How else could all these things be moved so easily in such a short time? How else could he transport my mom—a mermaid in a tank—to wherever he was hiding? And where the hell were McKenzie and Noah?

I started to turn around, but just then I heard footsteps coming from a dark corner I hadn't noticed before. It was behind a now empty display case, shoved to the side, well designed to stay inconspicuous no matter what angle someone stood in the room. Faint voices followed the steps, getting closer.

I ducked behind the desk, shaking. As I braced myself to encounter God knows what or who, I saw shadows nearing, and I peeked out to be absolutely relieved beyond belief when McKenzie emerged from the passageway. I stood up, and she rushed to me with arms wide open.

"Oh my god, I'm so glad to see you!" She cried, squeezing me tight. I wrapped my arms around her in response. "I'm so so sorry about your mom! We tried to stop him! And we tried to stop her from making his deal, but she wouldn't listen!"

"No, no, it's not your fault," I said, "I'm so glad you're okay! You shouldn't be down here, especially alone." I tried to keep my voice low, just in case we had company I didn't know about.

She released me from her embrace, pulling back to look over her shoulder. "I'm not alone." Noah appeared to her right and behind him trailed someone I would never have expected to see here of all places. The extra figure's eyes focused on mine and his withered hands were tucked firmly in his pockets, as usual. I was too stunned to speak, but I finally found the ability to utter one question as he and Noah stepped into the main room with us.

"Is that...Russell?" I stammered.

Noah's eyes hardened as he looked dead on into mine. "I didn't know who else to call. He's the only one besides us who knows about this world."

Russell hobbled forward. It was strange to see him in anything but his maintenance uniform from the school. But here he was in a sturdy pair of denims and loose button down work-shirt.

"Noah said you all needed help. I took the first flight to San Juan. I'm not sure what I can do, but I figure an old fisherman who believes in ghost stories is still an extra pair of hands."

I stood, unsure of what to say. Ultimately, I decided he wasn't wrong. The more bodies, the better, for rescuing my mom. But I had no idea what to tell him first. And what would he say when he saw Serena? How would he take it? It didn't matter, I decided. For now

I didn't have to explain all that. I just needed to make sure we were ready to face Bastian Drake.

DECOY

43

KATRINA

"I worried when you didn't come back this semester," Russell said, his old familiar voice bringing some strange sense of security.

"I had to save someone I love," I uttered.

A knowing twinkle appeared in Russell's eye. "I would do the same."

"Well now you might just have the chance," I said, yearning to tell him that his daughter he thought dead was just a few miles away sitting on the beach. But at the same time, I realized it was more important than ever to see that we won back Serena's crown. I couldn't bear to think of Russell having to relive losing her again if we failed. Which we wouldn't.

"What do you mean?" Russell tilted his head.

"I mean…" I couldn't get the words out. It just didn't feel right to tell him yet. Not here. It was too much at once. "I mean we need your help, but I don't want you to get hurt."

"Noah explained everything to me already. I'm not afraid of something happening to me. Not if it means helping you get your mother back."

I couldn't believe this was the same man who hysterically warned me to stay away from the pirates at all costs. Now here he was, ready to face a man marked by Davy Jones.

"I begged Noah to come home. But he wouldn't listen to me, not for nothing. So if he wasn't going to leave, I had to come to him. It's all I can do to keep him safe." Russell spoke as if he could read my thoughts. He looked at Noah, who offered him a subtle scowl.

"Well, I'm glad you're here either way," I said with my best attempt at a reassuring smile. "But I don't want to put anyone in harm's way. We can't just show up and attack Bastian when we find him. We've got to come up with a plan. Bastian will only let my mom go if we trade the sea goddess for her."

"You found her, too?" McKenzie beamed with wonder in her eyes.

"Yes, but we can't trade her. She's not strong enough to defeat Bastian without the Crown." My gaze bounced between Noah and McKenzie and then down the dark walkway that loomed behind them. "Where does this lead?"

McKenzie took a breath. "We followed it until we found where Bastian went...Don't worry, he didn't see us. We've been mapping out this tunnel system for the past couple of days. But the place he went...it looked like the inside of some old castle or something."

"Right, but it's easy to get lost in there. There are so many passages going in all sorts of directions. Not sure if it was an old irrigation system or a secret part of the fort. But it's a labyrinth." Noah looked around the corridor as if checking once more just to be sure. "I'd highly recommend a compass." He smirked, pulling out Milo's compass and displaying the face so that we could see the needle clearly pointing North.

"So where did Bastian go? Where does it lead?" I asked.

"All the tunnels we tracked were dead ends to the ocean. Except this one." McKenzie pulled up a map of San Juan on her phone, zooming in to show our location and followed the north path upward to a landmark directly above—a section of the old fort that jutted out from a corner into the edge of the ocean.

"Garita del Diablo," I uttered, focusing on the map. I recognized the little stone section that I'd heard legend of thanks to my dad and his Caribbean folklore that he'd randomly share with me as a kid. It was known for the mysterious disappearance of a guard posted there ages ago and other spooky occurrences. Noah and McKenzie watched me as if waiting for me to continue. "The Devil's Watchtower," I explained. "It's closed off to the public."

"Which would make it the perfect cover for another underground hideout," Noah crossed his arms.

I nodded, the significance of how this could help us slowly settling in. With the other tunnels leading out to the ocean, they could've been just what we needed. Bellamy and Milo could enter through those while we used the main tunnel, still allowing us to keep Bastian blind to our moves. But how I would communicate that to the boys was another challenge of its own.

"I have to let Bellamy and Milo know." I clenched a fist.

"You got Milo back?" Noah asked, the concern in his voice obvious despite his attempt to conceal it.

With a nod, I went on, careful to recount details as I remembered them. "He's back. But Bastian knows where Bellamy is at all times. And Milo is with him. He's tracking them to find S—," I cut myself off, looking at Russell before I accidentally let Serena's name slip from my lips. "He's tracking them to find the goddess, which is why I had to come here on my own."

Russell, McKenzie, and Noah all exchanged worried looks before Russell spoke. "Sounds like we're going to need to come up with a plan."

"Don't worry about it, grandpa, we've got this figured out," Noah held up a hand and shook his hand.

"Hey, you called me, remember?" Russell snapped. The tension between them was unbearable, and their backhanded bickering was the last thing I needed. "All I'm saying is, from what it sounds like, this guy is not one to be taking chances with, so you better make sure the one chance you got is as foolproof as possible."

"He's right," I said, earning a sour stare from Noah. "Bastian more than likely knows Bellamy and Milo are on their way here. But he doesn't know that I'm here with..." my words caught in my throat, and I looked away from Russell before finishing. "...with the goddess. Someone who needs to get the Crown back just as much as we do. If Bellamy and Milo serve as enough of a distraction, maybe it can buy us some time to figure out where he's keeping the Crown."

"And then what? Isn't this guy like indestructible?" Noah slapped his arms by his sides.

"Not if we get that crown. And that's what I'm thinking...We go in pretending to make the trade and get my mom, but we draw it out long enough to see if a few of us can find the Crown and get it to the goddess. Then hopefully Bellamy and Milo would arrive to stave off Bastian while we get the Crown and run."

McKenzie nodded the entire time I spoke, her orange waves bouncing like silk around her shoulders. "That sounds way easier said than done. And if the goddess is the one we trade, how do we get the Crown to her?"

I looked at her closely, an idea forming in my head as all three of them hung on my every word. "What if we create a decoy? Let him think we're agreeing to his deal...but really the goddess would be with us the whole time."

"So like a stand-in for the goddess?" Noah leaned forward, his impatience obvious by the tight jaw he clenched. My eyes swept over him and McKenzie and then fell on Russell.

I wanted to say it. I knew I'd have to sooner or later. But I couldn't say her name just yet. All in good time. "Does Bastian know what she looks like?"

"I'm pretty sure he does." I cringed, thinking of the clear physical differences between Serena and me. "But maybe we could use a veil or something. Just long enough to get him to let my mom go. What if I pretend to be her? We can make a disguise, and you all can escort me to Bastian's lair to trade me for my mom and get the Crown."

"He'll find that too suspicious," Noah chimed in. "If you're the one he wants to make the deal with, he's going to expect you to be the one to offer her."

I nodded, biting my lower lip as my thoughts raced and rearranged. I began to worry about leaving Serena unprotected back on the coast and felt the growing need to get back to her rising in my chest. My nerves felt shaky, and my stomach turned at the thought of the plan failing. McKenzie's voice ripped me out of my own head and away from my inner panic.

"I'll do it," she said firmly. "I'll be the decoy."

I blinked, as we all watched her with growing intensity. "No, McKenzie," I voiced my protest with a jolt. "Absolutely not. I'm not putting you in that position."

"I know you're not." Her back straightened and she made a point to address all three of us. "I'm putting myself there. We don't stand a chance if we hand over the only one of us who has magical powers."

The chamber filled with a silence greater than I could stand. Finally, Russell intervened. "How about we take this conversation elsewhere? Probably not the wisest to discuss our plans here."

"You're right. Good call," I muttered, my eyes not leaving McKenzie.

Back outside, we huddled in the main town plaza in an open seating area, careful to keep our voices low.

"There's no way I'm letting you walk in there and handing you over to that lunatic," I placed my hand on the table firmly, feeling my frustration growing. "If something goes wrong..."

"Then why did I come all this way?" McKenzie shot up, her chair nearly toppling over backwards. "Why did I forfeit this semester at ISA? Just to do nothing? I came to help you, and dammit Katrina, for once just let me do more for once than lend you a dress!"

The table was silent. I'd never seen McKenzie so worked up or determined. But the thought of sending her into Bastian's grasp was something I couldn't come to terms with.

"She's right," crooned Russell. "It'll seem suspicious if we go in there without you. He'll want to see *you* bringing this person he's bargaining for."

I watched him, somewhat shocked that he would suggest it, but realizing either way, someone was going to be offered up to Bastian like a stock animal. I opened my mouth to argue against McKenzie being the bait, but McKenzie stopped me before I could get any words out.

"Don't try to change this, Katrina." Her tone with me had never been more harsh. "I'm doing it, and it's going to be fine."

My jaw quivered as I fought not to say something stupid or rash. All three pairs of eyes pressed their gaze onto me, until I dropped my head and uttered a single syllable, laced with my distaste for the idea. "Fine."

"Glad we settled that," McKenzie's sunburnt face gleamed with pride at her win. "Now what about the goddess? Why didn't she come with you?"

"Because I couldn't risk Bastian seeing her and trying to kill her on sight. We have to keep her out of the way and hidden until we know for sure we have the Crown within reach." I stood up, gesturing for the others to do the same. "So we have to go. Now. She's left unguarded right now and I don't think we should push our luck." For all I knew, Bellamy and Milo were nearly here. And somehow I'd need to communicate this plan to them without alerting Bastian.

The trio followed me to the shore, a decent enough walk from town, made a touch more difficult by the sand and stone we trekked through. When we finally reached the coast where Serena awaited, I stopped, hesitating as I wondered what chaos would break loose once they saw her. But I couldn't keep wondering forever. Mom was waiting.

"Wait here," I told them. "I'm going to let her know what's going on first."

"Fair enough," Noah uttered.

With a nod, I turned and dove into the water, tossing my clothes back up at McKenzie from the water. "Hang on to these for me!" Not waiting for the reply, I took off, gliding through the water with ease back to the rock where I left the goddess.

"Took you long enough," Serena's playful yet calming voice was a welcome reassurance as I emerged from the water. "Are your friends all okay?"

"Yes," I looked up at her as water trickled down my soaked hair and neck. "And we came up with a plan to get into Bastian's lair and get your crown. But we have to warn Bellamy and Milo so they know what we're doing.

"Then tell them," Serena pushed at the air with her hand. I watched her, confused, urging her to continue. "Your Milo has the mark of the sun. It dampens Bastian's hold on him. He won't be able to hear you if you tell him."

"What do you mean *if I tell him*?"

"Your siren call. You and I in the water could communicate through the mind. It's because we are already linked to each other by nature, as all sirens are. And a skilled siren can also do that with those who are linked by her heart."

"So you're saying I can call him with my mind?" I blinked, flitting my tail in curiosity.

Serena nodded. "Yes, how do you think you were able to call him home with your song? You've been doing it all along."

Trying my best not to waste time, I hurried and closed my eyes, focusing on the way I sang to Milo at the Fountain's edge to bring him home. I reached for him once more, my voice swirling in my mind as it rose beyond the corners of myself and transcended into a place neither within me nor on the outside of me. I couldn't hold it for long, so I thought up my message as quickly as possible.

Bastian's hideout is beneath Garita del Diablo. We've come up with a plan to trick Bastian into letting my mom go and then...

...then you all will get the Crown. When his voice broke through to me, I nearly jumped at the sound of him in my head. And then I settled into the sound of him, cherishing the connection between us that superseded all others.

Yes, I'll let you know when we're at Bastian's lair. Maybe if he's distracted enough he won't have time to notice you and Bellamy coming. There is supposedly a system of tunnels leading in from the coast under the fort cliff. I wish I could tell you how to get to the hideout from there, but you'll have to figure it out. Noah says it's a total maze. Don't get lost.

Don't worry, Milo reassured with a chuckle. *Navigation is somewhat of a strong point for me. I'll tell Bellamy to sail in circles to throw the bastard off.*

"I take it by that smile that it worked." Serena's voice snatched me from my inner dialogue with Milo.

"Were you eavesdropping?" I asked with a grin, ducking down into the water so that only my head was out of it.

"Don't worry." Serena splashed some water my way with a flick of her tail. "Even I can't interfere with another siren's song-call."

"Hmm," I smirked. "Good to know." After a long pause, I pulled myself up to meet her on the rocks. "Now, you should know the plan."

I explained everything to her, ensuring to include the part about her potential body double.

"This girl is going to pretend to be me?" she raised an eyebrow.

I eyed her dark skin and thick braided hair. It'd be a lie to say I hadn't also wondered exactly how we would make my red-headed pale roommate look anything like her. "Well, she's going to try. I was hoping we could get creative with it."

Serena sighed, "Lucky for you, there are few limits on how creative magic can be." I didn't understand exactly what she meant, but I didn't feel like I had time to ask. I was just glad to have some form of approval from her for the plan. With Serena's blessing, I led her back to where the others waited. But when we neared the shore, I turned around to stop her.

"There's something you should know." I whirled around in the water, stopping Serena before we got too close. "Remember when you talked about Russell? You're about to see him again, and he's probably not going to know what to do when he sees you."

Serena's features tightened, her perfect lips separating to form the smallest inkling of a gasp. Then after a short moment, her look of surprise turned into a small warm smile as she glanced at the shore ahead. "You're full of surprises, little mermaid. You truly are." She dove forward, swimming past me toward the coast in the distance. She didn't even turn around as she called out, "Now let's hope you can save one for this crooked pirate lord."

What Does Water Do?

44

KATRINA

When we came ashore, the look on my friends' faces was exactly as I expected as my goddess friend neared. McKenzie stood mouth agape in awe of Serena's inhuman beauty. Noah narrowed his eyes in scrutiny, and Russell—Russell nearly stumbled backwards as his eyes widened in surprise.

"Dammit, who are you?" He called through a quivering chin. "What kind of trick is this?" He whipped his gaze to me, his voice cracking and eyes watery.

I stayed in the water as Serena rose up to the shoreline. Her tail effortlessly became legs once more, and she stepped out, the water following her like smoke, swirling around her waist and forming a flowing dress with each step. I stayed behind, tucked down in the comfort of the water as I gave this moment to them.

Russell still stood unmoving, nearly quaking as he watched this girl he believed to be his daughter walk towards him from the waves.

"Serena..." he choked. "Serena, sweetheart, is it really you?"

McKenzie and Noah stepped to the side as she passed, making her way right up to the man she'd called father in at least one lifetime. Her skin glistened in the sun as she reached forward to touch his face, a gentle brush of her palm sending Russell into full tears.

"It's me, Dad," she said softly.

Russell didn't waste time with words. Instead. He threw his arms around her, this grisly old man suddenly becoming soft right before my eyes.

"I don't understand, but I don't think I want to. All I care about is that you're here, now. Somehow."

Serena pulled back gently from his embrace. "I was bound to land in human form. Valdez returned me to the sea. This is where I've always belonged."

"So...you're the...the goddess Noah talked about?"

Serena nodded. Noah neared her, blinking in disbelief. "Wait," he stammered. "So this means you're like...my aunt?"

"I suppose it does." Serena laughed with a touch of her hand to his shoulder. "Hello, nephew."

Russell reached forward to take Serena's hand in both of his, his jaw clenched as pure resolve and determination settled on his face. "I may not fully understand what's going on, but I'm here to help you, sweetheart. Whatever it takes to keep from someone taking you from me again."

Something in my gut dropped as guilt gripped me again—how I had dragged so many people into this. And I worried that might mean dragging them beneath the waves with me if things went under. But here they stood, minds already made up and ready to face whatever destiny held next. And all I could do was let them. That, and try my hardest not to let them get killed in the process.

"Let's get this started, shall we? Before I change my mind." Serena's regal voice broke through as she turned from Russell and faced me.

I shot a pleading look at all three of them, my hair covering most of the front of me. "You guys...I have to get dressed."

"Oh, right." McKenzie pulled my clothes from the bag she carried and set them on the ground.

They awkwardly turned their backs to me as I climbed out of the water. My legs returned and I scrambled to put on the clothes. "Okay, I'm good now," I announced.

As they each turned back around to face me, Serena spoke, eyeing McKenzie. "All right, now it's time to set things in motion. We can start with my decoy. Because we have a lot of work to do in that area."

"Yeah," Noah chimed in, "How exactly are we supposed to pull off making her look like you? There's no way in hell."

"Maybe not without my help. But remember Katrina and I control water. And what does water do?"

She was met with a barrage of answers, while I kept silent, trying to think of what she was getting at.

"Umm, flows? Floods? Washes?"

"Drips?"

"Splashes? Drowns?"

"It reflects." Serena gently guided McKenzie to the water's edge, where she positioned her with a few nudges and turns. A crystal clear mirror image of both of them appeared on the water's surface. "Without my power, I can't perform this. It requires delicate mastery of the water. Detail and steadiness like a painter's hand." Serena looked at me. "You'll have to do this, Katrina."

"I'll try it, whatever it is. But how will I know what to do?" I asked, stepping near the water.

"Because you already do it by nature. Now it's just a matter of matching the water to the vision it reflects. And making sure it stays that way."

With a few gestures of her hand, she summoned up a bit of water, and up it streamed, like a grand ribbon twirling and twisting as she willed it. It coiled around her from bottom to top, and then snaked over to McKenzie, where it spread itself out thin like a veil and completely encompassed her body. Mere seconds later, an image began to form on the outside of the water cocoon. Broken glimpses of Serena formed like pieces of a shattered mirror, her reflection taking over whatever faint vision of McKenzie remained. As the water swirled gently, it closed in, attaching itself to McKenzie like a body-conforming shield. And on the outside, she was no longer McKenzie.

But then the façade vanished, the water falling into droplets like someone wrung out a soaked towel. And McKenzie was McKenzie again. "You must do that, and keep it like that." Serena said.

"Okay," I held out my hands, a bit nervous to try this new magic skill. But it couldn't be any more challenging than forming an image out of watercolors.

And it wasn't at all. My hands and mind knew what to do. I pulled the water back up, encompassing McKenzie in it once more as I formed each detail to reflect Serena. After a few slips, I realized half the challenge was positioning each water molecule just right in the light, to keep it reflecting the image I demanded—the image of Serena.

Aside from a small height difference, two identical Serena's stood before us, McKenzie only distinguishable by the slight glimmer of sunlight on water that sometimes rippled across her body.

"What just happened?" McKenzie spun around, attempting to see behind her own back as she craned her neck around. Her voice was the only thing about her unchanged.

"You look like me, now." Serena stepped back and looked her up and down as if admiring her work.

"Just don't talk and we should be good." Noah laughed.

We all stared in absolute amazement as the two Serenas, and I glanced over at the real one. "I can't believe that's possible."

"Just a bit of telling the water what to reflect and dispersing it out in all the right places." Serena winked. "Not so different than painting." I didn't even ask how she knew about that. I assumed as the Mother of Sirens she probably had the scoop on all of us.

I smiled softly. Then my focus shifted as Milo's voice called to me through my thoughts.

We've anchored. And we're scoping out the area. You were right. These tunnels are a mess. Don't face Bastian without us near, if you can. Give us one more hour. We don't want to leave you to do this alone.

Will do. I replied, looking back out at the friends surrounding me, and pulling in a deep breath. By the time we made it back down to the tunnels beneath the club and found Bastian's lair, it would be more than an hour. And saving my mom couldn't wait much longer.

"Okay people..." I said boldly. "It's almost time." Everyone huddled in closer as my heart pounded so loud, I figured they could hear it. "Are we ready to make a deal with the devil?"

CROSSWINDS

45

MILO

We'd left the boat moored as close as we could to the shore. Now we were climbing along the rocky cliff side of the coast where the old stone fort stood. We scaled the sides, looking in each crevice in the rocks for any sign of secret passageway. But nothing stood out as a hidden tunnel system entrance, and the setting sun only made it harder to see.

"Dammit, you gave them an hour. It's been way longer than that now," Bellamy grumbled behind me as we scaled the coastline.

"I couldn't ask her to keep waiting. You know she wouldn't have listened anyway," I snapped. "Calm down. If we don't keep our heads we'll never find this thing."

Bellamy hesitated. "I swear to god if something happens to Serena...I can't believe I let her go on without me. Why the hell did I let her go on without me?"

I whipped around. "If you hadn't, Bastian would've already been here waiting to snatch her up. You're protecting her. Don't forget that."

"If he wanted to kill her, why didn't he take her at the Fountain? I just don't get it." Bellamy scanned the area of the cliff we'd searched ten times over now, looking for this hidden entrance that eluded us.

I truly wondered the same, but the least I could do was to try putting Bellamy at ease about it. Little good wondering about it would do us here and now. "Maybe he can't kill her that easily. Maybe he couldn't truly fight us all at once to get to her. Maybe it's not as simple as we think. Whatever the reason, this is the only chance we have to end him for good."

Bellamy agreed with a grunt, his foot slipping and kicking a loose piece of rocks into the water below. My eyes followed the rocks, and I watched the waves at the foot of the cliff for a moment. I noticed a subtle suction of the water when the waves pulled back, different from the rest around it. "Look there!" I pointed. "The water's getting sucked down somewhere."

"That could be it. I'll check it out." Bellamy didn't hesitate a single second before sliding into the water below.

"Hurry," I said, "We don't have much light left."

He dove under, all of him disappearing beneath the waves except the hand holding onto the rock by the area where the water suctioned. Even though I wasn't the one underwater, I held my breath, eager to see if we'd found the tunnel.

Bellamy shot up, shaking the water from his eyes and hair. "There's definitely a passage there. But once we go in, there's no going back. It's tight. If we run out of air, we're screwed. I don't know if the whole 'mermaid's kiss' rule applies indefinitely."

My thoughts shuffled. "We have to find out somehow."

"I'll go check it out. If I don't come out in five minutes, don't follow me."

"I'm not agreeing to that."

"Of course you won't, golden boy." Bellamy mocked. "But if both of us are dead then who will be there for the girls? Do what I say. I'm the captain, remember?"

"Alright, fine, Calamari." I shook my head.

Bellamy vanished beneath the seawater once more, and I began the countdown. Like hell I wasn't going to go in after him if he didn't resurface. I counted the minutes down to the second, uneasiness rattling my nerves like the waves rattled the loose rocks around my feet. When Bellamy didn't come back up at the four minute mark, I refused to wait any longer. I went in after him.

The water shocked my system as I plunged down, taking a giant gulp of air with me. I found the tunnel entrance rather easily, though it was clearly eroded far from what it was originally meant to be. Claustrophobia gripped at me as I squeezed through, but I bit the inside of my cheek to keep myself calm and focused. This place kept out all light, and the pitch blackness smothered me as much as the flowing water around me.

Of course I didn't see Bellamy. He would've been much farther ahead by now. But the passage was so narrow, I wasn't even sure what ahead could've looked like. I squirmed my way through the small tunnel, jagged rock surfaces scraping against my skin as I wedged between them. The way ahead was dark as night, and the burning feeling rising in my lungs was a constant reminder of my time ticking away. And a reminder that a mermaid's kiss only worked for a little while. And I didn't have any recent refills.

I bumped into something, hoping it was Bellamy, but the feeling of human bone in my hand told me otherwise. With a shudder, I kept squeezing through, unsettled by the nothingness around me and the growing fear that I was going to stumble across Bellamy's lifeless body jammed in between some rocks. But then I felt the rock edges curve upwards. There was no more going backward. I wouldn't be able to make it out in time. My only hope was to follow the path. I crawled up, pulling myself up along the stone walls as they closed in on me further. I just wished I could see an inch in front of me.

My hands ran along the stone, and I felt where the opening curved above me, and there was air. I just had to find the strength to pull myself up. But the water was crashing around me every time a wave crested and filled the space. If I could just wait until the next swell, I could reach up and pull myself over. But as my lungs protested in pain, I didn't think I had quite that long.

I reached up, and a hand clasped over my arm, dragging me up just enough to get me out of the water and into the tiny crawl space higher than the rest. My feet scrambled as much as they could to boost me up the rest of the way where I caught glimpse of Bellamy pulling me up. My neck and shoulders scraped the top of a stone ceiling as I worked my way through the cramped nook. I breathed out my relief with a handful of coughs mixed in.

With just a bit more wiggling, I worked myself out the other side, where the tiny space dropped off into a full size tunnel, plenty tall and wide enough for standing. Bellamy stood with his arms crossed. "I told you not to follow me."

"After all this time I thought you'd know me better than that," I flashed a half-grin, pushing back my wet hair out of my eyes. The space was lit by a torch in Bellamy's hand, casting our shadows along the tunnel walls.

"Well now I've saved both you and your lass from drowning at some point or another. So you owe me." Bellamy turned around, shining the torch light down the black abyss of a path.

"How about I'll make it up to you by getting us out of here," I said, stepping forward, compass in hand. "Because God knows you're not going to be the one to do it."

"Would you shut up?" Bellamy groaned as I took up stride beside him. "Let's hurry before Katrina and Serena walk right into Bastian's hands."

"Don't worry," I said. "They know what they're doing." I did my best to put him at ease, knowing it frustrated him to not be able to know the girls' plan. We'd both agreed that it was for the best that I didn't share it with him in case Bastian was listening. But I knew that didn't make it any easier for him.

"I'll get us there." I looked ahead, merging the map in my head of the watchtower's location from the outside and the direction of the compass needle. "It won't be quick, but I'll get us there."

We stepped forward into the darkness, our path barely illuminated by the glow of Bellamy's torch. Of course I'd never tell him, but I was aching to find Bastian and the worry was beginning to set in. Even if Bastian fell for the girls' plan, I didn't imagine it would take him long to realize it. I knew we didn't stand a chance at killing him. But we sure as hell could go down fighting to slow him down. And if that's what it took to get Katrina out alive, it was good enough for me.

False Goddess

46

KATRINA

We crept forward, sneaking our way back through the tunnels that my friends had already mapped out, using our cell phones for light. I still hadn't gotten used to the fact that we were walking with two versions of Serena, and I tried not to think about it too hard. From down here, the glimmering sheen of water over McKenzie was no longer visible without the sunlight, making them the perfect spitting image of each other.

"McKenzie, when you found the hideout, could you see the Crown?" I asked, running over the plan in my head a million times over and then some.

"No," she sighed. "But he was sitting in a big chair surrounded by all kinds of things, like ocean knickknacks and just weird stuff. He has your mom in a tank behind the chair. The Crown has got to be somewhere in that collection."

"Why does he always have a big chair?" I groaned.

"It's his own personal throne where he can guard his toys," Serena rolled her eyes. "His ego's got to have somewhere to sit."

We neared a section where the tunnel widened, signaling our nearing of Bastian's new hideout. We came upon stone steps that spiraled upward, much like a tall tower of old—a watchtower. Between the watchtower entrance and the corridor we'd just come from, a door stood in plain sight, though it was more of a stone slab.

"This is it," Noah uttered, shoving the stone out of his way with all his might. I tried to look for a quick exit, some way we could leave without subjecting ourselves to being trapped down here. But I knew we wouldn't have that luxury in this winding system of tunnels and stone corridors.

"I'm staying with Serena," Russell said, directing his posture to Noah. "But don't you dare get hurt, Noah. I'm not losing either of you today."

"Give it a rest, grandpa," Noah groaned. "You don't have to keep acting worried about me." I watched the sunken look on Russell's face grow darker, his eyes downcast as his weary spirit. I understood Noah's resentment for the years lost all too well, but it was harder to see this way. Now as an onlooker to someone else's struggle, I saw the bitterness in myself I had to overcome with my own mom, and I hoped Noah could figure out how to do that for Russell.

We left Serena behind with Russell, hoping it'd be enough to keep Bastian blind to her whereabouts while still keeping her close enough to get the Crown to her. I pushed the doorway open, my chest full from a big breath of air I was too afraid to release. We were greeted by a gust of cool air and dim torchlight.

With a massive dome-shaped ceiling, this place really did look like a castle. Cracks in stone streaked like veins through the floors and ceiling. The walls glimmered with an array of items, some likely magic, some not—rare shells, golden statues, rare jewels and tribal masks, body parts in jars. I had to wonder how he'd managed to move all these things from his other hideaway spot in such a short time. Of course, it was likely magic. And in the center of the room, where the dome peaked with a hole through which the moonlight shone, there stood an eerily beautiful stone table with intricate paintings around it, but the images were faded and cracked. A short path of curved stairs led up to it, seeming more for decorative flair than function.

The dim chamber echoed with the taps of our footsteps as we worked around drips of blackened water that left a trail from the door to the front of the room. Bastian was nowhere in sight, but his throne certainly was. It sat empty, its velvet cushion seat nestled in a chair of bronze and gold, a puddle of more dark water pooling in the floor beside it. The Crown was nowhere to be seen, but my mother was.

Imprisoned in her tank, my mom swam to the glass, placing a hand against the glass, her face twisted in fear. I took a step forward to run to her, but the dark water on the floor converged into one mass and blocked my steps. I watched in horror and intrigue as the onyx black water rose up as if it had a life of its own. It grew to my height, then taller, until it towered over me and formed itself into the outline of a human. Bastian. It became Bastian.

"Hello, lovely Katrina," he grinned, the black water still dripping off his face like ink. "I see you did as I asked. Smart girl." His snake-like eyes flicked to McKenzie turned-Serena, who stood near the entrance with Noah. He pretended to hold her arm as though we'd forced her to come here.

"I did. I brought you Atargatis. Now let my mom go," I demanded, my fists balling up without me meaning for them to.

"Patience, little mermaid," he growled in my ear. "I make the rules, remember?"

"And the rule was that you take her and give me my mother. You made the offer. Now I'm taking you up on it."

Bastian let out a low laugh. "I bet dear Bellamy wasn't too thrilled with that decision. I'm guessing that's why you came without him. Poor fellow. He's been stabbed in the back so many times in life, and here you are adding your knife to the tally." He smiled, inky black lining his teeth. "And your beloved sailor. What of him? Did he side with his brother at sea?"

"Don't pretend you don't know where Bellamy is." I said, hoping to keep him distracted as long as possible while I scanned the room.

"Of course I do. If I cared to keep track of pirate scum. But I have no use for his whereabouts without the goddess. And fortunately for him, she's right where I want her." Bastian eyed McKenzie in her Serena form.

I called to Milo. *The Crown isn't anywhere we can see it. We'll have to find it. So when you get here, be careful. But we could certainly use your help. Bastian seems...stranger than before.*

*Of course. We're in the tunnels. *You* be careful.* Milo's voice was my only reassurance in this cold, hopeless place, and I clung to it like a buoy in a storm. My eyes studied the room, desperate for any hint at where the Crown might be, but I couldn't stop looking over at my mom in the tank. I was still grappling with the shock of seeing her with a tail, but then I wondered...since she was a siren, maybe I could communicate with her, too, the way I communicated with Serena underwater.

I called to her, throwing the voice in my head out to her, hoping for her to catch on to my words.

Mom, I'm here. We're going to free you.

I hoped she got the message, but I didn't have time to wait for a response as I stood before an impatient Bastian. "Bring the goddess forward," I motioned to Noah. He followed, hesitating in a way that looked so convincing I couldn't tell if he was truly afraid or just acting.

Noah stepped up beside me, pretending to drag McKenzie along as she put a convincing pull against him on display. They now stood beside me facing Bastian, whose shoes were still oozing in a puddle with the ink-water as it slowly ran down the sides of him.

He reached out to touch McKenzie's arm, but I lunged forward and blocked him.

"Let my mom go first," I demanded once more.

"Very well. After all, it's not like you could escape now." He straightened his shoulders, turned around, and then shattered the tank that held mom with a blast of black water from his hand. Mom flopped to the floor amongst the broken glass, her tail writhing. I ran to her and dropped down at her side.

"Are you okay, Mom?" I worked hard to control my breathing. I couldn't let Bastian sense my fear, especially now that I'd just handed over my roommate and best friend to him.

"I'm not hurt." Mom panted. "Just...just a little in shock. This...what is this? *How* is this?" She touched a trembling hand to her waist where her skin gave way to pearly scales.

"I know," I said. "You'll get used to it. But why did you do this? Why the hell would you do this, Mom?"

Her brown wet hair fell over her face as she leaned forward and hugged herself from the chill. Her chin quivered, distorting her words. "Your whole life I've never done anything to help you. This was me being a better mother. I made him promise he wouldn't harm you in exchange. I did this to help you."

Squeezing my eyes shut was the only way to stall the tears burning behind my sockets. I didn't know what to say. I wanted to be mad at her. And I was, but it would be useless to let her know that. And if things went awry and we didn't make it out of here, the last thing I wanted was for Mom to think I hated her. She'd had enough of that.

Suddenly her voice startled me, because I was looking right at her but her mouth wasn't moving.

Just so you know, I could hear you.

I sat upright, the jolt of her voice rattling me. I hadn't expected it.

Shhh! Listen, the Crown isn't here. But I heard him say he needs the Crown to complete the ritual. So it can't be far.

"What? What ritual?" I didn't mean to blurt out my surprise out loud, but it was an uncontrollable reaction.

She reached up and pulled my face to her so that I had no choice but to pull it together and focus. Her eyes pleaded with me as she went on.

To kill this goddess he's talking about. Katrina, He isn't human. He can transform into some type of...water shadow thing. I don't know. But he's made of that dark water. He controls it..

I should have known he would know better than to leave the Crown anywhere we would be able to see it. But if McKenzie could keep him distracted long enough, and Milo and Bellamy could show up to buy us more time, we just might have a chance at finding it.

I glanced over my shoulder to see Bastian taking McKenzie from Noah, leading her away to the base of the steps leading to the stone altar table. McKenzie stayed silent so that her voice wouldn't give her away, but I knew that she had to be terrified. They began to ascend the stairs. I had to think fast.

I quickly communicated to Milo what my mom just told me, and he responded just as surprised as I was. But he assured me that he and Bellamy weren't far. For now, I had to find a way to stall Bastian from harming McKenzie—or worse.

"Sit, dear Atargatis," Bastian breathed over McKenzie, trailing her collarbone with his finger. She obliged, probably unsure of what else to do. "Funny. I expected you to put up more of a fight. You certainly did all those years ago the first time I offered you my affections."

McKenzie stared at him through hardened eyes, and Noah watched them like a starving tiger waiting to pounce in an instant. His gaze whipped over to me for a second, and I could feel the desperation to intervene raging in him just from his expression and tense body alone. But I shook my head. Not yet. Bellamy and Milo should be here any moment...

"It seems our guests have overstayed their welcome," Bastian's voice cut through the cold stone space, even as he addressed McKenzie. He turned in my direction, leaving her sitting on the altar. "I believe you're no longer needed. Your mother's clothes are by the door. You can all leave now."

We stood, our eyes never leaving him. Things weren't supposed to get this far. We weren't supposed to have actually handed McKenzie over to him. Her purpose was to be a distraction, not a complete replacement. I couldn't let Bastian actually hurt her. So I braced, thoughts rushing through my head like an unhindered waterfall of what I could possibly do to stop him.

I bit my tongue so that a tear welled up, and I started to draw up the water that had spilled out from my mom's tank, slowly, so that Bastian wouldn't notice. It was difficult working with water so spread out across the stone floor, trying to find all the droplets and molecules and draw them back together. I wanted to call to Milo once more, but I found my mind could only manage to be occupied by one thing at a time. I hid my controlling hand behind my back, and kept talking to hold Bastian's attention.

"What are you going to do to her?" I spat. Any minute now Bellamy and Milo would be here...Any minute now.

"I think you know," he hissed, drawing up his hand to reveal the serpent symbol inked onto his hand. From it, more thick droplets of dark water formed, creating a stream, defying gravity and snaking its way across the open air to Noah, me, and my mom. It wrapped around us, its strength unimaginable, and forced us backwards. Everywhere it touched felt like burning oil on my skin. My head shook with pain as it slammed us against the wall, pinning us there to face the scene of Bastian and his false goddess. "But since you insist on specifics, Atargatis cannot be killed like a mortal. At least, not permanently. Valdez's foolishness proved that and simply returned her to her element. God knows she'll just keep on coming back in the next life. No. She must be destroyed once and for all with the power granted her by the gods, the same way it was given." He reached down and touched McKenzie's head, trailing down her tresses and coiling a lock around his finger. "The Crown? Check. The tail...we're getting to that. The things that made you a goddess must be destroyed together for you to become fully mortal..and fully killable."

A wave of relief flooded over me. At least he wouldn't try killing McKenzie where she stood—yet. Without a tail, she wouldn't quite be the piece he needed. That would buy us some more time as I focused on drawing the drying water on the floor to me. It was the only weapon I could think to make.

"It's a good thing your friends stayed after all. It'll be exciting to have an audience." He grinned, his eyes flashing with madness. With that, he commanded his dark water energy to crawl up my legs, slowly suctioning itself onto my leg. It crept upward, stinging my skin. As it worked its way up, the stinging became unbearable agony, burning like hot coal. "Now transform, Atargatis! Or watch your dear lover suffer."

A roaring sound of water filled the chamber, as shadow water flooded down the corridor, spilling in through the doorway and gushing into the room with us, carrying Milo and Bellamy within. As they choked and sputtered, I cried out. I couldn't break my focus, though. I gathered my emotions and forced myself to find the will to keep drawing the water together from my mom's tank. It was beginning to dry, so I had to work quickly before it was gone.

The rushing black water trapped them, pushing them with a force so hard against the wall, I winced at the sound of their backs hitting the rock. The water began to take its own form, filling up the space around them, as if suspending them in an invisible tank. As the water rose, lifting them higher off the ground, they gasped, struggling to breathe against the gushing rapids pounding over them.

"Let's find out if a siren's kiss helps them survive that!" Bastian laughed.

"No! Stop it!" I screamed.

"What? You really thought they could sneak up on me?" Bastian crooned. "It was a brave attempt, I'll give you that. But when you came alone, I knew better. Your lovesick sailors would never leave you to face me alone. And Bellamy? Thinking writing down his plans and sneaking around would keep me from knowing? I know his thoughts. His feelings. His every intention probably before he even knows it himself."

I felt so stupid, so gullible. We'd tried so hard to avoid this very thing and yet we had played right into Bastian's clutches. No matter what we could possibly think to try, his advantage was always too powerful.

The setback stole my focus, and I lost control of the water I was pulling from the ground. Did I really even think I could fight Bastian with it? His dark water would likely overpower mine with ease. And if it did, then what? My thoughts raced as I felt the water slipping from my mind's grip. I had to at least try.

"Noah," I said, still locked onto Bastian, "Take my mom and get out of here."

I drowned out the sound of my mother's protest as Noah rushed to cover her with his jacket and rushed her to the exit. The water around me pooled at my feet, siphoning to me through my sheer willpower. All around me, distractions screamed for my attention. Bastian grabbed McKenzie by the shoulders and shook her, shouting at her to change form as he threatened all of us with horrible deaths if she didn't. Mom's wailing faded in the background as Noah dragged her out of the room. And the water around Milo and Bellamy sloshed with a strange, looming sound as their muffled voices fought to break through it. And I was still supposed to be looking for the Crown.

I closed my eyes, trying to find solace in the sound of water trickling through my veins, the beat of my heart timing to the waves outside. As I concentrated, the water came to me all at once, the droplets combining to create a solid stream that wove around me like a lasso. And just as I prepared myself to send it lashing toward Bastian, a voice at the door stopped everything.

"Stop!" Serena's voice rose through the air like a queen's command. My eyes widened at the unexpected sight of her, standing tall and unmoving at the door, her water gown flowing around her and the gold woven in her hair glinting.

The silence was immediate, except for the soft swoosh of water. Bellamy and Milo dropped to the ground, released from their watery prison. I quickly eased my hold on the water I was conjuring, to keep Bastian unaware. Bastian turned to face the real Serena, the moonlight hitting half his face from the skylight above the stone table and illuminating his golden glowing eyes. His stone gaze flickered from the Serena in his grip and the one standing at the door, separated only by me standing in the gap between them.

"Well, now," he spat. "I'll admit, that's rather well-played of you. I certainly never expected a look-alike. But I don't see what benefit this brings you." His voice rose with agitation, and a strange crack that made it obvious he was trying to hide it.

"Your quarrel is not with them," Serena said, sticking out her chin. "Release them all and take me. Fulfill your dark destiny if you must. I can ignore the call of fate no longer."

An audible gasp escaped my lips as she stepped forward. Bellamy scrambled to his feet and chased after her. Milo leapt up to follow, but they were both met with a force as Bastian shielded her with a sheet of shadow water that they could not break through. "It's clear that this is what must be done." She stopped to look at Bellamy, only for a moment. "I'm sorry, my love."

"No it's not!" I cried. "What about all that stuff you told me about aligning the stars to form your own destiny? What about that?"

She kept walking, her eyes locked with Bastian's. "Serena!" I screamed. "If you do this, he'll have power over the seas and everything in it! He'll have power over *me*!"

"What else am I supposed to do, little mermaid?" She paused to look at me. "He's already won. I can't let him hurt you all, too. This is what is meant to happen. It's marked in stone."

"What?" I wanted her to explain. Where was this foretold? Why was she so willing to give up suddenly when all this time she'd been so stubborn?

Suddenly, Russell burst in, running after her as a defeated Noah stood behind him as the man tore from his grip. "No! Serena, no! I won't lose you again!"

"Grandpa, don't! You can't stop him! He can't be killed!" Noah called after him. I was relieved my mom was nowhere to be seen, assuming Noah had taken her somewhere safe for the time being.

Serena continued her walk to Bastian, trodding up the stairs to him like a princess about to be crowned. Only, she was heading to a chopping block.

Bastian snatched McKenzie by the arms and tossed her to the side, sending her tumbling down the old stone steps. Noah rushed to her as I called her name. I expected her reflection disguise to fade, but it didn't, and she remained in her form as Serena. I'd figure out how to undo that later, but right now it didn't matter. As Noah tended to her, I gritted my teeth in anger. I summoned my water once again, and sent it twisting and raging to Bastian, who deflected it with his black water with ease. "Nice try," he grinned. "But you don't possess half the power you need to fight me."

Serena was almost to the top of the steps, and Bastian was waiting with a literal open hand. She placed her hand in his. Russell ran up behind her screaming her name, arms grasping frantically as he reached for her. But Bastian sent a black wave to knock him back, pummeling him into the floor as Serena escaped his grasp.

The scene was set. The six of us watched in horror as Bastian took Serena's hand, guiding her to the altar on which he planned to kill her. "By the moon and sea you were created, and by the same you must end." A stream of moonlight poured down into the chamber from the opening in the ceiling above. As the white light encircled the stone like a spotlight, I remembered how Cordelia once said we draw our power from the moon. This was how Bastian intended to send it back. And I couldn't help but wonder, if the Mother of Sirens or her power didn't exist, would I?

Serena didn't struggle at all as she daintily sat herself on the table and leaned back. "All this because I would not love you."

"No, Atargatis. All this because the gods favored you and gave you the sea—something that should have been rightfully mine."

I looked around, frantic as the moonlight poured in. I strained to hear Serena and Bastian's exchange of words as Bastian pulled out an ancient-looking dagger with a skull mounted on the hilt. He touched the tip of the knife to his finger and twirled the hilt in his hand back and forth.

"At least let me see it," Serena begged. "One last time. Let me see what I've lost."

Bastian laughed, holding his knife to lift her chin. "I think I could honor that pitiful request. For a price."

"For a kiss, then?" Serena's words sung heavy and clear as she made the offer, hardly a question.

"Fair enough, lovely. Looks like we'll both be getting a taste of what we could've had." I felt a small gag tickle the back of my throat. Bastian wasn't only evil and manipulative...he had way too much fun with it. And it ignited a fury in my bones. But maybe Serena was onto something. If she could just get him to reveal where the Crown was...

Bastian snickered, his sharp eyes piercing right through her as he lowered his face to hers. "A kiss for a crown." He placed his lips on hers, forcing her head to him as he gripped the back of her neck. When he pulled away, Serena appeared struck by lightning, her body stiffening and jolting upright. With her head tilted back, she stared straight up, as if watching something above her intently. When the force holding her in place released her, her head fell forward and she gasped as though she'd been holding her breath. "Or rather, a glimpse of it. It's as close as you'll ever get." Bastian sneered.

A vision. Bastian had only shown her a vision of the Crown. Of course she should've known there was no way he would produce the actual crown in front of her. His deals always had a catch. This one was no different. What did that gain her? It was too late now.

So I was left with my jaw on the floor and my body charged, ready to react, but then Serena, up at the stone altar beside Bastian, frantically started yelling to McKenzie below. But the way she moved, screamed, and elbowed Bastian away to buy her just one extra second...it didn't seem like Serena. In fact, the more I watched her, the more clear it became that maybe it wasn't Serena at all.

"The Crown is in the West tunnel! In the floor beneath a half-heart shaped stone!" She cried.

The Serena beside Noah stood to her feet and shoved past him. She whipped past like a blur as she took off running back toward the way we came, disappearing into the stone tunnels that led back to Bastian's lair beneath the club.

It was so much to process that my mind was spinning trying to keep up. I glanced at Bellamy and Milo, who looked just as confused as I felt, but their eyes were fixated back on Bastian and the Serena he was about to sacrifice. Only this Serena was now transforming as a watery sheen ran down her body, peeling away into a puddle that revealed a pale, ginger-haired girl instead of the dark-skinned goddess that she had been just seconds before. It was McKenzie, and a heavy sensation dropped in my gut when I realized it'd been her up there all along.

BLACK WATER

47

KATRINA

"Conniving bitch!" Bastian struck McKenzie hard enough to send her toppling down the altar steps, where she rolled lifelessly past me. Noah and I ran to her, kneeling down and cupping her face in my hands. Noah shook her and I begged her to open her eyes.

"McKenzie!" Noah repeated, hovering over her body just as closely as I was, if not more. When she quickly came to, I breathed a sigh of relief.

Milo rushed to hold off Bastian before he could follow after the real Serena, while Bellamy ran after her as he called her name. One glance was all it took to see the disaster unfolding before us. The cave was beginning to groan and echo, tiny sandy bits of ceiling sprinkling us below. Something was beginning to crumble.

"You swapped places without telling us?" I asked, suppressing the slight feeling of betrayal I felt at McKenzie and Serena's secret plan.

"The fewer people who knew, the less chance to mess it up. It had to be believable." McKenzie raised an eyebrow as she sat up, holding the side of her face where Bastian struck. "It worked, didn't it?"

"You could've been killed. And how did you have Serena's voice?" My eyes drilled into her.

"Bastian's not the only one who can keep voices in his jewelry." She moved her hair away to reveal the necklace Serena normally wore—a white and blue piece of sea glass set in gold. "Looks like that acting class I took for an elective paid off."

I hesitated, debating whether to express my anger or save it for another day. I chose the latter. At the sight of Bastian knocking Milo back with his dark magic, I stuffed away my feelings about the secret plan and summoned my water back. This time it came to me fast, rushing like the blood pulsing in my veins. I drew it upright, and sent a cyclone at my command twisting toward Bastian like a raging cobra.

It only held him back for a moment as he met its force with his own shield of shadow and water, but I summoned all the water I could sense in this place and created an impenetrable wave that I sent rushing toward Bastian. I had to keep him away from Serena as long as possible. If she could find the Crown, this would be all over, I told myself as sweat formed on my brow from the effort. Bastian's power was strong, and it clashed against mine in an explosion of black and blue as he fought to break through

"Keep at it!" Milo shouted, charging toward Bastian. He tackled him with enough force to break his dark water hold on mine. With nothing holding it back, the water flowing from my hands shot forth, blasting Bastian across the room

In an uncomfortable silence, with only the sound of water dripping, I paused, watching a sopping wet Bastian groan as he stood slowly. The water in my hands felt like a weight, tangible, alive, and ready to be summoned again at a moment's notice as I drew back the water I'd just used. I couldn't afford to lose the strength of even a drop.

"Remember," Bastian licked a tiny drop of black liquid —either water or blood— from his curling lips. "You can't kill me. But I can certainly kill you."

"I don't need to kill you," I spat. "I just need to keep you away from the one who can."

Milo rushed to my side, and together we blocked the door through which Serena had escaped. Bastian growled, an unhinged rage in his breaths that came fast and hard. The black liquid streaming from his mouth grew heavier, dripping in thick clots. His shadow on the floor began to shift, forming into shapes and curves that didn't quite match Bastian himself.

Milo and I backed up as much as space would allow, our eyes fixated on the horrific transformation happening before us. Bastian grew larger, at least three feet taller and the rest of him in proportion as he shifted into a half-man half-monster before us. Wraith-like shadows curved from his back, writhing like snakes dripping with the same black venom as the liquid on the floor and from his mouth.

His already snake-like eyes began to glow like yellow pits of fire through the sludge of black water drenching his entire body. His voice morphed into a deep, growling version of something supernatural beyond recognition. After everything I'd seen, I thought I couldn't come across anything that truly scared me anymore. But this—this shadowy sea demon in front of me—left me frozen in place, short of breath as I tried to find the strength in my legs to keep from buckling.

"Good luck keeping me anywhere!" Bastian roared, his devilish voice grating against my ears as it shook the ground. He raised himself, lifting himself off the floor with nothing but black smoke and water beneath him. Hovering over us, he reached forward, his dark water reaching for me like a giant arm. Milo leapt in front of me, yelling for me to leave.

Just as the shadowy water struck, a burst of bright golden light sparked from Milo and sent Bastian's shadows flying back with a crackle. Bastian screamed in anger or pain, I couldn't tell which, as Milo stood staring up at him in shock, visibly shaken from what just happened. I noticed his sleeve had been torn off in the clash.

"Milo, your arm!" I pointed to the glowing sun tattoo on his arm. Yellow light lined the marking like golden, sacred veins—the same light that had deflected Bastian.

Milo gripped the marking with his other hand. "The sun. The Island. The light overcomes the dark." He spoke as if trying to remember something or rehearsing a line to himself.

"What?" I asked.

"It's protection. Protection from darkness—from the dark lord of the seas. Protection from Davy Jones." His eyes slowly shifted from his glowing tattoo up to a fuming Bastian. "Katrina, he isn't just controlled by Davy Jones..."

"He *is* Davy Jones," I muttered. It occurred to me all at once. The legend behind the strange cruelty of the seas. The one sailors feared for hundreds of years. The one who collected the souls of the dead at sea...

The Collector, I relayed my thoughts to Milo with my song call. *The things in his collection aren't just things. They're souls.*

Trapped souls. Milo reiterated.

"I am he!" Bastian boomed, stepping closer and closer with the inky sludge of his shadows cloaking him. "The dark lord of the seas. Cursed to this human form by Poseidon himself, but more powerful than any man."

"Poseidon cursed you once. What do you think he'll do to you if you kill her?" I spat.

"The gods of old are long gone. Without her, I'll be the last supreme being of the seas...as it could have been all along if she had chosen me instead of that useless mortal." Bastian snarled, sharpened teeth showing through the black water continually trickling down his face. "You may have the mark of the sun to shield you, but you're not the one I'm after." He struck the wall beside us with a burst of shadow and water from his hand, sending it crumbling to the floor and shaking the remaining walls.

"He'll collapse the whole fort." I watched the stony residue and pebbles dropping down on us from the ceiling.

"I don't think he's concerned about that." Milo uttered. Together we watched dumbfounded and completely baffled as he crashed through the wall and the shadows around him slithered across the floor, carrying him toward his destination—Serena and Bellamy.

BELLAMY

I couldn't think of a time when I'd run as fast as I did then, chasing after Serena—except maybe the night my father killed her and I ran to the pier, trying to save her...and failed.

"Serena!" I screamed, my voice echoing down the dark halls. There were passages snaking all throughout, leading to pitch black tunnels of nothing. I could barely see, as the torch I took from the wall was near to dying. "Serena!"

I called out her name again, stumbling my way through blindly, turning at every entrance and trying to decide which one I should follow. I finally chose a path and wandered into the dark, chasing an end I didn't even know existed and praying to a God I didn't believe in to help me find her. But the passageways around me kept multiplying, and each time I chose one, more would appear. I spun, surrounded by corridors that taunted me and spun alongside me, my vision blurring at the sight of the dark halls surrounding me. I no longer knew which way was left or right, north or south.

I wasn't one to panic, but in that moment, I felt my heart speeding up in a way that made my chest tighten. And the loud boom in the distance didn't do much to settle that feeling when I heard the sound of stone crumbling and the feeling of an earthquake beneath my feet. The chamber had become some strange illusion of tunnels, a maze that I didn't remember my way out of. Whatever Bastian was doing to my head, I wanted him out.

Find her, that's right. Lead me right to her. He laughed in the recesses of my mind, taunting me with the fact that the closer I got to her, so did he. *Poor Bellamy. The more you try to help her, the more you hurt her. It's always been that way. In this lifetime and the last. Yet you just can't stay away.*

"Shut up!" I screamed into the emptiness. "Shut up and go to hell!"

He didn't shut up. He kept on, making my head ache. I leaned against the wall, agonizing over every word, reaching up to my neck and digging in my fingernails in attempt to claw away his mark on my collarbone. The skin tore, burning at my desperate scratches, but it wasn't enough. I reached for a knife in my pocket and raised it to my neck.

Suddenly a hand caught my arm. "What the hell are you doing, boy?" I glanced up, my vision settling. There were no longer hundreds of tunnels. Just the two passages I was trying to choose between. And the person holding my arm was Russell.

"Nothing," I panted, trying to catch my breath in an attempt to look less insane. "Where's Serena?"

The look in his eyes told me he knew. "She found the Crown."

"She did?" I asked, a smile starting to form. "She's got her power back?"

Russell looked away, a heaviness overtaking his appearance. "Get out of this corner and come and see for yourself."

I followed him down one of the passages, a glowing in the distance as we approached.

"The West tunnel," I muttered, noting that the altar room was stark North of where I stood. "Damn. From North to West." I connected Serena's clue once again, baffled at how they'd been there all along, as Russell led me to the end of the passageway. It was a chamber, somehow inexplicably lit, showcasing even more of the thousands of Bastian's collected items lining the walls like a hidden treasure cove. And there in the center of the room was Serena, kneeling in front of a broken heart shaped opening in the floor from the stone that she'd pulled up, staring at the Crown in her hands with tears in her eyes.

"You got it!" I shouted, rushing to her side. "Wait, what's wrong?" I noticed her tears weren't from joy, but sorrow.

"I got it," Her voice squeaked, placing the Crown on her head. "But it didn't work. I'm still the same."

I didn't know what I expected would happen when she got that crown back. Maybe she would put it on her head and light would shoot out every which way, or maybe she would levitate and shine like the sun. I had no idea. But nothing even close to that was happening. And she made it clear that wasn't how it was supposed to be.

"What? No! Maybe it's a fake. Bastian probably switched the real one or—"

"I assure you, it's the real one." Bastian's voice interrupted me. He stepped into the room, a strange calm about him, though he was soaked completely with his dark water. Something seemed...different, more sinister...about him. He looked relieved as he watched Serena holding the Crown. He spoke so calmly it made me nervous. "So you see...you cannot stop this."

Katrina and Milo appeared behind him, but they didn't approach. They stood, just as mesmerized by the scene as the rest of us, waiting to see a goddess re-crowned. Bastian kept his distance, but he kept talking. "What now, Atargatis?"

"Very well," she said softly. "It's written in stone. How could I think I could defy that?"

"What's written in stone? What do you mean?" I took her hand, pleading for her to make sense.

"The altar is painted with pictures of my legend. The first, a weeping woman by her dead lover. The second, she's walking into the sea. The third, she emerges with a tail. And the fourth is meant to be the last. Her end. My end. I'm destined for this ending."

"The last picture is faded! I saw the altar. You don't know the ending!" Katrina screamed from where she stood.

"She's right!" I screamed. "You're going to let some damn pictures tell you what's supposed to happen to you?" I shuddered as I heard another boom in the distance, wondering what was happening, knowing it was just a matter of time before Bastian got tired of playing cat and mouse with us and made his next move.

"It's my destiny."

"No, Serena. No. You're *my* destiny! So what does that mean? We just give up?"

"What does it take to restore a goddess?" Bastian snickered. "Apparently more than it took to ruin her. Now come with me. Back to the altar, dear."

Something about the way Bastian said the words triggered a clue in my brain. And I carefully sorted through the thoughts in my head, almost afraid to think them because I knew he would be listening. But I couldn't help it. The thought came and I couldn't get it to leave. But I couldn't help but think maybe there was something more about that altar than we knew.

Stop trying. You'll only make this hurt worse.

With eyes clenched shut, I shook his voice away. I wanted to run, run far away from the hold he had on me. It wasn't fair that he could just appear any time and invade my thoughts. And all these years—had he been in my head the whole time? It made me sick that I couldn't escape it.

I'll always know. I'll always follow you. And when you fail once again to do what you failed to do before, I'll be chasing you, ready to remind you. No one has ever kept me out.

I fought like hell to get him out, closing my eyes to help me blockade my mind. But as he spoke into my thoughts, something he said made me finally believe him. He was right. I could never keep him out. No one ever had. So what happened if I stopped trying? What would happen if I just let him in? What if I played his game right back? What the hell did I have to lose?

Go right ahead, mate. Make yourself fucking comfortable. As I spoke back, I could almost feel the hesitation and utter surprise in Bastian's awkward response.

You're going to just open yourself up to me like that? How very bold of you.

Might as well surrender. It seems the only logical option, wouldn't you agree?

When there was no answer from Bastian, I knew that I had him. I was now in his head, as he was in mine, and if he insisted we share a highway between our thoughts, I was going to find out what his were. I was done running.

When I opened my eyes, I saw Bastian, looming with a clenched jaw and anger flashing in his gaze. Serena stood in the center of the collector's lair, facing a grim version of Bastian that I'd never before seen until now. He was taller than humanly possible, and black writhing shadows sprouted from all around him. He controlled some blackened water that burned to the touch, and he sent waves of it forward to wash us all back, separating us all from the one he wanted.

Serena screamed. I grunted with frustration, trying to break through the wall of black water he'd entrapped us in. Though it looked cold, it boiled like molten lava to the touch. Burn marks ate their way through my clothing and onto my arms from trying to break through the barrier. I screamed alongside a desperate Russell, who rammed the wall alongside me as Bastian dragged Serena away in his inky, shadowy clutches.

As Bastian swept her away and dragged her back toward the chamber with the stone altar, I stopped fighting the unbreakable water wall. I couldn't catch him. And I certainly couldn't stop him like this. Desperate and out of solutions, I looked inward again, reaching into my mind for an answer—or rather, reaching into his.

Why don't you just kill her right here? Why the need to keep dragging her back? Are you not strong enough? If I could figure out his secret—why he seemed to need her in that chamber so badly to kill her—maybe it would lead to an idea.

He fought me hard, closing off his thoughts as best he could without losing me entirely. I could feel it. His pride wouldn't let him give up the hold he had on me. Even if it meant I had access to him, however fleeting.

His thoughts flashed before me as I fought the mental battle to stay in his head and see what I could. I could only manage to see broken, fragmented, and fuzzy blurs of thoughts, but they were something. As he carried Serena, he was thinking about how he'd kill her. With a dagger he planned to stab through her...no, he planned to cut off her tail..to give...to give it back...to the gods?

What was given here must also be taken.

He had to kill her on the altar. He couldn't do it otherwise. Some kind of magical god rule, I'm sure. But wait...

On the throne of Atargatis must be her blood...To kill her once and for good.

Throne. Throne.

I reached for Bastian's memories. I knew I wasn't strong enough to be choosy. But I think the fact that we were now sharing a mind-link made him panic. I saw flashes, glimpses of what could have been bits of Bastian's life. I saw faces of the poor unfortunate souls he tricked into his deals. I saw pirate captains and kings. I saw glittering horizons and stormy seas. I saw love and loss, hate and war. And there I caught a glimpse—not even a second—of my life through his eyes. He watched us with envy. Serena and I, and the life we built millennia past.

She was mortal, but still just as beautiful. An ordinary girl with ordinary dreams. In a village built from stones and mud, at the earliest dawning of civilization. And there I was with her, in a life I didn't remember—a man clearly used to hard work and toil, rugged and dirt-covered, greeting her with a kiss as I entered our humble house. All this Bastian had watched, longing to be in my place.

And then I saw what he did to her. What he did to us.

He drove a dagger into my chest while I slept, and left the bloody knife in her hands. When she woke next to my body, holding the blade, she thought she'd lost her mind, and ran to the cliff by her village where she threw herself to the sea.

Centuries later he found her again, no longer a woman, but a goddess, a sea queen, rivaling his own power with her curse-turned-blessing. And he lured her to him, promising a power even she didn't hold—bringing me back in exchange for her crown. In a ritual under the full moon's light, he took her crown, sentencing her to a mortal rebirth, forever searching for the man she traded her power to bring back.

I shook away the visions of Bastian's memories. My legs threatened to buckle as I processed what I'd seen and learned in a matter of moments. What had passed as a lifetime in my mind was only a few seconds here in the real world. I'd hung on to every image. And I remembered the stone altar where Bastian ripped the Crown from Serena's head in exchange for restoring my life. It wasn't an altar. It was a throne. And thrones were used for coronations. We had to crown Serena on her throne. And I had to die to do it.

To Crown A Queen

49

If you crown her, you break my deal with her, and I take back what I'm owed—your life.

Bastian spoke to me even now, and I could sense the wicked smile on his disgusting face from his words alone. My blood turned to ice. I didn't mind dying. I'd already done it once. But losing a lifetime with Serena again...

No. I owed her this. I failed her before. Not again. I wouldn't do this for anyone but her. For her I'd rip out my own barely beating heart. And if I was the cost of her power, so be it. At least my death would be worth something this time.

I turned to my friends, all trapped here with me. "Help me get out of here. I know what to do to get Serena's power back. But I have to be the one to do it. Do you understand?"

As Katrina started to object, I repeated myself before she could finish. "Do you bloody understand?" I choked, my words coming out harsher than I meant them to.

"What are you planning, mate?" Milo stepped forward, a concerned look about him.

I stared at him. I wasn't going to share any of what I'd learned. I'd keep that all with me till the grave. No one else needed to be bothered with all that.

"You just need to know that I have to get to that throne room."

Katrina and Milo hesitated. I knew they cared, but right then I didn't want them to care. I wanted them to shut up and get me out of here. So I couldn't believe I'm admitting to this, but I was incredibly grateful when Russell stepped in.

"Just get him out." Russell blurted. "Katrina, you can do it. It's water, isn't it? Control it!"

Katrina sent a sideways glance my way. "It's dark water. It's different. I've never—"

"Try!" I screamed, my voice raking against the air.

Hesitating, she held out her hands, tears very clearly forming in her eyes. She groaned, sending forth her strongest effort to tame the black water swirling around us. As she fought to control it, her hands shook, but the wall of dark water remained untouched.

"Wait." Milo put his hands over hers. "Don't sirens draw their power from the moon? Let's try something."

She looked at him through heavy, shining eyes that had lost all hope as he guided her hand to the sun star marking on his arm. "Use me as a shield for your power."

Russell and I watched them, tense and hopeful, and terrified all at the same time. The clock was ticking. For all I knew Bastian had already killed her. I had to tell myself to breathe.

A golden light shone from Milo, culminating at the marking on his arm. Katrina held onto him, combining their power so that a golden light began to surround her. She reached forward and touched the dark water, Milo still at her side. Where her fingers met the water, it separated, a golden rim slicing through it as she created a small opening.

"The sun and moon must face the same darkness," Milo whispered beneath his breath. I would've asked him what he meant, but I was too busy rushing towards the growing hole in the water wall.

I went to escape, but stopped at the realization that Bastian would know my plan. He would know that I intended to kill myself for Serena and he wouldn't let me do it. Someone else would have to do it, at a time when he least expected.

My thoughts rushed like the water swirling around us. I turned to Milo and spoke low but urgent enough. "When I get in there...listen...when Serena is crowned, you have to kill me."

"What?" Milo's eyes flashed.

I gripped his shoulders. "I'm asking you this because it's the only way. My life for her power, that was the deal she made. I have to save her. You have to kill me. Do you understand? Kill me."

"I...I can't do what you're asking, Bellamy." Milo turned his head.

"Then I'm not asking. And I'm the captain, remember?" I breathed, my heart pounding.

"Bellamy, I—"

"Don't give me that golden boy shit right now. I already died once for Katrina. You think I won't do it again that much more for Serena?"

"That was different," Milo argued. "You didn't have a choice. We were cursed to hell. We were going to die anyway."

"Well my life's hell without her." I spat, meeting Milo's gaze with my own hardened stare. "I thought you of all people would understand. I thought you of all people would have my back on this. You said you'd have my back...on whatever came next."

He was silent, and I could tell I wasn't changing his mind. I couldn't waste any more time trying to convince him.

"To fucking hell with you, then, Milo. Don't forget to take your knife out of my back when I leave." I shoved him out of my way and ran to the water opening as Milo called for Katrina to close it.

She tried, but she wasn't fast enough. I leapt through, the edges of the water still managing to splash and singe my skin, but I didn't stop to notice. As fast as my feet would carry me, I ran to the Crown lying on the ground and scooped it up in my arms. Then I set off down those dark, empty tunnels, my fate literally in my own hands as I ran to crown my queen.

The walls blurred as I passed. The sounds in the distance became hollow wails that faded from my ears like the remnants of a ghost. I felt water in my eyes as I squeezed them shut to blink it back. I wouldn't let myself mourn this life, dammit. I finally knew what I was meant to do. I finally understood why I was here. And it was to save Serena, once and for all. Milo or not, I'd figure out how.

"Why the hell am I always dying?" I joked to myself. It was the only way to dull the sting of Milo's refusal to help me. I still couldn't believe he'd turned his back on me. I couldn't believe the coward he was.

As I entered the throne room, I heard footsteps behind me. I turned to see Russell, his arms splotched with burns just like mine, only worse. Of course he would've leapt through that opening right behind me. It couldn't have at least been Katrina or Noah, or hell, I would've even taken McKenzie. But Russell was the one standing in front of me, not them. I'd make it work.

"Good timing, old man," I said, scanning the layout of the room one more time. It was becoming clear to me that this would be a two-person job, since I would be dying at some point. I ducked low behind a stone pillar and motioned for Russell to do the same. Bastian was carrying Serena in his arms, shielded by the dripping veil of his dark power as he took her up the steps. She wasn't even fighting him anymore, and her body moved limp as a satin scarf as he laid her across the throne altar.

He ran forward, but I held out an arm to stop him. "Don't do anything stupid," I said. "We have to do this one way, with one chance to get it right. But he's going to know I'm coming because he's in my head."

I couldn't let myself think. Bastian was distracted with Serena at the moment but that didn't mean he was completely oblivious to me. I couldn't think. My only option was to act and act fast.

I placed the Crown in Russell's hands. "I'm going for Bastian. Make sure this gets back to her, no matter what. You go up there and you put it on her head as soon as you see me attack him. I have to let him kill me. It's the only way she's coming out of this alive."

I darted off before Russell could ask questions or say something useless to try to slow me down. But, by God, he'd better do what I said. At least, I thought, there was no one else here who wanted to save Serena as much as I did. Maybe, just maybe, it was for the best that Russell was the one who'd made it here with me. He might've been the only one who loved Serena enough to understand how to complete a mission I couldn't fully explain to him. Not if I wanted to keep Bastian unaware of it. Russell had no reason to give a shit about me, so he was likely the perfect one of the bunch to do this.

The chamber around me faded, becoming a mere haze to line the path before me. My focus homed in on Bastian and Serena. They were all I could see as I drew nearer, my footfalls speeding up with each frantic beat of my heart. I could make out the details now—the white terror in Serena's glistening eyes; the beading sweat above Bastian's brow as he lifted the skull-hilted dagger to kill her. I recognized it from the memory as the same one he'd used to kill me in my first life. And the same dagger my father gifted me. Knowing my next move, I couldn't help but realize it was once and forever intended for me.

With the moonlight pouring in from above, I nearly tumbled down the cracking stone steps as I climbed them. Bastian turned to me just as I ran up on him. He knew I planned to attack him. Of course he knew. I expected that. We were linked, and always would be, no matter how much I wanted to escape that. But did he know what the rest of the plan was? I'd fought so hard to separate it from my mind, to deny my own thoughts, hoping I could somehow hide my true intentions from him. I only had seconds to do it...

He whipped around to face me as I tackled him. Serena screamed.

"Bellamy, stop! Let him do this! Forget about me, please!" She begged through the tears flowing down her cheeks. I ignored her.

Bastian fought me with inhuman strength. My muscles groaned as I took a hit from him hard enough to crack a rib. I struck back, but my hits resulted in little damage. His skin was like armor, and his grip like iron shackles. He pinned me against the steps, the jagged corners of the stone bruising my spine. Perfect.

Mustering all the strength I could, I grabbed the wrist of the hand in which he held the dagger, fully intent on making him think I actually had some self-preservation left. His fingers loosened on the hilt, and I fought not to show my hope dwindling. He knew what I was trying to do. But I couldn't let him drop that knife. My tired arms ached as I inched my hands up over his, forcing each finger back down to keep the dagger in his grasp.

"I won't kill you, Bellamy. I know that's what you want." He laughed as his snake-eyes flashed gold. "But I'll certainly let you watch as I kill *her*." He gestured to the table, where Serena pleaded with me, begging me to leave.

Any minute now, Russell. Put the damn crown on her head.

"He can crown her all he likes, but it won't do any good."

"I know," I struggled to speak, my body shaking from fatigue as I fought to keep Bastian's hand closed around the dagger. "But this will."

I caught a glimpse of Russell, as he climbed up the other side of the altar with the Crown in his hands. He lunged forward, just barely reaching Serena as he secured the Crown onto her head. The moonlight struck the Crown, casting rays of its reflection across the room from the moment it touched the golden pearls and glimmering seashells lining the edge.

That moonlight was supposed to be the last image I would see. I was supposed to close my eyes forever to the sigh of Serena glowing with her restored power. But instead, I was still trembling with fatigue as I fought to pull the dagger closer to myself. Bastian resisted with ease, the supernatural strength in him enabling him to overpower me no matter what I did. I glanced over across the stone altar, where Russell pushed Serena aside as he scrambled to us. There was a determined look in his old eyes that made me hopeful he realized what I needed him to do. He practically jumped down the steps, colliding with Bastian's back and reaching over him to add his hand to the dagger we both gripped. With his strength and mine combined, I began to feel the knife lower. Bastian was weakening, and his shaking arm confirmed it.

I grunted from the sting as sweat dripped into my eyes. Bastian's breath tightened as he struggled against the two of us. The dead cool of this cavern wasn't enough to fight the burning in my muscles. But we were almost there...Just a few more inches and I'd have the tip of this blade in my chest.

But Serena...she leapt off the altar, still wearing the Crown, and threw herself on Russell. His grip slipped almost completely from the hilt. She wrestled against him, prying his hands finger by finger from the knife, and yanked him down with her as she pulled away.

"Dammit, Serena! Stop it!" I screamed, my dry voice spent.

"I won't let you—" The words hadn't fully escaped from her lips before her shriek tore through the air as I felt a sting between my ribs.

I took one slow, long look down at my chest, where the dagger was buried deep, held in place by a hand on the hilt overpowering Bastian's. A hand and arm with the mark of the sun. My eyes shifted up to Milo, whose eyes softened with a knowing, solemn nod. Bastian caught him with his elbow and flung him off in a rage. He staggered back, cursing us all as a light began to emanate from Serena's crown. I looked at Milo where he crouched on the steps.

"Thanks mate," I managed to utter as my breaths shortened and a scarlet warmth dampened my shirt.

"You're the captain," he said.

Serena's screams faded into muffled silence. Bastian filled the air with a flurry of curses that sounded like jumbled slurs to me. My head felt light, and a cruel chill dominated my body as my blood leaked out. This wasn't at all like dying in that cursed shipwreck. This was unsettling and slow. My eyes were too weak to move. I kept my focus on Milo. His eyes were full with budding tears, and they were the last thing I saw before the darkness swallowed me whole.

I'd just made it into the altar room as I screamed at the sight of Bellamy lying dead on the steps to the stone slab. Milo said he wouldn't do it. How could he do it?

"Bellamy!" I screamed. But it was too late. Bellamy was gone. I saw the knife in his chest and his lifeless body slumped across the steps. And behind him, Serena rose up, tears soaking her face and neck, reflecting a glistening light that showered her from the Crown on her head. The frame of the Crown grew downward, spiraling and weaving itself into her hair, joining the Crown to her as if it were a part of her. Her hair flowed, bits of blue intertwining with the rest of her full, dark locks. Bellamy was dead. And Serena was a goddess again.

I glanced at Bastian, who looked a lot like a man who knew his time was up. He quickly turned and summoned his shadow water, and it shot up from the ground, cloaking him in flowing midnight before it twisted into a cyclone that he drove into the walls. The whole place shook violently and sent chunks of stone raining down. I dodged them just barely, running to meet Milo as he worked to salvage Bellamy's body amidst the chaos. As he lifted him, the steps cracked between them, pulling apart and ripping Bellamy out of his reach. Milo's half gave way, and the only thing he could do to avoid falling to the churning water below was to throw himself to the only piece of solid floor left—the same piece on which I stood. He stumbled off the quaking steps toward me just as they collapsed behind him.

Serena knelt on the altar, face in her hands as she groaned Bellamy's name in agony. Through her tears, she paused long enough to catch Bellamy's body with a wave before he slid into the sea. The wave cradled him in place, holding his limp figure safely out of reach of the torrent. Serena cried his name, and drew it back to her, where she pulled him from the water and held him in her arms as everything around her toppled to pieces.

The squeal of McKenzie drew my attention from behind. I whipped around to see her with Noah, running as he tried to shield them both from the crumbling ceiling. The floor was giving way and pieces of it sloughed off into the ocean below the cliff it was built on.

"Both of you get out of here NOW!" I screamed.

"We're not leaving you!" McKenzie screamed.

"Yes you are!" I summoned water from the sea behind me and sent forth a blast that whisked them both away and back to safe, dry ground. I just hoped my mom had stayed put at least wherever Noah had taken her.

I'm okay. Don't worry, Trina.

I didn't expect to hear her voice in my head right then, but I couldn't have been more glad of it.

Good. I'll see you soon. I called back to her. *Just stay away from the sea right now.*

There was an unusually long pause.

I'm afraid I can't do that, Trina.

"Mom, what is that supposed to mean?" I blurted out loud. She never answered me.

Milo finally reached me and urged me to the exit back to the tunnel. "You need to go...What? What's wrong?" He panted, taking notice of the twisted look of confusion on my face.

"Nothing," I lied, shaking away the thoughts of Mom for a moment. "But I can't leave! Bastian's getting away."

"Serena will take care of him! It's not your fight anymore."

"Oh yeah? Where is she then?" I screamed, realizing she was no longer up on the altar. And neither was Bellamy's body. As I glanced up, the altar still somehow intact despite the rest of the fort having crumbled to pieces around it.

The watchtower above us had long fallen, leaving an open night sky above us and the sea before us. Milo and I stood on the open ledge, searching desperately for any sign of Serena or Bastian.

"I don't see them. What if Serena's too heartbroken to stop Bastian?" The ocean wind whipped my hair across my face, and I spat out the wild-blowing strands as I tried to talk through them.

"Surely she wouldn't let Bellamy die for nothing!" Milo screamed over the roar of the water that seemed to be crashing up against the cliff more and more loudly by the second.

There was a bubbling in the ocean, marked by a heavy darkness rising up from the bottom. It bloomed into a bubbling fountain of black, and the waves around it churned, parting to reveal the top of a charred mast. The water continued swirling, and the wind grew stronger as it lifted a ship from the depths. But this ship was in pieces, with wooden slats missing and broken mast poles and torn sails. It was coated in an inky black, similar to the dark matter around Bastian...almost like tar. And Bastian himself was at the helm, a vision of his true self. No longer an eccentric, vibrant club-owning collector, but a dark sea captain dripping with power and the decay of the souls he kept captive.

"His ship." Milo muttered, his eyes wide as he watched the ship rising up before him. "He's trying to run."

My eyes scanned the waters, and I remembered what my mom said. Was she down there? And more importantly, if she was, why would she be?

I suddenly felt a call to jump in as well. The sea tugged at my soul and my siren side was immediately in control. I resisted, though it was like trying to ignore an all-you-can-eat buffet on an empty stomach. Painful, tempting, and hard as hell.

Suddenly something burst forth from the water, glowing with a light that illuminated the crystal waters around it for meters. It was Serena, wearing the sea as a flowing gown, and no longer the size of a human. She was now a giant—at least two or three times the size of her normal height. The Crown on her head dripped with golden droplets, as if the water that touched it melted right into the precious metal.

The call of the ocean grew louder. I stepped forward, ready to let myself drop right in. Milo gripped my arm from behind. "What are you doing?"

"I don't know," I said, turning around to look at him. "I just have to go. I can't stop it."

He looked at me with a long pause. He pressed his lips together and released my arm. "Your eyes are blue. Go on and do what you have to do."

I nodded and with a leap forward, I dove off the cliff into the ocean. I'd never fallen from such a height before, but the need to be in the water below overrode the fear of the drop. Crashing into the waves, my lower half quickly morphed into a tail and all at once, I was at home.

SEAFOAM

51

KATRINA

Some strange instinct called me to it, drawing me to a force I didn't quite recognize, but couldn't resist. I didn't know where I was going, but I swam there with foreign confidence. As I followed the draw, I searched for my mom in the water without luck. Still I pressed on, following some innate primal instinct in me that I didn't know I had.

Chunks of stone from the old fort came floating down around me as they continued dropping into the water from above. I thought of Bellamy and shivered at the notion that he might just be lost in all this, cold and alone, drifting in the chaos. He deserved so much better. Milo once said life had always been unfair to him. He was right. I choked back some tears in sadness and anger, and I couldn't help but think to myself that if Serena didn't bring down justice on Bastian after that, I'd do it myself.

But Bastian was on a demon ship, sailing away to save his pathetic ass. And here I was, flipping my tail through some mystical pathway to answer a call only I could feel, unable to fight it. And through the ocean I swam, until I saw a light in the distance under the water. As I neared, the elegant shape of another mermaid welcomed me—my mom.

Mom, how did you get here, too? Where are we?

My mom tilted her head. She looked so rejuvenated in this form, as though she was still herself, but herself with an inhuman beauty about her. Especially here, suspended in the open ocean. Her brown hair framed her face that had been softened with an ethereal touch. Her eyes held some strange, feline charm that was never there before, and right now they were the same ocean blue hue as mine. It was almost hard to look away. Was that how I looked to others in my siren form?

I don't know. I just...came here, she said.

Great. So neither of us understood why we were drawn here.

Above us the water rippled, and a whirlpool formed, with the funnel's wide part at the surface. It spun and trailed down right before us, then whisked back up to reveal Serena in its place. She was in her mermaid form, her glorious tail nearly reaching the seabed, but this Serena wore a warrior queen's expression. Beneath a furrowed, tense brow, her sharp eyes flicked back and forth between my mom and me.

I've called all the sirens in the sea, and only you two remain. I prayed it wasn't so, but I had to know for sure.

Of course that made sense. We were drawn to Serena, our queen. She was the Mother of Sirens. It was impossible to resist her call. Whatever she asked of us, we would do.

I need you to protect him while I face Bastian. Take care of him and get him somewhere safe so that I can focus on destroying that bastard.

She waved a hand, revealing Bellamy secured in a giant bubble. His eyes closed, that black hair contrasting harshly against his deathly white face, and the dark red bloodstain across his chest, all untouched by the water around him—it was an image I didn't want to see. But we were charged with guarding him, and that was something I didn't need a siren queen's command to do.

My mother and I swam to Bellamy's body, taking up either side of him with knowing nods. Serena said nothing more but fixed her gaze on the dark shadow looming above on the water's surface in the distance. Bastian's ship I presumed. Serena took off toward it, but stopped to look back at us one last time as she entrusted us entirely with the body of her beloved.

I wasted no time telling Mom to help me carry Bellamy back to the surface. There was no safer place for him I could think of than with Milo. I used my song-call to tell Milo what was happening, and he planned to meet us at the shore.

We swam with Bellamy between us, one arm in each of ours, careful not to disturb his peaceful appearance. Up on the shore, Milo waited for us, and he'd managed to reunite with Noah and McKenzie. We passed Bellamy up to them, and together they laid him on the sand.

We were careful to stay out of sight, as the entire side of the fort crashing into the sea had obviously drawn attention of the locals and authorities. Nestled in a corner away from the flashing blue lights and police tape in the distance, we ensured no one saw the two mermaids with a dead body meeting their friends ashore.

"I can't just stay here," I said, unable to tear my eyes away from Bellamy. I couldn't make myself believe that I'd never hear that snarky accent or see that stupid, cocky smirk again. I'd just healed up from my grief from losing Milo. And now a new wound was created. Ripping at the still-healing seams of my heart.

I clenched my fists and closed my eyes as I allowed the reality of it all to set in. Losing Bellamy the first time was unfortunate, sad even. But I'd barely known the real him then. But now, now was different. We'd crossed oceans together. We'd stood by each other in pursuit of things others would call impossible. We'd watched each other's heart break and heal again. Losing him after all we'd been through together, even if it was technically his choice, just didn't seem fair. The tears burning behind my eyes reminded me how I first learned to control water aboard his ship. And the way he found me a blubbering mess on the pier in the twilight, mourning. And the way he faced Bastian even when he didn't want to, just for me to have the chance to get Milo back. He'd said it was a death sentence. I didn't think this was what he meant. And something told me he didn't either, at the time.

I opened my eyes and let them follow the ripple created from the tear that fell. A thirst for vengeance rose in me, and I wasn't sure if it was me or the siren, but I didn't try to resist it. "I've got to make sure I see Bastian pay for this."

We watched as in the distance a ship's silhouette flashed against a midnight sky, lights of gold and white bursting like fireworks around the masts. Explosions of water and light leapt forth from the sea as Serena and Bastian battled. From here, it almost just looked like an ordinary storm out at sea, instead of a duel between two oceanic immortals. It was probably a good thing, given the attention the crumbling fort was drawing.

Ignoring Milo and my friends' pleas against it, I dove down into the water and flipped my tail as swiftly as I could manage toward the ship in the distance. I couldn't help but wonder what was taking so long. Serena was supposed to be able to kill Bastian when she regained her power. Whatever this battle between them was, and however long it was supposed to last, I didn't have the patience for it. Bellamy deserved his justice now. And Serena had better truly be powerful enough to overthrow him or I'd try my hand at overthrowing them both. No—that was the siren talking.

My siren vision allowed me to see perfectly in the dark, so I could easily make out the scene of Serena, in her grand goddess power, held high as the ship's masts by the hand of the waves enrobing her from the waist down, fending off Bastian's attacks with her own. In a vortex of water I assumed was controlled by her, the ship bobbed in place, tilting and tipping as the water kept it from sailing out of Serena's reach. The sails in the masts strained against her hold, and the ship groaned with agonizing creaks as it drifted about.

In a clash of Bastian's black water against her golden waves, the forces of their waters raged on, turning the sea around them into a choppy, ominous abyss. Supernatural lightning struck between them each time their power collided, and the moon dripped its glow down upon it all as I neared. I was in awe at how easily Serena wielded her power, holding back Bastian's ship with the tide while striking him with magic waves streaked with golden lightning.

"I told you to guard Bellamy!" Without even turning around, Serena immediately knew of my presence, even as she dueled with Bastian from her post above the water.

"He's safe!" I shouted over the roar of the churning water around us and the creaking of Bastian's ship. "I came to help!"

"Your human side allows you to defy me." She shook her head, stopping just long enough to turn and make her point clear. "I don't need you, little mermaid! You possess no power that I don't already have tenfold."

As she spoke, a blast of darkness collided with her, knocking her into the water with me. As she resurfaced, she turned to me with a cold threat in her eyes that pierced me like harpoons. "You're distracting me! Leave now!"

A spout of black water came spinning toward me, but Serena launched it away with a burst of golden light from her hands. "If I have to waste time to protect you, you aren't helping!" She hissed.

"What's the matter, Atargatis?" Bastian's voice echoed around us in a cloud of shadow on the water. We looked to see him walking to the edge of his ship. He cocked his head and pretended to think. "Can't get your pet to behave? Perhaps if you'd spent more time protecting your mermaids in the first place they wouldn't all be extinct now would they?"

Serena flushed red that I could see burning in her cheeks even through her dark skin. Her eyes flashed with rage and panic, and she stilled in a way that made me nervous.

"That's right," Bastian went on, standing on the hull with his hand on the rigging. "Don't pretend you're better than me. We both fail to accomplish the tasks bestowed on us. You were willing to risk all your sirens, giving up the only thing you had to protect them, all for a man that still ended up dead anyway."

It was then that I realized Bastian not only took Serena's crown to take away her power, but to take away her army as well. It made sense that he took it in a time when pirates and greed ruled the seas. He was as responsible for the downfall of all mermaids as Cordelia was.

"Giving up my power for love is different than keeping souls captive for your sick collection." Serena shot back. "And you know it. That's why you're running. It's your only chance."

"I'll give you that, I thought it was." Bastian mocked. "But now I see you can't even control one testy little siren. So maybe you're not as powerful as I thought."

Serena bared her teeth, a flurry of water shooting up around her. The waves rolled and foamed around her, and the sight of it struck something in my brain. Something Cordelia once told me.

Seafoam.

I called to Serena with our siren connection while still keeping my eyes on Bastian.

She glanced at me with a raised eyebrow and tilted her head to one side, a look of half-aggravation and half-confusion. *What?*

I ran my fingers through the water, emphasizing the bubbles the movement created. *Is it true that when sirens die they become seafoam?*

Serena wrinkled her nose at me and looked away, continuing to send her golden waves toward Bastian. *Yes, but why are you asking me such a question at a time like this?*

"Because I don't think your army is gone." I shouted out loud.

Serena stopped short and her gaze fell on mine. She got it. With a nod she dove down under the water. I looked for her, waiting for her to resurface. An eerie whistle carried on the wind, sweeping in from all directions. The ocean shifted, and the waves reversed, sinking low and drawing down the entire water level with it. A rumble underneath created an endless stream of ripples across the surface, and I half expected a tsunami.

Bastian glanced around, his face white with fear as he realized the only one who could defeat the dark lord of the seas was about to fulfill that duty. I followed his gaze as he watched something in the distance. It was a wave rolling in—a foaming wave consisting not of water, but of the ghostly forms of sirens within the sea foam. Every single siren who'd ever lived and died at the hands of mermaid hunters, one unearthly chorus of their songs echoing in unison across the night air, as if their voices were infused in the sea spray itself. And in the middle of the siren wave, Serena swam amongst them, her magnificent tail flowing through the water like an iridescent rainbow and her crown glittering brighter than the moon.

The wave approached, and so did the sirens' wailing song. It was a sorrowful one, full of lament and mourning, but as it grew nearer, it turned to one of anger. I looked up to see Bastian running from one end of his ship to the other, desperate for a way out. As the wave crashed into his ship, he threw up his hands and shielded himself with a wall of black water, but the foaming siren wave wasn't hindered by it for even a second. It crashed through, engulfing him as the ghostly song grew so strong even I almost covered my ears. The wave took down his ship, specters of thrashing mermaids pulling it down to the depths, creating a whirlpool where Bastian remained. The sirens swept him up in their foaming tide, drawing him into them as they swirled around him like a cyclone, Serena amidst it all as she orchestrated their every move.

The cyclone of sirens spun faster and faster, creating a blur of Bastian behind them. And then, his shadow leaked out from him like ink as they drew it out. He cried out with a desperate scream as the water around him stained black.

"As you dethroned me, I now dethrone you." Serena's voice boomed like a clap of thunder, somehow beautiful and terrifying at the same time. Bastian groaned and cursed Serena as he writhed in the prison of the sirens. They encircled him in a blur, moving so fast as to draw out of him the source of his dark lordship, pulling from him the very spirit of Davy Jones that he'd been joined with all these years. Once more Bastian was a mortal man, stripped of his dark power, and the curse of Davy Jones was once again cast away to roam the seas, looking for its next willing host.

My eyes followed the dark shadow that loomed over the waters, erratic and frantic as the sea soaked it up like a stain. I shuddered to think who might welcome him next. But for now, at least it was no longer Bastian.

At last, the ghostly siren wave slowed, the spinning cyclone slowing as it lowered and pulled Bastian down. Davy Jones' power may have been his curse, but he was still wretched at heart all by himself, with or without the strength of a dark sea lord. And for that, he met his justice at the hands—and fins—of the vengeful mermaids that he'd indirectly slaughtered. They dragged him down with them as they crashed back into the ocean, leaving clouds of billowing sea foam in their wake. I thought at once of Cordelia, and wondered if she had been in there somewhere. She'd wanted to avenge the sirens and redeem herself. And now I guess she had, in a way.

The silence that followed was chilling. The water stilled, and the waves calmed. I drifted there alone, still taking in the fantastical event I'd just witnessed. I could almost still hear the haunting song of those sirens and I replayed their foreboding words in my head.

In future, in past

Our shadow is cast

Torn from the depths

Till nothing was left

One last time we rise

One last lullaby

Sun and moon unite

The wrongs of old made right

Thus ends the the ocean's night

The song echoed long after in my core, awakening my siren fully, and I couldn't shut her up fast enough. *Kill the queen. Take the Crown. Kill the queen. Take the Crown.*

My siren had an idea, and she wasn't polite about it. She insisted. She was clinging to something Serena said. That I was able to defy her, unlike other sirens. So that meant I could challenge her. And if I defeated her, I could become the new siren queen. I could have the powers of a goddess.

My mind was silenced. It screamed no in the back of my head, but it was silenced by the siren's overpowering commands. She was right. Serena didn't deserve the Crown. She didn't wield her power properly. If she had, sirens would still rule the seas.

Find her. Kill her. Take the Crown.

I had to follow. I had to.

I went to dive under, but something caught my arm. I hissed, my head snapping around to face my captor as I thrashed against him. It was Milo, who'd snuck up on me in a dinghy. But his voice and gentle eyes did nothing to calm my fury and power-mad desire. I hardly recognized him. And my siren wanted him out of the way.

KATRINA

"Katrina...listen to me!" Milo shouted as I ripped my arm from his grasp. He was trying quite desperately to tell me something but everything he said became muddled. Something about the siren magic surge under the moonlight strengthening my siren. But I didn't care why she was suddenly so powerful. I just needed to let her take control. I was tired of him and those mortals ashore holding me back when in reality, I was something so beautifully powerful. How dare I suppress it any longer!

I opened my mouth to sing a song I'd never heard before, but my siren was more than happy to teach me the words. From my lips came an ancient melody, the preferred siren song of old, used to lure sailors to their deaths. It flowed from me as naturally as breathing air into my human lungs. This song, not heard on these seas for centuries, now filled the air and Milo's ears.

"My heart searches for a sweet sailor bold,
Out on these seas and the depths untold,
A sailor who'll love me and follow me down,
A sailor to kiss is a sailor to drown."

Something primal in my blood boiled over, taking complete control. Milo had fallen under my spell. He leaned over the dinghy, his gaze helplessly entranced on me. I placed my hands on either side of his face as if to kiss him, and then, just before my lips touched his, I yanked him down and dragged him into the deep with me.

Finally.

He wriggled and struggled against me, but my strength easily overpowered his as I pushed him deeper and deeper. This was what it meant to be a siren. To commit such an act of irony so fitting on this perfect night of vengeance. I smiled as I thought of it—the last of the sirens, drowning one last worthless man.

But then something stopped me, and a flash of Katrina broke through. Warm lips against mine, and a gentle hand on my face. He was kissing me. He'd stopped fighting me and was kissing me. At first I recoiled, but he embraced me harder and deepened the kiss. And that was the moment I broke free.

This man—this was Milo. I loved him. What was I doing? Oh my god. Immediately I wrapped my arms around him, shooting upwards as fast as my fins would allow, back to the surface. No sooner had we just approached the surface of the water did I feel Milo's eyes on me. I'd expected him to be sputtering and coughing up seawater, but then I remembered the power of a mermaid's kiss.

"Milo, I'm so sorry!" My voice quaked frantically as I released him from my grip. "I didn't mean to—"

"I know," he said calmly as he caught his breath. "That's why I came to warn you. So you didn't just leave us all to disappear into the sea."

"Did you know kissing me would let you breathe underwater?"

"No," Milo's breaths were still short from wrestling against me. "Must've missed that bit of folklore somehow."

"Then why did you kiss me?" I blinked away some salty droplets from my wet lashes.

"Because it was the only way I knew to bring you back to me." He smiled that crooked half smile and I wanted to melt right into the water around me. "I'm just glad it worked."

"Me too," I swam near him and he flinched, making my heart twinge with guilt. "How...how did you know I would lose myself out here?"

Milo's eyes grew heavy and he turned his head away as if searching for his words. "Your mother...she couldn't resist the call of the sea. We tried to stop her but it happened so fast. She swam out and we haven't been able to find her."

"She just found out she was a siren. Of course she wasn't strong enough to fight it." My heart sank as I thought about what I could do to find her. I tried to use my song-call, but she didn't respond to it. She could be anywhere in the open ocean by now. The siren magic influence was too great for her to resist.

Neither of us said anything for a moment. There was too much to say, and too much to think about. I'd just almost killed Milo. My mom was a runaway mermaid. And that stupid siren song still kept ringing in my ears.

It was the last of siren songs I wanted to hear. It was unsettling, and gave me a twisted feeling in my gut. A feeling that reminded me why my siren side was just as much a curse to me as the power of Davy Jones was a curse to Bastian. The difference was, Bastian embraced it. He used it to magnify who he truly was at heart. But mine was a constant conflict. And the more time passed, the more I wasn't sure which side of me was stronger. But what happened tonight had brought an answer to that question once and for all. And I didn't like it.

So there in the dark, as Milo swam back to the dinghy, I stayed for a moment. With nothing but the ocean and me, my thoughts drifted. I'd forever be at war with the voice in my head. A voice that sought strife and destruction. A voice that would always threaten to overpower my own. A voice that could take everything and everyone from me eventually, if I ever lost control for too long. It would always make me choose the sea over anything and anyone else. It would always be a constant reminder of the soul I didn't have.

I made myself admit it out loud. I hated being half-siren. It wasn't an existence that was meant to be shared with a human side. I'd never be happy to walk—or swim—in both worlds. I needed to choose one. And I had one more idea in mind that I hoped Serena would be willing to hear.

DAUGHTER OF THE SEA

53

KATRINA

I followed Milo in the dinghy back to shore where everyone still waited. When we arrived, McKenzie, Noah, and Russell stood around Bellamy's body, their faces still downcast even though we'd technically won the battle for the seas. And I didn't blame them. Not much of it felt like winning when one of us didn't make it out alive and one of us was lost at sea, even if it was by her own accord. I hoped my plan would at least solve one of those problems.

"Where's Serena?" Russell asked, worry etched in his eyes.

"Don't worry," I said. "She'll be back for Bellamy. She wouldn't leave without him."

"How do we just go home after this?" McKenzie's voice sounded weak, and even from where I watched in the water I could see the tear marks on her face.

"It's going to be hard," I swallowed, looking at Bellamy. "But I try to just keep telling myself this is what he wanted."

Suddenly there was a swooshing of water behind me, and a soft light emerged from the surface as Serena lifted from the water. She stepped out, regal and elegant, the dress of seawater trailing behind her with a train like a waterfall. Her skin almost seemed to sparkle beneath her flowing hair tinged with blue. Across her waist, she carried a bag made of velvet and a sword hanging from a sheath.

But her face was dull with heartache. She stood, looking at each of us one at a time. "Thank you all for your help restoring my power. We've paid a great price for it." Her eyes dropped to Bellamy and she hesitated for a moment as we hung on her last words with anticipation. "I must return to the sea now, as there are no sirens left to rule, but there is always darkness to keep at bay. And before I depart, I have something for each of you, as a way to show my gratitude and to honor Bellamy's sacrifice."

First she walked to McKenzie, who she handed the sea glass necklace from around her neck. "A fitting keepsake to remind you of that time you impersonated a sea goddess." She and McKenzie exchanged smiles, and then McKenzie threw herself at Serena and embraced her in a hug, which didn't surprise me. I smiled to myself.

Next, she handed Noah something resembling a rolled up scroll. "A map of the seas, even the secret parts," she winked. "To remind you of the things you once didn't believe in." Noah nodded his thanks.

Next, she silently trudged over to Russell, placed a hand on his cheek, and uttered something just between them. I supposed she was helping him come to terms with the fact that his daughter was really an ocean goddess and maybe to ease the goodbye. Her gift to him, I couldn't see, but I believed that was sort of the point.

Last, she turned to Milo. She reached for the sword at her side and placed it in his hands. "This is—"

"Bellamy's cutlass." Milo cut her off, his voice catching between the words.

"Yes." She blinked. "Who else better to have it than the one he taught to wield it?"

Milo pressed his lips together with a dutiful nod. When Serena turned away, I caught him staring at the sword with hollow eyes. He held onto it for a long time before looking back up at us all.

With everyone on land dealt with, it was my turn. Serena turned around to face me standing with her feet in the surf as she looked down at me. "And you, little siren, what is it that I can give to you?"

I hesitated, my voice seemingly gone. I'd planned to ask Serena for this anyway, but I hoped it wouldn't anger her. Hell, I just hoped it was even possible. "Can...can you take away my siren form?" I spat it out, trembling.

Serena knelt down, her solemn expression unchanging. "Tell me. Why would you want that, Katrina?"

I looked at my friends standing behind her, and I looked for a long time at Milo. "Because of them. And because of my mom. I want to be fully human. I want a soul."

Serena stood back, and I fully expected her to deny me what I asked. I didn't even know if she *could* give me that. So when she spoke, I breathed a sigh of relief. "I can do what you ask, but not without something from you. The ocean demands a covenant of your sincerity for me to fulfill a task so great."

"Whatever you need," I said. "It wouldn't be the first deal I've made."

"It's not a deal," Serena snapped. "But it's the only way to relinquish all your siren qualities—your voice, your power, your strength. Just as Bastian needed to destroy the things that made me a goddess to kill me, the things that make you a siren must be destroyed for you to become fully human. And for you to gain a soul."

"So what is it that you need then?" I flipped my tail with impatience and a bit of nervousness.

Serena gave me a look that cut right through my core. "You must cut off your tail."

Smothering silence fell over us all like a wet blanket as I considered the condition. "Another mermaid before me cut off her tail, and that's what started all this."

"And now it must end with the same. Your great-grandmother did it to place a curse and spare herself. You do it to lift a curse and spare those you love."

"Fine." I sucked in a deep breath. "If that's what it takes, I'll do it."

"Katrina, you sure about this?" McKenzie asked, her face contorted in a grimace.

Once more I recalled all the times my siren had made me do something I regretted, and the answer came easily. Would I sever off a piece of me to rid myself of her influence? "Yes." I eyed Serena, anger rising in me for what she was about to make me do. Whether it was truly a requirement of the ocean laws or simply her own, I couldn't help but almost hate her in that moment. But that wouldn't change anything. My only choice was to get over it and grab a sword.

"Let's go somewhere a bit more...private," Serena looked out toward the sea. She was right. It was only a matter of time before someone noticed us down here. The shore and old town was already filled with commotion from the fort collapse. She turned and looked at me. "There's a small string of sandbars just east of here."

"I'll meet you there," I said firmly. My eyes flicked to Milo for a second, who watched me with a tense gaze and uneasy stance as he shifted from one foot to the other. "Will you come with me?" I asked.

"I was hoping you'd say that." He stepped forward immediately, but Serena stopped him. "She must do this alone."

"Why?" I tossed out the words with disdain and shock. "Why can't he come with me?"

"Because," Serena lifted her chin, "When you are at your weakest moment, and when you think that you can't go on for the pain, when your siren is begging you to stop, you must prove that your human strength truly is greater. I won't allow you to become something less than what you already are. If I remove your sirenhood, it must be because you are more powerful without it. And that, my little mermaid, you must prove."

I chewed my lip and flared my nostrils, unsure of what kind of response I could offer to such a twisted condition. But Serena was an ocean goddess, and like the sea itself, she was unpredictable, powerful, and clearly sometimes even ruthless. But if this was what I had to do to get rid of the side that made me much the same way, I wouldn't be deterred.

"See you at the sandbar," I announced loud enough for everyone to hear before diving under the surface and heading straight for the tiny islands just below the horizon. My siren's voice haunted me the entire way there.

Kill the queen. Take the Crown.

When I arrived, Serena was somehow already there, waiting waist-deep on the shoreline. The moon glittered on the water's surface like a beacon to mark the place where I'd give up half of myself. Behind her, on the island nestled crookedly in the surf was the stone altar, washed up from the collapse, I assumed. I swam up to her slowly. She offered not a word, but handed me a sword. Bellamy's sword.

"Milo thought it might help you," she uttered.

Now's the chance. Kill her with the sword. Kill her!

I took one look at the blade and thought of the bloodshed and combat on the seas it had lived through. How many lives had it taken? I wondered. Had it ever taken the life of a siren before tonight?

I slid myself across the sand and up onto the stone slab. My eyes lingered over the artwork lacing the edges of the altar, each a depiction of the story of how a woman became a siren. But now it would end with the reverse. And I thought how fitting it was that the last image was nearly erased. Because we'd forged our own endings, despite what legend demanded.

Serena followed me to the stone and lowered the sword into my open hands. It all felt very ceremonial and sacred, and it sent shivers down my spine and tail. As a silent sense of doom crept upon me I looked up at the stars for comfort.

Kill the queen.

Seated with my tail hanging down into the water, I stretched it out in front of me, straightening it out the same way I would if it were my legs. I raised the blade, studying the impossible lower half I'd been gifted and cursed with. Scales of silvery blue caught the moonlight and rivaled the stars themselves. It reminded me of the starlight dress I'd worn to the gala the night Milo admitted his love for me. And that was everything I needed to shut up the voice in my head. I wanted to dance with the man I loved beneath the stars and build a life with him. I wanted that night forever. And I never wanted to try to kill him again.

With that vision sustaining me, I raised the sword above my head with both hands, trembling as I squeezed the hilt, now slippery with my sweat and seawater. I looked above at the sky to pinpoint the North Star. When I found it, I fixed my gaze on it and drew in a breath.

What are you doing? Stop! STOP!

I plunged the sword down. I watched that star as I gritted my teeth against the pain so hard I thought my jaw would break. The blade dug in, slowly, shooting agony through my waist. I kept looking at the star.

Stop this, now! You're making a mistake! You're betraying yourself!

The siren screamed within me, begging and pleading, and finally demanding that I stop. The human side of me begged, too, because the searing torment of slicing through my own flesh was almost too much to bear. So much that I stopped halfway through, as the steel of the blade met bone. A shooting pain beyond comprehension paralyzed my body and mind. My tail writhed, and my arms shook in agony and exhaustion. The saltwater on my open flesh stung like the flames of hell as it seeped into every crevice of my raw, open tissue.

"I can't do it!" I screamed, the sword jutting out of me. I hung my head as my body quaked through my ragged breaths.

That's right. Listen to me.

I opened my eyes, drawing on the strength of the stars once more. I had to shut her up. I had to gain my soul.

I tightened my grip and slammed down, digging the blade into my very core, severing the connection between my torso and tail.

No! You fool!

The scream that burst from me might've shaken the depths, but the bleeding wail from my siren pierced my mind like an icepick to the brain. In twisted, cruel torture, I pushed on the hilt with every ounce of power I had left in my quivering, feeble arms until I broke through to the other side. The siren's wail died out as my head spun, and my vision of the stars grew dim. Every part of me tingled with icy numbness until I could no longer feel anything at all. I looked down at the vision of the waves washing up the stone over my waist, washing away the river of blood gushing out as fast as it flowed.

A flash of light blinded me, a prism shooting up from the water at my waist and shining to the heavens. My body felt hollow, and my head felt light and empty as my sight left me. The sound of crashing waves became nothing. I was awake. Barely. My consciousness was slipping away, drowning in the darkness of disorientation.

"Open your eyes, little mermaid." Serena's voice sounded underwater.

My weak eyes fluttered open with timid blinks. The white light died down, leaving behind the sight of the waves washing back to reveal my bare legs in place of where my tail had been.

"Well, you proved your strength. You're fully human now." She stood at my back, where she had been the whole time. I twisted around to look back over my shoulder, my body still wobbly and trembling from the trauma it'd just endured.

"Thank you," I managed to utter. I touched my fingers to my stomach and ran them down to my hips. My waist was smooth, except for a small scar in the shape of a cluster of scales just in front of my hip bone. I glanced at Serena with surprise.

"A little reminder for you. Of what you could've been. I'll be honest, I wasn't sure if you would really do it." She stepped forward, offering her hand to help me up. Getting to my feet was a task in itself, my legs shaking as if they'd never been used before.

I shivered, hugging myself in the night sea breeze. Serena motioned with her hand and summoned the tide. It washed up my legs, spiraling upwards around me until it formed a flowing dress, the top shimmering midnight blue, fading into a gradient silver cascading skirt for the bottom. "You'll always be a daughter of the sea."

To hear those words was a relief, somehow freeing, and yet a small bit of sadness lingered. Regardless of how much I hated it, and even though I'd only known about it for a few months, I'd still just given up a part of myself. There was a weird sort of heartbreak that came with goodbyes of any sort. My body felt regenerated, and though it was back to my normal human form, it was somehow different in a way I couldn't quite identify.

"I...I have a soul now?" I asked with timid breaths.

Serena nodded. "You do. And there's one more thing I think you've earned. A bit of a surprise I have for you." She gestured toward the water, and I squinted out to see a figure on the water, a shadow walking along the surface like a ghost. Finally, I could see the figure was that of a woman, clothed in a similar, more subtle dress than mine. And as she stepped through the night fog, closer to the shoreline, she locked her eyes with mine and I knew them right away.

"Mom!" I took off running on my wobbly legs, each step feeling like the first as my feet kicked up sand behind me. She flung her arms open and I met her embrace with possibly the tightest hug I'd ever given her. "Are you..."

"Fully human," Serena finished. "She asked me for this before you did."

"Is that where you were?" I studied my mother's face. She was still beautiful, still the same. But I noticed now that she had a few creases where she hadn't before. Just a tinge of sagging beneath her eyes held the promise of aging to come. She was aging normally now, as no one in our family line ever had the chance to do. She had a soul.

"I wasn't strong enough to do it, Trina." My mom slid her slender hands over my face, brushing my scar as she spoke in a tender voice that I hadn't heard since I was a child running to her from my nightmares. "But you, beautiful girl, once again, you saved the both of us."

I gulped back a lump in my throat. "No, Mom," I whispered. "You gave up yourself to save all of us. Into a world you only just found out about a few days ago. You were protecting us that whole time. Who knows what Bastian might have done to us if you hadn't?"

My mom pulled back long enough to look at me with a broken smile. The starlight reflected on the tiny teardrops rolling along her eyelashes. "I love you, Trina."

"I love you, Mom." I squeezed her in a tight hug and whatever rift was left between us seemed to drift away in the tide at our feet.

When we pulled away, I noticed Serena was gone. I followed the path of footprints in the sand only to find her a ways off, facing the other side of the shore. Turning, as if she knew I was watching her, she wore a tender smile beneath tired eyes that refused to meet my gaze.

"I like this little shoal," she uttered. "I think Bellamy would, too."

There was a long silence between us before I finally said something. "Let's get the others."

Serena bit her lip and looked away, the breeze catching a few loose unbraided strands of her hair. "Yes," She barely spoke loud enough for me to hear over the lapping of the waves. "Let's get the others."

She cupped her hands and dipped them in a small tide pool, lifting the handful of water to her lips where she whispered a message. She poured the water into the ocean, and it trickled down in droplets of gold and zipped away through the water back towards the mainland shore in a trail of light.

"Now we wait," she said.

Burial At Sea

54

I wasn't sure how much time had passed. I'd never been any good at keeping track. But dawn hadn't come yet. My mother and I sat on the shore watching for the others while Serena stood alone, unmoving, some meters away.

A small glow broke through the fog in the distance, burning from a lantern on a glass-clear canoe formed of water as it approached with the others on board. Their faces were somber, with Milo and McKenzie flanking one side of Bellamy's body and Noah and Russell on the other.

They slid ashore, bringing the enchanted boat in, where it dissipated back into the waves once everyone was out. No one uttered a sound. There was only the song of the waves and the patter of footsteps crunching wet sand as Milo and Noah carried Bellamy to Serena and laid him at her feet.

Serena looked down at her lifeless lover. With movements far too graceful for any human, she knelt down and kissed his forehead. We all stood encircling them, honoring this moment as best we knew how.

"A burial at sea, so that he can always be with me." Her whispers carried in the air like ghosts. "To love a siren is always a path to destruction." Then she began singing, a slightly different version of the siren lullaby.

"My heart found a sweet sailor bold,
Out on these seas and the depths untold,
A sailor who loved me and followed me down,
A sailor I kissed is a sailor I drowned."

Her voice cracked at the last word, and a tear rolled off the tip of her nose and fell onto Bellamy's pale cheek. I found myself holding back my own tears, still filled with more anger than I could contain at Bastian. He was long gone, but his damage was done.

Milo stepped forward and placed the sword on Bellamy, gently placing his hands over the hilt as though he was holding it himself. "For the locker, mate." He choked.

I gave him a moment, and then knelt down myself, placing my hand over Bellamy's. The cold stiffness of his fingers forced a sob out of me I didn't realize I'd been working so hard to keep in. With my head hung, I uttered my goodbyes.

Serena straightened her shoulders and summoned a patch of water that swirled nearby and reformed the crystal water jolly boat, this time just big enough for one. Another stream of water washed beneath Bellamy and began to gently lift him, pulling him into the boat. As we braced to send him off, a sudden shift in the wind caught everyone's attention. A harsh breeze blew in from the west, eradicating all the sea mist around us. And following it was a cloud of shadow, whisking right through us all and knocking the sword from Bellamy's hands.

"Davy Jones," Serena uttered with a scowl. "Even now he can't let us rest."

The black shadow moved aggressively, weaving between us and over Bellamy again and again before finally shooting out to sea and plunging in. Where it entered, a ripple of black formed that grew larger and larger until it was a slow-swirling black watery void—just big enough to swallow a small boat whole.

"Leave us!" Serena screamed, her desperate plea scathing my ears. But the shadow pool didn't leave. "I'll burn his body before I let you take him!"

We all looked at one another, not even Serena knowing what to do next. And for a moment, I missed my siren powers, because I felt helpless as the darkness raged off the shore.

DARK WATER

55

MILO

The strange dark whirlpool grumbled with hunger, drawing nearer and nearer to the shore of the sandbar. I ran to grab Bellamy, pulling him away from the waterline. In my struggle, Bellamy's arm shifted, revealing his open palm and a black snake marking on it. And I understood.

I stopped, still clinging to Bellamy as the realization settled into my bones.

"Serena," I called out. The look in her eyes pained me, but she had to know. "He's been chosen. He's the next to be Davy Jones."

"No, no!" She fell across Bellamy's body with her own. "No, he can't have him! I'll protect him. If he's the next chosen, Davy Jones will never stop pursuing him...so I will never stop protecting him." Each word was more frantic than the last. She struck the void with a blast of her golden water, and for a mere second it dwindled and vanished. But seconds later it returned unscathed.

The shadowy vortex continued spinning, sloshing and splashing like a growling lion waiting to devour. We all watched, all seven of us, stealing glances at one another as if perhaps one of us would know the answer to the question before us. Was it right to let Bellamy become Davy Jones, even if it seemed fate would deem it so? Or was Serena truly meant to guard him for eternity?

I looked at Katrina. Her gaze was already on me, and I knew what she was thinking—what we were *both* thinking. I cocked my head as if to make certain, and she replied with a solemn nod. So I spoke up. "The souls. The lost at sea that Bastian trapped. Bellamy could free them."

I expected the verbal lashing that followed as Serena turned red with rage at the very idea. Some of the others gasped or muttered amongst themselves.

"How could you even dare?" Her nostrils flared as she pierced me with a deathly stare. "That you would even suggest—"

"If there's anyone who could handle the power of Davy Jones, it's Bellamy," Katrina blurted out. "There's enough good in him to balance out the darkness. It has to be him. It has to be."

Serena whipped her head around from me to her, her face shining with tears. "No it doesn't!"

"She's right, Serena." I met Serena kneeling on the sand. "If it's not him, Jones might find someone with a truly black heart, maybe worse than Bastian. But Bellamy...Bellamy has enough good in him to balance the power. He'll fulfill the duty the gods gave Jones. He'll send the souls on." I placed Bellamy's lifeless hand in hers, truly believing my own words, and hopeful that it just may be the key to keep from losing Bellamy forever. "And he'll rule the seas with you, instead of against you."

That seemed to spur a reaction from her. She wiped her eyes with the back of her hand as she lowered her gaze to Bellamy's hand in hers. "With me," she sniffed. "With me, forever. He'd never age. Never die...never die." She repeated the words quietly as she stroked his cold skin with her thumb.

She pushed me aside and stood to her feet, facing the roaring black pool of shadows waiting in the water. She watched it for a moment as we hung on the suspense. If any one of us were breathing, it was impossible to tell.

"It's your decision, Serena." I stood up, too, before stepping away to resume my place at Katrina's side. "Do what you think is right."

Her eyes darted back and forth between me, then Bellamy and the whirlpool. Like a clock ticking, it beckoned, urging her to make her choice.

Finally, in one swift, sudden movement, she sent the crystal dinghy out to sea, into the path of the swirling black void. Gasps and screams erupted from our group as her power guided him to the heart of it. Though the water twisted and raged around him, his boat remained steady as though drifting on a calm sea. Ink-like water seeped into the boat, filling it to the brim until it covered Bellamy entirely, and pulled him slowly into its depths. The pool settled, becoming a ripple once more, moving in reverse—inward instead of out. And when it was all gone, nothing remained but a quiet, steady sea.

Dead Men Tell Tales After All

56

The sobs of Serena echoed in the silence as we waited ashore. McKenzie buried her face in Noah's shoulder, and Katrina and Grace stood huddled hand-in-hand, watching with anticipation. Russell and I glanced at each other, before he went back to wringing his hands and worriedly watching his daughter.

As the stillness lingered, I began to question if it was the right decision. Perhaps I shouldn't have spoken up. Perhaps Serena knew better, and it truly would've been best for her to spend the ages guarding Bellamy. Katrina and I might've made a grave misjudgment...and if we were, could we live with ourselves to see our friend return as a puppet of the sea's darkest force? The doubt gnawed at me, and I swayed uneasily, still watching the water that took Bellamy.

"I'm a fool for listening to you!" Serena wailed before lunging at me. "He's gone because of you! You were wrong!" I didn't stop her as she hit my chest and shoulders with the edge of her fists. I couldn't blame her.

"On the contrary, love, for once he was right." The voice that broke through Serena's rampage brought us all to a standstill. My head snapped to see Bellamy, taking form from a stream of shadow over the sand. He now wore the pirate lord's clothing, a long, black captain's coat and a skull medallion around his neck. His hair was long again, like our early days on the *Siren's Scorn*. He looked restored and rejuvenated in some ominous way, as though he'd been gifted a do-over of a life long past.

The smile that swept across my face was hindered by a gripping fear. I was certain we all had to be wondering the same thing. Bellamy stood before us, but was he still the Bellamy we knew?

He held his arms open wide as Serena ran to him, leaping into his embrace, weeping with joy. He spun her around and placed her down with a kiss. Katrina and I stood back as everyone else rushed to greet him with excitement and relief. He walked to me, to my surprise, and slapped me on the shoulder. "Don't stress yourself mate. I'm not completely evil."

I huffed out a sigh through my grin. "Still the same asshole as before, I see."

"With a few upgrades." He snapped his fingers and black water swirled from his hands and snaked its way around Katrina and me, wrapping around us loosely like a ribbon before Bellamy called it back with a motion of his finger.

"Bellamy!" Katrina stepped forward and threw her arms around him. "I've never been more glad to see you."

"You should know by now I don't stay dead for long, lass," he chuckled, patting her back in a friendly embrace, but then he gave her a protective squeeze, and I knew I could never thank him enough for keeping her safe.

"Thank you...for everything." I pulled his sword from where it hung at my side and offered it to him. "I believe this is yours."

He took a long look at the blade, and for a moment I thought he was at loss for words, as he dropped his guard for just a moment and allowed me to see beneath that aloof and sarcastic exterior. "You keep it, mate. I don't think I'll quite be needing a sword anymore." His eyes flashed silver and shadow swirled around his shoulders.

"You'll free the souls Bastian trapped?" Katrina asked, a hopeful look in her eye.

"If I must," he rolled his eyes with a sigh.

"Yes, you must," Serena stepped in with a chiding smirk. "That's kind of your new job."

"Aye. The deep sea undertaker. Could be worse, I suppose."

Katrina and I chuckled as the others drew in around us.

"So...will we ever see you guys again?" McKenzie asked.

Bellamy and Serena exchanged glances. "Maybe sometimes," Serena said gently. "Like when you come to the ocean just to get lost in the sunrise. When you're alone on the shore as the tide rolls in. When your soul is in true need of a breath of fresh sea air. We'll be there, watching over the ocean and those who've made it their grave. The last remnants of what the sea gods left behind."

"Then this is where we part ways?" I noted the dawn finally breaking over the horizon. Serena nodded.

"We'll miss you, you know." Katrina spoke to both of them, but she was focused on Bellamy. She stepped forward and embraced him in a hug, a burst of brightness clinging to his dark, looming figure. "It won't be the same without you."

"I know, lass." Bellamy said with more softness in his voice than I expected him to let break through. "But as long as you're by the sea, I'm never far away."

"Then you'll come visit us?"

"If Bastian can run an underground club, I'm sure I can squeeze in a visit to my best mates every now and then." They released their embrace, and Bellamy blinked a few times and swallowed. "Just bring along some rum and Dr. Pepper. Not sure they have much of that where I'm going."

Katrina laughed as she wiped a tear and sniffed. "Will do."

Bellamy turned away, leading Serena to the edge of the water. The tide was lowering, and the wet sand was cool with the promise of morning. Just before the dawn's light reached us, Bellamy waved a hand over the water, summoning the dark brigantine ship that had carried Bastian earlier. It rose up, ghostly black sails high, and almost seemed to levitate above the water.

We stood behind, waiting to see them off, but Bellamy turned around one last time and addressed me. "Turns out dead men tell tales after all. And what a tale you have to tell, brother." He went on with a half smile and a shake of his head. "I better not see you for a long while. Try to make it to the end of your life this time."

I nodded his direction and placed my hand on the hilt of his sword. "Aye. Till then, brother."

"Till then, indeed, mate."

With one last nod, he and Serena stepped hand in hand onto the ship, where they vanished with the sunrise in a stunning display of a splash of golden light mixed in a wave of shadows.

DAVY JONES

57

BELLAMY

I stood on the rocks as I watched the souls I'd freed leave the objects imprisoning them, taking the magic with them. On they went, to meet their so-deserved end at the bottom of the sea where they could rest once and for all. And once the last soul had gone, I clapped my hands and watched Bastian's collection shatter as two black waves crashed down on the once-enchanted items and ground them into dust. This was my show now.

What can I say? Becoming the next Davy Jones wasn't exactly in my plans. But somehow things all made sense for once. My father, Cordelia, the curse, Katrina, meeting and losing Serena, all lead to this. As weird and wild as it seemed, being the dark lord of the seas wasn't all that bad of a situation. I could be a captain of my own ship for eternity with my sea queen by my side...I just had to keep track of a few pathetic souls every now and then. How hard could it be?

Never mind that by the legend's design, we were meant to be sworn enemies. But we were making our own rules. Bending the laws of destiny, I like to think. A siren goddess as untamable and unpredictable as the sea spending forever with the ocean's grim reaper—what could go wrong?

Katrina and Milo might've chosen the mortal path, but I hoped they knew we'd always be there, on whatever shore they found themselves on.

"You know what we need?" Serena asked, placing her hand over mine on the helm.

"What's that?" I propped my leg up on the base of the wheel and pulled her onto my knee. She wrinkled her nose and nuzzled it against my cheek. "A pet. And I think I have the perfect one in mind."

I rolled my eyes with a shrug and a smile. "Your Kraken?"

She nodded with a grin and a giggle I once thought I'd never hear again.

I placed my hat on her head. "Captain's orders. Let's go get your beastie."

So we headed into the great horizon, two eternal guardians of the waters on which we sailed.

MAYBE SOMEDAY

58

KATRINA

Puerto Rico shrunk beneath us as the plane lifted, the blue sea so far below. It was foreign to be so separated from the water and not feel the siren call to it. I might not be a mermaid anymore, but my heart would always be drawn to the sea in its own way. Serena was right about that.

As we headed back home, back to Constantine, I hoped the school would let me pick up where I left off. But it could wait until the start of the next semester. For now, I just wanted to rest. Just to sit on the beach like a normal 19-year-old and enjoy the sand and sun. Maybe I would stay at my home again in Arkansas to reset a bit, but I knew in my heart I would always end up back on the coast. I wondered if life could ever be normal again. And if it couldn't, maybe that was okay. Milo placed a gentle hand on my thigh, reminding me that whatever came next, he was there with me. They all were—McKenzie, Noah and finally, Mom. I even had Russell to count on, in a way.

It was hell, but I'd do it all again to know it ends like this.

I jumped with a gasp, startled by Milo's voice in my head. "I could hear you just now!"

His eyes grew wide with surprise as I replied with my thoughts as well. *I guess Serena left one thing after all.* I laid my head on his shoulder.

Milo leaned in and kissed my forehead. *Or maybe she just couldn't take away what's written in the stars, fair lass.*

My elbow met his ribs with a light nudge and a laugh. *If only she took away your cheesiness.*

He chuckled softly.

I reached over to my wrist, feeling for a siren scale bracelet that wasn't there. I could still hardly wrap my head around all the fantastical things that had come as a result of moving to the little town of Constantine. Within the passing of only a few months, I felt as though

I had lived a thousand lives. Just a girl from a small town, who liked to paint, discovering she was a mermaid and finding her soulmate in a time-defying pirate. It wasn't exactly what I'd had in mind when I started college at ISA. But if anything had ever confirmed I was right where I was supposed to be, this was it. And I had every intention of returning and finishing what I began. I just hoped relinquishing my siren powers didn't also mean my watercolor abilities had gone with it. But I guess I'd find out soon enough. I already had so many ideas for the next piece I wanted to paint—the missing image that should've been on that last section of the painted stone table—a mermaid queen surrounded by her true power—the ones who crowned her.

I smiled, hearing Russell a few rows over gently teasing Noah about McKenzie and Noah nervously denying his feelings for her.

"No, no, it's not like that," Noah swore.

"Yeah, definitely not like that at all. We're just...really good friends." McKenzie fumbled with her words.

I laughed to myself as Russell pressed them, refusing to accept their obviously fake denials. It was plain as day to everyone except themselves. Maybe the old man poking fun at them might help them finally figure it out.

From the sound of it, Noah and Russell had begun to heal the rift between them, and I hoped Noah would continue to give his grandfather a chance now that he understood everything so much more.

My mom turned around from her seat in front of me, reaching her hand back for me to take. I took her fingers in mine and squeezed.

"So are we telling Dad about any of this?" I raised an eyebrow.

My mom paused, visibly in thought as she turned her face to the window beside her. "I've put him through enough..." She blinked. "But maybe someday."

"Maybe someday sounds good to me." My mouth twitched into a smile. Maybe we'd find a way to explain it all one day in the future, or maybe not. Because all that mattered was that what started as a nightmare had ended as a dream. And the things once torn apart, now mended.

Epilogue

Ten years later...

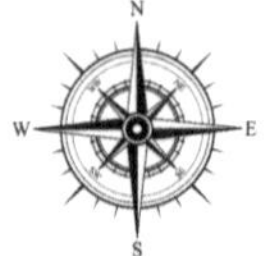

MILO

The sun would be setting in an hour, but those two just couldn't get their fill of the ocean. I watched from the beach as they picked up shells on the surf, throwing in the odd splash or two every now and then as the foaming tide rolled in. The beautiful barefoot woman and the starry-eyed child at her side who loved the sea as much as she did. My wife and son. My absolute greatest treasure.

"Katrina! Caspian!" I called from where I watched from the reeds by the boardwalk connecting our home to the beach. "The boat's ready when you are!"

"Five more minutes!" Katrina laughed, the wind sending her hair flowing as she danced in the wet sand with our little boy just shy of three years.

Five more minutes, Starlight. I told her with a warm smile at the sound of their laughter mixed with the crash of waves.

We'd planned a night on the sailboat for stargazing just off the coast, the three of us. I hoped to show Caspian the stars and tell him the tale of the mermaid who loved a pirate, and how they crossed time to find each other. And how the pirate found his greatest wealth in the life he built here by the ocean, where he could be the man he'd wished his own father had been. And years from now, I'd pass down my compass to him, to help guide him when his own storms came.

I reached up and felt the scar over my blind eye, a permanent reminder of my path. But I didn't need sight in both eyes to see I had everything I needed right in front of me here, in my final and most priceless life—one so much more than I deserved—as a port engineer married to a watercolor artist on the coasts of Cape Cod. Of course, we made sure to pay a visit to Constantine every couple of years to visit Noah and Russell, who owned a joint auto shop and boat repair shop, and where Katrina's paintings lined the halls of the school she once feared wouldn't accept her.

As Katrina approached with Caspian in tow, she smiled at me, and I was captivated by those deep brown eyes as much as every time before. I watched them walk back to the house, a trail of saltwater footprints, big and small. And I thought to myself that I'd cross oceans for a mere glimpse of this moment. But I didn't have to. It was mine. Full sail to the days ahead. No more curses. No more pirates and sirens. Just she and I and a lifetime.

"Have you checked the mail today? I'm waiting for a postcard from McKenzie. Last I talked to her she said she's loving London. She says she can't wait to—oh! Everything okay? Are you coming?" Katrina turned around with a grin as she released the hand of a giggling boy who ran to me.

I snapped out of my reverie and went to meet them, lifting Caspian onto my shoulders and kissing Katrina on the way.

"Of course I am." I smiled.

And I packed the Dr. Pepper. Just in case.

Follow the Author

To keep up with my current works and be the first to hear about new releases and special reader opportunities, follow me on social media @authorvalelane or sign up for my newsletter at authorvalelane.com